C.

much love

PROUD NEW FLAGS

Books by F. van Wyck Mason

PROUD NEW FLAGS

CUTLASS EMPIRE

EAGLE IN THE SKY

RIVERS OF GLORY

STARS ON THE SEA

THREE HARBOURS

CAPTAIN NEMESIS

THE MAJOR NORTH STORIES

THE CASTLE ISLAND CASE

Proud New Flags

Francis

F. van WYCK MASON

J. B. Lippincott Company

PHILADELPHIA AND NEW YORK

TO THOSE PEERLESS FRIENDS
HERBERT AND RUTH HARRINGTON
AND
TO THE MEMORY OF
THE OFFICERS AND SEAMEN
OF THE CONFEDERATE STATES NAVY
WHOSE INGENUITY AND DEVOTION TO THEIR CAUSE
WAS EQUALED BY FEW AND EXCELLED BY NONE

AUTHOR'S FOREWORD

It is as lamentable as it is astounding that so few Americans possess even the faintest knowledge or understanding of the great, and ultimately decisive, naval war that was fought between the Northern Union and the Southern Confederacy.

Why this is so, to me, remains baffling; especially since so many often-studied Civil War campaigns were decided by the use of naval power. Further, was it not sea power, exemplified in the Blockade, which eventually determined the fate of the Confederacy?

Had anything like the same understanding of the uses of a navy prevailed in Richmond that obtained in Washington, there seems little room for doubt that the South must have won late in 1862 or early in 1863.

Let us merely suppose that the Confederate Navy had been able to smash the Union blockade and so enable the Southern armies freely to draw arms, munitions and medicines from Europe. Is there much question that the magnificent armies of Lee, Jackson and Joseph E. Johnson could have failed to crush the badly organized and worse led armies of the North?

The South's failure to achieve naval supremacy, it appears, was due principally to the nature of President Jefferson Davis. His thinking, history reveals, lay on a tactical, rather than on a strategic plane. His stubborn opposition to a strong, all-out naval effort caused the Confederate Government to neglect, hamper and misuse a potentially powerful navy which came into being despite all manner of obstacles.

Alone in Stephen R. Mallory, only Secretary of the Confederate Navy, did the Southern cause find a Cabinet officer capable of appreciating the essential importance of sea power. The story of Stephen Mallory's dogged efforts to find ships and guns for that small core of first-rate former Federal naval officers who offered their services is a fascinating one. Such an account deserves the patience, skill and analytical genius of a Douglas S. Freeman.

This tale is intended to describe, in part, the South's early efforts to create a navy, also certain conflicts of that naval war as it was fought during the first year of the War Between the States.

To discover, and properly to evaluate accounts of Confederate naval activity, has proved difficult in the extreme for, with the end of the war, official records belonging to the Confederate Navy Department became widely dispersed—some of them even being carried off to Canada!

Many of the most useful memoirs I have consulted, alas, were written decades after the fact. Such recollections, written by extremely honorable gentlemen, for the most part were straightforward and generally accurate; but, too often, the passage of years had played such tricks on the writer's memory that one discovers truly amazing discrepancies as to fact and time. Such reports as were obtained from official Northern sources strove for accuracy but, inevitably, were tinged by partisanship.

I hasten to inform the reader that none of the fictional characters described in this book are based on actual people. Necessarily I have employed the family names of persons dwelling in the South at that period, but in no case are they to be confused with actual Southern families.

For my brief sketches of Southern society and the Confederate leaders I am indebted to Mrs. Chesnut's inimitable *Diary From Dixie* and Burton J. Hendrick's excellent *Statesmen of the Lost Cause.* Although replete with inaccuracies and tinged by a recognizable bias, Scharf's *History of the Confederate States Navy* has proved a veritable mine of information.

I wish further to acknowledge the invaluable assistance of Mr. Robert H. Haynes and his assistants, of Widener Library, Harvard College; the Enoch Pratt Library of Baltimore; and the cheerful and able assistance of my secretary, Jane West Tidwell.

F. van Wyck Mason

Gunners' Hill
Riderwood, Maryland
November 3, 1950.

Contents

BOOK THREE

THE SOUND AND FURY

BOOK FOUR
THE IRONCLADS

PROUD NEW FLAGS

BOOK ONE

The Uneasy Chesapeake

I

THE TELEGRAM

HIGH, THIN-LOOKING gray-white clouds scudding by suggested to Sylvia Seymour that snow might fall before long. After reassuring herself that the part in her golden-brown hair was smooth, she hurried down the precipitous flight of stairs leading to her tiny front hall. Who on earth would use a knocker so insistently? Certainly it was no well-bred person, nor was it likely to be the girl she was hiring from the Adams Family Machine Stitchery Rooms. She and the rented sewing machine she operated weren't expected to appear until after supper.

Who could it be? From delicately fashioned and rather pointed pink and white features she banished a frown and summoned a half smile. An exciting possibility had presented itself. Perhaps this was someone's servant with an invitation for the young Irad Seymours; apparently a good many very genteel balls and levees were held in Baltimore during the late winter and early spring.

Mechanically Mrs. Seymour smoothed the fullness of a gray moiré skirt, felt the many petticoats beneath it rustle reassuringly, then, as a lady should, drew her slender, slightly round-shouldered figure more erect.

Hesitantly Sylvia's fingers closed over the chill smooth brass of the front doorknob. Br-r-r. She braced herself, hated to let in even a little cold air. It was the Lord's special mercy that, thus far, none of her household had caught their death-cold in this miserably heated little dwelling.

She opened the door only a crack, hoped that nobody would notice that she, and not a servant, was answering. How silly. As if everyone along this stretch of Caroline Street didn't know that she and Irad could boast no servants beyond old Melissa, the one slave Irad had permitted her to fetch from Savannah.

A boy whose rheumy eyes, cold-pinched features and juicy red nose appeared above a ragged gray muffler, stood shivering on the stoop.

"Mr. Seymour live here, Ma'am?"

Sylvia's smile faded. "Yes. What is it?"

"Telegram, Ma'am," the messenger sniffled while fumbling for a pencil stub among his shaggy locks. "Please to sign here, Ma'am."

"A telegram!" Sudden anxiety quickened Sylvia's pulses and her fingers trembled a trifle while signing the receipt. How seldom did an unexpected telegram impart good news. Could anything have happened to Papa, Mamma? No, more likely it would concern Wilmer, her older brother, now on frontier duty in New Mexico with the First United States Dragoons. Could he have been wounded by those devilish Mexicans or equally barbarous Indians, or even killed—like Lucius Annable last year?

Snuffling loudly, the lad accepted her receipt, lingered a moment, then shrugged and turned away. Blowing on chapped hands, he went stumping off over the manure-splashed snow towards Central Avenue. Should have known better than to hope for a tip on such a poor-proud street. Now over on Park or Cathedral Streets, the folks there generally slipped a messenger boy a tip—sometimes as much as a dime, specially on a raw March afternoon like this.

Sylvia entered her living room and, hemmed in by handsome English mahogany furniture, stood fingering a flimsy blue envelope. Even while nervously considering the telegram, she decided that— cost what it might—Irad simply must find them a larger dwelling. Why not? Wasn't Mr. Reeder at the shipyard taking a favorable opinion of Irad's boldly original designs for the new coastal steam packet, *Martha Washington?*

Could this telegram be from Irad's mother? If so, it meant that complete catastrophe had befallen Irad's family. That product of thrifty New England would never waste money on good news.

Catching her breath, Sylvia suddenly ripped open the envelope and read the message transcribed in a careful Spencerian hand:

BROOKLYN, N. Y.
MR. & MRS. IRAD SEYMOUR, 33 CAROLINE STREET
BALTIMORE, MARYLAND—MARCH 15, 1861

CRUSADER DOCKEDIN NAVY NAVY YARD YESTERDAY. DAME FORTUNE NAVY DEPARTMENT WILLING WILL REACH BALTIMORE SOON. PAPA'S FONDEST LOVE TO ROBBIE. YOUR DEVOTED BROTHER

SAM'L SEYMOUR, LT., U.S.N.

Her delighted burst of laughter filled the room, resolved into a soft "How very wonderful. *Sam soon will be here!*"

To her shocked surprise blood had climbed streaming upwards to suffuse her face and neck and to fill her breasts. In a small Sheraton mirror she glimpsed herself. Curious. Had she been discovered in some lover's embrace she couldn't have appeared more guilty. Nonsense! She wasn't in love with Sam, or he with her. Not at all.

Petticoats snatched high like a small girl's, she pelted back towards the spice-scented warmth of the kitchen. "Robbie! Robbie! Your daddy's ship's in! He's coming home!"

Amid a swirl of full skirts, Sylvia caught up a yellow-haired two-year-old boy who quite solemnly had been playing at blocks within a warm area beside one of Mr. Bibb's patent hot-air cook stoves. She hugged him close.

When, all uncomprehending, the baby happened to emit a joyous gurgle, she kissed his soft cheek again and again. Mercy! Why—why —her heart was pounding like a battering ram.

"Melissa?" She called down the cellar stairs.

"Yas'm?"

"Mr. Samuel's ship is home from the West Indies!"

"Dat's good. Mebbe dat Misto Robbie he 'gin min' better." Tremulous jubilation was in the ancient Negress' tone, however.

The young woman's wedding band shone a deep yellow-red when she replaced Robbie amid his blocks. "There's Auntie Sylvia's little angel—just you play quietly till Uncle Irad comes home." Fervently, she hoped that he would.

When so-minded, which was often, Robert Ashton Seymour certainly could raise an impressive commotion for so small a body Sylvia reflected while returning upstairs. Certainly, Robbie had inherited not only his father's features but also his stocky build and tireless energy.

"It's absurd and lovely how much he's growing to resemble Sam," Sylvia reflected. Beyond any doubt he favored the blond, brown-eyed Seymours rather than his mother's family, the dark-complexioned and blue-eyed McKays who for three generations now had thrived in and around Portsmouth, New Hampshire.

Smiling a small private smile, she commenced to fold away sheets ironed just that afternoon by old Melissa. What she saw, rather than the linen in the wicker basket, was Samuel Seymour, as ruddy, clear-eyed and wind-tanned as ever in his double-breasted navy-blue uniform coat. Without interest she inspected for scorch marks the heap of too familiar and well-worn fabrics. Finding none, Sylvia vented a sigh of relief for, at seventy-odd, Melissa's eyesight had become nothing to brag over. Of course she might have been considerably older; few colored people possessed any real knowledge of their age.

Kneeling on the floor of that diminutive bedroom dominated by her bridal bed, Sylvia next counted out the napkins. Against these flyblown and putty-hued walls Grand-mère's lovely, satin-bright Directoire four-poster stood out like a Calvert Street aristocrat among scrubwomen. Its bed-posts really were too tall for so low a ceiling so its tester had had to be cramped downwards in order to be of use. The slim brass rods from which mosquito bars were slung in summertime needed a good polishing, but the bed's pale blue figured-chintz curtains had remained clean and new-looking despite three years of Baltimore's smoke and damp.

Sylvia paused and her naturally scarlet lips momentarily compressed themselves. How vividly those curtains recalled the big, comfortable and somewhat pretentious manor house Lucius Magoffin had built for himself on an oak-shaded bluff above the pale brown Savannah River! Sharply, she switched her thoughts away from home and its manifold comforts.

Winged brows merged, she inspected the least-mended of Irad's three ruffled dress shirts. Would it do for the Winans' ball? Her rather full nether lip crept in between her teeth; the fine lawn had become cracked between the shoulders, slightly, but enough to split under any stress at all. Botheration! She'd have to try to reinforce it, clumsy needlewoman though she was. But, wonderful possibility, maybe she could get that girl from the Adams Stitchery to do it.

How would Sam appear after the passage of nearly two years? Most naval officers returning from a tour of slave patrol duty in the West Indies looked gaunt and sallow as Spaniards.

A small smile curved Sylvia's mouth, emphasized the fascinating way in which her brief upper lip overhung its fellow. Most likely Sam's light brown sideburns would have become bleached almost white, especially near their ends. She hoped he hadn't given up shaving his chin as had so many young naval officers—trying to grow beards in their efforts to look older.

Irad, of course, wouldn't even dream of going clean-shaven. Among the Seymour clan, a beard had always been worn by the eldest son. How well she could recall his deep and precise voice drawling, "After all, honey, what's the difference? When we go abroad, 'tis you, not me, the people regard—as well they should."

Her slender, rather long neck straightened, and her head swung quickly like that of a wild duck startled while feeding. Did certain soft scraping sounds indicate that Master Robbie once again was attempting to scale the stairs? At least a hundred times she'd warned him against such ambitions but in matters like this Robbie undoubtedly had inherited much of his father's persistent and adventurous nature.

Keeping one ear cocked, Sylvia inspected her red-bordered supper napkins. Certainly another set must soon be bought. Even pin-poor folks such as she and Irad could not make out with less than a dozen; and to reflect that back home at Beau Rivage a week's wash never included less than a hundred serviettes!

Dear! Dear! There she went again. Really, she must train herself not— A series of thuds was followed first by a scraping sound, then by a choked scream which set tiny hairs to squirming on the nape of Sylvia's neck. She leaped up, sent the laundry flying all about. From the head of the staircase she forced herself to look down, and in breathless anguish beheld Sam's son sprawled at the foot of the stairs and yelling like a bluejay picked alive. Skirts frothing and billowing, Sylvia sped below. Praise the Merciful Saviour, he proved unhurt—although thoroughly outraged.

"Oh-h, you bad, sweet little demon!" she gasped, bestowing an angry kiss. "What kind of care will your daddy think I've given you if he finds you all black and blue?"

She rocked the child briefly, wondered, "Indeed, how *will* he think of me? Odd, I've not the remotest idea. Has he forgotten poor, dear Janet and her tragic death? Maybe. Two years is really a very long time." Sylvia's handkerchief appeared, mopped the baby's eyes and shiny button of a nose. "Of course, at Beau Ridgely's ball Sam did dance with me more than anyone else and, surely, he held me a trifle tighter when we were waltzing than he needed to— Or did he?"

Again, there was that occasion down in Norfolk when they all had been visiting the elder Seymours. Sam had seemed very pleased about trapping her under the mistletoe. To this moment she could re-experience her reaction, the unprecedented, indescribably delicious pressure of his lips. The caress had been perfectly innocent of course; only it had so chanced that she and Sam had come down to welcome overprompt guests so there had been no one else about— except Sam's mother.

"Hum," she dryly observed. " 'Pears to me like you're exchanging greetings for at least three years to come!"

Even now at the recollection of that cool voice from the pantry she flushed a little, but back in 1858 she'd gone crimson from her slippers all the way to her earrings and Sam had looked guilty as a schoolboy surprised at a cookie jar.

Absent-mindedly, Sylvia's finger tips gently caressed that wonderfully soft and always slightly damp hollow at the base of Robbie's skull. Yes, it had been a real joy to care for Sam's son; especially since the Lord in His mercy hadn't seen fit to bless Irad and her with issue. Why hadn't they had children? They had tried hard enough and really loved one another with deep devotion. Though he'd never mentioned the subject, she sensed Irad to be deeply troubled over this failure.

Once more, her roving thoughts returned to Robbie's mother who had survived Robbie's advent by less than a week before the dreaded childbed fever had slipped her from delirium into Eternity. A good thing that Sam's orders for the U.S.S. *Crusader* had arrived so promptly after the funeral. How well had Sam recovered? Was he seeking female companionship when ashore?

"He's taking his loss mighty hard. So far as any of us know, he's not glanced twice on any girl," Captain Maffitt aboard the *Crusader* had written Irad from Port of Spain. How had he put it in his quaint way? "Your brother is laboring like a modern Sisyphus, ever-toiling to thrust the rock of his Grief over the hilltop of Forgetfulness and always failing."

But that had been written nearly a year ago. Dear, sparkling Janet. How very like their Southern counterparts were the old, established New England families. To her deep surprise, Sylvia'd come to learn that manners, connections and traditions counted for quite as much in Portsmouth and Boston as in Charleston or Savannah. How quietly controlled and sure of herself Janet had been, but, merciful Heavens, how energetic!

Sylvia carried the boy back to the kitchen. There Melissa, all the while mumbling to herself, was making early preparations for supper.

"Aunt Meliss', just you mind Master Robbie and see he doesn't get out of here; I simply must finish sorting the laundry."

Purplish-blue gums and a few yellowed teeth glistened briefly in the light of a battered coal-oil lamp. " 'Deed Ah will, Miss Sylvia, but dat boy he got more laigs and travel faster'n any spiduh!" She hesitated. "Miss Sylvia, dat no-good butcher boy, he ent fotched Misto Irad's po'k chops."

"Oh dear, how vexing! And these days Mr. Irad wants his supper at six sharp!" The broad gold wedding band flashed when Sylvia passed an agitated hand over the smooth convexity of her forehead. "Well, if they aren't here in twenty minutes I—I guess I'll have to go get them." Angrily she lifted her skirts preparatory to climbing those wretchedly precipitous stairs; the idea of Lucius Magoffin's daughter running errands like a common mechanic's wife! Why had she ever let Irad talk her into refusing Pa's generous dowry? She must have been out of her mind.

"Misto Irad he do wuk mighty late nowadays," grumbled Melissa. "He keep it up, he gwine into a dee-cline."

"Sometimes I wonder if he knows I'm here at all," Sylvia murmured. "Oh, a plague take all ships, builders and their draughting offices!"

Sylvia, climbing the stairs, reckoned she wouldn't ever learn to become an efficient housekeeper—she simply couldn't manage without more servants. How could she be expected to? Until she'd married and come to Baltimore, Lucius Magoffin's daughter had never so much as had to pick up a dropped fan. In guilty haste, she assured herself that she'd never regret being wedded to Irad Seymour; of course not. For all that he was visionary and at the same time deeply practical, Irad was gentle, considerate and descended from a fine old Virginia family—now all but extinct through devoted service in too many wars. When she got Irad briefly to forget his eternal labors at Mr. Reeder's draughting office and dress up a little, he could, for so young a man—he was barely thirty—look positively distinguished.

Once, to her surprise, Sally Sasscer had fluttered: "My, Sylvia, maybe you haven't noticed it but yo' Irad's not only handsome but he—he's *noble* lookin'!" Sally wasn't wrong. Irad had a fine and thoughtful forehead, his mouth was even and determined—and the neat way his small, crisp ears laid flat against his head!

When, deliberately, she returned upstairs the fourth tread squeaked as usual. Beyond a ragged fringe of icicles dripping pallidly from the hall window frame darkness was settling in, early even for March. How could she have been such a great ninny as to imagine that Baltimore and Savannah enjoyed similar climates? Br-r. Right now, out in Caroline Street, dirty, well-trampled snow lay four inches deep.

Could three whole years really have elapsed since Irad had brought her to live in Maryland? Of course time went quickly when one was happy and liked one's surroundings as well as she liked Baltimore. With a population of two hundred and twelve thousand whites and over twenty-eight thousand blacks—of which only two thousand, two hundred and seventy were slaves—the Monumental City somehow had remained gracious, courteous and tolerant; a Southern metropolis and the biggest city in the South. For one thing, the summer fevers were less intense than at home but, heavenly days, how much it cost to run even a little house here!

Once more irritation clouded Sylvia's sherry-gold eyes. In some way, somehow, she must persuade Irad to modify his quixotic notions about their living on his earnings alone—or trying to. What a difference there would be if only she could use a little of that handsome dowry Papa had settled upon her. Why, in clinging to his convictions Irad was causing her to do servants' work, to pinch and scrape like a newly arrived immigrant.

She knew from whence had come that stubborn Yankee pride; from his mother, who had been Amanda Ashton of Boston. It was best not to allow her thoughts to dwell on her mother-in-law, Sylvia decided. Forthright, conscientious and impartially devoted to her three sons, Amanda Ashton Seymour would never become a person lightly to be considered.

She glanced at a tiny German silver watch secured by a chain about her neck. Although such were not uncommon here, it had been one of the first ever to have been seen in Savannah. Drat! Still no butcher's boy. Well, after ten minutes, she reckoned, she'd have to hurry through the freezing slush around to Helmholtz & Heimer's butcher shop on Pratt Street.

Fighting down a rising resentment, Sylvia closed her linen chest and repaired to the chamber she and Irad had dignified with the title of guest room. It was barely large enough to accommodate a trundle cot, a washstand and the smallest of imaginable wardrobes. On the bed lay that bolt of shimmering pale pink and gray silk from which the hired seamstress would fashion her a ball gown.

What wonderful luck to have this new gown in which to welcome Samuel home! Surely she'd see that it got finished in a big hurry. Her thoughts raced on—yes, she'd speak to Sally Sasscer and get Sam an invitation to Mr. Winans' cotillion. Moreover, she didn't give a hoot whether or not Irad were in the midst of designing some new and wonderful contrivance for the *Martha Washington*, that silly iron steamship Mr. Reeder was building.

Suddenly she beamed across the chilly little guest room, pictured herself making a grand entrance with Irad on one side and big, ruddy-faced Sam on the other. After all, the Seymours in Norfolk and the Magoffins of Savannah were far from social nonentities. Besides, if Irad intended ever to become a really successful businessman in Baltimore, it was only intelligent to establish proper and useful social connections. Everyone did. It was downright disgraceful that thus far Irad had failed to join even one of several gentleman's clubs, and not for want of invitations. True, he had become a member of the Mount Vernon Volunteer Hook and Ladder Fire Company, by far the most socially desirable of all the Fire Companies, but he'd joined merely to fulfill a sense of civic obligation.

Why, only last month Mr. Jerome Bonaparte himself had hinted that Irad would be welcomed into membership at the Maryland Club. Johnny Coulston declared that, although fairly new, this club already numbered among its members the very cream of Baltimore's bankers, landed gentry and genteel drinkers.

An impatient knocking sounded, this time at the side door. Praise Glory, the chops had been delivered! A sigh, eloquent of relief, lifted the gold and onyx brooch between Sylvia's erect and beautifully proportioned breasts. Now supper should be well out of the way before Mrs. Adams' seamstress would appear.

Even as she shook free a length of the silk to hold for inspection in a looking glass, Sylvia paused. Somewhere down Caroline Street music of a sort was being played; but there was what sounded like shouting, also. Soon she could distinguish dozens of hoarse voices bawling out stanza after stanza of "Dixie's Land"—that new tune so intensely popular throughout the Cotton States.

"Oh dear," she thought, "I hope there won't be trouble again. Those silly fellows ought to know that this whole upper end of Caroline Street is almost solidly pro-Union."

II

THE IRON WORKS

ON THE STOCKS of Reeder's Iron Works where the *Martha Washington* was taking shape the rhythmic clanging of sledge hammers driving home dully glowing rivets suddenly faltered, then ceased entirely. Presently the clatter and rasp of hammers and saws at work on the hull of a river steamer faded as shipwrights and joiners straightened to peer at the dirty gray water of Baltimore harbor.

The men composing Mr. Charles Reeder's draughting force looked up from their drawing boards, then stretched aching shoulders and backs, peered through a double rank of iron ribs thrusting stark and black against a yellow-gray sky.

Out yonder a gray-hulled side-wheel steamer was, with a yeasty thresh of her paddles, setting off down Patapsco channel toward Locust Point. Not until she reached Chesapeake Bay would she begin to set her sails. Behind the passenger ship's red and black funnel exploded a white bombshell of steam. An instant later came the prolonged scream of her steam trumpet sounding a valedictory blast. The *City of Kingston* was clearing for Europe and wanted all the waterfront to know it.

"She'll be for Liverpool or London," announced one of the draughtsmen.

"How can you tell?"

"By the British Jack at her forepeak."

Gradually, the beat of the steam packet's paddles quickened their rhythm and her lozenge-shaped walking beam tipped more rapidly, sending her smartly on a devious course through anchored shipping. She passed in rapid succession a big Brazilian barque, a shabby coasting schooner just arrived from Pensacola and, further out, a big British steam frigate, H.B.M.S. *Gladiator*, in to coal and let her crew ashore for some lusty doings along Baltimore's brawling, bawdy waterfront.

"Yon's a fine ship," observed the first speaker, knuckling eyes rendered weary by the rapidly failing light, "even if Fardy and Brothers did build her."

"A fine ship's a fine ship, no matter who built her," observed a short, reddish-haired individual whose small but remarkably piercing blue eyes seemed ever to view something at a great distance. "She's new and she's fast, sure enough, but within ten years she'll be conceded obsolete."

The tallest of the four designers picked up his bow pen, recharged it. "And all because she's not a screw ship, eh, Lachlan?"

Brunton, the red-haired draughtsman nodded soberly. "Aye. You numskulls may twit me from now till Doomsday, but sometime over here ye'll perceive the multiple advantages of propellers over paddles." From beneath thick sandy-red brows, he glared about. "More especially, aiblins ye've twin propellers—"

" '—Now aiblins ye've twin propellers!' " Mimicking the Scot, McMurray the senior draughtman rubbed a bald, gray-looking scalp, then stamped over to drop a few chunks of firewood into a pot-bellied stove. "Lord God, Lachlan, pray spare us another dissertation."

"Aye, that I will, for 'tis like throwing dice wi' a blind idiot to try to talk sense into ye."

"Brunton's right, though, Mr. McMurray." A trifle defiantly Irad Seymour shot black, cambric false sleeves protecting his cuffs. "Suppose you designed a pair of screws set close together—"

"Tuts! Not close, mon; they must be set well apar-r-t!" broke in Brunton. In his earnestness, the Scotch burr, ever-present in his speech, became more pronounced. "Twin screws musna be set too close, they'll lose traction, else. I tell ye they'll work stronger in water disturbed each by the other. 'Twas proved at James Watt's Yard two . . ."

The door banged open and gold-rimmed spectacles glimmered in the aperture. A sandy-haired, sharp-nosed individual appeared, watery blue eyes hard.

"Damme, Mr. Brunton! If you devoted half as much time to drawing as lecturing, you'd come nearer earning your wages. God damn it, those designs for the *Flora's* engine seats should have been completed a week since! And the rest of you, loafing as usual. Why in God's name Mr. Reeder keeps you on, escapes me!"

Mr. Nelson Swanson, Chief of Reeder's Moulding and Finishing Department, and a petty tyrant if ever there was one, paused, glowering in the draughting room door, watched the draughtsmen hurriedly retrieve pens and triangles.

"Mark my words! I'll have less chatter and more attention to duty in this department." He hawked and spat messily into a tin spittoon below Irad's desk. "Or else there'll be certain people, now present, hunting a situation."

The door banged shut.

Irad said, " 'Twould seem our dear Mr. Swanson prefers being disliked to being ignored."

"Ah, to hell with that old fool," growled McMurray. "Some day I'm going to kick his butt up on a level with his shoulders."

Even while his ink-blotched fingers closed over the bow pen, Irad bestowed a penetrating glance on the keel of a wooden hull just commencing to take shape on Reeder's Number Two ways. Hmm. Why had no work whatever been done on the *Comet* for two days? Could Mr. Reeder still be debating whether an out-and-out steam vessel should be designed with a blunt bow? Such a stem, Irad Seymour had argued, was more efficient in a steamship, pure and simple being less calculated to catch the water in an effort to turn at speed. Were she also to carry sail, that would be another matter and the conventional clipper bow more suitable.

Absently, he passed a square but not unsensitive hand over that short-trimmed yellow beard he wore in deference to family tradition. Sylvia hated it, but luckily, Mr. Reeder, like most merchants of the town, deemed such an hirsute adornment evidence of respectability and maturity.

"Did I go too far in conference yesterday?" Irad pondered. Certainly Lachlan Brunton had been too blunt, too impatient in advancing his ideas. Lord above! Mr. Reeder's chin whiskers had fairly quivered with outrage at being so plainly warned he was far behind the times —that his newest engines included certain principles long since abandoned in English and Scottish shipyards.

"Get out of my sight, you damned insolent Scotch braggart!" the owner had roared. "For all that you may have idled about some fine foreign shipyards I'll not have you preach to me of such foreign poppycock as variable pitch propellers! Out of my sight, you—you impudent jackanapes. You've tried my patience too far."

"Ye're master here, so I'll take my leave, sir-r. But some day, and soon, ye'll regret not having even conseedered my notions." And the bandy-legged little Scot had stalked out stiff-legged, like a dog on the verge of a fight.

Once Mr. Swanson's tread had faded along the hallway's gritty floorboards, old Mr. McMurray sighed, looked anxiously about. "Come lads, let's get cracking on the *Martha Washington's* cabin plan. By tomorrow the master carpenters will be yelling."

While using the tip of a goose quill to recharge his bow pen with India ink, Irad noted that today the light was fading faster than usual. Perhaps it was just as well. Try as he would, he simply couldn't concentrate on the *Martha Washington's* berth deck, a particularly uninspired piece of mechanical drawing.

There could be no denying Mr. Reeder's stubborn conservatism although he'd built his great reputation on boldly original hull designs and ships' engines. Small wonder John T. Fardy & Brothers' Shipyard and Marine Railway were now collaring the cream of new shipbuilding contracts.

How exasperating it was to survey from this point of vantage the Messers Fardys' busy yard situated only a few hundred feet distant at the foot of Montgomery Street and boasting a fine water frontage. Right now, Fardys', although comparative newcomers in the industry, were constructing no less than three good-sized vessels.

Irad narrowed deep-set gray eyes and frowned a little. By God, it appeared that that nearest ship, an iron one, was going to follow radically new lines. Yes, sir, eventually she would become a frank, if unlovely, departure from those graceful, sharp-stemmed and deep-hulled clipper types such as Baltimore shipwrights had been building for near a hundred years, to the envy and admiration of all the maritime Powers.

Reeder's, of course, was much the senior firm. Perhaps that was what was wrong, if, indeed, anything really was wrong. These new departures had yet to prove their worth—in America at least. Besides, Charles Reeder always had devoted his chiefest attention to the construction of fine marine engines; in that respect there wasn't any doubt that he was years ahead of Fardy.

Why, then, wouldn't Mr. Reeder consent to more than glance at young Lachlan Brunton's excellent drawings? Why had he not even considered Brunton's modifications of a Griffith propeller, for all that it had been proved that such a screw easily could be feathered while a ship was under way? This lack of propeller drag, constituted an invaluable advantage for any vessel expected to cruise long distances under sail alone—as a vast majority of modern ocean-going steamships still must.

Somewhere across the muddied busy waters of Baltimore harbor a steam whistle sputtered, gagged, but finally emitted a deep wail announcing through a cold gray gloom that five o'clock had been reached. Skilled workers finished their immediate task, as became true artisans, before lighting pipes and locking their tool boxes but the common laborers immediately quit work, stacked implements and went shuffling off towards the shipyard gate, Philpott Street and their sordid dwellings beyond City Dock.

Brunton corked his ink bottle, went over to warm his hands at the stove. "Well, lads," said he, blue eyes bright in the ruddy square formed by his features, "another day, another dollar and a domned cold walk for us all."

After removing the cambric over-sleeves Irad carefully cleaned his drawing instruments and locked them away; they were of fine French manufacture and almighty expensive. Sylvia had been a bit difficult about the extra money they'd cost, but then, she couldn't be expected to understand the importance of such an investment.

Sniffling because of a week-old cold, McMurray wound a two-yard-long muffler about his stringy, yellow-brown neck, then pulled a plug of tobacco from his pants pocket and wrenched off a generous chew. "See that you're all punctual tomorrow. That nosy bastard Swanson's aching to make trouble for this department. Thinks he's a small Caesar, I reckon."

All up and down the corridor and on the floor below, voices sounded, doors banged and feet descended clumping down broad stairs leading to the well-trampled mud and cobbles of Philpott Street.

Irad grinned at the young Scot. He liked him for his energy and independent ways as much as for his superior knowledge of steam engineering. "Care to take a lowly pork chop with my wife and me, or is your boarding house serving terrapin tonight?"

Brunton succeeded in struggling into a long brown coat showing neat patches at either elbow. It was much too big for him. "Aye, the Widow Gahagan has promised a tureenful o' that luscious creetur." He pulled on a well-worn tam-o'-shanter. "Somehow, I canna seem to get my fill."

"When you've been in Maryland another six months you'll flinch from it," Irad predicted. "Like canvasback duck, terrapin's so very rich—and cheap to come by. You'll not change your mind?"

"Alas," the Scot sighed. " 'Tis a trig little home and a bonny sweet wife ye have, but I've an appointment wi' an engineer fresh come over from the Old Country. He's recently come from Brunel's employ," Lachlan explained in some excitement. "We're discussing the proper thrust of propeller blades."

"Brunel?"

"Aye. Isambard Kingdom Brunel."

"What a name! Who's he?"

"Who *is* he?" Irregular but sound teeth shone beneath Brunton's modest red mustache. "Mon, he is only the greatest shipbuilder in all Europe. 'Tis his firm built the *Great Eastern*."

"Of course. I forgot. He's also the one who designed the famous *Great Britain*." Seymour's gray eyes lit. "Am I wrong, or doesn't he favor double bottoms for steamships?"

Brunton nodded. "Aye. I'll tell ye more, come tomorrow."

"Wish to God I could join you later."

"Why don't you?"

"My wife is left too much alone. We're both strangers here, you know, and without much money. So as usual we'll play cribbage I expect." He smiled. "Besides, it's a poor night to be abroad." He removed a gray cape from its peg and pulled on a brown felt cap.

"McMurray give you the draughting room key?"

"Aye. We'll leave it by the porter's lodge."

Brunton had just locked the door when a gangling youth whose pale face was splotched with enormous yellow freckles, came running down the corridor. "Oh, Mr. Seymour, thank goodness you're still here; I was 'feared you might have gone."

"What is it, Tommy?"

"It's Mr. Reeder. He wants a word with you."

A low whistle of alarm escaped Brunton while a sickening feeling of nausea welled up to sour Irad's mouth. So Mr. Reeder wanted him? Then the silly old goat had taken offense after all.

Brunton's lean shoulders squared themselves under the well-worn fabric of his coat and he thrust out a craggy jaw. "Speak up, Tommy. Doesn't Mr. Reeder want to see me, also?"

The errand boy looked his surprise. "Why, no, Mr. Brunton, 'twas only Mr. Seymour the Boss sent for."

"That's odd, indeed. Well, Irad," Brunton offered a consoling hand and look. "Stick by yer guns, man; yer right, and ye know it."

He was about to be fired, no doubt of that, and work so almighty hard to come by at this time of year. The worst of it was that, on twenty dollars a week, Sylvia and he had not been able to put aside anything to cover such an emergency. They'd tried, but it just wasn't possible if they were to exist in common decency.

After Brunton had departed, Irad stood quite still, trying to readjust, to see what could be done. While trying to regain mental equilibrium, he was thinking, "If worse comes to worst, Sylvia can always go home while I hunt employment. Probably she'll be glad to see her folks. Maybe Fardys' would take me on? No. They've never employed any of Reeder's cast-offs. What about Skinner and Sons, or maybe Moses Sanders' yard? Reckon they're too small. Of course I could ask Pa for a loan to tide me over, but I'm damned if I will. A retired naval officer doesn't draw much on half pay and Mother's entitled to all the comforts he can give her in her old age."

Cap in hand and carrying his cloak over one arm, Captain Felix Seymour's eldest son paused long enough to draw a deep breath before rapping at a door marked "Charles Reeder" in heavy Gothic gold letters. Odd, he hadn't experienced a similar sensation since that awful day when, down in Norfolk, the whole family, Mother included, had been summoned into the Captain's study to learn that Irad's eyesight had proved so deficient that the Board of Admissions at the Naval Academy could under no conditions consider him as candidate for the grade of midshipman.

Mr. Reeder sat ensconced behind a wide, green-topped desk, his heavily lined features and spade beard gilded by the warm orange glow of two coal-oil table lamps. That one of those lamps needed trimming was Irad's subconscious realization.

Charles Reeder was a very large man but, curiously enough, no one about the shipyard ever thought of him as such, because, even in his latter years, he was so well proportioned. The owner's nose was bold and big while his eyes peered out from cavernous sockets overshadowed by bushy gray brows. His squarish beard was almost pure white and betrayed no tobacco juice stains. Square-lensed golden spectacles attempted, but failed, to soften the severity of his aspect.

Breathing quickly, Irad Seymour halted in the exact center of a handsome Turkey red carpet. How pleasant it was in this atmosphere redolent of good seegars, furniture polish and slightly moldy leather. Coal gas, escaping from a small and highly ornamental stove, only faintly tinctured the atmosphere.

At various levels about the embossed brown and gold wallpaper were hung prints of various vessels which Reeder's had either built or had furnished with engines. Among these Seymour recognized the famous *Natchez*, largest merchant steamer thus far constructed in the United States; the coasters *Tennessee*, *Louisiana*, *Pocahontas* and perhaps half a dozen bay or river craft.

For several moments the owner remained silent, tilted back in his swivel chair and drew hard on a seegar. He made no gesture towards a chair.

"At least," Irad reflected, "the old goat has decency enough to discharge me by word of mouth. Well, let's have it."

"You wished to see me, sir?" He stood straighter and his fingers cramped down on the brim of his brown cap.

"Why else would I have sent for you?" Mr. Reeder paused, tugged gently at his beard then, with deliberate accuracy, pitched his seegar's well-gnawed stump into a tall and capacious brass spittoon.

"You're Virginian?"

"Yes, sir. My family has always served in the Navy," he stated not without pride. "My father's grandfather, Secundus Seymour, fought in the Revolution aboard the *Ranger*."

"Ha-hrumpf. I see."

Irad's stiff posture relaxed a trifle. Why should Reeder go into all this if he were only to be given the sack?

"Indeed? Why are you not in the Naval Service?"

Irad pulled out thick, steel-rimmed lenses. "Without these, sir, I can't see to read, let alone draw."

"Oh. Well, now, that's too bad—in some ways. Indeed it is." Reeder arranged a steeple from powerful pink forefingers and, from under shaggy tufts of brows, sat peering up at the tall figure before him. "Mr. Seymour, up until today, I've cared not a fig concerning the political opinions of my employees. Howsomever, I allow the time's come when I must know where they stand regarding this matter of Secession. You've read this afternoon's edition of *The Exchange?*" Reeder tapped a newspaper lying at his elbow.

"No, sir."

"Well, here's a report that this insane Southern Confederacy intends to build a navy—sometime. This is a very serious matter for anybody concerned in shipping." He picked up the newspaper, re-read the article, then said, "Mr. Seymour, the defection of Mississippi didn't much affect the commerce of this nation, even less did the rebellion of Florida and Alabama, but when Georgia joined Carolina and the rest, well, our entire coastal shipbuilding business faced ruin.

Still, I wasn't too upset, although nigh two-thirds of the vessels we construct are coasters."

"Yes, sir. I am aware of that," said Irad quietly. "Only a handful of seagoing vessels are owned and operated by firms located south of Wilmington, North Carolina."

"Precious few," Reeder agreed, "and that's a fact. But you miss my point. What alarms me is the prospect of the Rebels building men-of-war. So long as our Federal Government controls the sea I don't figure this Secession nonsense will amount to much."

Irad checked a hot reply barely in time, only inquired, "How much of a fleet do they expect to build, sir?"

The shipbuilder's heavy brows merged into a single silver line while he considered the newspaper for a second time.

"It says here that this so-called Confederate Congress is equipping United States vessels captured in Southern waters, about ten of them, for action against the Union. They're small, unimportant craft so near as I can make out, but that isn't the point—it's the principle behind this small effort." He paused, absently plucked a fresh seegar from a copper jar before him. "They also plan to purchase, or to build, ten more craft suitable for coastal gunboats, five of five hundred tons, five of a thousand. But here's what's really grave. Their naval Commissioners also announce plans to build big, sea-going men-of-war in England! Mark you, Mr. Seymour, I allow we'll all have call to remember this fifteenth of March, 1861!"

Gradually the weight of his coat lowered Irad's left arm. The dull and monotonous clanging of a not-distant locomotive bell penetrated the office. He was thinking furiously, attempting to deduce what old Reeder might really be driving at.

The master shipbuilder's big gray head jerked suddenly upwards.

"Young man, are you, or are you not, a Southern sympathizer?" he barked. "Answer me plainly."

Irad flushed, drew a deep breath. "To give you an honest answer, Mr. Reeder, I really don't know. Since the trouble began last December, I've tried not to make any decision."

"Why? You're Virginian aren't you?"

"I am, sir, and always will be, but Navy folk are trained to avoid politics and partisanship." The tall figure on the Turkey carpet stiffened perceptibly. "Such are for statesmen and newspaper writers."

"And what do your friends say?"

"We have few friends. Mrs. Seymour and I are new in Baltimore." He summoned a wry smile. "My salary, sir, scarcely puts me in a position to take an active place in society."

"Nevertheless, you are a Southerner?" Reeder insisted, lowering his head as if to level invisible horns.

Irad straightened again. "—And proud of it, sir. However, I assure you that my wife and I have adopted no position in this matter of Secession and will not, until there's no alternative. In fact, from the little I've learned through travels in the North and abroad, I wonder if any nation founded upon a purely agricultural economy—"

"—And slavery, can in all reason, succeed?" Mr. Reeder suggested softly. "Um. You've an uncommon level head, Seymour, or so it appears."

Lost in thought, oblivious to the figure isolated and uncomfortable in the center of his office, Charles Reeder revolved his seegar between powerful, blunt fingers.

"So far so good, but, Seymour, suppose this crisis resolves into an armed conflict, which side would you then favor?"

Well, here it came, that question someone was bound to ask. He spoke carefully, looked Mr. Reeder squarely in the eye. "If my State does not secede, sir, I will undoubtedly support the Union side. Too many of my family have fallen in its defense for me not to cherish it." He knew he was sounding dramatic, but he didn't give a damn. Two of his uncles had perished at sea during the Mexican War, and his great-grandfather had died aboard the U.S.S. Essex—to recall only his nearest relatives—and there were at least half a dozen others of near kin whom the Navy Department regretfully had reported as killed in action.

"Then, I take it I can count you for a Union sympathizer?"

"You may, sir," came the tall yellow-bearded figure's grave assurance, "so long as Virginia remains within the Union." It wasn't what Irad really had intended to say, but there it was.

"Good, good. Your Virginians are too level-headed to heed the clap-trap rantings of Cotton State agitators."

The older man stood up and, relighting his seegar at a lamp chimney, sent aromatic cloudlets of smoke whirling across the comfortable big office.

"Yes, Virginia will remain loyal, all right. For all the flag-waving down in Richmond and Norfolk the politicians there are damn' well aware of which side their bread's buttered on."

Charles Reeder arose, flicked a splash of seegar ash from the satin lapel of his frock coat. "Well, now that I'm satisfied about your good sense, I've something more to say to you."

From behind the desk Reeder marched up to his tall young employee. "Seymour, I'll confess that after yesterday's conference I deemed you both impudent and insubordinate; on reviewing your comments, however, I—well, I've decided that your want of tact was prompted through over-earnestness, rather than intended disrespect."

Like a discarded overcoat drenched by a cold winter rain, apprehension fell from Irad's being.

"Why, why, thank you, sir! I fear I was precipitate. Does this mean, Mr. Reeder, that you have taken favorable view of my suggestions concerning the Comet's design?"

Reeder marched to a window, stood staring down upon an irregular double line of drays, carts and wagons clumping and rattling homewards from docks and shipyards. Without turning about he said in a low voice, "For over thirty years, Mr. Seymour, I've toiled, and toiled mighty hard, to build up this concern. I started here in 1828 as boy run away from home—Newburyport. But that's of no matter; what does count is that I founded my chief reputation on excellent marine construction."

Irad saw him rubbing hairy hands slowly behind his back.

"I allow most shipping men along this coast will agree that I've turned out some mighty fine hulls, as sweet, sound and clean as any built this side of the Atlantic. On the other hand, as you so forcefully pointed out yesterday," he grunted, "maybe I don't understand the fashioning of hulls for true steamships not designed to carry canvas. I reckon maybe they do over at Fardys' and in Europe. I don't like being out-distanced; by them, especially." He nodded in the direction of the Fardys' yard above which rows of cranes, scaffolds and gantries could be seen in stark relief against dark, low-scudding clouds.

The big shipmaster suddenly faced about, buried hands under his coattails. "You mayn't think it, Seymour, but I'm not too old to learn, not yet. I'd hate to see my fine engines wasted in the wrong kind of hull."

Irad made bold to place cap and cape on a cane-bottomed chair. His arm was aching, but his imagination was alight. How could he have so misjudged this shrewd old man?

"No made-over clipper ship can ever be transformed into an efficient steam vessel, can she now?" Reeder demanded.

"No, sir. The cleverest shipwright in existence can't add twenty or thirty feet to a sailing ship hull without its weakening her fabric and altering the basic lines. What he gets is a sort of hermaphrodite; neither a fine sailer nor yet a successful steamer."

Reeder cocked his seegar ceilingwards. "I grant that, so—well, I am prepared to incorporate your suggestions concerning the *Comet*. After all, she's wooden and of but six hundred tons burden. If your near-flat-bottom, blunt-bow theory turns out addled, I'll buy her myself and sell her for a barge, for I'll be eternally damned before I'll turn over an inferior craft to the Merchants and Miners Line, or to anyone else, for that matter."

A warming uprush of gratitude flooded Irad's being. To know, to believe, at least, that those designs and calculations so doggedly arrived at during endless lamplit hours were about to achieve reality!

Impulsively, he grabbed Mr. Reeder's hand. "Thank you, thank you, sir! You won't regret this. I swear you won't." His deep voice swelled until the whole office resounded. "The most efficient steamship hull ever built in Baltimore will be launched from your yard next summer. You see, sir, I've been experimenting on a model and can prove that the sheer of the stem—"

Traces of a smile twitched at the master shipbuilder's mouth; to witness such enthusiasm made him feel as he had after his successful launching of the *Natchez*. "—Save the details for later. I hear my carriage below. I must be getting home."

Irad drew a deep breath. "Mr. Reeder, sir?"

"Well?"

"Er, would I appear presumptuous and ungrateful if I were to ask for a slight—"

"—Increase?" Charles Reeder actually chuckled. "Rest easy, young fellow. My chief bookkeeper's already been instructed to pay you thirty-five dollars a week."

Thirty-five dollars? Thirty-five a week! Glory *hallelujah!* How

Sylvia's smooth pink cheeks would glow, and then he would watch those lovely lips form that slow and wonderfully radiant smile so peculiarly hers. Of late it had not been much in evidence. What was Mr. Reeder saying?

"I expect finished drawings within the week." He snorted softly. "You'll find it easier to work since I'm firing that Scotch crackpot. Swanson says he's forever distracting the men in my draughting room."

Irad's smile faded.

"You—you're not really letting Lachlan Brunton go, are you, sir?"

"That I am. The fellow's a hopeless theorist—a lunatic!"

"But, sir, Brunton's theories are sound, sound as a dollar! He trained under the finest engineers at Laird's and—"

Charles Reeder's stubby fingers snapped loud as a pistol's report. "That will do, Mr. Seymour. I've decided to let him out. Don't try my good nature too far. Good night."

III

FREE FOR ALL

IN EASTERN AVENUE, torch in hand, a lamplighter was climbing a short ladder. As Irad Seymour hurried by, the yellow-white glare of a newly installed gas street light sprang into being and sparkled on icicle-draped near-by eaves, drew glittering reflections from store windows. Because of the delay occasioned by his interview with Mr. Reeder, Irad Seymour found the narrow, badly cobbled streets leading up from the waterfront to be nowhere nearly as crowded as usual. Still, there were a good many laborers, mechanics and clerks plodding homewards and attempting to maintain balance over icy patches of sidewalk.

Hands plunged deep in pockets, Irad strode along smiling. By Jiminy! Sylvia would be tickled. Yes sir, he reckoned they'd celebrate his luck with sherry at the General Wayne Inn. The shrilling of a locomotive's whistle in the distance sounded petulant, frail as an invalid's cry.

Presently he halted before a set of rails to permit the passage of a dingy yellow railway car drawn by a span of four horses. The steaming teams were dragging, at a snail's pace, the coach, passengers and all, across the heart of Baltimore from the Philadelphia, Wilmington & Baltimore Railroad Station to the Baltimore & Ohio's handsome new Mount Clare Station.

While striding along, ideas raced about Irad's brain like pups with cans tied to their tails. Should the *Comet* be built with a well for her propeller? The notion seemed sound. Behind his spectacles, Irad's gray eyes narrowed. Why should Brunton be so unalterably opposed to a deep propeller well? Was his claim well founded that the drag of a hull created an area of dead water in which the screw must operate?

He leaped over a gutter filled to overflowing by horse manure, garbage and half-melted snow. Would the theory of a retractable screw prove as practicable in a large vessel as in the river and channel types designed in England? He didn't think so while mentally computing stresses resultant from a worm gear transmission.

"Damned shame about Brunton," he mused. "But I'll not lose track of him—Reeder or no Reeder." Despite his lamentable lack of tact Brunton was a young engineer with excellent training and experience in the world-famous shipyards of Laird's and also of Messrs. Ravenhill & Hodgson. Maybe he and Lachlan might work out some kind of an association? He to plan the hulls, Brunton to design and build the engines? When it came to marine engineering the Scots were supposed to be unbeatable, provided you hadn't seen what bold new principles they were adopting at the Brooklyn Novelty Iron Works and Tom Rowland's Iron Works up in New York.

A brace of soldiers, probably on furlough from Fort McHenry, now invisible across the harbor, came weaving by, boisterous with drink. The capes of their dark blue greatcoats were turned back to reveal bright red revers. One of them was bawling:

> "A hundred years on the Eastern Shore
> O, yes O
> A hundred years is a very long time
> A hundred years ago."

He overtook an old Negro balancing a well-wrapped basket on his head; succulent odors of roast pork trailed after him like an aromatic comet's tail. At the thought that Sylvia had promised pork chops for supper, he brightened. Let those who would relish poultry, lamb or beef; nobody could even approach Melissa's inscrutable skill with any kind of hog meat.

His stride quickened. What a glorious, what a memorable evening!

Caroline Street was not important enough to boast gas illumination—only dim old kerosene lamps near fifty years old. Lights shining from dwelling windows, however, assisted in dispelling treacherous shadows. Discordant and raucous band music began to sound down the street—or just off it. Irad decided that, most likely, it was just another one of those three- or four-man German brass bands which of late had taken to pumping out tunes on convenient street corners.

"Damn!" His foot had slipped through a hole in the slippery wooden sidewalk and cold water commenced trickling into his shoe. He reckoned he really must buy a new pair; these wouldn't stand more patching.

A ragged newsboy came trotting up. "Thought you weren't never comin', Mr. Seymour. But I sho' saved yer a *American*—last one." His emaciated, young-old face appeared ghostly in this uncertain light. "Dunno why, but my stock's went like crab cakes at a fish fry."

"Thanks, Mortimer."

No, apparently it wasn't a band playing up the street, just a cornet and a drum.

"Why, there's a hull two pennies, sir."

"Buy a locomotive with them. Good night, Mort." Irad hurried on up Caroline Street, his smile broadening because home was almost in sight. Home? Of course it really wasn't home, just a shelter, cold, leaky, and rented. As Sylvia once had said, it was fit only for habitation by a family of indigent dwarfs. Well, Sylvia, he and little Robbie should now be able to enjoy something more suitable.

Sometime, after the *Comet's* efficient design had aroused speculation and imitation, he would rent a neat, brick house; maybe on Charles Street near Mount Royal. To be sure, Mount Royal Street lay pretty far out from the center of things, but some day Baltimore was bound to extend northwards—if the city kept on growing at its present rate.

In a few more years still he intended to build a quietly elegant residence, something like Mr. James Bartlett's, of brick and protected by a slate roof. No shingles for Irad Seymour. As a member of the Mount Vernon Volunteer Hook and Ladder Fire Company, he knew that fires were both common and disastrous in this largely wooden city.

Tucking the newspaper under his arm, he barely resisted the temptation of taking a quick nip at the corner saloon, since tonight Rafferty's sounded well patronized if one judged by an accordion's cheery wheezing and the loud laughter beating out from behind its battered doors. Long ago Sylvia firmly had declared that hard liquor would never be served in her house—had not Uncle Joel and Cousin Tom died drunkards' deaths? It was odd, Irad mused, how many men in the Deep South either drank more than was good for them or became uncompromising teetotalers.

Well, he didn't really mind, not with good whiskey costing all of a dollar a quart. Curse this mounting cost of living!

The wind, he noticed, had shifted into the northwest, which meant the coming of colder weather but at least would end this raw and penetrating chill. Um. Maybe, later tonight, he and Sylvia would drop in on Walter and Betty Abell, firm friends in all kinds of going. Besides, Walter had studied engineering with a Boston firm after graduating from Annapolis and so was well grounded in steamship design.

The old bitterness returned. Damn it. Why must he be cursed with such wretched near-sightedness that not even an Army medical officer would certify him? Granted normal vision he must by this time have become a lieutenant very senior on the promotion list. Young Sam, three years his junior, already had attained that grade. Loyally, Irad fought down an incipient jealousy which, during recent years, had soured him whenever he thought of how Sam, aided by good looks and abundant vitality, had been advanced so rapidly. As a midshipman he'd visited Europe, Africa and South America. Of course he'd been lucky, too, for during his captain's illness he'd commanded at twenty a sloop-of-war in action against Portuguese slave runners off the Bight of Benin.

Everyone in the Navy knew that Captain Felix Seymour's second son was uniformly popular both with his superiors and with his fellow officers. Down in Norfolk Captain Felix also kept ready to hand a

well-worn letter from Lieutenant Commander John N. Maffitt of the
U.S.S. *Crusader*, describing son Sam's able performance while prize
captain over the slaver *Echo*, captured August last in the Windward
Passage.

Irad quickened his gait. Poor Pa! For all that the veteran had never
complained, he must have found it mightily disappointing that only
one of his three sons had qualified to carry on the family naval tradition.

Irad's elation faded while he wondered what might recently have
chanced with his youngest brother Reynolds. None of the family had
received so much as a word since his expulsion from the University of
Virginia last autumn; a sad, miserable business! Apparently Reynolds'
trouble was attributable to much-too-consistent good luck at cards.
According to chance information he'd been seen in Savannah, working as a shipping agent.

So preoccupied was Irad Seymour that, before he realized it, he
had become entangled with a throng of men stealthily debouching
from the mouth of an alley. At first glance, he recognized them as
a party of Rip-Raps, a rowdy and lawless gang professing, for reasons
of profit only, profound sympathy for the Southern Cause. The foremost bravo, a bandy-legged, black-haired and bearded rogue, was waving on his followers while brandishing a flag of unfamiliar design;
undoubtedly a Confederate banner of which there were many variations.

A burly individual wearing an old Army tunic and a battered plug
hat surged up. Reeking of corn whiskey, he tried to thrust his arm
through Irad's. "Come along, Mister, and join in the fun. We air
going to take another crack at them nigger-lovin' Blood Tubs."

Irad pulled free. "Go on and have your fun, but leave me out. I've
no quarrel wth anyone."

"Ye'll come along," growled the leader. "We're 'way outnumbered.
Here. You'll fight all right when them Blood Tub rocks start flyin'."
Even as he thrust the butt of a broken whiffletree into Irad's hand,
two other gangsters closed in. "Don't try to run off, er we'll cream ye
good, Mister."

The Blood Tubs, Irad was aware from shipyard gossip, was another
group of waterfront hooligans, no different from these save in affecting Unionist principles. Actually, neither gang cared a hoot about

politics—but were a perpetual thorn in the side of the police. For many years they had seized on any excuse to start a riot as a prelude to pillage, mayhem and often murder. An election, a parade, a fire, or even an elaborate funeral would do.

"Come on, me Bucko, let's go," grunted the black-bearded leader. "Fer all them specs, yer big enough to be useful."

"You go to hell," snarled Irad and flung down the cudgel. "Go break your ugly heads, but let me be."

Shaggy, menacing faces closed in. Through the semi-darkness the sound of a pistol being cocked sounded crisp and ominous above a steadily increasing clamor.

"You Secesh?"

"I take no sides," Irad panted and tried to decide his chances of a break-away. This abrupt interruption to his workaday life was confusing, intolerable.

"The hell you don't, Four Eyes. Fer the next half hour yer fer States' Rights and Rebellion, see?"

A long-legged individual, the original shape of whose features had several times been altered, stung Irad's ribs with a sheath knife.

"Come on and yell for Secession else I'll spill yer guts."

Irad hesitated but an instant then common sense dictated immediate compliance. When he was handed the club again he hung on to it for a purpose. He shouted, "Hurray for Virginia and States' Rights," which seemed to satisfy this malodorous group. Two or three other belated and equally luckless householders also were impressed by Rip-Raps swarming like a dark torrent up Caroline Street.

Irad debated the feasibility of suddenly vaulting old Mrs. Howard's garden fence but found no opportunity, for, raising a series of murderous threats, curses and yells, a much larger party of Blood Tubs hurled a volley of brickbats and cudgels, then dashed from ambush amid the ruins of a burned-down building.

The thud of missiles striking wooden clapboards and a sharp jangle of breaking glass became intermingled with hoarse shouts. "Kill the dirty Rebel rats!" "Come on, Blood Tubs, tromp 'em flat!" "Here's fer you lousy Secesh bastards!"

A chunk of coal flung by a swirl of struggling men struck Irad's chin, sent his precious and expensive spectacles flying. The blow released a sense of outrage which further obscured Irad's vision in a whirling, crimson mist. In both hands he gripped the broken whiffle-tree and struck again and again in strange, savage satisfaction at any outline entering his vision. Yelps and groans coming at him through the dark argued that he had found more than a few targets.

The world degenerated into a confined area dominated by contorted brutish faces, yammering mouths and rolling eyes. Loud curses, groans and screams sounded over the dull thump of clubs landing hard, the clatter of trampling feet. Knives gave off feeble flashes under the kerosene street light. Back and forth swayed the rioters. A brickbat, shattering the nearest street light, so quieted the conflict that everyone could hear a woman screaming from a near-by window, "Murder! Po-lice! For God's sake somebody fetch the po-lice!"

An unfamiliar but strangely satisfying exhilaration surged ever more strongly through Irad's being. "Here's for you damn' hooligans!" He landed his heavy club with such savage effectiveness that the next man he hit collapsed, shuddering and silent, onto the slippery cobbles, another retreated before his onslaught, howling and draining blood over his face from a split scalp.

Then Irad tripped over a fallen figure, lost his balance and went down, instantly to become trampled by both gangs. When he managed to struggle again to his feet, his cap had vanished and his cloak was torn off just as someone armed with brass knuckles dealt him a savage glancing blow on the back of his head that made his teeth rattle.

As a result of that swipe he couldn't at once perceive that the sounds of battle were abruptly diminishing and that feet were racing off in all directions. Irad stood where he was, gasping and swaying like a drunken man, listening to a piercing shrill of police whistles which evidently had served to remind the Rip-Raps and Blood Tubs alike that "he who fights and runs away, may live to fight another day."

At any rate, Irad suddenly found himself standing like the lone survivor of a stricken battlefield, staring down upon a scattering of silent, or moaning and writhing fallen figures.

Unwisely Irad, in getting to his feet instinctively had picked up his heavy club and, to make matters worse, attempted to run.

"There goes one o' them Rip-Rap bastards!" yelled a householder, thrusting his bald head out of a second story window. " 'Twas him, the tall one what laid out three Unioners! I seen him!"

A pair of heavy-bellied Blood Tubs suddenly dashed out of the shadows and did their level best to knock Irad senseless. The draughts-man rallied, however, and lashed out so effectively that one of his assailants reeled sidewise, howling and clutching a broken arm. The other snarling horrible threats tried to close in but was checked by loud yells of "Clear out" and "Shake a leg! Coppers! Coppers!"

From the tail of his eye Irad caught a flash of brass buttons; then a squad of police wearing white belts, long blue overcoats and flat black caps, came pelting up Caroline Street.

A heavy hand closed over Irad's shoulder, jerked him about.

"Drop that club!" panted a beefy sergeant, ample red side whiskers abristle, "Yer under arrest, ye damned murderin' plug-ugly of a Reb! Won't be happy till ye've torn this town wide apart, will yez? Ah-r! No, you don't!" Irad had tried to twist free. "Keep still till the wagon comes, er I'll clout yez cold!"

The prisoner was not prepossessing in appearance. Blood from his hurt chin was dripping all over his shirt front, his jacket's collar had been ripped half off and his shoulder-long hair streaming wildly in all directions. Nevertheless he attempted to control his spasmodic breathing, to regain a measure of dignity. "Please listen to me, Officer. I swear I've taken no part in this business except to defend myself."

"Ah-h. Save that poop fer the magistrate."

More police came up hauling sullen prisoners along by the use of nippers.

A plainclothesman in stovepipe hat, appeared, notebook in hand. "This one fighting for the Rip-Raps?"

"Well, Cully," the sergeant snorted, "dast you deny you was?"

"I fought on no side," Irad panted. "I merely chanced to be in the street—on my way home—when this brawl began."

"He's a damn' liar. I seen him come up with the Rip-Raps," called the bald-headed man from above.

"Yep, he's a Rip-Rap for sure." More witnesses in aprons and shirt-sleeves began emerging from various dwellings and crowding about. "Me, I watched this tall feller fightin' from the start. He was leadin' the Seceshers!"

The detective demanded, "Who are you, anyways?"

Irad told him, his voice quivering with rage.

"You do talk mighty Southern, at that."

"But I tell you I'm no hooligan. I'm a marine architect. I live just three blocks down this street and was on my way home."

The persistent clang-clang of a gong, a loud clatter of hoofs and the rasping of iron tires over cobbles sounded from the direction of Lombard Street.

"Yah! Run like anythin'! It's the paddy wagon," shrilled a chorus of excited small boys. "Yay-y! Here comes the paddy wagon!"

No less than eight brawlers still lay limp and unresisting among the battle débris of stones, bricks and clubs. From under two of the fallen gruesome rivulets crept off over the filthy snow. Four more wounded hooligans, firmly in the clutches of blue-coated patrolmen, stood glowering and cursing one another.

Its team giving off clouds of silvery vapor, the police patrol wagon pulled up in the center of a rapidly growing crowd.

"Crummel's curse on you, get in before yer thrown. Git!" A patrolman pointed to the patrol wagon's rear step.

"In heaven's name, Sergeant, be reasonable," Irad begged. "I give you my word of honor as a gentleman that I was only a passerby who got swept into this brawl."

"Set that chatter to music and sing it to the magistrate." With a liberal use of his espantoon the sergeant began propelling his tallest prisoner up the patrol wagon's steps.

"Why, that's Mr. Seymour," a woman's voice called in surprise. "I'm sure it is! What is wrong?"

"He was fighting some Unionist rascals. Bully fer you, Mister Seymour!" yelled a deep voice on the outskirts of the throng. "Hurray for Jeff Davis and Secession!"

Immediately other onlookers began waving fists, yelled: "Let's tar and feather the damned Rebel!" "Naw! Hangin's too good for a slaver."

"Shut up, you goddam' stinkin' nigger-lovers."

Battered and still draining blood from his wounded chin but mortified, furious and humiliated beyond expression, Irad Seymour slumped onto a bench in the coverless patrol wagon. The other prisoners seemed quite at ease, familiar with this mode of transportation.

Once a quartet of burly patrolmen had clambered aboard, the driver called to his team, the gong recommenced its brazen clatter as the heavy vehicle lurched off to the brand-new City Jail. Baltimoreans

were vastly proud of that gray granite edifice thrusting its four
battlemented towers so high above Jones' Falls.

IV

A Dog's Bad Name

IN AN INCREASINGLY futile effort to fight down alarm over Irad's
failure to return from the shipyard, Sylvia Seymour again studied
the seamstress sent her by the Adams Family Stitchery. The girl
sat prim and straight, her narrow, silver-blond head bent over one
of Messrs. Wheeler & Wilson's patented stitching machines. She
wore an anxious, deadly serious expression.

"Mercy," Sylvia reflected, "Mrs. Adams ought to be ashamed
hiring out such a mere child."

"And how are you called, my dear?" Sylvia inquired through a
mouthful of pins she was using to attach her pattern to the gray
and pink striped silk. "And how old are you?"

"I am called Christina Reigler," the girl informed her in a low,
precise tone containing the barest hint of a foreign inflection. "I
became seventeen years of age last month." Anxiously she glanced at
her employer over the rented sewing machine. "But even Mr. Adams
says I work just as fast and well as any of—of his older girls."

"How long have you been in the Adams' employ?"

"A little over three weeks, Madame," the girl replied, then deftly
folded straighter the seam she was preparing to stitch.

"Where do you come from?" Sylvia really didn't care a rap; she
just needed to talk. Anything to divert her worry over Irad's failure
to come home. Never before had he been anywhere nearly so tardy.
Awful thought. Could he have taken one too many at the Fire
Company Club House? Husbands coming home tipsy and belated
weren't uncommon in Caroline Street—or in more fashionable
neighborhoods, either. Could that noisy riot down the street have
had any connection with this delay? She sighed, thinking of those

beautiful pork chops, grown cold and tough and Melissa's spoon bread spoiled. Mercy! The crone's lower lip had thrust itself out a full inch when she'd seen her pan gravy growing hard and greasy.

The seamstress' large China-blue eyes flickered up from her work. "I and Hermann, my young brother, we come from Waukegan, that is a very little city in Wisconsin," she informed Sylvia. Then using a small handle, she commenced to revolve a nickeled handwheel activating the machinery.

"She's clean and nice-looking, but not really pretty," Sylvia decided. "Her features are a bit sharp, but what truly beautiful hair!" By the light of a kerosene lamp the Reigler girl's hair, worn in fine double plaits bound tightly about her head, suggested a silver-gold crown. Her mouth was generously wide with pale pink lips that betrayed both sensitivity and tenderness. This shining young thing's manner suggested uncertainty and, at the same time, a certain quiet determination.

The machine whirred and clucked oilily on and on. Still no sign of Irad. Fear commenced to grope at her heart with icy claws. What *could* have gone wrong? "And when, Christina, did you come to Baltimore?"

Before making reply, the Reigler girl deliberately used blunt scissors to snip short her machine's thread, then knotted it with deft, slender fingers. She didn't intend this seam ever to unravel—which it would, granted half an opportunity.

"Last October." *Whir-r, shir-r.* "Our parents they both were dead of the typhoid fever. In Waukegan it was bad, very bad." *Whir-r, whir-r.* "Many people died," she stated without apparent emotion. "My father's brother, August, we thought lived in Baltimore. Together they had emigrated from Westphalen in the Old Country. They took part in the Student Revolution of 1848."

Sylvia momentarily became curious.

"You found your uncle?"

"No," came the young seamstress' even reply. *Whir-r, whir-r.* "My Uncle August, said his landlady, is purser on a clipper ship to China. It was too bad. His ship had sailed on a voyage one week before we came here."

Sylvia put down her shears.

"Oh, you poor children! You had no other friends?"

"No, Mrs. Seymour." Tina inspected the tension foot, pulled out a stray thread.

"What did you do? Did you appeal to the Humane Impartial Society?"

The clear blue eyes grew round. "Why? We had no more money, but I was not ill."

"But what did you do, you and your little brother?"

"I went to work. What else? For Hermann it was more difficult. Hermann is only fifteen years old—and not quick to learn."

Tina Reigler smiled happily. This machine was like magic. So quickly it sewed so many lovely, fine stitches. The only trouble was that unless one fastened off properly the silk, a seam would unravel even faster. "Mrs. Seymour, Ma'am, shall I these tiers closer together sew?"

"Yes. That should give the waist a firmer support. Not to find your uncle—wasn't it frightening?"

How could this pallid young creature be so matter-of-fact? Imagine finding yourself penniless, without friends, in a great city like Baltimore?

"To begin, it was not easy," the girl stated. *Whir-r, whir-r, whir-r!* "But I was lucky. I found this employment. Still, I am worried over Hermann."

"Worried? Why?"

"I do not know what to say." The seamstress hesitated, brushed some threads from her lap. "Perhaps, Mrs. Seymour, Ma'am, you will be so good as to advise? My brother wants he should take a job in Mr. Seeger's brewery."

"Why not? Seeger's is a big concern."

"Maybe I aim too high." Tina's smile was timid. "Better I think Hermann should study some other business, a business with a great future. I do not say that beer is not a fine drink, but our papa I do not think would like that Hermann should become a brewer." The shimmering silk passed and repassed under the needle. "My father was a carriage maker, but also a pastor on Sunday."

"Where would you like to send your brother, if you could?" Sylvia watched the seamstress' pitifully thin shoulders rise momentarily.

"—To the Baltimore Commercial College," came the instant response. "In their advertisements they say they teach bookkeeping, mercantile law and commercial eth—ethics." She sighed, shrugged. "Fine talk to be sure, but that is all. There is no money, so for Hermann to study is not possible. No. So I think he shall go to work as apprentice in the pattern and boiler shops of Mr. Denmead's Locomotive Works. They are on Monument Street near Holiday." The girl nodded above her machine and her pale lips compressed themselves.

"But why there?"

"In this country, distances are great. Will not many locomotives be needed?"

"I presume so. There is talk of building a railroad all the way to California."

A clock in the steeple of the First Presbyterian Church—her church —had just sounded eight shivering, sonorous notes. Eight o'clock. Irad not home yet! Panic flung small, icy darts at her heart. Should she seek a policeman? No. "Wait another half hour," she admonished herself. "Don't do anything silly or impulsive." Irad would be angry. Bother his Navy tradition! Aloud, she asked, "Do you earn much with Mr. and Mrs. Adams?"

Tina brightened, gave Sylvia a quick look that reminded her of a small bird—or a mouse. "Oh, yes, Mrs. Seymour. Since learning to use this sewing machine, I earn four dollars in a week."

"Can two of you live on such a sum?"

The slight brown-clad figure nodded. "Oh, yes, Mrs. Seymour. Besides Hermann's odd jobs bring in a little silver. He is a good worker. Today he runs errands for Mr. Hollingsworth, the apothecary."

Two people living on four, maybe six dollars a week? It seemed incredible. Why at Beau Rivage such a sum wouldn't buy coffee!

"We share an attic room at Mrs. Gahagan's boarding house. It is on Alice Anna Street near the waterfront, so it is not very expensive. For ten cents one can buy many fish or crabs."

Sylvia's troubled gaze sought the girl's black, buttoned shoes, and found them shapeless, patched and shiny—crinkled through long use. Numerous neat darns created extra-black areas in the seamstress' thick black cotton stockings and her full-skirted brown kersey dress certainly had never been intended for winter wear.

Christina's profile, sharply reproduced on the ugly wallpaper by the kerosene lamp, mimicked her nod. "Really, Mrs. Seymour, Ma'am, we have been most lucky. My work hours are not bad—only ten hours a day, and Mr. Adams and his wife are kind to me. Next week, they say, they may raise my wages fifty cents."

At the sound of rattling at the front door Sylvia leaped up, spilling spools, scissors, beeswax and other items of her sewing basket far and wide.

"There! Mr. Seymour is home at last!" Alarm began to give way to indignation. He'd no right to cause her such anxiety. "Pick up these things, like a good girl." Then as if to herself, "I have wonderful news for him!"

Sylvia fairly flew down the staircase, recognized the tall figure in the act of entering. Thank a merciful Providence, Irad was all right! "Mr. Seymour, is that you?"

"Yes, my dear," came his deep tones. "Or rather what is left of me."

The first thing wrong she noticed once he had turned up a lamp in their tiny hallway, was that his spectacles were missing and then that a smear of blood had discolored his left cheekbone. His jaw was swollen and darkened by a small gash. Good God! Why, his jacket sleeve was torn half off and dull red splotches of blood had splashed both the jacket's silk lapels and the shirt below. She forgot her news of Sam, darted down the remaining steps to fling both arms about him.

"Oh, my poor darling! Irad, darling! Are you all right? Are you badly hurt? What has happened?"

"There, there. I've been a bit banged up, my pet, but there's nothing really wrong with your husband."

His arms crept about her waist. For the thousandth time he noticed how ridiculously slim it was.

"But, but—how, what—?"

"It would appear," he explained wryly, "that, all within an hour, your husband from a respected householder and marine architect has degenerated into a dangerous Southern agitator, a common brawler and a ringleader of the Rip-Raps' gang."

Sylvia's great sherry-hued eyes swung up, widened in incredulity. "You? Rip-Raps? What in the world are they?"

"A band of dock rats, ex-convicts and hooligans who insult the Southern Cause by protesting sympathy for it."

Irad was securing his front door when out on Caroline Street deep voices shouted, "Yah! Traitor! Slave driver! You'd *better* hole up, you blasted Rebel rat." Another roared, "Get to hell out this neighborhood if you know what's good for your health! We want no traitors in this block."

Sylvia gasped, went a little pale. Oh dear, how angry, how menacing were those shouts from the chilly darkness.

When she noticed the skinned knuckles and swollen condition of his right hand, she began to get angry herself. "Shall I send Melissa for the police?"

"Let 'em yelp. It's the nature of curs."

Irad laughed mirthlessly, then pulled off and inspected his ruined jacket. "Don't appear quite so horrified, my dear. By unluckily being present, I became involved in a riot. Surely you must have heard it about an hour ago?"

"Oh, yes, yes! But there are so many these days—especially in this part of town—I didn't pay it attention. Oh, darling, what has become of your spectacles?"

"Gone, to keep my cloak, cap and wallet company." Irad tilted up the nacre-tinted oval of his wife's face, and kissed her hungrily on the lips.

"Why were those horrible people calling you a Rebel? A—a traitor—a—a Southern—?"

"It's all an absurd mischance," he reassured her, then added quietly, "Of course, everybody close by knows we're Southern born, while most artisans and working people are pro-Union. The police took me up and gave me a free ride in their fine new black Maria. A natural mistake." He smiled. "As soon as I identified myself to the lieutenant he was all apologies."

"Oh! Irad, how shameful!" Sylvia's expression was savage. "How dared they, and you a gentleman!"

In a small tarnished mirror Irad bent to inspect himself and grimaced while wiping specks of street dirt from his beard. "Your husband's a lovely sight, isn't he?"

"You'll always be fine and handsome in my eyes," she declared. "Irad, what do you think—?" She started to give the great news about Sam but he anticipated her.

"Madame, you may not realize it, but you now gaze upon the Assistant Senior Naval Architect of Charles Reeder's Shipyard and Marine Railway."

"*Assistant Senior?* What on earth are you talking about, you beloved idiot?"

He hugged her until he lifted her clear of the floor. "Mr. Reeder's not only given me full rein in the matter of designing the *Comet*, but, imagine it! He's raised me to thirty-five dollars a week! Now what do you think of that?"

"How grand!" She rubbed her cheek against his, felt the beard tickle her chin. "Oh, Irad, I'm so very proud of you!" she cried with such ardor that he flushed and wondered a little at her vehemence.

So Irad had been promoted! Here was his first strong step towards that goal she was determined he must reach. As a senior employee of a well-known firm he would attain a certain prominence and prestige that could be made useful socially. All kinds of possibilities suggested themselves.

After further congratulations she burst out, "Oh, I forgot my own good news. Sam telegraphed today that the *Crusader* has made port in Brooklyn. I expect he'll be visiting us within a week!"

"That's capital! I wonder if we'll find many changes in him?" His short-sighted gray gaze probed Sylvia's clear golden-brown one so intently that she colored a little. "Maybe he'll have got over poor Janet's passing away." He fondled her chin. "You'll make special efforts to cheer him, won't you? Invite around some attractive young ladies, perhaps. Robbie needs a mother."

V

ALONG THE WATERFRONT

A WEEK LATER the bad weather still prevailed. At the foot of Caroline Street, Christina Reigler bent her small, proud head against the gale and, crossing the Philadelphia, Wilmington & Baltimore Railroad tracks, turned left into Alice Anna Street. An especially vicious gust prompted the gathering of a coarse, woolen shawl more closely about her. Even in clement weather Tina had taken the precaution of concealing the pale sheen of her hair which, to her astonishment, so many men seemed to find alluring. The shawl not only disguised the proportions of her straight, virginal figure, but served to conceal a faggot she carried ready beneath the harsh gray wool.

A pair of hire-carriages overtook her, amber-hued side lamps clattering and patent-leather mudguards dripping slime. Deeply Christina pitied the miserable nags jolting stiff-kneed between their shafts; poor beasts, they weren't finding life easy or pleasant, either.

Despite her brave talk to Mrs. Seymour, she and Hermann went to bed hungry for nights on end after she had paid the room rent. An omnibus, rattling like a frightened skeleton, drew near on the way to Mount Clare Station, its driver slumped on his seat with head drawn, turtle-like, into the depths of a greenish black greatcoat. Dully she noted how the bus team set down their ungainly ill-shod hoofs in a loose fashion suggestive of approaching exhaustion.

Why, Tina pondered, must the Lord's world so often appear ugly? From the depths of the shawl she considered a succession of faces advancing along the sidewalk. Never a one of these visages revealed even a suggestion of kindliness, let alone sensitivity or beauty. Approaching the wharfs she could distinguish a familiar tangle of rigging, spars and masts, towering above chandlers' shops lining Philpott and Thames Streets.

By now Tina had learned the names of most of the commission merchants and shipriggers in the vicinity of Mrs. Gahagan's boarding house: Abrahams, Mathews, Mason and Greaves. Over what distant and exotic foreign lands must yonder house flags have waved?

As a rule this ever-varied vista of graceful spars and gaudily painted smokestacks stimulated her imagination. Tonight, however, the weather had grown so thick that only with difficulty could one discern the faint glow of lights marking Locust Point across the Patapsco River. Nearer by lay the famous shipyards of Baltimore, in one of which Mr. Seymour was employed. While quickening her pace Tina thought back on that night last week when pretty little Mrs. Seymour had been so worried.

"Ach," she thought in German, "*Herr Seymour* so beaten appeared with clothing spoiled and yet he was so full of happiness. *Warum?*"

Deftly as a cat avoiding unwanted attention Christina sidestepped the uncertain grab made by a ginger-whiskered seaman in a gray jersey and checkered pants who lurched suddenly from among a stack of empty oyster barrels.

"C'mere, honeybee. I'll gi' you a dollar, 'cause ye look real purty and I want—" Fortunately the sailor was so befuddled that he tripped and sat on the board sidewalk still slobbering obscene invitations until his voice was lost amid the clanking roar of a passing freight train.

Ever more rapidly Tina's feet carried her towards that chilly attic room at Mrs. Gahagan's. Her fingers closed tighter on the faggot.

She wondered. "Has *Bruder* really been seeking work at Mr. Denmead's locomotive factory? Of course, he shall be at home ahead of me. Have I not ordered him off the streets after seven o'clock?"

In lively interest, she watched a file of infantry under arms swing along towards the docks in cadence to the rattle of a lonely drum.

So many political troubles these days! Of them Tina understood nothing or wished to. *Ach!* Would a war really soon begin? Mister Adams only today had said that fighting was not likely even if those Southern people could not be conciliated and brought back into the Union.

A *tat-tat, rat-tat! tat! tat!* the drumming diminished, became lost.

Shafts of amber light escaped loosely hinged doors, together with snatches of Swedish, French and Spanish speech. Presently Tina halted, shivering happily because a chorus of rich German voices began roaring out: "*Ach, du lieber Augustin!*"

Wunderbar! Despite everything, was it not infinitely comforting to recognize the language of her childhood? Poor Papa! Pastor Reigler had not survived long enough to speak better than broken English. For all that he had insisted that, in his home, the children should speak only English.

"Mamma and me are German but you and Hermann are Americans and Americans speak English, not German." How many hundreds of times had Papa not said that? Mamma, always submissive, as became a good Rhenish *Hausfrau*, never ventured to disagree, especially since she spoke quite fine English. *Aber natürlich. Frau* Reigler, born Hildegarde Brünner, had been the eldest of *Herr Doktor* Waldemer Brünner's six daughters.

What might her maternal grandfather really have been like? A daguerreotype in Mamma's possession revealed this Professor of Semantics at Bonn University as a fierce, black-bearded individual.

No, it would never be proper to permit the *Herr Doktor's* grandson to become a loutish brewery boy. Poor, dear hard-working and uncomplaining Mamma! At the approach of death she had become frightened, not for herself—stout Lutheran that she was—but for her children.

"Tinschen, you must find your Uncle August if you can," Hildegarde Reigler had whispered through gray-colored lips. "Remember that without education you and Hermann will become nothings. You must set yourself a purpose and always work hard. So many great people forget that without work there can be no respectability or peace of mind."

She, Christina Hildegarde Reigler, would never forget Mamma's faint last words. "Trust in God, my child, be honest and work hard; then nothing very bad can befall you."

For once she felt no hunger while returning home. How good it had been of pretty, aristocratic Mrs. Seymour to have prepared with her own hands, cold meat, potatoes and, of all things, a cup of delicious hot chocolate for a servant! Christina felt very happy because the ball gown must require at least three more days of stitching. Not that she would dawdle; always she sewed as fast as she could. But, *Lieber Gott*, how fine it was to work among well-bred and quiet-spoken folk.

Just before she recognized the high-peaked roof and battered gray clapboard façade of Mrs. Gahagan's boarding establishment she had to avoid the amorous overtures of a pair of bearded blue jackets pursuing an unsteady course along Alice Anna Street. In so doing she stepped ankle-deep into a rut full of icy water.

Tina recognized the Widow's front yard by the skeleton of a gaunt sumac tree in the summit of which fluttered the remains of a kite entangled there long weeks ago. As quietly as she might, she entered the boarding house hallway faintly illumined by a kerosene table lamp whose red and yellow glass shade had lost a pie-shaped sector.

Dared she ask for a pail of hot water? When one's feet got cold Mamma had always made one soak them well. Alas, men's voices, raised in a very heated discussion, issued from that chamber which Mrs. Gahagan, in some grandiloquence, designated as her "parlor." In reality the room was a miserable, sour-smelling place equipped with chairs covered by black horsehair which invariably stuck into all but the best corseted posteriors, and a dejected davenport upholstered in scuffed green leather; its springs long ago had surrendered in an unequal struggle to support the backsides of several generations.

"That you, Tina?" Mrs. Gahagan's vast bosom preceded her untidy gray head and bloated red face out into the hallway; immediately its atmosphere became invaded by gin fumes.

"Yes, M-ma'm."

The Widow waddled out into the hall clucking like a monstrous brown Orpington hen. "*Tck! Tck!* Mary and all the Saints! And where have you been so late? Out on the streets after nine! A respectable girl might get into trouble and nobody's fault but her own. This here ain't Monument Place nor yet Charles Street, ye'll recall." Sharply Mrs. Gahagan's blood-injected eye swung to the floor. "Who's been tracking in this mud and watter? Mary love us! Yer feet is soakin' wet!"

"Yes. I just now stepped into a rut. I am sorry, Mrs. Gahagan, I will clean everything."

Mrs. Gahagan flopped a loose hand and sipped at the clear liquid in her glass. "Ah-hr, never ye mind—a bit more dirt won't hurt." Barely suppressing a hiccup, the Widow seized Tina by her arm. "Come along wid yez, Heart o' Corn."

Tina's teeth were chattering, but she hung back. *Himmel!* She didn't want to enter the parlor all wet and bedraggled like a lost kitten; there were at least three people yonder. The girl who was laughing so heartily must be Molly Sheridan, Mrs. Gahagan's niece, as glib of tongue as she was pert and self-assured. Older than Tina by a couple of years, she worked as waitress-chambermaid at the General Wayne Inn. A bright, merry creature, Molly never appeared concerned beyond the present. Tina squirmed free, smiled and removed her shawl.

"Please, Ma'am, let me tighten my braids. They've slipped. I'll come right in to the fire. Truly, I will."

Presently Tina entered an atmosphere heavy with a blend of stale cabbage, fried fish, pipe smoke and the reek of sea coal glowing in a broken grate.

From where she hesitated, timid and uncertain in the doorway, Tina noticed a small man distinguished by a shock of flaming auburn hair who, talking sixty to the minute, kept stabbing his forefinger at a sheet of paper marked by a mare's nest of overlapping lines, angles and ellipses.

"But, mon, I tell ye," he was growling, "a feathering propeller is no' so complicated a deevice. Since Maudesley pairfected the first one near fifteen years ago, such have been successfully employed in most English shipyards."

"For use in quiet canals and estuaries, I presume?"

"Now boys," Mrs. Gahagan wheezed affably, "we ain't none of us deef and shouting won't prove yer right. Tina, of course ye know Molly and Mr. Newton?"

Tina nodded to the buxom, black-haired waitress and smiled timidly at Mr. Newton. He was an assistant purchasing contractor for the Susquehanna Railroad and had been a fellow boarder for almost a month.

Mrs. Gahagan's thick hand, still clutching her gin and water, indicated the auburn-haired stranger. "This here is my new boarder, Mr. Brunton." Two black gaps mourning the departure of the landlady's front teeth were revealed by her loose smile. "Mr. Brunton, this here's my pet; been with me two months and never a complaint. Christina Reigler, and mind you treat her polite-like."

"She's a good girl and smarter than most—" Molly added as the new boarder got to his feet. "Like you see, Tina, there ain't much to Mr. Brunton, but what there is, I'd say is mightly noticeable." Molly rolled her eyes while fluffing a double row of ruffles adorning her generously filled shirtwaist.

Mr. Brunton, Tina perceived, was indeed short but well proportioned and stood straight in a threadbare business suit and a tartan waistcoat bound in black braid about its lapels and pockets. The only jewelry he wore was a Masonic ring, cheap agate cufflinks and a nickel-plated watch chain. The drawing fluttered from between Brunton's fingers while he managed an awkward bow towards that slight figure hesitating in the entrance. Tina, however, was chiefly aware of the brilliant blueness of the new boarder's small and steady eyes, his flaming hair and sideburns. His squarish features, although it was still early spring, showed a healthy red-brown.

A slight hiccup escaped Mrs. Gahagan. "Cat got yer tongue, Mr. Brunton?"

"I am honored and pleased," said the Scot carefully, "tae make yer acquaintance."

"Won't you come in, Miss Reigler?" Newton invited, then he laughed and winked while pushing forward a lumpy-looking chair. "Molly and I owe you thanks for this release. Plagued if these foreigners don't preen themselves on knowing everything there is to know about steam engineering. We have some pretty smart inventors ourselves, haven't we?"

"Why, I expect that we do, Mr. Newton," Tina murmured and, crossing to the fire, extended chapped red hands to the heat.

Immediately Christina Reigler attracted Brunton's attention. Unlike so many young women here in America, this pale-haired girl in the faded brown dress, standing so diffidently there before the fireplace, held her thin body erect, not in a defiant way, but in a manner suggesting innate self-respect.

He began fumbling with the bright brass buttons securing his tartan waistcoat.

" 'Tis braw outside," he observed. "I trust you've not taken a chill?"

"She's on the edge of it." Mrs. Gahagan reached for a tea kettle steaming comfortably on its trivet. "Look at her shivering like a stray cat. Well, I guess I'd better mix her a toddy."

"No thank you, Ma'am. I—I don't drink spirits." The girl's teeth chattered, for all her quick smile.

"Fiddle-faddle! Ye'll do as I say—else I'll smack yer stubborn German bottom fer yez." Mumbling, the Widow Gahagan stumped out carrying the teapot with her.

"She'll mainly fix herself one," grinned Mr. Newton. "Been waiting an excuse for some time."

A furious blush brightened Tina's cheeks when she realized that, for several instants, she and Mr. Brunton had been staring at each other for all the world as if mesmerized. Subconsciously she became aware that this ruddy-cheeked young fellow was scarcely taller than herself and of the same slight but wiry build. He might be twenty-eight years of age, maybe a little more. The first thing that she noticed, and liked, about this Mr. Brunton was a humorous quirk to his wide, thin-lipped mouth and the existence of good-natured crow's-feet at the outward corners of his brilliantly blue eyes. His regard, although intense, did not seem disrespectful; nothing like the way some men gawped when the wind pressed her skirts against her legs. She dropped her gaze to the muddied rag rug beneath her feet.

"You have been in Baltimore long, Mr. Brunton?" Tina inquired, as, presently, the damp and muddied hem of her skirt commenced to give off small feathers of steam.

"Near half a year," he replied. "You are a stranger here, too, I take it?"

"My brother and I have been here nearly six months. Oh!" She started, casting Mr. Newton an anxious look. "My brother! Hermann —has he come in?"

Mrs. Gahagan reappeared, shaking her untidy gray head. "Not yet. I expect the kid's landed himself a job rushing the growler."

"Rushing the—the what?" Tina's pale, coral-tinted lips formed a puzzled circle.

"Passing beer," supplied Newton. "Old Marty Grimm gives boys a quarter to pass trays at his Athletic Club."

The girl's thin body stiffened and she appealed to the red-haired stranger. "Hermann should not go to such places, should he? Better he should study at the Baltimore Commercial College as I want him to."

Brunton ceased tugging at short and curly sideburns. "Aye. A lad had better devote such time to schoolbooks."

Newton laughed a little, reached forward, and lit a paper spill which he held to a charred corncob pipe. "Nonsense! The poor boy can use a trifle of fun. Lord knows, Tina, you work him near as hard as you do yourself. A regular little tyrant in petticoats is what you've become. You Dutchies are too da—er—confounded serious."

The Scot raised a quizzical red brow. "In other words yer warning, 'God save the man Miss Reigler marries'?"

"Oh, no!" Tina flushed. "Not for one moment would I try to direct my husband. Not ever. Such is not respectful."

Newton's deep laugh rang out. "Respectful! I tell you, Lachlan, we'll never understand these Dutchies."

The girl directed troubled pale blue eyes at Brunton. "Please pay Mr. Newton no attention, he is not serious. Besides I am not a Dutchie."

From the pantry sounded the clink of a spoon against glass. "Ha! Auntie is brewing a poteen," laughed Molly.

"Please," Tina cried hurriedly, "I now must go and warn the landlady not to waste spirits on me. I am quite warm now and am going to bed. Good night, Mr. Newton and Molly. Good night, Mr. Brunton." The girl's limbs carried her quickly across the room and out of sight down the hall.

"What are you boys staring at?" Molly demanded in lazy amusement. "The kid's only a green peach and scared half to death!"

"True, but yon seems a lass o' rare spirit," Brunton observed as if he were alone in the room. "I wager there'll be no compromising wi' what she sets her mind on."

Newton slid back onto his seat and kicked Lachlan's chair into its previous position before the hearth.

"You'll learn that these Dutchies are a curious lot for all that they work like beavers. I know. I grew up among 'em in Hanover, Pennsylvania."

"Pale and thin as she is now, she'll be sonsie someday," Brunton predicted.

"That colorless kid?" Newton hooted. "Never! She reminds me of a fresh-picked spring chicken."

"Aye, but the bones o' her face are well designed and her eyes— Losh, they're steady as a compass." Brunton started to say something further, but only shrugged and retrieved the paper he and Newton had been discussing. "Speaking o' designs concairning yon bevel gear, I misdoot yer cogs o' lignum vitae would stand the stresses developed by an engine o' the horsepower ye've mentioned."

VI

HOME IS THE SAILOR

CLOUDS OF CANVASBACKS, redheads, scaups and marsh ducks, rose from various creeks and patches of water lying beneath a trestle conveying the Philadelphia, Wilmington & Baltimore Railroad's tracks southwards from Havre de Grace. Strident screams from the locomotive's whistle aroused other vast flocks feeding in the distance, sent them boiling into the sky like twisting pillars of black smoke. Geese, in unnumbered thousands, then lumbered into the air, creating black lacy patterns against unbroken lead-hued clouds.

Low and heavily wooded as a rule, the banks of these streams wound lazily eastwards to empty their contents at last into the not-distant Susquehanna. Every so often a silvery rain squall would erase all trace of the horizon.

The Baltimore Express clattered over yet another bridge, with chain couplings clanking a rhythmic accompaniment to the clatter of several loose brake shoes. Puffs of smoke swirled along the train windows and leaked in, to set passengers to coughing, for along this division locomotives used coal fuel rather than wood as was the rule further south, and a hail of cinders kept rattling along the coach roof. But all these noises quite failed to drown out the drunken bickering of a party of prize fighters and their hangers-on; this group occupied seats forward, and their boasting and lurid profanity had created a continual annoyance all the way down from Wilmington.

"Noisy brutes," grunted Lieutenant Samuel Seymour, U.S.N. Sourly, he bent forward extending hands towards a pot-bellied stove which, located near the center of the coach, accomplished little towards dispelling a penetrating chill.

"If they weren't pugs, I'd tell 'em off," declared the naval officer at Seymour's side, then settled deeper into a dark blue service overcoat the collar of which had been turned up about his ears.

"Wonder how big can a two-year-old boy grow?" Seymour was asking himself. "Hope to God Robbie's taken after Janet—about the eyes at least. How much will he talk? I suppose he can run now. Sylvia's last letter said something about that. Of course, he won't know me but if Sylvia—"

Sylvia? How wonderfully kind, thoughtful and generous she'd been at the time of poor Janet's death. Could he ever repay Irad and her for their two-year care of the new orphan? Jiminy! Wouldn't it be extra-fine to reach Baltimore and find Sylvia—er, well, in the family way? Irad did so yearn for a son of his own, or a daughter for that matter; a little girl who would grow up to become a demure and dainty replica of her lovely and spirited Georgian mother. To realize that within another two hours he'd actually be holding his son. *HIS SON!* He was surprised to find his vision blurring all at once.

"Hey! Your fire's about out," Seymour shouted at the brakeman; the fellow glowered but sullenly tossed a few damp pine chunks into the stove.

"No luck there, but let's have heat one way or another." Seymour laughed and a silver pocket flask slid into sight. "It's a poor welcome Maryland is giving you, Henry," he observed, while his companion swallowed a deep gulp of bourbon, coughed, then sat up.

" 'Twill be different in Baltimore, I promise," Seymour said. "There's a port where you'll never want for any kind of hospitality."

Lieutenant H. H. Lewis peered out of the grimy window at Gunpowder Creek. "Wish Ah had my fowling piece along. That's a right smart mess of canvasback yonder."

"I'll take you shooting if you like. Spring flight is at its peak. Phil Dorsey owns a shore at Grassy Point—it's near Baltimore. You'd like Phil."

"Reckon Ah cain't spend more'n a day in Balt'more; must get on home." Lieutenant Lewis, because of long black mustaches and generous mutton-chop whiskers, appeared considerably older than his real age.

Seymour frowned, spoke in deep earnest, "Really, Henry, are you dead set on applying for a commission down in Montgomery? This new Government may, or may not, last."

The other stiffened a trifle on the soiled green upholstery of their seat. "You bet Ah am, Sam! And Ah'll have plenty of company. Yo' heard Pelod and Captain Hallenquist turned in their commissions to join the Confederate Navy?"

"No, I hadn't," Seymour admitted. "But good God, man, they're throwing away a life's work. Now they'll not likely get promotions or retirement pay."

"Maybe they set patriotism above reward," Lewis snapped. "Damned if Ah understand yo'. You're Southern born and bred, so ain't it your duty to turn in yo' papers with me? Hell's fire, Sam, with yo' service record yo'll have no difficulty at all down in Montgomery. Hallenquist says Mr. Conrad, he's Chairman of the Provisional Commission on Naval Affairs, is handin' out appointments right and left." For emphasis, Lewis tapped the flask on his knee. "First come, first served, they say is the order of the day down there. Means a number on the promotion list. Yo'd better join up, Sam. Come along with us. Man alive, 'Old Beeswax' Semmes, Buchanan, 'Deep Sea' Maury and Maffitt, yo' own skipper, have shown yo' the way." Lewis frowned at raindrops pelting hard at the glass beside him. "The Confederacy is bound to build a navy and a powerful one. It's *got* to!"

The Virginian's big brown head inclined hesitantly.

"In time, yes. Still, I've not yet heard of any Old Navy man-of-war being surrendered into Southern hands."

"No, but—surely, a lot of them will be."

"I'm not so sure."

"Why?"

"Captain Maffitt, for all he's a red-hot Rebel, stood off a Secessionist mob in Pensacola to bring the *Crusader* safe in to Brooklyn Navy Yard before resigning. I was aboard. I know."

"If he did, 'twas a damned unpatriotic thing to do!" burst out Lewis. "The South needs every ship she can lay hands on."

"Just you tell John Maffitt that to his face and it'll be a case of pistols for two and coffee for one, my lad!"

Conversation died, perhaps fortunately, while the engineer commenced to whistle furiously for a crossing. The train lumbered past a row of dog-run cabins, then some ragged Negro children. A farm cart, the team of which was plunging wildly in snorting, white-eyed fright, showed a hatless driver clinging to their bits, and struggling to control them.

"Nobody could be more loyal to the South than John Maffitt," Seymour pointed out. "But, until his resignation had been accepted, he felt himself still obligated by his oath to the United States. No gentleman, Harry, could have done otherwise; I imagine his example will be widely followed."

Lewis' color rose and he spoke sharply. "There are loyalties and loyalties. God alone knows how badly the South needs every ship and cannon she can lay hands on. But, be that as it may, Ah still claim we'll get us a navy in jig time."

"You're right there," Seymour drawled, "provided Virginia secedes and the Gosport Navy Yard falls into our hands."

"Yo' just said 'our hands.' Exactly what do yo' intend to do in this business?" Lewis demanded. "Here yo' admit that yo're thinking of chucking the Old Service, yet yo' won't take a Confederate commission."

Absently Samuel Seymour's fingers began to drum against the round, gold-plated belt buckle of his overcoat. "When Virginia secedes, as I half expect she will, why then I'll resign and apply for a commission. In the meanwhile," he treated his companion to a steady look, "I imagine I can make myself pretty useful when on leave in Norfolk. My folk are all Old Navy, but Virginian through-and-through. I'll have free access to the Navy Yard and the officers' mess. I might learn some useful facts."

His companion sat up straighter.

"Yo' intend plotting to capture the Yard for the South?"

"Quiet! Keep your damned voice down, Harry," Seymour pleaded.

"But why? We're below the Mason-Dixon Line now."

"You mayn't believe it, but for all that, Maryland is at least two-thirds Union-minded, especially in the northern and western counties."

The Alabamian's enthusiasm mounted. "My God, so yo're really with us! Forgive my having underestimated yo'; Ah thought yo' weren't even luke-warm for the Cause." Lewis' excitement mounted. "Yo' said yo'r family lives in Norfolk?"

"Yes, my father's a retired captain." Seymour rubbed his chin. "Haven't yet learned where the old man stands on this matter of Secession. He's devoted his whole life to the Old Navy. Maybe you've noted that quite a few of our Southern friends would set the Union and their seniority above their State? Come here, you, boy!" He beckoned a gangling, ginger-haired Negro youth wearing an out-at-elbows coat, sizes too small for him. The boy advanced down the aisle offering a basket of soggy-looking pies, some apples and twists of chewing tobacco.

"Yas, suh. Deese pies is *fresh* baked, suh."

"Last week?" suggested Lewis. "How much are the apples?"

"One cent apiece, suh." He fumbled under his wares and he came upon a grimy cone of brown paper. "Got some lemon drops, heah, suh."

The drunken prize fighters' voices rose into a fresh dispute.

"Me work in a Washington office? Like hell! Once Ole Abe gets seated, my Congressman's gonna get me a job in foreign parts."

"Then I reckon you'll put in for our consulate in Turkey," suggested a battered and unlovely companion wearing a green velour cap.

When Samuel Seymour shifted his position to nap a little, his foot struck a parcel stowed beneath the seat. He hoped Robert Ashton would like that little yellow cart if not the jig-sawed, dappled-gray hobbyhorse, complete with a mane of frayed yarn, patent-leather bridle, reins and a short stick ending in a wheel. Would the boy have inherited Janet's fine fair hair and warm blue eyes? The last time he'd seen his son he'd been but a tiny red and mottled being which either slept most of the time or wailed like a lost kitten.

And what of Irad, literal and sober Irad? It came to Sam that the eldest child of most families had a careful, responsible way about him. Was this because they were the first of their generation to be experimented upon by inexperienced parents? For a fact, he'd avoided many a licking through observation of an unsuccessful social experiment on Irad's part. Poor, near-sighted Irad! He'd taken it quite as hard as Pa when the Board of Admissions finally rejected his application for appointment.

Sam settled deeper into his greatcoat of fine, warm serge. On the other hand, Irad surely had been lucky to marry a girl as bright and vivacious as Sylvia. "Um-m. Sylvia. Does she look at many men the way she did while I was packing my sea chest back in 'fifty-nine?" Of course, Sylvia was a skillful coquette, as was only natural and to be expected. Weren't well-bred girls down in Georgia instructed by their mothers in the subtle art of charming, teasing and flattering the opposite sex?

Wasn't it odd how some people could fall in love and become joined together in Holy Matrimony? Here was Sylvia, so warm and laughing and in love with life, married forever to Irad of the mathematical mind and scholarly philosophy. It seemed that, even in childhood, Irad had always been like a grown man. Somehow Sam couldn't picture Irad ever abrim with passionate declarations of love, ever completely losing his temper or consuming more than a suitable number of drinks. Not that Irad was a prig—far from it. He could tell, in male company of course, a number of clever but definitely salacious tales and he could ride and wing shoot better than the next man.

What could two such contrasting natures find in common? Probably, he warned himself, the last two years had wrought great changes in them both. How bitterly Sylvia must be lamenting her childlessness one could only estimate through the detailed descriptions she'd written of Robbie's various small accomplishments.

Wouldn't it be grand to see Sylvia again. Odd, right now he could recall the trick she had of quickly turning her head, then smiling over her shoulder. He dozed.

A commotion caused by passengers rising, readjusting mufflers and shawls and then collecting parcels, roused Lieutenant Seymour to wakefulness. A quartet of Army officers occupying seats across the aisle were brushing crumbs and cinders from their uniforms while resetting the pale blue or yellow capes of their greatcoats. These were Regulars —Federal officers—Sam recognized, not soft militiamen, but straight-backed, powerful-looking fellows with winter weather stained across their faces; three lieutenants and a captain. Had they been of field grade their belts undoubtedly would have been better filled, their whiskers fuller and their noses redder by several shades; the elder gentlemen of the Senior Service certainly knew which was the working end of a bottle.

In rapid succession rows of miserable shanties, then a coal yard, iron rolling mill, and a lumber yard glided by the window. Even in these last two years Baltimore must have grown, Sam decided. Everywhere the raw and yellow frames of houses were going up but because of this rain no one was working on them.

Regretfully, Sam recalled how fiercely the sun could beat down in the Grand Bahama Channel. Lord! Had it not been murderously hot that day the U.S.S. *Crusader* had overhauled the *Echo*, slaver? Some-time soon he should be touching a tidy sum of money out of that capture—provided open war didn't break out.

Of course, if it did, John Maffitt wasn't likely to collect his share. Again, Sam pondered that strength of conviction in men which caused them deliberately and forever for the sake of an ideal to forfeit hard-earned retirement pay, prize money and their whole livelihood.

The coach door banged open. A brakeman in a dingy gray overcoat bellowed, "Balt'more! Balt'more! End o' the run. Mind yo' baggage."

Lieutenant Lewis awakened, yawned and peered out of the window as the train slowed and, whistling furiously, commenced to roll down a street lined by dingy dwellings. It was raining quite hard now, so there wasn't much to be seen.

Seymour fumbled first for the brass luggage check they'd given him in Wilmington, then for his valise and sea chest. A locomotive topped by a huge, bell-shaped smokestack chugged by towing a long line of yellow or bright red freight cars in the opposite direction.

Lights—it was already growing dark—commenced to glow through the lashing rain. The engineer whistled loudly for another crossing and, through the open door, everyone watched the brakeman begin to whirl his wheel.

As usual, the passengers went crowding, pushing towards the forward exit as if an instant's delay would endanger their lives.

Henry Lewis lowered a bundle of Brazilian souvenirs wrapped in palm leaf matting, from the luggage rack. "Ah'll be lodgin' at the Howard House," he said, glancing at the Army officers busy buckling on their side arms. "Ah've Léon Duchesne and some other people to see befo'e Ah leave fo' Montgomery."

"Good," Sam Seymour smiled. "Give my regards to Duchesne. We once served in the *Susquehanna* together. I want to give you a letter to Commander Semmes. He's a close friend of my father's."

"He the Semmes commandin' the Lighthouse Board?"

"Yes."

VII

At the American Theatre

Molly Sheridan stamped her annoyance. "Really, Tina, why won't you give your looks a chance? You ain't pretty, but you're nice-lookin' and that frost-colored mop of yours—well, most of the girls would give their eye-teeth," she giggled, "and a lot more maybe, for hair like it. Come on, try doin' your hair in a waterfall. It's all the mode and I'll show you how. Those there flat braids may be fittin' for workin' hours," Molly laughed, "but if you aim to please Mr. Brunton—"

"I do not aim to please Mr. Brunton or any man wearing pants,"
Tina snapped. But she kept studying her reflection, distorted though
it was by an ancient mirror which lifted one of her slim brown brows
a good half inch out of its true position.

"Nonsense!" Molly's full black skirts swirled—she was in her
waitress uniform still—when she hurried forward. "Look, macushla,
I'm going to fix yer hair up a bit even though there ain't time to do it
up proper on curlers."

Christina attempted to rise, but the Irish girl easily pushed her
back onto a rickety stool. "No nonsense, m'dear. 'Tis I that's bigger
than you, so this once you'll do like I want!"

"All right, but, Molly, why should you bother?" Color invaded
Tina's smooth features and crept out along her rather prominent
cheekbones. The effect was flattering.

"Because, darlin' dear, I work in a hotel and, well, I—I guess I
see heaps of men; maybe I've learned to pick a good bet when
there's one about. Fellers like Mr. Brunton don't happen along
every day, believe you me. Here, hold these things." Swiftly Molly
plucked out two bone hairpins anchoring the braids on top of
Christina's head.

"But—but, Molly, I'll be late and Mr. Brunton hates unpunctu-
ality."

"That he will not when I'm through with you. Besides, he's only
just come in. He'll be puttin' on hair oil and changin' his cuffs now
the next half hour." The chambermaid shook her glossy black head.
"Dear! Dear! Ain't you got nothin', well—just a bit friller?"

Tina looked her embarrassment. "You know very well I have but
two dresses to my back. Besides, I wouldn't know how to wear
anything fancy."

Molly's fingers moved in expert patterns, parting, puffing and
pinning the silver-gold strands, although it was difficult because Tina's
hair was so very fine. "Nonsense. You'll learn how to wear fine
dimities and challis. Trust me to know what will please the boys,
and don't think I don't! But you, well, you're different. Me, I'm black
Irish with a ready laugh, a good-enough figger—as you can maybe tell.
But you, dearie, well, yer pure as moonbeams. Don't worry, I'll not
get you all tarted-up." She flicked a gold-filled lapel watch. "I'll bet
you a can of beer that Scotch feller won't be displeased."

"Oh-h, I hope not! Please hurry, I know I'll be late!" Back in Waukegan, tardiness was one of the few faults which had warranted the use of Mamma's old corset stay, and "on the bare," too.

"Will you stay quiet?" Molly threatened playfully with her hair brush. "Sit still, darlin', else I'll never get you ready." Through a mouthful of pins she demanded, "What's the great occasion?"

"Mr. Brunton," she explained carefully, "has—er—accepted a new position—a very good one, I think. He says this is in celebration."

"That's lucky. Yer friend's two weeks behind on his room rent, and my aunt was getting set to ask him to clear out." Molly rolled big, gray-blue eyes. "If you wasn't such a funny little sober-sides, I'd have invited you to come along to Mr. Foster's champagne supper. He's throwin' a big party at the Revety House for the Colonel of the McComas Riflemen."

Quite seriously Christina said, "Thank you, but really I wouldn't know how to act in such grand company. After all, Mr. Foster is very wealthy and a politician. They say he has traveled to Europe three times."

"Lord love us! You don't have to know how to act with the boys. They do all the acting."

To knot a thin blue ribbon about a few curls above Tina's forehead gave Molly a little trouble; what a pity she was so scrawny, so serious. A laugh couldn't hurt any girl no more than one—only one—glass of champagne, provided you drank it a little at a time. Mr. John Walter Foster's supper should be fun and very genteel by comparison with an Odd Fellows' smoker or the George Washington Marching and Chowder Club's annual picnic.

Mr. Foster's guests were older and because there would be people present they weren't sure about, they'd seldom progressed beyond pinching buttocks or snapping garters. A girl didn't really have to—not unless she wanted—and favors were given out all the same. Sometimes a silver locket, sometimes a brooch or maybe a tiny bracelet set with garnets. Jenny McCoy had her own carriage now and a pug dog.

Maybe, if Molly put it right, she'd persuade Tina to come along some night soon. Tina was ambitious and that thin handsome face and wonderful hair of hers sure would set some of the older men to thinking.

In the glass Christina cast a happy and a trifle envious glance at the cameo pin Molly had lent her, along with a slightly worn cashmere shawl.

" 'Tis fine, high-spirited gentlemen we have here in Baltimore, the Careys, the Blounts, the Lowndes, and their like," Molly declared, deftly clubbing the lustrous strands at the nape of Tina's neck. "Wait till ye've tasted really good cooking and learn how a fine French wine can warm the cockles o' yer heart."

Christina set her mouth. "Wine I shall never touch."

"Fiddle-faddle! All the fine ladies drink a little wine, unless her family is teetotal or Methodist."

Christina squirmed about until she could look up at the girl behind her. "You are not funning me? Do really grand ladies really drink wine? Mamma always said that only bad women drank anything stronger than—"

Molly laughed easily. "Your mother was German; I guess maybe she didn't know too much about high society. But I'll bet she wanted you to get on, which you'll have to do all by your lone, more's the pity. Tell me, Tina, what do you want out of life?"

While Tina debated, the distant hooting of a steamer's whistle penetrated her attic room.

"I want some day to become a fashionable lady and the wife of a great man," she stated serenely. "I intend to live in a big house like Mr. Brown, the banker. I do not know how I will, but I *will*, just as sure as my name is Christina Reigler!"

"Don't want much, do you?" Molly smiled, laughed a bit. "Well, duckie, maybe the next time Mr. Foster throws a party you had better come along."

Christina's China-blue eyes swung quickly upwards. Said she quietly, "You are very kind, Molly, but it must be my husband who will give me these things. But I will help him to earn them. Yes, I will plan and I will work very hard, for I am not afraid of working. We shall found a great and famous family, my husband and I. You will see."

"You poor kid! If that's really your notion, I'd say you're going about it in a mighty unlikely way." Molly smiled, patted the girl's gleaming head. "There now! You look less like an orphan fresh out o' Saint Agnes'!"

Most citizens of Baltimore saw in the American Theatre on Front Street only a garishly decorated and pretentious music hall but, in the smoky golden glow created by flaring kerosene sconces set to either side of the entrance and the glitter of many coal-oil lamps lining a pseudo-Moorish lobby, to Christina Reigler the American Theatre suggested a fairy queen's palace.

Her conscience had begun to trouble her. Surely, with Mr. Brunton not yet having landed his job for sure, she never should have permitted him to squander a whole dollar on tickets for this minstrel show.

The crowd, pushing noisily down the aisles, proved well liquored but in a jovial mood, forecasting a hearty reception for the entertainers. Men called loud and lusty greetings and occasionally offered elaborate bows to pretty painted girls garbed in such resplendent and revealing gowns that Lachlan Brunton's eyes widened and he began to look about.

Mr. Alex Carter's Black Face Minstrels proved to be no better or worse than the average. A pair of white artists with cork-blackened features clogged "Old Zip Coon" and "Possum Up a Gum Tree" with such noisy enthusiasm that the audience broke into gales of applause. "Misto' Interlocutuh" wagged his preposterous, woolly head and flung a series of conundrums to various members of his entourage. Why the crowd laughed so raucously over some of the sallies Christina couldn't understand but Brunton tugged at his auburn side whiskers, began to squirm and shine the patches on the seat of his pants.

"I'm sorry, Miss Reigler, I wasna aware a meenstrel show is no' like a music hall. Do ye wish to stay?" he demanded, half way through the performance. "I didna suspect the humor here would be so broad."

Christina treated him to a slow smile and replied in all seriousness, "But, Mr. Brunton, we can't leave now. You have paid out good money for these seats. Me, I am not offended by the jokes because I do not understand them." Her hand vanished into the cone of lemon drops in her lap. She wrinkled her nose at him just a little. "Please go ahead and laugh when you feel you want to."

Christina had never been so impressed or so curious. She sat straight, her large light blue eyes taking in every detail about the theatre. After all, this was the first she had ever seen from the inside. The realization troubled her somewhat. Pastor Hauser considered any and all theatres haunts of the Evil One. At the Lutheran church—

tomorrow was Sunday—she intended to pray extra-hard and maybe ask for forgiveness; but it wasn't every day a girl got invited to a real minstrel show. Mr. Brunton bought two large steins of beer from a tired-looking boy who served from a tray suspended about his neck.

At the end of an intermission the banjos resumed their foot-teasing twanging and jangling, and Mr. Alex Carter, also a white man wearing burnt cork make-up, appeared to sing, first, "Blue Juanita," a long sentimental ballad, and next a catchy tune called "Buffalo Gal." A pair of real Negroes then executed a very brisk buck and wing to the evident enjoyment of the audience which now was sweating but thoroughly comfortable owing to the surreptitious easing of various belts, laces and buckles.

"And now, Misto' Bones"—the Master of Ceremonies pranced forward, his enormous white bow tie wagging like a seesaw—"what am de mos' popular song of the day?"

The end man cackled, "Hyah! Hyah! Hyah! Why 'Dixie's Land,' ob co'se." Immediately the whole cast commenced to strum the tune as, slinging their banjos across their shoulders, a trio stepped forward to commence the first verse.

The gale of applause was making the dusty rafters shake and loose particles of plaster began to drift down like fine rain, when a quartet of soldiers, cavalrymen by their yellow collars and short, dark blue shell jackets, jumped up and began to shake their fists at the stage. A huge corporal bellowed in a parade-ground voice, "Cut out that Secesh caterwauling and play 'Yankee Doodle.' We've had our bellyful of that damned Rebel tune!"

While the musicians faltered and struck discords, men jumped to their feet all over the American Theatre.

"Throw 'em out!" people shouted. "Toss them Blue-bellies into the street!"

"Damn it, leave 'em be," came the counter-cry. "Maryland ain't no Secesh State."

"The hell she ain't!"

An enormously fat man swung suddenly at the last speaker and knocked him backwards over a row of seats whereupon a fiercely bearded individual, whose features looked as if they had been carved out of solid rawhide, grunted, "Shut up, you damned nigger lover!"

He then punched the fat man and joined in one of the fights breaking out all over the theatre.

Lachlan picked up his overcoat and stood quietly surveying the scene, deciding the best line of retreat. Unfortunately, he and Christina had occupied seats in the very middle of the fifth row and the mêlée was spreading about them with the rapidity of fire in a summer-dried forest.

"Please! Please!" implored the Interlocutor. "We'll sing something else."

A big, tanned bluejacket snatched away someone's umbrella and hurled it like a spear at Mr. Alex Carter. "You bet you will! Sing 'Hail Columbia,' you damned traitor!"

Christina clung desperately to Mr. Brunton's arm and neither said a word nor made any sound, for all that everywhere females were screaming, crying or whimpering in terror.

"Call the police!" arose the cry.

In the aisle at the end of the fifth row, Brunton saw three men dressed like clerks knock down a lean dark young man and start to kick him mercilessly.

"Halt there! Ye domned coowards. Yer killin' him." When they kept right on, Brunton dropped Tina's arm, uttered a growl and shot forward.

Although the Scot was small he certainly knew how to use his fists; they found their marks so effectively that the trio retreated and left their victim limp and huddled in the aisle.

Mechanically Christina rescued Mr. Brunton's overcoat then, with horrified hands pressed tight against colorless cheeks, stood rooted to the spot. How terrible! Nothing like this had ever happened in Waukegan. Oaths, the ringing smack of fists and hoarse yells reverberated under swaying kerosene lamps. Chairs and seats gave way, making a sharp crackling sound.

"*Du lieber Gott, er ist ein starker Kreiger!* Heavens, he is a real warrior!" She glimpsed Mr. Brunton, fighting like a red-headed terrier, knock down the sailor who had hurled the umbrella. While the tide of battle ebbed towards various exits, the thin young fellow Brunton had rescued struggled painfully to his hands and knees with blood dripping out of his mouth and staining his pointed black goatee.

"Are you badly hurt, sir?" Christina demanded, crouching beside him.

"*Merci, Mam'selle.* In a moment I will be all right. Some *goujat* must have kicked me on the jaw."

The furious shrilling of police whistles put an effective stop to the tumult; thinking only of escape, the combatants began to run aimlessly about. Tina was steadying the unknown to an upright position when Brunton, scarlet-faced and disheveled but grinning happily, reappeared.

"Quick noo, lass, and you sir-r. We'll try yon orchestra pit! Can you walk?"

"*Mais oui.*" Although still uncertain on his legs the stranger came reeling along.

As Brunton had hoped, the American Theatre's rear remained as yet unguarded, with the happy result that, presently, he and his companions found themselves floundering along a noisome alley in the general direction of Fawn Street.

"Well, my friend, are ye back on an even keel again?" Brunton inquired while dabbing at a swelling cheek.

"Quite," the other nodded. "It was a most brave assault that you made." The stranger's olive-brown features were long and sensitive and dominated by an aquiline nose, high cheekbones and two of the blackest and liveliest eyes imaginable. Employing a fine lawn handkerchief, he blotted gore from his pointed mustaches and goatee; then, despite slime-coated cobbles, managed an elegant bow, "May I present myself? I am Léon Duchesne, at your service, Monsieur, Madame."

The Scot's eyes narrowed in puzzlement over the other's mode of speech. "I am Lachlan Brunton, sir, and this is Mistress Reigler."

Christina's heart gave a queer little jump at hearing herself referred to as "Mistress" and on being formally presented to so elegant-appearing a gentleman. She inclined her head, and wished she knew how to curtsey. She decided to learn, and soon.

Mr. Duchesne flung about him a bottle-green cape topped by a plum-colored velvet collar and took matters in hand. "My benefactors, shall we repair to a locality in which I feel sure we may obtain refreshment adequate to us all?" His words were a question, but his manner constituted a polite command.

"To the Howard House," he instructed the gray-haired driver of a passing hackney.

"Yas, suh, di-reckly, suh."

Imagine it! She, poor little Christina Reigler, actually was riding in a hired carriage and being grandly escorted to supper by two handsome gentlemen. Happily she settled back on musty-smelling cushions. Oh dear! Why *hadn't* she worn that second-best gown of Molly's?

"From your mention of 'an even keel,' sir, may I venture that your occupation has to do with shipping?" Mr. Duchesne inquired once the vehicle's iron tires commenced to rasp over the uneven pavement of Fawn Street.

"Aye. I'm a marine engineer."

"—And a good one, sir," Tina was surprised to hear herself saying. "Mr. Brunton has worked in the best British yards."

"Indeed!" A subtle change came over Mr. Duchesne's manner. He left off attempting to straighten a flowing dark blue tie which had come undone during the fracas. "So, you understand the construction of engines for—er—seagoing vessels?"

In the gloom Brunton tried to read his host's expression. At what might this odd young gentleman be driving?

Sturdily he replied, "I'll no' claim I'm a genius, yet I've helped construct engines i' the finest shipyards of England and Scotland."

"Fortuitous," muttered Mr. Duchesne more to himself than to his companions. "How damned, astoundingly fortuitous!"

To her last day Christina could recall in detail the supper Mr. Duchesne ordered. Not too skimpy, not too heavy; they had oyster stew, luscious beyond description, apple cobbler and a fascinating dessert of cake and whipped cream—was it called a Charlotte Russe?

Mercy! How respectfully waiters bowed and gurgled, "How do, Misto' Duchesne? Glad to see yo' with us ag'in. Been a long time, suh." Mr. Upshur, the majestic headwaiter, hovered about, rubbed comfortably fat hands together. "I hardly knew you out of uniform, Mr. Duchesne. None of us will ever forget that party you gave when you were commissioned at Annapolis." He grinned. "—Nor the police, neither, I guess, sir."

Tina, meanwhile, lived a dream. She hadn't imagined that there were such huge mirrors in existence. How wonderful this room was with its flaring gaslights and spotless napery. Wonder of wonders, there were no stoves in evidence! The heat must be supplied from some central point in the building. She would have liked to inquire, but was too shy.

When at long last their waiter shuffled off, beneath a tray of used dishes, a small sigh escaped Tina.

"May I offer you a seegar, sir?" The dark young gentleman demanded, producing an alligator-skin case.

In evident regret Brunton shook his head as he settled back in a heavy walnut arm chair. "My thanks, sir. I've not ever been able to afford such luxury." He picked up the tiny glass before him. "Yon is elegant brandy."

"Would you deem it impertinent, sir"—Mr. Duchesne had not again employed the term "Monsieur" since recovering from the assault— "were I to inquire the name of your firm?" He smiled amiably. No less than three diamond rings graced those slim, olive-hued fingers with which he kept testing a heavy gold chain draped across a magnificent waistcoat of yellow and gray brocade depicting the scandalous antics of certain nymphs and satyrs.

"Not in the least," Brunton declared, but Tina noticed a thoughtful, even wary look, entering the Scot's vivid blue eyes. "For the moment, I have no employer."

The lean and supple young man started. "An alumnus of Laird and Son out of employment? Incredible!"

"Yet true, sir. Mr. Reeder, my former employer, took sharp exception to some plain truths I imparted concerning a proposed propeller-hoisting gear." Brunton's broad reddish face broke into a broad smile, "I am, therefore, as the actors say, 'at liberty.'"

"But not for long," Mr. Duchesne put in quickly.

Tina said, "In a day or two he will surely enter the employ of Mr. Fardy—one of our leading shipwrights. Mr. Brunton's abilities are too great to remain unrecognized."

"I wonder, now?" murmured their host, glancing quickly at the near-by tables. "I wonder."

The music of a string trio playing somewhere in a far corner of the dining room became momentarily noticeable.

Brunton hitched forward on his seat and surveyed his host with care. "You're a stranger here, I take it, yet not a stranger."

Duchesne smiled. "But yes."

"You're either a shipbuilder or, from what yon stuffed shirt implied, a naval officer?"

"I was graduated from the Naval Academy some years ago," replied the dark young man, a trifle stiffly, thought Tina, "and, I, er—am in Baltimore in behalf of—er, Governor Moore, on a very confidential matter."

"Governor Moore?"

"Of Louisiana, sir." Duchesne leaned forward, his seegar lifting delicate blue tendrils towards the ceiling. "It could be, Mr. Brunton, that we might converse further to—er—mutual advantage—in a business way." His gaze flickered sideways but found Tina patently absorbed in contemplation of a group of ladies in lustrous satin gowns garlanded and draped with French flowers. Just as Molly had stated, they were, ever so delicately, sipping wine while laughing and chatting lightly with their escorts.

"Business?" Brunton's easy manner evaporated. "Of what sort?"

"Come tomorrow at ten to my room at the Eutaw House and I will make you an offer that I do not think you will decline," was Duchesne's quiet reply. "Please remember, my friend, that I am in your debt. You are very sure you understand marine engines?"

Brunton started to flush. "Understand? Lord, man, I've been building all sorts and kinds the past ten years!"

"Your pardon."

He crooked an imperious finger to summon the headwaiter.

"Jules, *mon ami*, pray summon a carriage for my friends and see that its hire is charged on my account."

VIII

THE COMMISSIONERS

THE MODERN COMFORTS afforded by Mr. Léon Duchesne's suite of rooms at the Eutaw House proved a revelation to Lachlan Brunton.

At his knock a parlor door was opened by an immensely grave Negro wearing a slight gray mustache and beard; undoubtedly he was the Louisianan's body servant. He wore no livery but a suit of unrelieved black.

"Please to enter, M'sieu." Bowing deeply, the valet retreated leaving the Scot to view, open-mouthed, many evidences of elegance. The glass curtains, for instance, were of sparkling white *point* de Venise lace, and the russet velour draperies arranged before them looked very elegant for being fringed with tiny cloth balls. The furniture standing about a gleaming heavy oak table was of black walnut, heavily adorned by carving and upholstered in horsehair.

From the ceiling elaborate gas fixtures spouted like inverted fountains. Handsome English prints dealing with a multitude of hunting and coaching events decorated walls done in dark red and gold paper. There was even a small marble statue of some Roman deity sitting on a pedestal in one corner; and of well-polished shiny brass cuspidors there was indeed a lavish supply, each neatly centered in an India-rubber mat. These had hardly been used, Lachlan noticed, though the smell of strong seegars permeated the atmosphere.

"M'sieu Brunton, suh!" the valet announced and flung back a door giving into what must be a private dining room. No meal was being served, however in place of plates, papers, ink pots and pens littered the table.

"Ah! Welcome. Welcome. Here, *mes amis*, is my Scottish saviour." Hand outstretched, Léon Duchesne arose, the bruise on his jaw nearly matching in hue a house coat of plum-colored velvet, the black astrakhan collar of which stood so high as to graze the lobes of his small and flat ears. The other two men present also arose and stood waiting beside the table. One was a short and stocky individual whose bearing suggested no particular distinction, but the other presented one of the most unforgettable figures Brunton had ever laid eyes on.

"Gentlemen, I have the honor to present to you Mr. Lachlan Brunton, late of James Watt's and the Messers Lairds' shipyards. Mr. Brunton, this"—he indicated the shorter figure—"is Mr. James L. Semple. Yonder stands Commander Raphael Semmes." Brunton received an impression of craggy, weather-beaten features, of a tight ruler-mark of a mouth and black mustachios—they were long enough to be so termed—waxed into spikes only more pointed than the Commander's neat torpedo beard. Otherwise Commander Semmes looked a straight, spare individual in his early fifties wearing thick iron-gray hair brushed back straight from a high forehead and long enough to dangle over the collar of a well-cut brown sack suit. It was the Commander's eyes, however, which particularly attracted Brunton's attention. In their clear gray depths he read hints of sadness, of imagination, of tenderness, and yet the violent gleams of a zealot's fiery nature predominated.

"A pleasure, indeed, sir," Semmes declared in a deep yet soft voice. "My young friend Duchesne has been recounting your timely assistance last night. You seem to know how to fight."

"Aye. Precious few Highlanders do not, so 'tis no credit of mine."

Duchesne pushed forward a chair upon which Brunton gingerly seated himself. There was something disconcerting about the intentness of Semmes' gaze and the searching glances Mr. Semple was directing upon him.

"Do we understand correctly that you are, er—at the moment unemployed?" Semple drawled.

"Aye," the Scot admitted. "This morning, however, I've learned that Mr. Fardy wishes to interview me this afternoon."

"Commander Semmes and Mr. Semple," the host explained, slim fingers again fumbling at his watch chain, "are spending a few days in Baltimore on—well—call it a purchasing mission."

Raphael Semmes looked up suddenly. "Before we go further, Léon, we must determine one point beyond question or doubt. Mr. Brunton, how do your sympathies lie in regard to matters of Secession? Speak frankly, please."

Brunton began to perspire slightly; the Commander's eyes suggested the points of leveled bayonets.

"As a British subject, sir, I've taken no sides and express no preference one way or another." He paused, chose his words with care. "It does seem logical to me, however, that if yer various States entered freely into an Union, they should remain equally free to quit it." This expression of his sentiments was no more or less than what he actually felt.

When he had done, the three Southerners exchanged glances. Finally, Semmes twirled one of his mustachios, drawled, "I reckon you'll prove trustworthy, Mr. Brunton. Pray proceed, Mr. Semple."

Semple leaned forward, elbows on table. "Mr. Duchesne tells me you are a marine engineer, and a capable one. Could you, for instance, describe to me the various types of steam-jacket adheaters."

Appearing very earnest and sober in his knitted blue wool waistcoat, brown jacket and black serge trousers, Brunton spoke in deliberate, succinct tones for about five minutes, his broad red-brown features lit with enthusiasm. "The three adheating instruments most commonly employed are the coil, the tubular adheater and the steam-jacketed steampipe," he concluded.

"That's enough," Semple rumbled and relit a seegar he had let grow cold during his discourse. "So far as engineering knowledge goes, he'll do all right."

Semmes inquired, "Should it be made worth your while, would you be free to travel?"

Brunton hesitated the barest instant. "Aye. I've no family this side o' the Atlantic and, as ye know, no employment."

Both Duchesne and Semple frowned and sat straighter when Semmes' deep voice demanded, "Well, sir, what would you consider as a sufficient emolument?"

It was Brunton's turn to become wary. What the Devil were they about, these three oddly assorted gentlemen? Innate Caledonian caution restrained him, prompted him to fence. "Before we go into that, I feel I must know more concerning the nature of this employment ye seem about to offer."

"You'll learn that all in good time," growled Semple.

Duchesne, however, arose, crossed to toast long, closely pantalooned legs at the fire. "I don't agree with Mr. Semple. I think Mr. Brunton has a right to an explanation."

"Very well, tell him," Semmes directed.

"Mr. Semmes and Mr. Semple here have been dispatched to Baltimore—where I have the honor to be an agent of our Southern Confederacy—and to other cities, by Mr. Stephen R. Mallory, Secretary of the Navy. These gentlemen are commissioned to purchase all manner of war-like stores and to secure the services of persons calculated to be helpful in the building and arming of the Confederate States Navy."

"May God bless and further its creation!" A light flitted over Semmes' stern, almost ascetic features, then faded as he continued,

"My young friend has stated our mission quite exactly; we in the South stand in desperate need of marine architects, shipwrights, armorers and engineers. Unfortunately very few officials in Montgomery seem to appreciate that fact."

When a waiter brought in a bottle, ice and water and poured drinks, Brunton thought hard. How dared these men engage in what most people hereabouts would call treasonable activity within fifty miles of the Capital? Were these indeed responsible agents? How were they equipped financially?

An early fly commenced to buzz experimentally about the stamped-glass bowls protecting the gaslights.

Once the servant had shuffled out, Semple inquired, "Could you, Mr. Brunton, design an engineering yard capable of manufacturing engines suitable for men-of-war?"

Promptly Brunton's red head inclined. "Aye, that I could—granted time and the leave to import certain machineries and skilled mechanics from England or Scotland."

"That can and will be done," Semple promised. "My main consideration is whether you can at once tell me precisely what make of machinery you would require? You see, for us, time is of the essence."

"Aye. Rough plans and fundamental requirements I could give ye tomorrow. Jamie McFarland and George Leason I'd send for by the first packet."

"Do you think your friends might be persuaded to come as far as Mobile or New Orleans?"

"Aye. An' ye paid them well enough. I warn that ye'll have to dig deep, sirs; they're masters of their craft."

The end of an hour found tobacco smoke floating like a miasma in Léon Duchesne's private apartment, its occupants wearing unbuttoned waistcoats and bending over an ever-increasing pile of scribbled estimates and notations. Their most important achievement, decided Léon Duchesne, was the definite appointment of Lachlan Brunton as a Civilian Assistant Chief Engineer in the Navy Department of the Confederate States Government. His pay proved so munificent that that hard-headed Scot scarce could believe his ears. Two thousand, eight hundred and fifty dollars a year and payable in gold!

Mr. Semple left the room presently to reappear lugging a heavy canvas bag. Lips pursed, he set about stacking gold pieces to the amount of two hundred and thirty-seven dollars—the first month's wages. "Fifty dollars traveling expenses should get you to New Orleans in style."

"Aye," Brunton murmured, his head spinning at the gleam of those broad, red-gold coins.

IX

ROBERT ASHTON SEYMOUR

"TO THIRTY-THREE Caroline Street," Lieutenant Samuel Seymour directed, clambering into a ramshackle hackney cab. Although quite familiar with Baltimore as were most Annapolis graduates, Sam sat forward on the lumpy and mildewed upholstery of the carriage to study the busy streets, balancing a large bundle of presents on his lap. Baltimore, he decided, hadn't changed a great deal. Four-horse stages still rolled away from the General Wayne Inn heading for Bel Air, Emmitsburg and Reisterstown; horse cars still clanked along bulging with hoop skirts and stovepipe hats.

Um. There was Dukehart's, where, in the good old days, he'd purchased percussion caps, fowling powder and fishing tackle; but only disorderly black ruins marked the previous location of his favorite tobacconists. It seemed as if Baltimore must perpetually be taking fire, for at several other points brand-new buildings were in the process of erection.

Although somnolent of appearance, the cab driver quite skillfully guided his bony nag around large mudholes and breaks among the cobbles, and slipped between huge wains creaking down towards the docks.

The streets seemed to be jam-packed with pedestrians of every sort, color and condition. There were the usual farmers, merchants, errand boys and mechanics going about their business. He glimpsed broad-hatted Quakers, nuns, trollops, gamblers and many more soldiers than of yore. The sidewalks appeared blue with them. Soon enough, he arrived at an explanation. The arrival of Mr. Lincoln's administration had crowded travelers out of Washington, filling Baltimore's famous hotels to overflowing. Sam had noticed an indefinable uneasiness abroad shortly after registering at the Eutaw Hotel. Instead of that loud and general jollity so usual in a popular hostel, there had been substituted guarded conversation among the patrons who had gathered themselves into groups, talked in low voices, and kept glancing sidewise as if fearful of eavesdroppers.

For March the day was warm and icicles wept freely from eaves yet the desk clerk had claimed that this winter of 'sixty-one had been one of the most bitterly cold on record in Baltimore.

When the vehicle rattled into Salisbury Street, Sam drew a last puff from his seegar before flicking its stump into the street. Smiling, he settled back, surprised to discover his heart beginning to thump rapidly.

"In a very few minutes now," he told himself, "I'm going to see Robbie, my own son! Son! What a wonderful word! Wonder if Pa was ever as pleased to see Irad?"

Yes, this son of his might some day accomplish great things; his very existence was warming to the hearts of the old folks down in Norfolk, Captain Felix Seymour and Amanda, his wife. Of course, Mother, being New England, naturally wouldn't act downright silly the way Pa might; Sylvia had forwarded Pa's courtly but definite appreciation of his only grandson.

Being precious ignorant, like most seafaring men, concerning the growth of infants, Sam found himself desperately uneasy. Could a boy of two years be expected to talk? If so, how much? Did children of that age have any teeth, or did they still drink from a bottle? More important, would Robbie resemble his mother? The naval officer's weather-stained face contracted and his smile faded, as always, when he thought of Janet. How blissfully serene had been their all-too-short married life! Surely Janet must have become one of God's loveliest angels. He could still visualize her ever so clearly—especially that time they'd gone sailing on the Elizabeth River near Portsmouth.

The past two years had been busy ones, but mighty lonely, too, on occasion. A man who'd once been married found himself listening for the sound of a woman's voice speaking tenderly, for her quiet tread and gentle movements. Down in Matanzas and then again in

Nassau, he had been tempted to seek solace in the usual seafaring fashion—especially in Matanzas where a lovely, sloe-eyed young Creole named Lolita—well, he hadn't gone with her and now was glad of it.

Absently, his fingers drummed upon the brown-paper wrapping of the bundle held on his blue-serge-covered knee. All the same he guessed he was far from being a prig; as a midshipman on the Mediterranean station, he had accumulated an imposing tally of conquests.

Sam's daydreaming ended when the cab stopped and the Negro cabby dismounted, bowed and tipped a battered plug hat while opening the door.

"Heah you is, suh, Number Thutty-three Ca'line Street, suh."

Sam tossed the darky a half dollar, then turned, and narrowed his eyes in surprise. So this was where his son had been living for nearly two years! It was astonishing that Irad could not have afforded something better than this ill-painted and diminutive clapboard house; besides, Sylvia had money, lots of it by all accounts. On glancing up and down the street, he decided that, although this thoroughfare was narrow and ill-paved, it looked eminently respectable.

Mechanically Sam squared shoulders under his blue overcoat when starting for the door. He hoped both Irad and Sylvia would be on hand there to receive him; they all had so much to talk about.

While mounting steps of white-painted wood he thought to see a window curtain stir, but then a cheap, stoneware bell knob was beneath his gloved fingers and he gave a vigorous pull. A tiny jangle responded in the depths of the house, preluding the sound of hurriedly advancing footsteps. He clutched his bundle tighter, set a broad smile on his face and stood watching the front door swing slowly back.

To his amazement, there seemed to be no one in the hall. It was tenanted only by a slant of sunshine drawing a bright yellow streak across a badly worn, red runner carpet.

Sam set foot inside and caught breath to call out, when out of a doorway to the right a small figure dashed out. The child—it was a boy for all that absurd red tartan dress and those long gold-brown curls—halted with feet braced apart and raised a merry, round and pink face. As a parrot might he piped, "We'come home, Da-da."

During a long instant the tall uniformed figure remained stock-still staring down until, all at once, the lad's outline became indistinct.

Then the bundles thudded on the floor as Lieutenant Samuel Seymour sank to both knees, choking, "Son! Son!"

Startled, the child recoiled and made as if to flee, but halted when to a soft swishing sound Sylvia glided through that same door to the right. Keeping her gaze lowered she bent gracefully, guided the little figure into Samuel Seymour's white-gloved hands. "Don't be frightened of your father, Robbie dear."

"Oh, Son! Son! I'm so terribly glad to see you!" Sam whisked up the youngster, pressed him close and, for the first time, became aware of that curious sweet odor which is peculiar to very young children.

"Oh, Sylvia! Sylvia, you've taken wonderful care of him."

She made no reply only sailed forward, arms outstretched and a lovely radiance in her sherry-hued eyes.

"Sam, Sam! How wonderfully brown you look!"

Although his son's fat arms now were about his neck, he was able to fling an arm about his sister-in-law and draw her near. He read an impatience on those vividly red lips, then kissed Sylvia hard—on both cheeks. The child, being released, promptly scurried over to probe and tug at the bundle.

All at once Sam realized that he himself was clinging to both of Sylvia's hands and staring on her as if he had never seen her before.

"I didn't think you could grow more beautiful—but you have," he burst out.

"T-trust the Navy to—to flatter a p-poor-stay-at-home," Sylvia faltered. Lord above! How handsome and vital he was in that uniform which set off his bronzed skin, bleached gold sideburns and lively dark brown eyes.

A thousand words, often rehearsed, struggled for utterance. For the occasion, she had donned a dress of olive-green silk and cuffs and collar of fine Irish lace. There were little yellow bows securing the part in her hair and, above them, side combs of silver-mounted tortoise shell.

"If you don't intend to heat all Baltimore, perhaps I had better shut the door." He laughed while fumbling at the sparkling gold buttons of his overcoat. "Where's Irad?"

"Working as usual—or even harder," she explained over her shoulder while hanging his cap to a scruffy, deer-point hanger. "As I wrote you, Irad now occupies one of the most responsible positions at Mr. Reeder's shipyard."

"Bully for old Owlie!"

He noticed a curious twist to her mouth as she began her reply, but was too full of the moment to comment on it.

"I'm sure Irad will be home at any moment. When your message came from the hotel I sent a messenger for him to come at once."

"Good old Owlie! How is he? Rolling in wealth?" he queried and as quickly wished he hadn't. This house should have been answer enough.

Sylvia's firmly rounded chin elevated itself a trifle. "He's doing extremely well, now that Mr. Reeder has given him free rein to try out his theories. Irad works from dawn until late at night. He's most conscientious."

"Always was," Sam agreed, following her into the miniature living room.

"Da-da? Wha' here?" Crouched low, the child was trying to lift Sam's package.

"Yes, what's all this?" Sylvia demanded. "We're both consumed by curiosity."

He employed a sailor's clasp knife to slash undone the sturdy wrappings. "Call them belated Christmas presents. Here—son." His voice thickened over the word. He was about to present the boy with a lovely little model of a sloop-of-war—complete and authentic as to spars, hull and rigging—but Sylvia smilingly intervened.

"It's too fragile, Sam," she warned. "He'll crush it in two shakes of a lamb's tail. Haven't you anything sturdier?"

"Maybe this will do, then." Smiling broadly, Sam unwrapped the hobbyhorse which proved an immediate success. Emitting shrill whoops of joy, Master Robert promptly undertook to exercise his new steed up and down the hallway.

"This, my dearest sister"—Samuel held out an oblong package, limp in its French tissue and scarlet ribbon—"is yours and with it, my heart's gratitude."

The mantilla revealed by Sylvia's flying fingers was indeed an exquisite thing. It floated filmy and light as a summer cloud when she shook it out and saw that its pattern was executed with that infinite delicacy and patience peculiar to Latin peoples.

"Oh, Sam, darling, it's unbelievable it's so lovely!" Sylvia tossed the mantilla high into the air, rapturously watched its gossamer texture billow. "There'll not be another so fine in Savannah—or Baltimore either," she added quickly. "It's much too fine for me."

" 'Tis nothing," he assured her and, on impulse, kissed her glowing cheek once more. "When I think of all that you and Irad have done for Robbie, I consider myself forever in your debt!"

The brightness of her smile faded momentarily. "Your Rob's a wonderful baby. I—I hope, Sam, you won't mind that I have let him call me 'Mamma.' You see"—the light blond hair glistened when she bent to retrieve the French tissue wrappings—"I—we have so wanted a child of our own." She spoke in passionate emphasis and her gracefully sloping shoulders quivered beneath the puffed sleeves, "I want one so much I know the Lord won't deny me. I must carry on Irad's name. I know, I feel I'm not barren." She looked anxious. "Tell me, reassure me, Samuel. You—you don't intend to take Robbie from us?" The anxiety in her voice was genuine and touching.

"No. Of course not."

"I was afraid you might have met someone. After all, two years is a long time."

His gaze following the ruddy little boy's antics, Sam said quietly, "There is no one, Sylvia. To tell the truth I haven't even thought about remarriage."

"Oh, I'm glad, glad! So very glad!" The intensity of her manner astonished him. "All my friends—our friends," she corrected herself, "have babies. If it weren't for Robbie, all I could do at the Sewing Circle would be to sit and bite my lips while they talk children. As it is, I can worry with the best of them. Silly, aren't I?"

Sam Seymour patted her shoulder and the two gold stripes on his cuffs flashed briefly.

"Cheer up. Jim Jackson of the *Sabine* and his wife were married eleven years before they'd any tykes—now they've four."

"But I don't *want* to wait," protested Sylvia. "I won't! Why, in another eleven years, I—I'll be a withered old hag. There now, please forgive me. I'm so happy to see you I reckon I'm talking like a fool!"

Not knowing what to say Sam turned in a hurry to the other packages.

"These are for Christmas before last," said he, offering gloves of French glacé kid. "I—I hope they fit. I got them as small as I could." For Irad he told her he had purchased a pair of wonderfully engraved dueling pistols complete with case, powder flask, bullet mold and loading mallet.

"They were made in France," he explained, opening the flat leather case. "The man said there aren't any finer ones to be found."

Sylvia studied the weapons with genuine interest. "They must have cost a fortune, but do you think Irad will use them?"

His glance was at once mocking and steady. "Any man married to a woman half so beautiful is likely to find them useful."

The olive-green skirts swirled to Sylvia's derisive curtsy. "Heavens, Samuel, you have been in foreign parts!"

Sam laughed, strode over to survey his son's futile attempts to coax his hobbyhorse upstairs.

"Irad's always been my favorite brother—used to stick up for me at school."

A brief silence invaded the living room. Both were thinking of Reynolds, the scapegrace youngest brother.

"Are you—will you be ordered right away to a new ship?" Sylvia continued to stroke the mantilla.

"No. I'm on a forty-day leave."

"Naturally you'll want to spend some time with your parents."

"Naturally. Pa is getting on, and Mother, too. How are they?"

"Fine, the last we heard. You—you'll come back to Baltimore for a while before reporting back on duty?"

"Yes, but I don't know yet just when," he explained, sinking beside her onto the fine old Chippendale sofa she had fetched up from Savannah. "You see, I've some—well, I've some business down in Norfolk."

When, with curls flying and cheeks bright, Master Robbie charged his wooden horse into the parlor Sam caught him up and held him at arms' length studying every detail of his features. Think of it! This very solid child was his own—the next generation of Seymours. Some day he'd serve in the Navy, the fourth generation to do so. Beaming, he permitted the boy to stroke his sideburns, then fumble at the single golden star on each of his shoulder straps and at the glittering buttons that, in a double rank, ascended his broad blue chest.

The child squealed his delight so loudly that no one heard the front door open. Irad came striding into the room before anyone realized it.

"Sam!"

"Owlie!" They flung arms about each other, hugged and pounded each other between the shoulder blades in that curious manifestation of deep affection so peculiar to Anglo-Saxons. Irad, Sylvia noticed, stood almost a half head taller but was not so wide in the shoulders as his second brother. Restraining Robbie, she beamed on them, thinking, "They're both strong, good men; men on the verge of great accomplishments. I mustn't let Irad fall behind again. Is Reynolds Seymour like either of these two in character? I wonder. Why is his name mentioned only when it's unavoidable?"

The short day faded long before they had done talking and Master Robert was commencing to make imperative hungry noises.

"I think," Irad suggested to his wife, "that it might be fitting if I conduct our evening prayers before supper, while the four of us can pray together for the first time."

From a spool-legged table, he lifted the Book and briefly riffled pages worn by the fingers of three generations; then in a low grave voice, he commenced to read.

X

At the General Wayne Inn

Through clouds of pipe and seegar smoke blueing the General Wayne Inn's saloon, Irad cast his brother a searching look and took care to lower his voice before saying, "Sam, how do the bulk of you naval officers feel concerning Secession?"

Before replying Sam several times revolved a toddy glass bright with lemon peel. "Why, I suppose it's about the same as in the Regular Army. Where you hail from decides the matter for you. Only, in our service, the proportion of Southerners is about one Reb to three Northerners, almost the exact reverse of the Army."

"In other words," Irad muttered, "there hasn't been any general rush of naval officers to resign and go South?"

"Not exactly," Sam admitted earnestly. "Still, many of our very best threw in their commissions long ago and traveled to Montgomery; others are resigning the moment their ships make port. We've some of the very excellent seniors on our side, too: Josiah Tattnall, Henry Harstene, Franklin Buchanan and Matthew Maury, to name a few."

"You just now said 'we' in reference to the South," Irad remarked.

"Yes. We're Virginians after all, aren't we?"

"Of course. Tell me, Sam, are you fully convinced that this is Virginia's quarrel?"

"I expect our State will prefer being the head of the South to the tail of the North." He hunched further over their round marble-topped table. "Is it true that Commander Semmes has been seen around Baltimore?"

Irad looked away, fussed with his short yellow beard. "I really don't know. You see, Sam, I've made it a rule not to discuss politics when I can avoid it." He sighed. "But it's becoming near impossible for me to abide by my resolution because of something that's happened just recently."

Gray eyes grave behind their steel-rimmed spectacles, he described the brawl in Caroline Street. "As a result my name was published as a Southern sympathizer in connection with that riot."

"Where?"

"Oh, in the *Baltimore American*. It's suddenly become just as fervently pro-Southern as it was pro-Northern a while back."

"But weren't you in fact leading the pro-Southern element?"

"Southern element, my eye!" Irad burst out angrily. "It was a low-down gang fight between two sets of hoodlums. Neither side really cared a damn for the South—or North."

"More coffee!" Sam demanded, crooking his finger at their Negro waiter. "How does this newspaper account affect you? Thought you looked uncommon serious when you came in."

"Quite frankly, I am; because Mr. Reeder has come out into the open at last and as a Union sympathizer. He claims that no matter how many Southern States join the Confederacy, they'll never win."

"Then he's a fool!" Sam burst out sharply. "Our people know how to fight and the Yankees don't. There aren't many boys south of the Potomac who can't ride and shoot from the time they get out of diapers."

"True enough," Irad admitted slowly. "How many of these boys have we, though, compared to the North? Reeder, and most shipping men for that matter, point out further that we're quite without ships of war. Is that true?"

"For the moment, yes. All the same we'll build plenty of naval vessels—and damned good ones—should we have to fight Old Abe Lincoln's Abolitionists," Sam declared earnestly. "I suppose you've heard that Mr. Davis and the Confederate Congress recently have authorized the purchase and construction of ten heavily gunned and armored sloops? Five of them, mark you, are to displace a thousand tons!"

Irad's supple fingers selected and absently snapped several toothpicks from a jar set before them. "Yes, I'd heard of it. D'you know, Sam, I'd give a finger for the chance of designing one. You see, I've a theory that if a steamship's garboard strake—"

"Spare me the mechanical wonders in store!" Sam laughed, brushed crumbs from his lap. "Me, I'm a simple gunnery officer and can't tell a cylinder head from a camshaft. I declare, you're as full of ideas as an egg is of meat. You must take after Mother, and she's Yankee enough for the whole family, I expect."

Several times during their luncheon Sam was rendered hot and uneasy by unfriendly, even hostile, looks directed at him. Seated about the saloon he recognized many familiar types: local merchants richly but conservatively appareled, obvious gamblers sporting a profusion of pinchbeck jewelry and newspapermen locked in heated argument.

By far the most numerous patrons were buyers in from the Deep South to make a semi-annual purchase of hardware and other merchandise. Broad, drawling accents could be heard, too, from still another class of patron. These were the owners, or agents, of huge plantations in western Georgia, Alabama and Mississippi, in town to buy up essential manufactured goods which, traditionally, always had come from Baltimore. These gentlemen, already resplendent in gaily colored waistcoats, shirts and pantaloons, were further decked out by huge diamond shirt studs, ruby cufflinks and emerald stickpins. These were anything but subdued concerning their political views.

"Yes, suh. Ah know what Ah'm talking about," thundered a choleric old aristocrat. "Just let that Lincoln baboon tek one belligerent step, just one, then, suh, ouah armies will march and ouah generals will be dictatin' peace terms befo' summer sets in." But hotheaded talk from civilians was now commonplace.

Under the disturbed conditions it was only natural that an unusual number of uniforms should be in evidence. They offered an amazing variety—the handsomely distinctive uniforms of such units as the Baltimore City Guard, the McComas Riflemen, the Independent Grays and the Law Grays.

"Who's that headed this way?" Irad inquired. Spectacles gleaming, he indicated a tall, very handsome individual with curly black hair that tumbled down to the Lincoln-green velvet collar of a brown, long-tailed coat.

"Damned if it ain't Léon Duchesne!" Sam jumped up, upsetting his chair. "He's a real Creole, Owlie, from New Orleans. We served in the old *Susquehanna* together. I hear he resigned last winter. Damned good man despite his fancy duds."

Duchesne came swinging up to wring Sam's hand, then bow formally to the elder brother and declare himself vastly honored. At second glance Irad perceived what Sam did not, that the Louisianan must have been drinking freely.

"*Nom de Dieu!* Sam, what a wonderful surprise! You're headed South, I presume?" Chairs squealed and scraped about and a dozen heads swung in surprise at such a remark directed to an officer wearing Federal uniform. Duchesne settled a trifle unsteadily into a chair at the table.

Irad prayed that Sam would guard his reply. What he said was, "In that general direction."

"You are just in time," Duchesne declared in a soft, but carrying voice. "Great things afoot, great things. I can promise you, Sam, that within the year we—we'll have a navy second to none." He slapped the table sharply and so drew further attention. "Can't avoid it, can we? We've the cream of the Old Navy! Maury, the great oceanographer; Tattnall, best engineer our Navy ever had—"

"—Excepting, of course, Stockton, Ericsson and Isherwood," Sam Seymour corrected.

A graceful flourish of Duchesne's hand dismissed the suggestion, and he fell to toying with the clump of heavy gold seals dangling above his blue satin waistcoat. "Waiter! Toddies for three. No, *mon ami*, I insist."

That near-by tables were taking a deep interest and could hear everything disturbed Irad no little. There seemed to be nothing he could do about it, even though the Creole was saying in a conspiratorial undertone, "Take my advice, Sam, and board the first train to Montgomery. I'll give you a letter to Mr. Mallory and another to Rafe Semmes—you'll land a commission in jig time. We're short of gunnery experts and that's a fact!"

"Thanks."

"You are on your way, aren't you?"

"If Virginia secedes, I will resign," Lieutenant Seymour returned evenly. "I tell you, Léon, there's too much boasting talk from people like Edmund Rhett and those other South Carolina fire-eaters, from Toombes of Georgia and their like. They're talking too big for the size of the stick they carry."

Duchesne's lean features darkened and he flared right up, "Sir, I trust I do not misunderstand your true motives for such remarks?"

"You don't!" Sam Seymour declared heartily. "Should Virginia secede, I reckon the South will stand a good chance of winning."

"Bully for you, suh! That's talking," called someone from a near-by table. Obviously more than a few fellow patrons hailed from the Old Dominion State. "I trust you will permit me, suh, the honor of sending a round of drinks to your table. I hope the liquor, suh, will prove as sound as your sentiments," declared a plump, gray-haired gentleman, popping up and bowing from half way across the room.

Long white apron flapping like a loose jib, the waiter presently fetched a half bottle of truly noble bourbon together with a plate of curious little biscuits recently introduced by Baltimore's very sizable German colony. "They're called pretzels," Irad explained.

Duchesne's speech had thickened perceptibly when he inquired of Irad, "Have you noticed—er—unusual activity among Baltimore's shipyards?"

"Unusual, sir? I don't grasp your meaning."

"I mean are there no floating batteries, no sloops or gunboats under construction for the Federal Navy?" The Louisianan's attempt at casualness was painfully transparent.

"Not that I have heard of. You see, sir, Mr. Lincoln still believes our quarrel can be settled without recourse to arms."

"Never, never!" Duchesne burst out so loudly, so passionately that everyone in the whole mirror-lined room turned to stare. "War is unavoidable! Nor shall we flinch from a trial at arms."

Before either of the Seymours could divine his intention, the Creole had leaped up onto his chair and began waving his whiskey glass.

"To Southern liberties!" he shouted.

Hardly had he spoken when half the men present jumped up, raised their glasses and shouted, "Hoo-rah for the Stars and Bars!" "Down with the Rail Splitter!" "Hurray for Jeff Davis!"

Once the clamor had subsided—fortunately without incident—the headwaiter sidled up to the table. "Please, Mr. Duchesne, sir," he pleaded in agitation that extended even to his well-oiled sideburns. "I must beg you in the future to refrain from such provocative toasts. The management insists."

"Why, cer'ainly, my good man," Duchesne smiled loosely and fumbled out a half dollar. "We merely wished to make our sent'ments unmistakabl' clear. Besides I must leave. Impor'nt appointment. Ver' confidential matter."

Abruptly, he controlled himself, stood straight. "My service to you, Mr. Seymour and you, Sam." Duchesne bowed gravely. "My friends, I will be seeing you both before long," he predicted; then, summoning a gay smile, sauntered away among the tables and was lost to sight.

"Wish to God *that* hadn't happened," snapped Irad worriedly, polishing his spectacles.

"What happened?"

"That silly toast of Duchesne's."

"But why?" Sam was puzzled. "Expressions far more violent are heard all over Baltimore every day."

By means of the mirror, Irad, without turning, indicated an expressionless, hard-faced trio seated in the far corner. "The flat-faced one I know to be a detective officer of the police force, he with the pointed beard is Frank Byrnes of the Sun and I think the third is a Pinkerton man—anyway he's been nosing about the docks and shipyards for over a month. I don't like it. I can't afford to be seen with people talking like your Creole friend; it's risking the job I've worked damned hard to land."

"You always were a champion worrier, Owlie," Sam broke in. "By the bye, where does Pa stand on Secession?"

"So far, he's said nothing. You know he never opens his mouth till his mind's made up."

"—And Mother?"

"Flares right up in defense of the North, in her letters at least. I don't imagine she, or any dyed-in-the-wool Yankee for that matter, is overpopular around Norfolk these days." It became his turn to be curious. He studied his brother's powerful and windburned features with care while he inquired, "Sam, what do you aim really to do on your visit to Norfolk?"

Before making reply, Sam rubbed at his light brown sideburns, then stirred the sugar at the bottom of his toddy. "I'll look around, I expect," he admitted. "You see, I've several Southern classmates on duty at the Gosport Navy Yard who can tell me how the wind blows."

"I think you'll find they've been transferred," Irad predicted. "No Administration with the wits of a mouse would leave our most valuable Navy Yard at the mercy of disaffected officers."

"I wonder?" Sam drawled. "On the train coming down, Harry Lewis told me that our new President is so desperately afraid of offending Virginia that he has ordered Secretary Welles of the Navy to make no overt acts."

"But—but, surely," Irad insisted, "that particular shipyard is of critical importance?"

"We'll see," Sam Seymour smiled. "Somehow, I think it's important to understand the true situation in Gosport." He winked. "Might come in handy, you know, if our State goes out."

XI

The Ambrotype

For Christina Reigler, life these days was being transformed from mere drab existence into a realm replete with fascinating possibilities. Not only had she actually attended a theatre—even if the performance had ended in a riot—but now she was about to have her ambrotype taken, just as if she inhabited one of those impressive big houses lining Mount Vernon Place and Park Avenue.

"Now tilt the head upwards a trifle," suggested Mr. J. D. Marsters. "Ah! That's it! Really, Miss, you have such a lovely curve to the lips 'twould be a crime against Art not to do it full justice."

Tina complied, then felt the immobilizer close its kid-covered jaws at the nape of her neck. It would steady her head during the ten long seconds required to obtain a clear likeness.

"Smile a little more, Miss Reigler," pleaded Lachlan Brunton. "After all, is it no' yer birthday? Yer still young enough."

The engineer stood across the studio with hands lost in the slash pockets of his brand-new brown corduroy jacket. Tina was thinking what a change had come over her beau. She was beginning to believe that he really was such—not just a young man lonely in a foreign land. Auburn head cocked a little to one side, he was, with deep interest, watching bird-like Mr. Marsters perform esoteric rites about his camera.

Ever since he'd received employment three days ago now, he'd gone about grinning like a horse collar. It irritated her, however, that, no matter how tactfully she questioned, he steadfastly declined to disclose either the name of his employer or the nature of his new work. All that she'd been able to deduce was that it had to do with shipbuilding in far-off Louisiana.

"Steady now, Miss. No. Smile broader; hold!"

The shutter snapped open, remained so during a generous ten seconds, then clacked closed.

"Now that wasn't so bad, was it? Didn't hurt much, did it?" Mr. Marsters having pulled the last of his stock jokes, ran chemical-stained fingers through hair brilliant with Macassar oil.

"No," Tina declared seriously. "It was great fun."

"And where, sir, shall I deliver this little lady's picture? It will be ready in three days' time."

"Three days!" Brunton burst out in dismay. "Do you really need so much time?"

Mr. Marsters appeared affronted. "Why, sir, that's very quick for these days. My salon is always popular, but with all this war talk, it seems everybody wants to get photographed. Furthermore, I wish to devote my very best attention to this handsome little lady's portrait."

"Then I guess ye'd best forward it to Miss Reigler."

Tina got up, smoothed the skirt of a new dress she'd sewed during off hours. Certainly it had not been right to spend so much money on herself; still, the cloth *had* come extra-cheap for having been slightly watersoaked during a fire which had destroyed Mr. Elder's Elite Clothing Emporium—or so said the barrow man from whom she bought it. Of dark blue challis, set off by tiny little white crosses, the gown was essentially practical and warm.

Awkwardly, if gallantly, Brunton offered his arm. "And now, Miss Reigler, before I'm off to my train, suppose we try a dish of ice cream in honor of the day?"

"Yes, Mr. Brunton"—she still found it difficult to use his Christian name—"I would like to—very much. But first I must stop by Mrs. Adams' factory to pick up a parcel. I can deliver it on my way back from the railway station."

Brunton waited in the street while Christina lifted her skirts and flew up the stairs and into the common sewing room.

"Why Tina! What a lovely dress!" one of the girls called. "Wherever did you find such lovely material?"

The seamstresses crowded around, admiring, until Mrs. Adams suddenly appeared, parchment-hued features more drawn and worried-looking than ever.

"I declare, Tina, I don't know what's come over you this last week; mooning about over your work and here you are two minutes late! Quick, get this parcel to Mrs. Warfield's and don't you dast tarry on the way."

Suddenly Mrs. Adams' expression altered and she stared as if fascinated at Tina's modest new gown. Her heavy brows almost merged themselves, but she turned aside muttering something like, "I'd best make certain."

Tina never heard the remark, only sped downstairs and soon, in Mr. Brunton's company, was happily consuming a large dish of ice cream at Hopper's Confectionery.

Lachlan set down his spoon and his broad features went redder than usual. "Christina, my dear, I am about to speak of a matter that has been much on my mind. Ye see, yer such an uncommon sweet and clever and—and purposeful lass—" He faltered. "Well, would ye—if —I mean—"

Christina also put down her spoon, and, from across the table, raised China-blue eyes grown large and troubled. "Go ahead, Lachlan. If things were different, what would you ask of me?"

Oblivious to other patrons, to the clatter of a passing horse car and the presence of a near-by waitress, he blurted, "I, well, I'd ask ye to marry me."

"Oh-h. Mr. Brunton! Why, why I don't—"

"—I'm going far away, lass," he declared in a firm undertone. "Yes, wi' the Lord's help, Lachlan Brunton will some day become a great man, a rich man. And I'm in love with you, Tina. I've decided yer the lass for me." Under the table, he groped for and found her hand, pressed it strongly. "I notice we've many the same notions. That's true, isn't it?"

"Oh, yes, Lachlan, yes!" The fly-specked mirrors in their gilded frames seemed to be falling towards her, while the counters, piled high with loaves, cakes, buns and cookies, merged into a strange and general confusion. All else became blurred, everything except Lachlan's homely red-brown features, bright blue eyes and auburn hair.

"And I love you, Lachlan," she said quietly. "If you want I should wait, why, I will, for years if there is no other way. Will you send for me so soon as you can?"

To his last moment Lachlan would never forget the wondrous radiance which that moment beautified the girl's pale but cleanly modeled features.

"Aye, that I will and you may lay to that, as the sailors say. We'll get wedded the very first moment I'm sure I can provide for ye suitably. Here's my address in New Orleans and the name o' the shipyard I am to work at. Mind now, yer not to mention this to a soul," he continued softly. "And now, Dear Heart, I will be off."

"Oh, Lachlan." Her pink underlip quivered and the clear light blue eyes filled, "Is it time already?"

"I fear so." The grip of his hand became fierce. "You'll surely come when I send for ye?"

"On wings, if I had such." She looked pallid and frightened, not over sixteen at the moment. "Oh, Lachlan, I do love you so! Please, please don't make me wait very long."

"I won't," he promised. "I don't fancy the notion o' my promised wife slaving for an old clapperclaw like Mrs. Adams. No, Tina, I dinna favor the mien of her." From a change purse, he selected a dime, placed it on the table in payment for the ice cream. Tina arose, hugging Mrs. Warfield's parcel to her with both arms.

"When ye return to the Widow's," he said, "ye'll come across a wee bairthday present I left 'neath yer pillow. Yer to use it only if hardship befalls."

"But—but, Mr. Brunton—Lachlan dear—already you have made me a present of the wonderful ambrotype." Her pulses were throbbing and a wonderful unfamiliar warmth filled and lifted her small and pointed breasts.

Grinning, he shook his copper-colored head. "That was for me, so when it's ready, ye'll post it down to New Orleans like a good girl."

Out on the sidewalk he halted and turned to confront her. "And now, Christina dear, I must be bidding ye farewell. Ye'll be tardy with your errand, else."

"Oh, Lachlan! I—I would not let you go so far away!" She swayed blindly towards him; then, to the amusement of passersby, Lachlan Brunton kissed Christina Reigler for the first time, and awkwardly, too.

"There, lass, there. Now take good care of my girl. I'll soon be sending for ye. God bless ye, dear," he murmured, then broke away and went striding off down Charles Street as if the Devil were at his heels.

What could Lachlan have left as a birthday present? Tina fairly flew up hollow-sounding stairs to the attic room and beneath the cornhusk pillow of her lumpy little cot discovered a small cardboard box. It was so uncommonly heavy that her wonderment grew until she saw lying on a bed of cotton batting two gloriously gleaming double-eagles. The forty dollars in red-yellow gold was not so precious as that scrap of paper upon which Lachlan had written, "With these also goes my heart. L.B."

Tina sank onto the cot, and out of an unbearable happiness, cried a little, thinking, "This, Lachlan should not have done until I told him I would marry with him. But of course, he knew—I am such an obvious little goose!" She mopped her eyes but continued to cry out of sheer happiness. In search of a handkerchief she crossed to a rickety chest of drawers and only then perceived a square of common brown wrapping paper propped against her pincushion shaped like a tomato; it had been poor dear Mamma's last birthday present.

Tina's elation faded when she recognized Hermann's immature, sprawling script, and an odd, tingling sensation manifested itself between her shoulder blades. Her fingers commenced to tremble even as she unfolded the heavy paper. Lip caught between teeth, she read the penciled words:

Dear Sister: You have been a good and kind sister, and I thank you for all you have done, but I am no longer the little boy you imagine me. Today I have enlisted in the Naval Service. Buy the time you find this I will be on a ship, where, I will not tell you but you will here of me before long & you will be proud of your loving bruder Hermann Reigler.

XII

DEBACLE

HAD SHE TUMBLED down a flight of stairs, Chirstina Reigler could not have been more hurt and confused.

"*Oh, Bruder, warum?*" She felt the strength desert both legs. The husk mattress rustled slightly when she sank sobbing onto the cot. Was it not a sinful thing for any navy to accept a boy so young— only fifteen? Maybe, though, they didn't know the truth. No doubt Hermann had lied; he was big enough to look seventeen.

How sad a way to celebrate her own eighteenth birthday! Here was Lachlan off on his long, long journey to Louisiana, and now her baby brother had dashed off into the unknown. How terrible! Sailors were such rough, ungodly people. *Der kleiner Bruder* could not have had any conception of the real fate in store for him aboard a man-of-war; as a powder monkey or even as apprentice seaman, his life would be harsh.

Characteristically, Tina commenced to blame herself. "More care I should have taken," she sobbed. "He was left too much alone. Ach, dear Mamma in Heaven, please forgive me. I did the best I could, but it was not enough." She began to cry in earnest.

After a while her sobs diminished but not before she had got her eyes and nose thoroughly red. She sat up, set her jaw and told herself. "Tears never have mended a broken dish. There is nothing I can do about Hermann. Some day I will hear from him."

After she had cooled swollen eyes and features, Tina forced herself to go downstairs and cook her supper.

She had barely finished a plate of beef stew and a few turnips when a runny-nosed errand boy banged on the boarding house door. It was a note from Mrs. Adams directing Miss Reigler to repair at once to the Adams Family Machine Stitchery. At this prospect of extra work, Christina brightened. Of course her new employer wouldn't be half so sweet and considerate as that pretty Mrs. Seymour. It was largely due to her generosity that she had been able to afford the material for this new dress which everyone seemed to admire so much.

Night work would mean extra pay. A few dollars would be added to her slender but growing savings account in Mr. Alexander Brown's bank.

After having effectively removed all traces of her weeping, she boarded an omnibus at the foot of Central Avenue. Humming, she hurried up the broad stairs leading to the Stitchery's second floor where she hung up her cloak and removed a small round hat.

"Good evening, Ma'am," she called brightly as she hurried in. "I hope you are well."

Just inside the office she halted abruptly, so forbidding were the expressions of both Mr. and Mrs. Adams.

"I am astonished you should appear at all," snapped Mr. Adams through an imposing fringe of gray chin whiskers. "Close that door."

"Why—why, what is wrong, sir? I came just so fast as I could."

"Wrong? Oh you brazen, outrageous little hussy!" Mrs. Adams burst out. "Do you actually have the temerity to ask me what's wrong, you miserable creature?"

Fears rushed about Tina's mind like cats with their fur afire. Big-eyed, she commenced to tremble on the edge of tears for the second time that evening.

"Please, Mr. Adams, don't look at me like that. I try to work hard and I have nothing done to be ashamed of."

"Just listen to that! So innocent appearing." Mrs. Adams jumped up, rushed forward and seized Tina by the ear lobe and jerked her head so sharply that one of her long silver-blond braids came undone. "Don't you dast try to lie to me, you miserable thief!"

"But—but—before the Almighty," Tina panted after wrenching herself free, "I—I do not understand of what you are talking. At least tell me of what you suspect."

It was an unfortunate word.

"Suspect!" Little Mr. Adams' figure fairly swelled in outrage and his chin whiskers vibrated. " 'Suspect' is not the word! And you wearing the cloth you stole from this establishment." He pointed at the dark blue challis. "How dare you try to insult our intelligence like this?"

"S-s-stole?" Tina had backed up against the office door, a small terrified figure. "How could you ever think this possible of me?"

"I didn't," Mrs. Adams hissed, her black eyes hard and bright. "I took you for an uncommon clean, industrious and upright young female. The more fool I!"

"But—b-but, I have stolen nothing."

"Don't go on denying your crime," Mr. Adams rasped. "It only makes matters worse for you!"

To her own surprise Tina made herself cease being terrified. She felt a cold rage chilling her mind, but she didn't get so angry as not to appreciate her danger. "I have not stolen anything. I do not care what you say. I am the honest daughter of honest people. I have never taken so much as a pin that did not belong to me."

"Then where did you get this material?" thundered the proprietor.

"From a huckster on Light Street."

"A likely story!" sneered Mrs. Adams. "See how clever she is, Mr. Adams? Of course she would have bought from some nameless huckster, not in any reputable store that could bear out her story!"

Tina began to sob, more in outrage than in fear.

"But I did not steal it, I tell you, I did not! I paid five good dollars for it."

"That proves you are lying!" Mrs. Adams instantly put in. "That challis was worth fifteen dollars."

"But—but, it was water damaged. The barrow man said he got it at a fire sale." Eagerly she raised the hem. "Look, look here, you can see a little stain on the skirt."

"You spilled something on it. No, no, my girl," Mrs. Adams agitatedly folded arms over her thin breast. "Just you try to convince a magistrate with such a cock-and-bull story. You'd better think of a better one when your case is called."

"Case?"

"Certainly," Mr. Adams snapped. "You do not imagine we are going to permit an employee to rob us and go off scot free?" He wagged a menacing forefinger. "Now either you pay Mrs. Adams and me for the full value of the cloth, and," he added slyly, "five dollars for the trouble you've caused, or you will sleep this night in the City Jail."

"But—but, I swear, I did not steal it!" Tina's strength was beginning to give away. "Won't you please believe me?" Jail? *Herr Doktor* Brünner's granddaughter committed to a common jail! Oh, no, no!

A measure of Mrs. Adams' outrage subsided. She sniffed.

"It doesn't get me my cloth back to send you to prison so, young lady, we'll be practical. You fetch us twenty dollars by nine tomorrow morning, else it's jail for you."

In her acute distress Tina quite forgot about Lachlan's birthday present. "But—but—I have not got twenty dollars."

An unpleasant laugh escaped Mr. Adams. "You live down by the waterfront, don't you? 'Pears to me even a wench with your looks wouldn't find much trouble—"

"Aye, I'll warrant not," Mrs. Adams snapped. "Now don't go trying to run out on us. Try any nonsense like that and you'll be fetched back in jig time and spend a real long spell in City Prison."

XIII

Decisions

A RAW WIND howling seawards from the mountains of western Maryland brought realization that the bitter winter just past could yet administer a dying stab. Christina gasped under the sudden icy blasts, as she stumbled blindly out onto the sidewalk. For a space she felt too sick, too weakened to move on. Only the fear that one of her late employers might appear sent her tottering on down the ill-lit street. Whoever would have imagined this morning that the whole course of her life was thus to be so completely, so abruptly altered?

Gradually her terror again became subordinated by a sense of outrage.

"This is not right. I have not been fairly accused," she muttered to herself.

Although it was only eight o'clock the cold wind had driven nearly everyone indoors.

"Shall I go to the police and tell them the truth? That would forestall those dreadful people." She debated the notion a while, but, as usual, when the weather was bad, there wasn't a policeman to be seen anywhere; just a few pedestrians hurrying to get home.

She passed drunken men slumped, loose-limbed, on the sidewalk and, as she neared the waterfront, several of the "sisterhood," as Lachlan Brunton tolerantly designated the painted whores. These bedraggled and weary-looking creatures reminded Tina of Mr. Adams' all-too-pointed suggestion. Revulsion seized her. What sad mistaken fools these young creatures were to waste youth and perishable beauty for so little permanent reward.

The wind nipped savagely at her face and ankles and crept up under that skirt which had provoked this disaster. Maybe this was God's punishment for her having been so selfish as to buy that challis?

"To go to the police would not be wise." Her sense of practicality was warning her. "The Adamses no doubt believe themselves entirely right. Well, I am right, but it's my word against theirs. The only difference is that the Adamses are responsible merchants long-established in Baltimore, whilst I, Christina Reigler, am only a friendless lone young girl from Waukegan, Wisconsin, in a part of America nobody has ever heard of around here."

As shrewdly as any lawyer, Tina tallied up the odds, found them ranged hopelessly against her. However, not being guilty, she did not propose tamely to submit to injustice. Obviously she must leave town, and quickly, because Baltimore was not yet so big that reports of her supposed dishonesty would fail to make the rounds within a few hours.

Tina lowered her head wishing she owned even a cloth muff. This cloak was really much too light for such weather. Oh, if only this had happened yesterday and Lachlan were not at this moment traveling ever further away! Now Hermann was gone, too, God knew where. Still, in view of what had just occurred, maybe it was providential that her course was not to be encumbered by her brother.

By the time Tina entered Alice Anna Street, her well-developed common sense was functioning smoothly.

"Christina Reigler," she instructed herself, listening to the ring of her heels upon the familiar brown cobbles, "you must arrive at a grave decision—a wise decision. You will have to make this decision without advice from anyone. Remember always that you *did not* steal this material, that you have given to these awful Adams people only faithful and honest service. The Almighty alone knows how or where the huckster got that cloth, or why I came to buy just that piece. Who is Christina Reigler to understand the ways of the Almighty?"

Fortunately none of the boarders were about. Mr. Newton, who was a regular night owl, must be down to the corner saloon now that he lacked Lachlan's company for their interminable engineering discussions.

Tina's tin candlestick was waiting among a few others on the hall table. Tina lit it with a spill that quivered under the stress of her alarm, then tiptoed upstairs. She was especially quiet in passing the Widow Gahagan's door; now, above all times, she wished to avoid the garrulous old creature's gin-laden conversation.

Mercy, how cold it had grown in her attic room! She frowned on noting Hermann's letter lying on the floor where she had dropped it; then, following a practice established long ago, she commenced to think out loud, although her soft, clear voice was lost in the wind's wild rushing.

"Tina, you must decide your course and make no mistakes. First question: Shall you stay in Baltimore, or leave? You must leave— which is possible because for travel money you have Lachlan's birthday present. Forty dollars, gold, is enough to carry one a very long way, I think. Second: Shall you wait to draw out your savings from Mr. Brown's Bank? No. True there are seven dollars involved but delay of any sort is risky. Third question: Can you escape without being caught?"

Momentarily Tina's blue eyes strayed over to a wooden shutter which had commenced to rattle under the ever-increasing wind. Her fingers crept absently up to loosen her garters; they felt too tight after her long walk.

"It can be done, Tina, but you will have to be clever about it. Now what would a foolish person do? Probably she would try to board a train or a steamer from Baltimore. Therefor you will not do that."

The sound of her own voice in this chilly, dark little room she found encouraging, so continued the soliloquy. "You will take first the omnibus and ride out to Ellicott City, there and only there, will you get the train."

Gradually self-confidence reasserted itself. The first stage to Ellicott City, she knew, departed in the morning at seven from in front of the the General Wayne Inn. Few passengers were likely to rise so early and there would be even fewer people on the street. Both these likelihoods would militate against her being noticed, let alone recognized.

Even while talking to herself she arose and commenced methodically to pack.

She folded into the worn carpetbag, which Papa had brought over from Germany, her two other dresses, her few petticoats, cotton drawers and chemises. She hesitated about including a set of stays which had belonged to Mamma. These were heavy and her own scant figure did not by any stretch of the imagination require either restraint or support, but she packed them all the same.

"I hope Lachlan will not be angry, but I have no one else to turn to. I wonder just where Louisiana may be? How long will it take to reach New Orleans? That is a very pretty-sounding name. Have I enough money to reach that city?"

On completing her packing, she found the carpetbag neither full nor very heavy.

By the candle's draught-twisted flame she then penciled two letters; one was directed to Mrs. Adams, restating her complete guiltlessness and explaining that her only reason for departing to New England was because she knew that her word would not stand against that of such reputable persons as operated the Adams Family Stitchery.

After calculating her rent and board to a penny, she then composed a note for Mrs. Gahagan and again restated her intention of seeking employment in New York or maybe Boston. Having progressed thus far in her plans, Tina undressed, washed shiveringly at the basin before donning one of two Canton flannel nightgowns, then knelt beside her cot and fearfully prayed for half an hour; it was necessary, she felt, to implore forgiveness for those lies about going to New England.

XIV

THE TRANSFER CARS

TOGETHER WITH FRED Boykin and George Levering, Lieutenant Sam Seymour sauntered on this fine early spring day in the general direction of the Maryland Club.

"You'll like it there," Boykin predicted. "We haven't a large membership and though our premises are scarcely spacious we are very comfortably installed in the old Philip Rogers Hoffman residence."

Under a budding elm the trio halted to let a Madison Square omnibus rattle by. From its rear platform a small boy spied Sam's blue uniform and stuck out his tongue, then shrilled, "Yah! Yah! Lookit the Yankee nigger lover!"

"It would appear that your uniform grows less popular daily," George Levering observed, smiling. "Why don't you leave it off? Casual observers mightn't understand your true sentiments."

Seymour said, "Until I resign I'll wear it and not be ashamed."

"You're being stubborn as a blue-nosed mule," Boykin observed. "Why won't you admit the inevitable and go South with us next week? R. Snowden Andrews, W. F. Dement, J. B. Brockenborough, William H. Griffin, Henry B. Latrobe, Frederick O. Claiborne, William Thompson Patten, Walter S. Chew, William D. Brown, John E. Plater—we're all enlisting in the Confederate forces. 'Twill be grand sport."

Boykin lowered his voice. "We are all taking along sporting rifles, horses and body servants. We've been informed that there ain't too many rifles down South, so we're fetching along some bar lead and molds as well. Reckon I'll not find many balls fit to fire from my Enfield rifle."

At the intersection of Pratt and Hanover Streets, Seymour's head turned sharply to an undertone of voices.

"Say, George, what's going on over there?"

"Nothing much. Just people waiting for transfer cars to pass through, I reckon."

"Transfer cars?"

"Yes. Horse teams have to pull passenger coaches across the city between various terminals. Our august politicians won't permit locomotives to run across their fair city; seems they touch a nice piece of graft from transfer charges."

"Stand aside, my lad, you block our path." Employing his walking stick's gold knob, Boykin pushed aside a butcher's boy lugging a cluster of shrieking hens back from Lexington Market.

"Yessir. Sorry, sir." He and various ragged Negroes drew aside, permitting the broad-shouldered naval officer and his two fastidiously clad young companions to proceed to the curb of Pratt Street.

Boykin pushed a tall gray hat forward to keep the sun from his eyes, drawled, "I declare, must be something afoot." An obvious comment, since at every moment more people came pelting out of alleys and down side streets. They all looked angry, expectant. A shout went up. From the near-distance a curious clamor started, rolled like an ocean swell along Pratt Street. "Keep 'em out! Send 'em back!"

Tired as they were, a double team of horses towing a long passenger car commenced to snuffle and prick their furry ears. Within the slowly rumbling railroad car showed a mass of dark blue uniforms.

"Yah-h! Kill them Pennsylvania Black Republicans!"

A knot of roughs, mechanics and passersby grabbed at the tow horses and forced the lead car—there were four of them—to halt. Others pried at the pavement and succeeded in loosening a number of cobbles. Louder grew the crowd's menacing clamor and various missiles rattled against the dark red coach. Sam Seymour, never before having heard such a primitive outcry, found something in its pitch that chilled his blood.

An officer, red-faced and anxious, pushed his way out onto the besieged car's forward platform. "Patience, friends!" he shouted. "We're Regulars—Regular artillery."

"Hold on, fellers," a gangling fellow in a butcher's apron bellowed. "We're barkin' up the wrong tree. Them there are gunners, they ain't milishy; they're Regulars all right."

"Sho' enough are gunners," a tall, bald-headed grocer agreed. "I know, 'cause I served with the artillery back in 'forty-five."

A huge, bearded sergeant unfurled the scarlet and yellow guidon he had fetched out of the car. "See that, you damned yapping bastards? Save yer Irish confetti for the yellow-bellied milishy!"

Piped a small boy, "Hurray fer the Reg'lars! Hurray!"

Women among the crowd commenced to wave kerchiefs, and shouts of greeting arose. Levering growled, "What utter damn fools! They should hate anyone wearing a blue coat be they Regulars or Militia; they're all bound to try cramming Union and Abolition down our gullets."

"Git hup!" implored the railway car's teamster, his face streaked with anxious sweat. "Fer Crissake, boys, leggo them bridles!"

Heads lowered, haunches quivering and iron shoes rasping, the teams threw their weight into their collars and got the transfer cars rolling once more. Through coach windows grinning hard-bitten gunners derisively waved their kepis, cheered the Monumental City and blew elaborate kisses at pretty girls in the crowd. The enlisted men might act light-hearted, but, Seymour noticed, their officers did not. Tight-jawed, vigilant but calm, they remained on the car platforms, the broad red stripes on their trousers shining bright in the April sun. Their gold epaulettes and buttons blinked bravely, but they pulled down the brims of black felt campaign hats as if fearful of being recognized.

Four such cars rumbled along down the shining rails before there came a break and the traffic resumed its progress across Hanover Street.

Seymour and his companions had crossed the street, but halted, curious over a sudden alteration of pitch in the crowd's outcry. More cars were rolling along down Hanover Street. A jangle of trace chains and a ringing of horseshoes sounded very loud in a brief stillness which ended in a savage yell.

"Militia! Gaw-damned foreign Militia!" boomed a drover in a blanket coat and broad-brimmed hat. "Stone the bastards!"

"Go back to Pennsylvany, you Lincoln hirelings," someone else yelled in stentorian tones. "Who invited you into Maryland?"

Clouds of mud flew through the air and splashed a dark blue Pennsylvania State flag some color sergeant had unwisely displayed through a window.

"What in hell does that baboon in the White House intend?" demanded Boykin, hotly. "If he wishes to provoke hostilities he's on the right track."

"Yes," Levering agreed. "Under what right does Lincoln order his Dutch troops onto the Free State's soil?"

Seymour judged that a riot was imminent and, indeed, one would have taken place, had not a strong contingent of mounted police come clattering up. Patiently, the city policemen argued with the mob's leaders, and kept driving their horses through the more threatening concentrations. Their forbearance deserved more credit than it got.

The Pennsylvania troops looked scared, Sam thought, and well they might since breaking car windows were spraying them with glass. The militiamen were young fellows with farm boy written over most of them; the balance obviously were ex-clerks, professional men and merchants. They looked intelligent but bewildered, and encouraged the crowd by the clumsy and inefficient fashion in which they handled their weapons.

"Go back and tell your God-damn' Governor we will tolerate no more foreign troops passing through this city!" was the warning hurled by a tall individual who, fashionably dressed, wore a stovepipe hat, claw-hammer coat and a waistcoat of tabby velvet.

Thanks to the concerted efforts of the mounted police, the four cars of militiamen at length were allowed to proceed, but not before the dark red cars of the Susquehanna Railway were splattered with a liberal application of mud and horse manure.

"I had no idea," Seymour remarked, once he and his companions had resumed their progress towards the Maryland Club, "that pro-Southern feeling ran so high."

"You'd have seen some real Southern feeling if those damned police hadn't spoiled the sport," Levering insisted angrily.

Boykin's voice was low but charged with menace. "Just let that doddering old fool Winfield Scott try to send more foreign Militia across Baltimore, and, sure as sunrise, you'll see our gutters run red. We'll not be tyrannized over by Lincoln, Scott or anyone else!"

A gray-haired and very sedate Negro doorman called Richard, admitted them to the richly dark and pleasant-smelling lobby of a little club house on the northeast corner of Franklin and Cathedral Streets.

"Good afternoon, Mr. Levering, Mr. Boykin, suh. I trust you are well, Gem'men."

"Afternoon, Richard, reckon I'm bearing up," drawled Boykin.

Levering bowed politely to two elderly gentlemen on their way out. "Good day, Mr. Dobbin. Good afternoon, Mr. Carroll."

Once Sam had parted with his gold-braided officer's cap, Boykin guided him to a lounge on the second floor. Here, amid elegant surroundings, a large number of club members were smoking, sipping sherry or Madeira, or, more occasionally, a cocktail or some whiskey drink.

On the walls hung many handsome English sporting prints dealing mostly with fox hunting, but there were also some of Mr. Alken's excellent engravings of cock fighting, gunning and prize fighting. The antlered heads of deer, moose and elk glared with dusty glass eyes upon several elder numbers whose fiercely flaring mustaches suggested that their spread would not compare unfavorably if mounted in competition.

Potted palms occupied such corners as were not preempted by well-polished brass spittoons. Silver loving cups won by various members in point-to-point races or at live pigeon shooting competitions graced the mantels.

Sam was presented to a Mr. Columbus O'Donnel and to a Mr. John S. Hillen before Boykin touched a handbell summoning a light-complexioned Negro steward to fetch drinks. Although few voices were raised, Sam judged some pretty earnest arguments must be taking place.

"I say, Lev, do you aim to attend Tom Winans' cotillion?" inquired a tall young fellow named Swann.

"Yes. Why?"

"They say it'll be the last big affair until the Confederacy is recognized."

"Then I wouldn't miss it for a farm. Mr. Seymour here is interrupting a trip to Norfolk just to be present."

"Norfolk?"

As if a magic wand had struck everyone dumb, silence momentarily ruled this gracious, smoke-clouded lounge.

"And what sentiment, sir, do you expect to find prevailing at the Navy Yard?" quavered a handsome old man in a dark blue shad-belly coat.

"Hold hard, Mr. Howard," came O'Donnel's painfully civil tones. "Perhaps Mr. Seymour doesn't feel free to answer you. As you can see, he wears the Abolitionists' uniform."

Levering fired right up. "I fear I must resent that insinuation, Columbus. D'you imagine I'd introduce a guest who isn't a Southern sympathizer?" He stared deliberately about the crowded lounge. "No matter what uniform he wears for the present, Mr. Seymour is as good a Secessionist as any of us. After all he was born and brought up down in Norfolk."

Promptly Mr. O'Donnel offered his hand, his apologies and a tall glass of Brownelle's very best rye whiskey.

Until his reticence dissolved in a constant succession of drinks, Sam found it difficult to find answers to a flood of questions. All the same, he became aware that eight or ten members, August Bradford among them, remained aloof surveying him with no perceptible cordiality.

Mr. Charles Carroll of D arose from under a fine portrait of Jerome Bonaparte and, glancing at a heavy gold English hunting watch, remarked, "Well, I expect I had better be off." He bowed to the solid figure in naval blue and gold. "Pleasure to have met you, Mr. Seymour. Hope I'll find you at Tom Winans' party."

Levering lifted his glass. "Before you go, Charlie, let us drink to Maryland Secession and Southern Independence!"

To witness the alacrity with which a majority of these well-dressed and handsome young members jumped to their feet was impressive. An inspired gleam shone in most of their eyes and their expressions were jubilant. The older gentlemen responded less spontaneously, but their manner was marked by an earnestness that argued deep and responsible convictions. Yet, even as Levering's toast set the club house to ringing, not a few wooden-faced members claimed their hats and stalked angrily out into Franklin Street.

XV

LETTER FROM MONTGOMERY

TUCKED BENEATH THE door of his room at the Eutaw House, Sam Seymour discovered a slim blue envelope the address of which was written in a not-unfamiliar hand. What immediately captured and retained his attention was the fact that this missive had been dispatched from Montgomery, Alabama. Conscious of a tingle of excitement he inserted his thumbnail beneath the paper wafer seal and ripped it apart.

With one hand Sam commenced to tug gently at his sideburns, a habit he had when perplexed, while reading.

NAVY DEPARTMENT
Confederate States of America
Montgomery, Alabama
April 2, 1861

My dear Mr. Seymour:

You will recall, while commanding the U.S.S. *Crusader* during her recent cruise, I never permitted political discussions aboard, as is the custom of the Service. However, having regretfully resigned my commission in the United States Navy I feel I am now at liberty to express my views. I feel confident that, as a true-born Virginian, you will understand the grave dangers besetting our beloved Southland. Secession will win freedom from the Northern yoke only through the valor and patriotic endeavours of her sons. Most especially she needs the services of qualified and able officers.

Recently I submitted to Mr. Mallory a list of naval officers whom I feel will prove useful in advancing our *Just and Noble Cause*. I have just now received that gentleman's assurance that should you repair at once to Montgomery, you will be offered a Confederate Naval Commission in the same grade you now hold.

Sam's brows rose a little. So? Harry Lewis had spoken of sharp upgrading. He read on:

The President has decided, wisely I think, to offer no immediate improvement in grade to officers resigning from the Federal Service;

this is in order that we shall find in our midst no self-seekers who might seek thus to capitalize upon a transfer of loyalties. We do not want a *single officer* to join us who does not do so save from the strength of his patriotic convictions and the purest of motives.

Should you, friend Seymour, decide to transfer your allegiance—and *I earnestly trust that you will*—you have only to present this letter to Captain Franklin Buchanan, at the Bureau of Orders and Detail. Let haste be your watchword for, unfortunately, the number of vessels suitable to our new Service thus far are few. So, if you desire service afloat quickly, you must not tarry.

Trusting to have the honour of receiving you soon in this fair Capital of our new Republic, I am,

> Your sincere friend and former commander,
>
> John N. Maffitt,
> Lieutenant, C.S.N.

P.S. Should you chance to see your respected father, pray present him my compliments and assurances of continued friendship.

For a while, Lieutenant Sam Seymour, United States Navy, sat staring blankly out on irregular ranks of roofs and smoking chimneys marching gradually down to that forest of topmasts marking the harbor.

It came to him that this was a mighty serious moment—one that undoubtedly must determine the whole course of his future.

For ten years now, he had, he reflected, to the best of his ability served that flag which his forefathers had raised and shown to all the world. Should he resign, automatically his name would be stricken from the Navy lists and his seniority forever lost. He'd be tossing aside the certainty of a comfortable old age at half pay. Moreover, if he stayed in the Old Service an outbreak of war must mean certain and swift promotion. He reflected on the many Seymours who bravely had served and died under the Stars and Stripes following a tradition of naval service established by Secundus Seymour back in 1778. His great-great-grandfather, Sam reflected, had fought beside the immortal John Paul Jones when the U.S.S. *Ranger* so handily had thrashed H.M.S. *Drake*. He recalled also great-grandpa Pliny Seymour, killed when a new bridegroom aboard the U.S.S. *Niagara* at the Battle of Lake Erie. Grandpa Horace had been lost at sea when commanding the U.S.S. *Alligator*. Finally there was Pa, who had served the American flag with great distinction on all of Seven Seas, and had accompanied Commodore Matthew Calbraith Perry on his epoch-making second cruise to the Islands of Nippon.

Sam's fingers tugged ever more perplexedly at his short gold-brown sideburns. How *could* he turn his back on the Old Flag? At the same time, he wondered whether the Southern people were not expressing a very pure and true spirit of liberty in their efforts to secede. Was it right that they should be forced to bow to the dictates of their grimly determined Northern cousins simply because they were less numerous and less prosperous? Had not old Secundus, back in 1776, revolted against just such established power and arrogance?

As countless thousands of other Americans were doing, Sam wrestled the problem with heart and soul. Head bent, hands clenched behind him, he paced back and forth across his narrow bedroom. Surely, if such famous naval figures as Captains Maury, Buchanan, Tattnall and his own Captain John N. Maffitt felt impelled to abandon hard-won honors and security, would any valid reason exist why he should not follow their example?

Then, too, a career in the new Confederate Navy should offer enormous chances for distinction and promotion; it stood to reason that Secessia, as many had named the new Confederacy, must equip men-of-war, and in a hurry, if she hoped to keep open such ports as Norfolk, Savannah, Charleston and New Orleans. How else could the white gold of the South, uncounted cotton bales, reach Europe, there to create sound backing for the infant Confederacy's new currency?

Yes, time was of the essence all right, though the Federal Navy was known to be well dispersed, through the treasonable activity of Mr. Toucey, Ex-Secretary of the Federal Navy. At this very moment, Sam guessed that there were not nine men-of-war available for blockade duty.

In the end Sam drew a deep breath and, crossing to the desk, commenced the draft of a letter to the Honorable Gideon Welles, Secretary of the United States Navy.

> Baltimore, Maryland
> April 10, 1861
>
> Sir:
>
> I have the honor forthwith, to tender my resignation from the Service of the United States Navy. I trust that action terminating

my commission will be taken immediately and that whatever prize money due me will be forwarded in the care of Captain Felix Seymour, U.S.N. (Retired), Norfolk, Virginia.

Sir, I have the honor to be,
                    Your obedient servant,
                                        SAMUEL SEYMOUR
                                        Lieutenant, U.S.N.

Following a time-proven custom peculiar to his mother's family, the Ashtons of Boston, he decided "to sleep upon" this momentous decision and so postponed preparation of a final draft until morning.

XVI

A MOST GENTEEL AFFAIR

THANKS TO HANDSOMELY etched, amber-hued glass shades the new gaslights created a radiance peculiarly flattering to Mr. Thomas Winans' lady guests. Such illumination could be found in precious few private houses about Baltimore and Washington, although this great scientific advance had for some time been common enough in the more expensive hotels and modern public buildings. Prisms dangling below these glass shades cast fleeting miniature rainbows upon dancers whirling and gliding across the glistening parquet floor of the Winans' fabulous green and gold ballroom.

There were those among the guests who blushed and gasped but continued to survey certain marble statues depicting mythological figures as shamelessly unclad as the famous and bitterly protested "Greek Slave." Others, the ladies in particular, marveled over green velvet draperies recently imported from Paris. Intricately wrought Spanish ironwork decorated a broad staircase leading to the second floor and formed a balcony to accommodate musicians.

Banks of magnolias, camellias and other spring flowers, undoubtedly fetched up by fast packet from the Carolinas, created delicate rainbows of blossoms reaching to either end of the glistening dance floor and into every available corner.

Music played by Signor Tomaso D'Alessandro and his nine dark-faced and darker-haired virtuosos proved sprightly to the point of abandonment. Violas and violins sang like great nightingales, harps tinkled, flutes and oboes added a liquid accompaniment. Nothing so vulgar as a drum, accordion or banjo was in evidence.

To describe the dance floor as well patronized would have constituted a delightfully grave understatement. In order that reels and minuets might be danced, ushers flushed and handsome in their blue, chocolate or green claw-hammer coats, white silk waistcoats and black pantaloons, were forced to invite couples into the library, conservatory and dining room.

"Plague take these crinolines. They take up so much room," sighed George Levering while furtively employing an Irish lawn handkerchief to blot ungentlemanly beads of perspiration from his brow. "Thank God the silly mode is on its way out. Ah, good evening, Miss Marbury. May I have the next waltz?"

"Of course, George." She inclined a small dark head crowned with a delicate tiara of gold and pink coral. "Isn't this a perfectly glorious cotillion?"

To the strains of a waltz the dancing couples commenced to weave brilliant rhythmic patterns beneath the famous gaslights. The ladies, many of them almost startlingly décolleté, glowed in flowered and looped gowns of sapphire, yellow, pink, green and white.

By contrast the simple black worn by the older gentlemen afforded an effective relief. Of splendid dress uniforms there were a plenty. Among the dancers could be recognized shameless copies of French or British regimentals, hussars', dragoons', lancers', and Zouaves' tunics.

Very quickly Sam perceived that despite her less-than-modest income, Sylvia had won a definite position in Baltimore society. Everywhere gentlemen were bowing and young ladies calling greetings.

Samuel Seymour peeled off kid gloves through which perspiration at last had penetrated, and immediately felt better. Whew! A naval dress uniform might be satisfactory for formal occasions on shipboard, but certainly it had never been designed for dancing. The weight of heavy, gold bullion epaulettes dragged unmercifully at even his wide shoulders.

"So you're the brother Irad's been bragging about?" Trenholm greeted. "Well, here's to you."

"Irad's given to exaggeration, but he's a loyal soul."

"At the Alpha Fire House, he's a great favorite," said the tall militia officer. "When he talks or tells a joke everyone listens."

"For a simple naval officer," Sam said presently, "I'd say this cotillion is really magnificent. Are there many such during a season?"

"No," Trenholm admitted. "Few Baltimoreans can afford so genteel an affair. Of course, we do have cotillions all through the winter—members of the Bachelors' Society give them at their own homes. Good fun as a rule, but you'd not see half so many people."

"What uniform is that?" Sam inquired, indicating a very red-faced young officer.

"You mean John Dukehart's? Oh, that's the Baltimore Grays. He's departing early tomorrow morning, for—well, you can guess where. His parents are distracted because he's the only son among their five children. That's Jenny over there dancing with John Boykin and yonder is Eulalie.

"May as well look about," Trenholm advised, "and try to memorize this scene. I am."

"Why?"

"We'll not see anything similar for a long while, not until we've won our independence and established a prosperous Southern Republic."

To Sam's surprise this Secessionist atmosphere was beginning to excite him. "Our Virginia ancestors couldn't have been more determined than we in this matter." He drained a slender-stemmed glass of punch. "In my opinion, Captain, we shall win our independence all right, but it will cost us dear."

The scarlet plastron of Trenholm's lancer uniform swelled and his chin went up. "Why should it? We've not half the enemy our ancestors faced in 'seventy-six. When it comes to fighting Yankees and British Regulars, they ain't to be mentioned in the same breath."

Sam glanced curiously at his long-limbed companion. "Do you really believe, Captain, that the Yankees aren't going to fight?"

The music swelled louder and the air grew perceptibly warmer, while the perfume of flowers, and the scarcely less lovely ladies, more noticeable.

"They won't and can't," Trenholm replied earnestly. "When those Northern nigger lovers and money grubbers learn that we intend to go our own way they'll gladly call quits."

Sylvia came spinning by on the arm of a Lieutenant Charles Rich, a tall young fellow resplendent in a scarlet and gray lancer's uniform. She treated Sam to a slow but dazzling smile which only gradually parted her full, crimson lips.

Tonight Sylvia was happier than she had been in a long while. She and Major Donnel Smith were now waltzing easily, smoothly about the floor. The gallant major, aside from holding a commission in the Independent Grays, that most socially correct of all the militia companies, was influential both politically and socially. Like all women in a similar situation she knew that she was the target of envious as well as admiring glances.

Yes, she was inordinately happy. First, this ball gown she and that pallid little German girl had created was undeniably effective and more becoming than were most of gowns to their wearers. Next, Sam had really outdone himself in the matter of the large bouquet of pink roses which, like the rest of the dancers, she had placed on a long, marble-topped table destined to that use. The nosegay she was now carrying was a much smaller replica of his bouquet.

Her heart missed a beat, it seemed, when both Mrs. Symington and Mrs. Coulston, undisputed arbitresses of Baltimore society, nodded and called her "dear child." The Irad Seymours were getting on; if only Irad would let her use some of the dowry money to entertain, to dress more modishly. She felt more than ever resentful when she glimpsed Irad waltzing by with some tiny little woman who made him look taller than ever.

"Oh bother! He *is* a handsome dog!" Sylvia thought. "Why won't he use his good looks and manners to get ahead? Really, he has the social sense of a-a—well, a seal!"

When Signor D'Alessandro's music commenced to slow and couples began to desert the floor, Sylvia managed to guide Major Smith, quite without his realizing it, over to that spot where Sam's navy blue stood in company with a big lancer officer.

"Who's that with Sam?"

"Gustavus Trenholm," Smith replied. "Gus owns one of the biggest locomotive plants in the East."

"Oh, really?" Sylvia made another notation in the mental notebook she carried.

"Sam, I really must permit Major Donnel Smith his turn at that delectable punch." Once her partner had unwillingly departed, she considered her brother-in-law over the nosegay. "You see? I'm carrying your flowers, yet you've been neglecting me most shamelessly."

Sam bowed and laughingly offered a gold-striped sleeve. "It's only because I'm so unselfish. Come, let's try Mr. Winans' champagne. Trenholm was saying 'tis of a most excellent vintage."

In the conservatory, humid yet fragrant because of myriad ferns and potted flowers, Sam presently substituted their empty champagne glasses for fresh ones.

"I love champagne," Sylvia admitted, brilliant lips shiny with the liquid. "I wonder whether Irad's tried this?"

"Yes, I saw him. He's having a fine time." He lifted his bubbling glass. "Well, dear sister, here's a health to you and victory to the Southern arms!"

Her huge, sherry-colored eyes widened as she stepped very close and lifted her face. "Then you—you are going to resign?"

"Yes. I expect to."

"Oh, Sam! I'm so glad! So very glad! I was afraid you wouldn't see your duty that way. You Seymours are so odd sometimes. There!" She bent forward suddenly and pressed his cheek with warm and fragrant lips.

The contact proved electric, for his free hand caught her arm above its elbow-length kid gloves. Odd, that not until this moment had he appreciated the true depths of Sylvia's beauty. Seen like this against a background of fern, she was indeed a vision to recall in that low-cut, dove-gray-and-rose-striped ballgown. For the first time he noted how cleverly someone had sewed clusters of pink rosebuds to gather the fullness of her billowing skirt into festoons above a silk and lace petticoat that rustled to the least motion. Sylvia was wearing real rosebuds to secure her light brown hair at either side of her slightly prominent forehead; and a tiny dimple at the point of her chin had never seemed more bewitching.

Refilling their champagne glasses, he said, "I've decided to go south just as soon as the Navy Department accepts my resignation."

"Oh, I do hope you'll be ordered to Savannah! Papa, Mamma, my sisters and Wilmer, my brother, will do anything in the world for you. Oh, how I wish I could go with you!" Her eyes misted over. "I do miss Savannah so."

Over their glasses they watched a middle-aged couple enter the conservatory. The lady, gray ringlets a-tremble, dropped, rather than sat, on an iron bench and commenced to fan herself.

"Ah do declare, Foxley," she sighed, "I haven't felt so wickedly gay and giddy since—do yo' remember that Victory Ball following the Mexican War?" She fumbled in her reticule, produced a small silver vinaigrette and inhaled several deep sniffs. "A little sherry, Foxley. I believe it will quite restore me."

The straight-backed old gentleman hurried to a sideboard and drew smiles from Sylvia and Sam by the way he tossed off a quick bourbon before returning on his errand, and saying, "I expect, Florence, it's this martial air you're breathing. For a fact, I can almost feel epaulettes on my shoulders again." All at once the music was lost, became submerged by a sudden harsh and brazen clamor.

"It's a firebell—the tocsin," people explained to out-of-town guests as everyone stopped dancing to listen and count the sonorous, shivering strokes.

"Three and three, then two. That's a fire of the first degree in the Second Ward," Sylvia informed Sam.

"How the Devil do you know that?" Sam was astonished.

"You forget I've been married to a volunteer fireman for years."

Two or three younger men made hurried excuses and started for the door at a run.

"Oh dear," wailed Sylvia, "there would have to be a fire tonight of all nights, and this week Irad is Captain of the Mount Vernon Hook and Ladder Company."

"Owlie will have to go?" He found her distress oddly stimulating.

"Of course! Oh dear! Oh dear!" A glow of distant flames began beating through the Winans' windows. Irad appeared hurrying up, stripping off his white gloves as he came. Behind his spectacles the deep-set eyes were alight.

"Sorry, my dear"—he pecked at her cheek—"I must run. Sam, you'll beau Sylvia and see her home?" He went on without waiting for a reply, pushing apologetically among the guests.

XVII

Venture into Nirvana

Dawn was something more than a presentiment over Baltimore harbor and Fort McHenry beyond it when, as had recently become the fashion, Signor D'Alessandro's musicians struck up "Dixie's Land" and evoked a tremendous cheer that set the ballroom chandeliers trembling and swaying. Mr. Winans' wine cellar could not have become depleted in vain, so earnest were the boasts of military prowess and so tender were declarations made in obscure corners.

"I'll see you in Montgomery, Walter," promised Trenholm to Captain Chew. "Don't buy up all the decent sherry, will you?"

Levering was inquiring of Lieutenant Patten, "If you're catching the Arrow for Norfolk tomorrow you'll be short of time. I've a spare set of pistols. Want 'em?"

"Thanks, I can use 'em all right. Local gunsmiths are sold out."

Sam went to collect Sylvia's cloak through a golden aura that rendered his feet uncommonly light. His head was humming from considerably more than his customary two goblets of champagne and sang to the continued lilt of that final waltz. Jiminy! The perfume of Sylvia's hair still lingered on his cheek, indefinable, fascinating and stimulating.

Whew! How hot it was in here! His collar had wilted long ago and his cambric shirt was fairly sopping beneath his heavy, glittering dress jacket.

Hurrying out, he was lucky enough to find a disengaged hackney among those which had been patiently waiting since midnight.

As she settled her evening cloak in place and hurried down the Winans' walk, Sylvia emitted a soft sigh. Mercy, this had been just like the luxurious good old days down in Savannah. Compliments had flown to her like bees to their hive, social leaders had been friendly, even cordial, and she had danced, oh, how long and how happily she had danced! Most of her partners had proved far more accomplished than Sam, but in Sam's arms, somehow the world had appeared perfectly attuned. "And now," she whispered, "Cinderella must return to her ugly little house."

Undoubtedly Irad would be waiting up with brown-edged holes burned into his only suit of evening clothes. He would smell smoky and be streaked with dust, but possessed of a self-confidence he appeared to lack so much of the time. Fighting fires seemed to summon to the fore a latent leadership.

The blood leaped to her bosom when she recognized Sam waiting beside the Winans' cast-iron gate. Looking taller than he was because of his full dress cape, he came striding up a brick walk fringed by snowdrops and daffodils. The air was fresh but not cold when he handed her into the cab. An odor of brandy and seegars was on his breath she noticed.

"Thank you, Sam, dear. It—it's been a heavenly evening," she murmured, then settled back against the protection of the arm he put about her.

Odd how the musty saline smell of his uniform, so redolent of the sea and far-off lands, stirred her. She recognized in Sam an unfamiliar atmosphere of vitality. Here was a creator; a male creature in whose nature certainly must dwell furious, consuming fires.

All too soon that public hack's iron tires fell silent before Number 33 Caroline Street.

"Oh, Sam, I shall remember always!" she whispered while the cab driver was clambering down from his box. "Sam, forgive me but I—I must do this." Very quickly she slipped a slim arm about the velvet collar of his cape, pulled his head down and kissed his mouth with a passion engendered by long-sublimated desire.

Transported by a delicious floating sensation, Sam returned the caress; then, because their driver had commenced to fumble at the door handle, he straightened hurriedly.

He felt Sylvia's hand quivering violently when he assisted her to alight. "Come in, won't you? Irad will wish to offer you a night-cap and tell you all about the fire."

"Why, why, thank you, Sylvia. I—I'll be delighted. The walk back to my hotel should clear my head which, God knows, needs it."

A coal-oil lamp was burning down the hallway, but otherwise the little house was dark and, since no coat or hat was hanging on the hall tree, it was obvious that Irad had not yet returned.

Once Sam had closed the door, they stood facing each other, they hesitated, then kissed again and again before stepping breathlessly into the little parlor. He had removed her ostrich-trimmed evening cloak when suddenly her skirts gave a quick rustle and she spun about. By the hall-lamp's dim light he was aware of Sylvia's eyes suddenly becoming enormous, of her lips writhing apart to reveal the faint glint of teeth. As her head went back, she dragged down the ballgown's shoulder straps until she had freed swelling pointed breasts and a pallid tumultuous bosom.

"Ah-h—darling!" she gasped when he caught her so tight that his cold gold buttons dug deep into her flesh.

"Oh—Sam, Sam, take me, take me—please." She panted. At the same instant she was thinking, "I will have a child of my own—and of Irad's blood. This isn't wrong. Irad wants an heir almost as much as I."

To the soft rustling of skirts and petticoats Sam carried her over to the Chippendale sofa. "Sylvia, darling!" he panted. "You—I—"

Fingers soft as feathers sealed his mouth; then only the quick catching of their breaths disturbed the silence.

XVIII

NADIR

OF HIS RETURN to the Eutaw House, Lieutenant Seymour, U.S.N., had no recollection whatsoever. What had recalled him to consciousness was strong spring sunlight beating through the window shutters and creating across the counterpane a series of tigerish stripes. All the hammers of hell were beating against his temples just as they had the only other time he'd got so royally drunk—when he'd been granted his passed midshipman's commission.

What the hell had happened? His mouth tasted like the inside of an old felt slipper and his throat burned so intolerably that he lurched across to the washstand and swallowed several deep draughts from the pitcher.

Back on the top of the covers, he lay staring blankly at a brown water stain on the ceiling paper. What? Oh, yes, they were playing "Dixie's Land" at a dance. Whose dance? Oh, yes. Mr. Thomas Winans' cotillion. He was drinking champagne with his arms looped through a girl's. Which girl? There had been so many. Oh, yes, Sylvia! *Sylvia! SYLVIA!*

Gradually he recalled details of that breathless, reckless, and deplorable interlude in his brother's house. Sylvia's face incredibly lovely in the hackney; the hollow sound made by the front door closing; those hungry, wide and glistening eyes; lovely bare breasts and panted endearments; descent into a weird and lascivious maelstrom. Try as he would, he could not recall even an instant's debate, love-making or tender, redeeming vows; nothing of the sort.

Sam realized that he wore only a long-tailed dress shirt reeking of stale sweat. By raising his throbbing head he could see his dress uniform tunic sprawled on the floor where it had fallen from him.

Maybe this had all been a hideously distorted nightmare? Of course, of course! Comforted, he lay back breathing more equably until a small, harassing doubt drove him reluctantly to examine his memory with more care. God Almighty! Then, like a tidal wave, bitter, killing remorse engulfed him. He had committed a crime for which there could be no forgiveness. To have seduced a happily married gentlewoman would have been evil enough had she been an outsider, but to have tarnished his own brother's wife! What hell was hot enough to burn away such guilt?

"How could I!"

Never for a moment did it occur to Sam Seymour that perhaps he had not been entirely to blame, that the whole affair had not been of his contriving. What an utterly ignoble thing for a Seymour, for an officer and a gentleman, thus to repay those who so devotedly had cared for his motherless child.

After a while he got up and, taking care to avoid the shaving mirror, doused his head. What to do? One thing was sure. The slim black outline of a razor caught his eye. That? No. Only poor whites and niggers would use their razor for such a purpose. He'd never be able to face either Irad or Sylvia again. He went over to his sea chest and in it found one of his clumsy, brass-mounted pistols.

Using absurdly precise movements, he loaded the weapon, tamped home a gleaming leaden bullet and finally slipped a bright copper percussion cap over its nipple.

Drawing a deep breath he leveled the weapon in line with his temple; then lowered it wondering, "Is this the most fitting atonement?" He seemed to hear Amanda Seymour's even voice observing, "Only a weak coward would kill himself." An admitted suicide could cause his family only additional humiliation and grief. Many persons had watched Sylvia depart from the Winans' in his company and so could be able to add known facts into the correct and shameful sum.

The hammer clucked gently when Samuel Seymour uncocked his weapon and its percussion cap glared like a wicked eye when he removed it.

"Why not make my death of some account?" he asked of himself bitterly. Torn by indecision and mordant remorse, he hesitated in the center of the hotel room, a grotesque, blear-eyed and disheveled figure, until at length his eye encountered Lieutenant Maffitt's letter.

Once he had prepared the final draft of his resignation from the Federal Navy, he penned a note to Irad in which he explained that he had received, from the Navy Department in Montgomery, summonses so urgent that he could not ignore them. Since he had become convinced that Virginia was about to secede he was departing within the hour, which rendered it impossible for him to take leave in person of Robbie, Sylvia and himself. Lips colorless, he made over a pay check for three hundred dollars and promised to forward further sums towards Robbie's maintenance.

No matter what might chance, Irad was always to think of him as a truly devoted brother.

He found it extremely difficult not to conclude with a paragraph of bitter self-accusation.

That he was resigning his commission was just as well, he thought, while applying a signet to sealing wax. Certainly an officer who had fallen so low as he scarcely was fit to wear the honored blue uniform.

Hold on. Was he any more fit to don the Confederacy's gray? He found refuge in a sophistry. The old Sam Seymour would have nothing to do with this new loyalty. Perhaps, through devoted service to the South, his soul might achieve a rebirth and his mind surcease from the torments of conscience.

XIX

Exodus

When Sylvia Seymour finally aroused herself, Irad had long since departed to the shipyard. What a mercy it was that Master Robbie must have been taken marketing by old Melissa.

For a good while she lay utterly inert against the pillows amid the generous disorder of her long, light brown hair. Her mind had been in such a turmoil she'd not bothered to braid her hair as usual or secure it with pert little green bows.

A deep, deep yawn escaped her, then after stretching in almost feline grace she settled back again, smiling. She supposed she should feel guilty, immoral and abandoned to decency—but she didn't. Never had she felt better. Never had her body been more glowingly sensitive and its hungers so well satisfied.

"Well," she thought, "let's hope I've got what I want. Too bad Irad can't seem to give me a baby—but now I'll have one. I know I can. Now I can be like other women and have my own little darling to brag about and fuss over." She actually chuckled. "What's more, no one can ever truthfully say my child isn't a Seymour!"

What a lover Sam was. Among the covers she blinked like a sleepy kitten. No wonder poor dear Janet had always appeared so contented, pleased and proud.

"Of course," she promised softly, "I won't ever let anything like this happen again. Dear direct Sam seemed terribly flustered when he left me last night; reckon he was pretty jingled. Well, he's a seafaring man and won't get too penitent over our little affair, especially since it won't be repeated."

Her voluminous nightgown billowing about her, Sylvia slipped out of bed and went to consider herself in a mirror above her chiffonier.

"Lordy!" she thought, "it's just as well Irad's gone out!"

A distinctly unfamiliar expression shone in her wide and heavily lashed eyes and beneath them lay two, pale brown, feather-shaped shadows. Because of the weight of Mechlin lace ornamenting it, the gown fell apart and slipped until her elbows checked it. On impulse, she let the fine lawn robe fall all the way to the floor while she remained an erect, pale pillar in the center of that white pool it created.

Gently she tested upstanding pink-nippled and well-modeled breasts, found them still gorged and sensitive. Next she considered her abdomen. Its smooth surface was beautifully curved now in a flat ellipse, but what changes would pregnancy bring about? Some women grew into shapeless lumps, but there were others. Jane Turner, for instance, stood straight as a spruce for all that she'd given birth to four children. Maybe Jane would confide her secret if properly approached and flattered.

"He-e- cr-a-abs! Hi, ho, he-e-e cra-a-bs."

The singsong voice of a fish peddler advanced down an alley back of the house and aroused her from her daydreaming. Blushing suddenly at her nudity she pulled on a peignoir and knotted a ribbon about her hair. It was well she had done so for just then the doorbell jangled and its wire rasped dully as the pull was let go.

The caller proved to be a small black errand boy wearing the livery of the Eutaw House and conveying a letter unmistakably addressed in Sam's handwriting.

"A love letter already? Who'd have thought he'd prove so impetuous a gallant? Reckon I'll have to handle Mister Sam with kid gloves."

From a flower vase reserved for that purpose she selected a ten cent piece for the lad, whose eyes and teeth glistened at such munificence. Sylvia knew that she was being dreadfully extravagant but was so pleased with life she didn't care.

Then to her dismayed astonishment she noted that this missive was addressed not to her, but to Irad. That golden delicious haze into which she had awaked evaporated in a twinkle. For the first time it occurred to her that possibly Sam hadn't dismissed their dalliance as merely a gallant interlude. Come to think of it, the Seymour sons always had deemed their family honor as a mighty precious possession.

Irresolute, she paused in the hallway revolving the square yellow envelope between trembling fingers. What could Sam have written? Surely he wasn't being so colossal a fool as to make a clean breast of everything? God forbid! Such a move could wreck her marriage and set at naught her many subtle, far-reaching ambitions.

Panic began groping at her mind with cruelly sharp talons and her heart commenced hammering as if she had run up a very long flight of stairs. Pale lips pursed, she pressed Sam's letter to a windowpane and tried to read it, but alas the paper proved too thick.

After thrusting her head out of the front door to make certain that Melissa and Robbie were not in the street on their way home, she scurried to the kitchen—where, praise be, a kettle was steaming lazily. To ungum the flap without marring it required a distressing length of time, but at length Sylvia was able to pluck out the message.

When she had read it she dropped onto a stool, sobbing in relief. He hadn't made any confession, thank Heavens! A noise at the front stoop prompted her to replace the letter and enclosed bank draft and use a cold sad iron to reseal the still-gummy flap.

To all intents and purposes, Sylvia was airily peeling an apple when Melissa shuffled in, bent under her market basket. Master Robbie romped past her.

"Me some," pleaded the boy.

"Of course, dear. You shall have a whole apple to yourself." She then considered the child as if she'd never before seen him.

Her son, if she had one, very likely might come to resemble Robbie. Yes, she'd been really clever in this matter. Family resemblances were so easy of explanation.

"Trouble, trouble," mumbled Melissa, hanging up her shawl and depositing the wicker basket of provisions. "Dey say in de market de Gov'ment gwine send mo' sojers tuh Balt'mo'."

"Merciful Heavens! Why?"

"De Gov'ment suspecks dey's a powerful lot of—of—Sesech sentiment"—Melissa was obviously proud to use the term—"yere abouts."

"Robbie, dear, why don't you run along and play in the yard? It's a lovely warm day so you won't have to wear that heavy cap and coat. Keep an eye on him, please, Melissa. I really must get dressed."

"How was de cotillion?" The ancient Negress' curiosity was no longer to be contained. "Who was dere? De Gov'nor? Expeck yo' was the purtiest lady dere, wasn't you?"

Sylvia laughed a little loudly. "Maybe. Baltimore isn't Savannah. Oh, come up to my room and I'll tell you all about the party. You can watch Master Robbie from the window." This was just like old times, the good old days at Beau Rivage.

Sylvia spun a fine, vivid tale, made the new gaslights gleam, the uniforms glitter, the ballgowns glow, all to appropriate comments and criticism. For generations it had been the obligation of the Magoffin ladies to render such accounts to their servants, so she did it well.

"Laws, laws! Dat must have been a mos' ippicanarious a social occasion." Melissa sighed, then knelt to tie little tassels securing the laces to Sylvia's small gray Balmoral boots.

"Pity, Miss Sylvia, you ain't been to mo' sech elegant pa'ties. Misto' Irad he do look so grand when he git dressed up. Jus' like a Senatuh."

"Oh, from now on he and I will attend a lot of such affairs."

Sylvia was looking well, she realized, her color higher than usual. No one would guess that she had been up until dawn, that she'd experienced a very great event in her life. When, presently, she departed for the Tuesday Morning Sewing Circle she must look entirely serene.

All would have been well, so much easier, if Sam hadn't elected to disappear so abruptly. If only she could have talked with him she might perhaps have been able to dispel some of that distress so well concealed in his letter.

Where was Sam likely to be stationed? Wilmington or Charleston? She felt pretty sure of one thing—Savannah would scarcely be his destination, if he could help it.

Should she wear her mulberry cloak with its pretty gray squirrel collar or—she never arrived at a decision because at that moment the front door crashed back and Irad came storming upstairs wearing an expression which drained every trace of blood from her features.

"He knows!" was her thought on facing her husband's blazing eyes.

" 'Lissa, leave the room," Irad directed in harsh, flat and unfamiliar accents.

"God help me! He intends killing me!"

Irad Seymour had never stood taller. She stood waiting, anticipating the words which would blast her marriage forever. How could she have been such an utter little fool as to risk respectability, social advancement? How in the world had he found out? Some very early rising neighbor, no doubt.

To her vast amazement the starch went out of Irad's back and he crumpled into a sitting position on a black horsehair sofa. A measure of courage came welling back into her although she could not yet understand why he didn't rant and rage.

"What—what is wrong?" she stammered.

Hands twisting before his knees, he said without looking up, "It's rotten—damned unfair. The truth is, Sylvia, I—I don't know what to say. I've been discharged. I—I've lost my position."

"Oh! Is that all?" Sylvia burst out despite herself.

"All?" He gaped at her. "All? Don't you realize it means ruin? Absolute financial ruin for me?"

Tears of indescribable relief stung Sylvia's eyes as she flung herself onto the floor beside him.

"Oh, Irad, my darling. I didn't understand! Forgive me, please, forgive me." She crouched at his side pressing herself to him and kissing his forehead. "I—I was so surprised—but you looked so shattered and tragic." She slipped an arm about his shoulders. "Surely, my heart, there are other shipbuilders?"

"Yes, but Yankees and black Abolitionists to the man."

"But, dearest, what did happen?" Now that her breathing was easier her mental processes became alert, anticipatory.

"Reeder called me in. Seems some fool informed him book, chapter and verse, about Léon Duchesne's toast to Maryland's secession at the General Wayne Inn. He's convinced that I've been a Confederate secret agent all along and has threatened to have a United States marshal arrest me the minute hostilities break out."

Irad removed his glasses and commenced uselessly to polish them. "What am I to do?"

She would have answered save that he really wasn't asking her, but himself rather. "You know how hard-up we've been. I've not been able to save enough money to support us for a single month."

Sylvia nodded. "Yes, my darling. But, Irad, what do you intend doing?"

Her husband drew a deep, shuddering breath and heaved himself to his feet. A sudden impatience bordering on contempt seized Sylvia. Why hadn't he long ago foreseen this possibility and made plans? Really, Irad wasn't the least bit shrewd or far-sighted. Only weak and vacillating. Again she was in error.

"Since they've pinned a Secessionist label on to me," he growled, "by God I'll be one—one of the best! After all, I'm a Virginian and a Southerner." After restoring his spectacles to position he commenced to pace, much as had his brother earlier that fateful day.

"My dear, we must face the fact that I shan't be able to obtain a marine architect's post in or around Baltimore. That damned Reeder and his crowd will see to that, and I'm determined not to move further north."

"Why not?" Sylvia demanded. "Last night several people told me that in New York there are hundreds of Southern sympathizers. At this very minute influential men up there are buying equipment and arms for Confederate troops. Why, I was reading the *New York Herald* only the other day and, Irad, its editorials were so Secessionist you wouldn't have believed it had been published in New England."

"New York isn't a part of New England," Irad corrected subconsciously. "Up north you'll come across marine architects, draughtsmen and shipwrights to spare because nearly every English or Scotch engineer who comes to America settles north of the Mason-Dixon Line."

Stroking his short golden beard, Irad steadily considered his lovely young wife sitting stiff and pale across their room. "I intend going south, Sylvia, and there prove my shipbuilding theories. Perhaps in so doing I can serve my country better than a lot of fire-eaters rushing about in uniform. My principles are sound although some of them may seem revolutionary, but I know they are practical and their application to our new Navy would place it well ahead of the damned Yankees and their obsolete wooden tubs."

Never before had Sylvia beheld her husband so intense, so determined. Mercy, how little, after all, she appreciated the depths of this man she'd married!

Apparently it required a crisis like this to jar him out of his wellbred, tolerant and easygoing way of life. She ran up and flung both arms about him. So he did possess ambition after all. How wonderful! And she could, and would, help his star to rise in so many subtle, purely feminine ways. Family connections, which were legion, and still more numerous friends must be enlisted and allied—largely without Irad's knowledge; he was ridiculously touchy about being under obligation to anyone whomever.

Her arms tightened about him as she lifted a glowing countenance and offered Sam's letter.

As covertly intense as a defendant studying the foreman of a jury on the point of rendering a verdict, Sylvia scrutinized her husband while he read the communication through twice.

"Well, I'm damned," he said slowly. "Sam has beaten me to it. He's sent in his papers and started for Montgomery. Wonder what caused him to make up his mind so all-fired quickly? It's not like him."

"Oh, isn't it just the times, dear?" was Sylvia's suggestion. "People are doing so many things on impulse these days. Action is in the air."

"Well, good luck to him. Do wish we could have said goodbye." He reached for his tall stovepipe hat. "May not see each other again for a long time."

"Where are you going, dear?"

"To book us passage to Norfolk," he announced crisply. "I'll try for the Baltimore Steam Packet's *Georgeanna* tomorrow. You and Melissa had better get cracking."

XX

REVERBERATIONS: 12 APRIL 1861

BECAUSE OF WILD demonstrations inspired by news that a Federal fort in the harbor of Charleston, South Carolina, had refused to surrender and was under bombardment, the Baltimore Steam Packet's ship *Georgeanna* sailed at six-thirty in the evening—two hours late.

Wildly exaggerated rumors circulated that Carolina State troops had carried Fort Sumter at the point of their bayonets; that a Major Anderson, apparently the Federal commander, had touched off the magazine and had blown himself, the attackers and his whole garrison to glory.

Such was the excitement that, long after the steam calliope had finished a final asthmatic but deafening rendition of "Dixie's Land," very few of the *Georgeanna's* male passengers went to bed, but lingered in one or the other of the bay liner's spacious bars.

Long after Sylvia, her servant and the boy had retired to one of the Georgeanna's few staterooms, Irad Seymour continued to linger on the spar deck. Idly, he watched the great walking beam's jet outline rising and falling against the stars like a gigantic seesaw, followed the course of streams of sparks whirling off to leeward in their frenzied ephemeral course. Thank God, that infernal steam calliope had finally given up!

In bitterness, tinged with regret, he had watched the tangled silhouettes of the shipyards lining both banks of the Patapsco recede over lazy swells and a lacy wake created by the Georgeanna's massive paddle wheels. Ahead, a double line of small yellow-red lights indicated the ship channel out to Chesapeake Bay.

It went without saying that there would be several people aboard he knew; luckily these were acquaintances rather than friends. Nonetheless, in honor of the momentous news from South Carolina, these individuals had noisily insisted on standing him to drink after drink of Zeigler's and Brownelle's Baltimore Rye Whiskey, beer and brandy. With the third round he had become infected by raging partisanship emphasized sometimes by terrifying displays of pistols and daggers— every male aboard, himself excepted, appeared to go armed.

"Yes, gentlemen"—more than a bit soused at the moment, Irad had banged hard on the bar—"I tell you Ol' Federal Navy's obsolete an' wooden. Can't stand up to the new ironclads we're goin' build! *I* know!"

"*Viva!* Hurray for you!" A towering individual who claimed to come from Texas, described a glittering arc with a scalping knife above the cringing bartender. "Hi-ya-h-h!" he screeched. "We'll cut them goddam' Abolitionists inter kybobs and little rashers."

Far away and faint as if admitted by a pinhole puncturing the horizon, came noises made by huge flocks of ducks migrating northwards. These subtle sounds were terminated by the sudden barking roar of pistols. Some volunteers traveling south to join the Confederate Army were expressing their exuberance by discharging cap-and-ball Colt's revolvers at the sky. Frightened protests promptly arose from passengers sleeping in odd contorted positions about the deck.

When the Georgeanna had backed out of her slip, Fort Sumter had not been taken, nor had it surrendered, but still was firing. As near as Irad could ascertain with any degree of accuracy a whole nation was holding its breath, apprehensive as a person suffering the first pangs of some still undiagnosed disease. The communiqués forwarded from Charleston had sounded so biassed, so full of bombast, that obviously they must be the product of someone's overfertile imagination. The only non-participants in the almost general jubilation were a small party of naval officers and enlisted men, obviously returning from leave to Fortress Monroe or to the Gosport Navy Yard.

A captain of Marines was the only other occupant of the *Georgeanna's* spar deck. He was quietly smoking his pipe while thoughtfully gazing out over the starlit Chesapeake Bay.

At length the Marine officer arose and commenced to walk back and forth, every once in a while fanning at mosquitoes which, incredibly, appeared in droves. "Evening," he grunted, but Irad only nodded; he was still trying to clear his head.

From below resounded a volley of drunken shouts.

"Let 'em yelp and enjoy it," commented the Marine, illuminating smooth flat features in the glow of a long-stemmed German porcelain pipe. "Those braggarts will be howling a different tune before long."

"Indeed, sir?" Irad still felt belligerent. "And what, pray, leads you to such a conclusion?" He was surprised at his own pompousness and a trifle pleased.

"Why? Because, friend, even the few ships we maintain 'in ordinary' at Gosport can deny the whole of Chesapeake Bay to those noisy traitors. Our guns can batter Norfolk into a heap of smoking brickbats."

In monumental dignity Irad Seymour drew himself up, said stiffly, "I fear, sir, you address the wrong man."

The Marine shrugged. "Oh, so you're Secesh, too, are you? It's a wonder you're not getting drunk below. My mistake, good evening." The Marine captain, in no great hurry, turned on his heel and stalked off.

Irad thought he ought to call the fellow down but he felt too groggy and ended by venting his resentment on a mosquito stinging his cheek.

Lord! How much could happen in a short space of time! If anyone had predicted forty-eight hours ago that tonight he would be without employment, would have given up his career in Baltimore, and would be traveling south to join the Confederate Forces, he'd have thought that person plain demented. Yet here he was aboard the Georgeanna and bound for Norfolk!

Poor Sylvia. At first she'd been wonderfully brave and excited but when a van had appeared to load their trunks, valises and packing cases, she had cried and cried. Although 33 Caroline Street had been rented furnished, there were the fine Hepplewhite chairs, their big four-poster bed, the Magoffins' lovely Sheraton hunting board and the Chippendale sofa.

A uniformed bluejacket clumped by and spat tobacco juice over the rail. On the back of his hand he wiped bearded lips.

"Well, Mister, I allow the old Georgie won't be making this here run much longer. Seems like the Rebs sure have tipped over the apple cart today."

"Seems like it," Irad agreed. "You think Virginia will go out?"

The bluejacket stared, tugged embarrassedly at his wind-pulled neckerchief. "Why, no. Not if they ain't dumb-locks, they won't." The sailor spat again, then disappeared down a companionway beyond the busy port paddle box.

"What with all this commotion down in Carolina, Virginia may very well get carried away," Irad mused. "If so, there ought to be plenty of good construction jobs open—and near the top, too. Surely Mr. Mallory hasn't had extra many marine architects applying for commissions?"

Irad brightened at the prospect of finally wearing naval uniform. Wouldn't it be grand were Sam and he to find themselves on the same station? The steady tchunk! tchunk! of the Georgeanna's paddle wheels was having a steadying effect.

"Where can Sam be headed after Montgomery?" Irad wondered. "Funny for him not to have mentioned his destination when everybody at the Winans' was telling just where he was going."

Briefly Irad debated going below to occupy one of those bunks which, in tiers of three, lined the Georgeanna's forepeak—and decided against it. The sleeping compartments below he knew were separated only by dirty muslin curtains and torn netting, so every snore could be plainly heard. Moreover in their present mood some of his fellow passengers undoubtedly would prove to be fighting drunk or else getting sick all over the deck.

Dawn revealed huge clouds of ducks, geese and swans rising like smoke from the water at the *Georgeanna's* approach. Presently rows of tiny yellow lights appeared far off the starboard bow to mark the situation of Fortress Monroe. Last night there had been much speculation concerning its fate. Would the Virginians dare emulate the attack on Fort Sumter? Once Virginia seceded it was to be expected that there'd be plenty of violence; weren't the Virginians mighty handy fighters, and quick-tempered to boot?

In some excitement Irad observed a vertical string of signal lanterns climbing to a signal staff but, contrary to his expectations, neither of the two big steam frigates lying at anchor off the fortress appeared to have steam up. The smoke rose from their funnels only in sleepy slender threads. Soon the paddle steamer churned closer in to a dark, low-lying shore.

Paddle wheels splashing and threshing in reverse, the *Georgeanna* eventually coasted up and made fast to a strong wooden pier upon which glimmered the bayonets of Marines on duty below. Once a gangplank had been thrust into position, several Army officers and about thirty hilariously exhilarated or sodden soldiers stumbled off over the dew-wetted planking.

One of the officers on reaching the dock turned and, shaking his fist, called, "Come and call on us, ye dirty sneaking traitors and we'll teach you—" The balance of his promise was lost because the *Georgeanna's* steam trumpet roared as, creaking in every fibre, she backed well out into Hampton Roads before starting across that great estuary formed by the confluence of the Elizabeth and the James Rivers.

Pretty soon Irad was able to distinguish roofs of Norfolk bright with recent rain; some of the numerous church steeples appeared to be on fire so brilliantly did they glow in the sun's first rays.

How wonderfully familiar the distant city appeared! Yonder was where he and Sam and Reynolds had gone to school, had fished, sailed and shot and had teased the girls. Under one of those distant roofs his parents lay asleep. His eyes stung suddenly under this vivid, homely reminder that Virginia was his State.

From this distance Norfolk appeared to be as peaceful as usual, gracious hostess to myriad ships of all rigs and nationalities. By the dozen they rode anchor or lay tied up to a long series of docks.

It was a bitter business, to be returning jobless like this; Mother was certain to be disappointed. He guessed, too, she'd be far from happy at learning his decision to join the Confederate Naval Forces. Would Pa disapprove? True, he also was Virginia born but had he not served most of his career far removed from his native State?

Ahead and to starboard of the Georgeanna's present course lay Portsmouth and beyond it the barracks, ship houses and other buildings constituting the great United States Navy Yard at Gosport. Soon he recognized the grim, sable outlines of the many ships-of-war habitually anchored near the mouth of the Elizabeth River.

Easiest to identify, of course, were ships-of-the-line, distinguishable by their triple streaks of gunports. There were four of these obsolete behemoths. The U.S.S. *Delaware* and the U.S.S. *Columbus* lay idle in the stream but he was interested to perceive that the gigantic *Pennsylvania*, robbed of top spars and all but essential rigging, still was doing duty as receiving ship for the Naval Station. On this change of tide she was swinging sullenly to those same moorings which she had occupied for years. The poor old hulk presented a sad and expensive picture for, although her lofty sides had been pierced to mount one hundred and twenty guns, the *Pennsylvania* never yet had flown a commission pennant or spread sails to an ocean breeze.

He thought he recognized the *New York* lying in stocks over by Gosport. Anchored in the immediate vicinity and faithfully mirrored in the glassy river rode the modern steam frigates *Cumberland*, *Raritan*, *Columbia* and the old sailing frigate *United States*—that same gallant old paladin which, under the command of dashing young Stephen Decatur had pulverized H.B.M.S. *Macedonian* long ago during the War of 1812.

Smoke was rising from their funnels but the only activity noticeable among this silent, motionless armada was aboard the steam frigates *Cumberland* and what looked to be the *Merrimac*, forty guns. The latter vessel lay to a stone wharf to the east of the drydock where she must have been undergoing repair.

The first-class sloops *Germantown* and *Plymouth*, smart twenty-two-gun cruisers, and several other smaller vessels, seemed ready for sea. The minute hostilities commenced these should prove invaluable.

Steadily the big bay liner plowed on down the harbor. Could the Navy Yard be captured by some sudden foray? Probably not. Surely, the Federal Government must appreciate that here in Gosport was situated the principal naval shipyard in the United States. What could not be manufactured here wasn't worth troubling over.

Over the still and shining waters beat a sudden bray of Marine bugles blowing Assembly. Years ago, Irad had learned to recognize the various calls. He lingered, studying, reviewing the position of the Navy Yard's huge storage sheds, the three lofty ship houses, the rows of red brick barracks and those sinister piles of cannon and pyramids of shot.

Puffing pillars of woolly black smoke from her twin funnels and playing her steam calliope like mad, the *Georgeanna* continued up the Elizabeth River. More and more passengers came struggling up to the spar deck, for the most part unshaven, red-eyed and swollen of countenance; the women and children, however, seemed less travel worn.

Sylvia appeared, looking small and irritable.

"Oh, Irad, I've been looking all over for you. Come quickly or there won't be any breakfast left. Robbie is simply ravenous."

When they came up from below, the *Georgeanna* was nosing her way through a fleet of oyster boats lying gunwale-deep with those luscious bivalves so vastly appreciated along America's Eastern seaboard.

Also there were fishing sharpies, the masts of which were raked backwards to an almost ludicrous angle, pungies and all manner of produce sloops and lumber schooners. Some of these had bent weather-beaten United States colors on to their signal halyards, but most of the small craft showed no flag at all.

A faintly sour smell suggestive of wide mud flats, of spoiled oysters, fish and fruit, came rolling over the bay liner's rail like a noxious miasma.

XXI

The Honorable Judge Renders an Opinion

VERY LITTLE SEEMED to have changed, either about Norfolk or the Seymour home, a neat red brick and gray-trimmed residence standing by itself amid a spacious lot on the corner of Charlotte and Cumberland Streets. It was, by public opinion, far more modish and comfortable than most property owned by aging naval veterans. Captain Felix had never been spendthrift, and up in Boston, Amanda Ashton Seymour's family usually had earned more than "moderate bread," as they put it, as ship captains in the China trade; also Amanda had been a lone female child among seven stalwart sons.

To an observant caller the Seymour residence bespoke naval neatness and solidity plus a certain Yankee severity modified by good taste. During those sixteen years in which the Seymour family had lived here a series of handsome flower gardens had been laid out to surround the big, two-storied house with banks of blossoms. This was one reason Amanda always had mourned the lack of a daughter who might have been persuaded to take an interest and maybe help keep them up.

A heavy spring thunderstorm had come rumbling and grumbling up from the south—much like that political tempest commencing to stir and beset Virginia. Now it reached the environs of Portsmouth and Gosport and began rattling loose window frames and shutters and sending householders scurrying out-of-doors to retrieve perishable items.

An oppressive humidity prevailed in Captain Felix Seymour's big sitting room, a space quite as large as the parlor which was a chamber used only for such special occasions as when the minister or some foreign admiral or a friend from abroad came to call. Here the Seymour ladies sat stitching, making transparent efforts to avoid overhearing what deep masculine voices were saying in what Captain Seymour called his "quarterdeck." In reality that room was a library, cum trophy room, cum study, cum a retreat into which any female ventured at the risk of life and limb.

"You look flushed, my dear," observed old Mrs. Seymour in her crisp New England voice. "I fear the effects of the past week must have tired you greatly." She was rocking gently beneath a fine Gilbert Stuart portrait of Colonel Robert Ashton, her grandfather, as a student at Harvard College.

"How right she is," thought Sylvia, but she glanced up and directed a gay little smile at her mother-in-law. "Oh, Heavens, no! I really couldn't feel better."

As a matter of fact, she was feeling uncommonly well for this particular date. Normally, she would have been fretful, unusually pallid and conscious of dark semi-circles beneath both eyes. Until recently she hadn't dared to decide whether those moments in a certain small parlor up in Baltimore were going to cause physical, as well as mental, remembrances. Now being several whole days past due, she felt sure—a realization which proved to be at once reassuring and infinitely disturbing. To pretend to herself that nothing untoward had chanced on the night of the Winans' cotillion, she had found surprisingly easy. No hint of what had happened between Sam and herself had ever betrayed itself in her manner; of that she felt convinced. Therefore her needle flashed surely, delicately, back and forth through the embroidery she was working on a tambour frame.

"I assure you, suh, Virginia is being tricked, aye, tricked into this folly!" Judge Arthur Kenyon's deep voice rang so loudly down the corridor that Amanda Seymour discovered no difficulty in overhearing his every syllable.

"Perhaps then, Your Honor, you will be good enough to explain such an opinion?" That would be Lieutenant C. M. F. Spottswood, thought Sylvia. Intensely patriotic and excitable, the most violent Secessionist sentiments were ever on his lips.

"Young sir, I seldom elaborate upon the reasoning behind my opinions." The Judge sounded almost disdainful. "In this case, however, I will make an exception. What I mean is that this unhappy movement has been initiated not by the old, established Southern States, saving South Carolina—States which have fought two wars for freedom—but by a group of selfish, criminally ambitious parvenus from Alabama, Missouri, Mississippi, Louisiana and the western or new part of Georgia."

Captain Seymour's voice—it was still big and strong despite his seventy-odd years—rang out, "I fear, Arthur, that I fail to grasp your meaning."

Someone said, over a sudden drumming of rain against the shutters, "Why, Judge, you've just named the principle slavery extentionist States."

"Quite so," the Judge agreed. "What do we see in the far South, in the lower Mississippi Valley but a fixed determination to own more slaves and more land, in order to grow still more cotton, and so amass more power and riches? Why, damn it, we all know well that, for a long while, slaveholding has been on the wane not only in the Border States such as Delaware, Maryland, Kentucky and Tennessee, but in Virginia and North Carolina."

A sudden peal of thunder momentarily drowned out the jurist's declamation, permitting Sylvia to steal a sidewise look at Irad's mother. She seemed to be knitting extra-hard and sat bolt upright with lips set in a "prunes, prisms and persimmons" line.

"I maintain, suh, that if Virginia enters this Confederacy," Judge Kenyon resumed, "and as I fear she will, then she will become a cat's-paw, risking Northern fire to further the selfish schemes of cotton kings and sugar barons."

For a while no one spoke in "the quarterdeck" until Irad from his seat beside Pa's chart chest inquired, "But surely, Judge Kenyon, you don't contend that we should go on permitting the North to trample upon our rights?"

"The fulminations of ignorant demagogues to the contrary," came the even reply, "the North thus far hasn't trampled on our rights. Indeed, Irad, for some sixty-five out of the seventy-two years this nation has been independent, the South has controlled Congress and run the Government."

Captain Felix tugged perplexedly at his short white goatee. "Well, then, what's happened to change everything about so?"

"The South, Felix, that governed so long and so well was the Old South; a region represented by true patriots and able statesmen. Who speaks for the New South, gentlemen? I give you boors like Joe Brown and James M. Mason of Virginia, or downright charlatans and political chameleons like Tom Cobb or John Slidell."

A vivid flash of lightning converted the window frames into rectangles of silver-gold.

"Let us suppose, Your Honor"—Lieutenant Spottswood leaned forward, intense and handsome in his naval undress uniform—"that Virginia remains in the Union. Where will she stand with regard to her Northern neighbors? As a poor-relation State, sir! She'll be considered the very tail of the Union, whereas"—his voice rose—"should she elect to secede, she then can join this Great New Confederacy and queen it over all her lovely and valiant Sisters. Indeed, gentlemen, Virginia must stand at the head of the Southern Confederacy."

From a waistcoat pocket, Judge Kenyon produced a pair of little scissors with which he commenced very carefully to trim his finger-nails. His tone was bitter. "Exactly, Mr. Spottswood. You prognosti-cate extremely well. I fear we are allowing ourselves to be flattered and dazzled into accepting a leadership which may very well prove dis-astrous." His gaze shifted to Captain Felix's craggy, brown and mottled-pink features. "I believe myself to be a loyal and patriotic Virginian; therefore I intend to abide by the will of my fellow citizens and support our arms to the end.

"About our willingness to fight I entertain no doubts whatever—nor on our ability to do so. It is in the quality of the men controlling this new Government that I find the greatest dangers. Consider Jef-ferson Davis. He is able, no doubt, but possessed of so little loyalty as actively to conspire against the very Government he served *while still in office!* What of the Confederate Secretary of the Navy?" At this all three listeners stiffened, forgot to fan themselves. "Stephen B. Mallory possesses so little education that he can't even write a gram-matical letter. He's a second-rate politician from Florida, knows noth-ing whatever concerning naval matters."

"At least," Felix Seymour interjected, "you will concede that Davis' Vice President is able?"

"Aye, Alexander Stephens is clever, but do you know that he held out against Secession until the very last minute and only accepted his post with evident reluctance?"

Spottswood frowned. He wasn't enjoying this clear summation in the least. "We all hear the Secretary of State, Judah P. Benjamin, is shrewd and extremely able."

"My dear, Mr. Spottswood, 'shrewd' is a kindly term for men of Benjamin's kidney. If it is shrewd to be expelled from Yale for steal-ing his classmates' jewelry—then I will agree with you."

"That charge has never been fully substantiated, Arthur," Captain Seymour objected.

The Judge fixed a steady regard on his life-long friend. "I beg to differ, Felix. I was attending Yale at the time. I know that his name was expunged from the rolls, that Benjamin's abject application for readmission was rejected by the Board of Regents. Why has he made every effort to obliterate his early days?" The Judge was now in full cry. "If the Montgomery Convention had possessed a grain of political acumen, they would have elected Howell Cobb President, or possibly Robert Toombs. Both were Constitutional Unionists back in 'fifty-six.'"

"They made some pretty poor political choices during our Revolution, yet we seem to have survived."

Captain Seymour arose and in some agitation rang a bell. "Four mint juleps, Phillip," he instructed the servant. "Be sure to use only young leaves, and make them—er—convincing."

Thought Irad, eyes narrowed behind steel spectacles, "Pa really hasn't made up his mind yet—but when he does, he'll go Virginian. I've never seen him so upset, so undecided. Good thing he's too old for active duty. I wonder what Captain Farragut has told him? Old Davy Farragut's a Tennesseean, of course, so he'll likely send in his papers. What's Pa saying?"

"After all, Arthur, many of the ablest generals in the Old Army and many excellent naval officers have adhered to the Secessionist Cause." Pa looked older than usual standing there with his leonine shock of white hair and silvery beard but his jaw line still was jutting and firm. "When it comes to stupidity"—Captain Felix pointed at a copy of the Norfolk Day Book sprawled across the map chest's glistening mahogany top—"Mr. Lincoln must have gone completely mad to issue a call for seventy-five thousand volunteers at a delicate moment like this!" Irad's father scrutinized each of his guests in turn. "How dare he summon the citizens of one State to invade the territory of another?"

"That does appear a grave blunder," Judge Kenyon admitted and, opening an old-fashioned tortoise-shell box, helped himself to a pinch of snuff. A diamond glittered briefly among starched ruffles descending his shirt front. "But what other course could he adopt when South Carolina seizes and destroys Federal property belonging to all the States?"

Two Chinese porcelain Fô dogs, mementos of Captain Felix Seymour's service in the Far East, glared across the room at a row of Polynesian devil masks. Funny, that Irad should, at this instant, recall that the dog with a tiny chip off its scarlet tongue was his; the other slightly smaller one had always been considered Sam's.

"Legalize and rationalize as you will, gentlemen, hostilities had to start somewhere," Lieutenant Spottswood observed while lighting a paper spill from a lovely Japanese bronze lantern. A mirror behind the light reflecting Spottswood's buttons cast tiny reflections on the ceiling.

"But in the eyes of the world, Colonel Ruffin—I understand 'twas he who jerked the lanyard on the first cannon—and his supporters used extremely bad judgment. South Carolina stands branded as the aggressor," the Judge had time to point out, before averting his head to indulge in a very genteel snuff-sneeze.

"What does your friend, Captain Farragut, think?"

"I don't know, Arthur. I'm told that he's retired to his quarters and refuses to talk to anyone save on official business."

"That's a damned unpatriotic attitude for a Southerner," Spottswood broke out. "Even if he is only a Tennesseean."

A small silence ensued, in which the lively *thump-thump* of a mallet smashing ice for juleps could distinctly be heard.

Finally, Captain Seymour heaved erect his short stocky figure; despite habit and will power, its shoulders were commencing to bend under his seventy-three years.

"God knows where this all will end. Where in hell are those juleps?" he growled. Then, "I presume some unlicked puppy is going to tell me I'm too old for active service, me who helped open up Japan!" His gaze wandered to a series of outlandish prints purporting to depict the American arrival at Tokyo Bay. There they were, as seen by Oriental eyes, the United States ships *Mississippi*, *Plymouth*, *Saratoga* and his own vessel, the *Susquehanna*, all flying huge and absurdly incorrect versions of the Stars and Stripes. Dear Old Glory, revered emblem of American sovereignty and honor! The old man's throat closed spasmodically as he added, "I'll volunteer the moment Virginia goes out, but I must say that my heart won't be wholly in this quarrel."

"It will be, sir," Spottswood predicted warmly, "from the minute the Yankee President starts sending his troops across the Virginia line."

Phillip, grave and soft-footed, reappeared bearing a tray of greenly nodding juleps.

It was remarkable that no one offered a toast; they only chatted on trivialities until young Lieutenant Spottswood set down his cup. "That was most delicious, sir, and now, if you'll excuse me, I will go and make my manners to Mrs. Seymour. I must return to the Navy Yard by eleven o'clock." He smiled bleakly. "Commodore McCauley is taking all possible precautions. At your service, sir."

A trifle stiffly, he bowed to Judge Kenyon who surveyed him in obvious distaste before inclining his handsome silvery head.

At the door Spottswood made sure that the rain had ceased and only the water dripping from the chestnut trees caused the pattering sound. Then he touched Irad's arm. "Care to walk down to the corner?"

"Yes. I—I wanted a word with you, Charles."

The air was cooler and from the north, but a damp breeze redolent of the harbor had begun to stir young water oaks and myrtles. Taking care to skirt wide puddles, the two men started towards the river.

Spottswood said presently, "I didn't dare tell half of what I know before Judge Kenyon. As a Federal judge, I—well, I don't trust him too far, but let me ask you one thing. If invited, would you be willing to take part in—well, attempting to capture the Navy Yard for the South?"

"Yes. I know how badly we'll need its ordnance and facilities," came the thoughtful reply. "Have you made any plans?"

A slight hesitation marked the other's response. "Yes. They're quite complete. You see, an unusually large number of Southerners are on duty there—Ex-Secretary of the Navy Toucey saw to that. There are quite a few of us officers and many of the enlisted men," he continued, "who are Secesh to the heart and ready to risk all in capturing the Yard."

"I see." Irad nodded, his gaze following the furtive progress of a cat across Captain Farragut's narrow lawn. Lights were glowing in most of the rooms. "Charles, what of the ships? They could blow all Norfolk, Portsmouth and Gosport into rubbish."

"We have little to fear from that direction. They lie purposely undermanned," Spottswood replied promptly. "The minute Virginia secedes several trainloads of troops will start down from Richmond. Our local militia companies are well armed and craving action. Well, Irad, will you lend a hand?"

"Of course," came the instant reply. "As a marine architect I know how much this Navy Yard will mean to the Confederacy. You have only to instruct me."

Lieutenant Spottswood grinned and patted him on the shoulder.

"You'll soon be hearing from us." He strode off, the skirts of the blue naval uniform coat snapping briskly about his legs.

XXII

Various Plantings

ALTHOUGH SHE DESPISED the very sight of a rake or trowel, no one would have suspected that Sylvia Seymour took other than a passionate interest in gardening as, wearing a wide straw hat, gloves and a pretty blue denim apron, she worked over the nasturtium bed old Mrs. Seymour had planted, New England fashion, in a worn-out skiff.

"It must be such fun making different sorts of flowers blend together. Only I could never do it anywhere near as cleverly as you. Mamma always doted on heliotrope. It smells simply divine and looks so well with any kind of yellow flowers like—like primroses."

Old Mrs. Seymour smiled quietly. "Your mother must be very able to grow primroses so far south. I fear we shall have to wait a while for my heliotropes to come up." She eased herself down on her thin old knees, using a muddied pillow for protection.

Sylvia actually put some weight behind her trowel. "Oh, isn't it wonderful to be out-of-doors again after that horrid long winter?"

"It was a long and miserable winter, especially because one couldn't escape from the eternal discussion about Secession and war," Amanda Seymour said, deftly dividing a clump of chrysanthemums. "Wars! Wars! Seems as if I've never known anything else since I married Irad's father. First it was that expedition against Quallah Battoo. I can see you've never heard of it. Well, 'twas a punitive expedition against a Malayan sultan, a beastly heathen who had murdered some of our merchantmen. Then came the Mexican War and the troubles with various Spanish American republics—so-called. You can thank your lucky stars, my child, you haven't married into the Navy."

"But I have; at least, I think I'm going to be a Navy wife," Sylvia said diffidently as she commenced to weed a heart-shaped flower bed.

It was so cool Sylvia really didn't need her broad-brimmed straw hat, but she recalled that Mamma invariably wore something of the sort when gardening or playing at it—the black gardeners really did everything.

Before developing the subject of Irad's future career she deemed it wiser to wait; to permit Mrs. Seymour to wax enthusiastic over the fine manner in which her beloved sweet peas and nasturtiums were sprouting.

"Probably Mrs. Magoffin obtains wonderful results," Mrs. Seymour was hazarding between thrusts of a hand fork. "I have seen truly magnificent gardens about Wilmington, Charleston and Savannah; lovely dreamlands they were, but this soil is far from good. It's either too sandy or too heavy with clay."

"Oh, that's hard to credit, Mother Seymour. Your flower beds are so exquisite!" The younger woman's voice carried conviction and her animated, pointed features were quite devoid of guile.

Captain Felix's wife flushed with pleasure. "It's only a question of enough mulch and peatmoss. No matter where the Captain and I have been stationed, I have been able to produce flowers that none of my neighbors could."

"Of course, it must be the hardest kind of work to raise northern flowers so far south as Pensacola," Sylvia murmured and, sitting back upon her heels, wiped a beading of perspiration from her upper lip. In so doing she created a small muddy mark which, somehow, pleased Mrs. Seymour inordinately.

"You are a dear girl, Sylvia," she cried softly. "You always seem to guess how to please me. I can't tell you how nice it is to have a—a daughter take so intelligent an interest in my poor little gardenings. Now be sure you don't tire yourself, my dear. Your hands are so tiny and soft. You're to be careful, else you'll develop blisters."

"Oh, I'm quite all right so long as it doesn't get hot. How insufferably humid it must have been in Florida. Irad tells me that you and Captain Seymour were stationed at Pensacola when he was a little boy."

Amanda Seymour's coral-pink lips relaxed in a smile of reminiscence. "Mercy, yes! Captain Felix"—Mrs. Seymour always referred to her husband as such within the family—"was stationed there as Chief Ordnance Officer during eight years. That was where Irad and Samuel learned to speak Spanish. My dear, you never in the world could guess who taught them the language."

Sylvia knew very well, but it was not her intention to admit that knowledge.

"Of course, I couldn't. Do tell me!"

"None other than Mrs. Mallory, wife of the present so-called"— she sniffed—"Secretary of the Rebel Navy. Mrs. Mallory was a charming creature, though a full-blooded Spaniard. Coming from Spain itself, she spoke purest Castilian."

"Isn't that fascinating"—Sylvia ran to fetch a watering pot—"I don't suppose a busy lady like Mrs. Mallory would even remember Irad?"

Firmly, Mrs. Seymour drenched the newly planted chrysanthemum shoots. "Don't you doubt it! Manuela made a regular pet of him."

"Then you must have kept in touch with Mrs. Mallory?" Sylvia inquired softly.

"Only off and on. Mr. Mallory wasn't Navy, you understand. He was editor of the local paper and very able, as I recall."

"I suppose you know, Mother Seymour, that Irad is offering his services to the Confederate Navy?" Never had Sylvia's voice sounded richer, more charged with deep emotion.

Mrs. Seymour's petite and straight-backed figure relaxed into a sitting position and the thin shoulders drooped a fraction of an inch.

"Yes, Sylvia. I heard what you said a while ago about becoming a Navy wife."

Sylvia dropped her eyes in confusion. Then, "Why didn't you say anything, dear?"

"I wanted time to sort my notions, as we say up in New Hampshire." She brushed a scattering of pale green leaves from her apron and looked squarely into her daughter-in-law's great golden-brown eyes.

"It comes hard for me to say what I'm about to say, my dear, because I'm a New Englander born and bred and I have five brothers who'll soon be fighting for the Union. There'd be six of 'em, only one—Eliphalet—is dead."

"How awful this trouble must be for you," Sylvia murmured in genuine concern.

"It is. I've been married to a Virginian for near forty years—not that I've often regretted it—and during that time I've set foot in New

England only twice. So"—she sighed and looked at her wrinkled, earth-stained hands—"if my husband and my sons elect to support the Southern view, does it leave me any choice but to support them and give them all the love and comfort I find in me?" Here was no pathos, no plea for pity, merely a tragic resignation to fate.

Impulsively Sylvia rushed over to fling slim arms about the older woman and kiss a very soft and withered cheek that smelt faintly of lilac water.

"Dear Mother Seymour, please don't look so unhappy. I—I can't bear it. I'm certain you'll never regret your decision because"—her voice now rang rich and true—"our Southern Cause is righteous, almost holy!"

"I wish I could believe you," sighed Amanda Seymour. "But I don't know, I really don't know."

They fell to gardening again in a silence which endured until at length Sylvia said, "I've been thinking Irad would be wasted as a mere marine draughtsman assigned to some Navy Yard. I suppose he always has had very original ideas, but some of them were practical enough to interest a shipbuilder in Baltimore. Up there, Irad read and made detailed researches until I used to rage at him because for the sake of his work he wouldn't take me to parties."

"My eldest son always was studious." Mrs. Seymour's small eyes of faded gray narrowed. From the start she'd been pleased by Sylvia's brilliant charm and subtle flattery, although she hadn't been the least bit taken in by it. In fact, she had appraised her Georgian daughter-in-law far more accurately than that clever young woman ever suspected. She proved so now.

"I presume, my dear, that you wouldn't object to my writing a letter to Mrs. Mallory, possibly suggesting that her husband find some suitable post for Irad?"

"Why—why, yes." Sylvia stared in round-eyed astonishment. "But how ever did you guess it?"

A fleeting smile was all the answer she got before Amanda Seymour continued, "I believe you were about to remind me that, with Irad's eyesight being as bad as it is, he could prove far more valuable in the Reb—er, Confederate Navy Department rather than superintending construction or trying to serve at sea?"

As if surprised in the act of stealing, Sylvia could not have appeared more confused, more aghast at having her supposedly secret ambition thus anticipated and exposed.

"Why—why, yes," she faltered. "Is that so wrong of me?"

"I didn't say it was wrong, my dear." Mrs. Seymour gave her daughter's hand a reassuring pat. "Besides, life for you in the Confederate capital should prove far from dull, especially for a young lady of your particular talents—and charm. Why the Rebels picked a remote country town 'way off in Alabama for their capital I vow I'll never comprehend."

The old lady caught up her rake, commenced to smooth the ground where shortly clumps of bleeding hearts would glow.

Sylvia regarded this brisk, wren-like old lady with new respect. "And —what else am I thinking?"

"Shouldn't wonder but you've calculated that precious few officers of Naval Administration will get themselves killed in battle."

Such insight was as dismaying as it was uncanny! A furious flood of scarlet darkened Sylvia's cheeks. "Why, I declare!" she gasped. "I never thought such a thing, really I didn't! I wouldn't dream of encouraging Irad to shirk."

"Tut, my dear. Don't get your pretty self into such a swivet. I don't want him killed, either; not if I can help it, because Sam and Reynolds"—she broke off, turned abruptly away—"can't be stopped or cozened from sea service, not they!"

XXIII

THE CONSPIRATORS

LATER THAT SAME day, April the sixteenth, Mr. Mahone, principal proprietor of William Mahone & Sons, Wholesale Ship Chandlers, lingered in the rear of his well-stocked warehouse in Norfolk. In order that he might personally admit a number of individuals who appeared strolling, oh so innocently, down a back alley, he found tasks to occupy his shipping clerks in the sail lofts on the second story.

His callers approached, picking a gingerly route along a paving of crushed oyster shells, crab husks and other marine refuse. By five o'clock there had gathered in Mr. Mahone's stuffy little private office a group numbering ten men, of whom Irad Seymour could recognize about a half. What with the news of Fort Sumter's surrender he was feeling more than a little tense and excited and was perspiring under his sober brown frock coat.

"Joe, just you go and stand outside the back door," the merchant instructed his son. "If anything seems amiss, you'll knock twice, then three times. Understand? Tom, you'll not let anyone back of the rear counter, understand?

"All right, gents, find yerselves seats. Reckon there's enough chairs to go around."

A not-unpleasant blend of odors originating from cordage, pitch, canvas and paint filled the air; dust motes danced gaily across a beam of golden sunlight that intruded through a shutter to create a glowing puddle in the midst of a table about which the company was seating itself.

In rapid succession Mr. Mahone, a plump, apple-faced little man boasting enormously long, brown Dundreary whiskers, introduced Commander Robert G. Robb and Lieutenant Spottswood, from the Navy Yard; they appeared both embarrassed and uncomfortable in civilian garb that was by no means fashionably cut. Present also were a Major Tyler, a quick-eyed silent individual who, only that day, had traveled down from Richmond; one John McCarthy, Captain of the local militia company; an assistant editor of the *Norfolk Day Book*; and three officials from the muncipalities of Portsmouth and Norfolk.

Once the gathering had been presented all around, Mr. Mahone employed a businessman's directness and plunged quickly into the matter which had caused this oddly assorted group to congregate.

Irad felt his pulses quicken. After all these years he was about to enter upon active service; despite himself, his hand sought the butt of a revolver dragging at his coattail.

"Major Tyler, please repeat to these gentlemen what you've already told me," said Mr. Mahone.

"I came to inform you," said the Major and his hand crept up to stroke the carefully waxed points of bayonet-sharp mustaches, "that, as surely as the sun will rise tomorrow, so will the Virginia Convention pass an Ordinance of Secession."

"And exactly when, sir, may we expect to hear of this?" demanded Commander Robb, ill-suppressed tension in his voice. "For us at the Navy Yard, such information is absolutely essential."

"Barring unforeseen developments," gravely replied the Army officer, "the Ordinance will be passed in executive session late tonight." The speaker's chest swelled and his voice rang out, "Tomorrow, April the seventeenth, the Despot in Washington will learn that his direful threats have been hurled in vain; all Virginia will be crying as did the noble Brutus, 'Sic Semper Tyrannis!' "

In a low voice, the group echoed the motto of the Commonwealth of Virginia. Major Tyler, Irad was thinking, must once have been either a politician or an actor, so dramatically and effectively did he inflect his speech. All the same, Irad experienced a sharp tingling sensation in his finger tips. To think that, at this very instant, Virginia stood on the verge of the most fateful decision in her long and brilliant history!

Mr. Mahone arose, faced the two naval officers. "What Major Tyler has come from Richmond to learn is exactly what steps are planned towards gaining possession of the Navy Yard. Please to have your say, Commander."

Commander Robb, a big, ruddy-faced individual wearing his glossy, reddish brown hair at shoulder length, spoke crisply: "Mr. Spottswood and some other Southern gentlemen on duty at the Navy Yard have at last succeeded with some difficulty in persuading our Commandant, Commander McCauley, that nothing should be done which might serve in any way to excite the local population. Thanks to our efforts, he now vastly overrates their military power and belligerency." Robb shrugged. "In a way I really feel sorry for the poor old man, he's so desperately confused. They say he was a fine officer and a brave one in his day, but he's doddering now. Which is damned lucky for us."

"Then, I take it, all goes smoothly?" demanded the Richmond emissary.

Commander Robb shook his head. "It did until they sent Isherwood down from Washington—he's the Chief Engineer. We've had the Devil's own time since he came; the fellow's a positive mountain of energy."

"He's the one who's been refitting the *Merrimac*, ain't he?" demanded a Mr. Fenton, who owned a line of tugs and barges.

"Yes."

"But I thought repairs on her were to take a month and more?" Fenton persisted.

"That's what we reported to Washington," Spottswood interjected. "But now we've got to move quickly or Isherwood will get the *Merrimac* to sea despite all the delays McCauley and the rest of us can invent." The young naval officer's somber eyes circled the table. "Come what may, we simply cannot allow that ship to escape!"

"Why?" the militia Captain wanted to know.

"Why! Because the *Merrimac* is undoubtedly the most powerful single vessel and the most modern, in our—" he corrected himself, "—in the Federal fleet."

"Well, then, what's to be done?" demanded McCarthy, the militia Captain.

Irad watched Robb lean forward, elbows on the table. "For one thing, order those misguided zealots who are throwing up batteries on Sewall's Point and Craney Island to desist. The erection of those works are the most telling argument Isherwood can present towards forcing McCauley to carry out certain defensive measures he was ordered to take over two weeks ago."

Irad couldn't help asking, "But, Commander, how dares the Commandant ignore orders like this?"

"The poor devil's on the horns of a dilemma," Spottswood explained. "You see, in one breath Washington orders him to defend the Yard and ready the men-of-war for sea; then in the next he's instructed to offend Virginia in no way. Which is lucky, damned lucky, for us, I may say."

"Say, Mister Spottswood, what have you in the Navy Yard—aside from the ships, I mean?" drawled Jay Lewis. As became a good newspaperman, he had been listening, saying nothing thus far.

Commander Robb undertook to answer. "Over twelve hundred cannon, some of them modern Paixhans, Columbiads and Dahlgrens. There are mile upon mile of cables, sails enough to fit out a whole fleet, engine parts and propellers of all sizes. Regarding small arms, they are there by the tens of hundreds and ready for use. All this is in addition to huge stores of shot, shell and the finest machine shops and shipyards on this side of the Atlantic."

Commander Robb's voice quivered and all eyes attached themselves to that big rangy figure dominating this little office. "Gentlemen, we must not fail in securing these supplies—and those ships out in the river!" Dramatically, he swung open a shutter and pointed out of the window at the men-of-war dozing in the distance. "Mr. Ex-Secretary Toucey and the present Northern Government have as good as presented the Confederacy with a ready-made fleet!"

"You bet we'll take them vessels," boomed Fenton. "Next we'll take Washin'ton, then chase them nigger-lovin' Abolitionists clear back to New England."

For several moments the meeting degenerated into a pre-victory celebration. At length, Mr. Mahone rapped for order.

"Sure, we'll take the Yard, gents, but first we've got to do something to make sure them warships won't be towed off if the Yankees suddenly wake up. Right?"

Commander Robb's assent was vigorous. "Correct. It would prove an easy matter for the *Merrimac* alone to rescue at least three or four sailing ships or un-manned sloops such as the *Germantown* and *Plymouth*."

"We've one advantage," added Spottswood. His friend didn't like to be left out of things, Irad noticed. "All the ships-of-the-line lie in ordinary."

"Ordinary?" inquired Jay Lewis, making notes on the back of an envelope without looking up.

" 'In ordinary' means that a vessel is without a crew, mounts no armament and has had her yards and rigging sent down."

"In other words," Lewis said, "she is merely a helpless hulk."

Major Tyler's dark eyes lit. "How many ships, sir, are in ordinary?"

"The frigates *Raritan*, sixty guns; *Columbia*, fifty guns; and the old *United States*, forty-four."

Spottswood checked off the names on his fingers. "Then there are four line-of-battle ships; *Delaware*, seventy-four; *Columbus*, seventy-four; *Pennsylvania*, one hundred and twenty and the *New York*; she's even more helpless than the rest because she's in stocks at the moment."

"About how many ships you got ready for sea?" the freckle-faced and tow-haired militia Captain wanted to know. It was clear that he was greatly impressed, but definitely out of his depth.

"The Merrimac, forty guns; the Cumberland, twenty-four; the Germantown, Plymouth and the brig Dolphin. All of them, the Cumberland excepted, are seriously undermanned or almost without any crew at all."

"Glory be to God, what a rich haul!" exclaimed Major Tyler. "There'll soon be joy bells rung in Richmond and Montgomery."

"Could I point out, Major, that we haven't won them yet?" was Robb's wry reminder. "Now, following that line, here's what we in Gosport must know. What may we expect by way of support? How many troops can you guarantee ready to move"—he paused, glowered at a flyblown ceiling—"say by the twentieth?"

Tyler and Jay Lewis looked startled. "You don't plan on moving before the twentieth? I doubt that we can get the troops here until that day," said Tyler.

"No, that won't do. I tell you McCauley's so bewildered and contradicted he's taken to drink and just babbles. We, the Southern officers, tell him just what to expect." He squared his shoulders. "Again, Major Tyler, Captain McCarthy, what kind of support may we—Captain Rich of the Marine Corps and I—expect on the twentieth?"

"From us, not much," admitted the militia Captain, uneasily rumpling his hair. "We just got two companies of local boys who know how to vote and shoot—and that's just about all."

"Cheerful prospect," grunted Robb. "Can they drill?"

"Hell, no! Most of 'em won't even obey orders lest they argue."

"How many do you number?"

"Mebbe, two—three hundert if the weather's fine."

A slight choking sound escaped Commander Robb, but all he said to Major Tyler was, "And you, sir? What help will Richmond afford us?"

Major Tyler's chest again inflated itself. "I feel at liberty to inform you, sir, as a patriotic Southerner that once the Ordinance of Secession is made public, two fully armed and trained companies of Virginia State troops, four hundred men from the Richmond Grays and three companies of Georgia troops, will entrain at Richmond. You, sir," he bowed to Mr. Mahone, "must expect the early arrival of General Talliaferro and Captain Robert B. Pegram, C.S.N. Governor Letcher has—er, will—designate them to be Army and Navy Commanders over this District."

Two dogs chose that moment to initiate a gloriously noisy fight in the alley outside, which continued until someone, presumably young Mahone, settled the dispute by means of a couple of well-directed kicks.

"Doesn't seem there's much to be done, right off, except for two things," Mahone observed, once the racket had subsided into a series of shrill yelps. "First, this feller Isherwood has got to be shut up no later than tomorrow night."

"You can count on me," announced the tow-headed militia Captain. "I'll get the police to rig some charge and run him in. What else?"

"Some hulks ought to be sunk across the Elizabeth River blockin' the channel, say opposite McPhail's wharf."

Little Mr. Fenton jumped up. "Say, that ought to be easy. Up to my yard I've got some wore-out barges and a wuthless ol' schooner. They'd be easy to scuttle. Say, when you want 'em sunk?"

"Tonight and without fail," came Commander Robb's prompt reply. He mopped at his forehead. It was growing pretty hot in this office, what with all these people present. "It is quite as important that we prevent outside help from coming in as it is to keep those vessels lying off the Navy Yard from escaping."

There ensued an interval during which those present were assigned tasks.

"Say, Charles, what about me?" Irad demanded, a little chagrined at being ignored thus far. "I'm ready for anything."

Spottswood chuckled. "Eating fire, already, eh? Well, Irad, the instant the Yard is captured, you're to lead a party of dockyard people aboard the Merrimac and see that no harm is done. With her we can clear Chesapeake Bay in a week."

Irad blinked behind his steel-rimmed spectacles. "Thank you. You may rely upon it, gentlemen, that the Merrimac will be ready for duty when Virginia's flag climbs above Gosport."

A buzz of excitement circled the table.

"You claim that troops from Richmond can't possibly arrive here before the twentieth?" Robb cast Major Tyler a quizzical glance. "The twentieth? That won't do at all." Commander Robb bent over the council table. "As I've told you, old McCauley has grown timorous, though he was brave enough in his younger years, so I wish there were some way to fool him into believing, tomorrow, that a substantial number of troops has arrived from Richmond."

Mahone's bald head gleamed to an upward jerk. "Listen, fellows, I think maybe I have an answer. If Captain McCarthy"—he nodded to the militia Captain, "can fit out a few dozen of his boys in uniform of some kind, then I'll get Andrews of the Seaboard and Roanoke to couple up what'd look like a troop train. We can load the cars with volunteers ready to cheer and yell for Jeff Davis loud enough for old McCauley to hear. Will that do the trick?"

Commander Robb thought it would.

XXIV

HOLOCAUST

SLEEP SIMPLY WOULD not come to soothe Sylvia Seymour's troubled mind. Possibly this was because she missed the warmth and sense of security lent by Irad's presence in this huge, old-fashioned bed equipping the elder Seymours' guest room. Possibly it was because Robbie, for once, had become fretful—usually he slept as if drugged—waking it seemed every hour or so to demand a drink of water. She felt sure there was nothing more serious to blame than a change of food, water and habits.

Since the child's arrival in Norfolk, of course, he had formed a small center of attention. That old Mrs. Seymour should be inordinately proud of her one and only grandchild was only natural, but that Captain Felix should run on as he did was surprising when one considered his usually undemonstrative manner. Any number of white- and gray-headed captains and flag officers—there were no admirals these days—and their wives must call to pat the little fellow's long golden curls and admire his straight back and sturdy legs.

Or could this restlessness be ascribed to her becoming pregnant? Although now she felt convinced on the subject, she intended to make no mention of her condition for another twenty-six days. She must be absolutely certain for, on one previous occasion, she had been mistaken, thanks, no doubt, to a bad case of influenza. Besides, Irad was so tense, so overwrought, these days that she hardly recognized in him the self-possessed and methodical person she had lived with going on four years.

Not from him but from Charley Spottswood had she learned this evening of the militia's only partially successful effort to block the channel of the Elizabeth River, of Mr. Isherwood's mysterious escape from arrest and his flight to Washington on a bay boat.

"Some traitor must have warned him," Irad had declared when the matter came up. "Wish I could lay hands on the rascal."

She squirmed into a more comfortable position but lay more wide-awake than ever, staring at a pale, black-crossed rectangle cast on the ceiling by a light on the corner of Charlotte Street.

"Of course I can't sleep," she sighed. "Reckon I'm too excited. Wonder if that handsome Charley Spottswood is right? Will poor old Commander McCauley surrender the Yard tomorrow morning? Charley swore everything is arranged for the Virginia troops to take peaceable possession." She brushed a stray curl from her forehead. "How wonderful if the transfer comes about without any shooting or killing."

To her vast astonishment she began to experience pangs of increasingly sharp anxiety concerning Irad. Her husband must be among those partisans clutching their weapons, shivering and waiting to deliver an assault if one became necessary.

Probably there would be no fighting. If the Federals intended to defend so valuable a property, surely they would have sent more than a tug and the little *Pawnee* to McCauley's relief.

Sylvia turned again, plucked irritably at her voluminous nightgown which had become twisted into a series of hot and uncomfortable folds. Why, oh, why, couldn't she get to sleep and forget all the turmoil, doubts and alarms of the afternoon?

It surprised her to find how clearly she could recall every detail of what had happened since four o'clock. She and Captain Felix had mounted to a gazebo atop the house to see what was chancing over in Gosport. From the "widow's walk"—as old Mrs. Seymour called it —an excellent view of the harbor, of the river, and of even Hampton Roads, could be obtained and through use of the old officer's powerful spyglass few movements remained hidden from the watchers.

Old Mrs. Seymour had been all of a twit because it was seldom indeed that Captain Felix took more than a single julep or glass of wine before the midday meal. Today, however, he had taken to muttering to himself and gulping down such quantities of that old seafarer's drink, rum and water, that his usually florid face had turned a curious and unhealthy pinkish gray.

Hardly had they climbed the gazebo ladder than he uttered a sharp exclamation. "Look! Look, Sylvia, look! Look at the *Pennsylvania!* Am I crazy, or is she low by the head?"

Obediently Sylvia had raised her own little spyglass. Irad's father was quite right. It seemed that the great hull was slanting, her triple row of white stripes towards the surface.

"God in heaven!" gasped the old man. "She's sinking!"

"Look! Look!" Sylvia cried. "Aren't those small boats pulling away from the *Germantown?* What does that mean?"

A whistling groan escaped Captain Felix. He put down his spyglass and with both hands clutched the lookout rail.

Curiously Sylvia stared, watching the old man's shoulders commence to shake under his blue coat, then to heave as he bowed his head.

"Oh, my God! Those dirty, lily-livered cowards are scuttling the fleet!" He choked and tears commenced to form in his faded gray eyes. "Oh, Sylvia! Sylvia! I've lived too long." He commenced to sob. "Oh, G-God, please strike them d-dead! They're murdering those beautiful ships. T-there's my last command—the *Plymouth.*"

The trig little sloop's topmasts were assuming an ever-increasing slant to port, but, before she could roll over, the *Plymouth* had reached the bottom and so came to rest with decks awash, amid a mad tangle of floating gear. Her fighting tops and spars remained undamaged.

Cursing softly in savage undertones that employed many foreign words, Captain Felix grabbed out a blue bandanna. He said brokenly, "McCauley's accomplished what no naval power on earth could do! Sunk a whole American fleet. I—I guess I can't see— Sylvia, take my glass and tell me. Have the dastards harmed the *Merrimac?* Where is she?"

"Tied to the granite wharf— Ah, I see her now. She seems to be all right. There is smoke rising from her chimney."

"Funnel," absently corrected the stricken old man, "or 'stack,' if you must."

"Father, which are those huge ships moored nearest to the point?"

"The near one's the *Columbus.* The far one's the *Delaware.*"

"They're going down, too."

All over the Elizabeth River estuary, ships were sinking. One after the other, more than a dozen men-of-war commenced to settle, some by the head, some by the stern. Captain Felix turned aside and commenced to growl, "As a Southerner I—I suppose I should rejoice, but thank God I've never before seen the American flag go down without some sort of a fight. What miserable cravens they must have in the Navy Department nowadays. Imagine six millions' worth of ships lost without a shot fired in their defense or even an attempt made to tow them away!"

It was then that Sylvia noticed that the great liner *Pennsylvania* had ceased to go down. In fact she now lay with two of her three white streaks showing above the debris-littered river. So it was also with the other line-of-battle ships; the frigates as a rule managed to keep spar and quarterdecks and foc'sles above the surface.

Sylvia demanded breathlessly, "Why don't those vessels sink out of sight?"

"Because they can't sink any further," the veteran snuffled through his handkerchief. "The river's too damned shallow."

Angrily Captain Felix dashed aside tears of mortification, recovered his heavy, brass-bound telescope from Sylvia and once more surveyed the scene.

"The Federal commanders over there in Gosport are not only knaves but bunglers, which is worse," he snapped. "Despite everything, McCauley is making the South a really handsome present."

"I wonder where the militia is?" Sylvia inquired. "Shouldn't they be attacking the Yard?"

"I can't imagine! Now is the moment for such action."

In black throngs the people of Norfolk and Portsmouth could be seen crowding the water's edge, swarming out on piers and wharfs like gigantic insects. Others crowded rooftops or went sailing out in small boats and yachts to watch the last Federal crews go rowing ashore.

Why had neither the Cumberland nor the Merrimac shared the general fate of the squadron? There seemed no plausible explanation save that the powerful batteries of the latter vessel could be made useful in covering a retreat. The Merrimac lay secured to a wharf near the drydock from which she had emerged only a few days previously.

"At least she is going to make a run for it," predicted Captain Felix soberly. "Probably she'll take aboard the crews of the scuttled ships and then try to tow out the Cumberland."

How still it was at this hour! Sylvia realized that, in reconstructing the afternoon, she had all but fallen asleep. Where was Irad likely to be right now? She knew now she loved him—and dearly. She sighed. Tomorrow, if the Navy Yard hadn't surrendered, a general attack would be delivered now that the promised troops from Richmond had arrived.

Mr. Mahone's stratagem concerning the pseudo-troop trains had succeeded to perfection, convincing poor, addled, rum-soaked Commander McCauley that overwhelming forces were at hand a full day before the first company actually arrived from Richmond.

Towards sundown the wildest kind of rumors spread like water spilt on a hardwood floor. McCauley had committed suicide; Northern and Southern naval officers were shooting one another; a part of the Navy Yard had already fallen into Southern hands.

Sylvia finally lapsed into a light doze which must have lasted longer than she thought for when Robbie next wailed it was after four o'clock. She went down to warm some milk which had the desired effect for the child sank promptly into peaceful slumber.

Once more wide-awake, Sylvia sought a window facing the doomed Navy Yard. The reassuring possibility occurred that a transfer of authority might already have taken place. Perhaps the Federals had surrendered? Not to know just what was going on proved galling. She hoped Irad was using good sense in the matter of exposing himself to unnecessary danger. Certainly a considerable activity was taking place over yonder. There were a lot of lights, far more than normal, glowing at the Navy Yard.

She strained her eyes in the general vicinity of the scuttled ships and, by the clear starlight, seemed to distinguish a great many dark objects pulling about on the river. Suddenly, from the midst of those sombre islands created by the sunken fleet, what resembled a miniature comet appeared, climbed up, up, up into the sky until it burst into a frightening and garish splash of scarlet-gold flame.

"Why would the Yankees be sending up rockets at a time like this?" Sylvia wondered while gathering her nightrobe more closely about her. A terrible explanation was not long in presenting itself.

It looked as if the whole of Gosport were taking fire all at once. With the speed of a wind-fanned forest fire, flames soared into dazzling eminence not only throughout the Navy Yard, but among the scuttled ships as well.

Sheer terror froze Sylvia a long instant, then she screamed such a scream that Captain Felix turned out, nightshirt, cap and all, and came arunning with a cocked boarding pistol in either hand.

"What's wrong? Tell me, what's wrong?" shouted the old man. "Where is he?"

But Sylvia could only stand shaking, pointing numbly towards Gosport. Mother Seymour, pulling a cloak about her, came running down the corridor but stopped dead when she saw a throbbing pink highlight outlining her daughter-in-law's cheek.

"Well, seems as if there's a fire somewhere," Mrs. Seymour observed quite calmly, putting an arm about Sylvia. "Let's not get excited. There have been such fires before."

She was wrong. Never would anyone who lived through the next three hours again behold anything approaching the conflagration which grew, and spread until it bathed the whole city, the bay and even distant Newport News in a cruel, blood-colored glare.

Captain Seymour turned, muttered something, then pulled on an old watch coat and went toiling up the gazebo ladder. Presently he was joined by Sylvia.

In neighboring houses and from various slave quarters arose frightened wails and questioning shouts. The town's alarm bells wakened at last to fling their fearful, nerve-shaking clamor into the night. Lights blinked on, terror-stricken householders in night clothes ran out into the streets under the impression that the conflagration was near at hand. Children howled and men—volunteer firemen for the most part—commenced dashing off into the dark, shouting, dragging on their clothes as they went.

To old Captain Seymour's haggard eyes the scuttled ships suggested so many South Sea island volcanos spewing flame, sparks and smoke high into the heavens. He saw the consuming element run up a battleship's weathered shrouds, then race out along her yards revealing them as if penciled in glowing gold. Stunned, utterly aghast, he watched the end of the mighty *Pennsylvania* as she lay revealed to the least detail by fire spouting from her more than one hundred gunports.

Vessels such as the *Dolphin*, the *Germantown* and the *Plymouth*, his own old ship, that were fully rigged and possessing sails, burned with an especial brilliance. Like great flaming birds, huge shreds and tatters of burning canvas, propelled by the incandescent gases, went soaring upwards only to be overtaken and passed by smaller brands.

"Those yellow swine have fired the ship houses and barracks," Captain Felix muttered to himself. "Have they? Yes, there goes the rope walk, too."

Similar to but infinitely larger than that rocket which had initiated this terrifying holocaust, balls of combustible gas commenced to burst into blinding glory so high above that sea of flame engulfing Gosport that they illuminated all of lower Chesapeake Bay. "That will be the turpentine, benzine and coal-oil stores going up," Felix Seymour told himself. "My God, what'll happen if the magazines explode? If they take fire there'll surely be a long column of souls applying for admission to Heaven."

As if some pyrotechnical competition were under way, each ship and building appeared to be attempting to out-flame its neighbor.

"What of the *Merrimac*, Felix?" Mrs. Seymour called from the foot of the ladder.

"Why, why—she's safe. No! Oh-h my God! She's afire too!" His voice broke. To think that the *Merrimac*, the glorious *Merrimac*, pride of the United States Navy was about to die like Caesar—stabbed in the back.

As in a nightmare, he watched the little *Pawnee*, assisted by the Navy tug *Yankee*, lash herself alongside the *Cumberland*, and commence to tow that tall frigate out into the channel and towards the obstructions off the Naval Hospital.

Successive explosions momentarily silhouetted these fugitives to the ultimate detail, then they were revealed in full color, their disgraced Union flags fluttering crazily this way and that under the influence of violently conflicting air currents. The stumpy masts of the *Columbus* suddenly commenced to rock in deathly paroxysms until they fell overside, generating huge billows of rose-colored steam.

Towards midday of April the twentieth, only the charred ribs and a few blackened spars remained above water to mark the position of the wrecks, and all of the Gosport Navy Yard's combustible buildings had resolved themselves into piles of white-hot coals giving off trailing tendrils of gray-blue smoke.

Three facts of prime importance became known to everyone in Norfolk. The priceless granite drydock was still in existence. Some Southern sympathizer was reported, at the very last instant, to have severed the fuse leading to a series of mines which would have blown it sky-high. Secondly, nine millions of dollars' worth of heavy ordnance, chain, armor plate, ammunition and small arms, had not been consumed and so had survived to arm the new Confederacy.

Finally, at daybreak, Lieutenant C. M. F. Spottswood had hoisted the handsome white and blue banner of Virginia to that same signal mast from which the Stars and Stripes had been flying for nearly a hundred years.

BOOK TWO

The Turbulent Mississippi

I

QUEEN OF THE SOUTH

IN MID-MAY THE sun beats down upon New Orleans and the shipyards across the Mississippi at Algiers with an enervating severity which discourages, probably wisely, any activity during the middle of the day. This custom of knocking off work for nearly three hours had goaded Lachlan Brunton, Chief Construction Engineer for Hughes & Company's Algiers Yard, into many a futile outburst at easygoing subcontractors.

At this rate the Confederate Navy cruiser *Sumter* would never be built and ready for commissioning by the middle of June. To stride about the shipyard pleading with mechanics and shipwrights to go back to work proved futile; they simply wouldn't stir out of the shade while heat waves shimmered, danced and blurred the towers and steeples of New Orleans across the turgid Mississippi.

"Ah, well, a mon canna fashion a rope out of sand nor make vinegar taste like whiskey." Eventually he'd shrugged and, being an eminently sensible fellow, had taken to seeking the welcome coolness of a palmetto-thatched coffee shop situated not very far from the shipyard. Here he would sit fanning himself and looking out over the river, or contemplating the razed hulk of that fast little steamer which, until the war began, had fetched passengers and Cuban fruit to New Orleans and then returned deep-laden with cotton and manufactured goods.

· Thoughtfully Brunton surveyed spiderweb-like clumps of rigging created by idle coasting ships and brigs. Further downstream ten or eleven river boats had been tied up for lack of trade with the North and so lay idle, the rust growing brighter each day on their cold twin smokestacks.

Considerably more than a month seemed to have elapsed since he had arrived by rail from Baltimore with the ink barely dry on his contract and good gold dollars dragging at his money belt. During this period many changes, subtle but indicative of the future, had taken place. Each day more river steamers came panting down the Mississippi from the Red, the Yazoo and the Alabama with gunnels nearly awash under stacks of cotton bales which no one would buy; already the levees, sheds and warehouses were filled to overflowing. Consequently the number of smoke clouds hanging over the river were fewer and all except local traffic had thinned to a depressing trickle.

For some reason beyond the comprehension of Brunton and many astute Louisianans the authorities at Richmond—the Confederate Government recently had repaired thither—while not actually outlawing the export of cotton for fear of offending England and France, were employing every other means at their disposal to prevent shipment abroad of the precious stuff. Naturally, this absurd embargo enraged numerous neutrals who could easily elude the shaky and newly applied Federal blockade.

"We will cotton-starve the Britishers," reasoned Jeff Davis, "until they send for King Cotton with men-of-war. The Yankees will try to stop them, a fight and a declaration of war will then follow and the South will find the British Navy at her disposal." Except for one consideration, Brunton deemed this to be a logical bit of reasoning.

New Orleans, the young Scot had discovered to be as distinctive from other American cities as an egret among a flock of crows and was becoming increasingly fascinated by this great, sprawling metropolis and its polylingual many-hued population.

For instance, he experienced considerable difficulty in making himself understood by Madame Boileau, in whose boarding house on Dryades Street he had rented a large bedroom, cool because of its twelve-foot ceiling. This chamber even boasted a narrow balcony of cast-iron from which he could view not only the narrow and generally noisy thoroughfare below, but also the roofs and spires of the city.

About a great port such as this it stood to reason that he would encounter many Englishmen and Scots, mostly in shipping. Many, however, had become merchants or professional men. It was the first category which raged loudest and most bitterly against the Davis embargo on cotton shipments.

At the Anglo-Caledonian Club, a beet-complexioned sea captain had effectively summed up their bewilderment.

"Why don't the Rebels rush as much cotton abroad as fast as they can? Then, instead of rotting along the levees, it'll build their credit over in Europe which they'll need when the Yankees tighten their blockade about the mouths of the Mississippi."

No one could offer a satisfactory explanation, but certain pot-bellied and well-bejeweled cotton brokers remained smug of expression; they knew the answer but weren't going to tell. Mr. Davis intended cotton prices to rise mighty high before releasing a single one of the precious bales, although there were above two million on hand! In fact, the Richmond Government was advising planters, to their pained surprise, not to plant cotton this year but corn and other food-stuffs instead. A world cotton shortage, and a severe one, was about to occur if the Confederate Government had its way.

Brunton's humid meditations were interrupted by the appearance of a big, loose-jointed individual wearing a nondescript uniform coat. More than a little drunk, he came swaggering into the coffee house glaring about at the patrons and tapping significantly on the butt of a huge pepper-box revolver thrust along with a bowie knife into a wide rawhide belt.

"Iffin yer ain't showin' yer colors, I'm sellin' these cheap," he boomed, waving a dirty handful of crudely stitched red, white, red rosettes, the accepted Confederate design. He won only disdainful looks for, almost without exception, the patrons were wearing miniature Stars and Bars flags on their lapels. He came clumping over to Brunton's table, his single brass spur jingling loudly.

" 'Pears like this hyar's a right loyal lot." He swayed on booted feet. "Say, Mister, why ain't you displayin' yer sentiments?"

The Scot smiled, delved into a pocket and produced the cockade he had bought several days ago in self-defense.

"There you are."

"Well, then, just you put it on!" the vendor growled. "Yer wastin' a patriotic bearcat's time." Without waiting to see whether Brunton obeyed, the shaggy fellow tramped out, his huge figure momentarily darkening the entrance.

From up the street came strains of martial music which swelled until everyone ran out of the café to stand in the sunshine and cheer a file of youths in gaudy blue and yellow uniforms. They appeared, strutting behind a six-piece brass band. One of them perspired heavily under a placard reading, "Volunteers for the Louisiana Tigers! Join up before the fight is over!"

A horde of wild-looking, barefoot and screeching children were convoying this procession, all the while waving the Stars and Bars, a flag which, strangely and tragically, resembled the now well-hated Federal ensign. Its design consisted of two very broad red stripes separated by a single equally broad white one and a bright blue square in the canton corner. In this canton anywhere from six to nine white stars were arranged in a circle.

"Vive les engagés!" A handsome young woman—Creole by her dark complexion—caught up a bouquet she had been carrying and tossed its pink roses, forget-me-nots and cornflowers to a black-bearded lieutenant marching at the head of the volunteer detail. He broke step, and halted on the curb to bow, lift his kepi and blow the Creole girl a kiss. It was all very debonair and gallant.

Brunton had followed the proprietor out onto the sidewalk. Never was there such tireless enthusiasm, he decided. At any time, any day the Orléannais would drop everything to run out, wave, cheer and throw flowers at a military procession, no matter how unimportant or nondescript.

These particular volunteers proved an oddly assorted lot. Some were clad in rich and elegant garments while others slouched along under threadbare coats such as law or banking clerks might wear. The rear was brought up by perhaps three dozen swaggering, gap-toothed and sinewy fellows, beyond doubt the wildest-looking individuals Brunton thus far had encountered in America. Their belts and occasional bandoliers fairly bristled with weapons. They were not tall, but bandy-legged, and wore their tangled hair so long that it tumbled, mane-like, over their leather-clad shoulder blades.

As they went swinging by, Brunton noted that these fellows, without exception, were sallow, hollow of cheek and so restless of eye that they suggested newly trapped wildcats. Although a few wore ungainly big boots, a majority marched on dusty and callused bare feet.

These last volunteers lugged long-barreled Kentucky hunting rifles, fowling pieces or even antique flintlocks. Not a few carried Indian war hatchets jammed into their belts of rawhide. One volunteer, Brunton noticed, was equipped with no less than four hand guns of patterns ranging from tiny derringers to huge horse pistols.

Shouts arose above the shifting reddish road dust. "Hurray for Gov'ner Moore an' Jeff Davis!" "Down with the Abolitionist bloodsuckers!" "Vive Beauregard!"

Once the column had disappeared down a side street the café patrons returned unconcernedly to their tables, recovered newspapers and commenced noisily to sip strong black coffee grown cool during their absence.

In rising impatience Lachlan Brunton glanced at an *horloge* ticking placidly above the *patronne's* sleek black head. Full-bosomed to an almost alarming degree, Madame Bonnecaz possessed, in addition to alert and beady black eyes, a mustache more imposing than most of those shading the lips of certain youths at present on their way to join the Louisiana Tigers.

Only two o'clock. Damn, not until three would there be any use in returning to Hughes' shipyard, so Brunton fished out of his pocket a copy of Grantham's *Iron Shipbuilding* and from between its pages plucked a blue telegraph form, every word of which he knew by heart.

Dated Illinoistown, April fifteenth, in baffling simplicity it read:

MUST COME TO YOU. ON WAY. LOVE. CHRISTINA.

Why, oh, why, hadn't she amplified that message? What mischance could have befallen her? Nothing short of disaster would impel her to come without being sent for—he understood her that well. Since her telegram's arrival nearly a month had elapsed and the mail clerk at Mr. Hughes' shipyard was waxing facetious over Brunton's oft-repeated queries concerning a further message.

Why should Tina apparently have left Baltimore so precipitately, and so soon after his own departure? Again, why should so dependable a little person not have appeared within a reasonable length of time, or have failed to communicate further? When he considered her character this silence proved more than a little frightening.

He had prepared a letter to be dispatched to Tina the instant he obtained an address. In part, he had written in his crabbed Scottish fist:

> My decision to come to New Orleans has proved a wise one, I think. Here there exist facilities for a new yard designed to build ocean-going iron ships. Mark you, my own heart, the day of the wooden vessel is past, as I told you once in Baltimore. Strangely, although New Orleans is a great international port, the great majority of vessels built here are intended either for river use or are constructed as coasters.

> Tina, my own sweetheart, I am convinced that as quickly as this stupid war ends, I will found a modern shipyard. Capital I can obtain either from the North or from England. By use of studious application and industry combined with foresight, I feel convinced that riches lie within my grasp. For the moment iron still is cheap and easy to come by, but this situation cannot last long. There is a rolling mill to be built at Baton Rouge. The people of New Orleans are easygoing and friendly. Foreigners like ourselves are numerous and hardly noticed. You will be glad to know that many Germans have settled and do business here. They form an important and respected segment of this community.

He was roused from his brooding by a shadow falling across the table before him. He jumped to his feet.

"Losh, Commander Farrand, this is indeed an unexpected pleasure!"

Although he wore the brand-new gold and gray insignia of the Confederate Naval Service—two broad stripes on the cuff and two gold stars on either shoulder strap—Commander Farrand, like so many others had been forced to attach them to his old uniform of Federal blue, the Army having long since gobbled up every shred of cloth approaching any shade of gray.

Commander Eben Farrand, Senior Commissioner of the Confederate Navy Department in New Orleans, stood medium tall and was distinguished by thin, black-dyed hair and side whiskers. One of his mahogany-tinted cheeks had been bisected by a long white scar inflicted by the same keen weapon, a Mexican machete, which had driven a deep nick into the point of his chin.

"I trust, Mr. Brunton, that I do not intrude upon your leisure?"

"Not at all, sir; indeed, I welcome your company. I had rather be working over with the *Sumter*, ye ken, but—can *nothing* be done to keep the carpenters at work during midday?"

Commander Farrand seated his generous body, at the same time heaving a sigh eloquent of disgust. "No, and I wager you won't be pleased to learn that three more of your best engineers have listened to Army blandishments and are off to win laurels before the ration runs out." The aged naval officer's handsome head wagged slowly. "Silly fools seem fearful this war will be won before they can get their pot shot at some Yankee. Here, boy!" Farrand beckoned a waiter and ordered a brace of juleps although the Scot attempted to refuse.

"In all frankness, Mr. Brunton, tell me about the *Sumter's* engines; are they really worthless?"

"No. Such as they are, Commander, they are perfectly sound," came the prompt reply. "But, mon, they'll not develop near enough horsepower to meet the demands o' a true warship for all that we've razed off her top decks, shortened her spars and cut out her cabins."

The waiter reappeared bearing not only the juleps but also a great dish of chinquapins and almonds. Although the naval officer lifted his frosty glass in a silent toast Brunton kept right on talking; it wasn't always you came across a senior officer willing to listen to a mere civilian.

"On the other hand, Commander, we must allow for the weight not only of those thick beams installed to support the guns and their carriages, but also that of the ammunition and the other supplies a man-of-war carries on a long cruise."

Farrand's brow fell into wrinkles and absently he ran fingers through flowing and well-dyed sideburns.

"Speaking of supplies, Mr. Brunton," he lowered his voice, "is it true that the *Sumter* will not be able to stow coal for more than eight days of steady steaming?"

While sampling Commander Farrand's hospitality, Brunton nodded, wondering just how many hundreds of persons, Federal spies among them, had learned of the new cruiser's deficient bunker capacity.

"What, sir," pursued the older man, "were you able to devise for boiler protection? I'm told you have met with difficulties."

"Difficulties!" snorted Brunton. "Ye may well say that! Mr. Roy and I have combed not only this city but Baton Rouge as well in search of iron plates. There are none to be had, saving miserable three-quarter or one-inch thicknesses which give no adequate protection."

A gray and red parrot in a cage behind the cashier's rostrum commenced to burble, then tactlessly to sing a few bars of "Yankee Doodle." The patronne rushed to drop a silencing cloth over the offender.

"Therefore," Brunton continued, "I have devised a scheme of securing iron bars close together in oak frames. Such an arrangement will not stop solid shot of heavy calibre, but it will prevent shell fragments from reaching the boiler."

The waiter, a gaunt slave, was perspiring heavily when he fetched, with the compliments of M. Bonnecaz, additional juleps, crisp and most delectable of aroma.

To Brunton's surprise, Commander Farrand frowned, and remained lugubrious. "Alas, my friend, now that ice ships will be prevented from coming south, I fear we will not be enjoying many more of these lovely potations. Ah, well, 'sufficient unto the day'—I suppose. To your very good health, Mr. Brunton, which I offer in all sincerity. Captain Semmes has described the marvels of ingenuity you have devised. Now about contriving a carriage for the pivot gun?"

A brief silence ensued, since they both knew that no such thing as a carriage for a powerful eight-inch rifle existed nearer than Gosport and transportation from the East was cruelly slow and uncertain.

Brunton produced the stub of a pencil and commenced a sketch on the back of a menu. "Mr. Roy and I have been thinking that the only iron in plentiful supply heareabouts is railroad rails. Now we've the notion that at the Leeds' Foundry we'll find the equipment necessary to contrive a suitable carriage—maybe something of this nature."

He offered a rough but clear and proportionate drawing of what he intended.

Immediately the Navy Department's Commissioner brightened. "By God, sir, this seems feasible. Have you informed Captain Semmes?"

A flush of pleasure climbed towards the small Scot's flaming hairline. "Not yet, sir. I must feel more satisfied that this design is practical and contains no hidden errors. Yon poor gentleman already has met with far too many disappointments; what with our broadside guns a month overdue from Gosport, with our best shipwrights joining the Army, and, saving your presence, Commander, no competent direction from Richmond."

Farrand absently tinkled the ice in his drink and at the same time fanned away a nimbus of persistent flies. "Don't imagine that we higher-ups haven't even heavier problems—worse for being on a larger scale."

While watching the progress of a tug towing a series of lumber rafts upstream, Commander Farrand described the difficulties besieging the three naval Commissioners sent to Louisiana. For one thing, they had discovered a dearth of merchantmen suitable for conversion to men-of-war; next, there were in the vicinity of New Orleans no iron mills suitable for rolling armor plate over an inch and a half thick.

When a clock in the tower of a church struck three mellow, richly sonorous notes, Commander Farrand sighed, commenced to do up the gold buttons of his double-breasted blue tunic.

"May I ask ye a question, sir?" Brunton inquired.

"A dozen if you wish. I notice you've a purpose behind them."

The Scot settled back onto his chair—at the shipyard they never made trouble over late returners—and fixed brilliant blue eyes on Farrand's scarred countenance.

"Can ye not persuade Captain Semmes to delay till I can devise a hoisting gear for his propeller? Ye see, sir, the *Sumter* will move fast enough with the screw at work under a full head of steam, but remember yon cruiser carries dangerous little coal; she'll need to log hundreds of miles under sail alone. I need not point out that the drag exerted by an idle propeller is not trivial."

The Commissioner held up a hand. "Please say no more on the subject, sir. While Captain Semmes and I quite agree with you, he holds orders from Richmond to get to sea at the first possible moment, before more than a token blockade seals the mouths of the Mississippi."

Undaunted, Brunton persisted. "But, sir, do ye credit that the Yankees can blockade effectively? At last report the Federals had less than twenty-four men-of-war o' all classes available for such duty and is not the Confederacy's seacoast three thousand miles long?"

Earnestly he studied the Commissioner. "Tell me, sir, is it not worth losing a few weeks to send the *Sumter* to sea at her best?"

Farrand tossed a new Confederate bank note upon the marble and zinc-topped table. "Since you are not a naval officer, Mr. Brunton," said he stiffly, "you cannot be expected to understand that when a naval officer receives an order he complies, promptly and without question."

II

C.S.S. Sumter

Tied up at Mr. Hughes' construction dock that craft which was to become the Confederate States cruiser *Sumter* appeared depressingly small and inoffensive. This was so because only the stumps of three masts stood, her funnel was rusty and her superstructure had been only partially rebuilt. All the same she was designed along speedy lines.

Of only four hundred and thirty-seven tons burden, the new cruiser was one hundred and eighty-four feet long by thirty feet in her beam. In addition to barque-rigged sails, she was propelled by a single fixed screw driven by a horizontal, direct-acting engine. Due to the inventive bent of Messers Roy and Brunton, she had been blessed with a collapsible smokestack which might swiftly be lowered to permit the quick manipulation of her lower canvas.

By the fifteenth of May, 1861, any onlooker—not necessarily a Southern sympathizer, either—could note that this former passenger ship's bulwarks had been pierced to accommodate four guns to each broadside. Amidships, just forward of the smokestack, the carpenters further were completing a platform designed to support a long-range, deadly eight-inch rifled gun, if such a piece of ordnance ever did arrive from Norfolk.

As usual, Captain Raphael Semmes, stiffly erect, though in civilian clothes and wearing a broad-brimmed leghorn hat, prowled about his incompleted vessel. Occasionally his leonine shock of gray-streaked black hair stirred in a gentle breeze beating up the Mississippi from Pass à l'Outre, one of river's three principal exits.

Far below decks, Lachlan Brunton, greasy and sweat-bathed from efforts to recondition the engines, could hear Semmes' deep voice saying, "Mr. Kell, pray present my compliments to Mr. Yaggy at Leeds' Foundry and ask him why, in Heaven's name, they haven't yet delivered my water casks? Also, you're to warn him that I must have those copper tanks for the powder magazine tomorrow, no later. Mr. Hughes says he can't get ahead with the berth deck till we have them."

Like a torrent of molten gold, the sun poured its rays onto the ship-yard, intensifying the cleanly pungent odors of pitch, fresh-sawed timber, hemp and rosin. As usual, crowds of visitors, men, women and children, had taken the Algiers ferry from New Orleans in order to picnic and view this, the first vessel built to show a Confederate flag on the high seas.

These onlookers did not hesitate to question the shipwrights, to come aboard and look about as much as they pleased. Despite Captain Semmes' angry pleas, no attempt was being made to guard the vessel beyond the posting of a few somnolent militia sentries over the more valuable materials.

Captain Semmes was utilizing a red silk handkerchief to mop his high and slightly protuberant forehead when he noted a flash of blue and gold from his post of vantage on the *Sumter's* nearly completed quarterdeck. At the shipyard gate two militiamen on duty had roused themselves from conversation with a group of women and presented arms with a lack of precision that wrung Semmes' heart.

Presently, a single straight figure marched, rather than walked, through the yard, and smartly saluted the Stars and Bars flying above Mr. Hughes' main office. Picking a course among piles of cordage, chain and lumber, the stranger advanced to the foot of the gangway.

Um. Would the newcomer salute the quarterdeck of an uncommissioned man-of-war? If he did, he would be merely a reservist. There the newcomer merely paused, deliberately surveyed the vessel a moment, then hitched his sword higher and, grasping its scabbard, strode lightly up a laborers' gangplank and onto a deck littered with piles of sawdust and odds and ends of lumber.

Now Semmes was able to obtain his first clear impression of this solid-appearing young officer, a lieutenant by his single star and two stripes; he'd be nearing thirty years of age. Now he was climbing the quarterdeck companion, white-gloved hands bright in the blinding sunlight.

"Good day, sir. Can you direct me to Captain Semmes?"

"I am he."

"I beg your pardon, sir." The easy precision of the new arrival's smart salute was a hallmark of the professional.

"Lieutenant Samuel Seymour, sir, reporting for duty."

"Your orders, please?" Captain Semmes demanded, once he had returned the courtesy.

A white-gloved hand disappeared beneath Lieutenant Seymour's double-breasted blue tunic and reappeared with a document secured by a single strand of red tape.

Piercing gray eyes narrowed against the glare of sunlit paper, Semmes read the orders with care.

"Very good, Mr. Seymour, and where are your effects?"

"Aboard the receiving ship, Star of the West, sir."

"Very good, Mr. Seymour, glad to have you aboard. Please report yourself to my Executive, Mr. Kell. He will explain your duties as First Prize Master."

"Aye, aye, sir." Seymour was turning away when Semmes checked him, at the same time relaxing his formal manner.

"You were one of Johnnie Maffitt's prize captains, were you not?"

"Aye, aye, sir."

"Where is Lieutenant Maffitt at present?"

"At Port Royal, I believe, sir. He was sent down to assist Commodore Tattnall in fitting out a squadron."

"He was well when you last saw him?"

"His health was excellent, sir," replied the erect figure in the blue of the Old Navy. "He is determined to see that our Navy gets off to a good start."

The cursing of some riggers attempting in vain to fit small-boat davits into the Sumter's very narrow rail rang loud in the heated air. A look of distaste ruffled the serenity of Captain Semmes' expression.

"Very good, Mr. Seymour." He ran a finger around his sodden collar. "Oh, on second thought, you had best report back to the

g ship, but you have my permission to secure quarters in
"

, aye, sir. However, I would prefer—"

The floppy brim of Semmes' leghorn hat became twisted to the sharp shake of his head. "The *Star of the West* is overcrowded and I hear a case of yellow jack has been reported aboard. Can't jeopardize trained officers. That will be all, Mr. Seymour."

III

THE RIVER BOAT *Silver Wing*

DARK HAD FALLEN before the last of the freight accumulated in mounds on the wharf of Illinoistown—later to become East Saint Louis—had been manhandled aboard by chanting Negro stevedores. The river steamer *Silver Wing* was fairly new and so smart that each of her twin stacks, mounted abreast, was surmounted by an elegant crown cut from sheet iron. The points of these ornaments flared boldly outward like a morning-glory blossom, and so blew a million glowing sparks straight up into the sky. Anticipating quick departure, gangs of half-naked slave stokers had begun to toss logs into the furnaces.

"Quit scratchin' yerselves, you lazy black bastards, and git humpin'. Captain's hollerin' fer a full head of steam," the second engineer was bellowing, his hickory shirt already darkened by sour sweat.

"Loadin' all this extry freight we're shovin' off a hour late," the engineer explained to his chief oiler. "Christ! We're ridin' deeper than ever I see, but the Old Man will raise hell if we don't turn up sixteen knots. What he don't know about engines would fill a big book!"

Like the rest of the officers of the *Silver Wing*, the second engineer was impatient to cast loose; as never before speed meant money and time was of the essence for all hands. Because war clouds were piling up in the East ever more ominously, every steamboat owner, captain and crew on the Mississippi and its tributaries, was out to get in as many trips as possible before the storm broke and free navigation came to an end.

Of course the wildest kind of rumors were prevalent here in Illinoistown and even more so across the river in St. Louis. Over there street fighting was expected to break out at any moment and everywhere in Missouri black people went creeping about in fear and trembling.

It was reliably reported that the Confederate authorities were building all manner of forts and batteries further downstream. Soon they would permit no Northern vessels to pass. On the other hand, everyone swore that the Unionists were planning to build some iron-clad gunboats, a whole fleet of them, with which to convoy their trade down to New Orleans. Only yesterday a squad of blue-clad soldiers, gawky, self-conscious militiamen fresh from enlistment with the Illinois State Government, had appeared to guard the steamboat landings.

To a final rumbling of hand trucks and the thud of freight being dumped in a hurry, splintery gangways were hauled up into a vertical position on board and hawsers sent slithering over the rail like hairy brown serpents. After a few steamy discords the Silver Wing's calliope commenced to blare, "Columbia, the Gem of the Ocean." The middle "E" whistle got stuck and screeched like a damned soul in torment, but the operator—none dared call him a musician—kept blithely on playing the vessel out into the River.

Slowly at first, then faster and faster the steamboat's great stern wheel commenced to splash, sent the creaking of the Silver Wing's fabric into a rhythmic tempo. Captain McEnnis was justifiably proud of his command. Being comparatively new, only ten years old, she didn't groan and complain about the speed asked of her. After cutting a chew of his plug of "eatin'" tobacco, he turned to a pilot busily twirling the six-foot wheel. "Mister, this trip I aim to fetch N'Awlins in a big hurry. Make it in five days and there'll be a hundred dollars extry for you and yer mate, so look alive."

The pilot's shaggy head inclined. "Gimme th' speed, Mac, then me and Luther will fetch her in on tiptoes."

Captain McEnnis whistled down the speaking pipe to the engine room.

"Elmo? Yer to drive this old hooker like a bat outer hell," he announced. "Make them heavers o' yourn hump themselves even if you have to take a stick to 'em."

It was with considerable satisfaction that presently he surveyed a mass of humanity jamming the *Silver Wing's* foredeck. By God and by gravy, the profits of this run promised even to surpass the small fortune earned by his last trip. Stacked aboard was more than a capacity cargo of machinery, lumber and all manner of manufactured goods; some of this last would be ruined if it came up to rain really hard, but the owners were so keen to do business that they'd released the line of any and all responsibility.

Yep. One more round trip like this and then Frank McEnnis could quit the River and its damned shoals, bars and snags forever. Never before had so many passengers struggled to get aboard. Staterooms had brought double and triple the normal price and his overworked purser declared that he could have sold each cabin three times over.

"What with all them folks aboard, Josh is sure going to catch hell in the dining saloon," McEnnis observed to the pilot. "He's got a hell's mint of extry mouths to feed. Reckon he don't know how many." Captain McEnnis chuckled, addressed his first officer who unwisely had chosen this moment to appear. "Hank, just you trot below and say to Greenwood I want he should open up a temporary bar on the afterdeck. My God, the passengers already is five deep round the one on the promenade."

Mr. Verroux, the first officer, said, "Sure thing, Mac. Say, you don't really reckon them Rebs have guns mounted downstream?"

"Naw. Spoke to Joe Fithian o' the *Pacific* which got in from N'Awlins last night. He says he didn't see hide nor hair of any batteries all the way up."

"That's good," commented Verroux after picking an ample nose and inspecting the gleanings. "I sure hope them Southern heroes ain't movin' no faster nor they gin'rally do. I'd hate to feel a eight-pound cannon ball fannin' my coattails."

To Christina Reigler, seated not too uncomfortably on a bale of cargo, the departure at dusk proved a thrilling and memorable occasion. The screaming calliope, the diffident waving of the blue soldiers, the hoarse commands of shirt-sleeved deck officers and the mournful, re-echoed whistlings of other river boats—she enjoyed it all.

My, how lovely were the lights of St. Louis ever so far away across this vast river! She wished it had been possible to see St. Louis, but neither time nor the contents of her purse had permitted it. So, during eight long hours, she'd lingered, more than a little frightened, about the Ohio & Mississippi Railroad's western terminal. Not that she'd been bored; it was fun exploring small mountains of freight as varied as it was picturesque. Since most Southern governors had threatened immediate war on the North, many shippers had grown chary of using the railroads, and prompt confiscation of their property. In Marietta she had first heard reports that the Rebels were attacking a fort somewhere in the Carolinas. It had amazed her. Why should the act of firing on a piece of cloth, even if it was the Stars and Stripes, sting usually sensible people into such a frenzy of hate? Especially, she wondered, since it was reliably reported that no one had been killed on either side.

She couldn't believe her eyes when, in Parkersburg, she had watched strong, sober-appearing citizens assemble before the local telegraph with tears in their eyes and search their souls for curses to lay upon the Carolinians. A pack of murdering, boastful traitors, was the least opprobrious term.

Oddly enough, it was very seldom in the Middle West that she heard slavery or abolition even mentioned. What "riled people clear down to their corns," as a friendly brakeman put it, was the fact that a party of noisy Rebels had fired on and pulled down the National Flag. It seemed that to Northern folk the Flag constituted not only their symbol of national dignity, but also the spirit of Liberty and Freedom.

Tina slumped against the rough netting binding of the cargo bale at her back. Never in her whole life had she ever been half so dirty, or so bone-tired. A poignant twinge reminded her that her stomach had been empty nearly twelve hours now. Still, as a panacea there remained the wonderful realization that, from now on, she would be traveling straight in the direction of Lachlan Brunton's sheltering arms. If only she could be certain of the reception he'd give her. Plenty of men would be furious over a girl's turning up unsent-for.

"In another seven or maybe only six days, I shall be with Lachlan," she reassured herself happily. "The ticket seller promised that this is an extra-fast boat."

She hugged thin arms about her knees, watching the dark shore retreat steadily as powerfully thrusting machinery imparted to the deck and the bale behind her a gentle, jouncing motion.

What troubled Tina most was that she'd found she could no longer accurately visualize every detail of her intended husband's face.

Next loomed the problem of whether the two and a half dollars remaining in her cowhide change purse would suffice to keep her fed, no matter how meagerly, down to New Orleans? Despite the most drastic of economies the cost of her journey west had eaten steadily into the thirty-six odd dollars with which she had set out.

How long ago it seemed that she had ridden the stage out to Ellicott City where, providentially, no sheriff had been awaiting her. Washington to Harper's Ferry had proved perhaps the most exciting and picturesque segment of her journey largely because troop trains rolling in the opposite direction were numerous. From the Ferry she had ridden the Baltimore & Ohio to Marietta; a miserably slow, soot- and cinder-drenched trip from which she had emerged dark as any quadroon. To bathe in a public bathhouse had required the expenditure of fifty precious cents for towels and soap. Though she still had a sliver of the soap left, this had been sheer extravagance. Yet at the time she knew she'd fall sick or go mad without a bath and a change of underwear.

Once Washington lay behind, Tina had deemed herself reasonably secure from pursuit; the political situation was so serious that police officers weren't likely to take notice of a pale young girl walking quietly along with shawled head modestly bent.

Despite severe resolutions to the contrary she often would discover herself standing straight, as Papa had made her; and because the contents of her carpet bag were so light she had added a couple of bricks to remind her to walk stooped over.

Her meals, snatched at way stations whenever the engine paused to water and fuel up, never had cost more than ten or fifteen cents and they hadn't been worth even that. What the passengers generally were offered were grisly chunks of cold and greasy pork piled on sodden bread and lubricated with watery gravy. Sometimes, though, she'd been lucky enough to buy a mug of milk for a couple of pennies. A single meal ordered in that glittering new refectory car attached to the train at Harper's Ferry would have cost fifty cents at the very least.

Nothing of an adventurous nature occurred to her until, on a ferry conveying passengers from Parkersburg, Virginia, over the Ohio River to Moore's Junction near Marietta, a couple of drunken soldiers had pinched her buttocks, then patted her hard little breasts and had made such indecent suggestions that she'd burst out crying in shame and outrage.

They were attempting to kiss her and would have succeeded had not a black-bearded lieutenant of Ohio Militia interfered and sent her persecutors slinking away. It was he who had offered a very practical suggestion.

"Now, Missy, so long as you are traveling alone, just you keep that shawl pinned high and don't spruce up more than you have to."

Tina hated her present unkempt and malodorous state with a feline intensity. Lord, how she yearned to wash her hair, gone so dull and greasy; some fine railroad cinders still were lodged in her braids. First chance she got, she intended to wash her other set of underclothes.

IV

DECK PASSAGE

THE *Silver Wing* gained speed steadily until high white plumes spurted to either side of her low bow and trailed behind her a bridal veil of froth across a windless expanse of water. Through a low-hanging purplish haze stars commenced to wink and blink by the thousand and the tens of thousand. Christina Reigler was delighted by her discovery that while sparks whirling from the tall and slender smokestacks suggested red-gold stars, real ones shone silver-gold.

At long last the calliope emitted a final, wheezing gasp and, dribbling condensed steam, fell into a blissful silence. Then and only then was the girl aware of voices all about her. Most pleasing of all were the softly melodious tones of Negro deck hands gossiping with servants belonging to those lordly creatures who inhabited staterooms on both upper decks. From immediately above her head, sounded peals of laughter, liquor-heated voices raised in argument, and the cheery clinking of glassware. The bar up yonder must be doing a land-office business.

From her seat on the deck cargo Tina witnessed the appearance of a young couple who advanced to bend over the rail of the deck above and view that tangle of humanity of which she was a part. The girl was a lovely young creature wearing a gown of such light texture that it billowed gently, gracefully in the faint upriver breeze. Her companion, obviously her new husband, proved very solicitous and kept attempting to arrange a cloak about her shoulders.

Smiling, Tina thought of Lachlan. Would he ever fuss so delicately over her? No, she guessed not; he'd be too busy earning their living. By the time they could afford such clothes she'd be well on the way towards middle age and she knew that men didn't fuss like that over middle-aged women. Sighing, she turned away, determined that some-day she would travel in a stateroom, a big one, and have colored serv-ants waiting below to attend her.

She watched a lanky white man appear and use a flaming torch to ignite cressets or iron baskets already crammed full of pine knots. Once these took fire, they created a dramatic scarlet glare by the light of which the commoner sort of travelers brought out food baskets and prepared to sup.

Tina of course didn't have a basket, only a segment of some non-descript pie wrapped in newspaper and a bag of peppermint candy. The Negro peddler declared this pie to be chicken, but proof revealed it to be mostly dough enveloping a few shreds of stringy meat which might have been anything from veal to tomcat. Still she consumed her purchase with all the eagerness generated by a healthy young body of eighteen years.

Presently the air grew chillier and the breeze stronger. Being coun-try-bred enough to know that this sort of night precipitated heavy dew, Tina decided to look about, by-and-by, and learn whether some better shelter were not available.

For the present she felt too tired to institute an immediate search so remained viewing the black, low-lying silhouette of the eastern bank. Here and there the lights of some farm or a village glowed like fireflies, then gradually slipped out of sight.

A river steamer bound for St. Louis came pounding up, her lights blazing like a heap of stirred coals and her whistle stridently calling for recognition. Like the other passengers, Tina hurried to the rail and saw that the other was a big side-wheeler and apparently very new, if the brilliance of her white and gold paintwork meant anything.

To a courteous tootling of Captain McEnnis' steam trumpet, the stranger sped by, thin tongues of flame trailing gracefully aft from her stacks. Now whole rows of lights sprang into being and by them everyone could see fine spray misting about her paddle boxes. Christina could read the stranger's name in tall and elegant gold letters: *The Sultana of Baton Rouge.*

Sultana? The name so tickled Tina's fancy that she repeated it several times.

"My, she's lovely," Tina whispered. "Just like the fairy queen's palace."

A little later the *Silver Wing* overtook a lumber raft nearly a quarter of a mile long. This curious contrivance was secured by chains into a floating island with roughly pointed ends and supporting three wooden tents—"wigwams" someone called them—designed to shelter crews working hard at sweeps and steering oars.

The raftmen off duty had collected about a big fire burning in a sand box in its center. By its light Tina could see rough, wild-appearing fellows standing up to yell derisive comments and wave earthenware jugs at the steamboat's passengers.

By dint of waiting a half hour, Christina at last was able to enter the women's lavatory, where, with an old handkerchief, she scrubbed everywhere she could without indecently exposing herself. Her fellow voyagers looked far from prepossessing. Most of them were leather skinned, shrill creatures wearing shapeless dresses of calico or homespun, but others traveled in over-elaborate clothes and much cheap jewelry. These last ladies devoted great attention to their frizzed hair and the application of paint from the tiny pots they carried. Little brushes spread not only carmine on their lips but also tinted brows and eyelashes a bold and unconvincing black.

Tina found comfort in the presence at the washbasins of several severely garbed females who by their plain and decent appearance she guessed to be schoolteachers.

"This sure is a mighty fine ship," observed one tired-looking old lady. "With all this speed and travelin' down-current like we are, shouldn't wonder but we'll sight N'Orleans inside of six days."

Tina agreed, timidly inquired about food and learned that a counter for the accommodation of deck passengers was located just forward of the boiler room. "You kin buy a gre't big plate o' sausage, coffee and all the corn dodgers ye want fer fif'een cents. 'Tain't bad cooking, neither."

Tina felt vastly encouraged because her slender resources would not only feed her down to New Orleans but even leave her enough to buy a day's shelter in case Lachlan could not readily be found.

Clutching her carpetbag Tina returned on deck and presently was lucky enough to discover a narrow space between two bales which proved just wide enough to permit her to wriggle in.

By folding her other petticoat and placing it on her carpet bag she created a fair pillow. Her spare dress, the one which had caused her so much trouble, she used for a cover and presently fell into an uncomfortable doze from which she soon was aroused because the *Silver Wing* was about to make a landing. Such a bedlam ensued as she had never heard; engine bells clanged in short, irritable bursts, steam roared through the exhausts and, because the great stern wheel had been reversed too suddenly, the whole boat bucked and groaned like a speared leviathan.

Through a gap between the cargo that protected her, Tina, by the light of torches and cressets, could see cotton bales being carried aboard by gangs of Negroes. Eventually the *Silver Wing's* whistle screamed loud enough to wake the Seven Sleepers of Ephesus, and she backed out into the Mississippi once more.

V

Mrs. Ledoux Intervenes

THE NEXT TWO days of the voyage passed pleasantly enough, the weather having retained a spring-like mildness. Everybody declared it was the Lord's own mercy that the mosquitoes hadn't yet got started.

To Christina Reigler the river banks, all newly green and yellow, presented an endless succession of strange scenes and especial wonders, while the river itself proved an even more fascinating subject of observation. All manner of ducks and waterfowl were winging their way northwards and tempting otherwise languid gentlemen occupying the promenade deck to dash into their cabins and return in time for a quick shot at these migrants. More often than not they dropped a bird but perforce left it to drift uselessly onto a snag or sand bar where some buzzard would find it.

On the third day, however, Tina awoke aware of heavy, painful throbbings in her head and of a sour taste in her mouth. By the gripings in her bowels and stomach she judged she must have eaten something spoiled from the counter. To make matters worse, rain commenced to fall for the first time since leaving Illinoistown. To begin with the drops descended gently but soon came lashing down in blinding swirls that drove the ever-increasing crowd of deck passengers to fighting for any kind of shelter.

Twice, people tried to share Tina's crevice but, surprisingly enough, withdrew on finding it already occupied.

During the morning Tina's biliousness degenerated into waves of nausea so powerful that she was forced to quit her retreat in order to vomit over the rail amid the jeers or dispassionate interest of the nearer passengers. A second seizure left her so weak she had to cling to the rail, gasping for breath. Her knees began trembling so violently that they threatened to buckle at any moment.

A voice began calling from above, "Young woman! I say there, young woman; you in the gray shawl!" At length Tina found opportunity to glance upward over her shoulder. She beheld a very fat old lady in a big-brimmed straw hat and a magenta gown, topped by a yellow cashmere shawl peering down.

"Young woman! Can you hear me?"

Tina was just able to nod before yielding to a fresh series of agonized retchings. She wanted to be sick again but her stomach now was empty so she could accomplish nothing save to gag and pant.

At first she hardly realized that someone's hand had closed over her arm just below the shoulder. Tina rolled swollen eyes about and so caught a glimpse of a row of official-looking brass buttons, a blue coat and a new straw hat.

"Now then, Missy," the stranger commenced. "Don't take on."

"I—I couldn't help it," Tina gasped. "I—I'm so sorry, and I'll clean your deck. I—I just couldn't help it."

"Maybe not," the man in blue muttered while hurriedly she wiped mouth and chin. "Come along."

At this, Tina began to weep. Surely they didn't arrest people just for throwing up when they couldn't help it? The other passengers began crowding about.

"Reckon that there baggage must have tried pickin' someone's pockets," observed a sharp-featured female. "They's signs up all over this here boat warnin' against gamblers and sech."

By a miracle Tina found strength to stand straight and look this red-faced officer in the eye. "Please, Mister, I have not done anything wrong and I have paid for my passage." She coughed, kept on trying to clean the bosom of her faded cotton dress.

The big fellow behind those bright buttons grinned. "Who says you have? Just you come along quiet-like, Missy. Ain't nobody fixin' to hurt you." Still gripping Tina by the arm, he unlocked a white-painted door, pulled her inside, then reclosed it upon the curious crowd.

How vivid a contrast the saloon passengers' lounge presented to the hot and smelly foredeck. Here thick, dark green carpets felt ever so soft underfoot, potted palms, mirrors and chandeliers everywhere caught the eye, and clean odors of furniture and brass polish were strong in the air. At a piano a wispy-looking young strawberry blonde was playing Mr. Eugene Dawson's "Monterez Waltz."

Panic suddenly seized Tina and she tried to break away sobbing, "Please, Mister, please let me go. I have done nothing wrong."

"Quit strugglin', ye poor little starveling, and just come along," the officer advised. Presently he conducted her up a broad staircase and along a gallery lined by doors bearing the names of various states. "Maine, Ohio, Virginia" she read, then realized all at once why such accommodations had become known as "staterooms."

Before a door labeled "Vermont" in gold letters, the officer halted, rapped twice. A sharp voice called, "Who is that?"

"Mr. Greenwood, Mum. The purser."

"Oh. I must say you've taken your own good time. You found her?"

"Yessum."

A moment later Tina found herself inside a stateroom and under-going the scrutiny of that same woman who had called down from the boat deck. She wore jet, tightly curled ringlets on either side of plump and shiny red features. Two of the blackest and brightest eyes Tina had ever beheld took her in from patched and dusty shoes to be-draggled blond braids.

"Mercy, ain't you a sight! Sit down, you pore young thing." She waved to a red plush settee. "That'll be all, Mr. Greenwood, and thank you. Here." She passed over a carefully folded greenback.

Floppy straw hat in hand, the purser bowed so low that a big gold-filled watch chain across his black and white checkered waistcoat swung 'way forward. "Thanky, Mum. If you require me again, you've only to ring for old Becky."

Tina felt too weak to do more than mutter, "Find my bag. Please, it has all I own."

"Don't worry about your bag. Mr. Greenwood will find it," her hostess assured her cheerfully. "Now let's git acquainted. Me, I'm Flora Ledoux, otherwise Mrs. Aristide Ledoux. But I'm no Frenchy. Purser should have put me in the stateroom marked 'Maine,' 'cause that's where I hail from. Dear, dear, you certainly are a sight. What's your name?"

Tina told her and, feeling a trifle less queasy, made bold to say, "I did not ask to come here, Ma'am, and I would not have, only I feel so weak."

"Maybe so. I notice you've got spirit. Where I come from we set considerable store on spirit. Now tell me truthfully. Are you traveling alone?"

"Yes, Ma'am. I—I am going to New Orleans."

There was no hint of morbid curiosity in Mrs. Ledoux's voice. "You are a good girl? Of course. Don't know why I asked that because if you weren't you'd not be traveling all by yourself. Um-m. Let's see now. You've only a deck passage and no place to sleep. That's true, isn't it?"

Tina only nodded. She was too busy fighting down another parox-ysm of nausea. In so doing she must have turned very white, for Mrs.

Ledoux suddenly jumped up, grabbed a reticule lying atop a chest and produced a small cut-glass bottle.

"Smelling salts," she announced. "Breathe deep. Now tell me, dearie, what do you figure ails you?"

"My stomach," Tina replied when her head had cleared. "The stew last night tasted queer."

"Oh? Well now, Miss Reigler, paregoric will fix you up in two shakes of a lamb's tail."

"Oh, no. I—I feel all right now. Really." She struggled to rise, but Mrs. Ledoux's magenta, bombazine-clad arms proved to be powerful.

"Now just you listen to me," snapped the older woman. "I've paid in full for both berths in this cabin and since I am headed for New Orleans, too, why you're welcome to travel with me."

"But—but, I can't pay cabin rate," Tina protested weakly.

"Fiddlesticks! Ain't I just said I've paid for the hull cabin? Mr. Ledoux is very lavish with my travel money so I'll easy 'tend to the difference for your deck passage ticket."

To refuse such unexpected luxury came hard, but Tina's shoulders squared themselves. "You are very kind, Ma'am, but I cannot accept unless maybe you will let me do some sewing for you? Back in Baltimore—" She shuddered. Heavens! She'd let the cat out of the bag for sure by mentioning that town.

"All right, all right!" Mrs. Ledoux's sharp voice interrupted. "I'll find work enough to ease your conscience. Now I am going for Becky, my black maid, who'll wash you and put you into the extra berth. If you don't mind an old-fashioned nightgown, I guess I can spare you one."

Mrs. Ledoux rang, gave Becky instructions, then patted Tina on the shoulder. "I'm going to play whist in the lounging saloon so go to sleep and don't you dast stir out of that berth till I return."

VI

A Glow on the River

Considerable satisfaction, although tempered by regret, was manifest in Captain McEnnis' expression.

"Will you jes' look on that foredeck?" he invited. "The Twelve Apostles 'emselves couldn't stow another bale nor a barrel aboard." This was entirely correct. A scant four inches of freeboard was all that prevented the *Silver Wing's* cargo deck from disappearing beneath the Mississippi's tawny surface.

"Yes, sir, and a feller'd need a shoehorn to ship another decker," agreed the first officer, lantern jaw working on a fresh chew of tobacco. "I declar' there ain't room fer most of 'em to lie down. Yes, sir, this'll prove the most profitable trip ever!"

Both officers felt relieved now that Vicksburg lay astern and no effort had been made to halt the *Silver Wing;* especially because long streaks of raw, yellow-red earth had appeared to indicate the existence of gun emplacements and really impressive fortifications. Similar defenses had been remarked not only along the bluffs above Vicksburg, but also on several strategically situated islands.

The *Silver Wing* squattered past a huge flatboat lumbering downstream under a stained brown squaresail.

"With any luck, Hank, we'll fetch N'Awlins come the day after tomorrow," McEnnis remarked jovially. "Then we'll turn round right brisk. I figger maybe we kin log another round trip afore either side shoots at us."

"Yessir, we likely can—but we got to hurry. Memphis papers was talkin' mighty war-like."

McEnnis turned to his second officer. "Go below and tell them loafers in the engine room to feed them boilers more pitch knots."

The second mate hesitated on his way out of the Texas.

"Think we oughter? It's so mighty close below the passengers in

'California' and 'Virginia,' they're complainin' their staterooms is too hot to live in."

"Ah, the hell with them," grunted the Captain and watched the pilot guide his vessel past the drifting trunk of a huge tree. Upon its weed-draped limbs rested a trio of white herons. In delayed resentment they went flap-flapping in leisurely flight towards the Mississippi shore.

"Just you keep them complaints to yerself, Mister," Captain McEnnis drawled. "One more trip like this and we'll all walk down Easy Street. Me, I aim to quit the River afore I get shot at, and buy into my brother's feed business. He's making a mint outfitting waggin trains headed west."

Towards sundown the *Silver Wing* ran into the first bad weather she had thus far encountered. The wind mounted in velocity, drove huge banks of storm clouds boiling over the western shore. The Mississippi, nearly two miles across at this point, commenced to stir, then to froth and finally to writhe under terrifically violent squalls; some gusts proved strong enough to heel the steamboat 'way over on her port beam.

Soon solid sheets of rain commenced drumming down, beating the engine's smoke and curling streamers of flame low over the tumultuous water. Some of the passengers got so frightened that an itinerant preacher on the foredeck judged this to be an auspicious moment to hold a revival meeting and to circulate a plate.

At nine o'clock the engineer whistled up to the Texas.

"We're takin' too much water over the bow," he warned. "We'll have to slow down some."

This was true. The *Silver Wing* was so overloaded that she could no longer buck the storm waves without their leaping the low bow and flooding the freight piled on her foredeck. All this McEnnis could see by the almost continuous glare of lightning which hissed and crackled all about. But time was to be won.

He yelled down the speaking tube, "The pumps will keep her dry. Hold her at full speed, you yellow hound-dawg, or I'll knock yer ears."

By now the gale had risen to a tornado's velocity. Fierce squalls rattled stateroom windows, sent spray vaulting over the weather rail and so fed the engine drafts that long banderoles of flame streamed from the iron crowns atop the smokestacks. Reeling, plunging, relentlessly urged on by her huge stern wheel, the Silver Wing drove headlong through the wind-driven rain and darkness. The pilot knew the river to be wide and straight in this reach.

Mrs. Ledoux woke up, hot and sweaty as if she had taken a fever. She sniffed sharply and said aloud to herself, "That's wood smoke, sure as I'm born." At once she turned up the wick of the small kerosene light held in a bracket above the head of her berth. An icy dart shot the length of her back when she discovered little tendrils of blue-gray smoke working through a crack in the white-painted wainscoting beside her bunk. She was reaching for the call bell when a peculiar rushing noise drowned out the familiar sounds of a steamboat under way.

"Wake up!" For all her corpulence Mrs. Ledoux was out of bed in a flash and shaking her unconscious roommate. "Quick! Wake up!"

Christina roused up on an elbow, pushing hair out of her eyes—she'd felt too exhausted to braid it. "What?"

"This boat's taken fire!" Mrs. Ledoux cried over an ever-increasing roar. "Get some clothes on. Quick!"

There could be no doubt that a fire had broken out somewhere because heavy feet went racing down the passageway just outside. Then a gong commenced to clang-clang, made the whole hull reverberate to its brazen uproar; simultaneously the even throb of the Silver Wing's engines faltered, then died, and her steam trumpet commenced to screech hysterically.

Borrowed nightgown billowing up under her arms, Tina jumped down from the upper berth, saw Mrs. Ledoux stripping the case from her pillow. Into it she was shoveling rings, bracelets and other valuables. Her fat shoulders were shuddering to the violence of her movements.

"Put this cloak about you," Tina begged, holding out that garment. "Here are your shoes."

Mrs. Ledoux actually smiled through the graying air. "Wish you was my own daughter. I admire folks who keep their heads. Now let's figger what we'd best do."

Something must be done, and promptly. But what?

A low cry of fright escaped Tina's companion because, in appalling suddenness, a palpitating orange glare illumined the window's rain-streaked glass.

The shrill screams and screeching of humans aware that flaming death was about to close in upon them now began to sound over that infernal crackling roar.

Like most river boats of her type the *Silver Wing's* woodwork was heavy with oils through annual painting and therefore combustible as any torch. Although sluicing rain drenched her exterior it affected her vitals not at all. Tina was reaching for her worn and twisted shoes when a report like that of a cannon discharged at close range sent her quivering to her feet.

Mrs. Ledoux screamed, "We'd better try—" She got no further because someone set up a frantic hammering at their stateroom door.

Obedient to the older woman's command, Tina slid back a brass bolt only to be flung violently back by a gust of blinding hot gases which struck her with the force of a giant's fist. Pressed flat against the cabin's far wall Tina, as in a nightmare, beheld a woman's body slumped across the threshold with clothing and hair brightly burning.

Mrs. Ledoux must have been far stronger than she looked for, quite alone, she pushed the corpse back into the corridor, but it required the united efforts of both women to reclose their door. Even as Tina's fingers closed over the door bolt another tremendous gush of fire roared up the corridor and blew the door open again. Coughing amid the suffocating fumes, Mrs. Ledoux grabbed up a night pot and hurled it through the window.

"Out!" she screamed, a dim and grotesque figure amid the murk. "Out!"

Tina grabbed at the pillow case of valuables. "After you." But her companion's nightgown had exploded into a ball of flame and she tumbled face downward yammering and howling out her agony.

Another great explosion shook the dying river boat from stem to stern. Possibly it was the blast thus generated which propelled Tina bodily through the window just as she had grabbed at its jagged outline. Outrageous, intolerable heat beat at her back, something slashed at her arm and fire licked at her face before she was flung an immeasurable distance through the flame-filled dark.

VII

RIVER OF DREADFUL NIGHT

THE SHOCK OF sudden immersion in cold water cleared Christina Reigler's reeling senses sufficiently to permit her to realize that, although totally submerged, she was rising. When her head struck on some object and checked her progress towards the air a hideous panic gripped her. She struggled blindly until, magically, the obstruction overhead moved aside and fresh air suddenly gushed into her aching lungs.

For a while none of Tina's senses, saving that of touch, seemed able to function. Because she had learned to "dog paddle" on a cold lake back home in Wisconsin, she was able to thresh about, coughing and half-strangled until her hand came in contact with a rough surface capable of buoying her with head clear of the surface.

Gradually, like laggard and unwilling sentries, Tina's other senses returned to duty until she became aware of a dazzling scarlet-gold glare pulsating somewhere not far off. Its source, however, was effectively concealed by dense clouds of smoke hanging funereally low.

That the water was very rough and that great, icy raindrops kept lashing at her head was her next realization, along with the fact that beating through this rose and gray pall of smoke came appalling screams and despairing cries for help.

Gradually her vision improved so much that, when a slant of wind blew away the smoke, she was able to discern what appeared to be a flame-spouting island drifting along some two hundred yards downstream. A minute or so later this weird island erupted, was instantly disintegrated by a monstrous explosion which hurled flaming brands, small boats, timbers and huge sections of the steamboat high into the rain-lashed night. Then, as if by some magician's trick, the glare vanished all in an instant and the river flowed on dark, silent and terribly lonely.

Sobbing, Tina clung to what proved to be a bale of cotton. For a while it smoldered sullenly along its upper side, but presently rain extinguished the fire. Small pieces of wreckage, some still burning, dotted the water all about her, but the current must have snatched the larger pieces of flotsam away faster than her bale could travel.

Off somewhere to her left she heard someone floundering and a woman or a boy's voice yelling, "Help! For God's sake, help!"

When she tried to call out, "This way," all that resulted was a curious croaking sound. The hot gases she had inhaled had left her throat raw and seared.

Now she must be nearing the spot where the *Silver Wing* had blown up, for yells, cries, groans, sounded all about her. In the wind-filled darkness she could see nothing at all, however, so clung weakly to the bale after thrusting a wrist through a loop in its bindings. A swimmer came struggling out of the blackness towards her.

"This way, this way!" she managed to gasp. Someone must have reached the other side of the bale because she felt it turn a little.

"Hang on, help will come. This will keep us afloat." She had spoken in German, she was that frightened. *Du lieber Gott*, how her face stung!

"Dunno what ye said," came a feeble reply. "I think—whole back's burned off."

There sounded more splashing sounds close by, but gradually river noises and the lashing rain blotted them out.

Now that lightning no longer played to relieve the abysmal gloom there was no telling in which direction a shoal or an island might lie. Once Tina's breathing leveled out and a measure of self-possession had returned, she could feel the current tugging at her hair and became aware of an odd sensation along her left side. It wasn't hurting, only felt as if the skin had been stretched too tight.

Once Tina cried out sharply because the cotton bale almost snagged itself on a sunken tree and submerged branches suddenly clawed at her legs. The man on the other side of the bale emitted a hollow groan.

"Where are we? Can't last much longer."

"Right close to an island or something," Tina lied, trying to sound confident. "Just hang on a little longer. I can see it. Soon we will be safe on shore."

She had no idea how much longer the bale spun and bobbed downstream before her unknown companion gasped, "Oh, God," then the cotton bale rode higher in the water.

"You will not let go, Christina Reigler, you are still quite strong. Hang on! Hang on!" Endlessly she repeated those two words, first in English, then in German, until she drifted into a timeless void and was only dully aware that the rain had ceased and the waves were dropping.

How black and lonely it was in this weird and unlovely world where absolutely nothing was to be seen, not even the surface of her precious cotton bale. At length she roused to the fact that her support's bobbing motion had ceased. In fact, the bale was aground and soft mud lay beneath her feet.

In order to summon a measure of strength Tina had to draw many deep breaths and while so occupied became aware that a milky, gray-black quality was pervading the gloom.

Wisely, she remained clinging to the bale until she was able to see a tangle of branches not far away looking black and gnarled as the hands of a threatening witch. Some clouds must have been blown aside for all at once her immediate surroundings became clearly revealed in silver-gray tones. Beyond her cotton bale a stretch of sand climbed towards the tangle of trees she had noticed.

"Oh, my Heavenly Father, I thank Thee," she gasped, then reeled off towards the shore with sodden hair streaming pale and free over neck, shoulders and breasts.

Under a huge cottonwood she glimpsed a little gully choked by dead leaves and grass and into it she collapsed.

VIII

Wild Grape Island

Sunlight was beating so persistently upon Christina Reigler's closed eyelids that she reluctantly returned to consciousness and promptly became aware of a dull pain shooting through her left arm and shoulder. She roused surprisingly quickly and was appalled at the state in which she found herself.

She lay huddled on a bed of dried and sandy willow leaves as naked as she'd been when old Dr. Wagner had spanked the first breath into her tiny lungs. *Himmel!* To lie all exposed like this for all the world to see was horribly indecent. By raising her head a trifle, she could see her body stretching away, the view of her legs interrupted by the contours of her breasts. They and the rest of her were smeared with dried blue-gray clay.

Although her head still swam, Tina sat up and attempted to analyze the pain in her arm. No wonder it hurt; three long gashes ran redly across her upper arm. They weren't very deep and had largely stopped bleeding, though a few ruby drops still were oozing through scabs which had begun to form.

Her next discovery was that her face was so fearfully swollen that she could see hardly anything with her left eye; she learned also that practically the whole length of her left side had been scorched and blistered into a hideously tender area.

Wonderingly she tested her hair, found it amazingly short and its ends thick; she used finger tips to explore her forehead and learned that, where her eyebrows should have been, there remained no hair at all. A recurrent weakness forced her to lie back again permitting the sun to warm her and lend renewed vitality to her battered body. Two small, bright yellow and dark green birds settled in a creeper above and balanced there, surveying her with brilliant inquisitive eyes.

Gradually memory commenced to serve until she recalled Mrs. Ledoux's waking her up amid a hellish roaring of flames. Shuddering, she remembered that flaming corpse in the corridor and curiously enough remembered how Mrs. Ledoux's single black braid had dangled over her shoulder like a sable serpent.

She stiffened, for surprisingly near by a voice was rasping, "Aw, put yer Goddam' shoulder under it, Rufe. You too, Billy; we got to hurry. 'Twill be broad daylight soon."

"I'm doin' the best I kin," panted a nasal voice. "Wish to God we'd got us a mule. Come on, Billy, git yer feet sot an' give 'nother heave; these yere bales is wuth a hun'erd dollars each."

Men! Men, right close by! And here she lay in shameful nakedness.

Yip! Yip! A dog commenced a series of joyously excited barks descriptive of starting a cottontail.

Tina cringed, looked about for cover but, finding none, frantically tried to burrow under the leaves and grass, and almost immediately struck hard, sandy earth.

"Come on, ye lop-eared bastards. Heave, heave-ho!"

"Ah—to hell with the cotton! Water-soaked like this, them bales is too damn' heavy. Looky! Yonder's floatin' down a chest o' drawers. Me, I'm goin' after it."

Teeth chattering in terror, Tina struggled up onto her knees although the blistered skin of her side felt as though it must split.

Employing infinite care, she parted the undergrowth and saw, not fifty yards distant, three shaggy, half-dressed men hard at work. Two of them were using poles to lever a charred cotton bale up onto a sand spit; the third, younger and slighter of build, was splashing out over the shallows towards the river.

"Hi! Back yonder comes 'nother deader," shouted the youth, now up to his waist in the slow, coffee-colored current. "A man this time."

"Leave that chest be," directed a gruff voice. "It's groundit anyways and fetch that cadaver ashore. Mebbe we'll find a ring onto him."

Utterly aghast, Tina watched the boy wade further out and grab at a green-coated arm rising rigidly above the Mississippi.

"Gawd, Lord A'mighty, Buck, yer right! They's a sock-dologer big ring onto him."

Heart hammering in terror, Tina watched these wild, half-naked men—they were clad only in ragged breeches suspended from a single gallus—haul a corpse into shallow water.

"Christ! His fist's stiffer nor a poker. Billy jest you fetch that axe."

The axe flashed down *tchunk!* against a billet of driftwood and lopped off the extended claw-like hand.

"Go through the bastard's pockets 'fore ye push him off agin," directed the brown-bearded man the others called Rufe. "You, Buck, keep yer dad-burned eyes skint and we'll earn us a mint out o' this wreck."

Twice more the freckled, tousle-headed youth either waded or swam out to pull ashore stiff, unlovely relics of humanity.

The ghouls had levered three cotton bales into concealment amid the underbrush before their rabbit hound began racing along the beach in futile pursuit of some sandpipers. All at once he halted, swung a flea-bitten black and tan head towards Tina's refuge and began to sniff.

"*Herr Gott!* Please do not let them find me," prayed the girl, but to no avail. The little hound began raising a furious, excited clamor. At first the rivermen paid no attention, but at last the one called Billy asked, "What ails Snapper? Reckon must be a bobcat in thar."

Rufe straightened, used the heel of his hand to smear sweat from his leathery forehead. "That ain't no bobcat-rookus Snapper's raisin'."

The mongrel hound circled about Tina's thicket all the while raising a heart-stilling clamor.

"Billy, jes' you go see what that li'l son-of-a-bitch's found there."

The youth grunted protest, but came splashing along the beach.

"Come off that, Snapper, you danged fool!" Billy whistled several times but the dog only kept on raising an alarm.

Frantically, Tina squirmed down into the gully and tried to hide under the leaves. Branches threshed.

"Yo're a big fool, Snapper, come away— Glory! Here's a fee-male critter and—and, why she's nekkid as a egg!"

The other two came pounding up to stare down at the cowering, utterly terrified girl.

"Je-sus! It's a woman, all right, but ain't she a mess? Must've come offa that wreck," was Rufe's sublimely intelligent observation.

"Shucks!" grunted the one called Buck. " 'Tain't no woman, it's only a skinny young gal."

In utter terror, Tina used her arms to cover her breasts. Since she'd been six years of age, no one, not even her own mother, had ever beheld her completely unclothed.

Blue eyes, white-ringed in apprehension, stared fearfully upwards.

"Yer right, Rufe, she's sure been roasted to a turn."

Rufe, the biggest and the oldest-appearing of the three, scratched at his matted mane. "Damn' iffen' she don't look jest like a half-singed spring chicken—an' a damned scrawny one to boot. Billy, just you canter down an' fetch my shirt. Now look hyar, gal, don't git yourself so lathered up. We ain't fixin' to harm you. So pull on this shirt. Billy will fetch you down to our shack an' give yu sumpin' to eat."

IX

The Yeager Boys

A week dragged by before Christina Reigler felt able to move without biting her lips. Movement of any kind was painful in the extreme because not only had her side been burned to about the intensity of serious sunburn, but those cuts on her arm festered, took on proud flesh and for a while remained discolored, badly swollen and feverish.

By degrees her slim body commenced to mend, once her abundant and youthful vitality asserted itself. First the blisters subsided leaving shiny red patches, then her brows and eyelashes commenced to grow back during almost endless hours of sleep. Probably the factor which contributed most towards her recovery was the neglect accorded her by the Yeagers.

Buck and Rufe Yeager, she decided, must be brothers, while bucktoothed Billy was their first cousin. All three were coarse, primitive creatures always ready to brawl or to blaspheme anyone or anything in order to assert their manhood. Not one of them could so much as read or write a line.

Their talk was so larded by Indian words and river slang that half the time she couldn't understand what was being said as she lay limp and colorless on a pallet of dried cattails, her only covering an ancient and greasy quilt. Since no window graced this shack, whatever light penetrated its dim and musty interior entered through the door or beat down a mud and wattle chimney.

These rivermen had no regular meal hours. Whenever they got hungry they would fry themselves a mess of catfish, a muskrat or some kind of waterfowl. After sundown all three retired to lumpy, sour-smelling bunks, there to snore and grunt like a whole styful of pigs. The only one who manifested the least sympathy was young Billy; he smeared bear's grease on her burns and sometimes refilled the big gourd dipper of water she drank from.

Occasionally one of the older rivermen would pause to stare downwards from blank predatory eyes.

At the end of a week she was able to be about, garbed in a stained gingham gown which she suspected, because of a burned area on its sleeve, must have been stripped from a victim of the *Silver Wing* disaster.

Buck, grinning shyly, brought in a well-worn linsey-woolsey, a petticoat and Rufe produced a pair of water-soaked shoes. These last were obviously intended for a boy but still were several sizes too large. She rendered them serviceable by binding strands of manila rope over her instep.

Tina came to realize that these rivermen pretended to be trappers, but also worked on flatboats, rafts and occasionally had fought as jayhawkers in the terrible Border wars between Missouri and Kansas. Rufe she guessed must be a fugitive from justice, for every time he heard an unexpected noise outside the shack he moved over to the old-fashioned fowling piece he kept ready beside the door.

The loss of the *Silver Wing* must have been a fine windfall for even at the end of a week the Yeagers were still salvaging all manner of flotsam brought to Wild Grape Island by a favoring fluke of current.

By dint of scouring the bottom of a baking pan Tina was able to receive a dim impression of her likeness. *Himmel!* Was this the neat, clean creature Mr. Brunton had admired? At once horrified and relieved, she set down the pan. *Gewiss.* As long as she looked like the witch out of "Hansel and Gretel" no man in his right senses would dream of molesting her.

Of course Tina set about to make herself useful; every bit of clothing she came across she hung up to pegs driven into intersections between the cabin's twisted and mud-streaked logs. Next she swept out as much dirt as a birch-twig broom could move. She even stirred up a pan of corn pone and fried some catfish to greet her hosts upon their return from the river's edge.

"Wal, reckon yer tougher nor ye look," Buck observed that evening, while utilizing a broken fingernail to dislodge a troublesome shred of meat. "I'd not have risked two bits ye'd live to bury."

"Thank you. I feel very much better."

"That's good," rumbled Rufe, his eyes bright and predatory as a hawk's. "Ye can sew up my britches tommorrey."

"Why, of course. I'd be pleased to," Tina murmured, in her anxiety curling one dirty bare foot over the other.

"Ye'd better be. A wench had better keep on the jump come suppertime. When I gits hongry I don't admire waitin'."

Tina forced a tremulous smile. "Yes, sir. Mind if I go fetch a pail from the spring?"

Buck thrust out a long leg, halted her progress to the door. Large yellowish teeth shone in the candlelight. "Now jest don't you git no fine idees 'bout runnin' off. Why? 'Cause you cain't get off this island, and there ain't no place on it where us and Snapper cain't find you. That'd be plumb ongrateful and you'd earn a taste o' this." He tapped a heavy brass-studded belt securing shapeless trousers of brown home-spun. "I kin make a gal squeal real loud if I've the mind. See?"

He was so dirty, so bestial about the mouth that Tina shuddered but rallied enough to say quite calmly, "Oh, I wouldn't think of it, Mr. Yeager. You all have been so good to me, and—and—kind."

"That's as may be, Sis. Once ye get rid o' them scabs and fatten up, we got plans fer ye, me and Buck." Rufe it appeared was the leader of the group. "Yes, sir, you sure are a lucky gal, Teenie. Soon me and Buck is goin' over to town and cash some o' that there plunder. Iffen we gits good prices, why mebbe I'll buy ye a shimmy-shirt with red ribbons into it."

"And—and I, why, I'll buy ye a—a, well—a pretty blue and yaller calico dress, mebbe." Billy refused to be outdone in generosity.

"Never mind all that. What I—I really want is some soap and a comb."

"You'll take jest what we'll give ye," Rufe observed through a fresh chew of tobacco. "Come to me. I ain't had a real good look at ye yet."

Restive as a colt about to be saddled for the first time, Tina limped over to where Rufe sat on a salvaged cabin hassock, picking pone crumbs out of a ragged, brown-black beard.

"Stand closer, gal. Now let's look at them hacks in your arm. Um! Don't back away like that. I don't like it."

He peered at her scars. "Ain't no more proud flesh. That'll do." Awkwardly his fingers tested her unbound hair—she had deemed it wise not to make braids. "Damn' me, if ye don't look singed and shaggy like a she-coon fresh run o' a brush fire. How's the rest of them burns?"

"Healing very well," she cried hastily and would have stepped back except that his huge hand shot out and imprisoned both of hers. To admiring guffaws he held the girl helpless while with his free hand he flipped up the grimy skirt exposing the over-slender body all the way to its hips.

Billy goggled and Buck half arose at this vision of twisting nacre-pale legs and thighs.

"Don't!" she panted. "This is no way to treat a decent girl." She squirmed desperately to get away.

"Aw," cried Billy, "don't torment her. She cooks real good."

"Who says it ain't decent to see a pore gal's hurts? Damn it, Sissy, don't you dast try to lecture me." Rufe drew his hand back as if to slap her but let the skirt slip back into its place and allowed Tina to pelt frantically out into the dark sobbing and scarlet with outrage.

Two days later Rufe and Buck appeared from somewhere poling a solid, well-built raft. It was perhaps eighty feet long, crudely pointed at one end and equipped with a pair of ten-foot sweeps, rude affairs consisting of a peeled pole improved by a slab of board nailed to one end.

Onto this the Yeagers hauled four cotton bales, five chairs, a big brass hurricane lamp, two strips of slightly burned green carpet. Rufe carried the real loot in a leather poke; rings, bracelets, watches and such other jewelry as had been looted from the *Silver Wing's* luckless passengers.

Hope began to well up in Tina like a gratefully warm flood when all three Yeagers actually began to pull on crude rawhide boots, and crack coarse jokes; then they donned collarless shirts the fronts of which soon became stained by the tobacco juice they were forever squirting in all directions. Buck and Billy put bear's grease on their long sunburned hair and even attempted to comb with a twig brush. Rufe only jeered, called them dudes.

Unhappily Tina watched the trio haul their small dugout canoe aboard the raft; trust them to deprive her of that means of escape. Of course they had learned that she couldn't really swim. She noticed that, for some reason, the older men were guffawing a lot and winking behind Billy's back.

Heart lifting at the glorious prospect of being left alone for even a little while and afforded an opportunity to explore the island, Tina watched them lash down the last of their weirdly assorted cargo.

Buck turned to Billy. "Trot up to the shack, Bub," he drawled, "and fetch me a little ditty bag ye'll find under some rushes at the haid of my bed."

"Aw, no. I'm busy—send Teenie fer it."

"God damn! I said fer you to git it! Hump yerself or ye'll earn a clout on the jaw."

So menacing was Buck's beetle-browed scowl that Billy, cursing futilely, went shambling up the bank towards the cabin lying well-hidden in a hollow out of sight from the river traffic. The moment the boy had disappeared, the brothers put weight to their poles and quickly shoved the raft well out into the stream. By the time the youngest Yeager returned hopping mad because he had failed to locate the nonexistent ditty bag, the raft was well out and, gripped by the main current, was sliding rapidly away.

Not even along Alice Anna Street had Tina overheard such lurid profanity as was shouted by fifteen-year-old Billy.

"Come back for me, you sneakin' mother-seducin' bastards! Come back an' I'll cut yer dirty livers out." In his fury Billy trotted along the shore alternately shaking his fist and hurling rocks which fell far short of their mark.

Tauntingly Rufe's voice beat over the coffee-colored Mississippi. "Don't git yourself so lathered up, Bub, else you'll take to strangling. Besides, me and Buck will be back in mebbe two, three days. Iffen yer good, we'll mebbe bring yer a jug o' good forty-rod along with your money share."

"It's all fer yer own good," jeered Buck. "Yer too young to be hittin' the high spots of a wicked meetropolis like Bruinsburg."

"That's a damn' lie!" screamed the boy, now weeping in impotent rage. "I had me a high yaller last time. Come back, cuss yore guts, come back for me!"

Tina, wringing roughened hands in an agony of disappointment, could just hear Buck's reply.

"Naw. Now just ye mind the traps an' keep an eye on our female critter. Ye've got that there ash cat to keep ye company."

Billy paralleled the raft's smooth progress quite a distance all the while screeching his furious disappointment, but to no avail. Under application of the sweeps the raft continued gliding further and further out onto the shining expanse of the Mississippi until it resolved into a tiny black dot.

If she had to be left alone with any of the Yeagers, Tina philosophized, she'd prefer it to be Billy, although at fifteen he was as big and almost as powerful as his cousins.

He came stamping back, the little, greenish yellow eyes in his freckled red face aglitter with rage.

"That was a dirty mean trick," Tina tried to console him. "I—I'm ever so sorry."

"Ah-h, shut up!" he snarled and made as if to strike the slight figure in greasy calico. "It's all on yer account they crossed me; I've always went to Bruinsburg before."

Still spouting blasphemies, Billy jerked out his skinning knife and with a movement as smooth, swift and deadly as a rattlesnake's strike, flung it at a big sycamore stump. It lodged there, blue-white blade glimmering evilly in the hot morning sunlight.

After he had appeared to quiet a little, Tina brought him as appeasement a tin plate of doughcakes and a glass of water mixed with wild honey. "Am I mistaken, Billy, or haven't there been very few steamers go by here these last three days?"

The boy's long, sharp-chinned jaw worked steadily before he replied. "Dunno. Ginerally they's easy eight or ten go by each direction. I wonder what's up? Mebbe it's this war they bin talkin' about down to Bruinsburg."

Tina smiled and seated herself on the bole of a fallen cottonwood. "Were you born near here?"

"Naw, up Kansas way." Billy inspected the end of a sassafras twig he had been chewing. "Hull family got massacreed in that there Border war, five—six year ago."

Tina felt she was succeeding in her efforts to sooth the boy's outraged vanity.

"I guess you must be a better trapper than your cousins."

The flat, freckled features broke at last into the grin she had been hoping for. "Sure am. I can take coons, minks, otters and muskrats two for one 'gainst Buck any day, and he's a leetle smarter than Rufe; cuss their mangy hides." Angrily, Billy flung aside his chew-stick.

"Please, Billy, won't you show me how you set some of your traps?" Tina was thinking fast, but her manner was innocence itself.

"All right, but gals don't understand trappin'."

Before long he was leading the way through tangles of cane, poplar, cottonwood and gum trees. Among weed-festooned jungles caused by driftwood branches and trunks in various backwaters, he charmed and amazed her. Why, in traveling he made no more noise than the cottontails that went racing away! He kept warning, "Don't create such a gol-danged rumpus or we'll never see nuthin'."

Once he let her almost tread upon a huge, muddied black snake sunning itself beside a fallen sycamore and roared with laughter at her frightened shrieks. Presently he showed her a red-eyed vireo's delicate nest, that of a song sparrow containing four tiny chocolate-splashed eggs, and finally the huge, ungainly home some fish eagles had built atop a lightning-killed pine.

"The young ones is teeterin' up yander. Say," he said. "Yep. Say, you are interested in wild critters, ain't you?"

"Do you earn much money trapping?" she smiled. Thank fortune, things were going better than she dared hope.

"In the winter we do."

"And in the summer?"

"Sometimes we flatboat or fell timber. Mostly we jest loaf about."

By this time their tour found them walking along a wide and muddy beach curving towards the southern tip of Wild Grape Island. Billy rolled up the store pants he had expected to wear into Bruinsburg and waded out to inspect a promising-looking barrel lying half imbedded in the shoals. Tina, however, wandered on, her toes sinking comfortably into the soft warm mud. The sensation reminded her of childhood adventures around a muddy swimming hole back of Breyfogle's quiet mill.

Before she realized it Tina had emerged upon a miniature headland heavily crowned by muddy alders and willows. There she halted, heart in mouth, for yonder, on the very southern tip of this island, a party of men was digging, leisurely piling up the rich black earth into what appeared to be a series of small banks. A furtive glance over her sunburned shoulder revealed Billy busily scooping mud from beside the cask.

Obviously her companion had not heard the pounding or chopping. What were these men constructing? Every now and then an axe head or a spade flashed in the sunlight. She turned, tried not to hurry or betray her wild excitement.

"Danged barrel's full of molasses, but it's spoilt," he announced.

"Too bad. Say, Billy, I am getting very hungry. Let us go back to the cabin and I will fix us something good to eat."

He pulled out a charred corncob pipe and lit it before he drawled, "Reckon I'm a mite peckish myself. You'll fix up somethin' real tasty?"

X

BATTERY SIXTEEN

A MIDDAY MEAL of fried hominy grits and stewed rabbit passed pleasantly enough, although occasionally Billy would frown and curse beneath his breath, that loud and loutish youngster seeming to have become reconciled only with difficulty to his cousins' treachery.

Employing a pine splinter, he settled under a cottonwood beside the spring, alternately picking yellow, uneven teeth, and sucking at his noisome corncob. Freed of boots, his big broad toes spread themselves, then contracted.

"Yep, she hain't much of a shack," he said, "but she do keep the rain off and were ol' Miss' to riz up sudden-like—and she do, come springtime—and wash her away, we'd have no great loss, I reckon."

Tina sat, bare feet drawn up under her, in the shack doorway attempting for the first time to braid the dreadfully oily and tangled mane into which her hair had degenerated.

"My! Does the river actually rise up to cover this island?"

"This end, sure," Billy told her, lazily slapping at flies attempting to settle upon a sore above his leathery-looking ankle. He swung his head sharply, like a buck deer scenting some suspicious odor.

"Hear something?" Tina asked.

"Dogged if it didn't sound like somebody hammering. Didn't you hear nothing?"

"No, maybe it was only a woodpecker."

Presently Billy searched his pockets for the pig's bladder he used for a tobacco pouch.

"Danged, if she ain't empty." He arose and, belching noisily, shuffled into the shack and commenced poking around.

"That bastard Rufe's got some hidden somewheres."

All of a sudden a ringing whoop made the hollow resound. "Jesus! Hyar's a jug under his pallet!" Once in the open sunlight Billy shook the brown earthenware jug experimentally, then wrenched out its corncob stopper.

"Ol' son-of-a-bitch'll be plumb mad I found it," Billy chuckled. "Wal, reckon there's 'bout enough." He winked clumsily. "Buck and Rufe ain't the only ones gonna have a high ol' time, no siree. Now, Teenie, jest you trot over to the spring and fetch me a dipper o' cold water. This hyar snake-juice smells tolerable warm."

When she returned he had already set out a pair of battered tin cups on a piece of board. "Come on, Sissy, he'p yerself." He grinned, peering through a lock of sandy-colored hair falling low over his forehead. "Go ahead. They's plenty fer the both of us."

"Thank you, Billy, but I—I don't drink." She stood there miserably uncertain. Oh, if only he'd not come across that jug! How would the fiery Monongahela affect him? Probably he'd just get sick and go to sleep; a boy of his age would. Fervently she hoped so—or that he'd just get happy the way Buck did.

"Aw, come on," he waved the jug under her nose. "I'll l'arn ye. Shecks, you ain't no kid, yer a woman; yer eighteen year old, sure enough."

"But—but—to drink is against my religion."

"Ain't no religion around hyar. Leastways not so'd ye'd notice it."

Billy scowled, swung the jug to his shoulder, splashed out half a cup of the tea-colored fluid then swallowed a long pull and gulped water from the gourd dipper.

"Ha!" Billy coughed a couple of times then slapped his flat and naked belly. He had shed his go-to-town shirt and refilled the cup.

"S'yer turn." He hefted a skinning stick, pointed with it to the tin cup and gourd. " 'Tain't polite to leave a gen'man drink alone."

"Please no, Billy. I don't want to."

"Go on, *drink!*" His small green-yellow eyes commenced to narrow themselves as he took a step forward, with stick raised. There was nothing for it so she slopped in water until a fair amount of the whiskey overflowed.

"You—your good health." That was what she'd heard men saying that wonderful evening when Mr. Duchesne had taken Lachlan and her to supper. So long as she had to give in she might as well earn a full measure of good-will. Merciful Heavens! This drink was like liquid fire. Tina gasped, coughed and her eyes filled.

"Haw! Haw! Ho! Ho!" roared Billy and rolled on the ground in raucous bucolic amusement. "No need to drink so fast, Teenie." He patted the earthenware jug. "Plenty here fer the both o' us."

Only pleasantly stimulated, he made her join him under a locust tree where they could sit and look out over the river. Presently a towboat appeared from the direction of New Carthage spouting clouds of sooty smoke and dragging a big scow. Since it passed not a quarter of a mile distant, they both noticed that the scow was crowded with armed men. The sunlight kept glancing off musket barrels and other small arms, but what the color of their uniforms might be they couldn't tell because a shimmering heat haze kept distorting details.

" 'Pears like there mought be some fightin' somewheres," the youth drawled. "They're sure 'nuff headed up to Memphis. Ever see any fightin'—skirmishes, I mean? I have." Omitting no gory detail, he then launched into stories descriptive of the Kansas Border wars, including bloodcurdling accounts of wholesale murders that set Tina's already unhappy stomach to quivering.

He took another big drink out of the jug and this time his speech became slurred. At length he dug dirty knuckles into his eyes and gaped prodigiously.

"Reckon I'll jest take me a leetle snooze."

"That is a mighty good idea, Billy. A nap is just what you need." She must have agreed a little too readily for, somewhat unsteadily, he lumbered to his feet to stand peering down into her pointed and sunburned features.

"Say, why you so all-fired keen fer me to snooze? I'll bet yer figgerin' on runnin' away. Wal, ye cain't fool me!" His big hand shot out to close, trap-like, over her slender wrist. "Buck and Rufe shore would skin me alive iffen they find you gone when they gits back. Come along."

Despite her tearful entreaties and pitifully ineffective struggles, he employed a thong first to lash Tina's hands behind her, and then to tether her to a young pin oak. All the same she kept her head and strained to keep her wrists as far apart as possible while he was tying the knot.

"Please, Billy, I will be good," she quavered. "I won't run off."

"Not now, you won't." He stared stupidly at his handiwork. "Yes, sir. Yer gonna stay right there but yer rigged so's ye can set down iffen yer so minded."

Bare shoulders shining bronze-yellow in the hot sunlight, he swayed over into a patch of shade cast by the shack and tumbled onto the trampled earth to fall sound asleep. Presently his mouth sagged open. Bluebottle flies crawled freely in and out of it, while a smaller, black variety unmercifully bit and stung the helpless girl.

Billy had been in error, her lead thong was just too short to permit her sitting down. What did he intend when he roused? He didn't seem either cruel or vicious for a riverman; just stupid and suspicious. Fervently she implored Divine assistance in order to banish a sense of panic that continued rat-like to gnaw at her peace of mind.

"You must escape, Christina Reigler, you must! There is no telling what that young savage will think of if he goes on drinking." Meanwhile she flexed her wrists in all directions until the thongs nipped so hard that she had to pause.

Because the wind had died out the afternoon's heat grew so intense that, presently, trickles of perspiration commenced to slip down her arms and over the tender area along her side which had been scorched aboard the *Silver Wing*.

Was she actually creating a little play in the thongs? It seemed so. She blew desperately to drive those pestiferous flies from her face and continued to work and twist her wrists.

Granted just a little more opportunity, she felt sure she'd soon be able to slip a hand from under the encircling leather but probably at the cost of some skin. Sundown was not far off and Billy still lay snoring when Snapper, who had been off hunting in the bottoms, came trotting serenely back into the clearing.

The hound's moist brown nose sniffed at her knees, then he wandered over to his recumbent master. The youth must have splashed rabbit gravy or something equally desirable on his bare feet for the ribby little hound commenced to lick eagerly at them. Presently Billy shifted, curled his toes from the tickling.

"Snapper! Come here," she pleaded in a soft voice. "For Heaven's sake, please stop that. Here, Snapper, here!"

It proved sheer agony to watch her tormentor display unmistakable indications of waking, when she needed only another five minutes. The dog paid her frantic commands not the least attention.

Billy awoke to the continued tickling, reared upon an elbow. "Git! You tarnation pest!" He flung a stick at the dog, then yawned cavernously and foolishly grinned at his disheveled and despairing captive.

"Wal, that forty-rod shore do pack a wallop like the kick of a blue-nose mule." Accelerating Tina's rising fears, the first thing he did was to take a long drink from the jug; then he belched and came over to view her from red and owlish eyes. He was still drunk, but apparently no less amiable than before.

Billy giggled, scratched at his mop of tow-yellow hair.

"Come to think on it I never have seen a female critter close to," he remarked to Snapper, now busily crimping at a flea. "Leastways not by daylight."

"And you are not going to now, Billy Yeager. Don't you dare touch me!"

Though she flinched away to the end of her tether, he nevertheless undid buttons securing the front of her calico gown, hooked a rough finger inside and tested her bud-like nipples.

"Aw, stand still. I wun't hurt ye."

"God will punish you!" she choked, her throat closing from terror. "Let me be. Oh, please, be good. Let me alone."

"Don't take on so," he snickered. "Iffen you rile me I'll have to give you a good hiding. My, ain't you got softest skin! Just like a winter marten's pelt."

At the sudden wickedness in his expression she reeled backwards, wailing, and tearing frantically at her bonds.

"Le's see how them burns o' yourn is comin' along," he panted and, using both hands, pulled up her skirt. She commenced to scream.

At once he clamped a hand over her mouth.

"Let one more yip out o' you," he growled amid a fog of whiskey fumes, "and I'll shorely peel you jay nekkid. I tell ye I jest want to look careful at a female critter," and he yanked down the fragile cloth concealing her above the waist.

"G-gimme a kiss, Teenie." His freckled face and sun-cracked lips swooped down. Tina screamed again, then lurching aside, she felt the thongs suddenly give way. She leaped back so swiftly, so unexpectedly, that Billy, already unsteady, sprawled onto the trampled loam.

As if to atone for his previous ill deed, the dog romped up, yapping delightedly to join this horseplay and, for a priceless instant, got between the boy's legs and so delayed his rising that Tina was able to snatch up a stick of firewood. This she brought down with all her strength upon the back of that hateful, yellow-brown head.

Afterwards she recalled the queer, strangled grunt Billy emitted before he flopped back, face down onto the ground.

Pursued by the still-frolicking dog, Tina raced southwards along the shore, half expecting to hear Billy start in pursuit. How she ran! She kept driving her legs along until her breath came in like some scalding vapor.

A stitch in her side forced her to slow down after a little and lent opportunity for her first backwards view. Miraculously, no one was visible on that shoreline arching back towards the hollow. The only creature in sight was Snapper disconsolately trotting back towards the shack.

Sweat-drenched, trembling and exhausted, Tina sank onto a driftwood log and fought for breath while pulling up her dress into a decent state. Luckily, its buttonholes were large and thus had permitted the crude horn buttons to slip through instead of being ripped off.

Twilight was robing the Mississippi with a silver-blue mist, and long lines of raucous-voiced herons were flapping on their way to roost when Tina timidly neared a log earthenwork revetted by fascines of willow and alder. A party of soldiers left their cook pots and grabbed up muskets when her bare foot snapped a little branch.

"Halt! Who goes there?" challenged a tall young fellow wearing three scarlet chevrons on each sleeve.

Around the fires more soldiers—they turned out to be artillerists—jumped up and came running past stacks of shovels, picks and other entrenching tools.

"Please, sir. Don't shoot—I—I'm only a girl." Tina saw a dozen muskets aimed at the thicket in which she stood.

"You alone?" came the sharp query.

"Y-yes, sir."

"Then come out of there slowly," directed the tall young sergeant. "Anybody else'll get shot."

"Heyo, Sis," bellowed a big fellow wearing gray red-striped pants and a checkered black and white shirt. "Got any pies to sell?"

Everybody laughed at the ridiculousness of all those rifles trained on such a small, slim and pathetic figure.

"No, please. Please, I am in such trouble. Won't you help me?"

A tall, heavily mustached individual wearing a black slouch hat and a gray blouse set off by a scarlet collar came striding up from the center of the battery. Silvered spurs fastened to a pair of handsomely cut riding boots tinkled gently.

He peered through the dusk, motioned carelessly towards his hat brim.

"And who might you be, Ma'am?"

"I am Christina Reigler from—from—" again she almost said "Baltimore," but in time altered it to "from Washington. I am a survivor of the *Silver Wing* disaster!"

The new arrival, apparently an officer, came striding over the sand. "Welcome to Battery Sixteen, Ma'am. I am Lieutenant Robert MacQuarrie, Third Alabama Field Artillery, and at your service. What's wrong?"

In a dead faint, Christina Reigler had collapsed to lie like a small bundle of rags amid the light of the ruddy cook fires.

XI

Balcony in New Orleans

Now THAT NORTH Carolina and Arkansas had voted and adopted ordinances of Secession, albeit a trifle belatedly, the patriotic ladies of New Orleans were puzzled about how to add two more stars to various existing flags. Some odd variations of the Stars and Bars resulted, and everyone yearned for the arrival of that happy day when Maryland, Kentucky and Tennessee would join their revolted sisters and so justify use of the historic number thirteen.

To Lieutenant Samuel Seymour, somber of mien in these days and much given to taking long and solitary walks, it appeared touching that in every possible manner the new Government should cherish and imitate traditions reminiscent of the founding of the United States.

The Confederate Constitutional Convention had adopted in toto the original Federal Constitution with only one change, and that for the better. President Jefferson Davis was enabled to veto in detail objectionable sections of an otherwise acceptable bill, while endorsing the measure as a whole.

Drums nowadays were rattling louder and more frequently than ever along New Orleans' narrow, ill-ventilated streets, for, in almost every one of the city's faubourgs, various companies, troops and batteries could be viewed at drill. Private regiments by the dozens were being recruited—regiments which, alas, named on their rolls frequently less than a hundred men but provided color-loving Creoles with a valid excuse to adopt uniforms calculated to outshine all rivals.

The armies of His Imperial Majesty Napoleon the Third furnished such military tailors as M. S. Hedrick and M. Bouligny with satisfactory prototypes and soon to be seen on the streets were chasseurs, Zouaves, dragoons, spahis, hussars, and even lancers, although to what use lancers could be put amid the tangled forests and rough terrain of North America no one seemed quite able to explain.

Moodily, Sam Seymour lingered outside his bedroom upon a balcony of intricate iron grillework over which bougainvillea had draped itself, ever so gracefully. At this twilit hour before her night life really began, New Orleans seemed to be catching her breath.

His interest rose on discovering that, from this point of vantage, he could just discern the *Sumter's* topmasts. Um. Yonder trim little cruiser should, within a week's time, be ready for commissioning. But would she? Had so many delays ever before attended the completion of a man-of-war? Sam doubted it, chewed angrily on his seegar.

This big and noisy city, to his jaundiced eye, appeared to celebrate a perpetual succession of holidays. The Creoles especially possessed an inexhaustible capacity for amusing themselves in more or less dramatic fashion. Band concerts were offered every night, while the bars of all hotels, especially those of the Royale, the City and the celebrated St. Charles, were always jam-packed. In every square self-appointed orators spouted fire, brimstone and patriotism at anyone who was foolish enough to halt even for a moment.

Thanks to loosely cut linen pantaloons and the thinness of a ruffled cambric shirt, Sam was feeling cool and comfortable for the first time since sunup as he contemplated once more a letter received that day.

His brother's firm script informed him briefly that Reynolds, their scapegrace young brother, apparently owned and was selling shares in a privateer fitting out in Savannah. He wished Irad and Sam to see whether the services of some ex-naval officers might not be secured in that connection.

Where Reynolds has come across sufficient money to buy shares in so costly a venture, I have no idea but I do not intend to co-operate and imagine you also will refuse. Pa always has said that the principle of privateering interferes with a regular naval establishment. Do you not agree?

My immediate duties are to examine the remains of the *Merrimac* which soon is to be raised. To me her hull appears to be sound but her engines, by all reports, were far from satisfactory even before she was scuttled and burned. I doubt whether they have benefited through these long weeks under water.

Chief Constructor John L. Porter and Lieutenant John M. Brooke are hard at work planning radical changes both as to her armament and structure. From this sixteenth day of May I will have the honor of collaborating with these gentlemen.

Sam's lip crept in between his teeth. Always a sense of bitter shame stung him whenever Irad or Sylvia entered his thoughts. Another significant item imparted by Irad was that Sylvia was with child at long last! Despairingly Sam clung to the possibility that this baby might indeed be Irad's, but it was a tenuous hold. After all, had not Irad and Sylvia lived as man and wife without issue for nearly three and a half years?

He lingered on the balcony, staring with unseeing eyes at the sunset, his fingers tight on the settee's iron arms. How was Sylvia reacting to this knowledge now that the worst possible consequence of their folly had been realized?

Since that awful, soul-shattering morning in Baltimore, he had prayed on his knees for Divine forgiveness and understanding a full hour each morning and evening and whenever a service was held he attended the Lafayette Presbyterian Church.

Perhaps, by consequence, his sense of guilt had become somewhat less overpowering until receipt of Irad's letter. Surely an all-wise God could weigh the difference between an impulsive, unpremeditated outbreak of lust and a deliberately planned seduction?

"Oh, God," he groaned, softly. "So Robbie is to have a bastard for his half brother."

Again Sam deliberated seeking out his brother and making a complete confession in order that Irad might shoot him down as he deserved. He brooded so often that his fellow officers aboard the Sumter noticed and wondered, and nicknamed him "Silent Sam."

Two days later, however, Captain Semmes and the wardroom noticed an abrupt change for the better in Sam's demeanor. What brought this about was the arrival of a second missive from Norfolk; this time from Sylvia. She wrote that she and Irad were much concerned over his health. Wasn't New Orleans supposed to be a pestilential place aside from being a very sink of iniquity?

That she was going to bear Irad's child rendered her very proud and happy. Twice she had underlined her husband's name. Mercy, they had just about abandoned hope of having issue.

The writer then went on to dwell on family matters, of exciting days following the burning and surrender of Gosport Navy Yard. There was considerable rebuilding being done and Irad worked all hours designing an ironclad warship for the Confederate Navy which was in the process of being created.

Sam was not to worry over his son because Robbie was thriving; everyone thought him at least a year older than he really was. Every day the boy was learning new words and now chattered like a magpie. She remained his affectionate sister-in-law.

Written in pencil was a postscript which burned itself into Sam's mind as if written in fire.

> My child will be Irad's. It could
> not be otherwise. I KNOW!

This reassuring and emphatic intelligence lifted much weight from Sam's conscience; but still he did not cease to reproach himself for abysmal treachery towards those who had cared so tenderly for his motherless son.

On another evening Sam went out to lean over the railing of his little balcony, ignoring the few early mosquitoes abroad; later they were to become an intolerable pest, forcing him to anoint himself with lemon oil before resuming regular evening study of that dull Dutchman, Grotius' "Laws of War and Peace."

How pleasant it was to stand here fanned by a breeze and watching hundreds of lights wink into existence. Below pianofortes tinkled and violins commenced to sob out a waltz in Monsieur Pierre's popular café, located a bare half block down St. Charles Street.

As usual he ended his visit to the balcony by studying the distant Mississippi flowing violet-red in the sunset. It was mighty stimulating to reflect that, any day now, the Confederacy's first ocean-going man-of-war would be placed in commission.

To be sure the Privateering Act, published on April seventeenth, had sent some hastily manned, ill-adapted and badly armed privateers to sea. Such vessels as the *Savannah*, the *Lady Davis* and the *Gordon* were indeed to make some brilliant captures, yet their careers would soon end.

Far better than most of his associates he was aware of the heavy handicaps under which the *Sumter* must operate. Imagine being forced to close action with so powerful a steam frigate as the *Brooklyn*, the *Minnesota* or the *Wabash*, or any of a dozen others! He was too much of a realist to dream that anything but the Sumter's complete annihilation would result.

Along with a majority of his fellow officers, he agreed with Commander Josiah Tattnall's tenet that it was futile for the South to engage in a shipbuilding race against the numerous and well-equipped shipyards of New York and New England. Furthermore, everyone, except a few old die-hards, was aware that the age-old usefulness of wooden warships was ending. Construction of the Warrior by Her Britannic Majesty's Admiralty and of the French Emperor's equally powerful La Gloire—first of all armored ships—was pointing the way.

If a single ironclad of comparable construction were sent to sea flying the Confederate flag, she could send the lovely wooden frigates and sloops of the Northern Navy plunging down forever to rest among the cod and barracuda.

An exciting business, this, of participating in the birth of a navy which someday would rank with the world's foremost. Although the Sumter, mounting as she did a total of but nine guns, represented but a pitiful first effort, still her commissioning remained significant in that a Confederate man-of-war soon would be flaunting the Stars and Bars over the high seas.

No wonder that Raphael Semmes, who suggested a Rive Gauche poet or a latter-day prophet rather than a hard-bitten naval officer, fumed and fretted over the endless delays.

Of late, Sam Seymour had taken to spending his over-long midday meal period in the company of a likeable and highly intelligent young Scot. The fellow was a veritable bundle of energy and as full of engineering innovations as a round shot of iron.

This civilian dockyard employee could, and with any encouragement would, draw clever sketches of extraordinary engines, steering gears and—what principally interested Sam—pivot gun mountings.

Mr. Brunton discussed a ram under present construction at Henderson's Yard which he described as a low-lying, enormously powerful seegar-shaped vessel. She mounted but a single cannon to be fired through a Cyclopean gunport mounted forward, yet she was being so cleverly designed, and with so massive an iron beak, that inevitably she could stave in the toughest warship afloat.

Sam grew fond of the diminutive Scot, appreciating his realistic approach to problems at hand with the Sumter. Despite repeated rebuffs from Naval Commissioners Rousseau and Farrand, Brunton respected their gray beards, energy and patriotic purposes.

Sam exploded a blood-gorged mosquito on his cheek, heaved a reluctant sigh, then went indoors to turn up a kerosene lamp by which to refurbish his knowledge of the Spanish language and international law. Spanish quickly returned to him because he recalled readily Mrs. Mallory's liquid Castilian accents from boyhood days in Pensacola.

Perhaps more far-sighted than his fellow officers, Sam reckoned that a knowledge of these subjects might prove of inestimable value aboard a Confederate man-of-war.

XII

FINISHING TOUCHES

BY THE TWENTY-FIRST of May, 1861, an experienced observer could anticipate the cruiser's finished appearance. Barkentine-rigged with tall masts raking sharply aft, the *Sumter* further mounted Brunton's collapsible smokestack just forward of her mainmast. Shorn of cabins and upper works, the *Sumter's* silhouette lay low to the water, a very great advantage in a commerce destroyer.

His command, proudly thought Commander Raphael Semmes, already had assumed the aspect of a genuine naval vessel with black hull satisfactorily sleek and shrouds shiny from fresh tarring. Once the carpenters had largely completed their toil, he ordered the cruiser's crew aboard. Alas, few of these were men he had hand-picked nearly six weeks earlier when, fatuously, he had dreamed of getting the *Sumter* to sea by the middle of May; too many fine but impatient seamen had departed for the Army or had shipped aboard some neutral merchantman.

Consequently, at the cruiser's first muster, one recognized British, Scandinavian and German accents, for all that a majority of Semmes' ninety-odd men remained American, including certain Northerners who cared not a whit what flag they served so long as good food and prize money lay in prospect.

Every day visitors of all sorts, all ages and of both sexes, thronged John Hughes' shipyard, among them businessmen speculating upon the new cruiser's ability to destroy Union commerce. Also came politicians bent on foreseeing personal advantages to be derived from a knowledge of the ship's capabilities.

One afternoon Lachlan had worked later than usual, the adjustment of a lignum vitae propeller-shaft bearing having displeased him. By the time he reached the deck the yard proved all but deserted save for some Negroes throwing dice between a stack of pitch barrels and a pile of cannon awaiting their carriages.

Coat over arm, Brunton started down the gangplank. One of the sentries drawled, "They's been someone waitin' to see you." He leered a little. "A gal. Been here near' four hours."

"For God's sake why didn't you send word?"

"She wouldn't lemme," grunted the sentry. "Said you wasn't to be taken from your work."

Puzzled, Lachlan strode along the dock until he suddenly halted at the sight of a small, straight figure standing solitary beside the new cruiser's cutter. Being Scottish, Brunton neither called out nor ran, only quickened his pace until he came up to Christina Reigler and so could put arms about her slim body.

"Be kind, Lachlan," she pleaded softly. "Don't be angry. I had to come to you."

"Angry? Oh, Tina, Tina, my heart!" Succumbing to a rare impulsiveness he kissed her so hard on the lips that her blue eyes closed and, regardless of the grinning sentry, her slender arms crept up about his neck. She clung tight for a long while.

At length he was able to ask, "And where have ye yet been these past six weeks? 'Tis near dementit I've been."

"I was on the *Silver Wing*."

His small blue eyes grew very round amid the scarlet plane of his features. "So that's where ye came by yon burn?"

Tina flushed to the roots of her neat, silver-blond braids.

"Yes. Is—is it so very unsightly?"

"God bless ye, no, lass! But luckily I never dreamed you might have been aboard that ill-starred craft. I—why, I'd have gone mad!"

He slipped an arm about her waist. "Let's be finding some supper and tomorrow we'll see about getting married. A double room is no' so dear as two single ones."

XIII

ARRANGEMENTS

GENTLY BUT FIRMLY Christina Reigler refused to be married until she had obtained employment, which she did with Mr. Zogbaum, a German baker whose son had departed as a volunteer for the Washington Artillery.

"We are poor, Lachlan," she explained smilingly, "and so cannot afford to be idle—either of us."

During the week preceding their marriage, they tramped far and wide searching minimum quarters in which to set up housekeeping. One evening, during their still-futile search, she said, "We must keep on looking. It is worth while because you are an Englishman and so cannot be conscripted to fight in this senseless war."

Lachlan's auburn side whiskers fairly bristled. "Good God, lass! Never call a Scot an Englishman! But ye're right, we must search until we find exactly the house which suits our needs. Ye see, I have decided that New Orleans is where I will settle, where you will bring up our children. Of course," his voice deepened and he looked hard at this grave, pale girl across the table, "some day I will build us a fine big house that will be the envy of everyone."

Her China-blue eyes steadily returned his gaze. "And why, Lachlan, are you so sure that New Orleans is to be our home?"

"Think on it a bit, lass," he invited. "Where else in this great, rich country are foreigners so well respected? Not in Boston, New York or even in Baltimore. Look about ye. Here in New Orleans Frenchmen, Spaniards, Germans and Italians, even British"—he grinned—"are considered to be as good as the next man."

"Yes, that is so. Besides, most people here do not understand the

real meaning of work. We do, you and I." Beneath a red and white
table cloth on a table of Vonderbanck's Restaurant on Common
Street, her hand groped for and closed on his. "Then you have formed
plans—business plans?"

"Yes. No matter which way this war ends," Brunton lowered his
voice, "New Orleans cannot escape being a principal port of America.
One day seagoing vessels will be constructed here, they must be, and
I will be among the first to build them. All that is built now are
mere coasters and little river steamboats." He winked gravely. "Because of that, this war will drive existing yards out of business. Already
I've an eye on a fine big yard over in Algiers which will go bankrupt
before this year is out: also, I have made some few influential
friends.

"Maybe I can land a war contract. There are many here who are
disgusted with the Confederate Navy Department." Elbows on table,
he talked faster, more seriously. "Can you imagine it? The Confederate Navy contracts for so many million feet of lumber and so
much hardware, but Governor Moore o' this State orders such supplies
diverted to complete his State-built men-of-war. On top of all this
argy-bargy, private shipping contractors are defrauding and defying
both authorities for their ain profit."

Tina leaned closer over the table, her pale hair for once more
golden than silver beneath the gaslights.

"You said, Lachlan, that you have your eye on a shipyard?"

"Aye, Miss Nosey." He grinned. "But I'll not say more till the
deal is closed—if ever it is." He sat back. "And now, Miss Reigler,
ye'll have bought a dress for our wedding? Was ten dollars enough
for it?"

Tina flushed, glanced aside. "You were much too generous, Lachlan.
I did very well with seven dollars; the extra three I have put aside."

"Tish, tush! We'll be getting married but this once."

Before they had done talking Vonderbanck's Restaurant became
filled, emptied itself and then filled once more. There entered an
amazing variety of resplendent uniforms and ladies of pleasure
scarcely less brilliantly garbed than their escorts.

"I would like for us to marry in the Lutheran Church," Tina
announced as they prepared to depart. "I am told the Reverend
Predikant will be satisfied with a fee of two dollars."

Brunton stiffened, lost his carefree look. "May I remind you, Christina, that *I* am a Presbyterian? The Reverend Mr. MacNaughton of the Lafayette Church has already been bespoken by me for the ceremony."

Tina was on the verge of protest, but she recalled Mamma's warning that, in matters of first importance, the husband's decision must be respected.

"Very well, Lachlan," said she demurely. "If you wish. Have you found witnesses?"

"Aye. The *Sumter's* First Prize Mate is a fellow Presbyter. A sober, serious fellow who will appreciate the solemnity o' the occasion."

XIV

Léon Duchesne Provides

THAT BRUNTON, THE plain, hard-working Scottish engineer should have asked him of all people to witness his wedding had surprised and pleased Lieutenant Samuel Seymour.

So, on a sunny Thursday in late May, he repaired to a flower shop in search of a bridal bouquet. Momentarily he was distracted by a clatter of steel-shod hoofs and noted that a colored footman was with difficulty restraining a pair of sleek black carriage horses harnessed to a smart yellow and black town carriage. From it sprang Léon Duchesne.

"Ohé! Sam!"

Looking mighty handsome in the dazzling light blue uniform prescribed for the Louisiana Navy, the Creole's spotless teeth glinted in his dark and facile features. "And whither, my old friend, are you bound? Is that so-beautiful bouquet destined for the eye of some lovely quadroon of Rampart Street?"

"Nothing so romantic," Sam chuckled. "It's only that a civilian engineer at our dockyard is about to be married. He is Scotch and his bride, I gather, is from away, so they don't know a soul in town. I'm on my way up to help get them spliced."

"*Nom de Dieu!* Just poor little strangers in wicked old New Orleans, eh? This touches my heart. Ohé, Maman Zélé, tell Georges to load all your flowers into my carriage. We must encourage the bride."

"*Oui, M'sieu Léon, tout de suite!*" The old mulattress bobbed a curtsy, then her yellow *tignon* flashed as, hastily, she employed strands of raffia to bind a stock of roses and lilies into great glowing sheaves.

"And now," Léon announced, once he had pushed Sam into the carriage, "we shall find this bride an attendant." He snapped his fingers. "*Bigre!* I have it! We will call on my cousin Louise and see if she will not be amused to oblige us. One suspects that after six years in Paris, New Orleans bores her to extinction."

Although thoroughly embarrassed, Seymour could not dissuade his voluble comrade in arms and soon found himself in Conti Street gazing up at a handsome three-storied house of time-mellowed yellow brick. A moment later he was surveying the interior of a home such as he had not imagined could exist in America. Against walls of sage green, light blue and terracotta, crystal chandeliers and sconces glittered like frosty fountains in the dim light. The furniture was of the Louis XVI and Directoire periods, more delicate by far than the solid English mahogany pieces encountered around New England.

Léon vanished upstairs leaving Seymour to fret and glance anxiously at his watch. Damn Léon and his friendly bullying; that they would be late at the church was now inevitable.

Light footsteps sounded on an elaborate circular stone staircase protected by a handsome guard rail of Spanish wrought iron. Descending was a rather tall and slender-waisted young woman wearing a wide crinoline of lemon-yellow voile. Besides a reticule of yellow and black beading, she carried a long-handled, dark green silk parasol. For a moment Sam could discern nothing of her face because its features were concealed by a wide and floppy leghorn hat.

"Mademoiselle Louise Cottier!" Duchesne bowed gracefully on the staircase. "May I present Mr. Samuel Seymour of the Confederate States Navy?"

Miss Cottier paused, hand on newel post, smilingly to regard her cousin's square-shouldered friend. Sam for his part was deciding that he thought this proud young lady handsome rather than beautiful. Perhaps it was because of her rather heavy straight brows and strongly modeled features. Nonetheless he was captivated by the vivacity of her clear, amethyst-blue eyes shaded as they were by unusually long lashes. Curls, gathered into little clusters over each temple by small yellow bows, were the glossy blue-black of a grackle's wing.

"Your servant, Ma'am," he declared as Duchesne snatched up his cape.

"Shall we make our manners en route? I fear our bridal couple are waiting."

It proved a gay, hurried drive, through crowded, vividly colorful streets. Léon's flowers, roses, lilies, camellias, magnolias alike, lay in fragrant bundles upon the laps of the trio.

About Louise Cottier, Sam was discovering a pleasurable lack of affectation for when she regarded him she didn't peep up as if frightened half to death. He liked, too, the easy fashion with which she participated in the conversation.

The blacks were in a lather when Léon's footman jumped down to control them by the bridle handles. Recognizing the ingredients of romance, a vari-colored crowd had collected, for all that weddings were the order of wartime.

"*Ma foi!* Are all Protestant churches as somber as this?" breathed the Cottier girl on entering.

Sam found no time to reply, for out of the vestry strode Lachlan Brunton, perspiring heavily and looking definitely harassed.

"And where, Monsieur, shall I find your young lady?" Louise Cottier presently demanded, smiling at the Scot from under her leghorn's wide brim. "I presume she is unattended?"

Brunton indicated the vestry door. "Aye, aye, please go to her, Ma'am. She's in need of a female's comforting."

Just then Léon came running up the steps lugging a double armful of flowers and for the first time caught sight of Brunton.

"*Mon Dieu!* It cannot be! Sam, this is my rescuer at that *sacré* theatre in Baltimore." He tossed the bouquets to his breathless footman. "How quite impossible! Yet war makes so many impossibilities plausible, does it not? And your lady! Ah, how well I remember her Grecian profile and marble complexion. Oh, Sam, Louise, this is but *incrédible!*"

"Losh! I wouldna' ha' credited it," Brunton exclaimed pumping Duchesne's hand. "Sam! 'Tis him who got me my position doon here. Ye must ha' brought him a-purpose so that I'd have two friends on hand."

Léon Duchesne would entertain no demurring whatsoever about the newly wed couple's proceeding for an impromptu wedding breakfast at his residence, a pretty little Spanish-built house on a sleepy, oak-shaded square off Bourbon Street.

Tina, still dazed by the actuality of her marriage, for the first time in her life tasted champagne and commenced to enjoy Léon's gay gallantry and Miss Cottier's tactful suggestions.

Not since the catastrophic aftermath of Mr. Winans' ball had Sam Seymour drunk champagne, but he found it as fascinating as of yore.

Flushed pink and radiant with happy excitement, Tina clutched her glass and sat bolt upright on a gilded little Louis XVI chair, unconscious that her plain blue dress was singularly at harmony with its canary-yellow upholstery. *Himmel!* How could so many lovely things exist in one place? One day, she vowed to herself, that quite without envy, she and Lachlan would own such a room.

When Sam Seymour offered a plate of *petits fours* she said, shyly, "In Baltimore I once worked for a Mrs. Seymour, a very lovely lady. Is she by chance a relation?"

A tiny *ting!* drew Louise Cottier's attention to the fact that the stem of Lieutenant Seymour's glass had snapped. He said quietly, "Yes. Mrs. Seymour is my brother's wife."

"Oh." Tina's pointed features lit. "Then you must be that sweet little boy's father!"

A scarlet flush welled from under gold braid binding the collar of Sam's undress uniform. "You—you liked him?"

"Ach, yes! Robbie was so very good and how dear Mrs. Seymour adored him!"

The Cottier girl's slim fingers delicately smoothed a napkin on her knee as she laughed, "Trust Léon to forget mentioning that you are happily married, Mr. Seymour."

"Oh, no," Tina interrupted in sudden distress. "*This* Mr. Seymour is a widower."

"Indeed?" Louise Cottier turned quickly. "Your son is of what age?"

Sam drew a breath deep enough to lift his jacket's gilded buttons. "He will be three come next month. My brother and sister-in-law have cared for him since my wife died."

"Such kind people they are," Tina burst out. "You see, Miss Cottier, my—my husband and Mr. Irad Seymour worked for a time at the same shipyard." The bride blushed to the roots of her gleaming silver-blond tresses, smiled at Sam. "Please would you tell them about Mr. Brunton and me?"

While driving his cousin back to her home, Léon Duchesne forgot all about the bridal couple to hold forth on the *Manassas*, that strange new ram being built by private parties.

"Imagine," he cried, tooling his buggy about a dog lying asleep in the street, "this wonderful craft lies so low in the water that ordinary ships cannot hit her, and if they should, why, her back is turtle-shaped and so cannon balls will glance harmlessly aside. Further, she will be fitted with an iron beak and is to carry a single great gun."

He shot a sidewise glance at those serenely lovely features half concealed beneath the leghorn.

"*Misérable fille*, you do not listen to me."

"*Enfin*, my dear Léon, I own little interest in these engines with which you men so cleverly assassinate one another." She tilted her parasol to cut off the sunlight. "This Navy friend of yours? Were you aware he is a widower and has a little son?"

"But yes. What of that?"

Louise settled back after gracefully acknowledging the salutes of several friends on the sidewalk. "Just why should Monsieur Seymour snap the stem of a wine glass when his sister-in-law suddenly was mentioned?"

"Because he must be in love with her," Léon laughed. "Sylvia Seymour is most attractive." He twirled a bayonet-like mustache.

"I do not think he is in love, *mon cher*," the dark-haired girl observed over the cob's brittle-sounding hoof beats. "Again, if he is a Virginian, why does he not talk like one? *Mon Dieu!* I find him more like a Yankee."

"You had better not tell him so if you wish to see him again."

"And who says that I do, *mon cher cousin*?" laughed the Cottier girl.

"I do!" laughed Léon Duchesne, deftly guiding his buggy into myrtle-shaded Villière Street. "One is not so entirely absorbed with men-of-war as all that."

"Va-t'en, imbécile!" she cried and stuck out her tongue, small-girl fashion.

XV

Aide-toi et Dieu t'Aidera

THE NEW ORLÉANNAIS arose on the morning of June the third, 1861, in a state of ill-subdued excitement because today they would witness the commissioning of their Confederacy's first ocean-going man-of-war.

Such newspapers as the *Memphis Avalanche* and the *Galveston Civilian*, not to mention the local journals, had waxed so lyrical over the event that from surrounding plantations and villages crowds arrived by carriage, steamboat and rail. Everyone was keen to hear the patriotic address His Excellency Governor Moore would deliver following those of His Honor Mayor Monroe and Commander Rousseau, venerable Commissioner from the Richmond Navy Department.

Morning dawned disclosing, alas, an ominous gray bank lying in the southwest and it was still as frightfully hot as it had been all week. Armorers mounting the new cruiser's guns had had a miserable time. All the same, huge crowds made their way towards the waterfront.

The *Sumter* lay trim and neat as a yacht alongside Hughes & Company's construction dock. Her crew, through having come aboard several days earlier, evidently knew their way about and had got the feel of this smart little barkentine. The severest martinet of the Old Navy could justifiably have found nothing to criticize in the spotlessness of the *Sumter's* decks, the lustre of her brightwork nor in the smart bracing of her yards.

For this grand occasion the new cruiser's officers appeared for the first time wearing double-breasted, long-skirted coats of field gray over dark blue-striped gray trousers. A general atmosphere of high good humor became tempered by solemnity whenever Commander Semmes appeared. In the Captain's deep-set dark eyes, thought Lieutenant Seymour, gleamed the inspiration of a zealot dedicated to a high and holy cause.

Usually jovial Lieutenant Robert T. Chapman from Alabama for once was wearing a grave look while ranging himself beside his captain on the quarterdeck. Next to him stood Lieutenant J. M. Kell who was of medium height and seemed older than he was because of a few gray streaks in his brown hair, whiskers and mustaches. When he spoke it was with a flat and unmistakable Georgian accent.

John M. Stribling, Third Lieutenant, was probably the handsomest officer aboard, if it were not his fellow South Carolinian, Lieutenant William E. Evans. Only twenty-four years of age and very slim, young Evans was further distinguished by having a brother on duty as a major general in the South Carolina State Army.

Among the officers assembling amidst black and yellow shadow-patterns created in the rigging by the sun now forcing its way through the clouds stood Lieutenant Samuel Seymour, assigned to the anomalous duties of First Prize Master. How grand it was once more to tread a quarterdeck and feel the familiar tug of a dress sword at his belt. For the tenth time he inspected the cleanliness of his white kid gloves and exulted that, among hundreds applying, he should have found a post on this handsome little cruiser.

A Marine's bugle sounded a staccato warning that sent the crew, bravely clad in dark blue trousers, white shirts and pale blue scarfs, running to form up in the waist. A buzz of excitement arose from a huge crowd gathered on the quayside when bayonets glittered as the Marines presented arms in honor of Naval Commissioner Rousseau. The old hero's hair and beard shone frostily in the sunlight as he came striding up the Sumter's gangway bearing a long scroll secured with a gray, gold-edged ribbon.

While the bosun's silver pipe trilled and warbled, the cruiser's Executive Officer called all hands to attention. At the head of the gangway Commanders Rousseau and Farrand saluted the quarterdeck, then briskly the Commissioners advanced towards the foot of the mainmast. Awaiting them there stood Commander Semmes, his officers, Mr. Hughes and his partner in the shipbuilding business.

Once Semmes and the Commissioners had exchanged salutes, Commander Rousseau formally accepted the *Sumter* into naval service from the civilians who had rebuilt and armed her. From beneath his arm Commander Rousseau removed the cruiser's commission and solemnly gave it into her captain's hand.

A silence born of intense solemnity vaulted the man-of-war's rail and spread to the onlookers ranged alongside and crowding the rigging of near-by vessels. Everyone could hear Raphael Semmes read the Navy Department's order of commission in a penetrating and most impressive voice.

When he had concluded, a long red, white and blue commission pennant was hoisted to spiral lazily at the main top, Lieutenant Kell stepped forward bearing a neat compact parcel upon a black velvet cushion. No one on board had to be told that this was that ensign upon which ladies of New Orleans so long had been stitching.

At a curt command from Commander Semmes, the quartermaster saluted, accepted and bent the colors to a halyard. Then, while the music of the First Louisiana Zouaves played the "*Marseillaise*," field pieces boomed and the Stars and Bars soared smoothly to the signal gaff where, unfurling, it undulated gracefully to a gentle breeze beating up the mighty Mississippi.

Speeches followed, so charged with high spirit, self-confidence and defiance, that tears came to many eyes. Mayor Monroe touched the oratorical heights in picturing the *Sumter* as a gallant knight about to defend the fair city of New Orleans from a swarm of Abe Lincoln's licentious hirelings.

Later, in the privacy of his cabin Commander Semmes felt so moved that he wrote:

> And is he gone?—on sudden solitude
> How oft that fearful question will intrude!
> 'Twas but an instant past—and here he stood!
> And now!—without the portal's porch she rushed,
> And then at length her tears in freedom gushed;
> Big, bright, and fast, unknown to her they fell;
> But still her lips refused to send "farewell"!
> For in that word—that fatal word—howe'er
> We promise—hope—believe—there breathes despair.

When he had done, Semmes knelt and prayed, fiercely, like a prophet of the Old Testament for strength and wisdom with which to smite shrewdly the satanic minions of the Northern tyrants—in a courtly, honorable fashion, of course.

That evening the *Sumter's* officers were enjoying more-than-lavish hospitality and acclaim at Mayor Monroe's reception. Here the finest of vintages of France and Spain splashed freely into gleaming glasses and the refreshments were something to remember.

"Such confidences as were heard expressed this morning, I find sublime. Surely such spirit can never be daunted." Thus Mr. W. H. Russell, correspondent of the august London *Times* to Lieutenant Seymour.

"Enthusiasm undoubtedly has its uses," Seymour replied, nibbling at a *callas*—a doughnut of pecans. "However, I'd a damned sight rather see the money squandered on this affair devoted to the purchase of arms and ammunition."

The Englishman raised a white-kid-gloved hand to stroke very long and pale yellow side whiskers.

"Indeed, Mr. Seymour? Then you do not subscribe to the theory that one Southerner can whip five Yankees?"

The stare to which Seymour treated him brought color to Mr. Russell's lean, bright red features. Quickly he muttered, "I apologize, sir. During my visits to Charleston, Savannah and Mobile, I well— have heard so many, too many such boasts."

He accepted a glass of sherry offered by a liveried black footman. "I wonder, sir, whether you have any idea of the absurd misconceptions entertained by certain presumably well-educated Southerners?"

"As a neutral observer, Mr. Russell, what do you find to be our most grievous error?"

Although they occupied an obscure corner of Mr. Monroe's library, Russell glanced through the tall French doors, then quizzically considered this broad-shouldered young officer in the unfamiliar gray naval uniform.

"Do you prefer a frank, if unpleasant, answer or a tactful evasion?"

"I have made sufficient cruises in foreign waters, sir, to prefer an honest reply."

"Very well. I presume that you have read your President's recently

voiced opinion to the effect that the Confederacy needs no navy
because, within sixty days, the Federal Navy must find itself exchanging broadsides with British men-of-war fighting for the South?"

"I have." Sam frowned into his julep cup.

Mr. Russell delicately inhaled from a freshly lighted seegar. "You
appear to entertain some doubts as to the validity of that theorem?"

"I voice no doubts, sir, but I value your opinion."

"Since I have learned, to my sorrow, that every syllable I utter here
in the South too often is construed as British policy, I must secure
your promise not to repeat what I shall say."

"It is yours, sir."

"I am truly sympathetic with your Southern attempt to win
independence, Mr. Seymour; perhaps only because we British entertain a penchant for the underdog." Russell leaned forward and
lowered his voice. "Before long, the British Crown must decide
whether it prefers to have cotton, that staple which means bread for
a large part of its subjects or—"

"—What could outweigh such a consideration?" Sam interrupted
without shifting his gaze from the Englishman's long and impassive
features.

Russell answered quietly but impressively. "—The enslavement of
five million Negroes, Mr. Seymour. We can never forget that here in
your Southland five million human souls are being held in involuntary
servitude."

In the ensuing silence the music and the light laughter of many
ladies which penetrated the library's cool dimness sounded, somehow,
frivolous.

"Do you imagine that our desire, nay, need for cotton, will outweigh our detestation of slavery and all of its hideous and immoral
aspects?"

"It will," Sam replied slowly, "if it is true that the United Kingdom
is, as we are informed, ruled by merchants and the upper classes.
Surely our Confederacy will be recognized."

Mr. Russell combed his long side whiskers and smiled faintly.

"May I invite you to recall, my dear sir, that, at a cost of twenty
millions of pounds, slavery was abolished throughout the United
Kingdom and its possessions in 1833? And by the French in 1848?"

Seymour's white-kid-covered hands tightened.

"Are you sure slavery is abhorred to that extent? You must have seen that with a few exceptions our slaves are well and kindly treated."

"True, but most Europeans won't believe so; least of all the British public. No, Mr. Seymour, I very much doubt that England will ever ally herself with your Confederacy."

The newspaperman dropped his seegar into a tall cuspidor and looked towards the door. "Pray don't look so put-out and recall that you asked me the question. What do you say, shall we seek a cup of His Honor's claret punch?"

Sam's first impulse was to follow the correspondent out of the library, but instead he wandered out onto a balcony opening invitingly to his left.

It was cooler outside; besides he could watch the reception through open French doors, a brilliant spectacle, thanks to its bewildering variety of uniforms, banks of flowers and evening gowns even more splendid than any to be seen about Baltimore or New York.

How soon might the *Sumter* go to sea? Several days must elapse since the new cruiser had yet to conduct trial runs and charge her magazines and bunkers. Again, her raw gun crews must undergo further training and learn not only to load, point and fire, but also to pass powder boxes and serve her two small boat howitzers.

The *Sumter's* men had best learn their gunnery for, since the twenty-sixth of May, two and sometimes three, powerful Union mem-of-war had begun to cruise on blockade off the Delta some forty miles below New Orleans. It was reported that the U.S.S. *Brooklyn* was patrolling Pass à l'Outre, while the U.S.S. *Powhatan* was watching both the Southwest and Grand Pass exits. Sam knew from intimate knowledge of the Old Navy that the guns of either could easily sink the little *Sumter* ere her cruise had even begun.

Light issuing from the library momentarily became obscured by the passage of a couple entering the next balcony to his. Quickly he recognized the lady as Duchesne's cousin, Louise Cottier, radiant in a cerise evening gown cut daringly low, and wearing strands of seed pearls twisted through her glossy sable tresses. In easy Spanish she was conversing with her escort, a tall Spaniard darkly handsome in the somber blue and silver uniform of the Foreign Legion of New Orleans.

"*Qué calor!* At this moment," she declared, fanning gently, "I set fresh air above rubies and much fine gold."

"And your loveliness exceeds all three," fervently declared the Spaniard. "*Quién es?*"

Sam, aware that his presence had been noted, bowed and called, "Good evening, Miss Cottier."

Over the chatter of footmen and coachmen lounging in the court below he heard the Cottier girl saying, "It is chillier than I had expected, Señor Teniente, will you be good enough to fetch my scarf? It is of green silk and with silver sequins?"

"And where, Señorita, is this scarf to be sought?"

"Alas, I am not sure," the Cottier girl laughed carelessly. "Perhaps you will come across it in my carriage, or possibly I left it upon a sofa in the Honorable Monsieur Monroe's music room."

"Your wish is my command," declared the Lieutenant, then hurried off with lamplight glancing bravely from his ponderous epaulettes.

On her balcony, Louise Cottier deliberately faced about, moving her fan in graceful arcs. "Are you so difficult to please, Monsieur Seymour, that none of the ladies present can tempt you to dance?"

He hurried through the library to join her. "I would have begged a dance of you, but—but—your admirers were too many."

Her dark red lips curved slowly into a provocative smile. "If you fear odds—should you have joined our Navy?"

"There are odds—and odds. Your admirers would fight much more fiercely for you than for the Stars and Bars."

She lost a little of her light manner. "I hope not, for all that yours is a well-turned compliment. Perhaps you will dance later?"

"I would, save that I have danced very little since my wife died three years ago." Deliberately, he introduced the subject.

Her white-gloved hand crept out, came gently to rest upon the pointed loop and two gold bands indicating his grade.

"May one who is almost a stranger offer sympathy?" her rich tones softly demanded. "Your grief is written in more than your speech. Does your little boy resemble his *Maman?*"

"I am afraid not. Robbie looks deplorably like me."

Her teeth gleamed briefly in the starlight. "Of that he need not be ashamed. It appears that you view this war seriously, not like so many of my gallant but feather-headed friends."

"On the slave patrol I saw men killed," he explained. "I know something of what battle means. Besides, I know a great many Northerners."

"And how do you esteem them? Money-grubbers? Poltroons?"

"Why, the ones I've known are mostly unspectacular and slow to anger; once aroused, however, they fight bravely and, mark this well, are tenacious to the end."

"Will you fetch us some champagne?"

"But your Spanish friend?"

"That was a mere *ruse de coquette*; there was no scarf, *mon ami*, so he will be a long time finding it." Louise's laugh rippled like still water into which a stone has been cast. "Come. Fetch some champagne and then I shall wish to hear about your exploits at sea."

XVI

Pass à l'Outre

At the Head of Passes, the C.S.S. *Sumter*, reeking of new black paint, lazily swung to her anchors. Down in his cabin Commander Raphael Semmes was once more deliberating upon which of the three main exits into the Gulf of Mexico he would attempt. His answer, he was forced to admit, lay in the hands of Providence and the movements of the blockade ships *Brooklyn* and *Powhatan*.

For ten days now, his command had waited poised to make her bid for access to the high seas. Among the *Sumter's* afterguard was an officer who once had served aboard the *Brooklyn*; gloomily he informed his anxious fellows that, while proceeding from Tampico to Pensacola the year before, the *Federal* had steamed at an average of thirteen knots. No one knew for sure what the *Sumter* could do under steam alone since during her time-trials off Baton Rouge, she had either been checked or assisted by the Mississippi's swift current.

This Sunday, June the thirtieth, 1861, found the cruiser's Third Lieutenant, John M. Stribling on duty as officer of the deck and supervising the stowage of gear preparatory to the holding of Divine Services. The crew, unfeignedly grateful for a day's respite from "Old Beeswax's" eternal gun and boat drills, prepared for Sunday muster in heat so intense that, long since, ungainly gray-brown pelicans and sable cormorants had flapped off in search of shelter.

Presently, a small boat pulling over from the Pilot Station attracted Lieutenant Stribling's attention—something about the way her black oarsmen were bending their eight-foot sweeps bespoke urgency. Stribling, therefore, was at the head of the ladder to meet the caller, a gaunt and yellow-faced river pilot.

"Say, Lootenant, I just spoke the *Empire Destiny*," he panted. "Her skipper claims the *Brooklyn's* put out to sea after a blockade runner."

"He's positive?" snapped Stribling, black eyes lighting.

"As sure as God's above. Here's the chance you fellers been waitin' all week." The speaker's lantern jaw was working excitedly on his chew of tobacco.

Within five minutes the *Sumter* fairly seethed with activity as small-boat booms were swung in, crewmen dashed below, tearing off their Sunday uniforms and lugging sea bags back from inspection. Still in their Sunday best, the officers sped about their duties while from the barkentine's funnel dense columns of sooty smoke commenced to pour in volcanic fury; Engineering Officer M. J. Freeman, had orders to raise steam with all speed.

"On a still day like this so much smoke will be seen for miles," anxiously commented Lieutenant Kell. "Isn't it just our luck?"

Outwardly calm but with cavernous gray eyes snapping, Commander Semmes stood at the break of his brief quarterdeck listening to the capstan's pawls begin to click, clack, slowly at first, then faster.

Once her anchor had been broken out, the *Sumter* commenced gradually to yield to the current and swing her bowsprit downstream. The pilot demanded, "Which pass, Captain?"

"Pass à l'Outre and, as you value your life, Mr. Harrington, make no mistake."

Once he felt the deck commence to throb beneath his feet, Sam Seymour experienced a curious and unfamiliar thrill. Below the Delta lay no slaver but the United States steam frigate *Brooklyn*, swift and so heavily gunned that one well-directed broadside from her could

smash the little cruiser into a tangle of blood-streaked spars and timbers. Was this pilot's information correct? Once, previously, misin-
formation had induced the *Sumter* to waste precious coal.

The bare feet of seamen, furiously employed, *slap-slapped* about the
deck, and topmen swarmed aloft, ready at an instant's notice to set
the barkentine's canvas. The screw turned at increasing speed until the
barkentine's bow waves went curling whitely away across the placid
current.

The gun crews now began to cast off protecting tarpaulins, removing tompions from the guns and fetching powder boxes on deck. Additional shot and shell were fetched up from lockers below.

Lieutenant Seymour, Acting Gunnery Officer, superintended the
readying of that great pivot gun mounted amidships—an eight-inch
Paixhan capable of throwing shot some nineteen hundred yards. His
gaze mechanically checked the presence of the fifteen gunners serving
this princess of destruction—there should, by regulation, have been
twenty-five, but the *Sumter* was too small.

Both loaders, and all lever, springer and compression men were in
their assigned positions, but one tackle man was lacking, also a shell
man. The First Gun Captain soon located them, completing second-
ary duties; already stripped to the waist, their white torsos shone
silvery in the sunlight.

The departing man-of-war's course took her very near to the Pilot
Station, so close, indeed, that her crew cheered a pretty young girl
standing on an iron balcony there and waving a scarlet handkerchief.

"That's my woman," the pilot grinned. "She'll soon go to pray for
you."

Everyone watched Commander Semmes sweep off his cap and, as
the *Sumter* darted by, make a gallant bow in her direction. More petticoats swayed out onto Lighthouse Wharf and kerchiefs fluttered like
white butterflies above bright-colored Sunday dresses.

Mr. Harrington, the pilot, braced big feet against the horse block,
shot Semmes an anxious glance.

"You know, sir, they's a Bremen ship, sir, gone agrount half a mile
below? She's makin' ready to kedge and warp and will likely foul us
lest they slacken their hawsers in time. Mebbe ye'd better make signal?"

"I hardly think so," came the equable reply. "They will have observed our smoke."

An undertone of excitement arose from the ship's company when, on rounding a bend, they beheld the German vessel hard aground on a bar, but even as the Sumter appeared a taut line attached to her kedge commenced to slacken and to sag into an ever-deeper ellipse. When, moments later, the little cruiser thumped by her, the crew raised yells of gratitude to which the Germans answered with a ringing, "Hoch! Hoch der Sumter!"

Once he had conned the barkentine across the bar off Pass à l'Outre and the distinctive bright blue of the Mexican Gulf shimmered in the distance, the pilot departed flushed under the eloquent thanks of Commander Semmes. As Mr. Harrington set foot to the ladder he bawled up to the quarterdeck, "Now, Cap'n, you are all clear. Give them hell and let 'er go!"

The passage of only a few minutes was required before an anxious knot of officers on the C.S.S. Sumter's quarterdeck realized that, for a second time, they had been misled. The Brooklyn had not chased out of sight, but was cruising along under easy canvas perhaps four miles distant!

"Oh, God!" groaned Lieutenant Kell into his big beard. "She'll have the foot of us at by least five knots, and will you look at her stoke up?" Geysers of smoke came boiling from the Federal's squat single funnel.

Incisively Captain Semmes directed, "Heave the log, Mr. Seymour."

During the prescribed interval Sam watched the knots whirring over the stern rail, then stopped the reel and made a count. His broad brown face was sober when he called, "Eight and a half knots, sir."

Semmes' craggy features contracted. "You must be mistaken. Heave again."

When the result proved identical, expressions grew anxious among the afterguard.

To a midshipman Semmes barked, "My compliments to Mr. Freeman and will he report to the quarterdeck immediately!"

Red-faced, blackened by grease and coal dust, the Chief Engineer reported. "I'm doing my best, sir, but we suffer a drawback just now due to foaming in our boilers."

"Foaming?" rasped Commander Semmes. "What do you mean?"

"Such often occurs, sir, when steam is got up in a great hurry. When the foaming subsides we should be able to increase speed by half a knot."

"Thank you. Return to your post and coax your engines to their best efforts."

"Brooklyn's cracking on t'gallants, sir," called Lieutenant Chapman.

It proved depressing to observe the speed and precision with which the enemy frigate spread her canvas, then braced yards more sharply on to the starboard tack.

"Make all sail, Mr. Chapman," snapped Semmes. "We must gain as much headway as possible while the current still favors us."

To any but the experienced eyes of the ex-Union officers aboard, it would have appeared that the Sumter's courses, gallants and royal mizzen sheet were set and trimmed quite as expertly as those propelling the blockade ship; yet her topmen proved not quite so adept as their counterparts manning the Brooklyn.

Once the yards creaked under filling canvas and the Sumter heeled well over, Lieutenant Evans observed, "Curse it! They have a little the weather gauge of us." At the same time he glanced hopefully at a huge black rain squall rolling up from starboard.

"True enough," Seymour admitted after deliberation. "Still, we carry larger headsails and so should sail nearer the wind."

"Provided this wind holds yonder squall should overtake us in short order," Lieutenant Kell commented, nervously tugging at his whiskers. "Perhaps we can lose yonder damned big brute in it."

To everyone it became apparent that the great, high-sided Brooklyn was slowly, but perceptibly, overhauling her smaller antagonist, for all that the latter's black gang were so plying their shovels that ruddy fingers of fire came groping out of the Sumter's funnel.

Despite his mordant anxiety Sam felt fine to be at sea again, to feel the deck lift and sway, to hear the hiss!—hiss! of waves under the cutwater, the rhythmic creak of lofty spars and the soft thrumming of stays and shrouds.

All at once the Sumter seemed to gain speed, then an assistant engineer came running up to report that the foaming had ceased.

Barely had he done so when, with a whoop and a howl, the rain squall came roaring over the weather rail like an enemy boarder. In an instant such torrents of rain fell that a gray wall reduced visibility to a few yards and every man on deck was drenched. Under the wind's sudden savage assault the quartermaster and his mate were hard put to retain their grip on the wheel's handspokes. Even so the Confederate cruiser heeled dangerously far over to port.

Semmes clung to the weather rail, jet eyes fixed on the straining canvas although the barkentine listed over until a torrent of loose objects went tumbling across her rain-silvered decks. Still the wind's velocity increased, whipped lacy spindrift from the crests of rising waves. Of the *Brooklyn*, absolutely nothing was to be seen.

Lieutenant Stribling raised a streaming face and prayed aloud, "Oh, Great God, permit us to escape. We've got to teach those damned, arrogant Yankees a lesson."

As quickly as it had raced up, the rain squall howled off to leeward, magically clearing the horizon. Aboard the *Sumter* arose a concerted groan for, with the suddenness of a conjuring trick, the great, high-sided U.S.S. *Brooklyn* reappeared and undoubtedly much nearer.

Since the *Sumter* mounted no stern chasers there was nothing to be done save rely upon the slight sailing advantage afforded by her barkentine rig. Every instant the sodden group agonizing on the fugitive's quarterdeck expected to see the frigate's bow chaser let fly.

Stonily, Raphael Semmes turned to a midshipman. "My compliments to the paymaster. Direct him immediately to fetch up the public pay chest and our papers."

Presently Paymaster Henry Myers appeared carrying under his arm a canvas sack weighted with two bars of lead and heading two seamen who labored over a heavy iron chest.

Semmes, long hair whipping about his eyes, carefully studied the ship astern, then in a quivering undertone observed, "By God, Kell, we're beating her out of the wind. See, gentlemen? See! She's falling to leeward and we may yet win free. She will have to furl sail the minute she falls into our wake."

The paymaster waited breathlessly, his thick body swaying like an inverted pendulum to the cruiser's rolling.

Presently the inevitable occurred; the *Brooklyn*, unable to sail as closely into the wind as her adversary, was forced to let fly sheets and halyards, clew up and furl.

A ragged spontaneous cheer burst from the anxious men aboard the *Sumter's* decks. The *Brooklyn* began dropping astern so fast that, at half past three, the baffled blockader came about and commenced sullenly retracing her course to Pass à l'Outre, leaving the *Sumter* free to surge on towards the destiny awaiting her on the high seas.

XVII

THE *Golden Rocket*

THE *Sumter's* AFTERGUARD was aware that, according to the Letter of Instructions received by Commander Semmes, they were expected "to seek, burn, and destroy the commerce of the United States in a manner adjudged most practical to the current injury of the enemy's commerce in the shortest time"; but of where "Old Beeswax" intended to cruise they had as yet received no intimation.

The course set on the first day after the U.S.S. *Brooklyn* had been eluded was east-southeast, benefiting the cruiser with a slant of the northeast trade wind and, by use of sail, thus conserving her tiny coal supply. In the wardroom, officers calculated, from inspection of private charts, that the *Sumter* was heading over calm seas in the general direction of Cape San Antonio at the west end of Cuba.

Presently Commander Semmes made it known that his intention was to cruise along the southern shore of that Spanish possession, coal at some convenient point, then cruise to Barbados and there refuel before steering for rich pickings to be found off the Brazilian coast.

Sure enough, dawn of the second day revealed Cape Corrientes on the southern coast of Cuba lifting itself above sparkling, blue-green waters. Off to the cruiser's right lay the Isle of Pines, that former buccaneer paradise. Despite the drag of her non-retractable propeller, the *Sumter* proved speedy under sail, but all the same Chief Engineer Freeman often wished that the urgent warnings of a certain Scottish engineer named Brunton had not been disregarded.

Prize Master Sam Seymour, taking his turn as deck officer, reveled in the bracing, sunlit air free of the reek of mudflats, bayous and the eternal whine of mosquitoes. Still another school of silvery flying fish burst from the clear blue waves, flashed under the barkentine's foaming cutwater and disappeared into the back of an ultramarine roller.

Somewhat to his surprise, Sam found himself dwelling again on that last evening in New Orleans—and Louise Cottier. What a fascinating blend of intelligence, sweetness and coquetry! Had he found courage to beg an ambrotype of her, would she have—?

"Sail ho!" came ringing down from the foretop; various officers interrupted their duties to crane necks skywards.

Sam snatched up a leather speaking trumpet, bellowed, "Where away?" But, instead of answering, the lookout sang down, "I see two sails, sir, three points off the port bow!"

"How do they sail?"

"Towards us, sir."

Tucking a blue and white checkered shirt into his trousers, Raphael Semmes came running from below followed by his servant bearing an ordinary blue civilian coat. To his signal officer, Lieutenant Chapman, Semmes snapped, "Bend on and hoist a British ensign."

The foremost stranger proved to be a brig which, on demand heaved to, displaying the red and yellow colors of Spain.

Amid excited comments from the Sumter's crew, the launch was dispatched to inspect this stranger.

When the Elena proved indeed to be Spanish, out of Cadiz for Vera Cruz, Lieutenant Evans, despite deep chagrin, offered suitable apologies in a clipped British accent, then permitted the Spaniard to resume his course.

Without hoisting in her launch the Sumter got under way towards the second stranger, her British ensign flapping red and convincing in the sun-warmed breeze.

In a fever of excitement, the cruiser's rifled gun crew lined the rail, long since having drawn tompions, run in, loaded and primed. They stood ready to assume battle stations at the first roll of the Marine drummer's instrument. The Marines aboard, a tough, hard-bitten lot, numbered twenty, which was a good many for so small a man-of-war.

Supremely confident after witnessing the Spaniard's release, the second stranger altered her course not at all, but came sailing straight towards the Sumter. She proved to be a handsome bark with a New England look about her.

When the *Sumter* fired one of her eight-inch guns in warning, no one was surprised to see the Stars and Stripes rise proudly to the stranger's mizzen gaff. Despite himself, Sam Seymour felt a violent constriction in his throat. Could that once-revered ensign be an enemy flag? On the sun-darkened faces about him he read similar reactions, but Raphael Semmes' powerful features were set in fierce eagerness commingled with bitter hatred.

"Mr. Chapman, pray show our colors," came his icy command.

Down came the British flag and a spontaneous yell burst from the ninety-two men composing the *Sumter's* enlisted strength at beholding the Stars and Bars go streaming skywards.

Without awaiting a second gun, the bark's captain hove-to his lovely, clean-lined vessel and held her in the winds eye, with snowy sails slatting lazily.

This time Commander Semmes addressed his prize master. "Mr. Seymour, examine yonder vessel's papers and should she prove a legal enemy, take immediate possession."

Seymour experienced further unhappy twinges on approaching this vessel flying the beloved Old Flag. Somehow, he had never subscribed to that perfervid bit of poetry which Raphael Semmes forever kept repeating:

> Tear down that flaunting lie
> Half-mast the starry flag
> Insult no sunny sky
> With Hate's polluted rag.

The vessel's master, an ample-bellied middle-aged man wearing great, orange side whiskers, stood waiting in the gangway. His face was so long and crabbed-looking that he might well have posed for some caricaturist's typical Yankee. He was hopping mad at being halted like this, and said so.

The prize, so her papers revealed, proved to be the *Golden Rocket* of Bangor, Maine, and was spanking new. Of some seven hundred tons burden, she sailed in ballast in search of a cargo of Cuban sugar —a matter of keen disappointment to the boarding party.

Nonetheless here was a fair prize; Union-owned and manned, untainted by neutral cargo.

Mighty serious of mien, Seymour tucked the bark's papers under his arm, and announced briskly, "This vessel is herewith declared a prize to the Confederate States cruiser *Sumter*. Captain, you will accompany me aboard my vessel."

"But—but," sputtered Captain Snow, leathery face turning from purple to pink-gray, "there ain't no sech thing as a Confederate cruiser!"

By the time the *Sumter's* boarding party returned, Captain Semmes and his executive had donned uniform, and with broad smiles greeted the information that their prize hailed from the black Republican State of Maine.

"A clap of thunder from a cloudless sky could not have took me more aback than the sight of a Rebel flag in these here latitudes," Captain Snow mumbled from the depths of a miserable daze.

Semmes' dark eyes glittered as he jerked a stiff bow. "My duty, sir, is a painful one, to destroy so noble a ship as yours, but I must discharge it without vain regrets; and as for yourself, you will have only to do, as so many thousands have done before you, submit to the fortunes of war. Yourself and your crew will be well treated aboard my ship."

All through the afternoon, the little cruiser's boat crews toiled mightily in transferring from the prize such useful stores as food, sails, paint and cordage. Accordingly, not until ten o'clock at night was Lieutenant Seymour ordered to burn the *Golden Rocket*.

Instead of elation, Sam experienced only profound distaste in executing this duty, for the *Golden Rocket* was indeed a magnificently well-proportioned vessel and had been beautifully kept up. Although it was one of the darkest nights he had ever seen thanks to a high overcast blotting out all stars, Sam could make out the doomed vessel rocking gently on this Stygian sea with mainsail set aback and courses flapping loose.

Growled the coxswain, "Here's at least one damned Yankee won't carry no more freight fer the goddam' Blue-belly Armies."

Carrying a dark lantern, Sam swung aboard followed by the coxswain and a sergeant of Marines and found the once-orderly deck littered by a profusion of unwanted supplies and broken packing cases, but none of the captive crew's personal belongings had been touched. Captain Semmes' orders had been adamant on that score.

Sam Seymour paused long enough to watch his coxswain and the

Marine sergeant depart on their missions in foc'sle and main hold. The rustle of the canvas and the faint creak of yards against their parrels sounded so protesting and ghostly that he glanced apprehensively at the *Sumter* lying under easy canvas some three hundred yards distant, low, menacing and watchful. Only an occasional spark from her funnel spiraled up to reveal her exact position.

Papers littered the floor of Captain Snow's cabin but his bunk remained neat and white and his books ranged on their shelves. Sam sighed, gathered up a big, double armful of charts and heaped them on Captain Snow's berth, then he unscrewed a kerosene cabin lamp from its gimbals and sprinkled its supply of coal oil liberally about.

This accomplished, he removed the candle from his dark-lantern, touched it to the edge of a crumpled chart, then turned and hurried up the companion in time to see the first gray woolly serpents of smoke come writhing up from the main hatchway. The coxswain appeared, grinning from ear to ear. "Stove in a couple of barrels o' turpentine down there, sir; she'll burn like a bark wigwam."

The sergeant called, "I've set a blaze in her paint locker, sir. I'll bet she goes down by the head!"

Indeed, before the launch could shove off, vivid tongues of flame had already begun to lick up from foc'sle and main hatch, dyeing the bark's useless canvas a fatal and brilliant crimson.

Seen against this pitch-black background, the *Golden Rocket's* death throes remained forever stamped in the memory of the crews of both vessels. These crowded the cruiser's port rail but said nothing after the first dazzling flames appeared. Commander Semmes remained stern and stiff beside the *Sumter's* binnacle, but when the fire really got going Captain Snow turned aside, sobbing like a whipped schoolboy, "My ship! Oh, my poor beautiful ship. God punish these Rebel pirates!"

"Poor devil," muttered Lieutenant Kell. "Must be hard to see his livelihood lost for him by those damned tyrants in Washington."

Stribling, however, growled, "Damned if I understand why 'Old Beeswax' is so tender with a pack of Yankees. Didn't they fling the crew of our privateer, *Savannah*, into irons and bring 'em into New York charged with piracy?"

Again an unnatural silence descended, broken only by a savage, spine-tingling roar of flames beating across the water because the

Golden Rocket had been caulked with old-fashioned pitch and oakum, and so blazed extra-brilliantly.

Like fiery gymnasts, clumps of flame sped up well-tarred ratlines, thus outlining the shrouds in blazing relief. Like scarlet serpents, flames writhed out along the yards, touched off first the courses and spanker, then the dying bark's topsails, gallants and royals until the whole area was flooded by a hellish, throbbing light.

Great sections of burning canvas commenced to drive skywards under impulse of incandescent gases gushing from the main hold. Suggestive of great golden gulls, these shreds soared high, higher, above the conflagration. Even at a quarter-mile distance the roaring sounded like that of a mighty waterfall.

"That there's a foretaste o' what Abolitionist Abe and that bastard Stanton will find in the hereafter," hooted a voice on the main deck.

When its various stays, shrouds and braces had burned through, the victim's foremast commenced to sway in a peculiar circular motion until, raising a geyser of sparks and with a resounding crash, it toppled overboard soon to be followed by main and mizzen.

It was hardly noticeable when the *Golden Rocket* first commenced to sink by the head, but then she went down fast; and, raising a sound as of a hundred thousand angered snakes, she filled the night with whirling rose-colored steam clouds and disappeared, leaving behind only a few bits of smoldering wreckage. Darkness once more claimed the sea.

XVIII

Gray Wolf in the Sheepfold

THE DAY FOLLOWING, being July fourth, everyone wondered whether that hallowed date would be observed.

"Why not? After all, just as many Southern States as Northern signed the Declaration," Lieutenant Evans observed in his soft Carolinian drawl.

The question was resolved when Mr. Kell, as Senior Lieutenant, following an honored tradition, approached Captain Semmes and invited him to dine in the wardroom.

"Sir, we would be privileged if you—"

Semmes made an abrupt gesture. "Mr. Kell, today is not a national holiday in the Confederacy."

The big Georgian must have looked taken aback, for Semmes briskly twirled spike-like mustachios and gazed out over the emerald sea.

"I feel, sir, that the Declaration of Independence has proved but a specious device by which our loving Northern brethren enticed us into a so-called partnership, the better that they might, in the end, devour us."

The crew also was disappointed that the customary extra-ration of grog was not issued in honor of the day; several grumbled, said no good would come of such disrespect to the Founding Fathers.

Around midday of the fourth, with the south coast of Cuba five miles distant and half-veiled by heat haze, two sails hove into sight. Without showing any colors whatsoever, the C.S.S. *Sumter* headed straight towards them. They promised by their build to be of American origin.

Since the wind held light, these strangers could only attempt to run, but soon the *Sumter* ranged up between them and showed her Stars and Bars, then fired a single blank charge which caused both vessels to run up the United States flag and back their topsails.

Boats were called away presently to return with two luckless skippers and their ship's papers.

"Damned if we're not like pigs in clover!" chuckled Kell, fondling his bushy brown beard.

Upon examination the new prizes both proved to be deep-laden with molasses and sugar destined for British ports. Cross-examination revealed that but a short time ago the *Cuba* and the *Machias* had cleared from the island—a fact attested by small boats loaded with oranges, bananas, fruits and all manner of livestock.

These captive captains proved less philosophical than the skipper of the *Golden Rocket*. They raged, called Commander Semmes a buccaneer to his face and swore that they would see every man-jack aboard hanged and sun-dried for piracy. Quite unruffled, Semmes ordered the pair below decks under Marine guard.

"These cargoes, sir, unfortunately are protected by Certificates of Neutrality," Sam Seymour reported after a quick survey of manifests and bills of lading. "We cannot lawfully seize them."

"Blast!" Stribling scowled. "That means we can't sink these damned tubs, either."

"Quite correct," Semmes observed impassively. "However, this circumstance, gentlemen, will afford us occasion to test the disposition of the Spanish Queen towards our Cause."

His straight, iron-gray brows seemed to bristle. "As we all are aware, the English and French Governments have denied our enemies and ourselves use of their ports for prize condemnation proceedings, but I am hopeful of a favorable reception in Cuba. The Spanish have little love for these sister nations."

Everyone felt some anxiety because a recent proclamation by Queen Victoria's Foreign Minister had proved a mixed blessing. While it did concede to the Confederacy a belligerent's rights, it at the same time closed her ports to prizes made by either Northern or Southern men-of-war. This measure, of course, favored the North since precious few Southern merchant ships roamed the seas and Northern sea-borne commerce was second only to Britain's own.

In short order, Seymour detailed prize crews aboard the *Cuba* and the *Machias*. To the former, a small and badly found vessel, he sent only a midshipman and four rather ill-favored seamen, a fact which later proved a grave miscalculation, especially since her skipper was returned aboard; the *Sumter* was far too small to accommodate many prisoners in the degree of decency Semmes insisted upon.

For a while the *Sumter* attempted to tow both prizes, but the drag so reduced her speed that, before long, the *Cuba* was cast off and directed to make sail and join the *Sumter* in Cienfuegos Bay.

Around noon of July the fifth, the *Sumter* stood in towards Cuba, and those of the crew who had never before sailed the Caribbean hung over the bulwarks, peering down through the amazingly clear water off the shoals of Jardinillias. They found it difficult to credit that, although the lead line showed six fathoms of water, corals, shells and weed bank were distinctly visible. They also caught glimpses of huge and hideous yellow-green moray eels, big red Jewfish, groupers, and occasionally the deadly gray-white outline of a cruising shark.

With canvas furled and still towing the *Machias*, the *Sumter* steamed leisurely for that slender white finger suggested by Cienfuegos Lighthouse. Hardly had she neared the approaches to Jardinillias channel when a lookout reported the presence of two ships about eight miles' distant.

Could these be avenging Federal men-of-war? This was far from impossible, as Sam very well knew.

Immediately Commander Semmes ordered the Machias to be cast loose and instructed her to continue on into the neutral waters of Cienfuegos Bay. Her collapsible funnel spouting dense clouds of smoke, the cruiser then boldly stood out to sea with intention of intercepting safely beyond the three-mile limit.

Once again, the Sumter's luck was in. The strangers proved to be the Ben Dunning of Maine and the Albert Adams of Massachusetts, both fresh out of Cienfuegos but, alas, freighting Spanish property. Again Sam Seymour told off prize parties, sent them aboard the newest captures with orders to retrace their course into Cienfuegos Bay.

"Keep this up a little longer, then by God we'll be rich as old King Croesus," predicted Engineer Officer Freeman. On deck to catch a breath of cool air but black as any Moor with coal dust, he made a grotesque figure because rivulets of sweat had sketched minute white streaks and channels down his face and torso.

"Provided the Dons agree to condemn our prizes," Sam qualified. "There's the rub."

Freeman remained optimistic. " 'Old Beeswax' swears the Spanish Governor will not dare to refuse us either belligerent rights or a prize court. Spain is weak, hates England and knows that if she doesn't accommodate us, we'll annex Cuba and Puerto Rico after we've won."

From the starboard rail they could catch the glint of the Machias' sails already working up that passage which leads into the capacious and truly magnificent Bay of Cienfuegos.

"Before long we should sight the Cuba," predicted Senior Lieutenant Kell, scanning the stern horizon with a heavy brass spy glass. "Wonder where she is? Couldn't sail so slow as all that."

To all hands it seemed incredible that, within the space of some twenty-four hours, the Sumter, without firing a single shot at her victims, should have made five prizes, five ships now no longer able to serve in the Northern interest. When a banjo started a jubilant twangling in the forecastle, the deck officer was about to halt this indecorous exhibition, when Lieutenant Chapman called, "Let the lads have their fun; there'll be work and worry to spare when we make port."

Hardly anyone realized how astute was this remark.

The onshore wind proved too fickle, denying the cruiser and her quartet of prizes entrance into Jardinillias channel by daylight, so the *Sumter* lowered steam pressure and lay off and on, shepherding the sailing ships.

With dawn, however, the *Sumter's* screw commenced to revolve more rapidly and Mr. Evans sent up strings of butterfly-bright signal flags ordering the prize captains to form a column behind the triumphant man-of-war.

Gradually the Cuban coast line commenced to show in greater and more fascinating detail, disclosing palms and luxuriant vegetation marching down to the water's edge. Already the gilded tops of that grand central massif which forms the spine of Cuba were coming into view.

Almost as if by agreement, the sea breeze died away and wind off the land commenced to blow.

The quartermaster, standing beside Commander Semmes, who for once seemed pleased with the world, cried, "Look, sir, look yonder!"

From near the exit of the channel and floating over the emerald-green tops of jungle trees was rising a dense column of black smoke; it looked heavy, as if created by hard-worked engines.

Semmes' genial expression vanished in an instant. Tugging at his little goatee, he deliberated only briefly, then murmured, "Can the Yankees have a cruiser in there?"

It seemed impossible that an alarm should have been spread so promptly, yet the urgency of yonder smoke column appeared decidedly ominous.

He sent a midshipman aloft who reported, "Small steam tug with three vessels heading down-channel, sir!"

"Of what rig are her tows?"

"Two barks and a brig, sir, all Americans by their colors."

Sam pondered Semmes' next move. Three more prizes lay within easy grasp, yet to seize them here the *Sumter* must violate Spain's neutrality, since she now was steaming well within the three-mile limit.

As usual, Commander Semmes acted promptly, wisely and imaginatively. "Mr. Chapman, show Spanish colors, then run up the 'pilot needed' signal. Mr. Kell, send the topmen aloft, cockbill your yards a little and ease your stays. Mr. Evans, send below every man not immediately required on deck."

Stribling, the lean, black-eyed South Carolinian, looked worried while directing the lowering of the gunports. "What about our prizes?" he asked Seymour. "Won't they give us away? They only cleared here yesterday."

The various acting prize masters also proved quick to think and act by re-hoisting the Stars and Stripes and tacking lazily back towards the open sea as if they were on their way after being becalmed all night.

Presently the steam tug, a fussy little side-wheeler, rounded a bend opposite a stone fort guarding the entrance to Cienfuegos Bay and commenced to cast off her tows which immediately commenced to make canvas in obvious hope of catching the offshore breeze now blowing with increasing strength. With it the land wind brought odors of flowers, fruits and sun-baked earth. The tug whistled shrilly, dipped her red and yellow ensign in salute, then squattered back up the channel and out of sight.

Sam could see spy glasses at work on the newcomers now standing smartly out to sea. Apparently they beheld nothing more disturbing than a small merchant steamer awaiting a pilot and some familiar vessels getting under way.

The Sumter's company watched the sails of the three strangers fill; saw them heel over one after another and stand offshore. Some time passed before a battered and ill-painted pilot boat came bumping alongside to discharge a mulatto pilot whose lean, hatchet face had been horribly marked by smallpox. He came clambering across the rail in a faded seersucker uniform and on rope-soled sandals.

That the Spanish flag had deceived him quite completely became evident by his address to Commander Semmes in voluble Spanish. Sam Seymour's expert knowledge of that language—all thanks to Mrs. Mallory's patience—was called upon.

"But—but—" he sputtered, "how can those be your enemies? You are all Americanos del Norte."

"No. We are Confederados Americanos."

"Confederados!" The pilot displayed yellow broken teeth in a wide grin. "Válgame Dios! That is good. Too much have we suffered from the rapacity of arrogant Yanquis, those sister-milking puercos! Come, Señores, get up steam and I, Armando Gutiérrez, will guide you in pursuit."

"Remind this gentleman," Semmes directed in high good humor, "that Her Gracious Majesty the Queen of Spain owns these shores. Only when yonder merchantmen have sailed a good marine league offshore will we give chase."

To remain quiescent, while these three Union ships went scudding off under snowy clouds of sail in the wake of the Sumter's earlier victims, proved a distinct strain.

Sam Seymour, as First Prize Master, wondered why Commander Semmes had not ordered him into one of the more valuable ships, until Chapman explained that his services were being reserved until the Sumter should capture a prize valuable enough to risk sending into a Confederate port.

A shrill twitter from the boatswain's pipe was the signal which released the topmen from sweltering confinement below decks and transformed that lazy curl of smoke rising from the Sumter's funnel into a sable whirlwind. In diplomatic leisureliness the Spanish flag came down, then the Stars and Bars shot heavenwards and, like an eager hound slipped of his leash, the Sumter went racing in pursuit.

One after another, the unsuspecting merchantmen were overhauled and proved to be the bark Westwind of Rhode Island, the brigantine Naiad of New York and the bark Louisa Kilham from the Bay State.

To the surprise of none of the cruiser's afterguard these merchantmen also were found to be transporting neutral cargoes duly certified to Spanish and British owners. The ships, themselves, however, promised a rich haul in the prize courts.

The garrison of the little fort commanding Cienfuegos Narrows shortly was treated to an most unusual sight. Por Dios! Seven Americano ships, all of which had passed outward bound within forty-eight hours, were returning! Following these closely steamed a low, rakish man-of-war, flying a completely unfamiliar flag! Qué pasa?

Sorely perplexed the teniente on duty found courage to rout el Señor Comandante from his hammock.

"Ten thousand devils! How dare you interrupt my siesta?" roared the Commandant. "You disgrace of your mother, I—I'll—"

"But, Señor Comandante, this warship flies a flag never before beheld by any of us. She may be a *pirata* chasing the *Yanqui* ships. Six of them have just sailed by, ships we all recognize."

El Señor Comandante vented a purple oath but remained wakeful enough to shake out his sandals before donning them. Still yawning and blue-jowled, Major Don Ernesto de Jiménez y Sánchez pulled on a wrinkled blue and white striped uniform, buckled on a huge sword, then sought the parapet of his *castillo*.

Plowing up the narrow channel to Cienfuegos Bay was steaming a low, black-hulled barkentine characterized by raked-back masts and swift lines. The fact that her guns were run out, and of large calibre, persuaded *el Comandante* to countermand his original order to fire a shot across the bow of this sinister stranger.

"Two of you misbegotten dogs fire your muskets in warning, but take care not to strike yonder *vapor*, else I'll make your filthy backs into razor strops."

Once the little *soldados* had obeyed, much to the annoyance of various pelicans, the strange vessel's propeller slowed to a stop and thrice she dipped her unfamiliar ensign in salute.

"*Nombre de puta!* What is this but a corruption of the *Yanqui* flag?" The worthy Major rubbed plump brown hands in satisfaction at having caused this uncomfortably powerful man-of-war to halt. Now she let go her starboard anchor and commenced to swing to it proudly, gracefully.

In the stern of the captain's gig Sam Seymour wearing his best gold and gray uniform experienced a thrill of pride at the expert way its crew tossed oars and rounded smoothly up alongside a small stone jetty.

Commander Semmes cleared his throat and brushed an imagined speck from his triple-gold-ringed cuff. "Mr. Seymour, I need not warn you to be most considered in what you say. This moment is historic, for undoubtedly we are the first Confederate naval officers to land on foreign shores."

In the *castillo's* guard room Commander Semmes and his lieutenant-interpreter were invited to wait briefly because Don Ernesto, having viewed the landing party through a glass, had decided it was only politic to improve upon his appearance.

He strode in and attempted to appear impressive but succeeded only in being pompous. Sam saluted briskly and performed introductions. Undoubtedly His Excellency had learned of a war being fought between the *Federales* and the *Confederados?*

The Commandant nodded. "This vessel, then, is a Confederate ship-of-war?"

"Your Excellency's astuteness is as apparent as it is to be admired," murmured Seymour.

Don Ernesto's sweaty brown countenance relaxed. Would the so distinguished *Capitán* Semmes deign to drink the wine of friendship?

"Friendship? Ha! It's as I thought," smiled Semmes, once Sam had translated. "We'll accept, Seymour, but please convey to this gentleman that we can linger but a short while."

While Sam was translating the first part, but not the last, of his captain's message, Semmes glanced uneasily out of the glassless, barred window and was relieved at the sight of his seven prizes standing obediently up the bay towards Cienfuegos City.

"Mr. Seymour," Semmes directed, when a black servant padded in bearing glasses and a decanter of Malaga, "please inform our host that I desire to drink the first glass in honor of his most illustrious Queen, and," he added quickly, "see if he can't be induced to fire a national salute to our flag? Such a gesture would constitute a most valuable precedent." He spoke urgently for, thus far, no foreign Power had so honored the Stars and Bars.

In a courtly gesture Captain Semmes elevated his glass. "Mr. Jefferson Davis, our President," said he pointedly, "I am sure would wish me to drink long life and happiness for your most gracious Queen."

A similar response thus was deftly invited but Don Ernesto was not to be beguiled. Commander Semmes' toast, he acknowledged by a bland, "To our honored guests in Cuban waters."

Sam could read disappointment and humiliation on Semmes' powerfully chiseled and weather-beaten features, as he said in a conversational tone, "I think, Mr. Seymour, you had best not broach the matter of a salute but request this gentleman's permission immediately to proceed to Cienfuegos."

The *Comandante's* rotund, saddle-hued face brightened at once. "Your Honor may proceed at your pleasure. In Cienfuegos you are certain to receive warm welcome."

"Then the Confederacy is popular with the Cuban authorities?" Seymour hazarded.

The Cuban spread apologetic hands. "Alas, that we know so little of your new nation, *Señores*, but *los Americanos del Norte* for generations have displayed a lack of courtesy only exceeded by their deplorable greed."

After an exchange of florid compliments the Southerners departed and, presently, the audacious little *Sumter* dipped her colors in salute to the mildewed red and gold-yellow ensign hanging limp to a flagstaff above the ancient gray *castillo* and started slowly up the channel.

XIX

Diplomatic Representations

Cienfuegos Bay, so named by certain early Spanish adventurers because of the hundred fires they had observed burning along its shores, affords a magnificent landlocked anchorage—one of the best and largest in the world. As a rule its wide waters are clear, placid and the color of strong tea, and upon it innumerable flights of pelicans, murres, ducks, gulls and other seafowl, preen themselves and fish for food.

News of the inexplicably prompt return to port of no less than seven Yanqui merchantmen accompanied by a foreign ship-of-war caused a disorderly flotilla of yachts, piraguas, fishing canoes and bumboats to come tumbling out of Cienfuegos harbor. Because the victors lacked enough Confederate flags to raise above their prizes, several prize masters either displayed no colors at all or ordered the Union flag reversed and flown to half mast.

White topsails billowing gently, the prizes bore down on the city in the wake of that lean, black barkentine, much like obedient ducklings following their mother, until they dropped anchor along the harbor's outer perimeter.

Yellow quarantine flags flying on the new arrivals brought the port doctor pulling out to confer with Dr. Galt, the ship's surgeon, on the subject of granting *pratique*. He reached the *Sumter's* spotless quarterdeck just in time to witness a scene bordering on the quixotic.

During the last four days Captain Snow had appeared so utterly glum and despondent that without exception the *Sumter's* officers had become touched by the New Englander's distress. Snow had already lost one ship, so his mate had reported in an aside, through no fault of his own. Now that the *Golden Rocket* had gone down in flames he faced ruin—no one would employ so unlucky a skipper, no matter how able he might be.

Roly-poly Bob Chapman and good-natured John Kell were the first to suggest that a purse be made up for the unfortunate captain. Every member of the cruiser's afterguard contributed, and right liberally for the most part.

"God bless you all, gentlemen," quavered Captain Snow, red-rimmed blue eyes bright with tears. "I'll never forget this."

Indeed he did not; by way of gratitude he gave to the New York newspapers next month a lurid account of insult and maltreatment at the hands of the *Sumter's* crew!

Once the *Sumter* rounded up to her anchors, Commander Semmes repaired below to pen a letter ostensibly for the attention of the Governor of the Port, but actually designed to win favorable consideration from the Captain-General of Cuba.

Selecting each word with infinite care the *Sumter's* master pointed out, and emphasized, the legality of his position, especially that all of his prizes had been captured well out of Spanish jurisdiction. Semmes wrote:

> Confederate States Steamer *Sumter*
> Island of Cuba
> July 6, 1861

To His Excellency the Governor:

I have the honor, sir, to inform Your Excellency of my arrival in the port of Cienfuegos, with seven prizes of war. The barkentines *Cuba*, *Machias*, *Ben Dunning*, *Albert Adams* and *Naiad*, the barks *Westwind* and *Louisa Kilham*, property of the citizens of the United States, which States as Your Excellency is aware, are waging an aggressive and unjust war upon the Confederate States, which I have the honor, with this ship under my command, to represent.

I have sought a port of Cuba with these prizes with the expectation that Spain will extend, to the cruisers of the Confederate States, the same friendly reception that in similar circumstances she would extend to the cruisers of the enemy; in other words, that you permit me to leave the captured vessels within your jurisdiction until they can be adjudicated by a Court of Admiralty of the Confederate States.

As a people maintaining a government *de facto*, and not only holding the enemy in check but gaining advantages over him, we are entitled to all the rights of belligerents and I confidently rely upon the friendly disposition of Spain. . . .

It is well known to Your Excellency that the United States are a manufacturing and commercial people. The consequences of this dissimilarity of our pursuits was that, at the breaking out of a war, the former had within their limits and control almost all the naval forces of the old Government. This naval force they had dishonestly seized, turned against the Confederate States regardless of a just claim of the latter to a large portion of it. As taxpayers out of whose contributions to the common treasury it was created. . . .

Supposing there would be no dispute about the title to the cargoes, how are they to be unladen and delivered to the neutral claimant unless the captive ship can make a port? Indeed one of the motives which influenced me in making a Spanish port was the fact that the bulk of these cargoes are claimed to be Spanish property.

Raphael Semmes smiled a little grimly as he drove his Spencerian pen further.

It will be for Your Excellency to consider and act upon these grave questions touching the like interests of both our Governments.

I have the honor to be Your Excellency's most humble, obedient servant,

RAPHAEL SEMMES, Commander,
Confederate States Navy

Making precise gestures, Semmes affixed a smear of new wax and used as a seal one of his new Confederate naval buttons. This depicted a full-rigged ship at sea, surrounded by a circlet of eleven stars within a circle of rope; all in all a very pretty design.

To his orderly, Semmes said, "Convey my compliments to Mr. Seymour, direct him to don his best uniform and prepare to carry this letter ashore within twenty minutes."

Semmes sighed, mopped his high and narrow forehead. Never robust, he felt strangely fatigued, nay, on the verge of exhaustion. Now that the ship lay motionless the heat was growing oppressive, for all that her crew had rigged a variety of wind sails.

Head in hands, he slumped forward until Chief Engineer Freeman appeared. "Sir, may I remind you that our coal bunkers are all but empty, and we've but the forty-eight hours permitted a belligerent in port?"

"Thank you, Mr. Freeman, you will have received an ample supply before our time limit expires. I intend to act legally to the minute. It is of first importance that our Confederacy shall become favorably known among our sister nations."

Public curiosity reached such a pitch that soon the *Sumter* became completely ringed in by boats and canoes bearing cheerfully noisy and colorfully clad natives, black, brown and white. On the decks of neutral merchantmen in port—two Britishers, a Frenchman and a Hollander—telescopes and binoculars could be noticed in use.

Wearing his best gray uniform brave with a double row of glittering buttons, gold-trimmed shoulder straps and a broad, dark blue sash beneath his sword belt, Lieutenant Seymour made his way on deck. There the brilliant afternoon sunshine drew flashes from the single golden stars adorning his shoulder straps, from the rings and diamond-shaped loop decorating his cuffs.

His brown hair he had permitted to grow longer than he ever had during service in the Old Navy—perhaps in deference to their commander's example, he and most of his fellow officers were affecting regular manes. He wore his cap tilted just a trifle to one side, its ornament showing a chaplet of fat-looking laurel leaves surrounding a fouled anchor placed slantwise beneath the single star of his grade.

Waiting below the ladder bobbed Commander Semmes' own gig, flying a small Stars and Bars. Somehow a boat's crew had been got together in the uniform prescribed by the captain, light blue shirts, white duck trousers and straw hats; thus far no official garb for Confederate seamen had been announced.

"*Viva los Confederados!*" Shrill cheers arose when Lieutenant Seymour, stiff and serious, stepped into the gig. From a broad-beamed English brig, anchored hard by, came deep shouts of "Hurrah for

Jeff Davis! Go it, you Rebels! Teach 'e bloody Yanks a sharp lesson. We're for ye. Hurrah! Hurrah!"

Hopefully, the *Sumter's* officers kept an eye upon a flagstaff rising above the Governor's Palace situated upon a rise above the red and yellow tile roofs of this disorderly little port. Would the water battery fire a salute? Alas, nothing occurred to disturb those great black buzzards soaring patiently, gracefully, above Cienfuegos, but others, perched on warehouse roofs whitened by their droppings, craned hideous, scabby necks in suspicion of the unwonted activity on the Royal Government's moss-grown stone pier.

Several squads of infantry wearing uniforms of stained bedticking formed up upon the landing stage but were not even ordered to attention by a big yellow-faced sergeant in command when the gig's crew tossed oars, made fast and discharged two officers onto the broad and well-worn watersteps.

The Spanish noncommissioned officer, at a sharp glance from the larger of the two strangers, finally did draw himself up and managed to execute a lackadaisical salute. At the land end of the official jetty, however, a large group of white-clad individuals was seen to be waiting.

"Sure wish I could speak this parrot talk," piped little Midshipman Thomas, sent to accompany Lieutenant Seymour.

"It's just as well you don't," grinned Sam. "It would only get you into trouble."

The midshipman sniffed. "Good God! What a four-cornered stink! Do all Spanish towns smell like this?"

"When it doesn't rain." Sam squared shoulders and assumed an impassive expression at the approach of a tall individual distinguished by a very red face and enormous bags lurking beneath yellowish brown eyes.

"Sir," the stranger began, lifting a broad leghorn hat, "may I present myself? I am Walter Harris, a merchant of this town and honored, indeed, to welcome ashore officers of a brave nation fighting so valiantly against long odds."

At the genuineness of the Englishman's welcome Seymour's heart lifted. A Monsieur Moiroux then presented himself and declared himself no less charmed to welcome the officers and men of a Confederate warship.

"You'll both come for a dish of tea at our club?" Harris urged presently.

Seymour deliberated, chiefly because various well-dressed Cubans could be seen hovering in the background. Were invitations to be forthcoming from these dark-faced gentlemen and well-bejeweled persons, it stood to reason that these should have preference in matters social.

"I regret, Mr. Harris, that Mr. Thomas and I can make no commitments until I have presented Commander Semmes' respects to His Excellency the Governor. I would appreciate it, however, if you would show us a route to the Palace."

The Englishman turned to a tall, very thin individual who stood smiling uncertainly a pace or two behind him. "I'd be delighted, my dear fellow. This is Don Fréderico Isnaga, a leading shipping agent of Cienfuegos."

Don Fréderico declared himself immeasurably flattered, extended a long, pale brown hand, then turned to indicate an enormously fat Cuban wearing rat-tail mustaches and golden spectacles the lenses of which must have been a quarter-inch thick. "My cousin and partner, Don Mariano Días."

"We will deem it an honor, Don Fréderico and I," the latter declared in mellifluous Spanish, "to extend to the officers of your noble vessel guest privileges at el Círculo Deportivo—our Sports Club, during your stay in port." He bowed profoundly, at the same time sweeping off his panama and placing it over his heart. "We are eager to make welcome the valiant sailors of your glorious new republic."

"You'll find better food at the Anglo-Cuban Club," murmured Harris and then displayed insight by adding, "Come when you can, but by all means accept Don Mariano's invitation." He smiled faintly. "I quite understand your position. Shall we move on? The crowd is increasing."

To Mr. Harris, Seymour again mentioned the matter of Commander Semmes' communication, at the same time confessing a dilemma of which he had just become aware. Should he deliver the missive in person? Suppose that Governor Roxas refused to receive it? To receive a rebuff at this delicate moment would certainly seriously harm the Sumter's and the Confederacy's prestige.

Harris was one of those Englishmen who, instead of tanning, always burns and peels. He cast a quick glance at Midshipman Thomas. "Why not dispatch this young gentleman to the Governor's Palace?" He looked Seymour in the eye a long instant. "I feel confident His Excellency will receive your Captain's communication with all speed."

And so it came about that Mr. Midshipman Thomas, very straight and solemn in gray uniform and conscious of his brass-mounted dirk, went driving off in Mr. Harris' own *volante* with Commander Semmes' letter firmly clasped in white-gloved hands.

To Sam Seymour it came as a cheering revelation that the Southern Cause appeared to be wildly popular not only in Cuba, but in all the Spanish domains. Moreover, the French, Dutch and South American merchants of the town seemed to stop at nothing to demonstrate their affection for the Confederate States.

Throughout the entire afternoon Seymour met with only one unpleasant incident. At the Círculo Deportivo, a large group of members, inescapably Americans, drew themselves up when the Confederate entered and with one exception, ostentatiously turned their backs.

A lanky, black-bearded individual, whose white linens could have been more spotless, remained where he was, slowly fanning himself with a palm leaf. As the Confederate passed by, this lanky member stared as if wishing to memorize the least details of his appearance. Undiluted malice shone in the fellow's steel-gray eyes.

"And who might that be?" Seymour inquired.

"Jabez Sheppard, a former countryman of yours and United States Consul in Cienfuegos," Harris chuckled. "He was simply dancing with rage and humiliation when you were seen sailing up the bay with all those prizes. You people should touch a pretty sum in prize money."

He led the way to a wide window affording a magnificent view over the harbor lying glassily green beyond the white walls and red roofs of the town. At this distance the trim little *Sumter* suggested one of those wonderfully exact models made by Napoleonic prisoners in England. Clustered about her lay the *Louisa Kilham, Naiad, Ben Dunning, Albert Adams, Westwind* and *Machias* still flying their flags union downwards, or showing Confederate colors.

In the street below arose the familiar shriek of ungreased axles preluding the appearance of a huge, two-wheeled cane cart drawn by three spans of great, wide-horned white oxen.

"And now, Señores," that soul of hospitality Don Mariano exclaimed, "let us drink champagne to the gallant Sumter and her officers! May she bring many more prizes back to Cienfuegos!"

This was the first of plentiful toasts and just plain drinks. By the time the sun had disappeared to bathe city and bay in a glowing violet, gold-sprinkled twilight, Seymour was clinging to sobriety thanks only to determination and previous experiences in foreign ports.

Another sobering factor was that, thus far, no reply had been dispatched from the Governor's Palace, although Mr. Midshipman Thomas had reported having duly delivered the all-important document to the Governor's own secretary.

"Glory day, Mr. Seymour," that young Texan grinned. "Reckon the Confederacy's mighty popular in these parts. Two of the prettiest gals Ah ever have seen kissed me on the way up heah. How long we stayin' in port, suh?"

"Not longer than forty-eight hours, according to international law," Seymour laughed. "You'll have to work fast.

Later, from below the veranda, sounded the lively music of guitars, violins and maracas, curiously shaped dried gourds, which, swung in intricate rhythms, made pleasing swishing noises because of the seeds within them.

By ten o'clock Sam Seymour felt definitely apprehensive at a continued silence from the gubernatorial Palace. Also it was becoming difficult tactfully to decline the plethora of chilled wines and rare liqueurs pressed upon him by almost the entire membership of el Círculo Deportivo.

He was about to fear the worst when a squad of cavalry in white uniforms clattered to the club's front door. A lieutenant, evidently an aide to the Governor, by his smart blue uniform, jingled spurs right up to the Confederate officer and saluted briskly.

"El Teniente Seymour?"

"I am he." Sam's heart commenced to hammer wildly. "And at your service, Señor."

"His Excellency sends greetings, but regrets that he can make no reply to your Capitán at present. He awaits the pleasure of instructions from His Illustrious Excellency, the Captain-General at Habana. Once they arrive you will immediately be informed."

From the aide's manner and expression, Seymour was able to deduce absolutely nothing concerning the Governor's sympathies or intentions.

The Englishman, Harris, drew him aside. "Don't feel downcast, old chap. That his nibs, the Governor, has referred Commander Semmes' communication to Havana is a step in the right direction. Meanwhile, I suggest that it will advance your chances of success to remain ashore and show your uniform. Besides, certain practical considerations concerning possible condemnation proceedings need to be discussed with Don Fréderico, Don Mariano and myself."

"Practical considerations?"

"I feel confident, my dear fellow, that Commander Semmes soon will find himself in need of reliable prize agents."

A few moments later Midshipman Thomas clicked his heels, regretfully said good night and departed for the official jetty with the understanding that, should the captain require Mr. Seymour's immediate return, he need only order a green lantern to the foretop.

XX

AFFAIR IN A SIDE STREET

SUNLIGHT SLANTING THROUGH green jalousies sketched across a yellow wall beyond Sam Seymour's bed a vivid pattern of alternating black and red-gold bars. It required several minutes for him to recall where he found himself. He drew a deep breath, looked out through a snowy mosquito bar and found wonderfully pleasant repose once more in a wide bed. His bunk aboard the *Sumter* certainly must have been designed to accommodate some half-grown midshipman!

Because his temples were throbbing like tom-toms, he grunted when, engulfed in one of Don Fréderico's massive and lace-trimmed nightgowns, he reached for his heavy German-silver watch.

Gradually his head cleared until he recalled how, cheering loudly, dark-faced club members had unhitched horses to draw him in triumph to the handsome residence of Don Fréderico Isnaga. His host, Sam estimated, must be extremely well off, for towering *palmas reales* shaded the lovely patio of this big, two-storied house. When he got up he glimpsed flower beds glowing with an infinite variety of blooms. The bedroom floor and furniture moreover, all were of rich, wine-red San Domingo mahogany and, through the glass-less but elaborately barred windows, the last of the sea breeze stirred curtains of yellow Sevillian damask.

He hoped Commander Semmes would approve of the prize agents he'd selected: Messers Harris, Isnaga and Días; also of the arrangements arrived at. The two Cubans, it appeared, had suffered considerably through the inaccurate estimates of sharp-dealing Yankee sea captains.

If only it were possible immediately to convey homewards news that the Southern Cause was so wildly popular in these latitudes!

Lacking shaving water, Sam rang a bell and was horrified when the *mestizo* valet who appeared not only insisted upon shaving him but also on assisting him into his uniform.

Breakfast was served at six o'clock but already Cienfuegos' narrow streets were thronged; Don Fréderico had mentioned that many inhabitants of the interior were traveling considerable distances to view this strange man-of-war and her bevy of prizes. While awaiting the arrival of his host, Sam sat listening to the musical dripping of an *olla* and essaying further to clear his head through gulping deep breaths of this cool and faintly scented morning air.

Don Fréderico Isnaga apparently possessed no family beyond a very aged and nearly toothless wife; at least there were no younger persons in evidence at an *almuerzo* served in the serene green patio where caged birds trilled and warbled. As he recalled, Louise Cottier kept some very similar songsters. What might she be doing? Probably like her companions she would be devoting long hours to picking lint and rolling bandages at the Ladies Benevolent Society.

On arrival at Mr. Harris' office he found that beet-complexioned Englishman deeply perturbed. Offering some papers, he said, "Here are copies of certain telegrams dispatched to Havana by your friend Mr. Sheppard."

Seymour scanned them, a frown deepening on his features. Mr. Sheppard, it appeared, had urged his superior, the American Consul-General at Havana, to demand of His Illustrious Excellency, the

Captain-General of Cuba, the immediate arrest and imprisonment of the *Sumter's* company on charges of piracy. Failing such action, Sheppard advised that every effort be exerted to purchase all coal available in Cienfuegos. Further, the fleetest screw sloops in the Union Navy should immediately be dispatched to hound down this gray wolf of the sea.

"Of course," Harris reminded him, "what our Yankee friend doesn't know, and would give a mint to learn, is the *Sumter's* intended course from here on."

"Might I inquire how you came by these?" Seymour asked, returning the telegrams.

Harris smiled, averted yellowish brown eyes. "You may; and I'll simply reply that we British in foreign parts find peculiar ways and means. The main point remains: thus far Mr. Sheppard has not been able to damage the *Sumter* or her purposes.

"However"—the raw features loomed suddenly closer and Harris' voice dropped to a whisper—"Sheppard's a damn resourceful fellow, determined and, I suspect, patriotic to the point of discounting scruples—so watch out!"

On one score the United States Consul definitely had been thwarted, for shortly after sunup a pair of coal barges lumbered out to the *Sumter* as she lay with yards braced man-o'-war style and the Stars and Bars curling gracefully from her mizzen gaff. Despite the cruiser's desperate shortage of coal, Commander Semmes had not deemed it expedient either to order his fires drawn, or to grant any of his crew shore leave. There were so many foreigners among them.

When would the Captain-General's decision arrive?

Throughout the siesta hour of the cruiser's second day in port Seymour fretted about Don Fréderico's office. Long since he had written letters home: to Irad and Duchesne in the hope that the latter might pass on certain data to his lovely cousin and to his friend Brunton. The little Scot certainly must be eager to learn how well the *Sumter's* engines had performed.

When he had done writing nothing remained save to watch lively little green and brown lizards dart about the ceiling gorging themselves on a plentiful supply of flies and mosquitoes. By five o'clock the *Sumter* lay fully coaled and provisioned but still lacking a reply from the Captain-General. Commander Semmes, openly apprehensive of treachery inspired by Yankee gold, decided to delay his departure until sundown—a few hours before his belligerent's time limit expired. After that he must trust in Providence and depart leaving his prizes in the uncertain custody of Messers Harris, Isnaga and Días.

Through Lieutenant Kell, enjoying the luxury of stretching legs ashore, Seymour received his captain's instructions to tarry in Don Fréderico's offices until seven o'clock. Then, if no reply had been received, Seymour was to return aboard as, win or lose, the *Sumter* would weigh anchor at eight.

At six-thirty Don Mariano sighed, "*Amigo*, I fear that *los Americanos del Norte* have so prevailed that you will receive no answer before tomorrow—after your time limit has elapsed."

Mr. Harris appeared, listened to the negative reports and shook his narrow head. "I'm off to the Governor's Palace where I'll attempt to learn how the wind blows. If I've not returned here by seven, Seymour, you'll understand I've nothing to report and go your way." He offered a thin, yellowish hand to be warmly shaken by Sam's big bronzed fist. "I pray God your gallant cruise continues successful."

Blue-black shadows had begun to darken the narrow and refuse-littered streets of Cienfuegos when the gilded hour hands of the Cathedral clock swung upwards to indicate the hour of seven. No communication whatsoever having arrived from the Governor, Sam dreaded the necessity of returning aboard with his mission so inconclusively accomplished. Yet what more could he have done than to heed Mr. Harris?

Guitars and castanets playing "*El Lisonjero*" in a *cantina* down the street preluded the almost simultaneous appearance on the Plaza Mayor of slim, dark-eyed young girls, their duennas and sundry gay young blades. The señoritas, oddly enough, took the cool evening air while moving about the square in a clockwise direction while the white-clad caballeros sauntered in the opposite direction. In the side streets, soldiers and planters, prostitutes and their pimps, sailors and merchants were all represented.

Reluctantly Lieutenant Seymour arose, buttoned his jacket with care, then set his naval cap squarely in place.

"Don Fréderico, I regret that I must return aboard ship empty-handed. Should the Captain-General's message arrive before eight, will you please show two red lanterns on your private wharf?"

"But certainly; and *por el amor de Dios* do not disquiet your noble nature, *amigo*. Don Mariano and I have every reason to believe that with a certain—er—contribution"—Don Fréderico's eyelid fluttered— "we can persuade His Illustrious Excellency to grant you prize-court proceedings. May I accompany you to the jetty?"

"Thank you. I know the way." Fervently Sam wished to be by himself, if only for a brief period. He bowed, Don Fréderico bowed, Don Mariano bowed, then all three bowed once more before raising hearty *vivas* for the Confederacy.

In truth Sam had been haggling over the purchase of a tall tortoise-shell comb, gold-filigreed and adorned by much lustrous coral which might look extremely becoming above a dark head like that, say, of Mademoiselle Louise Cottier.

Sam's heels rang along a narrow, stone-paved avenue slanting gradually towards the harbor úntil he reached a side street down which dwelt a jeweler who now was ready to admit that a certain *teniente Confederado* was no mean haggler. Sam twice had sauntered in to work down the price of that lovely comb until it was within his reach. This time he felt more hopeful of success. Surely Don Iago Mendoza must have heard that the *Sumter* was to sail within the hour.

Whistling, Sam entered the side street, cheered by the sudden realization that his share of prize money already won must, eventually, amount to several thousands of dollars.

In a shadow-ruled courtyard to Sam's left suddenly sounded the quick stamping of feet, of blows and sibilant curses; then a woman raised a series of breathless, ear-piercing screams.

"*Ayuda! Por el amor de Jesús, asistencia!*" someone wailed in accents so charged with terror that Seymour's scalp tingled.

Immediately he wheeled and darted into the court in time to glimpse a small female fighting desperately to free herself from an assault attempted by a trio of white-clad figures.

"*Asistencia! Ayuda—*" The girl's scream was cut dramatically short by the pressure of a hand over her mouth, but the victim must have bitten her attacker for he screeched and flinched away, permitting the girl to reach under her full, madly whirling skirts. A long blade flashed, but promptly was knocked spinning across the court.

Sam charged in and as promptly discovered that it was impossible to see much in this fetid semi-darkness. However, he felt his fist land so solidly that he heard the breath go whistling out of someone's lungs. While ducking a volley of blows he grinned, tried to select one particular opponent. Ever since Annapolis days he had relished a Donnybrook and this promised to be one of the best.

Expertly he flattened the nose of a big fellow and sent him reeling back off balance, then dealt a spidery-looking individual a stinging crack on the cheek. Sam was about to follow this advantage when the big man still writhing about on the cobbles managed to trip him. In struggling to rise something must have struck the Confederate's head violently, for suddenly great meteors exploded before his eyes and sent him whirling across a fiery lake into a black oblivion.

XXI

La Cárcel

THE DEATHLY STILLNESS prevailing in Lieutenant Seymour's cell became shattered by a faint screech of hinges, which prompted the prisoner to assume a sitting position upon the pile of rotting sisal leaves serving him as a bed. In the glare of the lantern Sam blinked and dug dirty knuckles into his eyes until at length he could discern a white-clad figure standing in the cell door with the tips of two bayonets flashing like evil eyes beyond.

"Good evening, Mr. Seymour," came a nasal, high-pitched voice. "I trust I find you well?" That down-East twang could belong to none other than the United States Consul.

Painfully Sam got up, peered short-sightedly on his visitor.

"It is generous of you, Mr. Sheppard, to come to the assistance of an unfortunate enemy."

Sheppard chuckled, pinched his hawk's beak of a nose against the awful stench. "Glad to find my good natur' appreciated for once."

The Consul then borrowed a lantern from the turnkey and held it on high. "Can't say's they've made you extry-comfortable."

"Hardly. Mr. Sheppard, I assume that I've been made the victim of an intolerable outrage. Thus far the authorities have not even charged me with an offense—and I assure you that I have committed none. I haven't even an idea of how long I've been kept here. No one heeds anything I say. Mr. Sheppard, it—it's ghastly being locked up like this, and denied all communication." He drew a deep breath. "Has—has the *Sumter* sailed?"

"Oh yes, several days ago," Mr. Sheppard drawled, jaws working steadily on a chew of tobacco. "Her skipper delayed sailing an hour hopin' you'd turn up. I'm told he was mighty put out. Naow your bein' in here is a downright shame. Wish I'd heard about it sooner."

Mr. Sheppard leaned against the wall, but recoiled with a greasy smudge showing on his jacket sleeve.

"Am I to assume," Sam demanded in poignant anxiety, "that you are here to release me from this hellhole?"

The Consul's bright black eyes ceased probing this disheveled scarecrow clad only in a pair of stained and badly ripped gray trousers. "I allow you've come pretty nigh the mark, Mr. Seymour. I sure hate to see a live young feller like you lost in a backhouse like this. Yep, I'll see what can be done towards getting you out of here."

An uprush of gratitude warmed Sam's being. "Will you? Will you, really?"

"Yes siree. I'll have you out o' here inside of five hours and mebbe find you some clothes and a little cash money, if—" Sheppard's rather Indian-like features lost their mobility, set themselves.

"—If what, Mr. Sheppard?"

"If you'll answer me a few reasonable questions," replied the down-Easter. After spitting out his cud the Consul offered a pigskin case fairly bristling with thin brown panatelas. "Smoke a seegar?"

"I'd like one all right," Sam admitted, "but first I'd better hear your questions."

"Why, they're nawthin' extry, Mr. Seymour. I'd just like some idea of where your skipper might be fixin' to cruise."

"Commander Semmes never has stated his intentions, and that's God's truth," Sam snapped, although his legs were beginning to tremble under a combination of weakness and rage.

"Well, naow, he don't, at that. Mister, when I was factorin' the Chiney trade, I never allowed my skippers to let on about their cruises

—not in port." He inhaled several deep puffs, sent fragrant clouds billowing across the cell. "This ain't a bad seegar, if I do say so. Wal, now, let's see. What else was there? Oh, yes. How many days' steaming coal can your packet bunker?" Silence. "Wall, then, how fast does she log under steam?" Silence. "What's her armament?"

Seymour gathered himself, wishing he were stronger than a single daily bowl of soup had left him. "Get out of here, you damn' Yankee buzzard! I could kick myself for imagining you any part of a gentleman."

Mr. Sheppard stepped hastily aside and the two bayonets swung to a menacing horizontal, behind them a pair of brutal-appearing barefooted *soldados*.

"Naow, naow! Don't you take on so, young feller," urged the Consul. "Speak up and you'll go free tonight. My proposition's entirely reasonable."

"To one of your sort, no doubt," Sam growled, pushing a greasy mass of hair from his eyes. "I'll thank you to clear to hell out of my quarters! They smell bad enough as it is."

"Well, well," gibed the Consul, "so it's 'quarters' is it? Well, my fine Southern cavalier, let's see if I can't find you a place where you can enjoy a little exercise such as pumping out the tide if you want to lie down."

Sheppard drew himself up and flicked the ash from his panatela. "I'm mighty sorry, son, you seem bound to act so mighty foolish, because we'll sink your damned ship anyhow. Howsomever, if you change your mind enough to answer them few simple questions just say the word 'libertad' to your turnkey. I'll so inform him."

"You know damned well I'll rot first!" Sam shouted, but felt his heart sink at the prospect of continued damp, cold darkness and starvation rations.

The turnkey's lantern wrought a mimicking silhouette of Mr. Sheppard's grave nod. "Shouldn't be surprised but you will. You hotheaded Rebels are too damned proud for your own good."

Sheppard flung his glowing seegar butt at the prisoner's naked feet. "Don't forget one thing, Mister Seymour. Northern ice will put out Southern fire—like that!" Loudly he snapped his fingers, then the iron door clanged shut.

XXII

A Hand in the Dark

ONE DAY MUST have followed its predecessor, but when one ended and the other began Seymour entertained no idea at all. The turnkey who fetched the gaunt wretch his supper never spoke, only regarded him from blank onyx eyes. Mr. Sheppard *must* be paying well! To have no idea of where his ship might be cruising, or whether she yet had fought a Federal warship or what disposition was being made of the *Sumter's* prizes proved maddening.

To a naturally active person like Sam, this deadening incarceration proved particularly torturing. There was nothing to do save pray, then doze for long hours dreaming of life aboard the *Crusader*, of Norfolk, dear dead Janet and their son. Sometimes lovely visions of Louise Cottier haunted him, and several times he was astonished to discover that he retained such vivid recollections of that fateful evening in Irad's parlor.

Occasionally he heard voices, but only at a distance. For one thing at least he could be grateful; rats and other vermin must have discovered more profitable fields of activity. "It's so damned poor around here," he once muttered in order to hear the sound of a voice, "even a louse won't drop in for supper."

During the interminable hours of silence he took to reciting aloud nursery verses committed to memory during childhood, Ordnance Regulations for small-boat drill, classics of poetry and bawdy rhymes.

What might have happened to Irad and his wife? By now Sylvia must be growing big with child. What a blessed consolation to know that her infant would be indeed Irad's!

Would he leave this humid hellhole with a sound mind? At times bitter tides of despair engulfed him and he would want to commence yammering as did some of his fellow prisoners, but somehow he never did.

He invented a number of weird and pathetic time-killers such as counting and recounting of the moldy sisal leaves composing his pallet. By a sense of touch alone he had learned that his cell's floor consisted of exactly twenty-eight slabs of limestone and that two hundred and two bricks constituted the right-hand wall of his cell.

At the end of nearly three months—so he estimated the term of his imprisonment—Sam's beard had sprouted enough to rival Johnnie Kell's, and it particularly irked him that his finger and toenails had grown claw-like. But what most worried Sam was the fact that he was sleeping longer and longer, except that his unconsciousness really wasn't sleep, but a species of stupor induced by gnawing hunger aggravated by lack of light and exercise.

As more endless weeks of maddening inactivity dragged by, he cared less about that single daily dish of food he had so ravenously anticipated in the past. Finally his senses became dulled to the point that he began leaving his earthenware bowl of soup and rice on the shelf just inside a peephole let into the cell's massive iron door.

During indeterminable periods he lay thinking of his son, staring into unrelieved gloom and attempting to remember the least details of Robbie's appearance.

Damn and double damn Sheppard and all others of his kind!

Were any of his former shipmates in the Federal Navy suffering a like situation? He knew well enough it wasn't impossible, there were plenty of blindly, cruelly prejudiced people in the South.

At the end of a fourth month he had grown so weak, so lethargic that his imagination commenced to play curious tricks. For instance, he saw Robert Ashton as a handsome young midshipman attending his first cotillion. Again, he found himself waltzing about a gardenia-scented garden with Louise Cottier, paying her subtle compliments, and holding her so close that he could sense the soft undulations of her bosom. But, no, it wasn't Louise he was holding; it was Sylvia—Sylvia with small proud head thrown back and dark red lips parted in invitation. Next, Sylvia and Louise would seem to be dancing together, laughing gaily and mocking him.

"This," he would mutter heavily, "is ridiculous because ladies don't dance together."

And what of the *Sumter?* Sometimes she loomed in his fevered imagination as large as a ship-of-the-line spewing smoke from three tall funnels and firing thunderous broadsides in all directions.

To escape from these bewildering fancies, this perpetual chill and filth, he had only to say a single word, "*Libertad*." Besides, by now Mr. Sheppard undoubtedly had learned all he needed to know concerning the C.S.S. *Sumter*.

Sam was roused from the increasing confusion of his dreams by the impact of a hand upon his shoulder and a voice saying softly, "Señor, señor! Please to wake quietly. You are to come with me."

So the end had come and a bullet-pitted wall was waiting? Mr. Sheppard's methods were certainly thorough. Sam shrugged away the hand and, by the light of a dark-lantern, made out a boyish private wearing the palm-leaf hat and baggy striped uniform of a Guardia Civil. Weakness engulfed him and he sank back.

"Señor, *por el amor de Dios!* Awake! I have come to release you; not much time remains."

Stumbling, but assisted by the young soldier's grip on his elbow, Sam was guided along what appeared to be an endless succession of dim and damp-smelling corridors. All at once a passage ended and, through a grilled door, he beheld the miracle of stars—a whole skyful of them, glowing like white-hot nails hammered into the purple-black heavens.

"*Aquí.* For your life, make no noise!" Sam felt a cape flung about his skinny, grimy shoulders and a kepi crammed down upon his shoulder-length mat of hair. Only with difficulty was he able to rid himself of the conviction that he was being prepared for secret execution.

Again the Spaniard cautioned in sibilant whispers, "Quiet, as you love life."

Because he was barefooted Sam made no noise in crossing a narrow courtyard, but from his post on a high, whitewashed wall a sentry challenged sharply, "*Quién pasa?*"

"*Amigos, hijo de tontos! Vamos al retrete.*"

From his belt Sam's guide presently produced a key with which he unlocked a small, sheet-iron door. He opened it barely enough to permit Seymour's slipping through.

"*Vaya con Dios,*" whispered the guide. "Your guide waits beneath yonder ceiba tree, but do not move until I have gone."

Sam heard the lock *cluck* gently, then the sound of retreating footsteps. Dazed through weakness and still utterly bewildered, he remained crouched in the gloom of a small arch and tried to think coherently. To stimulate his thinking he rubbed hard at his forehead, then at the base of his skull until he had recalled a measure of intelligence.

At the sound of a step he quivered and recoiled. God, to think that this paralyzing weakness had robbed him of strength even to defend himself. A woman, muffled in a heavy shawl, drifted up to him silently as an owl in flight.

"*Silencio,*" she breathed, then took his hand and led him some distance parallel to the prison wall, across a muddy street and into the lightless security of an alley.

Such was Sam's overwhelming weakness that he began to breathe as if he had just lost a foot race and clung like a drowning man to his guide's soft small hand.

"*Por piedad,*" he gasped, "*más despacio.* Slower please."

Of their course he later retained no clear recollection because it proved a great task simply to remain on his feet. God above! The earth swayed beneath his naked feet like the deck of a ship in a sea way.

At the end of an eternity his guide paused and pushed open a heavy wooden door which, once they stood inside, she promptly bolted.

XXIII

Coralita

Only after she had made sure that her shutters had been secured against a rainstorm blowing up from the bay did this girl speak in characteristic Cuban-Spanish. "Some rum and coconut milk, perhaps? You look exhausted, *pobrecito.*"

His companion hesitated, a short but not ungraceful figure still shrouded in her mantilla. There was something saucy about her despite bare and mud-stained feet and her large, dark eyes seemed extraordinarily expressive of good humor, her small mouth restless to break into a smile. The girl turned up a cheap little kerosene lamp the better to view her guest who had swayed over to warm claw-like hands at a charcoal fire glowing upon a knee-high hearth.

She spoke slowly in a rather hoarse voice, slowly, as if to a child and pointing at herself. "Coralita—Coralita Menéndez."

"Mil gracias, Señorita," Seymour mumbled. "I speak Spanish. Is there—could I drink some rum mixed in hot coffee, or have you tea?"

"Coffee and rum, sí, all you want; but there is no tea." The girl shrugged, and a vigorous shake of her small black head set earrings of coral and imitation gold to bobbing. "Tea is not for this street; it is too expensive. Señor, I think rice and egg cake for you will be good."

While she busied herself with various spiders and earthenware pots Sam's faculties, dulled by endless hours of silence and dark, reluctantly returned to duty. For example, he deduced that Coralita Menéndez must be wearing at least four petticoats beneath her somewhat spotted green cotton skirt; nothing else could cause so much rustling.

Next he studied her feet and noticed that, although unblemished, they were wide like those of a person well accustomed to going barefoot. Above Coralita's full, green skirt she wore a loose bodice of a gay red and yellow calico somewhat stained under the arms. Evidently it was far from new. Long, blue-black hair trailed in a single, neatly plaited rope between her shoulders and was secured by a length of brilliant yellow ribbon. Obviously several Indians must have played their part among Coralita's ancestors—if the high line of her softly rounded cheek and a curious golden-brown cast to her complexion meant anything.

Yearning for strength to get up and wash his hands and face, the gaunt, half-naked figure could only sit watching his hostess flit about, busy as a catbird. She thrust egg cakes into the ashes, then fetched a badly chipped pottery tumbler of goat's milk.

Often she smiled, stole quick, sidewise glances as if trying to anticipate this starveling's wants.

As for Sam, he reveled in these simplest of comforts until he found strength to seek a washbasin and make efforts at cleansing himself. God above! How glorious to feel water on his face once more! Dirty rivulets splashed onto the red tile floor and stained the towel she gave him.

"Coralita—it is a very pretty name."

"You find it so?" Over a bare brown shoulder the girl flashed a fugitive smile. "I am glad. I chose it myself, last year when I became sixteen years of age. Before I was called Yqueri, such an ugly Indian name!"

Presently the girl brought a pannikin of fragrant black coffee generously laced with rum. Teeth shining behind darkly restless lips, Coralita placed beside him a wicker-covered bottle.

"Here is all the rum you can want—and here is goat's milk. You can milk a goat?"

"A sailor learns to do almost everything," he mumbled through a mouthful of egg cakes. "But I reckon goat milking is beyond me."

"You can learn, no? But I forget. My nannies are in that yard and you must never go out-of-doors for any reason." She sobered with mercurial speed, and squatted inelegantly upon a three-legged stool at his side. "Señor Seymour, do you know that you remain in the gravest of danger?"

He laughed apologetically and patted the hand she placed anxiously upon his filthy, gray-clad knee. "I feel so profoundly grateful—so—so wonderfully comfortable I, well, I can't think about danger."

"But you must, amigo mío! When the Governor learns of your escape he will become very frightened. No corner of this city will escape a search and if you are found—bam! You will have attempted to resist arrest."

"Won't the police hunt me here?"

A pinchbeck cross at Coralita's throat glinted to her shrug.

"The Agente de Policía for this district is my amador—one of them."

The spoon halted half way to Sam's ragged mustache. "Your lover! You are—a—a courtesan?"

"And a good one," she admitted simply. "What else is a girl of my station to do if she dances well, is pretty and can neither read nor write? Besides, there is el Viejo, my grandfather, who must be fed and clothed." She flashed him a reassuring smile. "No, no need to worry, señor. El Viejo is very, very old, blind and almost deaf."

For all that he had cruised the Caribbean many times and had spent weeks, even months, in various Latin American ports, Sam felt shaken to realize that this very young creature already had become accomplished in the profession of pleasing men. That she indeed must be popular he could not doubt; that quick smile of hers was infinitely winning and subtle, and the way she swung her hips! There was provocation also in the way her generous but firm young breasts rode beneath that overly loose calico bodice.

"Yes, I am well favored by the caballeros," she admitted seriously. "But always I go to Mass on Friday and Sunday and make confession." She broke off, counting the strokes of a distant bell. She made a little "face" of annoyance.

"Nine o'clock already!" She commenced to gather their supper things onto a copper tray. She pointed. "That staircase leads to a little room directly above. Warm water is in this iron pot. Open the door for nobody—*nobody*, you understand?"

"How can I begin to thank you? You—you are an angel, Coralita." He found it amazing that, with his stomach warm and full once more, blood began stirring so quickly, strongly through his veins.

"Just one question. Who sent you to free me from that infernal *cárcel?*"

The girl's rounded, cream-colored features became expressionless. "That I will not tell you—now."

"Was it an Englishman?"

"Englishman? *Diablo!* I know no Englishmen. They value liquor before girls."

From a cupboard Coralita produced a tiny brush, a pot of lip rouge and with it sketched a pair of broad vermilion lips over her naturally dark ones, then employed a stick of charcoal to lengthen the line of her brows. As a last preparation she pulled on some scuffed yellow slippers and doused her neck and armpits with patchouli.

He was shocked at the transformation from a young girl into a bold, self-confident baggage appearing ten years older.

"*Buenas noches,*" she called and blew him a kiss from her finger tips, then slipped through a door leading to the front of her house; a key rasped in its lock.

Returning strength brought with it awakened caution, so he reconnoitered the little *casa*; Coralita Menéndez undoubtedly was correct in predicting that the Governor would wish to avoid explaining the summary imprisonment and detention, incommunicado, of a naval officer belonging to a friendly Power. Mr. Sheppard, of course, must have paid the Governor handsomely for risking so grave a breach of neutrality and international law.

Curiously enough, Sam found he retained no great personal resentment towards the Consul for this maneuver; he had intended to solicit intelligence while also depriving the Confederate Navy of a fully trained officer.

Of course he would attempt to rejoin the *Sumter* with all speed. Failing this, he must, in some fashion, return to the Confederate States. Taking care first to blow into the lamp chimney, he then pushed open the shutters, massive iron-bound affairs. He was forced to wait so that his eyes could adjust themselves to the outer gloom, but presently he discerned, by lights streaming from adjoining habitations, a microscopic back yard where two sheds and a chicken coop stood under a frayed-looking coconut palm. All seemed entirely peaceful.

Then and only then did he relight the lamp and turn to inspect himself in a tarnished mirror adorned by a frame of gilded cardboard.

God above! What a sight met his gaze. Simply because this late November night was unduly warm had he failed to realize that he stood only in the deplorable remnants of those uniform trousers he had worn ashore so many miserable weeks ago.

On silent feet, he climbed upstairs to be confronted by a whitewashed chamber resembling a cell more than a room. Here mosquitoes were whining in a minor key about a crudely earnest lithograph of the Virgin and Child adorned by preposterously high and gaudy gold crowns.

To complete the furniture there was a wooden stool, an earthenware chamber pot, and a narrow cot seemingly resplendent because of its clean bolster and single folded sheet.

What really mystified and touched the scarecrow was the presence on the cot of a blue cotton shirt and a pair of those white linen drawers such as serve also as trousers for Cuban *paisanos*. Why should she have gone to all this trouble? Despite her undeniable, if purely animal charms, Coralita could not earn a great deal about a third-rate seaport such as Cienfuegos.

XXIV

Resurrection

Despite the fact that he had spent the best part of the past four months asleep or drowsing, Sam Seymour failed to open his eyes before the sun had lifted well over the mountains and only then did he become aware of a sweet odor pervading the atmosphere. He attributed it to a huge sheaf of flowers standing in a red clay jar beside the head of his cot. Coralita must have been here, quite undeterred by the fact that during his slumbers he had kicked off the sheet constituting his only covering! He could hear her bustling about downstairs and singing softly to herself.

Presently came further homely sounds such as the bleating of goats in the back yard and the cackling of a hen proud of a newly delivered egg. Both the coarse blue shirt and drawers-like trousers proved rather small, yet Sam, being clean again, felt finer than silk as he slapped water onto his face, then used a section of tortoise-shell comb to urge his light brown mane into something like order.

His enigmatic hostess he discovered speeding about and clad in nothing beyond a very loose cotton wrapper, which must have been cool indeed since it concealed but little of her short, solid-appearing figure. With sable hair flowing unbound and the crude cosmetics removed, Coralita again was looking her true age.

"You slept well? You were not cold?" Mocking little devils danced in her great liquid brown eyes.

"Yes, admirably. A bath and a clean bed work wonders."

"Then you will have appetite for eggs and hot milk?"

To a sudden fumbling at the back door he wheeled, poised for instant retreat upstairs.

"It is only *el Viejo*," laughed Coralita, stepping over to unbar a door powerful enough to resist an assault by those buccaneers who had terrorized the city more than once. Coralita's grandfather stood even shorter than she, blinking blank white eyes and mouthing something through toothless gums. The bosom of his collarless shirt was splattered by such food as had not reached his lap. Unerringly, he pattered across the room towards a sagging cane-bottomed chair in which he sat hunched like some strange marine creature too abruptly brought up from the deep.

Coralita stooped, thrust a bowl of stew into his hands, at the same time shouting, "Abuelo! I have visiting me a friend from Santiago. He is a mercader, a very rich merchant."

The old man gabbled a comment of some sort, then fell eagerly to ladling up the stew. When he had eaten his fill, the girl wiped her grandfather's chin, then utilized the back of a knife to scrape off his clothes as much as she could of the spilled stew before guiding him out into the sunlight and over to a rattan chair set beneath the ragged coconut palm tree. Promptly the ancient's head canted forward and he lapsed into snoring slumber.

"As you see, amigo, he is no trouble," Coralita explained cheerfully; then, in effortless grace, bent to blow on the fire.

While preparing their breakfast she chattered gaily and without reservation concerning the night before—describing a baile at which she had performed. The girl even executed several illustrative pirouettes violent enough to send the wrapper whirling waist-high.

"Few can dance the jota better than I," explained Coralita quite modestly. "Some time you shall see me dance."

"I am afraid not," Seymour contradicted over the saliva-inducing crackle of eggs dropped onto a smoking skillet. "You see, I must return to duty immediately."

Spatula poised, she turned a frightened countenance. "No! No, you cannot soon leave; the risk is too great. When your escape was discovered this morning the Yanqui Consul was furious." She surveyed him curiously. "You must be even more important than I had deemed you—and I thought you very distinguished, even in your rags. Imagine it, Don Esteban de Vasconcelos, our Governor, offers fifty pesos for your capture. That is much money, amigo. More than most of us poor girls will ever see in our lifetime. Here, however, you will remain unfound, because it was I who brought about your escape." Coralita winked, placing his breakfast of eggs and beans before him.

"But, but, who paid for it?"

"I," replied the girl, steadily meeting the probing of his sunken brown eyes. "With the help of certain niñas who also find employment at the Casa Azul."

"But why? What does our Confederacy mean to you?"

"Nada," laughed Coralita. "Less than nothing. It is that I felt ashamed of my part in luring you into that patio. Did I not scream and fight convincingly?"

"You! It was you who called for help?" Utterly taken aback, Sam started to his feet.

"Oh, amigo mío." Bare brown legs flashed across the kitchen and she flung herself onto her knees before him with hands raised in supplication. "Do not look on me so, I implore you. True, I was wicked, but how could I know my victim would be a caballero, that he would fight for me, a poor puta, with all the valor of el Cid Campeador?"

She flung arms about his waist and clung sobbing, despite his reassurances and efforts to raise her. "Oh, beat me! Please beat me. Then I shall feel better than I have since I beheld you lying there bleeding, senseless but, oh, so handsome, across the bodies of the two strong men you struck down with your bare fists. All these weeks I have felt like a Judas in petticoats."

"Who paid you and your playmates?" Sam demanded, much relieved when at length Coralita arose and commenced to dry her eyes on her sleeve.

"Who but Señor Sheppard, the Yanqui Consul? See? I spit on his soul." And indeed she spat viciously onto the pile of firewood. "He offered el Borracho, me and his men, ten pesos if we would see you safely into the cárcel. This runt of an Americano paid us gold, true enough, but in clipped Portuguese escudos." Her head came to rest upon his blue-clad shoulder. "Oh, Señor Seymour, had I but known what you were like I would not have played bait, not for all the riches of Mexico."

"But these other girls? Why should they help me?"

"Because at the Casa Azul we do not like the Yanquis. Captains and sailors alike get so drunk they fight and often they break our furniture. Also, they beat our protectors and sometimes us girls as well. Therefore we favor los Confederados—like most Cubans."

"But you really haven't met any of us," came his half-humorous protest.

The girl shrugged. "*Qué importa?* We have nothing against you, then."

"You have taught me much, Coralita, a great deal that I hadn't even suspected about you and other ladies of your profession."

After the repast was concluded they sat comfortably watching some half-grown game chickens scratch and strut among the three brown nanny goats roaming the back yard.

"Tell me," he invited through a halo of tobacco smoke, "is anything known in the town about my ship?"

One of Coralita's brown big toes scratched absently at her ankle. "There has come no news save from the *Yanqui* newspapers which report her to be cruising off the coast of Brazil, sinking, burning and carrying on your war."

Sam sat up, looking very pale and thin in this glaring sunlight. "Good old *Sumter!* What of the prizes we brought in?"

"Prizes?" Coralita repeated, while casually parting her wrapper enough to blow upon chubby but well-proportioned breasts.

"The six prisoner-ships we brought into port with us."

"Oh! The Captain-General sent orders for all those vessels to be returned to their owners."

"*What!*" Utterly aghast, Sam glared at his startled companion. "Then that crooked old bastard must have refused us a prize court?"

"I am sorry, *amigo*," the girl cried softly. "Please do not look so unhappy."

To look any other way was impossible when Sam thought of losing all those fine prizes. Worse still, a crippling precedent had thus been set—one which eventually must cost the Confederacy dear.

"Was any reason given for this—this outrage?"

Coralita thought back an instant. "A pilot swore your last three captures were made inside Spanish waters."

"That's an outrageous lie!" exploded Sam. "We were at least five miles offshore before we overtook the first one. And to think that that perjured pilot acted so friendly. The damned Yankees must be pouring out gold by the handful."

A frightened look appeared on Coralita's good-humored countenance.

"Señor, please, this at least is not my fault."

"Of course, it isn't. Please forgive me, *niña*."

The assimilation of her information proved a bitter task; to think of the brave little *Sumter* faring so brilliantly and against such a multitude of enemies only to have her prizes snatched away by a corrupt Power! Naturally he also hated losing his share of that badly needed prize money; he had no intention of permitting Irad to support Robbie, especially since he and Sylvia were expecting a child of their own.

She came over briefly to stroke his long brown hair, clean for the first time in months.

"When you do not frown you are most handsome, Señor Seymour. None of the other girls at the Casa Azul have an *amador* like—" she broke off giggling. "Of course, you are not my *amador*, but I shall say so." The girl snatched up a tangerine and began to tear at it with strong white teeth, then on her toes whirled across the tiny kitchen. "Am I not light?" She cocked her head to one side in a bird-like motion. "Am I not pleasing to look upon?"

Sam felt sudden perspiration breaking out all over his forehead. "You are indeed beautiful, Coralita, light and gay as those butterflies dancing about yonder trumpet vines."

When she had completed her impromptu *pas seul* he fell to peeling a small, reddish banana—it seemed that he simply could not eat enough fruit—then inquired, "How long do you imagine the Captain-General's men will hunt me?"

"*Quién sabe?* For a reward of fifty pesos his soldiers will search far, and for many days. *Gracias a Dios!*" She laughed lightly, then reached through the window bars and broke off two scarlet hibiscus blossoms.

"Señor Sam, I think I must call you so, you must dress for the occasion." She laughed, and parted his shaggy hair enough to tuck the blossom over an ear. She placed a similar bloom over her own ear, then slipped an arm about his shoulders. "If we were Indians we would now be considered as *novios*. It is a pretty tradition, no?"

Enormously embarrassed, yet increasingly captivated, Sam flushed. How impossible it was becoming to remain reserved in the presence of so natural, so gay, so kind a little creature!

"I shall be charmed to remain your guest," he grinned, and was surprised to find himself feeling happier than he had in many a blue moon; no responsibilities, no worries, no striving, no necessity of earning a living. "However, I cannot eat you out of house and home indefinitely."

"A friend, who is sergeant at the *cárcel*, will let me know when the search falters. In the meantime"—like a flying squirrel Coralita scampered across the little *cocina* to land on his lap—"promise that you will not frown any more—that you will only be gay?"

Quite subconsciously he put an arm about her shoulder. "You are a pet! If only I could find words to express how eternally grateful I am for all you've done, for your sweetness to a luckless and quite penniless stranger."

She yawned softly. "Money does not matter when a man pleases a girl. Soon I must go to sleep. You see, we who live at night, must rest during the day."

"Before you go," Sam begged, "will you find me a pencil and paper?"

"Old Luisa next door may have a pencil, and I have a piece of paper." Her merry laugh tinkled in the increasingly hot air. "The *caballero* who gave me his address did not know that I cannot read. You wish a letter sent somewhere?"

"Sí, to a Señor George Harris who does business in the Calle Santa Isabel."

Silently she vowed that no letter would reach the Englishman before a week's time, for like most of her profession she had suffered through the cleverness of the Captain-General's all-seeing secret police.

XXV

Dance by Candlelight

During all of eight days Sam existed in a turmoil of suspense and apprehension until, late one night, a little envelope was poked furtively under Coralita's door by a ragged Negro boy who scuttled off with the speed of a frightened lizard.

Mr. Harris had written:

November the 11th, 1861.

My dear Lieutenant Seymour:

I am completely dumbfounded and outraged at this news of your miserable and wholly illegal imprisonment. Really, the villainy of these Yankees is scarcely to be surpassed. After dark I will forward to you suitable clothes, and some money. We have been wondering why Friend Sheppard has been acting sourer than usual.

You dated your missive the seventh so where it has been all this time I cannot imagine, except that your messenger may have been overcautious.

I wish that I could reward your sufferings with wholly good news, but, alas, I cannot. The lying and malicious representations—and gold—of the United States Consul-General in Havana, and your special friend Sheppard, have lost the *Sumter* her prizes; one and all have been returned to their owners! But as an unwilling tribute to your cruiser's prowess these brave (?) merchants have, like most of their fellows, transferred the registry of their vessels to the Spanish flag!

Of course you must be anxious over the fate of your gallant little man-of-war. Well, rest assured that, according to latest advices, the *Sumter* is proving a veritable scourge to Yankee shipping, snapping up prizes right and left off Curaçao, Martinique and Maranhão in the Empire of Brazil. She burns them all, save for an occasional cartel to convey her prisoners to safety.

Seymour's hands trembled. So the *Sumter* was prolonging her ever-victorious cruise! What a costly shame that the neutral nations, one and all, evidently had followed England's lead in refusing to harbor prizes and so rob the hard-pressed Confederate Treasury of badly needed credits. Sam continued reading:

During conversation yesterday with a Mr. Bannister, a compatriot of mine doing business in Habana, he mentioned the existence of a group of Southern sympathizers. These gentlemen, six or seven in number, are seeking to purchase a small sloop with the intent of braving the Federal blockade and sailing into some Southern port.

Should you care to attempt the hazardous journey to Habana with a view of joining your compatriots, please prepare to leave at dawn tomorrow. I will arrange for your transportation.

If arrangements are to go forward, kindly reply at your earliest convenience.

A passage home? A return to service! He broke into an exultant war dance about the *cocina*. Happily he read and re-read the good, the magnificent, Mr. Harris' letter. On its reverse he penciled in quivering eagerness:

Dear Mr. Harris:

May God reward you for this manifestation of true friendship for our Cause. My country may, but I can never, repay your generous assistance. I am all impatience to join the expedition you mention and will be ready to leave when called for.

Your grateful and obed't serv't,

S. SEYMOUR

To forward his reply without risk of perhaps fatal delays would entail taking a calculated risk. God alone knew when Coralita might return—her movements were as unpredictable as those of a feather in a wind. Since he possessed not even a centavo, he wrote on the back of the envelope, "Please reward bearer." His debts to Coralita and Harris would be settled with the first of his back pay.

El Viejo he knew to be snoring in his hut out back, so he helped himself to one of the old man's huge frayed hats of palm fibres, then appropriated a sort of crutch which would keep him bent well over and so disguise his height, unusual in Cuba.

The tethered goats merely got to their feet and stared when he traversed the yard and a few game chickens, perched on a scruffy bush, clucked sleepily. He would have liked to approach George Harris directly, but there was no use jeopardizing his escape at the last minute.

After paralleling a main street for two blocks, he emerged from an alley and stood blinking under the street lights, studying the passersby, almost uniformly dressed in white.

At length a none-too-bright-looking youth paused to light a *cigarro* and savor its doubtful fragrance. Sam touched his hat, quavered in a poor counterfeit of an old man's cracked voice, "Amigo? I feel very ill. To win favor of the Virgin will you render me a very small service for which you will be well paid?"

The youth rolled sleepy black eyes in his direction. "What can one do for you, *Señor Extranjero?*"

Extranjero? Foreigner? Disquiet stabbed Seymour's mind. For all Mrs. Mallory's drilling his accent then must be noticeable.

"You have merely to deliver this little *carta* into the hand of Señor Harris, the Englishman in the Calle Santa Isabel. You know this *caballero?*"

"*Verdad.* He is the rich *Inglés.*"

"Good. He will pay you well. *Vaya con Dios.*"

The youth was accepting the letter when, amid a blaze of cruelly brilliant light, the door of a *cantina* opened not three yards distant, revealing a *carabinero* in the familiar act of wiping beer from his mustachios. The envelope must have flashed and so attracted his attention, for he paused in readjusting the bandolier supporting his heavy machete.

Reaching an instant decision, Seymour turned his back, thus surrendering all opportunity of observing the policeman's reactions, to go shambling off down this busy street until, sweating with more than the heat, he could turn into the mouth of the alley he had descended.

Only then did he dare cast a backward look down the street. He was in time to glimpse the white-clad figure of the youth hurrying along with the *carabinero* striding after him. He felt a trifle reassured when his messenger darted suddenly into a side street, but the policeman's shout of "*Alto! Alto!*" rang clearly down the main street and directed every face in that direction.

Still hunched over, but hobbling along fast for all that, Sam pushed open Coralita's back door to be immediately embraced by his nearly hysterical hostess.

"Oh, *Jesús, María y José*, how you have frightened me!" Coralita flung hands about his neck and pressed a tear-wetted cheek to his. "When I came in and found our house empty, my heart turned to stone," she sobbed. "Oh, Señor Sam! *Por el amor de Dios* never frighten a poor girl like this again." She quivered like a bird dog on point. "I could not bear to have you leave me."

A miserable confusion welled into him. How could he hurt this warm-hearted creature? It would be like punishing a trustful but overly playful puppy.

She received in good part the intelligence of his immediate departure—if the messenger had not been arrested. For all that he had tried to be tactful and gentle in his approach, he feared at first that she might weep again but, instead, Coralita straightened, threw back her shoulders and looked him full in the face.

"What a great *tonta* I was to dream of keeping you with me. You would not be a *gran caballero* were you to remain away from your war. Oh, Señor Sam," she wailed, "for weeks I shall weep and pray for you."

"There's a good girl," seemed an inadequate response, yet it was all he could find to say while patting her small dark head.

Mercurially, she brightened, "If we must part tomorrow, then we shall make *fiesta*, just you and I, and perhaps blind Miguel."

"Miguel?"

"Sí. Miguel is a most excellent player of the guitar. I will run out and buy cakes and ron. No! We will drink real Spanish Malaga!" she cried excitedly. "Later, Señor Sam, I will dance for you as before the Captain-General himself!"

A fresh deluge of tears greeted the delivery of a laundry basket containing clothing and equipment necessary for Sam's journey to Habana. What especially pleased him was a big revolver and a bag containing all of fifty pesos, together with some useful silver coins.

Sam had expected that Coralita's eyes would light when those rich, red-yellow coins fell, clinking, onto the table, but all she said was, "It is well you have this *dinero*."

By the candlelight he entreated, "Let me try to repay your generosity, *caríssima*. With how much did you bribe that young soldier?"

Coralita's eyes squeezed themselves shut and stubbornly she shook her head.

"I will never tell you. Your imprisonment was on my conscience." She stuck out a bright nether lip. "I did not know that you have other friends in Cienfuegos."

He caught her in his arms.

"Coralita, *mía*. You did not betray me, but a complete stranger, so you will make me feel more honorable if you permit me to repay the bribe."

"No! No! And no!" She stamped her foot loudly—since it was now night she was wearing her high-heeled slippers.

"It is as you wish, then," Sam smiled, patted her shoulder, and decided to leave half of his travel money under her pillow.

His farewell meal proved memorable. Seasoning of saffron, bay leaves, mace and curry powder spiced plump young kid for the main dish. This was followed by a heaping platter of rice and camarones, luscious shrimps fried in olive oil.

From a brief excursion Coralita returned triumphantly bearing a jug of Malaga and a huge armful of flowers. She chattered brightly, almost feverishly, throughout their farewell meal—by the standards of Baltimore and New Orleans a rather meager repast, yet, in Sam's still hollow eyes, a feast fit for the gods of high Olympus.

Deep-toned Cathedral bells had tolled the hour of twelve and many a jovial toast had been drunk in warmly fragrant Malaga before Coralita jumped up and made him an exaggeratedly deep curtsy. "You will excuse me for a little? I must dress."

"Don't go," he begged. "You are so lovely, so real, as you are. Like a ruby, all warm dark flame."

"*Paciencia!* Heart of my heart." She pressed a swift kiss on his cheek instead of upon his lips, even at this hour obeying one of the most ancient rules of her profession. She darted across the kitchen and disappeared. Then, and only then, did he glance at a note found in the new coat's pocket.

Be ready at five. Up the Stars and Bars! Good luck. G. H.

Sam sighed and commenced to dress. He wished he could see himself and determine whether Coralita's tonsorial efforts that morning had been skillful or not; at any rate it meant much to have lost that shaggy beard and find his hair trimmed to a level with his ear lobes.

He was still inspecting the big, pepper-box revolver when a brisk tapping began at the front door. His heart leaped. The secret police? His hand was on the door latch when he heard Coralita's lilting voice call, "Patience, *amigo.*" Then the door reclosed and a male voice was offering salutations and excuses for tardiness.

Presently Coralita's door swung back and, for the first time, Sam Seymour beheld her bed chamber brave with light blue walls, yellow curtains, a tall, gaily painted armoire and, dominating the whole scene, a wide, brass-headed bed. Upon a bidet-chest set against the opposite wall perhaps a dozen candle flames flickered above a wide variety of holders and revealed a young musician who, like so many unfortunates in these latitudes, had gone blind from one of the various eye infections prevalent along the shores of the Caribbean. His was a singularly gentle expression, despite the fact that only sunken skin pockets existed where his eyeballs should have been; his smile was so winning that one quickly forgot his sightlessness.

For the guitarist Coralita produced a half bottle of *aguardiente*, so, for a space, the oddly assorted trio only talked and drank sparingly, slowly. Never before had Sam beheld Coralita in her dancing costume, a saucy, full-length affair of many scarlet frills set above a base material of black and yellow striped silk. Her many, heavily ruffled petticoats were of a matching scarlet while the black silk stockings slimming Coralita's sturdy legs bore long lace inserts. Slippers of black satin boasted enormously high red heels and were garnished by fetching little paste buckles.

That *aguardiente* is far more potent than Malaga, Sam rapidly discovered, for soon he was experiencing a fascinating sense of lightness, a complete and delicious freedom from worry and responsibility.

First, Coralita performed a simple little Aragonese country dance to the sole accompaniment of her castanets, and her red-heeled slippers moved with such lightning rapidity that their paste buckles resembled fireworks playing just above the red tile floor.

When, flushed and panting, Coralita had done, she gave her companions cool drinks of milk of coconuts and delicious little honey cakes. After a bit, Miguel's guitar strummed, then exploded into a tarantella which sent the little dancer whirling, leaping back and forth, her castanets crackling like volleys of musket fire. Without realizing it, Sam yielded to the furious invitation of the music and began swaying and clapping time.

There followed more *aguardiente*, more music to which Miguel sang, permitting Coralita to catch her breath and blot the perspiration from her flushed face and neck. Gradually the number of candle flames multiplied themselves before Sam's fascinated eyes until suddenly he leaped up and ripped open his shirt half way down to his belt.

"Miguel, can you play something to this rhythm?"

Hands clasped delightedly, the girl stared in amazement to see this tall *Americano*, eyes brilliant and thin cheeks flaming, beat out a slow stamping tempo with his feet, meanwhile throwing his arms violently on high.

Thanks to that adeptness peculiar to musicians who play only by ear, Miguel quickly mastered the indicated tempo and, improvising, set Sam Seymour to treading a Polynesian war dance learned 'way back in the early 'fifties as a midshipman on duty among the Sandwich Islands.

Surprisingly the Malaga and *aguardiente* restored suppleness to Sam's limbs even while raising the flood gates of memory. Coralita's huge eyes began to sparkle when, laughing exultantly, he first flung his shirt into a corner, then kicked off his shoes; the *Haākaa* never could be danced by performers hampered by such encumbrances.

Coralita looked on enchanted, utterly dumfounded. *Nombre de Dios!* Was there ever any understanding these *Americanos?* Who could ever have suspected this courteous, self-controlled individual capable of such magnificently barbaric dancing? The twisting of his body over the closed fan he had caught up to simulate a war club, the furious flourishes he gave it never missed the exact moment for completion. Swift and light on his feet, he pretended to defy, to attack, to retreat from, and eventually to vanquish, some invisible foe.

Finally, Sam set up a peculiar wailing chant, then dropped crosslegged onto the floor and fell silent save for great gasping breaths.

Blind Miguel grinned and cried, "*Bravo! Magnífico!*" while groping for his mug of spirits. Coralita ran over to kiss Sam with a passionate intensity.

"Oh, *mi corazón!* That you, too, love dancing as much as I is a miracle! If only I could learn those dances from the Southern Sea's islands." She lifted a carved coconut shell to his lips and held it while he drank in deep, thirsty gulps. "And now, *mi amador*—my own dance. Very few ever have seen it."

What followed was not a characteristically Castilian, an Aragonese nor yet a Sevillian dance, but suggested elements of all three blended with distinctly West Indian and African elements. So violent were the little figure's movements that, presently, her hair comb fell out leaving her hair free to fly like a sable gonfalon above some hotly disputed skirmish.

At the start of the dance's second phase Coralita discarded her footgear, then wriggled her shoulders until her frilled blouse hung at a level with her elbows. Miguel evidently had accompanied the dance before, for, disregarding his instrument's strings, he reversed it to slap out an intricate and foot-tingling rhythm on the sound box.

The tempo slowed, emphasized itself by quick, half-beats which subtly titillated Sam's senses. In a gesture of supreme impatience, Coralita tore off the blouse. Never, anywhere, had Sam witnessed such supple undulations, such sinuous gyrations. By the golden glare of the candles her shoulders and breasts gleamed smoothly warm, like old ivory.

She kept her eyes upon the lean Southerner, her crimson lips silently inviting, imploring, until suddenly he sprang up, caught her about the waist and guided her into a wildly whirling waltz. Everything became confusion until, all at once, Sam realized that the only music to which they were dancing was played in their hearts. Her head thrown back, Coralita whirled her skirts until her raven hair licked about his neck like fragrant lashes. Miguel disappeared and a hundred tom-toms commenced to thud in Sam Seymour's brain when he gathered Coralita close, closer.

XXVI

The Blockade Ship

The seas below Cape Hatteras in late November are only a little less tumultuous than during the hurricane season, yet for over five days the ex-pilot boat *Sirena*, late of Havana, had been thrusting her aged bows into bright blue rollers while plowing across great marine pastures of bright yellow Gulf weed.

True, the little sloop had encountered a few fierce squalls which strained her ancient fabric until, on occasion, water had come spurting liberally in through her freeboard and sun-dried deck. Since her single pump had proved defective beyond repair nothing remained for the seven men aboard her but to bail by hand.

Thanks to five days of placid seas, the crew dried their sodden garments and in so doing had become badly sunburned, for all their long exposure to the fierce Cuban sun. One and all they turned red as so many crayfish dropped into a seething cauldron.

On duty at the *Sirena's* tiller sat a lean, black-haired individual whose intense dark eyes restlessly probed the horizon as if seeking to detect an insult somewhere along it. Actually, John Alan Maxwell of Dickenson County, Virginia, was only attempting a landfall. If the navigation of Messers John Grimble and Samuel Seymour were even only approximately correct, the coast of South Carolina should soon appear as a dim gray-blue streak to the northwest.

Since the day preceding, land signs had been plentiful in the Gulf Stream. First some driftwood appeared, then branches with leaves still green upon them, then the even more stimulating sight of an empty cask and a stove-in lifeboat. Excitement aboard the ill-painted old pilot boat had risen to a fever pitch once it was noticed that this derelict undoubtedly had been shattered by gunfire.

Since morning pathetic, lost land birds such as robins, mocking-birds and warblers, had fluttered up to circle and sometimes to fall exhausted onto the deck or to take precarious refuge in the sloop's weather-bleached rigging.

Maxwell stroked a ragged goatee, glanced impatiently at two civilian adventurers dozing under the bulwarks: Alphonso Barbot and J. W. Billups. Both were fired by a determination to serve in the Southern Navy. Those veterans, Seymour, Grimble and the rest, having maintained the night watch, lay sleeping below, enjoying a dubious shelter from the blazing sun. Thank the Lord, the weather was remaining fair, although at sunup the glass had commenced to fall.

John Maxwell shifted to a more comfortabe position on the broad stern locker, then cocked an eye at the remnants of a home-made Confederate flag which, long since, had blown itself into little more than a collection of rags and tatters because Barbot, who had borne the chief expense of the *Sirena's* purchase, insisted that their flag remain aloft, day and night, for all that it might better have been preserved to fly intact at a possibly critical moment. Not while he remained alive, that fire-breathing Carolinian had roared, would yonder ensign come down!

An exhausted bluebird tried to land in the rigging, but its wings collapsed and the unhappy bird fell onto the back of a long, brilliantly azure swell. It remained afloat until a hissing wave crest mercifully ended its struggles.

Maxwell was raising his eyes from the tragedy when he noticed a dark smudge very low on the horizon; undoubtedly it was coal smoke. He debated an alarm but deemed his fellows far too weary to be aroused at this particular juncture; besides, the *Sirena* was sailing her course at a smart clip. At the end of half an hour, however, the smoke smudge had grown so much blacker against a bank of high, silver-yellow clouds that Maxwell caught up a verdigris-encrusted telescope and tried fruitlessly to focus it while also controlling the tiller.

"Grimble! There's a suspicious smoke raising off our starboard beam."

Presently Mr. Grimble came on deck, a piratical-appearing figure in a black and yellow striped jersey and filthy, bell-bottomed canvas trousers supported by a broad leather belt. Accepting the glasses and still yawning, he swung up into the shrouds.

"It's a steamer," he announced presently. "Can't make out any masts, but she carries a big funnel. Hey, you below! Rouse out of there. Looks like we're maybe in for trouble."

With amazing speed a low, squat hull materialized upon the horizon, all the while spouting clouds of sooty smoke.

"What in God's name is she?" grunted Seymour. "Never saw a seagoing vessel without masts of some kind."

Presently the lookout, a Georgian named Peed, declared the stranger to be a side-wheeler and, before long, she was cruising close enough for all to distinguish enormously high paddle boxes and the gleam of spray flying from them.

"Damned wind *would* have to die out right now," growled Billups. "Can't we do anything?"

"Only pray that she's Confed," remarked Seymour, when, as elected skipper, he put the old pilot boat broad to the wind and away from this queer-looking vessel steaming up on the *Sirena's* starboard quarter.

Louder and more anxious arose the curses of the adventurers when the wind slacked and weakened into irritating puffs which alternately lifted and dipped the sloop's long boom and caused her dingy gray mainsheet to sag like an old woman's cheek.

Seymour lifted the spy glass again, ejaculated, "As God's my judge, what's chasing us is a steam ferry!"

Peed uttered a strained laugh. "You've a touch of sun, Sam. Ferryboats don't go cruising out of sight of land."

But Peed was mistaken, for when this incredible craft revealed herself in greater detail everyone could see that her port, then her starboard, paddles squattered wildly as the ungainly hull lifted too high and so prevented the blades from biting deeply enough into the ocean.

"Douse those colors!" At the moment the adventurers could have throttled Barbot for his quixotic insistence on keeping the Confederate flag aloft, for, too late, that weather-stained ensign came whirring down. Glasses aboard yonder inexplicable stranger must have recognized the Stars and Bars because she immediately ran up Union colors.

"It would appear," observed Michael Sprigg, an ex-passed midshipman, U.S.N., "that we are due for an extended vacation in a nice cool Yankee prison."

Nothing remained for the disreputable old *Sirena* but humbly to await her fate. She could only wallow on the graying waters with sails gone slack, hopefully awaiting the arrival of a rain squall, curling up blue-black from the south-southeast.

"Maybe they won't bother us," Maxwell suggested tensely. "Such a craft simply *couldn't* be serving as a naval vessel."

Their bewilderment increased as, very rapidly the ferryboat threshed nearer and nearer, trailing a sable train of smoke through the hot and completely lifeless air. Seymour leveled his glass again.

"I don't know whose crazy notion it is, but she's got what looks like a three-inch field artillery piece mounted behind iron plates in her bows!"

"Then she *is* a blockader!" groaned Barbot. "But what in hell is a craft like that doing twenty miles offshore?"

"God only knows," Grimble replied. "Comes up half a gale that old relic won't last an hour. They've either plain damned fools or very brave men manning her!"

What the *Sirena's* company had taken for a simple rain squall—of which there were many in these latitudes—proved to be more than just that. Astern, a peculiar haze commenced to materialize under low-scudding black clouds. To a man the fugitives could see water boiling white under the force of the wind.

As Billups, a former merchant captain, and Peed, ex-engineer of a British transatlantic steamer, knew, such small fierce storms were particularly dangerous in the vicinity of Cape Hatteras. Still, that dull red-brown painted ferryboat kept churning relentlessly towards them with her long, diamond-shaped walking beam rising and falling monotonously amid feathers of steam.

"Her engines can't be any too sound," encouraged Peed. "Will you look at all that steam escaping about her smokestack?" In a short while the crew of the old pilot boat could make out a tarnished eagle stretching its wings above the stranger's wheel house and then were able to read the name *Canarsie* painted in faded gold letters across the bridge of this outlandish craft.

They discovered also through the glasses that this makeshift man-of-war's bulwarks were improvised of oak planks bolted to braces, and faced with thin sheet iron; frail protection, indeed. Soon they could distinguish figures in blue moving about the blockader's deck and collecting about the field piece.

When she had steamed to within half a mile of the helpless *Sirena*, a string of bright and variegated signal flags climbed to a signal jack atop the ferry's glass-enclosed pilot house.

Seymour laughed bitterly. " 'Heave-to or take the consequences,' he says."

"It's bad enough to get caught," groaned Grimble amid sulphurous curses rising all about. "But to be run down by a cross-eyed bathtub like that!"

The *Canarsie* came up until they could hear the loud *tchunk-tchunk* of her paddles through air growing steadily colder. She had steamed to within a few hundred yards when a thundering jet of white steam burst from the base of her funnel, and the dejected men aboard the *Sirena* listened to the wild jangling of bells. Peed rapped out a delighted oath.

"By God, her engines have quit!"

"But they'll collar us all the same," Sprigg predicted. "Why couldn't that goddam' valve have blown twenty minutes earlier?"

The ferryboat's headway proved sufficient to bring her, rising and falling slowly, within a hundred yards of the helpless ex-pilot boat.

A young naval officer on the *Canarsie's* bridge raised his speaking trumpet and called, "Do you surrender?"

"Never, by God!" roared Barbot and, of all things, ran up his flag in a gesture of defiance as sublime as it was futile.

"Then I shall have to board you. Boatswain!" The lieutenant leaned far out over the bridge. "Call away your boat crew and look alive. That squall's coming up fast!"

Every detail of this makeshift man-of-war now was to be noticed. Apparently the *Canarsie's* only armament was a three-inch wheeled howitzer served by a crew of field artillerymen. The broad red stripes descending their dark blue trouser legs were as unmistakable as those red-topped kepis.

As the Federal had noticed, the squall was fairly roaring up and, even while a party of uniformed seamen awkwardly attempted to swing out one of the ferry's two lifeboats, the *Sirena's* main sheet stirred.

Even in the midst of this tension Seymour couldn't help muttering, "What kind of a flag officer would order a floating barn like that to patrol offshore?"

"The Yankees must be pretty hard up," Grimble agreed, "to try blockading with such a rattletrap."

A ringing sound of hammers at work below and even the curses of engineers toiling to restore the *Canarsie's* engine to usefulness, were plainly audible.

At the identical instant that the enemy's small boat struck water the *Sirena's* mainsheet filled, lifted and, all but imperceptibly, she commenced to slide on through the water. Colder air beat in gusts on sunburned faces damp with the sweat of a mordant anxiety.

Had the *Canarsie's* boat crew proved at all well-trained, they might have overhauled the *Sirena*, but their oarsmanship was so lubberly that the pilot boat drew away at gradually increasing speed.

"Come about, else I'll fire!" warned the lieutenant from his bridge.

"Going to chance it?" Grimble inquired.

"Damned right," Seymour nodded. "I've no curiosity left about prisons."

Stony-eyed and swallowing hard on nothing, the adventurers watched a rammer staff flash.

"Pray God it's ball they're loading, not grape," Seymour breathed, aware that for even an experienced gun crew, to hit so small a target was no easy matter, especially from such a swaying, unsteady platform as that presented by the Canarsie's foredeck.

Only faintly did a second summons to surrender reach the Sirena, now sliding along very rapidly.

"Fire!" Instinctively, the seven men flung themselves flat, heard a tremendous crash; then a roundshot went screaming by just wide of the main sheet.

"Let go the main sheet!" Seymour snapped. "That'll give him only our stern to shoot at. Thank God, the fool's using roundshot!"

The Canarsie's next shot whistled through deepening gloom to raise a tall waterspout from a roller so close as to drench the fugitive's deck. Smoke from the disabled ferry's field piece came drifting downwind, bitter and pungent but harmless. Then, raising a whoop and a roar, the squall struck at the two vessels and in an instant churned the sea into a frothing turmoil.

"Quick! Down the mainsail!" shouted Seymour over the tumult. "Double reef when she steadies."

Wind-driven spume and stinging sheets of rain narrowed visibility to a few yards. The last they saw of the Canarsie she was heeled 'way over, broadside to the blast and her people desperately attempting to recover her small boat's party.

Swirls of spray dashed triumphantly over the Sirena cowering on the surface of the sea like a duck terrified by the swoop of an eagle, and careened her so violently that her crew tumbled in a struggling mass into the lee scuppers. Her jib, however, held by a miracle and kept steerage way, while the wind, howling like a tormented demon, buffeted the sea with a succession of stunning slaps and in no time at all raised a series of mighty billows.

Half drowned by pelting rain and whirling spindrift, Sam Seymour kept his little sloop running before the wind until she ran in danger of becoming pooped—she could not carry enough sail to outrun the rollers that came racing up from astern. To bring the Sirena into the wind and riding to sea anchor proved no mean feat of seamanship but, with the help of Sprigg and Grimble, Sam accomplished it.

When the rain suddenly ceased and only the screaming wind remained, no trace of the Canarsie was to be seen.

"Poor devils," Grimble said, wringing sea water from his beard. "It's five to one she's either swamped or turned turtle."

"Ah, to hell with all damn' Yanks," Barbot growled. "They'll feel at home in hell."

"They're brave men to take such a floating hencoop so far offshore," Seymour insisted. "They must have known the risk they were running."

"If she's typical of the blockade ship Mr. Lincoln is using," Sprigg said grimly, "by God, we'll win this war before the year's out!"

"Aye," agreed Billups, "the Union must be hard-put to send such deathtraps to sea."

"Anyhow, let's be thankful we've won clear," Maxwell pointed out as he returned from below bearing a wicker-covered jug of Cuban rum. "Let's hope we'll find a fleet building in Charleston. I can't wait to take a crack at the Blue-bellies."

Soon they were able to hoist the main sheet, although reefed down to the proportions of a large leg-of-mutton sail. Twisting, plunging and lurching, the *Sirena* resumed her course towards the yet invisible coast of South Carolina.

BOOK THREE

The Sound and Fury

I

SEATS OF THE MIGHTY

LIKE ANOTHER, AND much more ancient capital, Richmond sprawled her habitations over seven distinct hills—a coincidence not lost upon certain perfervid orators given to holding forth when even three or four were gathered together.

All in all, this young capital of the Confederate States of America radiated confidence, pomp and high purpose. By now a horde of office-seekers had departed, some satisfied, some raging with disappointment; but still more remained in town to besiege and harass Government officials who were becoming appalled both by the magnitude of the tasks set before them and by the inadequacy of means afforded to carry out their assignments.

Now that the sick and wounded, those tragic reminders of the gloriously victorious Bull Run campaign, had more or less disappeared from the streets, and with Christmas less than a week off, people felt cheerier.

Every day new regiments from the Deep South and North Carolina paused in the capital to rest, change trains and round out their equipment before moving on towards the northern front. The shops did so much business and at such prices that their owners were in despair because little was available with which to replenish their stocks.

At first there had been considerable uncertainty about the new

Confederate currency. To be sure only one million dollars of paper notes had been issued, to be eagerly snapped up by the patriotic citizens and firms who willingly paid United States greenbacks, silver and gold for Confederate Government bonds.

Far-sighted merchants and bankers, however, wore troubled frowns within the privacy of their offices; such sure assets must soon become exhausted or go into hiding and what then would there be to back up the Confederate dollar?

One and all they cursed Jefferson Davis' stubborn refusal to ship cotton while the Lincoln blockade remained ineffective. Cotton in Europe meant gold credits abroad—credits necessary for the purchase of guns, medicines and other essential military supplies. But right now, it wouldn't do to act suspicious of Mr. Secretary Christopher Memminger's new currency.

Although the Union blockade had proved laughably sieve-like in some respects, Lord John Russell, the British Queen's Foreign Secretary, unexpectedly had elected to respect that blockade established by what the Southern writers contemptuously dubbed "Uncle Gideon Welles' pitiful soap-box fleet."

Still and all, there remained more than enough in big stores like Bulkley's and Gwatkins' with which to celebrate a real, old-fashioned Christmas. Glossy phaetons, broughams and carriages, belonging to the wealthy and to high Government functionaries, drove away deep with bundles.

Despite the loss of the forts commanding Hatteras Inlet, the capture of New Bern and the Yankee Captain Du Pont's victory at Port Royal Sound, a cheery atmosphere pervaded the Confederate Navy Department. Commander Irad Seymour was among the first to notice optimism stemming from the good tidings dispatched from England by Captain James D. Bulloch. In fine Captain Bulloch had reported brilliant success in his negotiations for the construction of three additional powerful seagoing cruisers. Moreover, the *Oreto* and *Number Two Ninety* rapidly were taking shape in Messers Laird & Company's shipyards and soon would be ready for launching. Once the two vessels got clear of neutral British waters, Mr. Secretary Mallory confided, these men-of-war would become known as the C.S.S. *Florida* and the C.S.S. *Alabama*.

And then, aside from the *Sumter's* staggeringly successful cruise,

work was progressing rapidly upon the former United States frigate
Merrimac, the same which had been scuttled and burned to the
water's edge during the capture of Gosport. Her hull had been pronounced as sound as ever, but her never-very-satisfactory engines, according to Chief Engineer William P. Williamson, were scarcely
operable.

At a cost of six thousand dollars the Merrimac had been raised and
a staggering $172,523 had been appropriated to convert her into the
ironclad ram Virginia. Oddly enough, no one ever referred to the ram
by her new name in other than official reports.

Chief Engineer Williamson and Lieutenant John M. Brooke, Chief
of the Ordnance Bureau, spent half their time on the James River
traveling between Richmond and Norfolk while the whole nation, and
sundry Federal spies, waited with bated breath for the new ironclad's
completion.

"Lord knows the Merrimac's the big thing these days," Irad Seymour remarked, "but I can't understand why the press hasn't paid
more attention to the Manassas and what she's accomplished."

"Manassas?" Lieutenant McBride, a civilian recently commissioned
and detailed to the Bureau of Construction, glanced up short-sightedly
from his drawing board. "You mean the battle?"

Assistant Chief Engineer Petre shook a grizzled head. "Seymour's
referring to a double-ender ram they've built by private subscription
down in New Orleans."

"Well, what about her?"

"Plenty." Seymour pushed gold-rimmed spectacles up onto his forehead. "So far she's accomplished more in home waters than any other
Confederate man-of-war."

"And just what has she done?" Glad of the excuse to straighten his
back, McBride got off his draughtsman's stool and strolled to stand
looking out upon the sleet-shiny gray roofs of Richmond.

"She's only defeated and driven a Union fleet from Head of Passes
back to the mouths of the Mississippi—single-handed!"

"The devil you say!" McBride ejaculated. "What's her design?"

"If you'll come over here," Irad told his suddenly intrigued companions, "I can give you a rough idea of her lines."

"How do you know so much about her?" Petre wanted to know.

"I've a Scottish friend who is a marine engineer in New Orleans." A soft pencil commenced to sketch out one of the most unusual vessels either onlooker had ever beheld. "You see? This Manassas is a true ram; a complete departure from previous types of naval vessels. Looks like a damned overgrown torpedo, doesn't she?"

Petre shook his head. "She's no more original than our Merrimac."

"You're in error there," corrected McBride. "The French and British had armored floating batteries in action at Kinburn during the Crimean War. The only difference between them and the Merrimac is that our conception is self-powered, instead of being towed like the floating batteries."

He broke off, watching Irad fill in the outlines of a craft which, indeed, resembled no other in naval history.

"This is a ram in the truest sense of the term," Irad explained through puffs drawn from a low-slung porcelain pipe. "Ramming is what she's built for. You see? She's shaped just like a seegar and her back is so rounded and armored as to deflect any roundshot that may strike her; shells won't even tickle such a craft."

"But where are her guns?" McBride demanded.

"She carries only one—a little nine-pounder forward of her smokestacks." Irad looked up. "Can't imagine it's of much use since the gun obviously can't be pointed except by turning the whole ship."

"Who built her?"

"Fellow named John Stephenson," Irad explained. "Her original hull was that of an ocean-going tugboat called the Enoch Train. That's why she develops so much horsepower and has an eleven-foot propeller. My friend Brunton sent me her dimensions, so I can tell you that her length on deck is one hundred twenty-eight feet, her beam's twenty-six feet and her draught of hull is eleven feet."

Petre whistled, "Eleven feet? Ain't too much for river fighting? What of her engines?"

"Brunton says they're of the inclined type with thirty-six-inch cylinders and stroke of piston two feet, eight inches."

"Sounds formidable," McBride muttered over the sound of voices and tramp of feet in the corridor outside. "What about her funnels?"

"She has two and, I believe, rigged to telescope out of harm's way when she's in action."

Definitely intrigued, McBride bent low over Irad's sketch.

"One of the most ingenious things about the Manassas is her defense against boarding," explained Irad, fingering his short golden beard. "Her builder's rigged jets so placed as to bathe the whole deck area with steam and scalding water."

Over his shoulder Irad's deep-set gray eyes viewed the intent faces above him.

"I'll wager not one man of ten in this Bureau has even heard about what the *Manassas* did below New Orleans early last October."

"You've already told us she chased the Union fleet down to the Delta."

"Yes. She broke the Yankee blockade where it was completely efficient, rammed a great hole in the *Richmond's* side and chased the *Vincennes* aground. Her turtle-back design deflected every shot the Federals fired at her. If she'd been half way backed up, she'd have destroyed both vessels. Anyhow, the Yankees pulled foot and still are lying down in the Gulf."

Petre rubbed his forehead and left behind an ink smudge. "You say she was heavily fired upon?"

"Yes. They did hit her smokestacks," Irad stated. "Only thing I can't understand is how can she get draught enough to keep up steam if her stacks are lowered or shot away. As I understand it, the *Manassas'* engines were relocated *below* the water line when Stephenson rebuilt her, so how she finds air to keep her fires burning when the funnels are out of commission, beats me."

A considerable discussion ensued until, by twos and threes, the balance of the staff of the Bureau of Construction returned from eating dinner. One and all blew to warm their fingers before returning to their draughting boards. No one delayed since Mr. Secretary Mallory himself had stressed the fact that the *Merrimac's* reconstruction plans must be completed with all speed. Unhappily no hope remained of purchasing the French Emperor's *La Gloire*, an ironclad which, reportedly, could smash the Union blockade all by herself.

Presently a page boy came hurrying down the corridor and banged open the draughting room door.

"Commander Seymour, sir, Mr. Mallory's compliments and would you report to his office at once?"

Irad pulled off the Osnaburg apron with which he protected his uniform jacket and quickly presented himself at the Navy Secretary's office.

Stephen R. Mallory of Florida much more resembled a New England country doctor than the first, and only, Secretary of the Confederate States Navy. His was a big, squarish countenance distinguished by clear blue eyes sparkling from behind square spectacles, and a widely humorous mouth surrounded by whiskers clipped quite short indeed. His hair also was trimmed much shorter than was the current fashion.

There were those, Irad reflected, who claimed that Mallory had not always been completely loyal to Southern interests and no wonder. After all, had he not prevented the seizure of Fort Pickens by a Secessionist mob back in January?

Like many others, Irad had not much admired his chief to begin with, but, as the weeks and months had rolled by he had come to appreciate that Stephen Mallory was about the only Cabinet member capable of viewing this contest as a single problem. In short his approach was strategical rather than tactical.

"Pray take a chair, Irad," the Secretary invited, pushing a stack of papers to an aide. "And how does the Merrimac progress?"

"Very slowly, I'm afraid, sir. I have driven out to the Tredegar Works twice this week and have found them working at half capacity."

The Secretary's chunky figure rose and he commenced to pace slowly about his desk, stubby fingers playing at a heavy watch chain draped across the imposing façade presented by his abdomen. "Why half capacity?"

"The shortage of mechanics I previously have mentioned continues to exist, sir. The Corps of Army Engineers has bribed and weaned away still more of the foundry's ablest employees."

A mahogany stain tinctured Secretary Mallory's countenance and, for several moments, he swore in a surprisingly fluent and versatile fashion.

"This nonsense must stop!" he growled. "I refuse to go on being blocked at every turn by those damned self-important, greedy Army jackasses in gold braid! By God, I'll take this up immediately with Mr. Davis."

He bent to scribble something on a pad and evidently came across a notation. "Oh, by the bye, Irad, I am not entirely sure that Mrs. Mallory and I will be able to attend your soirée, but we'll try." He smiled. "Mrs. Mallory, you know, is very fond of your lovely wife. Who'd have thought, back in the old days when you and Sam were obstreperous little boys in Pensacola, that you'd turn up with so clever a girl? It's mighty seldom, Irad, that I've noticed a wife so wholly and intelligently devoted to her husband's interests."

Irad swallowed, murmured something deprecatingly, for it was only too true that, like a trickle expanding into a freshet, had been Sylvia's growing interference in his affairs and career. If she hadn't been so nearly always correct, far-sighted and well-advised, it would have been easy to put an end to her meddling.

Nowadays Sylvia was forever intriguing with the wife of this captain, of that Cabinet officer, and even with Varina Davis herself! Shamelessly she'd flattered vain old Captain Ingraham and cajoled such naval bigwigs as Tattnall, Buchanan and Maury.

He was recalled to the present by Mr. Mallory saying, "The principal reason I sent for you is this," he plucked a telegram from a wicker basket full of them. "Your brother Sam apparently is sufficiently recovered to travel. That fever he contracted upon landing in Charleston has left him weak, but Captain Ingraham declares him fit for duty. I am, therefore, ordering him to Richmond for re-assignment—and the holidays." He grinned broadly and winked. "I imagine you and Sylvia will be glad to welcome him home, eh, what?"

II

Ashforth House

According a final pat to her modishly coiffed light brown hair, Sylvia Seymour paused before the pier glass, opened her peignoir and by a flaring gaslight smilingly inspected her once-more-lithe body with meticulous attention.

"My dear," she told herself, "I reckon you really must deserve all those compliments about having kept your figure. Who could suspect that you've had a baby just three weeks ago?"

Although sorely tempted to linger in bed and revel in the solicitude and flattery of Irad, his friends and relations, the urge to be up and participating in the innumerable intrigues and the gossip of the capital had proved more compelling. She had regained her slim ankles and demurely smooth buttocks; true, her abdomen was more noticeable than before, but only a trifle so, and her pink-pointed breasts were definitely rather globular for all that she had engaged a wet nurse for young Jeff's benefit. She hoped that Madame Dulac's advice about applying compresses of ice water, morning and night, to reduce them to their normal proportions was well founded.

Her gently sloping shoulders glistened as white and young-looking as ever, and those feather marks of pale brown beneath her eyes which so many men, especially the older ones, found irresistible had grown no more pronounced.

While re-tying the broad pink ribbon sash of her peignoir she laughed in satisfaction, for certainly she had come through the ordeal of childbirth in a triumph accorded to few of her sex.

Eagerly she approached that huge double bed which she again was sharing with Irad. Minerva, her angular, "high-yellow" personal maid, already had laid out her evening gown upon it. What a shame that the Ashforths hadn't built a more spacious ballroom, thought Sylvia, for desperately she yearned to include additional couples to her list of guests invited to hear Mlle. Esterhazy, the celebrated European harpist, give a recital.

By securing the appearance of that lovely Hungarian virtuoso Sylvia had scored one of the major coups of Richmond's holiday season; everyone was aware that Mrs. Robert Toombs and Mrs. Judah P. Benjamin both had angled in vain.

A small and private smile curved Sylvia's dark lips. Mrs. Toombs was on the outs with Varina Davis, so her success in the matter shouldn't harm Irad's prospects—provided that President Davis and his popular young wife attended her soirée.

Thought Sylvia while making selections from her jewel casket, "Of course, it won't do to become high-handed with the opposition. Who can tell which way the political cats may jump?" Already there were rumors of impending replacements in the Cabinet. For instance, a mighty outcry was rising against that poor, bedeviled soul Mr. Walker, Secretary of War. Neither had dour, pickle-faced Christopher Memminger gained popularity through his efforts to check speculation and find sound backing for Confederate currency. Sylvia resolved to be especially attentive to socially prominent Mrs. Northrop for all that her husband, in charge of Army Supply, was being bitterly reviled in the columns of the Richmond Examiner. To stand by Mrs. Northrop at this time would lend a proper air of loyalty—and earn gratitude useful at some later date.

She rang a bell for Minerva and, seating herself before her dressing table, curled her toes inside slippers lined with rabbit fur. Despite all efforts this big, white-columned house remained dreadfully cold and damp after its years of unoccupancy.

Tom Farraday and Becky, his famously beautiful wife, should be able to further not only Irad's prospects, but also those of Reynolds Seymour. How was it possible that Captain Felix and Amanda Seymour could have produced three sons so totally dissimilar as Irad, Sam and Reynolds?

She hardly realized it when Minerva entered the room; that tall reserved creature could at times move so quietly as to be quite disconcerting. Minerva resembled no other Negro Sylvia had known. An officer, recently returned from duty with the slave patrol off the Bight of Benin, declared her to be a pure Somali type. Certainly Minerva's features were more Arabic than negroid and she had proved uncommonly quick to learn. What a stroke of luck to have picked her up so cheaply at that auction following the death of Colonel Montrose from the heavy wound he had taken at Manassas.

Minerva now knew exactly what was expected as she set about heating the curling tongs over a small spirit lamp after removing from her mistress' hair bits of wire covered with kidskin. Expertly, the slave rolled Sylvia's white silk stockings up her hand preparatory to slipping them over on her mistress' toes and so guiding them smoothly upwards until they could be gartered with lengths of that wonderful new elastic webbing which was now being imported from France.

As Sylvia recalled, Reynolds Seymour—until recently met only at her wedding—no more resembled his brothers than a Chinese. High-strung and nervous as a blooded two-year-old, his smile had been ready and most engaging. Dark of complexion and slight of build, he had suggested a lithe black panther in the company of two young lions. His mental processes and sometimes stinging repartee were too quick for comfort, reflected Sylvia; yet everyone in Richmond was describing the youngest Seymour as able, fascinating and prodigiously ambitious.

"I wonder what really happened at the University of Virginia?" Sylvia pondered, while stepping into a lace-edged petticoat, grateful that she had survived the torture of being laced into corsets strong enough to restore the virginal slimness of her waist.

How awkward poor Irad had appeared on being informed that his brother had arrived in Richmond bearing letters not only from the Magoffins of Beau Rivage, but from many friends in Savannah. For Irad to ignore his brother before all Richmond had been unthinkable particularly since the Seymour family had denied all aspersions on Reynolds, had ascribed the unhappy incident to a calumny attributable to certain envious classmates.

So Reynolds was here in the capital and, by all accounts, brave in the silvered buttons and pale green regimentals worn by the Cape Chatham Fencibles. Despite all conjecture such a unit must exist because Mamma had written to that effect; also old Colonel Mason returning from duty in Savannah recalled having seen some unit of that name parading about Savannah. All the same, no one in Richmond had ever beheld anything quite so handsome as Reynolds' Fencible uniform with its unique silver epaulettes and buttons which, in a triple row, descended a claret plastron.

Comfortably, Sylvia could hear her servants moving furniture in preparation for the influx due to begin about nine o'clock. She smiled at her little finger, reddened through the discreet use of lip salve; most ladies dared not use cosmetics—openly. Now, to complicate things, Samuel Seymour was due to appear at any hour—what a nuisance! The trains nowadays were so wretchedly slow and irregular.

Sylvia's smile softened gradually. Dear, sweet Sam! She hoped her letter had rescued him from that mental agony in which she guessed he must have existed. A good thing that she had been so determined to have a baby of her own. How much would Sam have changed? What would be his reaction when they met? More important, could she successfully conceal her own anticipation? After all, Sam had been her one and only lover.

Poor Sam! Apparently he'd been very ill of the fever down in Charleston and after having been held prisoner, too. Long ago Sylvia had guessed that Sam's failure ever to write indicated that he despised her only less than himself. Naturally, he would remain polite through gratitude for all she had been to young Robbie.

Unconsciously Sylvia straightened before her dressing table; nobody ever could say that she'd not treated Sam's son just as tenderly as if he'd been her own. Now that young Jeff had arrived to perpetuate her blood and Irad's name, she hoped that Robbie might be taken elsewhere. Impatiently she glanced at a French gold-and-crystal pendule, and frowned that Irad again should be so late. Why, in Heaven's name must he linger so long up in that forlorn and chilly draughting office?

To control a rising impatience she let her thoughts revert to Reynolds Seymour. Only one year in Savannah had made him the intimate of so many families among which she had grown up. Why, he was familiar with the Bartows, Hudgsons, Lockes, Wards and even Judge Burns' family. Wasn't it simply fortuitous that Papa, never anybody's fool, should hold so high an opinion of Irad's youngest brother? Apparently some kind of a blockade-breaking scheme was in the making and, although she had attempted, ever so dexterously, to ascertain details from Reynolds, for once she had been politely but definitively foiled.

By the time Commander Seymour's carriage pulled up before Ashforth House, the turtle soup was cold and Sylvia was in a bad mood, although Irad had completed his drawing of the *Merrimac's* aftershield.

Across a card table Sylvia had caused to be set up in the library she said through slightly flattened lips, "Really, Irad, you might have made a special effort to be on time tonight. Edouard's fricandeau of veal is spoiled and he'll become difficult." Her lower lip quivered. "Must you always remain such a complete slave to that stupid Bureau? Just look at your hands! Ink all over them and our guests due within half an hour."

He made no immediate reply, and, had Sylvia not been quite so irritated, she might have taken warning from a certain tightening of cloth about Irad's shoulders.

"I find this an inspirational supper," he announced at length. "I wish, my dear, that we were free to enjoy it at our leisure."

The butler fetched in and offered the fricandeau by the light of four tall candles set in massive holders of solid silver.

"Bah!" he grunted. "More fancy French swill! Can't we ever have some honest-to-God chops, or beef?"

Something about her husband's expression warned Sylvia to bite off a sharp retort and simply say, "Beef, my dear, must go to the brave men who are defending us to the north."

"Damn little of it gets to them, from what I hear." He pushed back his chair, making an angry, grating noise. "Sylvia, this must be our last party—holiday season or no holiday season. I simply can't afford such extravagance."

"Perhaps you can't," she declared in a trembling undertone, her sherry-hued eyes narrowing themselves, "but we can."

Irad snapped, "Please remember that it's you, not 'we,' who can afford this social campaign. Oh, God! Why was I ever such a fool as to permit you to draw upon your dowry?"

"Because, dearest husband"—Sylvia swept to her feet, placed lovely pallid arms about his neck—"for the sake of our son and his heirs it is imperative that you become a great man in this new Confederacy! I beg you to consider the George Masons of Virginia and the Sampson Masons of Boston; they made a mark in equally new communities near two centuries ago, and today their descendants stand as leaders in the land!"

She bent to kiss her husband's cheek and permit her French scent to linger in his hair. "Thus far, darling, we've not done badly. Do you know that you are being considered for the post of Assistant Chief Engineer of the Navy? Tonight, after only five short months, the wealth, aristocracy and power of the South will come flocking to our home."

Irad tried to contain his sense of righteous indignation, but couldn't. He was too fatigued.

"Wealth and power may perhaps appear, but the aristocracy won't. This capital reeks of adventurers, political ruffians and pompous windbags from the Cotton States. Confound it, Madam, we Virginians are being led down the garden path for fair!"

"Oh, yes, I know the speech. Your friend Mr. Edmonston made it," Sylvia said bitterly, then struck a mock-heroic attitude; "'Virginia wards the blow from her weaker sisters, though the quarrel is none of hers!'"

Irad, red-faced, got to his feet. "You mayn't agree, but what Edmonston said is true. You'll find fewer real aristocrats about Richmond nowadays than snowbirds in hell!" He was angry as she had never seen him, his gray eyes chill behind those spectacles she so hated. "Do you know what your precious Davis Government consists of? A parcel of greedy cotton brokers, slave-sellers, ambitious charlatans and self-seeking, dog-leg politicians!"

"Irad! For Heaven's sake lower your voice. How dare you talk such treason?" She quailed. What lay behind this outburst? Could Sam have written anything?

"I dare say so, because it's God's truth. Mrs. Seymour, pray resume your seat and attend what I say. Once this holiday season is over, there will be no more social campaigning. When I observe so many splendid naval officers serving as simple lieutenants, I—I'm damned well ashamed to be wearing these commander's stars!"

Sylvia knew better than to argue, only smiled sweetly.

"You may be quite right, dear, and already I know you are going to say that the money spent on a soirée such as this would buy several cannon for your precious men-of-war."

"And so it would. When will you, and the rest of this zany capital, realize that the Confederacy's very existence lies upon the scales of time?" He commenced to stride back and forth. "We must make every sacrifice if we are to survive, especially since the very principle upon which this nation has been founded is one which may eventually destroy it."

"What principle, dear?"

"That of State Sovereignty being carried to the nth degree. Good God, Madam! Can't you realize that the Confederate Navy Department wields so little power over Louisiana that, instead of building ships critically needed by the national navy, she is frittering away money, men and resources on a crack-pot River Defense Flotilla?

"All our State Governments are building private ships and so robbing us of hulls, guns, men, which to the Confederacy are like pearls and fine gold. Our Navy Department," he went on, his shoulders suddenly very wide, "has become neglected, a stepchild, a wretched pawn in a game played by self-named Napoleons, Alexanders and Caesars among our governors!"

Sylvia could have sobbed in relief when the butler rapped and en-

tered. "Mrs. Seymour, Ma'am, de orchestra leader want to know which
end de ballroom he goin' to play?"

"Very well, Zeno. Commander Seymour and I will take coffee in
our apartment."

With heels clicking briskly and sapphire-blue house robe flowing,
Sylvia hurriedly made for mahogany double doors leading to her not-
too-spacious ballroom; in it, candles already had begun to glisten in
crystal sconces and chandeliers arranged with tasteful decorations of
laurel, mistletoe and holly.

III

Soirée

SHORTLY AFTER NINE o'clock the first carriages commenced to roll up
to Ashforth House with lanterns flashing and spans stepping lively
because of a nipping westerly breeze. The teams kept silvered curb
chains jingling like so many Christmas bells, prompting guests to observe that the threat of snow was becoming very real. Gallantly the
gentlemen assisted their ladies in managing hoops through carriage
doors and up a privet-lined brick walk to a neo-classical Greek portico.

"That clever Seymour girl really has transformed this gloomy old
place," declared Mrs. Trenholm to her tall and sedate husband. "Ever
since poor Billy Ashforth drank himself to death the house has resembled a mausoleum."

"Yes, my dear. Good evening, Miss Howell." The Charlestonian
lifted his tall silk hat and bowed to a lovely young woman wearing a
Lincoln-green capuchin cloak edged with sable.

"What a lovely girl," declared Mr. George Trenholm. "There aren't
many in Richmond half as lovely as she and Mary Horning. A good
evening to you, Mrs. Northrop, and you, my dear General." With his
hat he saluted the Commissary-General who, despite able and sincere
efforts, rapidly was becoming the most bitterly criticized official in
Jefferson Davis' Government.

To Sylvia it brought a vast gratification, mingled with an honest surprise, that so many high officials should have elected to attend Mlle. Esterhazy's recital.

Looking quite small in a gown of pale blue watered-silk looped with pink ribbon and tiny blue flowers, Sylvia Seymour had never seemed more radiant than as, paired with her tall, yellow-haired husband, she welcomed their guests.

Irad felt hot and uncomfortable in a new overly tight gray naval uniform and, as always, found difficulty in recalling names. Despite Sylvia's patient coaching, he reckoned he would never acquire the politician's knack of associating names with faces.

Gradually the ballroom became filled by a brilliant and often over-dressed throng; rumors and gossip commenced to circulate and the hum of voices swelled until, presently, violins, violas and flutes struck up a sentimental air called "Casta Diva."

Among the earliest to arrive was Mr. Pollard, irascible editor of the Richmond *Examiner* and inveterate critic of President Jefferson Davis and all his works. Sylvia was inordinately pleased by his attendance; it meant, of course, that her *soirée* would receive ample and friendly attention in tomorrow's *Examiner.* Just as well that Mr. Davis probably would not attend, now that Mr. Pollard was present.

Dark-faced Manuela Mallory came sailing up in a gown of topaz satin trimmed in green velvet.

"Good evening, dear child." The Navy Secretary's wife pecked Sylvia's cheek, then acknowledged Irad's deep bow. "Your Spanish, *amigo*, you have not let it grow rusty?"

"I trust not, Aunt Manuela."

"Your Uncle Stephen tells me you are making a great success at the Bureau."

Irad turned beet-red. "We—we do the best we can, all of us."

Bright black bird-like eyes twinkled. "*Bueno*. When the *Merrimac* is at last commissioned," she lowered her voice, "I am told that you will receive a suitable reward and promotion."

Mr. Secretary Stephen Mallory looked shorter, more insignificant than ever, in a high collar and broad white stock, but shook hands vigorously before hurrying over to the *Examiner's* editor. "Ah, there, friend Pollard, I trust you won't be as severe on my Department as you have been with State."

More and more guests arrived including the Tognos and Louisiana's General Gonzales who looked so lean and saturnine that he more resembled a Spanish than an American officer. Also appeared fiery Edmund Rhett, Jr., Robert and Mrs. Hunter of Virginia.

Several celebrated belles eyed each other in honeyed venom from as great a distance as possible. It was a pity, Mrs. Mallory sighed, that lively and observant Mrs. James Chesnut was down in Camden where reports had it that her health had given away due to unstinting labor in various hospitals.

Generals and colonels arrived by the dozen, but a considerable stir arose when Zeno, on duty at the door, called out, "His Honuh, de Secretary of War and Mrs. Benjamin!"

For all that he was a Hebrew, Judah P. Benjamin by popular agreement was the most brilliant mind included in Jefferson Davis' Cabinet, becoming known on Capitol Hill not only as "the Brains of the Confederacy" but also as the President's *alter ego*.

These latest arrivals commenced immediately to circulate. Mr. Benjamin shook a multitude of hands, cracked clever jokes and radiated confident good nature. To Irad it was astonishing that Secretary Benjamin could greet even the least exalted of his guests by name.

"Damned if I trust the fellow. He's too confounded glib," growled a dark-faced major of artillery. "You know that the New York *Independent* published an article by Dr. D. Francis Bacon, a distinguished physician, accusing Benjamin of having been expelled from Yale for stealing?"

"Come, come. Dr. Bacon must have been mistaken," mildly objected Mr. Trenholm.

"If so, why has our Jewish genius never sued the reverend gentleman for libel or even publicly denied the charge, for that matter?"

"Probably he dismissed it as malicious gossip not worth refutation," suggested General Gonzales. "Mr. Benjamin, sir, is a highly regarded citizen of Louisiana."

"Speaking of gossip," a sparrow-like little woman began fluttering her fan to attract attention, "have you *heard* the latest rumor from Washington? It is reported and on good authority, mind you, that that odious Mrs. Lincoln has discharged many servants who have served the White House for years.

"My Cousin Fanny writes from Washington that Mary Todd Lincoln is so pinch-penny that she has been seen doing her own marketing! Moreover, the outrageous hussy has declared her intention of saving twelve thousand dollars out of Old Abe's salary each year. I think she'll find it difficult because everyone knows that both she and that backwoods ape she married drink like fishes."

Quickly the atmosphere of Sylvia's little ballroom grew warmer, redolent of pine boughs and many perfumes combined with the pungent, distinctive odors of wool uniforms.

Once her receiving line was dispersed, Sylvia's instinct sent her gliding up to the pale, plump and affable Secretary of War. Were anyone likely to wheedle naval appropriations out of President Davis, here was the man.

Diamonds set in Judah Benjamin's frilled shirt front flashed when he bent low over her hand, at the same time declaring himself privileged to be sharing the most precious territory within the Confederacy.

"And why, dear Mr. Secretary, is my ballroom floor so very valuable?"

"Because, dear lady, you stand upon it. Indeed, Mrs. Seymour, everything you touch betrays the excellence of your taste."

"Then pray give me your opinion of our champagne." Flushed with pleasure, Sylvia offered Mr. Benjamin a glass, then drifted smilingly on to converse with Mr. Pollard.

Inevitably, groups of guests commenced to speculate on the proportions of the Magoffin fortune until Irad had overheard enough to tighten his jaws.

"My dear! Have you ever seen such a variety of wines in wartime? And just *look* at all that lovely icing on those cakes! It's certain-sure Sylvia Seymour can't entertain like this on a commander's pay. I know, and my husband's a captain."

Other snatches of conversation came to trouble Irad.

"Look at Mrs. Mallory! Why, she's dark as any Arab."

"It's no wonder. They say she's a pure-bred Spaniard and a Catholic, of course; they both are."

"What! Is Stephen Mallory a Romanist?"

"My dear, you positively astonish me. Haven't you heard about Stephen Mallory? His mother was an ignorant Irish immigrant to Key West—really a nobody. She ran a boarding house after her husband was lost at sea."

"Then I wonder why Mr. Davis should select such an unknown to be his Secretary of the Navy."

"Oh, I suppose Florida had to have at least one Cabinet member even though Mr. Mallory possesses no knowledge of ships or naval affairs."

"Oh, but you're wrong there, darling. Mr. Mallory did serve as Under-Secretary of the Navy during dear President Buchanan's Administration."

"Really? Tell me, dear, is it true that he and Secretary of War Walker are at daggers drawn over the Army's stealing men away from the Navy?"

"Maybe, but they do say General Walker was replaced at the War Department over his failure to follow up our wonderful victory at Manassas."

"I simply can't believe it, my pet. Did you know that Mrs. Edward Johnston is intriguing to win the post for her husband?"

And so it went until Irad felt sick, and hungry for fresh air and silence.

Imported candles of clear French beeswax gave off a clear and smokeless light which was so much more flattering, everyone said, to evening gowns and uniforms than the garish glare of gaslights.

Sylvia became aware, as a good hostess should, of an unusual stir at the entrance to her ballroom.

Someone murmured, "It's that lovely Becky Romaine from Atlanta. They say her father owns a steel mill and is making a fortune out of this war."

"Really? Who's that handsome officer escorting her?"

"I don't recognize his uniform."

"He's our host's brother, darling, and a captain in the Cape Chatham Fencibles, wherever they are!"

Before Sylvia realized it she was acknowledging Reynolds Seymour's graceful bow and his partner's sweeping curtsy.

"Please, Mrs. Seymour, do forgive our being so inexcusably tardy," pleaded Miss Romaine. "Our coachman had such trouble with my horses."

Sylvia assured her lovely young guest that Mlle. Esterhazy had not yet put in an appearance.

Irad came up, offered his hand and presently conducted Reynolds to a well-stocked sideboard.

"Brandy? Port? Chartreuse?"

"Brandy, please, and not in a damned glass thimble, either. It's growing mighty cold outdoors; real Christmas weather. Thanks! Here's health to you, Owlie, and to hell with all Yankees!"

Over his champagne glass Irad regarded this darkly handsome youngest brother in his dashing green and claret regalia.

"Weren't you returning to Savannah two days ago?"

Reynolds glanced quickly about. "So I was, but a rather delicate matter has arisen." He winked. "A matter concerning some, er, rather important Army contracts."

Irad brightened. "Since you have stayed over, Rey, I hope you'll join us here for Christmas dinner and meet your two nephews under the Christmas mantelpiece." He grinned. "There'll be five of us young Seymours together for the first time."

"Five?" Reynolds' dark brown brows elevated themselves. "You can't mean that old Sambo will be on deck?"

"Yes."

"How wonderful! I haven't seen Sam in a donkey's years." Reynolds spoke easily, as if there weren't any reason at all for Sam's having avoided him. "Just think how pleased dear old Pa would be if he should chance in and find us all three wearing uniform. How is he, by the way?"

"Poorly. I'm afraid he got into a pretty bitter dispute with Matt Maury because old 'Deep Sea' turned down his application on account of age. Mother says he was furious and threatened to go with Captain Farragut; you know Farragut's joined the Yankees?"

"So I heard. When is Sam due to appear?" Thoughtfully, Reynolds' lively gaze surveyed the company so gaily milling about the ballroom.

"Perhaps tomorrow, maybe the day after, depends upon the trains, but he promises definitely to be on hand to celebrate Christmas and we'll have a grand old time."

Despite himself Irad flung an affectionate arm about his brother's silver-decked shoulders and gave him a little hug. Somehow, he had never been able to remain angry with Reynolds for very long.

Preparations for the recital got under way, with musicians tuning like a quartet of stomachaches and Mlle. Esterhazy's big golden harp being trundled out from a corner to have its green baize cover removed. The guests had begun to seat themselves when a young officer wearing the golden aiguillettes of an aide made his way up to Sylvia and said in an undertone, "Madam, His Excellency the President and Mrs. Davis are on their way and will appear within a few moments."

"The—the—President is coming?" Sylvia uttered a low, rich laugh expressive of delighted astonishment. Incredibly the President of the Confederacy and Varina Davis were about to attend her soirée! Now the most stiff-necked grandes dames in Richmond must travel to Canossa!

When in radiant triumph she conveyed the news to Irad he turned brick-red.

"Good God! Sylvia, what are we to do?" Unhappily he blinked behind his golden-rimmed spectacles. "Pollard and many of the President's bitterest political enemies are present."

Sylvia found an instant solution. "Don't worry, dear. The moment His Excellency arrives I will order the orchestra to strike up 'Dixie's Land.' That should give Pollard and his sort sufficient warning in case they care to withdraw." She smiled charmingly at Reynolds. "Perhaps you will suggest that Pollard and Company will find brandy and seegars in Irad's study?"

"Sister dear," Reynolds assured them, "you may count on me to the bitter, diplomatic death. I'll shepherd 'em out so slick that no one will notice."

The instant Jefferson Davis' aide reappeared, Sylvia signaled the orchestra leader to strike up "Dixie's Land," that heart-lifting tune which fast was becoming the Confederacy's unofficial anthem. Startled, the guests arose and hastily drew aside their chairs in order to create a passage the length of the ballroom.

"Irad!" urged Sylvia in a sibilant whisper. "Take my arm, you great idiot! We must advance to greet them."

She wished now that certain haughty dowagers back in Baltimore who had patronized "poor sweet little Mrs. Seymour" less than a year ago could have watched her tall, distinguished-appearing husband and herself proceed to the ballroom's center at the precise moment it was being approached by the President and his lovely lady—she who had been born Varina Howell of Mississippi.

Volleys of cheers, as sincere as they were loud, made candle flames

dance. The ovation persisted until the presidential pair occupied arm-
chairs reserved for their uses. Everyone noticed that Mr. Davis had
limped noticeably.

"It's that old wound he took at the battle of Buena Vista," murmured Mrs. Togno. "Bleak weather like this always bothers the poor
soul."

Irad for once stood in awe of this sweetly efficient young hostess
who was also his wife. That she could have maneuvered the foremost
couple of the South into thus honoring the home of a not-very-im-
portant naval commander was indeed a remarkable achievement.

When cheers faded and the music stopped, Jefferson Davis briefly
greeted his Cabinet officers, but his manner was so reserved as to indicate his displeasure over something. He did not see, or pretended
not to notice, how promptly Mr. Pollard and certain other gentlemen, including General Gonzales, disappeared into a library opening
off the ballroom.

Presently Mlle. Esterhazy arrived to curtsey profoundly before the
President and Mrs. Davis, who appeared graciously regal in a small
tiara and a handsome evening gown of magenta silk—a color furiously
fashionable at the moment. The musicale consisted of selections from
the works of Arnadeno and Mozart, interspersed with sprightly Hungarian peasant airs. Everyone was charmed, especially when the artiste
closed her recital with a spirited rendition of "The Bonnie Blue Flag."

Scarcely five minutes following the program's conclusion, President
Davis sent for his carriage and, with ascetic, lean features set in their
customary immobile expression, conducted his wife out of Sylvia Seymour's ballroom.

IV

Recessional

ONLY ONE MINOR incident served to mar the greatest triumph of
Sylvia Seymour's life. In taking his departure, Mr. Benjamin, a dumpy
yet somehow impressive figure, unfortunately raised his voice in say-

ing, "My dear Mrs. Seymour, how pleased I am to inform you that I've persuaded Colonel Dabney's widow to sell you those carriage horses in which you were so interested."

The Secretary's bright black eyes sparkled. "You not only are blessed with a most charming partner, Commander Seymour, but you've married a shrewd trader as well."

"Oh, how very good of you!" Sylvia's breath entered sharply and she avoided Irad's startled look. Possible purchase of the Dabney carriage horses had aroused considerable acrimony; Irad irately maintaining that their present pair of dappled grays was entirely satisfactory. Why couldn't he be made to see that Mrs. Dabney's blooded blacks would look ever so much smarter than those tame old grays which never snorted, pawed or threw their heads?

Once the Secretary had moved on, Irad said in a furious undertone, "By God, Madam, after I strictly forbade you! You know we can't afford— Good evening, Mrs. Gonzales, it was so good of you to appear."

"Oh, must you go so soon, Colonel?" Sylvia's voice fairly trilled. "There's to be a buffet supper. No? Please don't apologize. Of course, you warriors have such heavy responsibilities these days I know you must be dead-tired. Oh, Major Graham, I'm delighted to see you looking so perfectly splendid. Your poor arm is healing well I trust?"

Of necessity Irad forced a smile and joined in the amenities, yet underneath his cordial manner he was in a boiling rage. Why, oh why, had he ever been such a great fool as to let Sylvia touch her own money? He'd no idea, of course, that old Lucius Magoffin was so boundlessly rich.

The purchase of these carriage horses he felt to be in deplorable taste; all fit mounts should go either to the cavalry or to the field artillery. Everyone knew that Remount Service officers were wailing like scalded cats for replacements.

By the Lord Harry, he swore silently, he'd put an end to this sort of nonsense; yet, at the same time, he knew he could not. Now that she had produced an heir, Sylvia would do as she pleased and when she wanted something she would get it. Hadn't she set up housekeeping in Richmond; won him a most promising appointment in the Navy Department—and produced a son, Jefferson Davis Seymour?

He heard her engaging the lovely Miss Romaine in conversation.

"My dear Miss Romaine, you and Reynolds simply must stay for supper. It's been such a long while since Commander Seymour has had a chance really to visit with his brother. I just won't hear of a refusal."

Becky Romaine ended by declaring herself delighted to linger. At eighteen, she was no little impressed; after all, Sylvia Seymour just possibly might become her sister-in-law if Pa, and brother Randolph, grew less consistently unreasonable. Why did they feel it incumbent upon them to disparage Reynolds at every turn and ridicule his military efforts? Perhaps the Cape Chatham Fencibles weren't the South's most distinguished regiment. What if he hadn't gone rushing off to Northern Virginia once the bugles had commenced to sound? There were plenty of other well-born young men who hadn't, either, but had kept on serving in less glamorous fashions. Was it any disgrace that Reynolds Seymour should have purchased a few shares in a blockade runner? Certainly not. Everyone, even Mr. Trenholm, was doing similarly.

Sylvia, covertly studying the Romaine girl, decided, "Becky's face is really beautiful, but her ankles are heavy and she could benefit from a few lessons in carriage. Doesn't seem too clever, either, but maybe that's because she's head-over-heels in love with Reynolds."

She watched her brother-in-law and his partner across the supper table set up in the walnut-paneled library. Curious, how well she understood Reynolds, for all that they'd not met more than two or three times and then always in a crowd.

That curious disparity between characters of the three brothers returned, struck her even more forcibly. Irad was almost devoid of humor but was as dependable as the tides and the sun; Sam was full of humor and sensitivity while possessing much of Irad's simple and earnest directness. A fine full-blooded fellow, Sam, who physically would make almost two of Reynolds. To her, the youngest Seymour brother suggested a darkly vital and precious stone, beautifully cut and mounted. One never caught Reynolds making an awkward gesture, he was much too alert. His manners she found impeccable; certainly, she'd met no one in a very long while who could offer more convincing flattery. His mind she analyzed as restless and as penetrating as it was retentive. All in all, this was quite a family into which Sylvia Magoffin had married.

V

Carry Me Back to Ole Virginny

Lieutenant Samuel Seymour found his way out of the dim, grimy Byrd Street Station of the Richmond & Petersburg Railroad carrying a bag containing all his worldly possessions.

After the stuffy reek of the railway coach the air proved wonderfully invigorating and this fall of fine snow seemed friendly, even caressing.

It being near eleven o'clock, Eighth Street looked dark and empty, but by hurrying he managed to overtake an ancient hackney driven by an equally aged Negro.

"Wheh to, suh?"

"Do you know where the Ashforth place is on Leigh Street?"

The old man slewed around on his seat. " 'Deed I do, suh! Useter belong to old Miz Ashforth till she willed me free." He coughed while gathering up leather reins patched with wire. "Wish't I wuz huh slave agin."

"You do? Why's that, uncle?"

"Mighty hard fo' a free nigger make his livin' round Richmond. Yassuh, ol' Miz Ashforth she feed us berry fine, and come every Christmas a new suit of clo'es. Don't get nuthin fo' Christmas no mo'." He craned about again. "You come to Ashforth House in de ol' days, suh?"

"No. I'm afraid not."

"Too bad, dem wuz gran' good times when ol' Miz wuz still alive, suh. Giddup, Meteor," he clucked to a raw-boned skate drowsing between the shafts.

Sam groped beneath a blue watch coat, then took a pull of brandy from a convex flask. Still feeble from his illness, he had commenced to shiver. Absently he passed his hand over a two days' beard. "Must be a pretty sight," he mused. "My collar's probably gray as my coat."

At the prospect of holding Robbie before long, he brightened. It would be grand to see Irad again, too, but how would he react on coming face to face with Sylvia? Could they pretend that nothing whatever had chanced that dawn after Mr. Winans' cotillion?

Praise God, good old Owlie wasn't overly observant. Sam intended to remain on his guard and linger in Richmond only long enough to receive orders. Should he relieve his brother of Robbie's care? Mother and Captain Felix would take him and gladly—but they were so old and tired.

The poor beast struggled up a long hill, then clattered down its reverse slope. The driver sat hunched well forward and apparently asleep, with battered plug hat canted forward to keep flour-fine snow out of his eyes.

Which was the taller, Louise Cottier or Sylvia? Curiously enough, in a good many respects, they were quite similar. Both had small hands, tiny feet, the same lively glance and ready, heart-warming smile.

At length the empty-sounding *clack-clop* of hoofs halted and the driver shrugged snow from bent shoulders.

"Heah we is, suh. Dis de Ashforth place." With his whip he pointed to four pillars looming through the gentle snow like attenuated white ghosts.

It was infinitely reassuring to notice several lights sketching golden ruler-marks across the snow as, a moment later, Sam tugged at a silvered bellknob. A spray of holly secured to the front door fell away.

"De guests all done gone home, suh," a heavy-eyed butler informed. "De pahty's over, suh."

"No doubt. Here, take my bag and go fetch your master. I am his brother."

Zeno's eyes became ringed in white. This large, hollow-cheeked apparition with fatigue sketching deep black lines all over his countenance was a different sort of guest.

"Come in, Mister Seymour, suh, come right in!"

He started away, but Sam restrained him by inquiring, "My brother still up?"

"Yassah. De Commander and de Missus an' a pair of guests is still partakin' of some eatments."

Somewhere a bell was being rung impatiently. Grinning, Sam caught up the tray Zeno must have deserted to answer the door. Imitating a Negro's dragging footsteps, he pushed open the door, drawling, "Yas, suh, yassuh! I's comin' mos' direc'ly."

"Put your tray on the side—" Irad got no further. "My God! Sam!"

He barely allowed Sam time to put down the tray before the two entered into a bear-hug and pounded each other wildly between the shoulder blades.

Before he could do anything about it, Sylvia had slipped arms about his neck and the fragrance of her mouth was on his.

"Oh, Sam! Sam! What a very wonderful surprise!"

Tiny electrical impulses shot through him. Damn! This wasn't what he had planned at all.

"Sam! Dear old boy." Dark features alight, Reynolds also flung arms about his brother and hugged hard, just as they had in the old days. Everyone commenced talking at once and nobody listened until Sylvia's breathless voice predominated.

"Miss Romaine, may I present Lieutenant Seymour, my elder brother-in-law? He's sailed aboard the famous *Sumter!*"

Deep sincerity in her tone, Becky Romaine said, "I am privileged, sir, to meet so distinguished a defender of our sacred Cause," and curtseyed all the way to the floor.

They crowded about him: grave, yellow-bearded Irad; Reynolds glittering and gay, and the ladies lovely as wood ducks in fall plumage.

"Mercy! What are we thinking of?" cried Sylvia at length. "You must be starved, poor dear."

"I'd enjoy a bite," admitted the unshaven and travel-stained figure in gray. "Had only a slab of greasy pork and cold potatoes between Petersburg and here." He flushed guiltily. "Is Robbie all right?"

"Never better," boomed Irad. "You'll find him grown huge, and almost disgustingly healthy."

"Could I—when may I see him?" Just in time he remembered. "And little Jeff." Sylvia's glance met his and clung a perceptible second.

Irad chuckled. "Of course, all in good time, but first come up to my room and wash. Reynolds, will you please entertain the ladies during our defection?"

VI

Noël! Noël!

CHRISTMAS DAY OF 1861 forever remained a vivid recollection in the memories of all gathered in Ashforth House; family and slaves as well. Although certain gaps had appeared among supplies ranging the dozens of pantry shelves, there remained a fine stock of delicacies and, when the servants appeared crowding about the foot of the big white staircase chanting, "Chris'mus gif'! Chris'mus gif'!" there were plenty of bandannas, Osnaburg shirts, pipes, tobacco twists, sugar candy, oranges and even choice items of cast-off finery.

Still, by comparison with Christmas celebrations at Beau Rivage down in Savannah, Sylvia found the jollification decidedly modest. Next month she intended to insist on sending home for her slave Juliet, twin sister of Romeo, who had been presented to brother Wilmer. Juliet was clever with babies and certainly would make an ideal nursemaid for little Jeff.

The usual Christmas breakfast proved enormously gay, with Master Robbie prancing about the table beating a drum and wearing a diminutive Scottish kilt and bonnet presented by his Uncle Reynolds.

Thought Sylvia, "I wonder if Irad will ever love Jeff the way Sam worships his son? You can read pride in his every glance."

She experienced a pang of resentment that Jefferson was still so tiny he could not be present and so share in the admiration and affection being lavished on his cousin. Was he too little to be taken for an airing in her new yellow and black chariotee? One of Messers Hitchcock & Osborn's best, it boasted a glossy black-and-cane body mounted on spider-thin canary-colored wheels. She was pretending to all and sundry that Irad had bestowed it upon her.

Sylvia lay upon her great bed with stays unlaced as a penalty for having consumed unlady-like portions of that Christmas goose, which at three of the afternoon had appeared to grace the gaily decorated Christmas board.

What great events had taken place during this dying year! That successfully managed affair with Sam, the outbreak of war, the move to Richmond and finally the birth of a son and heir. A smile crept over Sylvia's delicate pink and white features. Just to think that last year at this time she'd been wife to a struggling and obscure young marine architect, occupying a miserable little dwelling in a most unfashionable quarter of Baltimore.

In those days she'd had but a nodding acquaintance with less than a dozen socially acceptable ladies. And now, she had slaves galore, was mistress of Ashforth House and an intimate of the chief officials of the Confederacy and their wives. She settled luxuriously upon an incredibly soft swan's down pillow.

If only Irad could be made a little more up and pushing, like—well, like his youngest brother. If only he'd an ear for significant and profitable gossip, but he hadn't. How much easier it would have been for her to forge continued success, had she married quick, handsome and supple young Reynolds!

She sighed, drew a lace and pink satin coverlet up higher over the twin mounds of her bosom—a bosom which she was glad to note had not lost its shape.

Imagine Sam's being taken in by that silly, melodramatic letter she'd sent him last spring! He must believe the baby undoubtedly to be Irad's, else, never in the world, would he have come this near. She found herself wishing that Sam would get his orders quickly and depart before anything chanced to upset the delicate balance of their relationship.

Had she been married to Reynolds she would never have dared take so terrible a chance, his was too shrewd and noticing a nature; every now and then she glimpsed devils dancing at the backs of those expressive sea-green eyes.

Well, come another year, she intended to own a Paris ball gown as smart as Varina Davis' just as surely as she'd see Irad become Chief of the Navy Department's Bureau of Orders and Detail. It should not prove overly difficult to displace slow and painfully methodical old Commander Minor. By George! Irad would become Chief, whether he wanted it or not!

Such a post surely would lead to his having a flag before long. True, the present Tables of Organization for the Confederate Navy provided for no higher rank than that of Flag Officer—an anomalous grade often confused with that of commodore.

Everyone predicted, however, that if this war continued much longer some admirals would have to be created; in that connection the names of Buchanan, Bulloch, Maury and possibly Tattnall were those most frequently mentioned.

Sylvia drowsed. Samuel Seymour, Secretary of the Navy? Would it be possible eventually to unseat Stephen R. Mallory? A great many still suspected that quiet Floridian of secret Northern sympathies. Um-m. Madam Secretary? The title sounded well as she dropped off to sleep.

In the walnut-paneled library below, Sam sat sprawled all over a deep armchair, legs thrust far out and with close-cropped head tilted away back the more perfectly to savor a selection from that magnificent box of Havana seegars Sylvia had presented.

Irad, meanwhile, was doing a sentry-go back and forth before the fireplace. He had replaced his uniform tunic with a house coat of tabby velvet set off by rich crimson lapels and on his head wore a tasseled fez of the same hue.

"I loathe wearing those damned commander's stars," said he ruefully, "when you're still only a lieutenant."

"Nonsense." Sam, supremely comfortable and gorged with Christmas dinner, grinned small-boy-like at his elder brother. "You've earned them all right! I'd sooner tackle a Malay gone amok than the rat-souled politicians and crooked commissioners you deal with. No, Owlie, I wouldn't swap posts with you for a captaincy. No, sir."

Irad, towering above the mantelpiece, removed and polished his spectacles, cast his still-haggard brother a look of deep affection.

"Seems odd us having children, doesn't it? We'd about given up hope, Sylvia and I. Somehow I can't get used to being a father to a boy of my own."

Sam's gaze flickered to and away from his brother's grave and impassive features—having read nothing.

"You will!" he assured his brother, smothering a small belch. "And I hope Jeff will just be the start of a procession. You ought to have three boys—just like Pa and Ma."

Irad folded his arms, watched smoke curling upwards from that long-stemmed porcelain pipe which was his favorite. Sylvia discouraged his using it, declaring that the fumes smelled up her Irish lace curtains.

Sam undid the last button securing his tunic, shot Irad a quizzical glance and demanded, "What about Reynolds? Has he really seen the light?"

Slowly Irad passed a hand over his jaw, making invisible bristles crackle.

"I really don't know. Rey secured advance information and was smart enough to sell out his privateering venture when the Europeans closed their ports to prizes. As near as I can find out, he's busy outfitting blockade runners in Savannah."

"How much time does he devote to military duty?"

Irad shrugged. "Not too much; at least that's Captain Crockett's opinion. He told me, among other things, that Rey's maintaining a high yellow, which may be the accepted thing in New Orleans, but in Savannah such goings on aren't condoned."

Sam, sensing that his seegar's ashes were about to fall, flicked them into the fireplace. Frowning, he studied the glowing coal thus revealed.

"Is there more to it?"

"If it weren't old Captain Crockett himself who'd told me, I'd not credit the report that when Rey gets really liquored up he beats this girl so hard that she shrieks."

"Reynolds beat a woman?" Sam's jaw dropped and he sat bolt upright. "Of course, he's always been wild as a hawk, but he simply couldn't do such a thing!"

"Have you ever seen Reynolds well awash?" queried Irad. "I have, and he's not a pretty piece of work at such times."

"I still don't believe Crockett's gossip. Rey's always the soul of gallantry. Didn't you notice how considerate he was of the Romaine girl?"

A brief silence pervaded the library, which was terminated by the loud and irregular clatter of hoofs. From a window overlooking the stable yard Sam watched a small colored groom wrestling to control a restive horse rearing and striking out with its front feet. The darky hung on, talking until the beast quieted and condescended to drink from a long stone trough.

"Those horses you gave Sylvia for Christmas look quite a handful."

A *click* made by Irad's jaws made Sam turn.

"I didn't give Sylvia those horses."

"You didn't?"

"God no, man! Where would I find the money on a commander's pay? Sylvia bought them. I had to put up with it, just as I have had to put up with all the rest of this."

"How come you broke down and allowed her the use of her dowry?"

Irad looked a little helplessly at his brother. "I was out of a job when the war began, and prices were soaring. What else was I to do?"

Hating to read the misery on Irad's face, Sam kept eyes on his gradually lengthening seegar ash.

"Sylvia's very gracious about it and you're not to imagine that I have ceased to love her; she's everything in the world to me. I don't know what I would do if anything went wrong between us. If ever I were to catch anybody trying to trifle with Sylvia, I—I'd—kill him!"

A rivulet cold as ice water seemed to trickle down Sam's spine while his brother continued.

"That's what makes it so damnably difficult. Here she is, throwing away her money in putting up this front. It's not only uneconomical, but it's damned bad taste." Irad tugged angrily at his short, golden beard and commenced to walk more rapidly before the fireplace. "Consider what that same sum would buy in medical supplies."

Sam bent, eased off his sea boots, then wriggled a stockinged foot before he said cautiously, "I'm sure Sylvia means only to help you; look where you've gotten, a full commander in only seven short months!"

"Oh, to be sure, to be sure!" jeered Irad. "And I'm on intimate terms with dozens of purblind politicians and grafting contractors. God above, Sam! You've no conception of the selfish intrigue, the crass greed prevalent on Capitol Hill. No power on earth seems able to render Mr. Davis sensible of the Navy's desperate needs."

The library fire crackled comfortably, sleepily.

"Aren't you stressing the black side? I know we've a great many capable officers eager to serve our Cause."

"We've good officers as you say," Irad admitted. "But where will we find ships for them to command—and seamen? When you come for your interview with Mr. Mallory perhaps you'll better understand our difficulties. Speaking of the interview, what sort of a post would you prefer?"

"First, and above everything, I want sea duty in a fighting ship. If possible, I'd like the independent command of a cruiser—like the Sumter."

They talked until there came a knock at the door and Robbie, wearing a miniature Confederate naval uniform, rushed in and pelted over to his father's wide-opened arms. Sam swung his son high towards the ceiling.

"We Seymours do get on," Irad laughed. "Bob is already a midshipman by the anchors on his lapels."

"Mis' Sylvia done 'broidered dem hersef'," Melissa proudly announced from the doorway, nodding violently to show off her principal Christmas gift, a pair of gold-wire earrings. It was like Sylvia to think of that.

Father and Uncle went to don their uniforms and were still teaching Robbie to salute when Sylvia, looking livelier than ever, appeared.

"I see you two are grounding our future admiral with due attention to detail," she smiled. "But perhaps you seadogs had better get ready."

Irad groaned. "Good Lord, Sylvia, we're not going out?"

"Heavens, yes, the Memmingers are giving a tea; our absence might possibly be misinterpreted."

VII

Mr. Secretary Mallory

For a mere lieutenant in the Old Navy to be received by the Secretary was almost undreamed of, so Sam Seymour's manner was diffident for all that his brother appeared entirely at ease when rapping on Secretary Mallory's door.

"Here goes. I'll linger a bit, then leave and let you talk with Uncle Steve."

The Honorable Stephen R. Mallory, Sam discovered, was much as he remembered him from Pensacola days, of below average height, pink of cheek and possessed of an imposing abdomen draped in a silk tartan waistcoat. His beard was gray now and clipped neatly short, as was his sandy-gray hair. The Secretary arose, beaming, and came striding forward with hands outstretched.

"It's a great pleasure, Sam, at once to welcome an old friend, an officer of the *Sumter* and the brother of a most dependable assistant." His pale blue eyes twinkled. "Not to mention a brother-in-law to the enchanting Mrs. Seymour."

Sam could feel Irad wincing, hurrying his departure.

Over the *Sumter's* successes and subsequent legal difficulties with the Captain-General of Cuba, Secretary Mallory became particularly inquisitive. He posed endless questions concerning Semmes' representations and the Yankee Consul's counter-measures.

"Returning the *Sumter's* prizes to their owners was a sad blow," Mallory sighed, "but, until we win recognition abroad, I fear that is what we must expect. And now, Sam, can you give me some specific and practical recommendations concerning the outfitting of cruisers now being constructed for this Department in France and England?"

Behind the great desk he listened carefully and made occasional notes. When Sam had concluded, Mallory created a steeple of stubby forefingers amid his chin whiskers.

"Sam, what you've told me sounds so practical and valuable that I'd like to order you abroad to supervise the construction of our new commerce raiders. After all, you have had considerable experience."

"You seem to forget, sir, that I was imprisoned in Cienfuegos after the *Sumter* had been at sea for less than a week," Sam pointed out.

"True, true." Stephen Mallory hunched forward, flexing a paper knife between plump but powerful hands. Small nuggets of raw gold gleamed at his cuffs. "You spent some time in New Orleans last spring, didn't you?"

"Yes, sir, almost two months. We sailed July first."

Secretary Mallory consulted a small pile of documents. "Umhum. Then you must have missed subsequent developments and don't know that Congress has authorized me to construct at once ten gun-boats for service on the Mississippi; propellers, of about a thousand tons displacement and to be armed with one ten-inch gun and four eight-inch guns apiece."

The Secretary glanced up with a wry smile. "Trouble is, Sam, we're totally unable and unequipped to complete any such gunboats within the legal time limit. We just haven't the necessary yards or skilled mechanics—the Army has gobbled them. We, therefore, have been forced to convert a number of steamers to meet our pressing need. We've the *Livingston*, for instance, undergoing reconstruction by Hughes and Company, which will prove useful and there are some other promising rebuilt river steamers; they mount, let's see now, six guns each. Naval Constructor Sidney Porter, who is supervising this project, reports the rest of our river fleet to be miserable makeshift cotton clads, such as the *General Polk*, the *Ivy*, the *Maurepas* and others."

"We'll do better soon, sir," Sam predicted, while he balanced on the edge of his chair with eyes riveted on Mr. Mallory's features.

"Aside from this difficulty the situation in and about New Orleans is deplorable."

"Deplorable?"

Bitterness hardened Stephen Mallory's voice. "Because the sovereign State of Louisiana has been encouraged by certain contractors and speculators to believe that this Department does not sufficiently appreciate her danger, nor the gravity of the Federal fleet's threat to New Orleans.

"This is sheer buncombe inspired by selfishness or mistaken concepts of State's Rights. From the beginning, this Government has fully appreciated the vital importance of New Orleans. That's why I have ordered to Louisiana many of my most experienced officers; men such as Rousseau, Farrand and, more recently, Captain George N. Hollins.

"President Davis, as a brilliant former Army officer, fully recognizes the peril of allowing a Yankee fleet to detach Texas and the other Confederate States west of the Mississippi River from communication with their eastern sisters.

"That the Richmond Government has not produced enough naval power adequately to defend New Orleans unfortunately is quite true.

But, to correct this, I am at present doing everything in my power. Unfortunately I must have better cooperation from the Louisiana authorities before I can make real progress."

Sam hesitated, caught his breath. "But haven't I heard rumors about a so-called 'Mississippi River Defense Squadron' being equipped down there and designed to serve under Army orders only? Surely the President hasn't countenanced such ruinous folly? I trust I'm mistaken, Uncle Steve."

A dark flush appeared above the Secretary's high collar.

"Unfortunately, Mr. Davis has," growled the Secretary, "thanks to the persuasiveness of General Leonidas Polk, who may have made an excellent Episcopal bishop but, as a general, however, he lacks quite a number of desirable qualities." He sighed. "And that's not all, Sam. Governor Moore sedulously has lured men and officers away from our ships and shipyards in order to build an independent Louisiana State Navy."

"But, sir, how can a government hope to succeed by maintaining three fleets on a single river, all acting independently?"

"Go inquire of Mr. Davis," Mallory advised and his pale eyes glittered. "For the Army—everything—for the Navy, crumbs from the banquet table. You've no conception of how I've had to intrigue, beg, plead and threaten, to secure a mere eight hundred thousand dollars with which to lay down the ironclads *Louisiana* and *Mississippi*."

Sudden enthusiasm brightened Mr. Mallory's expression. "This last vessel, Sam, we figure will prove the most destructive warship ever launched. Imagine it, she's designed to be of about six thousand-ton displacement, two hundred seventy feet in length and with a sixty-foot beam, and—" he added in ringing tones—"this super-gun-boat will be completely sheathed in four-inch armor especially reinforced at critical points. She'll be driven by four engines turning three propellers."

Sam blinked. Four engines turning three propellers? Here was an innovation all right, possibly an excellent one.

"She's to cost two million dollars," Mallory was continuing, "so it's as well I have such a sum certified by the Treasury. The *Mississippi* is being constructed by Nelson and Asa Tift of New Orleans, while her engines are to be installed and modified, on your brother's rec-

ommendation, by a Scotchman named Brunton. You've heard of this
Lachlan Brunton?"

"Yes, sir," replied the broad-shouldered figure in gray and gold.
"I took part in his wedding last spring. Irad knows him better and
deems him extremely capable."

The Secretary's square spectacles flashed as he bent over his desk
and linked fingers. "And now, Sam, I'll tell you what I have in mind
for you." He smiled. "How would you like to become the Mississippi's
ordnance and gunnery officer?"

Sam's heart leaped like a speared dolphin. "I'd admire to, sir. Who
wouldn't want to serve in the greatest ironclad afloat?"

"Good. The Bureau of Orders and Construction will issue instructions clothing you with power to supervise the installation of her
armament and magazines."

An indescribable exhilaration warmed Sam.

"This Department will require from you at the first possible instant
recommendations concerning the most suitable weights and character
of her battery, the design of their carriages and the placing thereof. Do
you feel qualified?"

"Gunnery and ordnance has always been my specialty, sir," came
Sam's eager assurance. "I believe Commander Maffitt would be willing to vouch for my efficiency."

"Good." Mallory's chair creaked under his weight as he settled back,
eyes suddenly shrewd and penetrating. "One fact you must never
lose sight of is that, for us, time is like rubies and pearls and much
fine gold. We understand that the Federals are well along in constructing a powerful river fleet at St. Louis. James B. Eads, their
supervisor, is being afforded every facility. Our espionage agents
further report that a powerful Union squadron is being collected in
the Gulf with a view to smashing the forts below New Orleans and
seizing that city.

"To prevent such a disaster, the Mississippi must be got ready in
time. Must! You understand? Your task will not be easy. The Army
contractors for that asinine River Defense Flotilla often outbid us for
essential materials and even foment strikes among our workers. You
must be determined; even ruthless. Do you think you can be?"

"With a necessity so great, that will be easy, sir. Persistence and diligence you shall have as a matter of course; trickery I shall resort to if that's required to accomplish the *Mississippi's* completion."

Sam arose, bowed, and would have taken his leave had not Mr. Mallory smilingly pulled out of his desk a cylinder of stiff white paper secured by a broad, navy-blue ribbon. "Here, Sam, you'd better take this along. As a lieutenant commander you will accomplish results far more quickly and efficiently."

VIII

Sunday Airing

THE SUNDAY FOLLOWING Christmas proved to be one of those unseasonably warm and pleasant days with which the inhabitants of Maryland and northern Virginia occasionally are blessed. Gradually the sun's beneficent intensity increased until it began to melt the snow away in great patches and enabled deeply embarrassed soldiers to remove those detested civilian overcoats which were all they had been issued.

This gentle warmth quickened the blood and evoked general good humor as, on the hilly streets of Richmond, appeared quantities of citizens clad in their Sunday best. Along Clay Street, as well as on Broad Street below the Capitol, a variegated procession of citizens sauntered; families including numerous children were strung out like steps on a staircase.

Energetic young cavalry and artillery officers felt prompted to mount chargers and canter along, gravely saluting their superiors and flirting gallantly with bright-eyed young ladies in huge hoop skirts. Even members of the Congress risked their top hats to snowball-hurling urchins and hired carriages for a drive into the suburbs.

Sylvia Seymour was delighted. On such a glorious day it would be entirely proper to show off the new span of blacks and her chariotee. Yes, she and Irad would take a drive, with old Melissa holding little Jeff for all Richmond to see and to admire.

Moses, her newly hired coachman, had given his charges an extra currying and also seen to it that their well-scrubbed hoofs glistened with varnish. What a pity that, as yet, her pair would wear no fancy brass-mounted bridles boasting crown pieces bearing the family monogram. Still, it would be mighty pleasant to roll along Broad Street toward Chimborazo Hill wearing her new plum-colored cloak and a tiny blue pill-box hat.

The glossy pelt of a bearskin laprobe would match her horses, and few such slender, canary-yellow carriage wheels had ever been seen about the Confederate capital.

Irad felt sleepy from his Sunday meal, but the baby was making happy gurgling noises characteristic of a well-fed infant. As for Melissa, her withered slate-gray cheeks swelled with pride when she was given the young master to hold upon a pillow trimmed with rich Flemish lace.

"This is all damn' silly and pretentious," Irad fumed, "but since it's such a fine day I'll go this once. What about this new coachman?"

"He belonged to the Clingman family," Sylvia replied sweetly, "and you know how horsey they are."

Several strollers paused to watch the chariotee draw up to the granite mounting steps before Ashforth House. The blacks, too, evidently were inspired by this sunshine; they snorted, pawed and danced until Irad cast them a doubtful look. Despite their fractious behavior Sylvia's purchases indeed were lovely to look upon with their manes and tails neatly braided and secured by a series of little yellow ribbons; besides, he knew precious little concerning horseflesh.

"Which way did Sam head?" Irad demanded, settling himself on the back seat beside his wife. Melissa and her charge sat opposite. "We should have made him accompany us. Really, my dear, isn't Jeff pretty young to take out of doors?"

"Nonsense! A breath of air will do him good. Besides, I want everyone to appreciate our son and Sam insisted on taking Robbie for a walk. Heavens! What a delightful picture they made, both in naval uniforms."

The coachman glanced over his shoulder anxious to let this restive span get going. They were fighting their bits so hard that his shoulders were commencing to ache.

Sam's pride swelled when, after walking ten long blocks, Robbie Seymour still kept on as strongly as ever. The boy's curiosity proved as boundless as his friendliness was unquenchable. More than once Sam was forced to stand, flushing and uncomfortable, when females attracted by the miniature uniform, would cry, "What an adorable little angel! I simply must kiss him," and promptly did so.

A big cavalry general in jack boots and loudly jingling spurs gravely returned Robbie's cheery salute, halted and spoke in a broad Georgian accent.

"Reminds me so much of my own son, suh, when he was little," he declared softly to Sam. His face worked strangely. "Billy fell at Manassas. I hope, suh, your son will prove more fortunate."

"—And as nobly inspired," Sam returned quickly.

"Thank you, suh," the General smiled and stalked on, even straighter of back than before.

Somewhere away down the street another of those seemingly numberless military bands began to bray.

"Rob, would you like to go listen to the pretty music?"

Robbie having given enthusiastic assent, his father swung him up onto his shoulder and strode along beneath the bare and scabrous branches of sycamores lining the sidewalk.

Everywhere, it seemed, he encountered gray- or brown-clad casualties wearing empty sleeves or being pushed along in improvised wheelchairs or set out, swathed in blankets, to enjoy the sunshine.

From nearly every window fluttered the newly popular, but not officially recognized, Beauregard flag, that banner distinguished by a blood-red field and white-edged Saint Andrew's cross done in blue and spaced with white stars.

"That's a beautiful flag," Sam thought, "and none but a fool could ever confuse it with 'Old Glory.'" A moment later his sailor's eye detected a flaw, and a grave one, in the Beauregard flag's design; such an ensign should never fly over a man-of-war because its perfectly balanced design precluded inverting it to indicate distress.

They were drawing nearer to the bandstand when the music struck up a martial overture commencing with a great roll of drums and the startling clash of several cymbals.

It was this fanfare which caused Sylvia Seymour's horses momentarily to snort, then recoil in quivering terror upon their glossy haunches. The next instant they had bounded forward with such irresistible power as to rip their reins from Moses' grasp. All restraint removed, they hurtled, white-eyed, off down Broad Street.

Sylvia shrieked even as Irad flung a restraining arm about her, for, under the furious speed of the high-strung blacks, the little chariotee commenced to lurch like a ship laboring in a cross-current.

Fast, faster and faster still, drummed the flying hoofs before the vehicle careening along Broad Street. Men shouted, women screamed, while Sylvia received the weird impression of Melissa hanging desperately on with one hand while hugging the pillow and its precious burden with the other, her eyes grown white and large as dinner plates. A sickening sensation of utter helplessness pervaded her. Ignoring his wildly flying reins, Moses only clung to the box, yammering out his mortal terror.

"Get those reins, damn you!" Irad was yelling.

Unhampered by two or three cavalrymen spurring in vain pursuit, the blacks raced on with nostrils flaring scarlet. First they swerved over the left-hand curb, bowling down or scattering various pedestrians.

"Jeff! Save Jeff!" Sylvia heard her own voice screaming.

A horseman riding in the opposite direction charged bravely straight at the frantic carriage horses, but only succeeded in causing them to swerve onto the sidewalk.

There followed a sickening, cracking, splintering sound when the chariotee locked a front wheel about the trunk of a young tree and was slewed violently around. The wheels gave way hurling a cloud of shattered and flying spokes at the crowd but permitting the chariotee to bump onwards, strewing its passengers onto the cobbles with a sickening violence.

"There's been a runaway, an awful one!" Sam heard someone yelling from the vicinity of the bandstand. "Music must ha' frightened them carriage hosses."

"What kind of a carriage was it?" Sam felt the skin on his forearms beginning to chill and tingle.

"Why, 'twere what some calls a chariotee, sir," called a wounded soldier. "It was black wi' yellow wheels."

"Oh, my God!" Tucking his son under one arm as if he had been a bundle, Sam disregarded the child's frightened outcry, to pelt down Broad Street until he came up with the first of three separate knots of pedestrians. This group was bending over a baby which lay with its long white gown growing momentarily a brighter crimson. A little further on an aged colored woman lay like a sack of soiled laundry, a bluish tinge spreading over her wrinkled features.

Gasping, utterly dismayed, Sam ran along to the next group. A deep sob, wrenched from the depths of his soul, escaped him when, on pushing through the crowd, he found Irad lying flat on the muddied cobbles with his uniform torn and his yellow head twisted at so grotesque an angle to his body that he must have died instantly, his neck broken.

All manner of shouts and yells for doctors, for shutters, for bandages were arising. Brain seething, Sam lurched on another ten yards to where Sylvia's slight figure lay with head resting on some gentleman's coat. A pair of capable-appearing older women were rubbing her wrists. Even as Sam crouched at her side Sylvia's great, topaz-colored eyes opened; but it was evident that she remained dazed.

"Sylvia! Sylvia, do you know me? Stand back, this is my sister-in-law!" he snapped, passing Robbie on to an onlooker.

Her eyes could not yet focus themselves, but her voice sounded both clear and low. "Yes, oh, Sam, Sam my darling. I'm so glad you're here."

"You don't understand," Sam cried harshly. "Irad's dead."

Still hopelessly bewildered, Sylvia stared up into his face a long instant. "Oh, wha—what's happened?"

"There's been an accident, lady—" cried an onlooker.

All at once Sylvia remembered, clutched at Sam's sleeve. "Oh, Sam! Go find Jeff, we mustn't let anything happen to our baby!"

BOOK FOUR

The Ironclads

I

LA RUE CONTI

A CLOCK IN the spire of the Cathedral of St. Charles clanged sleepily, resonantly, five times. Other church bells disputed the exact moment of five o'clock as far away as Jefferson City and in Algiers on the opposite and western bank of the Mississippi. Immediately various roosters and cockerels contributed their own opinions of the hour.

Within the confines of her massive four-poster, Louise Cottier stirred, yawned and peered through mosquito bars of filmy white to glimpse dawn-light sketching pale rectangles on the wall opposite. Subconsciously, she listened for those first street noises which always had delighted and stimulated her imagination. Alas, they were growing fewer and further between, now that New Orleans' commercial sinews had commenced to atrophy owing to interruption of traffic both with the Gulf and with the North.

She shifted position by deftly concentrating her weight between feet and shoulders in order to pull down and smooth a voluminous lawn nightgown. This done, she pushed aside long twin braids dividing her breasts like sable cross-belts.

For all that she still felt fatigued and wished to sleep longer, Louise found that she could not, so lay listening to the *clip-clop* of some horse resound hollowly, lonesomely in empty Conti Street.

A good hour yet must elapse before kitchen noises would rise from across the patio, before hawkers would commence to sing-sing melodiously, for all that their supplies of fish, fruits, vegetables and milk were diminishing at an alarming rate.

"*Bigre!* Why can't I sleep?" she muttered in French. She was tired from having been detailed all yesterday, together with the Dunois and the Claiborne girls, to the Ursuline Sisters' Dispensary down by the levee.

Since fighting along the upper Mississippi had grown in intensity, it seemed that nearly every steamboat bound downstream discharged a small army of sick and disabled and as yet there had been no really great battles! It was well for the New Orléannais that they remained unsuspecting of the blood baths of Forts Donelson, Henry and Island Number Ten, which were yet to come.

Here it was only the eleventh of January but, for all that, the weather had grown unseasonably hot, emphasizing the unbearable stench of gangrene and badly healing wounds.

How luxurious it was to lie in this wonderfully soft bed and dwell, without interruption, upon Sam Seymour and that amazing telegram he'd sent after a silence so long that she had been hurt far deeper than she cared to admit. She knew the wire by heart, just as she could have quoted whole paragraphs exactly from the only two letters she had received from him.

ASSIGNED DUTY IN NEW ORLEANS. DUE SUDDEN DEATHS IN FAMILY BRINGING SON. PLEASE BE GOOD ENOUGH ENGAGE SUITABLE GOVERNESS. ARRIVE JANUARY 11TH. MY HUMBLE RESPECTS TO YOU AND YOUR FAMILY. PROFOUND GRATITUDE IN ADVANCE.
/S/ SAMUEL SEYMOUR

RICHMOND, VIRGINIA
7 JANUARY 1862

Louise lay with great blue eyes wide open—darkly vital pools amid the gentle oval of her features. To think that sometime today—this being the eleventh—she would meet Sam once more—and his child. Louise wondered just what would be her reaction to the youngster's presence.

"*Mon Dieu,* was there ever before an affair so bizarre? Only three times have I met this Samuel Seymour and even then never truly alone, and yet I—I, well, am I not absurd to permit him to enter my thoughts so often?"

Briefly she speculated on why Sam's son had not been dispatched to live with his grandparents. That Sam's telegram should have been so delayed, over forty-eight hours, was entirely normal; communications within the Confederacy were deteriorating at alarming rate. One never could be sure whether a letter would even reach its destination.

Beneath her coverlet she felt warm, so lifted the sheet and pumped in cool air beneath, expelling warm air redolent of moss roses and her own body's peculiarly fragrant aura.

She told herself, "Madame Soult is just the one to become *gouvernante*; since the so-sad death by typhoid of little Sylvestre Peynac she has lacked employment."

Would Sam have changed much? In one of his letters he had, in direct and unflowery language, described a long and illegal imprisonment in Cuba, his experience in the hospitals of Charleston. And now had happened these deaths. Who could have died so suddenly? Obviously Sam's brother and sister-in-law, since the boy had been living with them.

A mockingbird commenced to trill and warble an oriole's notes in a treetop above the patio. How wonderfully sweet and clear his fluting notes sounded in the morning's empty stillness! She could hear somebody, probably Papa, snoring, but again it might be her cousin Antoine. Big, hearty and practically rotund Antoine had ridden in from his plantation in search of salt fish with which to feed his enormous gangs of slaves. He wasn't going to find any, Louise felt sure, because salt fish came either from New England or the West Indies.

On the other hand, the snorer might be her brother Étienne, now on duty as an aide to dashing, but not overly brilliant, Major General Mansfield Lovell. Poor Étienne had never been very hale and so was forced to meet the demands made by his duties by drafts upon a slender stock of nervous energy.

What a pity this awful war had dragged him away from Cythère, the enormously rich Cottier plantation down in Terrebonne Parish. Certainly 'Tienne looked far more natural at his easel, painting the mournful, lush landscapes he so favored, than galloping about city and countryside on the commanding general's business.

Yes, the tide of Cottier business was ebbing fast indeed. Only last week Papa had ordered closed his counting offices in Tchapitoulas Street, remarking bitterly that he perceived small sense paying clerks merely to count rats, mice and roaches. There wasn't, he'd declared, enough merchandise left in all those great warehouses along the levee to fill even the smallest of them; also supplies of cotton and sugar kept piling up and up until their price dropped to unheard-of levels and even then found no buyers.

Louise turned on to her side, idly studying a detail of her beautifully carved San Domingo mahogany bedstead. Could it be that Sam really was in love with her? She hoped not, because Mamma and Papa most certainly would offer the most fervent objections to serious attentions from an American. Like so many of their generation and descent, they still clung proudly to the delusion that they were French gentlefolk chancing to reside in America.

Again, the obstacle of incompatible religions presented itself. Why was it that Samuel Seymour's simple, direct manner and speech to her seemed so appealing, so reassuring? She supposed it must be because, since birth, she had been accustomed to flowery compliments and elaborate courtesies from every male who drew near.

Smiling, Louise recalled the curious thrill she had derived from Sam's, "You're looking pretty as a speckled pup, tonight." To be compared to a speckled puppy at first had seemed so inordinately funny that she had quite shocked Cousin Antoine by employing the very same simile with regard to pretty Marianne de Tadoussac.

He had stared, then rumbled, "Really, Louise, I find it in the most deplorable of taste to compare a lovely, well-bred lady with a dog. One fears that you have been consorting too much with Americans."

It being still too early to ring for bed-coffee, strong and black as Lucifer, Louise arose, poured a glass of water, then crossed to peer down the length of Conti Street.

After her long absence in France, these pale blue, pink, and ochre façades looked wonderfully soft, friendly and familiar; so also the iron grillework balconies, although they were of Spanish origin. Here and there she noticed slender threads of blue woodsmoke beginning to rise from certain blackened chimney pots. *Hélas*, the sky was clouding up in the southwest which argued a rainy day for Commander

Seymour's return. She returned to sprawl lazily upon the bedclothes, idly flexing her toes.

What should she wear? Of course, there was nothing new. Um, possibly that powder-blue gown with the pale yellow bolero and a wide straw hat would do.

Somewhere away down by the levee, a bugle began to sound First Call; then others reiterated the summons to be up and doing. Nowadays nearly eight thousand troops were quartered in the city or bivouacking about that great crescent of the Mississippi upon which New Orleans had been constructed.

Would Sam's child have inherited his robust frame, light brown hair and direct gaze? No telling. For all she knew, small Robert's mother might have been dark as herself.

For two days now she had been debating the most tactful manner in which she could inform Maman that she, a maiden, actually had received a telegram requesting her to find a governess for the child of a widower—and an American at that!

Only one element might alleviate her problem; since the advent of hostilities many rigid values were becoming modified. On the Place des Armes people were speaking these days, even exchanging gossip, who never previously had more than nodded.

Maman, definitely and permanently old school, would resist every innovation until the bitter end. Papa might prove more tolerant.

Ha! From downstairs came the clank of a saucepan and the welcome sound of a hatchet at work.

"Grace à Dieu, the domestics are up." At last she could send for her breakfast. Would Sam and his son arrive by train from Montgomery, or down from Memphis by river boat? The train seemed more likely. Most of the packet lines, such as the St. Louis, Cairo & New Orleans and the Red River, had about quit operation, what with traffic between plantation and city so reduced.

II

En Famille

Cousin Antoine appeared at breakfast, beefy, florid and incorrigibly humorous. He wore a long black goatee and mustaches trained into fancied resemblance to those affected by His Imperial Majesty, Louis Napoleon, Emperor of the French. That the Confederate Guards uniform the planter was wearing proved a bad fit was probably because Mr. Breaux, the tailor, had scamped precious cloth and so caused ugly, little spoon-shaped wrinkles to appear about its buttonholes.

Brother Étienne looked as if he had slept poorly, for pale blue patches lurked beneath either eye, and without comment he accepted a cup of café au lait.

In satisfaction Cousin Antoine consumed four eggs en cocotte, but grumbled over his not-so-generous ration of bacon.

"Ma foi, Louise, what is this? A child's tid-bit or a grown man's portion?" Heavy jet brows climbed.

"Mon cher, have you tried to buy bacon recently?" Louise briskly demanded while tucking back the cuffs of her blouse.

"No, do I look like some sacré grocer?"

"Well, then," she advised serenely, "count yourself lucky to find even this much on your plate."

She passed a silver bowl of fruit to her brother. "Étienne, you look tired. Don't let that General Lovell work you into a prostration. Must you be so busy?"

Étienne sighed, wearily dipping into the shirred eggs. "I fear so; it's all a silly business."

"Then it certainly originates in Richmond," remarked Antoine, his mouth full.

"What new species of imbecility is our bon Président Davis about to inflict upon us?"

Étienne delayed making reply long enough to select a flaky golden-brown croissant from a cloth-covered basket. "I understand little of high strategy, Toine, but it appears that our General Leonidas Polk before becoming Episcopal Bishop of Louisiana unfortunately attended West Point. Therefore he has consulted with and persuaded *le bon Président* Davis that our Confederate Navy is unable to defend New Orleans."

Half-forgotten dissertations by Sam immediately returned to Louise's memory. Said she, "That is true, indeed; our Navy *has* been most criminally neglected. But why should a general, of all people, persuade the Administration to strengthen it?"

"But he has not!" Étienne exploded. "*Morbleu!* We, the Army, have been ordered *independently* to fit out a fleet of our own!"

Cousin Antoine's heavy, blue-shadowed jaw sagged so far open that a bit of egg fell onto the point of his spike-like imperial.

"Surely you are making pleasantries, Étienne?"

"I am not," gloomily returned the aide. "General Lovell is beside himself with rage. What does he know about gunboats, of naval strategy? Is it not enough that he must strengthen and garrison those river forts which are our real protection?"

"You are sure of this?" Louise demanded.

"Positive. Already those great idiots in our Congress have diverted nearly a million dollars towards this absurd scheme. What do we soldiers understand of the management of warships? No more than those loud-mouthed river captains understand of gunnery or discipline!"

"We soldiers." A sad little smile flattened Louise's dark red lips. Less than six months ago Étienne could not have distinguished between a major general and a corporal except, perhaps, by the amount of gold lace they wore.

"All day General Lovell rides along the levees examining this laid-up steamboat and that one." He shrugged. "God knows there are plenty to choose from. A veritable marine graveyard extends all the way to Slaughterhouse Point."

A graveyard? The simile struck Louise with full force. Although the hour was now nearly seven, from outside came no sounds of wheels grinding against cobblestones, no patter of hurrying feet and only an occasional vendor's thin cry.

"Some strawberry preserve, Étienne? Oh! And, by the bye, who is the new Commandant of this Naval District?"

Her brother hesitated. "I believe the gentleman's name is Whittle. At Headquarters we have seen but little of him, he is so very occupied hurrying those new rams called *Mississippi* and *Louisiana*."

Presently Étienne excused himself, kissed Louise, then departed to mount a horse awaiting him in the courtyard.

"Toine," Louise began cautiously, "would you do me a favor?"

"But of course, chèrie."

"Would you secure a guest card to the Cercle Saint Philippe for a friend of mine?"

"Naturally, Louise; why so prettily diffident?"

"He is an American," she explained. "But a very nice one."

"American! *Mon Dieu.* Louise, have you gone mad?"

Her full skirts rustled briskly as she arose. "Not at all, *mon cher* cousin. You will do this for my sake, and ask no questions."

"As you wish. Today all manner of impossibilities become actualities. And what is this paragon's name?"

"Samuel Seymour, of the Confederate States Navy."

III

A. Schniewind & Company

To August Schniewind, ship chandler and ironmonger, the silence prevailing in New Levee Street was becoming funereal and its crushed oyster-shell paving, after last night's cleansing rain, suggested a long and dirty white shroud. Here and there small brilliantly green tufts of grass had begun to thrust tender exploratory fingers between cobbles reinforcing the crossroads.

The fact that the air, for a wonder, smelled clean and fresh was about the only happy result of this war, for when August Franz Schniewind reached New Orleans back in 1852, quite a good while elapsed before he became accustomed to the Crescent City's appalling variety of stenches.

In the family quarters, located above his store, August could hear

Maggie scolding, getting the children ready for school. *Ach, Maggie!*
What a fine, sweet and uncomplaining helpmate—despite occasional
exhibitions of Hibernian temperament. Not once during these dismal
past months had his wife complained while they watched his business
falter, sicken and finally collapse, another victim of the blockade.

Out of habit the big German sought a desk upon which rows of
ledgers, darkened and greasy from use, stood ranged as of yore. Until
three months ago, Schniewind and Company had never employed less
than three busy bookkeepers, four freight handlers and a number of
black teamsters. All these had either enlisted or been discharged as,
inexorably, various bins and shelves emptied themselves to their
bottoms.

Frowning, Schniewind went out onto the sidewalk and commenced
to take down a series of ponderous wooden shutters, but paused.

"Why do I bother?" he muttered in German, then peered back
into the cavernous gloom created by what once had been a leading
ship chandler's warehouse.

Across the street little Mr. Peron was going through the motions of
opening his chinaware and bric-a-brac shop—just as if he had something to sell.

The sun was climbing a little higher now, and revealing in full
detail dozens of river steamers tied parallel to the levee. How forlorn
they looked with stacks rusting, with paint and goldwork fading
and their small-boat davits trailing uselessly in the current.

Save for small mountains of cotton bales commencing to rot
through exposure, the great wharves and piers, usually crammed chock-
a-block with an infinite assortment of merchandise, lay barren—a
playground for Negro children and their ribby curs. The only visible
sign of activity was a quartermaster's tug churning over to supply the
McRae, flagship to Commodore George Hollins' little Regular Navy
squadron.

What a wicked thing was war, thus to nullify long years of planning,
toil and self-denial. August glanced at his hands—found them broad,
powerful and equipped with clever, blunt fingers; still the hands of
a master carpenter.

A peddler's pushcart turned into New Levee Street. "Po'gies!
Po'gies! Fresh fish!"

"Any meat?" August called.

"Naw, sar," replied the Negro. "Mought mebbe have some come next week, iffen de sodgers doan' tek it all."

"You're sure those porgies are fresh?" Maggie had suddenly appeared.

"Yas'm. Cotched dis bery mo'nin'."

Maggie's dark blue eyes sought her husband's plump red features.

"I despise serving fish again, dear, but—"

"I know, I know." Schniewind produced a wallet bloated with many pale brown and gray bills.

"Ain' you please, mebbe got jist one li'l bit ob silver, sar?" The gaunt slave blinked anxiously. "Massa doan' like me come back 'thout no silver at all."

August shook his head and passed over a greasy, limp bill, then produced what had once been a horse car ticket, the only available form of small change.

As the Schniewinds retired into the cool gloom of their store, Maggie inquired, "And will you be attending the Foreign Legion's drill tonight?"

"Ja. I vill drill."

Maggie was pleased. August, thanks to three years' service in the Royal Bavarian Army, had already been created a sergeant and looked really soldierly in the handsome dark blue uniform of a corps composed of French, Spanish, German and Irish residents. Exempt from service as foreigners, they nonetheless had been forced by public opinion to organize themselves into a home defense corps which, with so many of the regular police gone into service, already had proved its worth.

"Yes. I vill go to drill and draw mine pay, Margaret," he announced heavily, "I haff decided to close out mine business." The wildness of his laugh rendered her stare uneasy.

"As if there vass any business left to close up. Look! Look, vill you? Vhy didn't those verdammt idiots up in Richmond ship dot cotton ven they could?" Contemptuously, he flung his bulging wallet onto the dusty counter. "Den dot bum-plaster maybe vould buy us somethings."

As usual, when he became excited or angered, August's German accent broadened.

Maggie put down the fish, ran to fling arms about those brawny shoulders she so loved. Gently she cried, "Don't take on so, dear heart. The children and I won't go hungry. We still own a dray and two pair o' fine draft horses."

"Vun pair," Schniewind corrected heavily. "The browns I sold last veek. *Mein Gott*, Maggie, such a miserable price for those fine big Flemish horses, but I got greenbacks."

"August, did you *have* to sell them?"

"Vot else? Bills I had to meet, although no vun seems ready to pay mine. No, *Liebchen*, today der advice of *mein Freund* Brunton I vill take, and a master carpenter become at der big shipyard near Jefferson City."

Quietly, Maggie picked up the porgies. "That's where they are building that monstrous great warship?"

"*Ja*. Brunton swears those Tift brothers iss solid and pays good."

"I know it's a bitter pill you're swallowing, darling, but I think you are being wise and far-sighted," said Maggie and patted his broad hand. "Christina tells me that Lachlan's told her the Tifts do everything for their master carpenters."

"How is Tina, by the way?"

Maggie managed a little laugh, felt relieved to see that desperate drawn look departing from her husband's features.

"Bigger than Mother O'Toole's sow the day before she farrowed. And speaking of angels—"

Heels clacking briskly, a small, compact figure appeared striding along in their direction. Lachlan Brunton doffed a small visored cap, then mopped a face reddened by his pace.

Once commonplace greetings had been exchanged, Brunton demanded, "August, have ye told Maggie yet?"

"*Ja*. That haff I just done."

Lachlan observed sympathetically, "After the way ye've worked all these years 'tis hard to see so fine a business go to pot. Well, we must bend to the blast, and many others, besides. I've news for ye."

"Tina's had her baby?" exclaimed Maggie.

"Not yet, besides 'tis you, Maggie, she'll be sending for when her time comes. We'll have none o' those dirty old midwives. Have you not born six and lost never a one?"

He grinned like a friendly terrier. "No, my news is that the first o' the *Mississippi*'s armor has arrived from Richmond after six mortal weeks of waiting! Only reason 'tis here even now is because 'twas put in charge o' a regular naval officer. Also there's a crying need at Tift's for two more master carpenters. When I gave yer name to Mr. Asa Tift last night he said he knew you."

"Natürlich. It vass me fitted out his last two river steamers before this *verdammt* war," August rumbled. "Dot big ram iss progressing?"

"Aye. 'Tis a miracle we're accomplishing, Gus, but we'd do better had we the men who are wasting time working on that crank's delight called the *Louisiana!* When will you report at Jefferson?"

"Very soon," August replied in a doleful voice, "ven I haff sold vot little remains of my stock." A contemptuous sweep of his hand indicated a few blocks, tackles and some hogsheads of spikes and nails.

IV

JOURNEY'S END

A FINE RAIN slanting steadily downwards applied a temporary patina to huge and ungainly slabs of four-inch armor lying on flatcars newly arrived in the Mobile yards of the New Orleans & Jackson Railroad. Sodden sentries, posted to guard the precious shipment, were bitterly cursing the day they had volunteered.

"Better send more guards soon as you can, sir," advised their commander, "or Leeds and Company's agents will be grabbing this armor for the *Louisiana*, or maybe for that confounded River Defense Flotilla. They've stronger influence in the Capitol and at City Hall than we poor outcasts of the regular service."

Lieutenant Commander Seymour nodded agreement. "Thank you. I'll report to Commodore Hollins and send reinforcements at once. You will be glad to hear that I carry Mr. Secretary Mallory's instructions that these plates are for the *Mississippi*, and none other."

"Aye, aye, sir," Lieutenant Harley saluted, then bent and tipped a wink at Master Robbie, waiting grimy, round-eyed and weary on a bunk of the caboose.

Normally, Robbie would have jumped up and saluted, but long days of travel at a top speed of ten miles an hour—the maximum permitted by law on any Southern railroad—had left him much fatigued.

After dispatching a soldier to fetch the yard master, Sam sought a little stove rigged to warm the caboose and tested a pan of water steaming gently upon it.

"Come on, Rob. We don't want Miss Cottier to imagine I'd fetch a mulatto into her home."

She must have been vexed by his wire, dispatched from Jackson and reporting his supply train delayed nearly three days by late winter washouts along the line.

The Navy Department, he felt, had been unusually prescient in detailing him to convey this precious armor to its destination, for in almost every freight yard along his route he had noticed sidings crowded with cars full of cannon, shot, and all manner of critical material, apparently forgotten or abandoned.

Inexpressively cheered at the thought of once more beholding Louise Cottier's serenely warm features, Sam scrubbed Robbie thoroughly despite whimpered protests at the raw chill pervading the grimy old caboose.

Although he hated the necessity, Sam was forced to dress his son in the miniature naval uniform made by Sylvia for Robbie's Christmas present; it constituted his cleanest and most presentable attire.

"Come, son, we'd better get your hair really dry. It's a mean day we've picked to land here."

A pinched look about Robbie's mouth worried him. This journey west, though alleviated by the spartan comforts offered by an extra caboose, had drawn deep on a three-year-old's stamina.

At the end of half an hour father and son were perceptibly sprucer than they had been in many days and buoyed by the lively expectancy of hospitality in generous New Orleans proportions.

Robbie said, "I hungry, Daddy. Please, can I have candy?"

"Yes, dear, but first we are going aboard a launch which will carry us down to the city."

Robbie suddenly looked up from the important business of stowing his few toys into a little canvas sack. "Daddy, is Miss Cottier pretty?"

Sam interrupted strapping a telescope case to smile at the small figure. "Son, whether a lady is pretty or not is a matter every man must learn to decide for himself. Suppose we wait and you tell me what you think?"

Half an hour later they watched, through lashing rain, the dome of the new opera house, the still-unfinished Mint and various church steeples materialize above restless current.

"Look! Rob, look over yonder," said Sam. "There's the famous *Manassas!*" His own excitement mounted on recognizing, tied up to the levee, that seegar-shaped ironclad which, almost single-handed, had driven the U.S.S. *Richmond* and her mighty consorts in ignominious headlong retreat to the Gulf of Mexico. Like a weird and ungainly marine monster, the ram lay quiescent, her sleekly rounded back glistening in the wet.

Since no thread of smoke rose from either of her squat twin funnels, Sam concluded that her captain must have ordered her fires drawn. The smokestacks, he noticed, had been mounted so close together as to suggest but a single funnel; a poor notion in his estimation, because a single shot might level them both and so disable her engines for lack of draft.

Increasingly he became depressed at the obvious deterioration during the past eight months of this great city's commerce. Dozens upon dozens of ships of all rigs and design lay tied up to the levee, and he could hardly credit his eyes that the only other vessel to be seen under way at this mid-afternoon hour was a superannuated revenue cutter standing downstream in the direction of Forts Jackson and Saint Philip guarding the river some fourteen miles below.

The only further activity was the reluctant departure of a few disgusted-looking pelicans flapping out of the launch's course, and the dispersal of a big raft of green-head mallards.

The Navy Department's ramshackle and bird-whitened wharf proved deserted, but luckily a cabriolet came rattling by shortly after Sam had led Robbie ashore, lugging their telescope case in his free hand.

Once they started driving through the frigid downpour towards Conti Street, Robbie insisted upon standing up to peer out of the loudly rattling window.

At the prospect of encountering Louise Cottier after all these months a sense of panic seized Sam. Strange how much her rich and gentle personality had obtruded upon his thoughts; yet now he was faced by the disconcerting fact that he knew her not at all well. How could he have been such a great, forward idiot as to trespass so far upon Miss Cottier's good nature?

True, the one letter he had received from her during his convalescence in Charleston had, to his eager eyes, appeared warm and sympathetic to the verge of affection. Yet while reviewing those well-remembered phrases at this moment it seemed to have been definitely impersonal as to salutation and conclusion.

The moldy smelling cab plodded on through street after narrow street encountering but little traffic. The few pedestrians in sight were wearing rubber coats or attempting to shelter themselves under umbrellas.

The downpour increased until it became almost impossible to see more than a few yards and the driver grumbled, "Lawd, Lawd! It sho' fixin' fo' to drown de frawgs!"

By the time the cab had rattled to a halt Robbie lay fast asleep, with tousled head pillowed upon his father's lap.

To Sam's surprise two carriages stood waiting before the Cottier residence. Robbie, still plunged in the profound slumber of exhaustion, lay limp under the partial shelter of Sam's long rubber coat, while he reached for an ornate bell handle of bronze.

"Is Miss Cottier at home?" he inquired of a colored servant who cautiously opened the door a crack.

"Yas, suh, Miz Cottier's at home. An' who shall I say am callin'?"

"Commander Samuel Seymour. Open that door wider, it's wet out here."

His voice was sharp because rain was pouring down inside his rubber coat.

"Yassuh, yassuh, come right in, suh."

Sam removed his naval cap but hesitated to put Robbie down because the upholstery about him looked too elegant to bear a wetting.

It was not Louise who appeared but a sharp-faced, wren-like little old lady whose features suggested parchment or old ivory. She inquired sharply, "Well, Monsieur, and what is it that you require?"

"Your pardon, Ma'am, it was *Miss* Cottier I inquired for," he explained. "I'm sorry to have inconvenienced you."

"Ah, that Alexandre is so hopelessly stupid," she complained in accents faintly tinged with French. "I am Madame Cottier. I repeat, what is it you wish?" Deliberately, her vitreous black eyes surveyed the caller and his sleeping burden.

"I—I am Commander Seymour, a friend of your daughter's."

"Oh! So you are that American?" Madame Cottier stiffened, deliberately placed one withered hand upon its fellow. "My daughter anticipated your call three days ago. Really, Monsieur, you have been most inconsiderate. She is much upset."

"I regret that, Ma'am," Sam explained, reddening under her uncompromising glare. "I have been on duty convoying naval supplies from Virginia. Three days ago I sent Miss Cottier a telegram from Jackson, explaining that my supply train had been delayed."

Madame Cottier sniffed. Clearly, she took a poor view of this big stranger and the child dripping water all over the well-polished parquet flooring of her foyer.

"Is Miss Cottier at home?"

"Yes, but she is—indisposed and will see no one."

Sam paused, incredulous that the old lady wasn't going to offer assistance of some kind. After all, this was wartime and patently he was an officer on active duty.

"I am very sorry to appear so unexpectedly, but my son here, well, I, uh, had hoped—"

"—You had hoped what?" Small, silvery and symmetrical ringlets dangling from below Madame Cottier's lace cap quivered aggressively.

"I had hoped that Lou—Miss Cottier had found me a suitable governess and quarters. As you can see, my son is very tired. We have been riding a freight train for over a week." He attempted a smile.

"If you expect my daughter to run errands for a mere acquaintance, you are in error."

Water dripped steadily from his raincoat as, wearily, Sam replied, "Of course, I didn't, and I'm sorry she feels put-upon. Now, if you will permit me to leave my son here out of the rain, I will go in search of another cab."

"You may do as you please," observed the uncompromising old creature. "I am having guests for tea and whist; you have interrupted our game."

Sam drew himself up, mad clear through. "Pray return to your guests with an easy mind, Ma'am. I would rather take my son out into the weather than leave him under a roof which shelters so little appreciation of the sacrifices made by some of us in the armed forces."

"How dare you address me in such terms!"

"Already I have dared more serious dangers than your displeasure, Ma'am," he replied evenly, "and am likely to dare much more."

Madame Cottier's piercing black eyes wavered for the first time. "If you wish, you may both stay here until the rain ceases."

"You're being too generous, Ma'am, but I prefer to seek a hotel where I may be assured of a welcome—even though it be paid for. My services to your daughter, Ma'am. Good day."

Somehow, he managed to lug Robbie beneath his heavy rubber coat and also to carry the heavy telescope bag, but it was hot, hard work.

The two carriages waiting outside had been hired by Madame Cottier's guests and their drivers sullenly refused to drive him even in search of another conveyance. Before he had tramped a block water had begun again to trickle down Sam's neck and his feet quickly became soaked in generously overflowing gutters.

Through his previous visit to New Orleans, he recalled that the Carondelet House must be situated within five or six blocks, but as to its exact location he could not be certain.

Like a Stygian tide, gloom invaded his spirit as he splashed along bent under his portmanteau and Robbie's leaden weight. Both he and the child were sopping wet when, through the pale gray downpour, he recognized the hotel's entrance.

"Welcome to New Orleans!" he muttered bitterly and started up its wide and well-worn steps.

V

MR. MILLANDON'S PASTURE

LONG BEFORE DISTRICT Commandant George N. Hollins' steam launch nosed into the busy landing of Mr. Millandon's plantation, the *thuck, thump* of lustily swung axes, the scraping of gang saws and the chromatically rising ring of hammers had drowned the rhythmic *hiss-hiss* made by a leak in the engine's cylinder packing.

The C.S.S. *Mississippi*, taking form in what until recently had been an ordinary cow pasture, but little resembled any vessel previously beheld by either Sam Seymour or William C. Whittle. At this stage of her construction the new ironclad's square superstructure and flat, barge-like sides suggested nothing more than a modern but much lower Noah's Ark. All yellow ribs, she lay amid a tangle of scaffolds, huge, impressive in dimensions which dwarfed the humans working on her like Lilliputians over prostrate Gulliver.

A number of scows, deep-laden with heavy timbers freshly hewed out of oak and cypress forests upstream, lay alongside a brand-new wharf.

On the bluff above, an irregular row of weather-beaten canvas tents revealed how at least part of the construction gangs were finding shelter. Further back Sam later noticed a regular village of shacks, stables and storehouses.

The launch presently made a landing under the counters of a pair of decrepit river steamers straining at permanent moorings. These, the newcomer soon ascertained, housed designers, engineers, armorers and the elite among the construction crew, such as Chief Constructor E. M. Ivens, Acting-Chief Engineer E. Warner and Naval Superintendent Pierce. Others among the technicians, however, had elected to find billets in a hamlet grandiloquently named Jefferson City, lying just above Mr. Millandon's property.

But such family men as Lachlan Brunton and his big, boss carpenter August Schniewind, together with many others, came up from New Orleans every day aboard an old stern-wheeler ferry chartered for that purpose.

Raw and yellow, the gigantic ram's timbers towered loftily up into the watery January sunlight as Commander Whittle turned a handsome, well-modeled head. "Well, Seymour, and what do you make of her design?"

Honestly perplexed, Sam hesitated. "Well, Billy"—he and Whittle had been shipmates aboard the *Susquehanna*—"I'd expected to find something unusual, but I'm damned if I've ever seen anything like her before."

The tall Georgian laughed. "You'll find in her a classic example of 'needs must when the Devil drives.' It proves that our contractors, Messers Tift, are resourceful to a degree. When they discovered that New Orleans had become almost destitute of trained shipwrights as well as of marine designers and engineers, they determined to plan their ironclad with such modifications that it could be, and is being, built by *ordinary house carpenters*, as you can see." A wave of Whittle's hand indicated a number of lumber rafts anchored and straining against the clay-colored current.

"All the *Mississippi's* surfaces, therefore, are designed to be flat and contained within four straight lines with the exception of her bow and stern sections. These curved areas, of course, will have to be rabbeted to the usual knees and ribs. Since any house carpenter can build along straight lines, and very few are able to shape ribs, let alone lay down a proper keel, the Tift brothers have been most ingenious, I think."

Sam looked his incredulity as they mounted muddy stairs leading up onto the bluff. "Do you mean to tell me that this vessel has no frame?"

"No more than is required for a successful scow. You see, Sam, this ram's strongly built. Her bottom consists of solid wood, twenty-two inches thick, and her sides," he smiled faintly, "I suppose we had better call 'em 'walls,' are two feet thick before the application of that four-inch armor you brought— My God, weren't we glad to see it!"

A nearer inspection revealed the complete accuracy of Commander Whittle's description; the *Mississippi* indeed was being most massively constructed and her casement certainly looked able to support those ponderous iron plates he had convoyed from the Tredegar Works in Richmond.

All in all this tremendous, if ungainly appearing, craft proved a most impressive and inspiring sight. Two hundred and seventy feet in length, she was sixty feet in the beam and almost equaled in displacement the Old Navy's *Colorado* and *Roanoke*, but those vessels were wooden, while the *Mississippi* would be protected by four inches of tough, wrought-iron armor. Inspiring, too, was the fact that workmen of all sorts were laboring as if their very lives depended upon the big ram's immediate completion.

In rapid succession Sam was presented to Chief Constructor Ivens and Mr. Pierce, the Navy Department's superintendent, a genial individual who kept squirting pencil-thick streams of tobacco juice onto the chip-littered mud.

"Right glad to meet you, Commander," he declared, pumping Sam's hand. "Been losin' sleep 'bout them plates. I'll ask Asa to send down flatboats to load 'em tomorrow. Yes sir, I'm sure pleased to meet you."

Commander Whittle called, "Come here, Mr. Brunton. I want you to meet our new ordnance officer."

Lachlan strode up grinning widely through a fine red beard. "Well, I'll be damned if it isn't my best man! Sam, yer welcome to these sinful eyes as a shower o' whiskey at a costers' picnic. This is chancey!"

"Glad to find you here." Beaming, Sam offered his hand. "And how is that sweet little lady of yours?"

"Little no longer," Lachlan chuckled, then added with a hint of pride, "She's so big we're expecting twins at the very least. And if they prove boys, one shall be called Sam. Ye see, Tina and I will never forget you and your lady's kindness to us on our wedding day."

"She's not my lady," Sam corrected shortly. "Tell me, what about the engines? I heard something about them in Richmond."

Joyousness faded from Lachlan's ruddy features. "And well may ye ask. Lieutenant— Losh! I ken you're a leftenant-commander the now."

Sam smiled. "Through a mistaken notion on the part of the Bureau of Orders and Construction."

Whittle departed to attend a conference being held aboard one of the decrepit river boats. Apparently certain bolts, specifically forged for the *Mississippi*, had been diverted for the use of the *Louisiana's* builders, which ironclad vessel was much nearer completion—thanks to Mr. E. C. Murray's unremitting efforts.

"What about this other ram?" Sam queried.

"She's a fine freak," Lachlan burst out. "Yon engineers are zaney, looney, to hope so heavy a craft can be propelled by such tin-pot machinery as they've specified." He broke off, waving agitated, greasy hands. "Mon, ye should hear what they contemplate! The good Lord deliver us, they're constructing two paddle wheels inboard!"

"*Inboard?*"

"Aye, there's to be one big paddle wheel mounted amidships and a second smaller one forward o' it. Sam, yon demented device will move a ram as heavy as the *Louisiana* no further than a fly can pull my hat!"

Climbing ladders and leading across unsteady plank walkways, Brunton undertook to show the newcomer about. The familiar clean smells of boiling pitch, pine wood and sawdust filled the air.

"Coming along handsomely, isn't she?" Lachlan shouted over the ringing of sledge hammers driving home foot-long spikes. "Her frame will be complete well ahead of schedule."

"When is she due to be commissioned?" Already Sam's eye had begun roving the length of this skeleton's deck, estimating structurally advantageous locations for various guns.

Brunton shrugged. "As near April first as God wills. 'Tis all a question of engines, engines, engines! That and the installation of yer armament, Mister Ordnance Officer."

With satisfaction, Sam noted that the *Mississippi's* decks could support the heaviest naval pieces ever employed by the Old Navy, and, still more satisfactory, his gun crews had been allotted maximum space in which to serve those sixteen powerful guns with which she was designed to blast the Federal Navy into a watery grave. And well she might! To the best of Sam Seymour's not inconsiderable knowledge, no projectile at present in the possession of the Union fleet could penetrate such a monster's sides.

Teams of oxen, horses and gangs of slaves puffed and sweated in fetching up timbers which, scarcely a month ago, had been trees of the forest. No sooner had the bulks come to rest than crews of expert axemen and trimmers set to work—an inspiring sight. Here being displayed was the sort of energy which could match the Yankees' best efforts.

VI

KITTY

THE ADVENT OF Mrs. Pingree came as if to break for Sam Seymour an over-long succession of unhappy events. He had, on the night of his arrival in New Orleans, noticed her as a pensive and somber figure occupying an obscure corner of the Carondelet House's dining salon. Both by her manner and her garb of unrelieved black he judged this young auburn-haired woman to be a new widow.

The next morning she had sat opposite Robbie and his father, reading a copy of the *Picayune* and quietly partaking of a modest breakfast.

Robbie had not slept well, and although the hotel keeper's plump wife kindly had volunteered to mind the boy, that poor lady already was badgered by a numerous brood of her own.

Robbie proved unusually fractious and indifferent to his porridge and twice had pulled off and flung onto the floor a napkin Sam had tied about his neck.

Sam's temper began to mount and attained the boiling point when Master Robert decided to see how far across the room he could blow a spoonful of soft-boiled egg.

"Why, you outrageous young pup—" Sam surged to his feet, but, even more quickly, the young woman in black reached Robbie's side.

"Please," she smiled, wiping the boy's chin. "Both of you seem— well, somewhat inexperienced. If you will allow me, sir, perhaps I can persuade your son to dine a little less dramatically."

Nothing in her speech afforded the least clue to her origin. Her English was clear and quite unaccented.

"Thank you, Ma'am, thank you indeed!" Sam burst out. "I reckon we can do with some assistance. My son, Robert Ashton Seymour; I am Lieutenant Commander Samuel Seymour and very much in your debt."

"Thank you. I'll confess I had been wondering what your grade might be," this fresh-complexioned young woman admitted. "I can recognize most of our Army's insignia, but there are so few naval officers about I—I well, I haven't been able to learn. . . . Oh, yes, I am Mrs. Pingree, Katherine Pingree. My home is, or was, in St. Louis."

Her gaze dropped and she set about re-tying Robbie's napkin.

"Your husband—or a brother?"

"My husband," she replied in a low tone. "Shot by a Union sharp-shooter near Fort Henry."

"I'm awfully sorry," seemed an inadequate thing to say, yet what else was there?

By degrees, he learned that Mrs. Pingree herself came originally from Michigan, that her husband had been a civil engineer practicing in St. Louis until, immediately following the fall of Fort Sumter, he had volunteered. Archibald Pingree was of Louisiana origin, she told him, then added that the shock of her son's death had killed old Mrs. Pingree, his only relative—the rest of the family had perished in 1856 during an epidemic of the dreaded yellow fever.

The talk quickened, especially once Robbie commenced obediently to absorb nourishment, but without any great relish, under Mrs. Pingree's tactful guidance. He appeared quite reassured by her voice and the slow firm grace of her motions.

"You are interested in the *Louisiana?*" she inquired brightly.

"No. It's the other one, the *Mississippi*."

After treating the child to a final slice of bread and strawberry preserve, she settled back on her seat.

"I've overheard people say that she will be the most formidable man-of-war ever launched. Is she to be only a river boat?"

"No, Ma'am. The *Mississippi* is designed to go to sea; at least along our coasts."

Presently it came out that the Pingree family had been far from well off and that the sale of their small plantation, already fully mortgaged and debtridden, had brought barely enough to afford her mother-in-law a decent interment. Further, he deduced that young Mrs. Pingree was in New Orleans awaiting the arrival of funds from her family which would afford her the means of returning to Michigan.

"Then you are not remaining in Louisiana?"

"Why should I?" she inquired, fixing him with a steady regard of dark brown eyes. "Coming from Michigan as I do, I have not been made to feel too welcome here, for all that both my parents come from Tennessee and are strong Southern sympathizers."

"And what are your opinions?" Sam inquired evenly.

"I entertain no political opinions, Commander," came her sad reply. "All I hate is broken homes, broken hearts and countless wasted lives and fortunes. Why can't presumably civilized men resolve differences without murdering one another?"

From the tail of his eye, Sam glimpsed several heads at near-by tables swing in their direction; a fat old man wearing a tobacco-stained white goatee commenced to scowl.

Sam nodded, "I wish there had been more like-minded people about last year," he nodded, then stared so fixedly upon the fat old man that he muttered something and returned to his coffee.

At length Sam drew a deep breath. "Mrs. Pingree, I wonder if you can help me. Robbie requires a governess, someone to care for him while I'm on duty at the shipyard."

"Why," her whole face lit up, "I'd be delighted. It would give me something to do besides wait for that confounded letter."

Before breakfast was over, it had been resolved that Robbie should move with Mrs. Pingree into a two-room suite which Sam insisted on substituting for her own modest quarters. This tall young widow would make sure that the boy received the proper food, clothing and care. She had had no children of her own, Katherine Pingree explained, but had helped to bring up numerous small brothers in the turbulent lumbering town of Saginaw.

It was, therefore, with a much lighter heart that, on the second evening of his arrival in New Orleans, Sam set to work analyzing a set of plans for the *Mississippi's* construction. He found them crude, really elementary, and foresaw long hours of calculation necessary, so to place his armament that the battery neither altered the iron-clad's balance nor her designated speed. Apparently none of her builders had devoted much thought to anything save that the *Mississippi* must be ready for commissioning on or before the first of April.

The next familiar person he encountered upon his return to New Orleans was Léon Duchesne by whom he was warmly greeted in the bar of the new St. Charles Hotel. With the second round of *rhum flambé* he first heard news which was plunging all Louisiana into deep anxiety. Up in St. Louis a certain Mr. Eads was completing a fleet of formidable ironclads designed especially for river work by a gentleman boasting the euphonious name of Samuel Pook—all seven were reported by Southern agents to be double-enders, a faculty inval-uable in narrow waters since it obviated the necessity of turning about to engage some new enemy.

"Our agents swear these gunboats are practically ready for launch-ing, and after only ninety days!" Duchesne exclaimed. "*Ma foi!* Once these are afloat, our forts upriver will find themselves well occupied!"

They had seated themselves at a small, marble-topped table and settled down to another drink.

Presently, Sam was depressed to learn that, discouraged by the incompetence, neglect and dilatory methods of the Confederate Navy Department, Lieutenant Higgins and several other Louisiana officers of the regular service had resigned in order to accept promotion and commissions in the State Navy.

Moodily, Sam looked about and decided that, war or no war, the St. Charles bar was as usual filled to overflowing by a cheery and colorful throng of patrons.

Louise's cousin forever was breaking off in mid-sentence to greet passing friends and pass the time of day.

"Sorry I must leave, Sam," explained he, twirling his mustache. "The—er—Committee of Safety meets tonight, Cupid presiding."

As Sam entered the lobby of his hotel a liveried footman came forward, hat under elbow and offered an envelope.

"*M'sieur le Commandant Seymour?*" While fumbling for a *pourboire* Sam recognized Louise Cottier's foreign-style writing.

"Mademoiselle tell me wait for the reply." By his accent this messenger undoubtedly was a native of Haiti.

"Very well, you may wait in the hallway." In the act of turning Sam asked, "How did you find me?"

"Why, M'sieu, Mademoiselle 'as sent me to inquire everywhere."

In the Carondelet House's musty-smelling writing room, Sam broke a seal of blue wax and read:

My dear Samuel:

I am utterly desolated that you should have met with so sorry a welcome on your return to New Orleans. Your telegram dispatched from Jackson arrived only yesterday; where it can have been all this time is a matter for wonder. I shall be delighted to receive you and your son at your earliest convenience.

> Faithfully yours,
> Louise Cottier

" 'Faithfully yours!' " Not a word of apology over his having been, to all intents and purposes, turned out of her home? So she'd be "delighted to receive" him, would she? Jaw outthrust, he wrote:

My dear Miss Cottier:

It was indeed a sharp disappointment both to my son and to myself that you were unable to receive us the other day. Please believe that I appreciate whatever efforts you may have made towards securing a governess. Pray do not concern yourself further in that regard since I have been successful in concluding other arrangements.

When my duties at the shipyard are less exacting, I shall give myself the pleasure of calling upon you.

Very truly yours,
Samuel Seymour

The footman revealed big yellow teeth in a grin. "*Merci*, M'sieu. One is relieved to have found M'sieu. Mademoiselle Cottier will be most happy."

"I wonder!" Sam grunted, then swung away to climb creaking old stairs.

Before Mrs. Pingree's door, he paused long enough to recognize her brisk, unaccented voice concluding a fairy tale, so he delayed long enough to seek his own room and spruce up.

"Robbie has just gone to bed," she declared, wide mouth set in a completely disingenuous smile.

"How is he?"

A worried V appeared between the girl's slender auburn brows. "Not well, I fear. He ate hardly any supper. Did he get very wet yesterday?"

"I'm afraid so. Why?" He caught his breath.

"He seemed a bit feverish just now." Quickly Mrs. Pingree added, "Probably he's taken no more than a sniffle, but if he shows any temperature, I will dose him with a quarter-grain of quinine."

"A quarter-grain of quinine? How do you know about such things?"

Katherine Pingree's usually very white features colored. "Oh, my father's a doctor," she laughed. "I used to help him mix prescriptions. You'd be surprised to know how much I've learned about the simpler facts of medicine."

"Thank God for that. You'll inform me the minute he runs a fever, won't you?"

"Naturally. Good night, sir."

VII

SIXES AND SEVENS

A MORNING SPENT in Commodore George Hollins' Headquarters at the old St. Charles Hotel gave Lieutenant Commander Seymour his first real inkling of the extraordinary muddle prevailing in Naval District Number One. The Regular Navy Headquarters consisted of bleak former bedrooms stripped of all appointments and equipped only with cuspidors, maps, rough desks and a few tables and cane-bottomed chairs.

From Arthur Warley, an old acquaintance of West African slave patrol days, he received valuable information concerning the truly chaotic conditions prevailing over naval affairs in New Orleans.

Commander Whittle, Warley explained, was nearing his wit's end, plagued as he was by an unending stream of impossible instructions from Richmond, suspicion and selfishness from the State Naval authorities and hostility at Army Headquarters.

"Can't imagine what they're thinking of," growled Warley. "Do you know that Mr. Davis has ordered the entire river squadron upstream, excepting my ship, the *Manassas*?"

"What does this squadron consist of?"

"The *General Polk*, the *Ivy*, the *Maurepas*, the *McRae* and that God-awful monstrosity called the *Livingston*."

"Why leave the *Manassas* behind? Isn't she the best we've got?"

"She is, and by a damned wide margin," Warley snapped. "Trouble is my engines are too sluggish, won't turn up three knots an hour against the current. You've heard how we got her last October?"

Sam nodded, Whittle already having described how this same Lieutenant A. F. Warley had led a naval boarding party to take over the *Manassas* by force from Captain Stephenson and her civilian owners. The only consolation was to find around Headquarters such able veterans as Huger, Read, Commander Kennon and the rest.

It being the dinner hour, the two found themselves alone save for a single blue-nosed clerk stolidly penning a batch of telegrams.

Sam settled back, offered his tobacco pouch. "The outlook seems scarcely encouraging."

"We're trying to accomplish something despite the grossest misunderstanding and lack of perception," Warley sighed. "Imagine it, we've got two other rams building, and very nearly completed, at Memphis; the *Arkansas* and the *Tennessee*. But will old Mallory order them down here where they'd be some use against the blockade ships? Hell's fire, no! The Army wants 'em around to protect their flanks."

A small, terrier-like figure with very black hair and a lean jutting jaw, Warley commenced to stride nervously back and forth.

"God! What criminal stupidity it is to keep trained naval officers in the East to command river batteries or fighting land battles! Can't those idiots strutting about Richmond comprehend that if New Orleans should fall, then Texas, Arkansas, Missouri—the whole West is lost to us?"

Sam lit his pipe from a spill ignited at the grate. "Some people do, and that includes Mr. Mallory. The poor devil is interfered with at every turn by the Army. Generals such as Beauregard, the two Johnstons, Bragg, Hood and the rest, it appears, can do no wrong. Do they ever consult poor Mallory while planning a campaign? Never! Do they understand the Navy's problems? They do not! Let any dispute arise, then the generals go running to the President and always he sides with them! That's why, time and again, our ordnance is pulled off flatcars as it leaves Richmond and Norfolk."

Warley treated his companion to a sidewise glance. "What do you make of the *Mississippi?*"

"At first sight I was dumfounded," Sam admitted. "Now, I'm not so sure. One thing is certain; her engines will be powerful enough if Lachlan Brunton has luck and his way."

"You mean that queer, little carrot-topped Scotchman?"

"The same."

Briefly they then discussed rumors concerning a weird man-of-war the Yankees were reported to be building in Brooklyn; Confederate spies even had prepared some rough drawings.

Warley picked up a pencil, commenced sketching rapidly. "She's supposed to look something like this. Only thing I find in her favor is that revolving turret and her low freeboard."

"She'll sink," Sam predicted. "And if she doesn't, she'll never ever amount to much unless her designers give her more freeboard. Besides, she mounts only two guns."

"The Merrimac's broadside ought to blow her clean out of the water."

"How is the Merrimac progressing?"

"Should be finished come mid-March. Wish to God we had her here now along with the Arkansas and the Tennessee. Then we'd soon smash the blockade."

At Warley's suggestion they made their way to a small restaurant much esteemed by bons vivants. They found it crowded largely by Army officers, who, as they entered, grinned derisively or uttered jibes concerning the Navy and all its futility just softly enough to avoid provoking overt action.

"Who in God's name is that?" Warley demanded, shaking out a napkin and tucking it under his powerful chin; he was peering curiously at a sky-blue Louisiana State Navy uniform similar to Léon Duchesne's.

"Why, I'm damned if it ain't Beverly Kennon! What's he doing in such a rig?" Quickly Sam explained about Kennon's resignation from the Regular service.

"Well, I can't blame him much," grunted Warley. "Sometimes we don't get paid for weeks." They were agreed, however, about the dangerous precedent set by the President's creation of the Army's so-called River Defense Flotilla. Warley turned purple when Sam told of what he had heard in Richmond.

"It can't be so! Surely, the President won't go through with so insane a project when he hears how desperately short of men and supplies we are around here. I'll bet you that damned Mansfield Lovell's at the bottom of this!"

He mentioned the Commanding General's name so loudly that several Army officers turned on their seats and glared balefully in his direction. As it turned out, Arthur Warley was entirely in error on that point. Major General Lovell held no love for this undesired and misbegotten flotilla, which already was causing him grief, embarrassment and confusion in Homeric proportions.

Sam spent the balance of the afternoon examining records and attempting to list the ever-increasing so-called shipyards which were springing up in all directions, the names of the dealers in marine supplies and, most important of all, the identity of such men as seemed able to get things accomplished for the *Louisiana.*

He learned also, through the course of his researches, that, due to the cessation of river traffic, the city was becoming troubled by a great influx of river pirates, slave thieves, deserters, sharpers and other outlaws. Stews along the waterfront, or so the *Bee* reported, were becoming dangerously overcrowded, affording to the whores and madams who swarmed there a rich harvest. The Crescent City's murder rate, never very low, mounted steadily.

By the time Sam was ready to return to the unstylish but eminently respectable old Carondelet House, he was feeling uncommonly depressed—save for one realization: it should be entirely possible to complete the *Mississippi* within a reasonable length of time.

Guiltily, he realized that he hadn't even given either Robbie or Mrs. Pingree a thought since that morning, a fact borne upon him when she greeted him with an anxious expression.

"I fear your son is in for a siege, Commander," she informed quietly. "Due to that wetting the other day he has taken at the least a very heavy cold." Her coral-hued lips forced a smile. "When his temperature went up, I called a doctor who declares that Robbie is uncommonly robust so we have nothing, thus far, to cause us worry, serious worry, that is."

Anxiously Sam surveyed this trim black-clad young woman, found her calm manner infinitely reassuring. "How can I begin to thank you? Why didn't you send a message to the St. Charles?"

"It would only have worried you and wasted your time," Kitty Pingree pointed out. "Believe me, Doctor Toutant is capable and has prescribed well," she smiled faintly. "—Just as Papa would have. I'll watch Robbie and the minute his temperature mounts, I'll call you and the Doctor."

"Would you—er, care to join me for dinner?" Starved for feminine companionship, he hoped she would accept.

"That would be agreeable—very." A shadow crossed her vividly white features. "It has been terribly lonely here."

He was about to climb to his own quarters on the third floor when a bellboy came trotting up.

"Commander Seymour, sir, they's a lady been waitin' for you to come in."

"A lady?" Who in the world?

In a dim writing room to the right of the hotel's entrance, he found Louise Cottier.

"Oh, Sam!" Louise Cottier, darkly handsome in a small round hat, dark blue silk dress and a yellow plaid shawl, came hurrying forward offering both hands. "Oh, Sam," she cried, "I have been simply miserable. What can you think of me?"

He bowed formally. "Nothing, Miss Cottier, save that apparently I presumed too much upon our slight acquaintance."

She fell back a step, her eager smile fading. "If only I had known! I—I wasn't well and no one told me you had arrived until the next morning."

"I regret your indisposition and the inefficiency of your servants," he said, standing very straight. "However, you occupy your parents' residence and your mother has made it unmistakably evident that there will be no welcome there for me or my like."

"Oh, Sam! Please! Please. Let me atone for Mother's rudeness. She is old and—and well, *planté là*. I have engaged a nice old lady to care for your son. How is he?"

"Thanks to the drenching he got after leaving your house, he is ill. How ill, remains to be seen."

Louise Cottier's tawny features crumpled and she extended a slim hand shaking in agitation. "But this is dreadful! How could *Maman* have been so uncivil!"

"Why not inquire of her?" was Sam's cool suggestion. "In the meantime I thank you for your trouble in finding a governess. However, I prefer not to have my son brought up by a Creole, but by someone who does not consider loyal Southern officers as coarse foreigners or 'Americans,' as I believe your mother terms us."

Louise flinched and her great dark eyes grew even larger. "Are you being entirely fair, Monsieur?"

"Possibly not," he returned, looking steadily into her features. "I only know that my son is very ill and that I should be with him."

"At least please credit that I am most regretful for what has chanced," she murmured lifting the yellow shawl into position. Her voice faltered, then abruptly she lifted her head and summoned a bleak smile. "Since obviously I can be of no service, I will detain you no longer. I shall pray that your little boy recovers. Good evening, Monsieur."

VIII

RECAPITULATIONS

CONSIDERING THAT THESE were wartimes and that Lachlan Brunton had arrived in New Orleans less than a year ago, he had done remarkably well, decided Christina as she reposed, still weak and spent, in the double bed of handsome carved walnut she had bought for a song on Rampart Street.

Her recollection of the transaction remained vivid and pleasing, for the old woman who ran that ramshackle little shop possessed no idea concerning the bed's real value, her energies being more thoroughly occupied by the purchase and consumption of cognac. Red-eyed and craving her tipple, the harridan incredibly had let her beautiful old French bedstead go for a paltry fifty dollars, and in Confederate currency!

Now and then, Tina's conscience had troubled her over the deal and, when the war ended, she intended to rectify the price paid. Meanwhile she took care never to approach the shop again. How pleasant to lie thus in the semi-dark, luxuriating in regained slimness.

Soon big, good-hearted Maggie Schniewind must appear to bring little Adam—named after Lachlan's father—for suckling. At first it had seemed to her impossible that she could have grown so big over so small a baby. When first viewing the infant, Lachlan chuckled, muttered something about "not even having got his bait back." Maggie had acted shocked, but Tina had laughed faintly since Lachlan wasn't so very big himself.

When massive and yellow-bearded August had come clumping in, awkward and embarrassed, he employed German—which he and Tina loved to speak—in suggesting that a mountain had labored to bring forth a mouse. Tina had laughed at that, too. It had been fortunate that her child was small since she was not of sturdy German peasant stock, but narrow of hips and dangerously slender of body.

Now she recognized the sounds of Maggie bustling about downstairs; her own children were being cared for by young Hilda, who, being all of fourteen, was held perfectly competent to discipline and care for five younger brothers. Secretly Maggie was very pleased that her family had arrived in just that order; too many boys were running off to enlist; especially, if big for their years.

Tina stirred. Rain again was falling but she didn't mind, because this steady *drip, drip* off the shingles was a reminder that she and Lachlan soon would own this little house on Thalia Street altogether. Yes, barring some catastrophe such as a plague or a Yankee invasion, they would own their home, lock, stock and barrel, come another two or three months.

Lachlan indeed was proving, as August Schniewind had not, to be both astute and far-sighted, and how he had worked! For that matter how hard they both had worked until she'd grown so big she'd had reluctantly to resign her position.

When the Confederacy's currency first appeared, Lachlan had done the patriotic and politic thing by investing half of their small capital in Confederate Treasury notes. With patriotism at a fever heat, none dared, for a time, to refuse to accept the Richmond Government's crudely printed promises to pay so, with these, he had been able to purchase a few well-built marine engines, some sets of driving gears, screw propellers and other items which he foresaw soon would be in sharp demand.

After the first fine glow of self-sacrifice, Tina recalled, depreciation inevitably had set in but found Lachlan established in the role of a firm patriot, a distinction not shared by many of his countrymen.

Lachlan, she knew, was also making small investments in munitions, transactions which insured him only a decent profit. It wasn't right to bleed the new Government, he held, even though many of the best-born people in the city were making fortunes.

Their chief concern, both Bruntons realized, was the growing shakiness of this new currency. Because of it Lachlan was willing to pay top price for any commodity that would promise to retain its value in the face of a sinking Confederate dollar.

Without saying anything to her husband, Tina had employed savings from her housekeeping to emulate his tactics on a smaller scale. Right now a couple of lockers under the eaves held several bolts of silks, satins and lengths of cashmeres that, some day, might yield a pretty profit.

If their calculations proved correct and the business district expanded in the direction of Thalia Street, they eventually should be able to turn over this old-but-sound brick house for half again what they'd paid for it and rear their newly commenced family on the healthful shores of Lake Ponchartrain.

When she considered how her situation had changed, Tina impulsively joined thin hands, closed her eyes and offered grateful thanks to the dear Lord. Why, last year at this time she'd been a miserable, lonely orphan shivering in a draughty attic back in Baltimore and frequently uncertain as to where her next meal might come from.

Briefly she pondered on Hermann's fate. If her brother had, indeed, enlisted in the Federal Navy, God alone knew where to find him; conceivably he might be serving aboard one of those grimly tenacious men-of-war engaged in blockading the Delta. She felt very sad over the fact of having completely lost contact with her strong young brother.

From time to time, Lachlan would, if he could get part of his price by barter, sell some piece of mechanism desperately needed by one of the many new shipyards. Of course, like everyone else with anything to sell, he made enormous paper profits, which he invested at an appalling discount in real property.

Whenever his duties at the shipyards permitted, and at no other time, he would make long excursions along both shores of the Mississippi in patient search of marine supplies of any description. At one remote plantation he came across a generous coil of fine three-inch hemp cable; at another, he discovered a dozen scarcely used blocks and falls, all of which had to be stored somewhere.

He had recently formed a company with Gus Schniewind as his junior partner; being German, he, too, would be exempt from the draft. Despite loud denials in the press there were too many able-bodied men parading about the Southland in *opéra bouffe* uniforms and troubling themselves no more about the war than half-heartedly to attend an occasional drill.

The night of Adam's arrival on earth the red-haired Scot had taken his wife's sweat-spangled hand and stroked it gently, saying, "It will cheer you to learn, lass, that, whatever befalls, our bairn will have the best this brave new country offers."

"Then he an *Universität* will attend?"

"Aye. The best in America—and that I hear is Harvard College."

"*Mein Mann.*" She was still a little light-headed. "*Das ist meine höchste Zufriedenheit.*"

He'd continued in a soft, half-frightened voice. Once a stable currency reappeared, as eventually it must, he planned to convert his real properties into cash.

"I intend," he solemnly assured her, "eventually to become the greatest shipmaster in the South."

"In the Confederacy, you mean?"

He hesitated just an instant, then smiled a flat, mirthless smile, repeating, "In the South, my bonnie."

For a while she'd felt uneasy at these confidences; did Lachlan imagine that she was going to die and wished to set her mind at rest? If so, he was gravely mistaken; having come this far she had no intention of giving up the ghost.

She was recalled to the present by hurried clumping noises; Maggie came flying up the staircase.

"Tina! Tina! Something terrible has happened!"

Fear for her baby raised granulations on Tina's forearms.

"What has gone wrong?"

"The Yankees have captured Fort Henry!"

A small gasp of relief escaped the prostrate young mother before she murmured, "That is bad. Lachlan says Fort Henry controls an important river up in Tennessee. But, surely, that Fort Donelson will turn back the Blue coats and their dreadful ironclads."

Tina was being optimistic for, ten days later, Fort Donelson also was surrendered and with it fifteen thousand good Gray soldiers. A depression descended upon New Orleans, but not so dense as appreciably to diminish the number of concerts, balls, and horse races being held.

IX

Ironclad

NOTHING COULD HAVE more profoundly shocked the population, as well as the military and naval hierarchy of New Orleans, than loss of Forts Henry and Donelson. Now the invaluable communication routes afforded by the Tennessee and the Cumberland Rivers lay at the enemy's disposal.

When the casualty lists were posted at the City Hall, Post Office and various police stations, there were many who turned aside weeping or stony-eyed; besides, many Louisianans had been among the surrendered troops.

One result was intensified recruiting for such mushroom military organizations as the Calhoun Guards, the Rough and Ready Rangers, the Crescent Blues and the Screwmen's Guard of which a Mr. S. J. Risk was captain; further, they actually stepped up their scheduled exercises to twice a week.

Many comfortably obese merchants, lawyers and bankers felt it incumbent upon them to join the Confederate Home Guard and so ordered uniforms from the fast-vanishing stocks of Messers Theodore Danzinger and M. S. Hedrick of Canal Street. They also combed the town for modern revolvers and rifles, but usually had to content themselves with antique, flintlock pistols and fowling pieces from the all-but-depleted cabinets of Messers Taylor & Churchill on Magazine Street.

Enormously serious, and sublimely oblivious to their ludicrous appearance, these worthy burghers, bald, grizzled and gray, waddled through various simple infantry evolutions. Hands which, in many a year, had performed no heavier labor than the carving of a turkey swelled and sweated through coarse white cotton gloves in repeated performance of the manual of arms.

In the already-busy shipyards efforts became redoubled. A three-sided struggle to obtain supplies and labor developed between Naval Constructor E. C. Murray and his fellow contractors for the *Louisiana*, the Brothers Tift and Naval Inspector Pierce of the *Mississippi's* builders, and Captains Stephenson, Montgomery and Gilbert, sponsors of that River Defense Flotilla conceived by Major General Leonidas Polk. These last only nominally obeyed orders from a Captain Higgins, formerly of the United States Navy.

Unfortunately, this maverick Higgins proved to be as resourceful as he was energetic, and probed into corners unexpectedly to snatch previous items of supply away from the hard-pressed Regular Navy.

Despite all obstacles work progressed so rapidly on the two ironclads that, by the middle of February, workmen had commenced armoring the *Louisiana*, while the massive *Mississippi* had been completely framed in, with her casemate about ready to receive those iron plates Sam had fetched down from Richmond.

Aboard the decrepit river steamboat *Iatan*, that floating draughting office in which the *Mississippi's* plan continually was being modified, midnight oil regularly was burned.

Happy in the possession of at least two sound engines out of the four required to propel the *Mississippi*, Messers Pierce, Brunton and Seymour drove bow pens until the owls grew tired of hunting the marshes above Mr. Millandon's meadow.

The remaining engines were under urgent construction at Patterson's Iron Works under the personal supervision of the Brothers Jackson, Scottish, grave and short-spoken.

What chiefly harassed Christina's husband was the fact that no amount of requisitioning, rummaging or negotiation had produced suitable propeller shafts. Such as Brunton did uncover either were too short, or too slender, to drive the weight of a giant ironclad.

He who worked latest as a rule was Samuel Seymour. Hour after hour he would analyze the construction and ordnance plans for the *Arkansas* and *Tennessee*. Thanks to Mr. Mallory's cooperation he further was blessed with details of the *Merrimac's* armament.

By patient calculation he felt able to eliminate various mistakes committed in the construction of these earlier ironclads. For instance he would not repeat an obvious error on the part of the *Louisiana's* ordnance officer who had not insisted upon wide gunports; further, when the *Mississippi* went into action her cannon would not be mounted so close together that her gunners could not readily traverse their pieces.

At present the new ironclad's main battery was intended to consist of four seven-inch pivot guns. He intended to mount a pair of these rifles, bow and stern, where they should prove useful while chasing or in running away.

For the rest Sam decided on ten nine-inch smooth bore guns, for close-range action such as one might normally expect in river fighting. Thus the *Mississippi* would mount in all fourteen carriage guns.

To a nicety, Seymour calculated not only the weight of the pieces themselves but also that of their carriages. After all, rammers, shot and training tackles weighed far more than a careless officer might suppose; further, he designed an efficient system of scuttle chains to the magazines and closely computed stresses on the deck beams. It proved no mean task.

His careful planning brought tired smiles of satisfaction from the Brothers Tift.

"By God, sir," declared Nelson Tift, raising weary, red-rimmed eyes, "if only your Department will send us a few more officers like you we'll have this river cleared in no time! And now, Commander, I'd appreciate your comments on our drawings for the conning place."

It was near ten o'clock before Sam wiped his bow pen and put away his drawing instruments. Pulling on and slowly buttoning his gray tunic, he departed from what had been the *Iatan's* lounging saloon where the kerosene lights had begun to burn red and smoky.

At the *Iatan's* scarred rail he paused before descending a shaky gangplank. From where he stood he found that he could visualize the completed *Mississippi* lying yonder beneath a small forest of cranes and hoists. By the deceptive light of a full moon, gunports, already let into her massively thick casemate, appeared black and menacing and smooth bed-planking lent the illusion that her armor already was in place.

Piled all about this unborn Titan rose mounds of machinery, armor plate, gun carriages and other gear. Over by that sawmill which the Tifts had constructed—together with a small foundry—on Mr. Millandon's meadow, stood tall piles of logs awaiting their turn to be cut, shaped and fitted into her hull.

Of course they'd get her done in time—they must. The *Mississippi*, figured the Tifts, should be ready for launching within a fortnight; after that she would lie to their construction dock to receive her battery and permit the completion of her engines about two of which Brunton was commencing to have qualms. There must be no question about the *Mississippi's* ability to maneuver; and that could only be assured if the tremendous two thousand horsepower demanded of her engines actually were developed.

A belated heron, gorged at last with frogs, croaked and beat out over the moon-silvered current towards the distant, sleepily sparkling lights of New Orleans. Sam sighed and cursed his fate. Here was another late night and no supper in the cheery company of Mrs. Pingree and his son.

What a quietly charming and utterly dependable person this young widow was proving! He was ashamed to find himself hoping that the arrival of her money from Michigan might remain indefinitely delayed. Robbie became as devoted to Kitty Pingree as ever he had been to Sylvia, and was fine and frisky despite ten days in bed with influenza taken on that unforgettable day of arrival.

The morrow being a Sunday and winter well advanced, he reckoned he might hire a carriage and take them for a picnic out at People's Park. All the newspapers had been playing up a running race arranged between a horse rechristened Jeff Davis and a celebrated racer called Battle Axe, the latter being owned by Mr. Jay Miller and the former by a Mr. McCreary.

Although Sam knew less than nothing concerning horse racing, the match promised to afford some thrills, for betting over the outcome was rife in New Orleans' multitude of cafés, bars and brothels.

For a youngster there should be such attendant amusements as jugglers, rope dancers, puppets and just possibly a carrousel. Sam was very hopeful that there might be one; to this day, he could recall the pure ecstasy of his first ride on a merry-go-round.

It would be pleasant, also, to enjoy Kitty Pingree's company, to admire her auburn hair, white complexion and lively brown eyes. This girl from Michigan pleased him, too, by her air of self-sufficiency, unaffected speech and cheerful, energetic manner.

X

PEOPLE'S PARK

As IF TO atone for a week of wet and chilly weather caused by a norther beating down the Mississippi Valley, the fourth Sunday of February dawned fair and warm, thanks to a breeze off the Mexican Gulf. Magically, streets and roofs dried themselves and the fresh green of magnolias, water oaks and camellias glistened to gladden the eye.

It was hard to say which of the prospective picnickers felt most elated at this prospect of escaping to the country. Robbie, pink of feature and with long golden curls flying at odds with his miniature naval uniform, was bursting with energy.

"Mercy!" thought Kitty Pingree. "Sam Seymour's never seen me out of my weeds." So, in honor of the occasion she had exchanged her mourning for a simple gray crinoline, and even went so far as to pin a modest white magnolia to the front of her dress and clasped on a slender strand of seed pearls Archie had bestowed the night before he'd gone marching so bravely away with replacements for the Washington Artillery Regiment.

What wonderful fun they'd found in deciding upon the ingredients for their picnic lunch. With the realization that Commander Seymour actually would be with her all day long Kitty had found it difficult to concentrate on cookies and cold chicken.

Flushing a trifle she had told herself, "I just can't go on thinking of him as 'Commander' and I do wish he'd stop calling me 'Mrs. Pingree.' He makes me feel like a paid governess even if he has presented me with two books and a box of pralines."

The hired carriage turned out to be a glossy affair of dark blue with salmon-colored wheels; undoubtedly a private vehicle leased out by some owner feeling the pinch of wartimes. Drawn by a pair of bays too aged for military purposes, the vehicle was a handsome affair boasting well-polished brass mountings and lamps of German silver. The driver, a grinning, half-grown slave boy, wore a livery coat sizes too big, but was not any the less proud of his appearance.

Yes, there was every indication that this would prove to be a wonderful adventure for the sky hadn't appeared so softly blue in weeks, and New Orleans, cleansed by the past week's downpour, wore a scrubbed look.

Robbie wriggled between the grownups, pointing to this or that wonder or waving vigorously to such round-eyed children as he noticed by the roadside.

Thought Kitty, "For all that Sam must be dog-tired from working till all hours, he's confounded good-looking. I'm glad he can act so carefree."

"So we're going to witness a horse race?" Kitty commented. "My chambermaid said it's to be quite an important match."

"Judging by all the to-do in the newspaper, I expect she's correct." Sam leaned closer in order to see under the wide-brimmed straw Kitty had secured by means of a Lincoln-green ribbon.

Exactly as though he had been reading her thoughts, he turned suddenly. "Do you mind very much, Mrs. Pingree, if—well, if I were to call you by your Christian name?"

Her laugh rippled and she smiled happily. "I've been wondering just how long naval etiquette must be observed. You see, in Michigan we begin to use given names almost on sight."

The carriage spun comfortably out Kerterec Street past handsome brick mansions and a long succession of high walls topped by spikes or broken glass set in cement.

"If you've no religious scruples against betting a few dollars, I'm sure I can help you to lose them."

Her teeth flashed in the bright spring sunlight. "And on whom shall I wager?"

"Jeff Davis," he advised in mock gravity. "I'm reliably informed by Léon Duchesne—who is friendly with Jeff Davis' owner—it is a certainty that Jeff will win the first and last heats and therefore the match."

"Léon Duchesne?" Kitty repeated, while increasing her grasp on the slack of Master Robbie's pants. He had risen on the seat in order to wave joyfully at a cavalry officer about to overtake the carriage. Easy in the saddle, long black hair flying, the gallant rode by with light bravely glancing from the gold braid and buttons of his short shell jacket.

"I have been meaning to tell you," Sam said presently, "how deeply I appreciate the care you gave Robbie during his illness. You've quite won his heart."

"I'll confess my secret," she laughed. "Mother told me, years ago, that if you feed any male well enough and often enough, he's bound to fall in love with you."

"Rob's a lucky boy," Sam chuckled, then in fresh interest considered his companion and thus, for the first time, became aware of a delicate powdering of freckles crossing her short and faintly upturned nose. He noticed also a small scar on the point of her chin which she explained she had earned years ago while attempting to lead a stubborn calf out to pasture.

As they approached the racecourse, traffic increased. Sharing the road were forage wagons full of hilarious soldiers on furlough and carriages conveying flashily dressed gamblers and their harlots. There were also many ordinary citizens, most of whom were riding in work carts of varying description.

Among these dust-provoking vehicles trotted numerous well-dressed cavaliers astride nervous thoroughbreds; elaborately languid of manner, these gay blades were forever lifting their caps to some lovely lady or reining beside the shiny equipages of Wealth and Power.

If anyone in this holiday throng recalled the tragedies of Forts Henry and Donelson, no one could have guessed it. Winter grass grew green and lush on the outskirts of People's Park, where catch-penny entertainments were flourishing. Yonder, acrobats in frayed, spangled tights were tumbling about a canvas ground cloth; a moth-eaten brown bear danced to the squeaky accompaniment of an accordion and the thumping tambourines of a family of brown-faced Romany gypsies. Beyond these a quack was, at the top of his lungs, bawling out the merits of his "Choctaw Elicampane and Sovereign Remedy."

Now Sam's rented carriage commenced to pick a leisurely course among holiday-makers who already had unhitched their teams and were sitting about tablecloths and quilts spread on the moist grass with their luncheon baskets disgorging a fine variety of eatables.

Off to one side, a group of pleasantly liquored young gentlemen were noisily attempting to arrange an impromptu horse race.

Presently the blue and salmon carriage passed a one-legged man in a disreputable gray uniform. He was hobbling painfully along on a crutch and holding out a kepi to solicit alms. Slung from his neck was a placard reading, "Pleez help a hero of Manassas."

As Kitty reached into her purse their driver warned over his shoulder, "Doan waste your pity, Mist'ess, I seen dat racsal beggin' longst Rampart Street all de last five years."

"I declare that villain ought to be whipped," hotly declared Kitty. "The idea of his trading on the sufferings of our valiant troops."

At last on the outskirts of the park they came upon a suitable picnic site beneath a gigantic live oak where they could sun themselves, feast and witness Robbie's manful efforts to capture a variety of gaudy butterflies.

When they had finished the last of their crab cakes, fried chicken and celeste figs, Kitty delicately licked her fingers, settled back against the silver-gray tree trunk and then wrinkled her pointed little nose at her companion.

"Life's full of surprises, isn't it?" she demanded smilingly.

"What do you mean, my dear?"

"Why, I never imagined I could ever enjoy myself half so much again."

Sam nodded, thrust long, gray-clad legs out before him and prepared to ignite a seegar with the help of a sulphur friction match.

"A lot of people will need to discover the same thing before we've whipped the Yankees."

They took turns feeding Robbie sugar cookies until he became torpid and sleepy. At length Kitty inquired, "Do you plan to attend the Military Fair tonight?"

"Hadn't even heard of it. Why?"

"Someone said that, for a miracle, there's to be a booth in the interests of our Navy."

He emitted a derisive laugh. "You don't mean to tell me that the good people of New Orleans are becoming aware that they own a navy? Where did you hear this?"

"The wife of a captain in the State Navy, Mrs. Alexander Grant, told me so at supper last night."

A blind, very scrawny Negro led by a couple of gap-toothed pick-aninnies advanced uncertainly over the grass. "Please, suh, shall us dance fo' you?" pleaded the larger of the children. "We hongry."

When Sam nodded the old man unslung a banjo and played "Possum Up a Gum Tree," a jangling jig, to which the two boys executed a loose-jointed, shuffling dance so grotesque that Robbie broke into giggles of delighted laughter and Kitty chuckled as she poured out cups of cold chocolate.

The two white-eyed little Negroes kept on until a single horseman astride a magnificent gray stallion came riding up.

"Hi, Sam! Thought I recognized those yellow side whiskers!"

Léon Duchesne was wearing a gray top hat and most elegantly cut civilian riding clothes. His silver-buttoned coat was of bottle-green velvet and fawn-colored overhauls were strapped over well-varnished black shoes into the heels of which slender spur shanks had been screwed. In almost a single easy gesture he dismounted, looped bridle reins over his arm and came striding up.

"Afternoon, Léon. Wonderful day."

"Yes. Isn't it. You betting on Jeff Davis?" His gaze sought and lingered on Kitty, who, with quick graceful movements, had commenced to repack the picnic things. Belatedly, Sam remembered his manners and presented them.

Commander Duchesne declared himself absolutely overwhelmed at the pleasure of meeting Mrs. Pingree and gladly accepted Sam's invitation to partake of a glass of cool Canary after securing his stallion to the tip of the carriage tongue where he could not assault the aged bays placidly munching oats out of a small wooden trencher.

"Mon Dieu, Sam, what a surprise to find you out here," Duchesne cried, offering Robbie his riding crop to play with. "Somehow I never imagined you able to waste time on a horse race. So this is your son? You are new in New Orleans, Mrs. Pingree?"

Gradually People's Park became dotted by dozens on dozens of carriages and by swarms of folk more eager to escape the city and enjoy the sunshine than to witness a racing match. The crowd, colorful and varied, occupied acre on acre all around the course.

At last a military band in the distance struck up a lively tune, terminating Duchesne's cheerful and generally successful efforts to attract Kitty's favorable consideration.

"We'd better be moving," Sam suggested, although he hated to rouse himself. "Come on, youngster. Wake up and I'll give you a pick-a-back over to the track."

Through the crowd wandered weasel-faced bookmakers, most of whom Duchesne appeared to know more than casually.

"Let's lay our bets with Wroxton Ted," the Creole suggested. "He's lame and can't run too fast," he explained to Kitty. "May I place your wager? The dog will give you good odds; ought to, he's battened off me for ten years or more."

Quite without seeming to, Duchesne took over the expedition, guided Sam's party to an old-fashioned coach about which a very lively party of handsomely dressed young people were congregated around a tub of champagne on ice. Loud and sincere were their welcomes to Duchesne's guests and everyone seemed eager to make the most of this fling—perhaps their last for many a year.

The afternoon flashed by, Kitty radiant over a plethora of Creole compliments and Sam dazzled by languorous glances and the adulation bestowed on an officer of the now-famous *Sumter*. Presently Robbie fell so fast asleep on a seat in the old coach that not even the tumult raised by the crowd over Battle Axe's success in the first heat could rouse him.

For Kitty the afternoon proved memorable. The ladies, when they heard of her recent widowhood, made efforts to be cordial and friendly and witty Commander Duchesne hardly left her side. In fact, she became faintly irritated at Sam Seymour's failure to notice the Creole's pointed attentiveness. Always he seemed ready to indicate some celebrated figure or to offer choice items of refreshment.

"For once that flaneur Duchesne is wasting his time," observed Jeanette Dufour in an aside to her sister Laure. "That pretty little widow appears to listen to him, but always she looks at this Commander Seymour."

At that moment, Duchesne was pleading with Kitty Pingree. "Will you not accord me the honor this evening of attending the Military Fair? Sam has just told me he must work on those accursed drawings for the *Mississippi*. As most of this party will attend, you will not be without friends." Duchesne hesitated. "Of course, Mrs. Pingree, if you have—how shall I say it?—an understanding—"

Kitty went a bright pink. "Oh, no, Commander Seymour is only a—a good friend, while I am what amounts to governess for his son."

His deeply tanned features lit. "Bon! Then there is no reason why I should not call for you, say at eight?"

"It will be a real pleasure, Mr. Duchesne, to patronize so worthy an affair."

"Perhaps," she later assured herself, "it will do no harm to give Sam a gentle prod. Confound it, he's more than a little fond of me, and yet he's never so much as taken my hand."

XI

The Benevolent Society

The recesses and rafters of Odd Fellows Hall reverberated to the trample of many feet, to the tapping of tack hammers and, most of all, to the high-pitched babble of women's voices. Mrs. Monroe, the Mayor's wife, glared at Madame Seynac, wife to the Chairman of the City Council of New Orleans.

"Mr. Davis' portrait must be the very first thing one notices on entering this hall," she was insisting. "After all, Mr. Davis is our President and the raffle for his likeness will constitute our main attraction."

In sharp disagreement Madame Seynac sniffed, wrinkled a thin, beak-like nose. "Ma chère, if you esteem that raffle as our principal source of income, I fear you are in error. Mark well my words, even the prettiest of our young ladies will discover difficulty in selling chances to a majority of our patrons. Jeff Davis? Mais non!"

The little old Creole lady sniffed again, then signaled her footman to pick up her contribution—a hamper of purposeless knickknacks, excellent preserves and books nobody would read outside of solitary confinement.

Hoop skirts and crinolines bobbed and swayed in all directions, directed the efforts of sweating black servants climbing ladders in order to drape garlands of oleander, cedar and magnolia. About a gallery completely surrounding the main floor hung oil paintings, pen-and-ink sketches and lithographs of such of Louisiana's heroes as Generals P. G. T. Beauregard, Polk and Albert Sidney Johnston. These had been arranged to form the center of huge rosettes contrived of magnolia and camellia blossoms. Occupying the place of honor above a jerry-built speaker's rostrum shone a very fine Peale painting of General George Washington.

Interspacing these portraits dangled dozens of banners, the most numerous among these, of course, were the State flag and the Stars and Bars. Also popular to an extreme was that curious and unofficial new ensign which had inspired that popular Southern war song entitled "The Bonnie Blue Flag."

"What an atrociously bad design!" exclaimed Étienne Cottier. "And why do they call it a blue flag? You observe that it boasts but a tiny little patch of blue in its upper corner?"

His companion, Véronique Deloques, obediently raised eyes to perceive that her escort was entirely correct in that the banner's field was white enclosed in a narrow red frame; further it showed in its canton a blue rectangle with a single yellow star. In the very center of the field its designer, for no apparent reason, had called for a conventionalized magnolia tree!

Through a mouthful of pins, Véronique replied that she had no idea and would Étienne please hold the bunting with which she was trying to decorate the bandstand upon which the Crescent Blues' band was scheduled to play.

Handsomest of all the flags was that ensign soon to be known as the Battle Flag, showing a blood-red field and a white-edged blue Saint Andrew's cross, star-dotted.

Reverently, a delegation of Virginia-born ladies occupied themselves in draping about a booth their own State flag; a white field showing three golden Ionic pillars labeled, "Wisdom, Justice and Moderation" to support a lintel marked "Constitution."

Louise Cottier and Thérèse d'Ancoy were attaching to the front of their booth a device done in dark gray and gold which was attracting considerable curiosity. The seal displayed a laurel wreath enclosing a fouled anchor slanted diagonally across it. Above this wreath were arched two large five-pointed stars and a pair of smaller ones, all neatly executed in gold leaf.

"That's a handsome design all right, but what in the world does it stand for?" was the public's general reaction.

"This booth," Louise informed them, "is to secure funds for the relief of officers and seamen serving in our Navy. Mrs. Kennon, Mrs. Warley, Mrs. Whittle and I agree that, while nothing is too good for our heroes fighting on land, we feel," her chin went up a little, "that the public is neglecting, most shamefully, our first line of defense, the Navy!"

Henrietta Warley smiled a little. "My dear, what a wonderfully impassioned declaration. But then, I forget that your cousin Léon serves in the State Navy."

Olive cheeks suddenly suffused, Louise turned aside. Why, oh why, hadn't Sam come to call? Hadn't she outrageously humbled herself? At the same time she reckoned he must still be blaming her for his son's severe attack of grippe. Her expression relaxed. Perhaps Léon would succeed in fetching Sam to the Fair?

Among the masses of unregarded, ugly and wholly useless articles donated for the Fair there were also to be found a surprising number of good antique silver pieces, lovely old laces, fragile wine glasses, decanters and case on case of excellent wines and liqueurs. The chief offering of the naval booth was a model of the *Constitution*; also there were a hopelessly out-of-proportion miniature reproduction of the C.S.S. *Manassas* and the model of some unknown steamer upon which the name *Sumter* had been painted.

Could she possibly persuade Sam to come to the booth and help for a while? Lieutenant Warley had promised to help and Commander Whittle briefly would address the Fair following Major General Mansfield Lovell's address.

Already patrons were commencing to appear, although the real crowd was not expected until People's Park had emptied itself. In sharp distinction to other Southern cities, Sunday was an ideal day for the Benevolent Society's Fair; no trace of Sabbatarianism was to be found in the Creole character.

"Mademoiselle Louise?"

She recognized her footman. "Yes, Alphonse?"

"Dis yere letter just 'rive. Messenguh said it was 'potent."

Thinking to recognize that big, sprawling handwriting on the envelope Louise hurried to the rear of her booth and read:

16 February 1862

My dear Miss Cottier:

This is simply to beg your forgiveness for my churlish behavior since my return to New Orleans. Now that my son is fully recovered and I have had opportunity to think clearly, I realize that you could have had nothing whatsoever to do with our rather awkward reception at your home. If you can be persuaded to forget and forgive please let me know when and where I may see you.

Penitently,
Samuel Seymour

That was all. How very like Sam was this letter; direct, sincere, and completely devoid of dramatic declarations.

Full skirts of dark yellow billowed because Louise had sat down suddenly to indulge in a fit of relieved laughter. She hoped Letitia Kennon wasn't noticing the pair of joyous tears which had commenced to parallel her nose.

To come across pen and paper proved a considerable task but, twenty minutes later, her footman pattered off to the Carondelet House. Smilingly, Louise watched Alphonse depart, strangely convinced that Sam would attend the Fair and later drive her home. By then her parents must have retired.

XII

THE NAVY BOOTH

IN HIS LITTLE room at the Carondelet House, Lieutenant Commander Samuel Seymour struggled into his one freshly starched shirt, at the same time attempting to reread a note delivered shortly after he and Kitty Pingree had returned from the races.

My dear Samuel:

Please let us forget those unhappy circumstances under which you returned to New Orleans.

It would afford me great pleasure should you consent to assist me this evening at our Navy booth. If you can spare the time from your duties, I would be much pleased if you would appear by nine o'clock of this same evening. Will you be good enough to inform me whether this is possible? I am aware that this is disgracefully short notice but I deem the cause for which I enlist your aid to be a worthy one. Lieutenant Warley has kindly volunteered to remain if you cannot make an appearance.

Trusting that this finds you well and your little boy fully recovered, I am,

Yours faithfully,
Louise C.

"Damn!" He had discovered a loose button on the breast of his best tunic, but already it was a quarter to nine so he'd have to chance its loss. A glance in the mirror reassured him that he had regained most of the weight lost during dreary weeks in the *cárcel* of Cienfuegos and the hospital in Charleston. His light brown hair appeared a trifle long he decided, and the sideburns descending half way to his jaw could be improved by trimming, but there was no time.

Employing unaccustomed care, he knotted a wide, dark blue sash about him, then clasped his sword belt above it. Brightly shone the letters CSN picked out in silver against the buckle's gilt background. He considered it inane to wear a sword on such an occasion, yet it was the custom, locally.

He considered bidding Mrs. Pingree good night but he decided against it. She must have become more fatigued than he realized, for hardly had they returned to the Carondelet House, than she smiled sweetly and departed to her rooms declaring that she and Robbie were almost as weary as they were happy.

From a tin box lined with lead foil Sam removed the most precious item of his military wardrobe, a pair of fine white kid gloves for which he had to thank Sylvia. Sylvia? Resolutely, he diverted his thoughts from that subject.

Humming a little, he tried on his officer's straight-visored cap, gray with a dark blue top so depressed that the contrasting color was difficult to observe. The gold-framed twin stars indicative of his new rank glistened satisfactorily in the light of a kerosene lamp—gaslights were not to be expected in so decrepit a hostelry.

On impulse he lifted from his sea chest a small package wrapped in

French tissue containing a Spanish comb of much the same type he
had intended purchasing in Cuba. He'd come across this one while
convalescing in Charleston.

Within Odd Fellows Hall the music of the Crescent Blues and the
Quitman Guards alternated in pumping out such popular airs as
"Lorena," "Old Dog Tray," "Wait for the Wagon" and "Ben Bolt."
Voluminous skirts sailed, careened and scudded in all directions and
gorgeous full-dress uniforms vied with the dazzling effect of several
hundred evening dresses. Perspiring old gentlemen in evening clothes
were producing thick wads of the new money and, with a sigh, passing it over to wives, daughters and, occasionally, to some more
sprightly female.

The blaze of lights and the density of the crowd at first proved as
definitely disorienting to Sam as the bevy of pretty girls selling cock-
ades for the benefit of the Louisiana Volunteers, the Washington
Artillery, the Calhoun Guards and the Rough and Ready Rangers.

Here and there he recognized a familiar face, and bowed to Mrs.
Legendre, sashed about with Confederate colors and selling rosettes
from a tray suspended from her shoulders by little yellow ribbons.
Everywhere ladies were selling miniature battle flags or the colors of
their favorite volunteer organizations. Sam only eventually located the
Navy booth. It was, in the face of the Army's competition, scarcely
well patronized, and Louise Cottier was looking a trifle unhappy.

Nougat, pralines and other candies seemed to be the chief items of
her trade although there were some fine Spanish coffee spoons and,
resting alongside the rough representations of the *Sumter* and
Manassas, an exquisite little model of the famous frigate *Constitution*
done in Peruvian silver and priced at the astronomical sum of five
thousand dollars! Also offered for sale were some lovely examples of
crystal, Sèvres and Dresden china.

"Oh, Sam, how good of you to come!" Louise's great dark eyes met
his, lingered. "I had commenced to despair."

"We are doomed to be star-crossed, it somehow seems," Sam explained, bowing low over her hand. "Your sweet little reply to my
note arrived while I was attending the races."

Warmly he greeted his good friend Arthur Warley, who, though
courteous as usual, was impatient to patronize an adjoining booth at

which all manner of fine liqueurs, wines and whiskeys were being sold at thrice their normal value.

Sam inquired, "How does the Navy fare tonight?"

Warley's answer was a tight smile.

"It don't appear, Sam, that anybody in New Orleans cares a thin damn—begging your pardon Miss Cottier—about the Navy."

Louise's shoulders, fully revealed in their smooth and rounded beauty by the low cut of her chartreuse-green evening gown, rose in a little shrug.

"I fear I begin to understand why you gentlemen complain about indifference. Look here—and there!" She indicated first the well-stocked trestle before her—then the booths to either side at which but few objects remained unsold.

Sam treated Louise to a hungry glance, then drew a deep breath.

"Much as I hate to seem to sound off, Arthur," said he, "I think a few people here might be interested to hear about the *Sumter's* success off Cuba."

"Oh, Sam, *will* you speak?" Louise clapped hands in gentle enthusiasm before sending Warley over to request the Crescent Blues' bandmaster to order a long roll beaten on his snare drums.

Commander Kennon of the State Navy appeared fortuitously, just in time to ascend a chair and roar in a deep, quarterdeck bellow, "Ladies and gentlemen! Please! Your attention long enough to present our first naval hero in this struggle for independence."

Silence spread like sudden fog.

"You all recall how the *Sumter*, commissioned in this very port, tricked the Yankees and in one week captured no less than seven enemy ships! Let our friend Commander Seymour, here, describe the feats of Captain Semmes, whom we all love and respect, and his gallant company."

Upon Odd Fellows Hall descended the stillness of deep curiosity. Sam cast Louise a quick look, then his deep, clear voice described the *Sumter's* escape and made his audience relive those anxious moments when capture by the *Brooklyn* had seemed inevitable.

His audience roared with laughter over his description of how the *Golden Rocket's* captain stubbornly had refused to believe that any such a thing as a Confederate Navy was in existence and raged over the scurvy fashion in which that same Yankee captain had repaid

Southern generosity with slanders dictated to New York newspapers. Everyone in the great lantern-lit hall shared, vicariously, in the thrill of the chase, and the sight of a tall enemy ship burning upon a glassy sea.

An innate eloquence surprising to Sam himself found for him telling words with which to plead for public support. After all, was not the Navy just as much a first line of defense as ever it had been for the Old Union? People listened surprised and a little ashamed at their complete preoccupation with the Army and its problems.

Within half an hour most of the Navy booth's offerings had become translated into encouragingly thick sheaves of gray-brown bills. Much of this patronage came from former naval officers, some of them so old that they had served in such historic men-of-war as the *United States*, the *Essex*, the *Constellation* and the *Constitution*. They crowded about to offer gnarled, brown-splotched hands and longwinded reminiscences.

At length other attractions claimed the crowd and Sam found himself alone with Louise. Once while they counted receipts their fingers touched and their glances had engaged when Louise Cottier turned so hurriedly away that Sam glanced up to find himself confronted by the uncompromisingly hostile stare of Mme. Cottier. Accompanying her was a tall, thin old man wearing a magnificent snowy spade beard. He looked confused, as if he entertained no clear idea of where he was, or why. Mme. Cottier so trembled with rage that diamond pendants in her ears began to sparkle.

Sam drew a deep breath, remembered Robbie's illness and fought to keep level his voice as he inquired, "Madame, is there anything here that you would care to buy for the benefit of the families of naval folk?"

"I will buy not a sou's worth from you," snapped the old creature. "The Navy indeed! A parcel of semi-pirates. They're drunken and lecherous, too, so I have heard. Your presumption at entering my daughter's booth passes belief. Is there no—"

"*Maman!*" Louise cut in, dark eyes beginning to snap and her olive complexion deepening. "I especially invited Commander Seymour to assist me."

"Miserable child, how dare you ignore my wishes!"

M. Cottier unexpectedly intervened. "Come, come, my dear. You are forgetting yourself. Louise is no longer a child. She is entitled to friends of her own. Young man," he fumbled in his pocket, indicated the little silver model of the *Constitution*, "and what is the price on that?"

"Five thousand dollars, sir," Sam replied and half-wondered what a tiny rosette of scarlet ribbon was doing in the old gentleman's buttonhole.

"What a lovely thing," commented Louis Cottier, stroking his glistening beard. "I am sure that it must have been made in France. I will buy it, Monsieur."

Mme. Cottier's black diminutive figure fluttered like an agitated blackbird's.

"Louis, I forbid such nonsense. You know the rents from the properties have—"

The old gentleman's manner altered abruptly and he fixed a frosty gaze on Louise's mother.

"That vessel pleases me. I will have it, and you, Madame, pray remember your duties."

Louise gasped. Never before had she heard Papa address his wife in such a tone. Mme. Cottier stiffened, turned aside, her fan in furious activity.

"I once was a naval officer," he explained to Sam.

Considerable comment arose from the crowd when M. Cottier presented the purchase price.

"There," he observed loudly. "Besides I will pray *le bon Dieu* to support these brave fellows whom everybody appears to neglect."

Casting his wife a defiant glare, Louise's father offered his hand.

"I hope, Monsieur, that you will deign to accept the homage of a former lieutenant in the Navy of His Imperial Majesty, Napoleon the First, Emperor of the French."

A small cheer arose as the old aristocrat stalked away carrying the silver frigate beneath an arm and with his ivory and ebony cane tapping loudly on the floor. A general rush began in the direction of the Navy booth.

"Do you know," Louise admitted in a wondering undertone, "that to this day, I never knew that Papa once had been a naval officer?"

"He certainly has done wonders for your booth," Sam smiled.

"No, it was that fine speech you made," Louise insisted. "If only the people would listen to men of your sort instead of gawping at loud-mouthed orators and self-seeking political hacks. What is it?" She had noticed Sam staring out into the crowd.

Yonder, peering up at President Jefferson Davis' portrait, and apparently escorted by Léon Duchesne, stood Kitty Pingree! Sublimely ignorant of the implications, Louise called out, "Léon! Léon! Come right over here and buy my last two coffee spoons; they're just the thing for your wardroom on the Governor Moore."

Duchesne turned, goggled a little at recognizing Sam Seymour at his cousin's side—naturally, he had heard both versions of the contretemps in Mme. Cottier's foyer, but, being an astute young man he had refused to become a partisan.

Only when they had started forward, did Mrs. Pingree recognize Louise Cottier's companion. She met his eyes, half smiled, and then pretended to inspect the contents of a reticule while thinking, "If Sam is working on his drawings for the Mississippi, he's selected an odd place to do it."

At the same time, she recalled that her last words with him had been to declare her intention of retiring early. Heavens above! What a pretty how-d'you-do! Outwardly, Kitty remained serenity personified, although she was coming to understand many things.

The widow studied Louise Cottier far more thoroughly than even that sensitive individual could have guessed and decided that here was a rival who would be difficult to overcome. This Creole girl radiated gentility, imagination and taste; and what had Kitty Pingree to offer by comparison? Anglo-Saxon blood, a sturdy physique, a sense of practicality which undoubtedly must be lacking in this lovely Creole's make-up and, most important, similar religion, for, judging by her ancestry and the presence of a gold cross dangling from a dark blue velvet ribbon about the Cottier girl's throat, she undoubtedly must be a Roman Catholic.

Presently Kitty recognized a further advantage; Sam's son was in her charge and had come to love her even more than that increasingly nebulous Aunt Sylvia. For some reason Sam seemed pleased over it. Her graciousness therefore was wholly genuine when Mlle. Cottier offered a slim pale hand.

In turn, Louise indulged in an estimate. A flash of feminine intuition told her that before her was smiling the reason why Sam so long had delayed his note of apology. "She's attractive, this pretty young widow. Probably she can cook and sew and order a household; moreover, she is strong, while I am not, and, on account of Maman's prejudices, she enjoys an enormous advantage."

"Mrs. Pingree," she invited, smiling her sweetest, "won't you condescend to help me dispose of these last few articles? I am convinced that Commander Seymour and Lieutenant Warley must be consumed by thirst."

Any possibility of further contretemps was avoided by a sudden flourish of trumpets, announcing the arrival of His Excellency Governor Thomas E. Moore to draw the number winning President Jefferson Davis' portrait.

Frantic applause greeted the conclusion of Governor Moore's fiery address in which he had assured his audience that important improvements on Forts Jackson and Saint Philip had rendered them invulnerable to Union attack.

"Thought you were working tonight," gibed Duchesne, while Sam mentally consigned him to a particularly torrid corner of Hades.

"I had fully intended to," Sam replied evenly, keeping his gaze on Kitty. "My presence here was most unexpected."

Louise was inquiring very innocently, "I hope, Mrs. Pingree, you didn't miss Commander Seymour's thrilling discourse upon the cruise of the *Sumter?*"

For the first time Kitty evinced confusion. "I'm afraid so. On our way here Léon and I stopped in for an ice at Raymond's."

"Would you care to join us at the wine booth?" Sam invited.

"Thank you, no, old chap." Duchesne's grin expressed pure devilment. "Mrs. Pingree and I have promised to join the Whittles for a cup of coffee and a liqueur."

Kitty treated Sam to an inscrutable smile before obediently accepting Duchesne's proffered arm. A moment later they had become lost in the crowd.

"Aren't you going to invite me to drink a cup of coffee?" Louise queried. "I've been on my feet all day."

"Why, of course. There's Bev Kennon; let's ask him to join us. He's one of the most amusing naval officers on duty here."

"But not *the* most amusing," Louise observed and, laughing softly, picked up her cloak.

Purposely, Kitty Pingree delayed final preparations for bed by donning a pale blue dressing gown and loosing the coppery hair of which she was justly proud. The vague hope persisted that Sam just might rap on her door to inquire about Robbie so her eyes kept straying to the pocket watch that had been Archie's.

"I haven't done anything that Sam reasonably can take exception to," she reassured herself. "After all, he didn't ask *me* to the Fair. Oh, dear! If only that Cottier creature weren't so lovely, so aristocratic, so dratted well-dressed."

The rhythm of her comb strokes faltered and ceased when she recognized Sam's footsteps in the hall. Surely he must notice the light under her door? To make assurance doubly sure, she commenced to hum "The Bonnie Blue Flag" just loud enough to make sure he could hear her.

His footsteps slowed opposite her door, died away. She drew breath to say, "Oh, Sam, I wanted to thank you so much for that lovely afternoon." But then his footfalls resumed their course to the staircase and, while they diminished towards the floor above an uncontrollable flood of tears stung Kitty's eyes.

XIII

So Little Time

In consequence of the disasters at Forts Henry and Donelson in February and the lively threat presented by that Federal armored flotilla commissioning in St. Louis, the Confederate Navy redoubled its efforts to complete the four great ironclads with which they intended to clear the Mississippi and restore New Orleans to usefulness as the South's principal port.

By the end of that month the authorities in Richmond felt that naval prospects were vastly improved, for at Memphis the Arkansas lay practically complete and the Tennessee had donned her armor and wanted only a week or two more to be called ready.

Hopes of the hard-worked Naval Commissioners in New Orleans also mounted while they watched the last of the Louisiana's armor applied—an ingenious makeshift protection devised of railroad rails bolted close together and secured to a wooden casemate of solid live oak. It was on the huge Mississippi, however, that public attention and hopes were centered. Certainly, the damned Yankees could produce nothing to match her destructive power and invulnerability.

Supplied with further funds by impatient Stephen Mallory, the Brothers Tift could afford to hire mechanics away from other projects. So many eager workers appeared that they got into fights over the better paying jobs and guards had to be posted to prevent interference.

Alongside that crude jetty below Mr. Millandon's former pasture flatboats came and went fetching all manner of supplies and machinery. Under protective tarpaulins lay gauges, valves, sections of steering gear and various adjuncts to the ironclad's battery.

Throughout the last of February and during early March the work went forward by day and by the light of huge, wrought-iron cressets crammed full of lightwood and pine knots. At other points tall bonfires, fed by refuse from the construction, created an infernal glare at night.

Every day excursion boats brought curious, anxious crowds to view the giant ironclad. Lachlan Brunton, Chief Naval Designer Ivens, Sam Seymour and the rest worked themselves hollow-eyed improvising, redesigning and hurriedly attempting to correct or to compromise with deficiencies.

Sam experienced a distinct thrill when up from New Orleans appeared one day a big barge pushed by the Navy tug Mosher. Upon it, like glistening and sleeping monsters, reposed eight brand-new, nine-inch smooth-bore cannon and four seven-inch banded rifled guns procured through the good offices of Commander Terry Sinclair, new Chief of Ordnance at the Gosport Navy Yard.

To have received mounts for such magnificent pieces, of course, was too much to expect, so Sam Seymour summoned Assistant Head Carpenter Schniewind and the Tifts' master blacksmith to learn whether they could assemble crews capable of constructing such all-important items of equipment as trunnion plates, eccentric axles, compressor battens and journal plates.

"*Ja*. I think so. If ever ve finish that after-fantail. *Ach!* So much trouble ve find now because us joiners and house carpenters of curving surfaces understand little."

Sam rubbed a pink row of mosquito bites strung across his forehead. This day had dawned so very hot and humid to boot that smoke from a dozen portable forges climbed, column-straight, into a brassy sky. Men and mules which operated the cranes and hoists sweated and grew increasingly ill-tempered. From where he stood on the great ironclad's bow, Sam watched the rhythmic bunching of the back muscles of a carpenter employing a huge pod auger to drill a passage for one of the myriad bolts intended to secure the lowest course of armor—massive four-inch plates—about the expected water line.

From a patched and stained hospital tent, situated down on the shore, commenced a series of hair-lifting screams. Sam reckoned they must be amputating a laborer's leg crushed by the sudden collapse of a constructor's stage. No one paid much attention since accidents were commonplace, thanks to a complete disregard or contempt of even basic safety precautions.

Sam stood visualizing his bow division both in section and in profile. Yonder twenty-four inches of live oak supporting four inches of the best grade rolled armor should prove impervious to the heaviest shot mounted by a Union man-of-war. Still, there remained an unpleasant possibility that unprecedentedly powerful types of ordnance might have been developed by the Federals since the outbreak of war.

Behind this shield he intended to mount two of his seven-inch rifled pivot guns; here the gunners would find plenty of room in which to traverse their guns on the flat iron tracks which, at this very moment, were being spiked into place within the noisy gloom of the stifling hot casemate.

Last week he and Mr. Ivens had dropped downstream for a surreptitious inspection of the much more advanced *Louisiana* and when they had shoved off after their visit, Ivens and Sam reckoned they understood a certain reticence on the part of Mr. Murray in encouraging visitors.

Lips compressed, Sam shook his head. "I can't conceive of what Murray thinks he's doing."

"You mean these gunports?" Ivens asked. "Or those silly teapot engines he's installed?"

"The gunports," came Sam's acid reply. "Her designers must have been daft to have built 'em so narrow; why her broadside guns won't be able either to traverse or elevate more than five degrees! And the way her ordnance people have arranged her battery!" He shrugged. "I've known passed-midshipmen who could lay down a more respectable plan!"

The sound of brassy band music floating over the river attracted Sam's attention.

"More zany sightseers!" grunted a leather-faced armorer. "Wisht to Gawd the passel of 'em would go to the bottom."

"Amen!" Sam said, but hastily retracted his agreement when, a few moments later, a party of elaborately gowned ladies and plump gentlemen in stovepipe hats, frock coats and elegant pantaloons advanced, picking an uncertain course over the tool-littered deck.

Among them Kitty Pingree was leading Master Robbie along. Hurriedly he buttoned a sweaty blue and white checked shirt, and lamented that his tunic was inaccessible, aboard the *Iatan*. Garbed in sweat-stained white ducks and a frayed straw hat Sam guessed himself far from presentable.

As usual, when he spied his father, Robbie came pelting forward with arms outstretched and eager to be swung up on high.

"Well, Kitty," he called, smiling as she drew near with yellow parasol raised against the sun. "It *is* a pleasant surprise."

He was flattered on deducing that Kitty apparently wished to become better able to understand those matters he discussed so often over the supper table. Kitty posed innumerable questions and intelligent ones for the most part. She proved alert to understand various construction problems—it turned out that, in school, she had excelled at geometry. To his astonishment he learned that, in Michigan, young ladies were even encouraged to study advanced mathematics!

Although, during the past two months, they had been constantly together, it was astonishing how many new facts concerning Kitty came to light every day.

No doubt remained in his mind that she might make an eminently satisfactory wife and foster mother. This robust, auburn-haired girl was so fair-minded, so honest in her reactions and speech. She was possessed also of a lively sense of humor, sharpened by an acute appreciation of the ridiculous. Her best attribute lay in that Kitty was wholly dependable and as logical in her mental processes as any female could ever hope to become.

On the other hand, his attentions to Louise had been marred by a series of conflicting obligations and purely accidental contretemps which left them both thinking themselves star-crossed. Certainly neither of them wanted to break appointments, yet so often they were left with no other choice. And then there was always that unrelenting hostility on the part of Mme. Cottier.

Robbie was fairly bubbling with excitement. "This biggest ship in the world, Daddy?"

Sam laughed, ruffling the lad's long yellow curls. "Hardly. But some day, son, maybe you'll command one like her."

Nelson Tift beckoned him from an absorbed conversation with Mr. Monroe, Mayor of New Orleans.

"Your Honor, may I present Commander Seymour, the Navy Department's ordnance officer over this construction?"

"You must find it a heavy responsibility, sir, to be responsible for our watchdog's teeth. We count on them to bite hard and deep!" Mr. Monroe observed loudly, but kept his eyes on Kitty.

"We are all doing our best, Your Honor. All we need is time and support."

"You may count on that!" boomed the dignitary. "Your lovely young wife and child, I presume?"

"The boy is mine," Sam explained, smiling at Kitty, "and I wish that Mrs. Pingree, here, were indeed his mother."

Due to the sudden blast of a tug's whistle which attracted Sam's attention, he missed noticing that furious tide of color which came surging into Kitty's even white features, as well as the way her breath came rushing in.

"I wish Mrs. Pingree were indeed his mother!" What a way to propose! Kitty commenced to laugh softly, happily. Who'd ever have deemed Sam so dreadfully bashful as to adopt such a stratagem? Looking him full in the eyes she nodded slowly, deeply, and he smiled back.

"I could wish, sir," Mayor Monroe was booming, "that our Louisiana flag were flying above this yard in company with the Stars and Bars."

Nelson Tift frowned. "This, sir, is a Navy Department yard and not State property." Quickly he added, "If you and your committee care to brave the heat below I will show you our progress—and problems—with the engines."

"Ahem. I—er—think we had better remain on deck. We must soon return to attend a—a function in town."

"Very well, sir." Tift went over to shout down a gaping hatchway. "Mr. Brunton! Please come on deck."

That bandy-legged Scot presently appeared mopping heavy sweat from a broad red forehead.

"Have you all your engines installed, sir?" wheezed one of the committee.

The Scot winced. "God love ye, no! Ainly their beds. So far only two engines have arrived from Patterson's Iron Works."

"What! Only two engines here and those not even installed?" exploded an enormously fat committeeman. "What have you been doing all this time?"

"Attempting to remedy offeecial neglect, my friend, and local short-sightedness."

"You are impudent, sir," puffed the fat man.

"No. I'm overly-patient conseedering that twice yer precious State Navy has snatched awa' engines I'd contracted for."

Mayor Monroe looked horrified. "I wish I had been informed. Have you located replacements?"

"Aye, but at the cost o' a fortnight's delay. The now I seek my fourth engine."

"Four engines! Merciful heavens, the *Mississippi* will outrun any ship on this river."

Brunton, still sour of aspect, spat resoundingly. "That we shall presently see. Ye spoke of asseestance just now?"

"Mr. Brunton, I stand ready to do anything in my power to hurry completion of this magnificent craft. These gentlemen and I mean to demonstrate, despite past mistakes, that the fair city of New Orleans is truly anxious to assist your splendid efforts. What can I do?"

Sam knew what was coming and stood grinning in anticipation, scarcely aware that Kitty, having slipped her arm through his, was hugging it. She murmured, "Oh, Sam, how wonderful! I'm so very happy."

"I'm convinced things will work out well for us," said he, concentrating on the *Mississippi*.

"Our most serious defeeciency, yer Honor, is adequate propellers and then driving shafts."

Mr. Monroe's plentiful whiskers quivered. "Surely there must be scores available aboard those idle river steamers? I'll gladly countersign your requisition and—what's more, see that it's honored, sir!"

Brunton scratched his red pate, looked mighty downcast.

"We've thought of that long ago, but such shafts are of cast iron and seldom run twenty feet in length, whereas we need wrought-iron shafts, three forty feet long and no less than nine inches in diameter. To be sure Messers Leeds and Company have one under the hammers, but 'twill not be delivered till the nineteenth o' this month."

The pink and portly gentlemen goggled.

"Good God!" expostulated a committeeman to Nelson Tift. "Your contract calls for commissioning on April eighteenth and here it is the sixth already."

Tift grunted; he was almighty sick of such stupidity. "The mere existence of a contract doesn't forge propeller shafts from non-existent foundries. That's why Mr. Brunton is asking you to conduct a thorough search for two more suitable shafts. We'll pay *anything* for them. Second-hand shafts are as acceptable as new—you simply must find some if you expect this ram to defend New Orleans!"

The Mayor beckoned his secretary. "Mr. Baker, please make a note of this gentleman's exact requirements. You may rely upon it, Tift, ever-patriotic New Orleans will move mountains to assure the *Mississippi's* being completed in time. And now, gentlemen, shall we continue our inspection?"

When Kitty held Robbie up to be kissed, she murmured. "Good-by for now, darling, and don't be too late tonight because I'll wait up for you."

Her cool lips pressed themselves against his sweaty cheek, then, yellow parasol ablaze in the torrid sunshine, she hurried off down the deck after the rest of the visitors.

XIV

Dispatches from Hampton Roads

Sam Seymour failed to fall asleep immediately, a most unusual circumstance. Generally when he tumbled into bed he slept as if slugged. Perhaps, because he had worked all day and half the night under a pressure, his nerves had become drawn too taut.

Designs, including some innovations to improve pivot-gun mounts on the *Mississippi*, had demanded the most profound concentration. In the old Gosport days an ordnance officer could have drawn upon a corps of specialists to calculate the recoil and stresses generated by all the various charges and projectiles usable in a seven-inch banded rifle. But now it wouldn't do to leave any consideration unexplored; not with so much dependent upon this ironclad's success.

Well, he told himself, staring into the ghostly space created by mosquito curtains, he wasn't going to be able to sleep for quite a while, so, cursing under his breath, Sam got up and lit first a coal-oil lamp, then a little fire in the grate.

Feet thrust into carpet slippers and bundled into an old watch cloak he settled into a rocker and picked up his copy of *Ordnance Instructions for the United States Navy.*

Whatever else might be found wanting in the *Mississippi*, her battery and its arrangement must prove above criticism. How short did he dare design the shifting trucks? Were the loading tools properly placed? God knew that in even this great ram's spacious casemate her gun crews would find little room to spare. Amid the uproar of an engagement when burned powder smoke began to billow back through the gunports in blinding, choking clouds, every unnecessary movement must be eliminated.

The fire flared, tinted his drawn features and short brown side whiskers with a golden brush. The book remained unopened on his lap while he sat staring, mesmerized by a furious dance executed by those sprightly little flames in the grate. Their brilliant play reminded him of Coralita; fiery, generous and contradictory little Coralita!

A mosquito, sounding incredibly loud amid the room's stillness, commenced to whine about his head. By the time he had flattened this pest with a slap that would have jolted a bull he had forgotten Coralita, to mull over a most perplexing question. Why had Louise Cottier not deigned to acknowledge even one of the two carefully worded notes he'd dispatched to the Rue Conti during the past four days?

He sighed. Undoubtedly Kitty Pingree was much more what Pa would call "his own breed of cats."

Only because his duties interfered had he been unable to see more of her. Certainly she had taken a most affectionate turn. Had he not been so drugged by fatigue he might have wondered over this sudden tenderness. As it was, he found her kisses of greeting and parting most comforting.

"Yes," he told himself, "Kitty's desirable all right—mightily so. Her charms aren't yet full-blown and that short upper lip of hers argues an ardent nature. Wonder how she looks with no clothes on? Funny, in a good many ways she reminds me of Janet, although this girl's bigger and isn't so graceful."

The play of flames and some coal glowing like angry eyes in the gray-white ashes were occupying his attention when he heard a thud like that of a single stroke on a huge and distant bass drum. Then a second.

"That's cannon fire," he said aloud. "What on earth?"

He ascribed the shots to some jackasses among the wholly undisciplined crews of the River Defense Flotilla. Often they would get roaring drunk and amuse themselves by discharging their pieces. But at that moment a whole battery let go, making the windows rattle and raising a tremendous report to go ricocheting about New Orleans' narrow streets and faubourgs.

Jumping up, Sam glanced at his big, nickel-plated watch. Five-thirty. Boom! Bo—oo—oom! Bom! Bang! Salvo on salvo, undoubtedly fired by batteries guarding the levees, made the night quiver. A chill hand closed over his heart. By God, the Federal fleet must suddenly have mounted the river and were attacking the city!

Second thought rendered this explanation unacceptable. The enemy first would have had to engage Forts Saint Philip and Jackson and such an action would easily have been heard on so still a night. What then?

He commenced to dress with all speed, aware that the city's deep-toned church bells had commenced to clang and bang, tossing their bronze, quivering notes about with a reckless abandon which invited still other bells to join in the general clamor.

There occurred a terribly logical explanation. "It's the waterfront thugs! Those hellions have broken loose at last."

A sudden rapping began at his door. It proved to be caused by Major Trowbridge of the Twelfth Louisiana Flying Artillery, who occupied a room down the hall.

"You awake, Seymour?" he called. "Open up, quick."

Regardless of his grotesque, un-naval appearance, Sam stuffed the tails of his nightshirt into the top of the first pantaloons he came across, strapped on a pistol and jerked back the arm bolt.

"What's up?" he flung at a group of wildly excited and similarly attired officers.

"By God, Sam," bellowed Trowbridge. "We've won a decisive victory! And your Navy boys did it!"

More doors banged back and disheveled night-capped heads were thrust out into the hallway.

"Victory? Navy? What the hell, are you all drunk?" Sam demanded.

"You've done it! The telegrams came in only a little while ago. By God, our Navy has blasted, sunk and destroyed the Federal fleet at Hampton Roads."

This half information was infuriating. Sam grabbed Trowbridge by his shirt front. "Damn it, man. What ships? What's happened?"

Someone caterwauled, "Hooray for the Merrimac! The Merrimac's broken old Abe's blockade."

"You said the Merrimac?" Glorious exultation swept Sam's being. During those harried, uncertain weeks in Richmond, unavoidably he had come to learn many intimate details concerning the Merrimac's bold new design—in many ways the prototype of his own Mississippi. Poor dear old Irad! How hard he had labored for this victory. Maybe in God's Heaven he knew about it?

More half-clad men came hurrying up, bewildered but belligerent. Everyone soon clustered about Lieutenant Belknap, a signal officer on duty at Major General Lovell's Headquarters.

"Quiet! Quiet!" voices pleaded. Sam, ever suspicious of overwhelmingly good news, invited, "Come on, Belknap, give us the facts."

From a coattail pocket the signal officer produced a yellow form and at the top of his voice announced, "A telegram received from Richmond at three o'clock of this morning. Message.

YESTERDAY OFF FORTRESS MONROE IN VIRGINIA THE C.S.S. RAM MERRIMAC FOUGHT AND SANK THE U.S.S. STEAM FRIGATE CONGRESS, FIFTY GUNS.

Pandemonium made the old Carondelet House resound up to its heat-warped rafters.

SHE THEN ATTACKED AND CAPTURED THE U.S.S. SLOOP CUMBERLAND, 24 GUNS. TOMORROW THE MERRIMAC IS EXPECTED TO SINK OR DESTROY THE ENTIRE ENEMY FLEET OFF NORFOLK.

Sam batted his eyes and shook his head. "There must be some mistake. I know those ships well. Why, why, they're two of the most powerful vessels in the whole Union fleet!"

"Nevertheless it's true. And in addition our ironclad has driven the U.S.S. Minnesota, frigate, hard aground." Belknap raised his voice. "There is no doubt she is being destroyed at this very moment."

He waved the telegram. "This message declares that nothing the Abolitionists have produced can stand up to our Merrimac and survive. Gentlemen, the South has become invincible on the sea!"

A tremendous resounding shout swelled in the corridor outside of Sam Seymour's room—that of the only naval officer resident in the hotel. Down in the street cheer after cheer began to rise for the Confederacy, for the Merrimac and her gallant crew. Unfortunately, nobody seemed to know who had commanded the victorious ironclad. The church bells kept on ringing like mad and the cannon were thundering unceasingly.

"If you want to cheer her captain, folks, then sing out for Franklin Buchanan," Sam yelled. His head was swimming. God above, if the weak-engined experimentally built Merrimac could accomplish so much, what then might the much more powerful *Mississippi* not do?

"Hurray for Buchanan! The blockade's broken!" went the shout. "We've got those infernal Blue-bellies on the run!"

Somebody thrust a glass of raw whiskey into Sam's hand, panted, "Come on, Navy, drink up!" The wild enthusiasm of these tousled, unshaven, and red-eyed people was unforgettable.

"To our Navy!" yelled a lanky, leathery cavalry colonel. "Let 'em run the Yankees clear off the oceans."

New Orleans went wild that day. Not since the arrival of the news last July describing the overwhelming rout of Lincoln's conscripts at Manassas had there been anything approaching so spontaneous an outbreak of rejoicing. Hardly anyone ate breakfast. Complete strangers danced the carmagnole, shook hands and beat each other between the shoulder blades. Otherwise circumspect and reserved young women kissed anyone wearing what they conceived to be a naval uniform. As one woman declared, "Good news makes a body feel like she'd got rid of a pair of tight stays."

When Sam rapped at Kitty's door she flung ecstatic arms about his shoulders while Robbie, brave in his tiny midshipman's uniform, clung to his father's knees.

"Oh, dearest, what wonderful, what glorious news!" Kitty exulted. "It must mean so much to you and all Navy men!"

Gripped by overwhelming satisfaction and emotion, Sam caught Kitty Pingree's softly firm body close and kissed her hard on her warm, coral-tinted mouth.

"At last!" he cried, swinging her about in a wild, capering dance. "At last the Confederacy understands the meaning and taste of sea power. Just think! Now all Chesapeake Bay lies open to us. Next the Potomac and Washington will tremble under the *Merrimac's* broadsides.

"Kitty! Kitty! Can you understand what this means? The value of ironclads is proved." In fierce tenderness he gripped her by the shoulders. "Why, within a few days we'll be throwing nine-inch shells into Abe Lincoln's lap!"

"Down with Ol' Abe Lincoln!" piped Robbie. "Down with all Blue-backed bas'ards!"

"Robbie!" gasped Kitty in utter dismay. "Such language! Where ever did you hear such?"

The child stared, puckered up his face. "Why, A'nt Kitty, everybody calls 'em so."

Suddenly sobered, Sam dropped on one knee and put a hand under his son's chin. "Robert, I want you to listen to me. The Federals are our bitter enemies, true enough, but all the same they are brave fellows, Americans who believe in the righteousness of their cause as earnestly as we. Promise that you'll never use such a word again."

"Yes, Daddy. Is it all right to call them baboons?"

Kitty and Sam broke into peals of overwrought laughter.

All day a dense and jubilant crowd lingered before notice boards erected outside the offices of the *Bee,* the *Delta* and the *Picayune* thirsting for further details which came in slowly but proved reassuring beyond all expectation. Everyone learned how, single-handed to all practical purposes, the *Merrimac,* otherwise the *Virginia,* had engaged a whole Union fleet, ten guns against nearly two hundred! Brave Captain Buchanan had ordered an express messenger to place the *Cumberland's* flag at President Davis' feet.

"The Yanks ain't seen nuthin' yet," was the word in the grog shops. "Wait till we sic the *Mississipp'* onto 'em."

Fireworks and parades released the pent-up emotions of a city which, for weeks, had existed in the chill shadow of Fear. Churches of all denominations were filled by thankful worshipers, no less the city's two synagogues; was not Mr. Judah P. Benjamin, about to become Secretary of State, a former resident of New Orleans?

At Naval Headquarters in the St. Charles Hotel, champagne and brandies flowed in unprecedented quantities. It was the Navy's day of glory. Dark features alight, Léon Duchesne came hurrying up to wring Sam by the hand.

"What glory! What an achievement. Sam, you must come to my *pied-à-terre* off Bourbon Street and no refusals. *Silence, mon vieux.* Tomorrow, to be sure, we will labor as usual—maybe day-after-tomorrow, but tonight I intend to empty two of the best bins in my wine cellar. You will attend my *fête.* I exact your promise. It will not be a large party—just good friends of the naval service."

Sam said, "May I include Mrs. Pingree?"

The readiness of Duchesne's assent came as a surprise. "But, of course, my dear fellow. I found her to be one of the most charming ladies I have ever encountered. By all means, bring her."

Duchesne hesitated, narrowly considered his friend as he added, "By the bye, my cousin Louise will be present."

"Louise Cottier?"

"How many Louises do you know? The poor girl has been very ill for nearly a fortnight, in bed with some sort of low fever, you know."

"I didn't know," Sam replied quietly and became convinced that either Louise had been too sick to write, or that her harpy of a mother had intercepted her replies to his notes.

All the way back to the hotel, he mulled over the implications raised by Duchesne's information.

Obviously Kitty Pingree considered herself engaged to him and he had done precious little to dispel that impression—maybe he had even encouraged it. Kitty knew that he admired her clean good looks, her quick intelligence and above all her ability to sense his mood. There wasn't the least doubt in the world that she would make him a capable, energetic and affectionate wife—moreover, she was head over heels in love with him.

In a way he was relieved when her money had failed to arrive from the North by the last prisoner-exchange cartel from upriver. What would Robbie do without her care and guidance?

A frayed-looking gray pigeon hopped lazily out of his path as he cut across a small park.

"I'll stick to Kitty," he decided suddenly. "We'll get married next week, if I can find the time."

As, slowly, he forced his way through still another rejoicing throng, he noted that, all at once, the State flag of Louisiana was becoming popular. For the first time he viewed its composition with care and noted that it boasted thirteen stripes, four of blue, six of white and three of red. The union was red and bore a single, pale yellow five-pointed star. This was the ensign which flew from the signal gaffs of such State naval vessels as the *Governor Moore* and the *General Quitman*.

He found Kitty Pingree looking unusually lovely in an unfamiliar gown of apple-green which made the most of her auburn tresses. When he told her of Duchesne's invitation, she cried out her delight and flung both arms about his neck and yielded, warm and radiant-eyed, to his embrace.

It was on his lips formally to ask her hand when a sudden screech from Robbie sent them leaping across Kitty's suite to find that youngster howling and holding up a finger stung by some drowsy wasp. By the time Robbie had quieted and his outraged feelings were soothed by the rare treat of a dish of ice cream, the moment to speak out seemed unpropitious. Tonight, at Léon Duchesne's town house he would find, or make, an opportunity for his declaration.

XV

The Music Room

WHEN KITTY PINGREE and her escort arrived at Duchesne's town house off Bourbon Street, it was to find a trio of whitely grinning Negroes playing a lively mazurka on banjos and a concertina; and Émile, Léon Duchesne's butler, gravely mixing champagne punch in a huge silver bowl.

Nearly every naval officer on duty in New Orleans was present from Commodore W. C. Whittle down to Johnnie Morgan, a little midshipman on leave from service aboard the McRae. Big, broad-shouldered Commodore Beverly Kennon of the State Navy's Governor Moore was there, his huge walrus mustache fairly bristling; also Lieutenants Huger, Fry and C. W. Read. With them they had brought sisters, wives and sweethearts.

Pretty little Mrs. Whittle had pleased Duchesne enormously by consenting to act as hostess. Applause greeted Sam Seymour's entrance; apparently no one had forgotten his stirring impromptu address at the Military Fair.

On an enormous sideboard lay hams, cold ducks, turkeys and a huge pasty of ortolans. Flanking them steamed such favorite Creole dishes as courtbouillon, pappabottes, pompano en papillotte and there were veritable mounds of callas, pecans and pralines. From graceful chandeliers of pale blue glass, pure beeswax candles cast a mellow lustre over the guests.

The Duchesne house proved to be not large at all but was graced by an ample, magnolia-shaded patio which absorbed excess numbers of guests.

Léon Duchesne, with dark hair swept back into a gleaming mane, hurried forward, offering both hands to Kitty. "I declare, Mrs. Pingree, if you hadn't appeared I would have abducted you," he declared in an earnest undertone.

"Had I not arrived with Commander Seymour," she replied lightly, "I fear you would have had to have done without me. What a perfectly exquisite little house!"

Innumerable toasts were drunk to Captain Buchanan of the *Merrimac*, to Lieutenant Brooke, her designer and, at Sam's instigation, to Chief Engineer Williamson, who had, so Irad claimed, done most of the hard work. After a little, one of the ladies stepped to a piano, struck a few tentative chords, then all the sweet and powerful voices were raised first in the "*Marseillaise*" and then "Dixie's Land." The little house off Bourbon Street fairly rocked under the singers' fervor. Later, old-time songs such as "Blue-Eyed Mary" and "The Lowbacked Car" were sung again and again.

When a fourth Negro musician appeared carrying a battered clarinet, Duchesne waved towards French doors opening into his courtyard. "Out with you all and we'll dance."

For the first time since her husband's death, Kitty Pingree joined in a quadrille which she danced none-too-certainly until Duchesne undertook to guide her. Sam, watching her bright head flash under the rows of Chinese paper lanterns, resolved that at the first opportunity he would seek a secluded corner and say his mind.

Presently a waltz set hoops and crinolines to swinging and weather-beaten Lieutenant Warley begged the favor of Kitty's partnership. Happier than he had been since he had arrived in Baltimore a year ago, Sam sought the buffet.

He was sampling the punch and enjoying it when suddenly its bouquet evoked memory of that unforgettable night of Mr. Winans' ball! He'd drunk champagne then—plenty of it. He was replacing his half-empty glass on the buffet when a rich voice mocked, "Dear me! So the champagne isn't good enough? Most of Léon's guests are tossing it off right hand against left."

Louise had appeared, radiantly lovely in a gleaming gown of yellow silk decorated by a row of small scarlet roses running diagonally from one shoulder to her waist. More tiny French cloth roses gathered loops of material upon her skirt, and atop sable hair drawn into a bold chignon glinted the comb he had presented.

"Sam! Oh, my good friend." Louise extended hands gloved in elbow-length white kid.

All in an instant his whole being seemed to dissolve within him. "Louise, my dear."

By silent consent they sought a tiny music room, at that moment mercifully deserted.

"Of your letters," she explained, "I received only one. It arrived the day I fell ill again—those fevers are so unpredictable." She smiled apologetically. "I suppose *Maman* intercepted my reply?"

He nodded; then, as if activated by a force as irresistible as it was invisible, swept the lovely Creole into his arms. There could be no other way. No, not ever.

Louise surrendered her lips willingly, returned his embrace with caresses so ardent that his head swam like that of a schoolboy seized by the first fevers of puppy love.

"Oh, Sam! Sam! What shall I say?" she breathed, cheek pressed tight to his. "Of obstacles and sound objections a thousand exist, but I know only that I love you so greatly that nothing else in creation matters at all." She swayed and seemed to go a little faint, so he placed an arm under her shoulders and rained kisses upon the soft throat thus sweetly exposed. So completely disoriented and self-absorbed had the couple become that they quite failed to notice either approaching footsteps or Kitty Pingree hesitating in the doorway. She lingered there a long minute, looking on with stricken and tragic eyes. A queer little noise escaped her as, blindly, she started towards Duchesne's front door but recoiled on discovering the sidewalk crowded with revelers. A narrow flight of stairs seemed to offer a haven towards which she fled on blundering feet.

Kitty wanted to cry but was too numbed to achieve even this pitiful relief. Characteristically honest, she endeavored to conquer her raging anger and a profound sense of humiliation. Deep in her heart she knew that Sam had not ever really asked her to marry him. She'd only been indulging in wishful thinking in so construing his words on the *Mississippi's* lumber-littered deck.

No, if Sam were well and truly in love with her he must long since have spoken out. A sound of women's voices on the stairs set her to dabbing at her eyes and rearranging her coiffure.

When she returned to the patio, she crossed at once to Léon Duchesne, wearing a stiff smile mercifully softened by the Chinese lantern light.

"I'm afraid I was pretty awkward in that quadrille," said she, "but I really can waltz."

The Creole's dark eyes lit, "Ma chère, this I must learn for myself. Ho! Émile, tell them to play the 'Monterez Waltz.' " And from that moment he never left her side.

XVI

Smoke Clouds Downriver

Christina Brunton had no cause to complain over the weight of her big wicker market basket. As recompense for a three-hour search through various markets she carried no more than a dozen crabs, a short string of onions and a half peck of yams, scarcely nourishing provender and ill-suited to the needs of a hearty man who was toiling sixteen hours a day. If only there had been even a few other qualified engineers at Mr. Millandon's! As it was, Lachlan needs must supervise the simplest phases of engine installation.

A further concern was the fact that Lachlan had taken to worrying over the indecisive results of the famous Merrimac's recent encounter with that strange new Union gunboat known as the Monitor.

One night he had grumbled, "Ah. My dear, I fear yon revolving turret in the Monitor will revolutionize naval construction and it's no' so new a notion as ye might think. This same Swede, Ericsson, tried to interest that great windbag, the French Emperor, in his invention, but got nowhere."

Christina sank wearily upon a public bench. Where could she discover food likely to keep her milk going? Due to this long hunt, her breasts felt swollen, hot and sore. If only she could come across a ham! Apparently only the very rich had any left.

"You must think," she instructed herself. "What have we to offer to exchange with some rich person for a ham?"

Abruptly she recalled an ever-growing shortage of refined sugar. Locked away in a mouseproof tin trunk, she had, last autumn, stored two dozen gleaming, marble-hard sugar cones.

Employing the heel of her hand to dash perspiration from her forehead, Tina glanced at a near-by church steeple. There would, she calculated, be just about time to reach home and nurse Adam before hurrying to that nice Cottier girl's residence.

Miss Cottier was most gracious and declared herself entirely pleased indeed to exchange a ham for a cone of sugar. Would Mrs. Brunton care to stop for a cup of tea?

"I would very much like to," Tina was frankly replying, "but I must speed home to make Lachlan's—my husband's—supper. This ham will prove a pleasant surprise."

Her head whirling in triumph, she decided to stop by and beg a few eggs of Maggie Schniewind, who, of late, had taken to keeping her flock of chickens in Gus' disused sail loft. Robbers and sneakthieves had grown so bold that no chicken was safe on the ground nowadays.

Because she had no idea of when Lachlan might return, she decided to boil a generous slice of ham with which to surprise him and cut off only a tiny sliver for her own supper.

When at last she recognized Lachlan's voice in the darkness she was horrified to hear someone with him. "*Gott im Himmel!* An extra mouth to feed!" She went very red, standing there in her kitchen; Lachlan, of course, must have found good reason for inviting a guest in these lean times.

The visitor, to her great delight, turned out to be Commander Seymour. Theirs was a firm friendship based upon the fact that both were experts in their speciality; there was nothing hit-or-miss about their planning, designs or execution.

Both were as grimy as field hands, for undoubtedly Commander Seymour had been helping to assemble and to adjust the engines about which something had gone very wrong, judging by their sour expressions and the weary sag of their shoulders.

She kissed her husband fondly and attempted to inject a note of cheeriness into her tone as she said, "A glorious surprise I have for you, Lachlan. I'm so glad the Commander is to share it with us."

Lachlan lifted his broad and ruddy stub of a nose, sniffed like a questing hound. "That canna be ham?" Sniff. "By God's glory, it *is* ham!" He hugged Tina so hard that he lifted her clear off the floor and made her apron flutter. "What a wee magician ye are! Did I no' tell you, Sam, my Tina can hook fish off a bare stone floor?"

"Ham?" Sam Seymour brightened perceptibly. For weeks now the Carondelet House had served precious little beyond fish, shrimps and an occasional stringy chicken.

"Wherever now did ye manage to find it?" Brunton demanded while crossing to pump washing water into a basin in the kitchen sink.

Tina's pointed features made a little face over the shoulder of her blue gingham dress. "As you say often, Mr. B., 'Ask me no questions and I will tell you no lies.'"

During the course of the meal Tina ascertained the reason for those worried expressions the men had worn. She, too, looked grave when she learned that a naval dispatch boat had sighted dense black smoke raised by at least fifteen steam vessels advancing westward along the Gulf and converging upon Pass à l'Outre.

"'Tis the Union's invasion squadron, at last," Sam explained, while chewing slowly in order to savor every bit of fat and flesh. "We've been warned repeatedly from Richmond that the Federals have been collecting and readying a powerful fleet at Pensacola."

Lachlan put down his fork and studied his superior's sun-bronzed features. "How soon d'ye estimate they may attempt to pass the forts?"

"The minute they have conducted preliminary reconnaissance and talked to their spies of which there are plenty among us—especially at the shipyards."

"Pray God, they delay till the end of April," Lachlan growled. "Then we'll have had opportunity to launch our giant and gi'e her at least one shakedown run."

"—And my gun crews a chance to do some practice firing," Sam added. "I've got one gun mounted ashore and am drilling my gun captains at it. Wish they'd forward the rest of my gunners from the East—they should be already trained."

Venting a sigh of satisfaction, Sam pushed back his chair, and, on considering Tina's dining room, found it almost painfully neat. If it looked a little bare, it was because Tina had refused to install anything which was not well made and of excellent quality. One encountered the certainty that, in Lachlan Brunton's home, everything had its place. You knew for instance that baby Adam was sleeping dry, well-fed and sensibly dressed.

How in the world could so luxuriously reared a girl as Louise ever make-do on a Lieutenant Commander's twenty-two hundred seventy-five dollars a year? Especially when paid in sadly depreciated Confederate currency?

His doubting was interrupted by Lachlan's producing a small earthenware jug of Holland gin.

He explained, "It's been a long day, Tina, and tomorrow I fear will prove worse." Carefully he measured off two small drinks and added water before lighting a long clay pipe. "That was a rare fine supper, Mrs. B., dear. Now go do the dishes. Mr. Seymour and I must have the serious talk I brought him home for.

"Friend Sam," said he eyeing his gin and water, "ye ken my engines are taking recognizable shape, but I'm at my wit's end where to come across that third propeller shaft. And I must have it before the *Mississippi* takes to water."

"Third? Then you've found a second one."

"Aye," he said, "in an old Red River boat I located a pair of nine-inch shafts."

"Thought you said no river boat ever used a shaft long enough for your needs," objected Sam.

"They don't." Lachlan passed a worried hand over greasy red hair. "Still, I figure yon two short shafts could be welded into a single long one if I can find the right iron workers."

"What about Leeds and Company?"

"Their mechanics still are occupied wi' my first shaft and all their hammer men are busy finishing the *Louisiana*. Damn yon top-heavy abortion to Tophet! Never in this world will those poor apologies for engines ever drive her upstream. But ye were saying—?"

"Brunton, I intend to telegraph Mr. Mallory himself explaining your desperate need and requesting him to dispatch expert welders from the East with all speed."

Brunton's stubby forefinger dislodged a bit of ham from between his teeth. "Then don't delay, friend Sam, because I've learned that

yon damned silly River Defense is fair deluging our President wi'
requisitions."

The two lingered over the supper table listening to Tina hum as
she washed the crockery. Heartily they cursed the Army's project of
strengthening the prows of twelve powerful river towboats with
numerous strips of railway iron under the delusion that this would
transform them into rams capable of sinking small Federal men-of-
war. Each was being armed with a single gun, mounted aft; on the
singular theory that this cannon would only prove useful when running away after ramming the enemy!

At ten o'clock Sam sighed, heaved himself to his feet. He reckoned
he would proceed directly to the military telegraphist's office, it being
much too late for the exchange of a few tender words with Louise.
Undoubtedly she must have retired for, every day, she and her inti-
mates devoted long hours to the wounded fetched downriver by nearly
every Government boat. Increased numbers of casualties were being
expected in consequence of a heavy clash between the Union's river
ironclads—nicknamed "Pook's Mudturtles"—and the enormously
powerful Southern batteries erected on Island Number Ten below
New Madrid.

Hollowly, Sam's heels resounded along a succession of deserted and
grass-grown streets in which cats had become rare since "Ragout of
Rabbit" and "Squirrel Hash" had begun to appear upon restaurant
menus.

Had Sam been less near exhaustion these past two weeks, undoubtedly he would have found occasion to deliberate upon a gradual
change in Kitty Pingree who, though remaining as sweet as ever and
as entirely devoted to Robbie, seemed to have withdrawn into a subtle
reserve. No longer did she offer her lips and ask about ordnance problems when he returned from the shipyard.

While striding along Shell Road it came to him that Léon
Duchesne's frequent visits to the Carondelet House might have something to do with Kitty's metamorphosis. A small frown sketched a V
between his brows. So experienced a *boulevardier* as Léon must very
well understand how to stimulate a young widow's interests, especially
after his own half-hearted and gauche attempt to fall in love with her.

Would it accomplish any useful purpose for him to drop Kitty a
word concerning Léon? She, of course, was no raw school girl, but on

the other hand Kitty was amazingly unworldly and romantically inclined in certain respects. How could she be made to understand that, no matter how persuasively Léon courted and made love, he never in the world would marry her? Kitty had nothing but her own sweet and honest self to offer, while Duchesne, still enormously wealthy, was inordinately proud of his undiluted Creole blood.

The more Sam deliberated the matter, the more troubled he became, remembering all at once, various and elaborate bouquets and baskets of flowers delivered to Mrs. Pingree's rooms. Of late she had taken to wearing bright colors again, and what about a certain pair of mighty fetching coral and pearl earrings? The sooner she departed for Michigan the better, he was thinking when the faded façade of his hotel loomed through the tall water oaks before it.

On impulse, Sam paused at the hotel desk and queried of the night clerk, "When was the last mail received from the North?"

"Le'me see, sir; 'twas maybe two weeks back. I remember because there was a letter for your friend"—he was careful not to smile—"Mrs. Pingree. It was fat and done up with red tape and sealing wax."

"How long ago did you say this letter arrived? Try to recall exactly."

The clerk, digging assiduously at his ear all the while, considered. "I think 'twas just ten days ago. Yep, it was two weeks last Friday. Mrs. Pingree seemed right pleased, maybe on account of it was full of greenbacks."

"Greenbacks? Are you sure?"

"Positive, Commander, 'cause I watched her rip open one corner and peek in," grinned the clerk. "Me, I got one mighty sharp nose fer a greenback. Though I hate Ol' Abe worse'n Satan, I sure do admire the color of his money."

Why hadn't Kitty mentioned receiving her long-expected money?

Um-m. By rapid calculation Sam decided that her remittance had arrived after they all had gone out to the horse race.

He found himself both perplexed and resentful but then he brightened somewhat. So this was the source of those earrings and her new clothes! And to think he had been maligning Léon Duchesne!

XVII

RISING FEVER

APPREHENSION CONCERNING THE strength and intentions of the Union squadron still gathering strength below Pass à l'Outre caused the wildest sort of rumors to circulate about New Orleans. Even more alarming, came the intelligence that Flag Officer Foote's Yankee river-ironclads from St. Louis had successfully attacked and run past supposedly overwhelming batteries defending Island Number Ten. Thus they had severed the principal line of retreat practicable for the Gray garrison in that great bastion.

A dense and bitter gloom, relieved only by a grim determination to retrieve this disaster, settled over the Crescent City while telegraph receivers click-clacked details concerning the abandonment of Island Number Ten. Twenty invaluable cannon, seven thousand stand of arms and other precious stores had fallen into Yankee hands along with five thousand prisoners.

This meant that only the ironclads Tennessee and Arkansas—the latter still not completed—Vicksburg and certain minor fortifications such as that battery Christina had seen built on Wild Grape Island, stood between the Union forces from the north and New Orleans.

Once the initial shock was over, the Louisianans reappraised their situation and took heart, for there was much on the bright side to be remembered. Vicksburg's defenses were infinitely stronger than those on Island Number Ten and the Mississippi there ran narrow and was full of shoals and rapids.

The bulk of Commodore Hollins' Confederate River Fleet was, against his bitter opposition, ordered north from New Orleans, but General Mansfield Lovell felt encouraged enough to predict that not a single Union gunboat ever would live to pass Vicksburg.

Reassuring articles written by veterans of former wars appeared by the dozen in local papers. New batteries were going up and older

ones, such as those at Chalmette and English Point, were being reinforced and strengthened, while militia by the hundreds came pouring
in from Texas, Mississippi and the back parishes.

The *Picayune*, for instance, published a hard-and-fast report that
Forts Saint Philip and Jackson were manned by no less than three
thousand veteran troops among whom served many former ex-naval
gunners, men trained to shoot at, and hit, a moving target. It claimed
that a new battery on a Mr. Janin's plantation was armed with rifle
cannon which could blast Blue warships at a range of five miles and
more!

The *Bee*, not to be outdone in solemn optimism, reported that, in
and about New Orleans, above thirty thousand well-trained and well-
equipped troops were encamped and that an equal number had been
stationed within easy marching distance of that great, uneasy city.
Therefore, if by some miracle, the Yankees did manage to squeeze
past the barrier forts downstream, this huge force promptly would
hurl the Blue coats back aboard their transports, while Confederate
artillery played havoc with the invading men-of-war.

An "expert" on the *Delta* contributed to resurgent confidence by
writing, "We are under the protection of active and able leaders such
as Major General Mansfield Lovell and Brigadier General Johnson
K. Duncan, gentlemen who possess our entire confidence." There followed a further account of such Confederate naval strength that most
New Orléannais found ground for hope, for was not their lovely city
defended by the already-victorious and well-tested *Manassas*?

In addition, the city further was guarded by two State Navy ships:
the *Governor Moore* and the *General Quitman*, and, of course, by
the Army's River Defense Flotilla.

"We may be sure," wrote an editor of the *Picayune*, "that at the
first hint of approaching danger our River Fleet, now below Memphis,
will return to our defense together with the powerful new rams
Arkansas and *Tennessee*.

"Lift up your hearts," the editor entreated. "We all are familiar
with the fine fighting qualities of the *Ivy*, the *McRae* and other com-
ponents of our gallant Regular Navy. Next week the Father of Waters
will welcome two mighty mail-clad champions which alone can rid our
beloved river of Abolitionist pollution. Reliable reports have it that
the *Louisiana* already has mounted her battery and that the giant *Mis-*

sissippi is ready for launching and will be able to fight within a week."

Sitting in the sun-dappled patio of the Cottier home, Sam found it strangely silent since all save two servants had accompanied their owners into safe seclusion at Cythère, the family plantation. A puzzled little frown marking the accustomed smoothness of her brow, Louise put aside a late copy of the *Bee*.

"Sam, if even half of these reports are true, what can we possibly have to fear?"

Unhappily, the naval officer shot a glance at a near-by church tower and read the time as four o'clock. Um. That left him forty minutes to board a launch which would carry him and certain essential supplies down to the great forts guarding a most difficult bend in the Mississippi.

"Darling," he replied, "I will answer you on condition that you promise to repeat nothing of what I am about to say. About troops, batteries and forts, I know less than nothing. Pray God *that* information is correct. But when that editor fellow writes as he does about the *Mississippi*, he's a plain and fancy liar."

Louise's small head swung quickly about, the blue eyes widened. "What do you mean?"

"The *Mississippi* can't possibly be readied for action next week. My guns all have arrived, praise God, and their carriages, but we lack all manner of loading tools, primers, fuse wrenches and, oh, a hundred necessary items. We have received nowhere near enough powder, so in a little while I must leave you to go to beg the commander of Fort Jackson for some projectiles useable in my rifled guns."

He gulped cooling coffee, then continued. "As for recalling Flag Officer Hollins and his ships to New Orleans, those chuckleheads in Richmond will never agree to it because Mr. Davis entertains the notion that the enemy's threat to the Mississippi is more serious from the north than from the Delta."

Louise stirred on her seat, bent forward. "And why is Mr. Davis wrong?"

A small silence fell in the patio during which an obese tiger cat appeared to sniff, in bored fashion, at fingers Louise absently wiggled for his benefit.

"Because, my dear, our present naval strength can accomplish little against Foote's ironclads. If the *Louisiana* and my ship aren't ready for action, vessels like the *McRae*, the *Ivy* and the *Governor Moore* can't stand toe-to-toe and hope to slug it out with powerful ships like Pook's Mudturtles. Our existing gunboats carry practically no armor beyond cotton bales."

"Then why should our Navy fare any better against this dreadful new fleet collecting off the Delta? What do they say is their Admiral's name?"

"Farragut. I wish it were anyone but Pa's old friend," Sam added sadly. "The reason we stand a slight chance against him is because Farragut's fleet is composed entirely of old-style, wooden men-of-war, such as the *Manassas* whipped last fall."

Sam drew a slow, deep breath. "If the vessels of the Regular service —the *Maurepas*, the *General Polk* and so on—were stationed here, we could win after all. I can't imagine what the Union's thinking about in sending wooden ships against such tremendously powerful forts as Saint Philip and Jackson—and at short range."

"Then you don't believe the Yankee ships will be able to get by?"

"Well, Louise, we *might* be able to sink them piecemeal. Especially if Hollins' whole squadron appears to reinforce us."

"What about those—those River Defense boats?"

"We'd be better off if those damn—I beg your pardon, dear—misfits were at the bottom of the river. Those ex-steamboat captains commanding them are so thoroughly insubordinate that they won't even heed orders from Stephenson, their own elected superior."

"But, the *Mississippi*? Can you get her ready in time?"

Sam arose, brushed a mosquito from his chin.

"Possibly. It all depends upon the intentions of Providence and Flag Officer David G. Farragut."

While preparing to leave, he outlined the *Mississippi's* present state: her lower armor belt was all in place and even a few of the casemate plates. Her engines were all assembled, her smokestack mounted and three propellers lay ready for attaching—alas, to still non-existent driving shafts.

Louise's facile dark features drew near, her eyes poignant and anxious, as were so many feminine eyes these days.

"When shall I see you again, *mon coeur*?"

He caught her close, kissed those troubled eyes and faintly parted lips. "God only knows. Soon perhaps, because we've some fine, capable officers arriving from the East at any moment to take over the *Mississippi*. They're all experienced officers like Frank Dawson, Clarence Carey and Commander Pegram. God grant us just three, even two, weeks and we'll be ready."

Under a flowering almond he folded Louise close, close, kissed her eyes, then stepped back intently to gaze upon the dark, sunlit loveliness of her features as if he feared never again to behold them.

XVIII

THE GUARDIANS

BECAUSE, IN THE early spring, the Mississippi's current flows at approximately four knots, a steam launch conveying Brigadier General Johnson K. Duncan, commander over both forts downstream, made such good time that the sun was still high when, around a sharp bend, appeared the low silhouettes of Fort Saint Philip dominating the river from its northeast bank. At a glance it became patent that the original builders had selected a position which permitted these twin forts to enfilade the river for a good mile and a half.

During the course of the trip, Sam Seymour learned that Fort Jackson was much the more powerful, mounting two ten-inch and three eight-inch Columbiads and an assortment of other cannon ranging from seven-inch rifles to twelve-pound howitzers. All in all, Fort Jackson was showing the muzzles of seventy-four guns capable of raining destruction upon any enemy foolhardy enough to approach within range. The garrison numbered roughly six hundred men including many German or Irish artillerists; in this, at least, the newspapers had not erred.

The nearer the launch steamed to the brick ramparts and salients of Fort Jackson the higher grew Sam Seymour's hopes. Surely, yonder water battery, equipped with a ten-inch Columbiad and two thirty-two-pound rifles, alone should be able to destroy any wooden vessel Uncle Davy Farragut might risk against it. As a further and very potent means of defense there lay in the river above the forts some thirty so-called "fire rafts." Actually these were not rafts at all, but flatboats heaped high with brush, tar, sulphur and other combustibles which at a critical moment could be loosed against the Federals.

These humble engines of destruction strained at their moorings, as if impatient to spread flame and destruction upon an enemy laboring up against the river's tawny spring current.

While his launch was pulling into the water court, General Duncan pointed out still another defense.

Slightly downstream from Fort Jackson Confederate Army engineers had contrived a barrier composed of eight tired old hulks supporting a heavy chain. Surely a steamer already struggling against the current must find it difficult indeed to snap such an obstacle, particularly since the chain would be capable of considerable snubbing power. Situated within close range of both forts, this arrangement must create a veritable deathtrap.

Presently the party from New Orleans crossed a drawbridge over a broad moat swarming with huge alligators and tramped into Fort Jackson where Sam was to find the Fort's ordnance officer ready to honor his requisitions.

Once Sam had signed his requisitions he bent a curious glance on the big, red-faced ordnance major. "Do you mind if I say, Major Turner, that I'm amazed at your allowing the Navy these supplies so readily?"

An arc of pale brown tobacco juice described a graceful parabola across the dimly lit casemate to disappear into a sandbox.

"Well, Commander," he drawled, "whatever we got that I kin spare goes to the Regulars. Yessir, them so-called 'rams' of Stephenson's ain't wuth a poop in a gale of wind. Wanter climb the ramparts?"

Delighted at this opportunity, Sam followed his guide onto a wide emplacement, there to become absorbed by furious activity evident in all directions. Parties of shirt-sleeved or half-naked soldiers were briskly digging entrenchments or constructing new firing platforms. Everywhere tension was evident—absurdly similar to that which seizes a household when a thunderstorm draws near. Even while Major Turner was explaining the additions to his works, a group of officers appeared and commenced to level spy glasses towards the south.

"Well, dogged if them Yankees ain't headed this way again," remarked Major Turner, offering Sam a chew. "They bin fussin' about below the bend right reg'lar. Cain't do much harm down there."

By the density of that black cloud the Federals must have been present in force, but all sight of the river below the bend in question was obscured by a dense, olive-green and gray forest which, on this reach of the river, advanced to crown a series of high bluffs.

"What's the range from this fort to yonder bend?"

"Wal, we figger it near three thousand yards. Why?"

For a long moment the broad-shouldered naval officer scanned that distant smoke cloud through a borrowed telescope and became somewhat embarrassed to find himself surrounded by a group of lean and fierce-eyed artillery officers.

"Well, gentlemen, I just happen to know that a thirteen-inch mortar gun can be made to hit pretty accurately at nearly four thousand yards."

"The hell you say!" snorted a tall Mississippian.

"The hell I say," Sam insisted pleasantly. "I've seen 'em do it on the Old Navy's proving grounds."

"Navy, eh? Well, reckon we-uns got no need to worry."

Despite those twisting columns of sable smoke rising downriver, no diminution of confidence was written on the expressions about him. Sam was so pleased over the unexpected success of his visit that he hadn't the heart to explore with these painfully courteous officers an awful possibility suggested to his well-trained eye.

An orderly, spic and span in a brand-new uniform, approached and saluted. "Would Commander Seymour care to mess with General Duncan and Colonel Higgins?"

By consequence, it was near eleven o'clock of a warm April evening when Commander Seymour, feeling finer than Italian silk, stepped ashore in New Orleans.

XIX

Unexpected Light

Thanks to General Duncan's more than lavish hospitality and the contents of a stone jug produced aboard the launch, Sam could find small cause for complaint with life, even if the pavement did tilt unexpectedly now and then.

Just imagine coming across all that rifle-gun ammunition when it was scarcer than crowing hens! Such projectiles in all reason should have been shipped west along with the guns themselves, but they hadn't been; probably they lay in some sidetracked freight cars.

Yes, sir, if Sam Seymour recalled anything about the Federal Navy's passion for red tape, there'd be enough time to complete the *Mississippi* before Uncle Davy Farragut tried smashing his way upstream.

After what he had seen today Sam felt easier in his mind. The Federals in their wooden ships never could win by the forts.

Yes, sir, once the *Mississippi* was commissioned she'd make a name for the whole world to admire. Somewhat unsteadily, Sam set foot to the Carondelet House's boot-chewed wooden steps and made his way across the veranda past would-be patrons asleep in chairs.

On the hotel's billiard tables reposed other unfortunates, among them an enormously fat infantry officer. There was something inordinately funny about the miniature mountain range suggested by his body where foothills rising at the fellow's boots sank, then climbed to a summit of a vast belly, only to relapse into a valley and climb again over an unshaven chin towards a shiny and rubicund nose. Blubbering noises escaping this sleeper's lips and set Sam to snickering.

Like a jaundiced ghost arising from its tomb, the attenuated figure of a night clerk suddenly appeared above the hotel desk. He offered a thin pale blue envelope. "Came in, suh, this mo'nin'."

Sam made an effort to steady himself, then sobered perceptibly on recognizing Reynolds' handsome, rather florid script. Attempting to ignore a gentle but persistent swaying of the floor, he entered that same dingy little writing room in which he had received Louise.

While he bent to turn up a kerosene night lamp smoldering weakly on a battered desk, his thoughts whirled back to Richmond. How curious that, despite their intimate relationship, he should not have devoted to Sylvia more than a few brief thoughts since his return to New Orleans.

The last he had seen of Irad's widow she had been lying, a tiny, pallid and big-eyed figure in a great four-poster bed. In mute, darkened Ashforth house she had lingered for two days in a light delirium during which she had emitted some sentiments mighty embarrassing to them both.

Half the time she would plead for Irad's presence, then, in amazingly passionate terms, call for himself. Later, as her shock diminished, Sylvia had demanded irritably that little Jeff should be brought for her inspection and admiration.

He regretted that he hadn't been able to delay in Richmond until she was able to be up and about and better able to control her frequent floods of tears.

He had been puzzled, and still was, grievously so, over the paradox that while she had truly and deeply loved Irad—of that there could not exist the least doubt in the world—yet it was his own name that she had coupled with the most compromising of endearments.

Sam dropped, rather than seated himself, upon a shiny, lumpy, leather-upholstered chair, and stared at Reynolds' letter. Um. The envelope was of good quality, a rare thing these days. The letter, he noted, had been postmarked in Savannah. And Savannah was where Sylvia had been born and reared. Catching his breath, Sam ripped off the envelope's end and blew into it.

Fortunately Reynolds' writing was large, clear and therefore easy to read.

Savannah, Georgia
March 23, 1862

My dear Bro:

I am writing to offer you again shares in a swift blockade runner now building. I would like very much to operate this craft as a Seymour family undertaking.

I know that your pay as a lieutenant commander is small, but because you are my brother, I am willing to accept Confederate money for the thirty shares I herewith offer you in the *Endeavour.* Surely you can pick up plenty around New Orleans? I hear conditions are most distressful. Praise God, the local merchants are still willing to accept Confederate Treasury notes at only 10% discount, but you must act promptly as public confidence in our first money is waning. The sum required would be in the neighborhood of twenty thousand dollars.

Please believe that I would not sell these thirty shares to anyone else for less than thrice that sum.

Sam suppressed a hiccup, put down the letter and dug knuckles into his eyes. What the hell was Reynolds up to? Despite the scamp's harum-scarum background, he still seemed to remain loyal to the family. The written words wavered a bit when Sam picked up the letter once more.

It may encourage you to know that Sylvia, our very charming sister-in-law, is purchasing forty shares on her own account and is traveling down from Richmond this week in order to consummate the sale. Of course she also will visit her parents whom she has not seen in over three years.

Sylvia has made a most remarkable recovery from her tragic losses of last winter—I number you among them. It is inescapable that she mourns your absence in the West.

Like so many good and noble ladies of Richmond, she has decided not to wear mourning. Nothing is more dispiriting to our troops, say the newspapers, than for them to see black everywhere they go. Dr. Robert McCullom declares that the swiftness of her recovery, both mental and physical, is one of the most remarkable in his experience. Sylvia tells me that she conceives it to be her duty to Irad's memory to continue exactly as if the Grim Reaper had not snatched him and their child away.

She even gave a brilliant *soirée* for General Beauregard two months to the day of Irad's unhappy death. Although she was much criticized in the more conservative quarters, public opinion could not but applaud the dear girl's courage. You may imagine that I was delighted to be of assistance to her on this and on several similar occasions. In fact, my dear brother, I discover in our charming, widowed sister-in-law, so many estimable qualities that I do not frequently deny myself the pleasure of her company.

"I'll bet not," Sam muttered thickly. "By God, it's a wonder she didn't go dancing on Irad's coffin lid! And yet, and yet, Sylvia probably does do an infinite amount of good about the hospitals."

A curious, bitter humor pervaded his being. "It would appear," he assured himself in alcoholic gravity, "that we Seymours hold a certain fascination for dear Sylvia. Well, let's see what else Rey has to say."

Can you not obtain leave of absence from your naval duties? I promise you, Sam, great, even huge, fortunes are to be made in running the Yankee blockade. If only you would consent to captain the *Endeavour*, you soon could bank your profits in England and become rich for the rest of your life. Indeed, if you will accept command of the runner I will give you ten shares in her *gratis*.

How's that, Bro? After all, there's your son to provide for and you already have done more than your fair share for our Navy. Sylvia joins me in sending you earnest supplications to return East— perhaps in time for a joyous and tender occasion which concerns us both.

Do let me hear from you immediately as there are dozens of subscribers panting for the shares I am offering you.

> Your dutiful younger brother,
> Reynolds

Had Sam's head been clearer, he would have re-read the letter to make sure of the amazing implications he sensed it to contain. As it was, he felt at once touched and outraged.

According to his lights, Reynolds probably was acting as a loyal brother should; yet to attempt to bribe an officer away from his duty in wartime—well, only Reynolds could have proposed such a thing!

Sylvia, lovely, passionate, yet self-possessed, Sylvia! Would she really marry so soon again? Lord, what exquisite lights could play in those sherry-clear eyes. No! He mustn't start thinking about her; not after having successfully locked her out of his thoughts during all these weeks.

Again General Duncan's good liquor stirred within him and re-kindled his normal good nature; so, cramming Reynolds' letter into a side pocket, he started up to his room.

God A'mighty! Not in months had he felt half so jingled. By force of habit he glanced at Kitty's door in passing but noticed no ray of light to tell him that the widow still was awake.

Humming cheerily, Sam tiptoed along the corridor's bare and gritty flooring and was half way up to his room on the floor above when the faint click-clack of a bolt being slid back caused him to halt on the staircase.

Kitty Pingree's door was opening just a dark inch or two. It remained motionless a good half minute, then opened wider—enough to admit the passage of Kitty's head and a single green-clad shoulder.

Twin braids swaying over her shoulders gleamed copper-red in the hall light while she peered both up and down the hall. Then she drew back, leaving the slim black rectangle created by the doorway unoccupied.

"Must have imagined she heard something," Sam started to assure himself, but broke off the explanation when, swiftly and very silently, a male figure slipped through the doorway and tiptoed off towards the staircase.

No second look was required for Sam to recognize Léon Duchesne's supple, dangerously lithe figure. As if nailed against the wall, Sam remained half way upstairs long after Kitty Pingree's door had erased the black oblong created by it.

"Better not try to think things out now," he warned himself. "Mustn't do anything, not right away. Kitty is no real responsibility of yours except that she's caring for Robbie— Oh, to hell with it! Tomorrow's time enough to think this thing out."

But it wasn't. In spite of everything, Sam slept briefly, badly and got up at dawn. Hitherto unimportant incidents were returning to plague his conscience. Could he really have lied to Kitty? In meticulous deliberation he thought back, day by day, and decided that he had not, but, standing before his shaving glass, he remained troubled.

Kitty deserved any true happiness which might come her way; she was too generous, too fine, not to. Duchesne, also, was fundamentally an admirable character; only trouble was the difference in his background. Since coming to New Orleans Sam recognized that, to the Creole mind, blue so to speak did not always appear the same shade of color in Anglo-Saxon eyes.

"This is awful," he told himself. "Kitty's so level-headed and a Christian in the true sense of the term. Can't she understand that

Léon won't ever marry her? If I try to interfere, he'll remind me that Kitty is no inexperienced child and invite me to mind my own business; then I'll call him a blackguard and knock him down, after which he will call me out and we'll fight a duel in which either he or I will get killed—and that won't mend matters for Mrs. Pingree."

He bent and slapped water onto dry-feeling features. It stood to reason that by this time Kitty must have spent the bulk of her remittance money. Could this have had anything to do with last night's affair? As quickly as it had presented itself, he rejected the notion.

"Good Lord!" he moaned. "What's to be done?"

A solution occurred. "I'll take Robbie to Louise. It will please her to have him in her charge. After all that big empty house must be pretty depressing, especially since her health prevents her going to the hospital every day. Yes, that's the ticket."

The young widow was giving Robbie his breakfast when Sam appeared to stand looking on, rather red-eyed. An initial sensation of sympathy cooled on observing how thoroughly natural was Kitty's manner. Who, looking on her, so demure and ever so calm, could suspect that last night she most likely had rested in a lover's arms?

"I must talk with you," he announced so abruptly that Kitty started. "Please send Robbie to play in your other room."

She obeyed without comment and returned untying her ruffled apron. She stood quite still, smiling a little and with warm brown eyes seeking to read behind his expression. "Why this extra-martial bearing, Sam?"

He said, gripping his cap by its visor, "Don't you think you should have informed me when your—er—money arrived from the North?"

She said, coloring, "Am I in error? I believe that my financial status is really my own affair." Kitty's gaze wavered downwards. "I have kept enough to see me home—provided I can find passage."

"I am glad of that," Sam burst out a shade too promptly.

"So you seem. Why, may I ask?"

Essentially forthright, he found it vastly difficult to dissemble. "Well, Kitty, you'll be going soon, anyhow, so I've decided to take Robbie to—"

"—To whom?" Kitty's always pallid features began to take on color. "That snobbish Louise Cottier, I shouldn't wonder." She could hardly have employed an unwiser term.

Sam's back stiffened and his jaw line hardened. "Some envious persons might deem her snobbish, but Miss Cottier at least observes our rules of moral conduct."

Kitty's hands crept out to steady her against the back of a black horsehair-covered chair.

"I think, Commander," said she in a small taut voice, "that you had better explain your meaning."

Sam looked most unhappy. After all, who was he to cast stones? "I'd rather not explain, but since you demand to know, I tell you that I chanced to return from a trip to Fort Jackson very late last night."

Vivid scarlet rushed up from the top of the young widow's dress. "Then it was your step I heard in the hall?"

"Yes. You understand now why I prefer my son to—"

"—To grow up into an insufferable, self-satisfied prig like his father?" Her eyes commenced to glow. "Is that what you mean?"

"I regret that you deem me such. Personally, I'm not qualified to sit in judgment and I know it, but Robbie's training is my sole consideration in even mentioning the matter. Again, I may have misunderstood Duchesne's presence—"

"Thank you for that," she sighed wanly, "but I won't lie—Léon made love to me; I wanted him to. You see I love him—well and truly. Not in the silly half-hearted way I tried to love you—and got what I deserved."

"Did he ask you to marry him?" Sam rapped the question as before a court-martial.

"No, but he might just as well have," Kitty flared. "Léon is a gentleman. He knows me for what I am—no matter what you think—a thoroughly decent and respectable woman." She floundered, picked nervously at her apron's frilly hem. "We will be married very soon, I'm sure; Léon has implied as much."

"Look, my dear, I've known Léon Duchesne ever since we served as midshipmen in the old *United States*. I also have come to understand something of the Creole code of morality—believe me, for the men, at least, it differs widely from ours. So, if Léon didn't propose marriage in so many words, you'd best stand by for a severe shock."

"I don't believe it! Léon means to marry me. *I* know."

He took a step forward and awkwardly put an arm about her quiver-

ing shoulders; he'd far sooner lead a charge up a beach swept by howitzer fire than to listen to a woman's weeping.

"I'm not blaming or reproaching you, Kitty, really I'm not. How
could I when you've been so confounded good and kind to Robbie—
and me. Somehow I've botched my original intention which was
simply to remove Robbie from among your considerations. If Léon
really does intend to marry you, it will be easier for you both not to
have Robbie under foot; if he doesn't—well, the boy's absence will
make it easier for you to start north."

She fumbled a handkerchief from her sleeve and raised a blind, tear-
stained face. "Forgive this idiotic outburst," she sobbed. "I already
know what you think of me."

"But you don't!" he contradicted miserably. "Nothing on earth
could alter my fondness for you or my gratitude. Please, please, stop
crying. Of course, I'll never let anyone, least of all Léon, ever know
what I learned last night."

"W-won't you l-let Robbie s-stay?"

Yielding to a sensibility rare with him, he murmured, "For another
two days, Kitty. I expect we'll have to get him used to the idea of being separated from you."

Before he realized it, she had flung herself upon his chest and clung
there, her firm body racked with sobs. "You are good," she whispered.
"That was a very gentle thing to do. And now, if you will let me give
you one last kiss, I believe I'll be better able to face this new scheme
of things."

XX

THE MORTARS

NEWS THAT A very powerful Federal fleet had churned up the Mississippi to cast anchor only three miles below the guardian forts spread
like wildfire. On a still evening their smoke created quite a black
smudge against the sunset with the result that still more faint hearts
quit New Orleans pell-mell, whole families of them. Some departed
by rail, some in small boats and more still in carriages.

Such farmers, fishermen and hucksters as had persisted in trying to supply the city took alarm when bands of roughs and deserters, emboldened by the consequent disorder, took to raiding their wagons. They merely stayed home and let the townsfolk go hungry.

Food prices soared so high the poor became desperate, ready tools for leadership by large gangs of the lawless. Mobs cruised the threatened city and grew so bold that Mayor Monroe was forced to order out the Foreign Legion.

The wildest kind of rumors commenced to fly. The moment the *Louisiana* and the *Mississippi* got crews aboard they would steam down to administer to the Abolitionists a decisive thrashing. Public confidence in the impregnability of their forts, the efficiency of their fire rafts and the usefulness of that great chain to smash the Yankees, remained unshaken, even when soft-handed militiamen shed their gorgeous uniforms and commenced to throw up breastworks along the levees.

Major General Lovell's orderlies galloped about the suburbs carrying orders for outlying units to concentrate and be ready to move at short notice. Renewed courage came with the great news that the *Louisiana* actually had got her battery and gun crews aboard and was now under the command of handsome Captain Charles F. McIntosh.

Meanwhile the entire Confederate naval force, in and about New Orleans, passed under the orders of Commander John K. Mitchell, which came as a last-minute surprise. Curtly and unfairly, Commodore Hollins had been relieved of his command for over-insisting upon the strategically sensible move of committing his entire Mississippi fleet to the defense of vitally important New Orleans.

What principally had evoked Secretary Mallory's wrath was that Hollins had, on his own responsibility, detached the little *Ivy* and the *McRae* and had sent them down from Memphis to reinforce the weird assortment of gunboats composing Whittle's old command.

Faces fell and grew thoughtful when reports arrived at naval Headquarters concerning the *Louisiana's* first efforts to maneuver under her own steam. As Chief Constructor Ivens and Lachlan Brunton had all-too-accurately predicted, the new ironclad proved about as handy as a lumber raft, those absurd internal paddle wheels of hers not generating enough power to move her against the current.

Purple-faced with humiliation, Sidney Porter, her constructor, planned hurriedly to install two small propellers driven by auxiliary engines at the opposite ends of her stern.

"They may improve her steering a wee bit," Brunton grunted, while toiling over a delicate adjustment to the *Mississippi's* principal shaft bearings, "but yon toy engines will not increase her speed by half a knot."

That bandy-legged little Scot's eyes were red rimmed and he was gaunt and unshaven, through days and nights of unremitting labor. For that matter "fatigue" was written harsh and bold all over the Tift brothers, Constructor Ivens, Ordnance Supervisor Seymour and, to lesser degree, upon Captain Arthur Sinclair, recently arrived from Richmond in company with a hand-picked staff. The night before there had been a furious wrangle. To launch now, or to delay until the engines were able to turn their screws, was the burning question. The hull was tight and the main propeller shaft in place but still lacking satisfactory bearings.

The remaining two shafts still lay in Leeds' foundry where the process of uniting and tapering four original units into two had proved to be unexpectedly difficult. By no stretch of the imagination could those all-important units be readied for delivery by the nineteenth, for all that, downstream, the enemy were concentrating in overwhelming force.

"Put her into the water," urged Captain Sinclair and the Richmond officers. "Put her in and then place your driving shafts and mount her battery."

Growing short-tempered to the verge of insubordination, Sam acidly explained how far simpler and speedier it was to mount at least part of the battery prior to launching. Ivens and Brunton, being civilians, swore mightily in pointing out that the two remaining propellers probably couldn't be rigged once the *Mississippi* lay afloat.

About ten on the morning of April the sixteenth a gang of armorers, driving home bolts as if the Devil himself held a lash over them, hesitated, then abruptly interrupted their work on the ram's steel gunport covers. For, far away, a sound like that of a giant's hand clap came beating up the sun-lashed river. *Bam!* There was another report. Eyes sought, met one another. "What the hell?"

Because the day was almost windless a succession of distant reports were clearly to be heard.

Lieutenant Dawson, newly arrived from the East, shot Sam Seymour an inquiring glance.

"Sounds like mortar fire," Sam sighed.

An irregular succession of explosions began to thud out a deadly obligato until it seemed as if the Yankee gunners were beating titanic kettle drums. Beyond doubt a furious bombardment had begun.

Asa Tift raged, literally tore his hair. "That settles it, Nelson. We will have to launch at once. Mr. Seymour, you'd better get aboard what guns you can."

All day long the multitude of men worked in renewed anxiety on Mr. Millandon's former meadow, subconsciously heeding that steady rumble. Occasionally they would look up during a particularly furious salvo which indicated that the forts must be returning the fire.

Not until late afternoon did a Navy dispatch boat arrive bringing intelligence that the Yankees had begun to shell Fort Jackson, but with what result nobody knew. To a group of wildly excited questioners the messenger could only state that some seventeen mortar ships, all of them small schooners or light draft sloops, were now in action, and that as he had passed New Orleans watchers from church steeples had called out that, about five o'clock, huge billows of blue-black smoke had commenced to rise in the general direction of Fort Jackson.

"By Grabs! We've set the Yankee fleet afire!" Someone yelled and a mighty cheer went ringing up into the hot and windless sky, prompting mules sweating beneath the cranes to tilt their long and furry ears.

XXI

The River Defense Flotilla

In the Pallas Athena Restaurant, long a favored rendezvous among the more successful steamboat captains, voices resounded, billowed through a miasma of pipe and seegar smoke.

Captain John A. Stephenson, Chief Captain elected by the Confederate Army's Navy, was holding forth to certain subordinate captains, among whom lounged gangling, loose-limbed Tad Phillips, one-eyed Joe Hooper, pug-faced Larry McCoy and a dozen others. They were a hearty, quarrelsome and hard-bitten lot, scarcely a man among them not scarred or marked by some vicious waterfront encounter.

Red-faced and half-drunk, Stephenson had climbed onto a chair and begun waving his arms. "Sure, we'll fight them goddam' Abolitionist ships, but, by gravy, it'll be in our way and in our own time. Ye can bet I'll take no orders from any snot-nosed Navy cockerel. B'Jesus, I'll relay orders from General Lovell only! So mind you bastards don't heed any brass-bound Navy son-of-a-bitch, no matter how loud he bellows!"

Everybody present could understand Captain Stephenson's insensate hatred of the Regular Navy and all its works. After all, it had been he, more than anyone else, who had conceived and outfitted the Manassas—only to see her requisitioned just after completion by the Navy Department.

It was proving a serious blunder to have denied him command of his creation, and many had begun to rue the day that the Naval Commissioners had sent Lieutenant Warley at the head of some Marines to take possession. These, using contemptuous language and leveling bayonets, had driven Stephenson and his outraged civilian crew helter-skelter over the side.

Monongahela whiskey circulated more freely than ever, perhaps thanks to the distant thud-thudding of those mortars so mercilessly pounding away at Fort Jackson.

Stephenson suddenly spied a new arrival. "Here's Mike Simonds, by God! Boys, let's raise our glasses to one o' the smartest captains ever to tread a Texas or kick a lazy nigger overboard."

"Good old Mike!" roared a barrel-chested captain across the saloon. "Keerist! As if I don't remember that free-for-all we had in Natchez-under-the-Hill back in 'fifty-eight."

Mr. Aeneas Spiradon, swarthy and pop-eyed proprietor of the Pallas Athena, silently appeared, wiping dust from a pair of enormous black bottles. Captain Simonds he hailed jovially in Greek and clapped hard on the back before calling for a corkscrew.

Grinning and belching, the river captains flocked over to crowd about the newcomer, a large, brown-featured man distinguished by a glossy spade beard showing occasional streaks of gray.

"You're back just in time, Mike," Stephenson shouted and thrust forward a mug of livid-colored wine.

"So? Een time for wot, heh?"

"To take command of the Army river ram *R. J. Breckinridge*, one of the best we got. Yes, sir, the *Breckinridge* is damn' fast and useful for a skipper with real guts."

"What happened to her old skipper?" thickly demanded Captain McCoy.

"Reckon the bastard's got drunk or yellow—maybe both. Anyhow, his first mate swears he ain't been seen in three days."

"How're things over in Texas, Mike?" gap-toothed Captain Hooper wanted to know. "We been missing your fruit boats 'round here."

Mike Simonds directed liquid black eyes to the speaker.

"Until thees trobles I been doin' fine; make plenty, plenty money. Now ees nottings. Yonkees capture my goddam' leettle steamers so fast as they go to sea. George, come over here." He beckoned to a slender olive-featured youth. "Thees George, my oldest boy. He big for eighteen, no?"

"Sure is. Why've you come back to New Orleans, Mike? There ain't no business bein' done."

"Sure, sure. I know, I know." Simonds' shoulders rose in a typically Mediterranean shrug—after all, his name originally had been Michael Georgi Popalogolous Simonides. "Twenty-fi' years thees country been goddam' good to me. At Galveston I own plenty fine vineyards, fruit and grain fields. Also, before goddam' Northern gunboats come my fruit steamers run to Cuba and here." He flung a look at Stephenson towering big and hawk-faced amid the drifting tobacco smoke. "You serious, John? You want I really command that *Breckinridge*?"

"You're damn' right, Mike. Reckon you ain't forgot how to handle a crew of rivermen."

"What I get for hands? Full crew?" Simonds' bushy black brows rose sharply.

"Now as to that, I ain't too sure," Stephenson admitted. "But I'll guarantee you'll find plenty of river rats aboard by sundown. Hear them Yankee cannons? We're going to work right away, I reckon."

"She armed?"

"Sure, like the rest o' us," McCoy told him through a series of hiccups. "You've a thirty-two-pound pivot gun mounted aft, but your main weapon is a beak of bar iron for ramming. You will find the old *Breck's* boilers protected by a double thickness of oak planks packed in between with cotton."

"Ees good. But Jesus, boys, who going load and fire that damn' big cannon?" Simonds scratched at his shaggy pate. "Brass knuckles? Knife? Derringer? Hokay, but cannons, *pfui!*"

A deep guffaw made the saloon resound, sent various stray dogs flying out onto the street.

"Aw, hell, Mike, dear Gen'ral Lovell will send some militia artillerists aboard us to fire them pieces, so there ain't nawthing to fret about."

The host's fiery Chios wine continued to circulate until the steamboat men forgot all about the monotonous *boom! bang!* of mortar shells bursting over Fort Jackson.

XXII

C.S.S. *Mississippi*

ON THE AFTERNOON of April 19, 1862, the Father of Waters received the C.S.S. *Mississippi* upon his troubled bosom to practically no accompanying fanfare or ceremony beyond a Navy chaplain's earnest prayer that her career might prove ever-victorious. Her armor gleaming a smooth brown-black, the new ironclad lay secured to a construction jetty upon which had been piled the first of the materials necessary to complete her.

Down by the water's edge lay the greased timbers from the launching ways, and loud rang the hammers of mechanics at work securing chains to support the great ironclad's single squat funnel. Gangs of laborers also were busy transporting cranes from the abandoned stagings above to re-erect them at the water's edge. Deep within the newly launched monster sounded the rasp of saws, the clanging of mauls and the sulphurous curses of riggers, gunners and carpenters getting into one another's way.

That the new ironclad rode the café-au-lait-colored current uncommon easily was the delighted conviction of all who viewed her.

Up on Mr. Millandon's ravaged and well-trampled pasture a small army of workmen were packing oblong wooden tool boxes and other impedimenta while bidding one another farewell among the slovenly shacks and tents which had been their home for so many long weeks. A majority boarded carts or mounted weary, lop-eared mules and took the rutted road down to New Orleans. Occasionally these travelers directed anxious glances to the southwest because it had grown dark enough now to disclose the faint flash of those bombs which, for two days now, continually had been lobbed into Fort Jackson.

Anxiously, Sam Seymour paced the ironclad's foredeck. What in God's name could have happened to those shifting trucks and compressor screws Leeds' had promised to deliver three days ago? He strode over to view his guns again, lying, ready for mounting, on a flatboat alongside. Already a skim of dew had settled upon them because some petty officer had neglected to rig a covering.

Up a double gangway illumined by cressets of pine knots shuffled dozens of workers carrying an incredible variety of finishing materials: doors, bolts, copper sections of magazine lining. Below the water line Brunton and his fellow engineers were working like maniacs to assemble and adjust various gears which, one after another, were lowered into the bowels of this naval colossus.

Another scow rode low in the water under its load of high grade coal for the Mississippi's fire boxes. Awaiting their turn anchors, steering gear and cook stoves, lay on the bank. Granted time enough, Southern determination and energy would get them installed in short order.

Despite everything, Sam experienced a sense of exultation to see the great ram water-borne. Messers Ivens and Brunton had calculated that, with the aid of many powerful blocks and tackles, the Mississippi's stern just might be elevated enough to permit the two missing driving shafts to be slid into place.

He noticed certain of the gun crews freshly arrived from the East standing on the bluff and studying this vessel in which they were about to fight and possibly die.

Those among the Mississippi's officers who had managed to visit the Louisiana were congratulating each other. They, at least, were being ordered aboard a ship that could be fought and should show speed. Certainly her gunports looked large enough. Moreover, her ordnance supervisor had known his job as thoroughly as the *Louisiana's* had not. Imagine arranging a man-of-war's battery so that out of three hundred and sixty degrees she could be approached from three hundred and forty of them with impunity?

Nevertheless all New Orleans had turned out to cheer when, this same morning, the *Louisiana* had threshed past the city with dense smoke pouring from her funnel and seeming very efficient and war-like for all that the sustained efforts of two tugs were required to guide her along anything approaching her intended course. True, half her guns remained to be mounted, but aboard her the new ironclad transported the necessary carriages. Bitterly, Sam suspected that these mountings had originally been destined for the *Mississippi*.

Yes, the *Louisiana* must have presented an inspiring sight while paralleling the crowded levees, disappearing and reappearing through the drifting smoke of salutes fired by wildly enthusiastic militia batteries. People beamed on their neighbors and stood them drinks now that the first of their iron champions actually had departed to play a part in the Homeric struggle about to take place.

Downstream more salutes were fired by Louisiana State Navy vessels and, aboard the *Governor Moore*, Léon Duchesne cheered himself hoarser than any of his fellow officers.

"When will the Federals most likely make their attempt?" was the primary question confronting the drawn-faced staff met in conference at Naval Headquarters in the St. Charles Hotel.

"Exactly what is Farragut's strength?" Lieutenant Thomas B. Huger, commanding the C.S.S. *McRae*, was attempting to ascertain.

"Only wooden ships which the forts will sink piecemeal and in short order if they're fools to try conclusions," boomed pudgy little Captain Grant of the State Navy.

When, however, Commander Mitchell's orderly brought over a list of Union ships already identified, Huger's lean lips pursed into a soundless whistle. Like all officers out of the Old Navy, he was soberly recalling the tremendous hitting power of the batteries mounted by such first-line vessels as *Brooklyn*, *Hartford*, *Richmond*, *Mississippi* and *Pensacola*. However, such names as *Iroquois*, *Cayuga*, *Pinola*, *Wissahickon* and *Kennebec* meant little to him.

"Gentlemen, they'll never live to get by those forts," burly Beverly Kennon of the State Navy kept repeating. "The Yankees will be bucking a four-mile current and so can't move at any real speed; why, they'll be regular sitting ducks. If a few should manage to win by, why then, gentlemen, our river squadron can pick them off with ease."

"I hope you're right, Bev," grunted Sam Seymour. "Farragut's biting off a big piece of battle with those forts."

Huger looked about, then inquired, "Can anyone tell me whether the *Louisiana* is able yet to maneuver under her own power?"

Someone said, "Not yet, but they're installing auxiliary engines at this minute."

An orderly presented the Commanding Officer's compliments and would Commander Seymour please report immediately to Commander Mitchell's office?

Never had Sam felt more galled than while he was reporting that, short of a major miracle, not a single cannon could be placed aboard his ironclad earlier than April the twenty-fourth.

"Dear God! This is far worse than I'd been led to believe." Commander Mitchell passed a quivering hand over his eyes, then reached for another cup of coffee. "You're certain she can't be armed sooner?"

"I'd be stating a deliberate lie if I said anything else. You see, sir, her engines aren't nearly finished and I can't proceed until they are. My guns would block entrances through which parts must be passed."

At Sam's disconsolate expression the Commanding Officer sighed. "You have done everything possible, Commander, I am confident of that." He settled heavily back in his chair. "I am counting on you, Seymour, to see that the *Mississippi*'s battery is mounted in time to be of use."

Sam Seymour made his way downstairs through a saloon in which groups of pot-valiant militia and home guard officers were offering bloodthirsty predictions about what they were going to do to the damned Yankees.

XXIII

Peaceful Interlude

After the eternal din and hammering at Mr. Millandon's pasture and the reverberation of voices raised in heated dispute it seemed sheer heaven to find oneself in the Cottier patio on Conti Street. The surroundings seemed also to please Master Robert Ashton Seymour who was finding infinite amusement in futile attempts to clutch gold-fish circulating in a waterlily-grown pool built against a mossy wall.

"I fear," Louise remarked while turning a small silver pot, "that this will be the last coffee we shall enjoy until the port is reopened. There is none left anywhere in the city."

Sam nodded but found it entirely blissful merely to recline in this comfortable Chinese wicker chair and gaze alternately upon Louise and his son. How bright the setting sun was tinting yonder bougain-villea-crowned ochre and pink wall.

He marshaled his attention. What was Louise drawling?

"The very idea of my sitting with you and never a chaperone in sight!" She laughed lazily, dabbling fingers in the pool and then flicking crystalline drops at the lilypads. "What changes this year of war has brought about! My mother considers me no longer a daughter of hers because I refused to follow her to Cythère."

Sam looked his concern. "Your father?"

The faintest imaginable shrug lifted Louise's gently sloping shoulders. "Poor dear, out of habit he renders lip service to Maman but, unless he has suddenly grown too old, he still thinks and loves for himself."

"Then would he object to me as a son-in-law?"

"Most assuredly not, my darling, excepting for the matter of—" The dark-haired girl fell silent, but they both knew that she was re-ferring to the difference in their religions.

"After all we are both Christians," he said, leaning forward elbows on knees, "worshiping the same God and observing identical ethics. Isn't that enough?"

"Perhaps—we shall soon see," came Louise's soft response. "War changes many viewpoints."

Hurriedly she continued. "I apologize for there being so few flowers on the table, but Tante Thérèse is so old and Joseph has all he can do to cook and clean."

Robbie came tearing back from the fishpool, clutching a small green frog and shrieking in triumph. With honest devotion, he promptly deposited it upon Louise's lap. Had it been a bouquet that slender, young woman could not have appeared more appreciative.

"Oh, Robbie, it is indeed a very lovely frog," she declared. "Now let's see how far you can make him leap."

"I can jump further," announced the lad.

"Maybe, but I reckon you've not yet tickled him in the right place."

"What is the right place?"

Louise laughed. "That's a dark secret which I'll some day confide, but right now why don't you return Johnny to his pool?"

"Johnny?" Robbie raised fair eyebrows. "Is his name Johnny?"

"Oh, yes, 'Johnny Crapaud,' or 'John Frog' is what most Americans call a Frenchman—or us Creoles."

Sam failed to detect any hint of bitterness in the explanation and was glad of it. Presently he took her hand, stroked it slowly. "Louise dear, I must leave very soon and I can't even guess when I'll see you again."

The bright expression vanished from Louise's features, became supplanted by drawn, ageing lines. "Then a fight is not far off?"

"Yes. The Union fleet will attack and very shortly."

The lovely Creole's palmetto fan checked itself in mid-motion. "And what will be the result, besides dead and wounded men?"

"God alone knows. Logically, the gunners in our forts should sink every Union vessel that approaches. We also have fire rafts and our River Squadron and our barrier chain. Darling, the only reason I trouble you with this is because, if the battle starts as soon as I think, I've no notion where I may be sent to serve. We've so very few trained naval officers here in New Orleans."

"But surely, Samuel, you will fight aboard your beloved *Mississippi?*"

"Nowhere else, if the *Mississippi* can be readied in time. If only the Yankees will delay—and it's entirely possible—just five more days!"

Louise's skirts swirled when suddenly she crossed to kneel at his side. "Oh, Sam! I—I can't bear having you leave like this, my dearest one. Everything is so disjointed, so uncertain! What am I to do—if the forts should fail?"

"Stay here—or at least don't cut yourself away from this house. I must know where to reach you and my son, though I wouldn't for a moment have you quit your duties at the hospital."

Her fingers slid up to touch his soft yellow-brown sideburns. "As if I would, even for you, *chéri*."

XXIV

Bourbon Street

To judge by this dinner prepared by Émile, Léon Duchesne's butler-valet and sole remaining servant, no one would have divined that stark hunger stalked the grass-grown streets of New Orleans. Today no clouds of buzzards wheeled above, or perched upon, the beleaguered city's red-tiled roofs, with eyes cocked for tasty morsels of garbage.

By the light of tall wax candles set in sticks of antique silver, Émile served Commander Duchesne and that frequent guest, Mrs. Pingree, little brown oysters, the flavor of which had been improved by a squirt of lime juice. There followed in order an exquisite bisque of crayfish and a *casserole de pouissin*—chicken prepared with green olives, almonds, peppers and saffron.

"To you, my dear love!" Teeth glinting beneath carefully pointed and waxed mustaches, Léon Duchesne delicately raised a glass of chilled chablis.

"To you, darling," responded Kitty Pingree's low, sweet voice. "But why do we dine so early? It is only seven o'clock."

Duchesne circled back of her chair to press a lingering kiss on a fragrant little hollow at the base of her neck. The day having been warm, Kitty had donned a most fetching dress of violet dotted dimity and the candlelight worked coppery wonders in her auburn tresses. His hands slipped over her arms, and Léon raised her that he might avidly press lips the color of oxblood cherries.

They drank coffee beneath a hoary and twisted old olive tree in the patio, then lolled upon a huge, well-cushioned banquette facing a wall upon which white climbing roses created sweet confusion.

"Léon, darling, do you know that you have not yet answered my question?" Kitty reminded, stirring her cup.

"Only because I have heavy news for you—for us both."

Her eyes flew wide open. "Bad news?"

His hand slipped into the bosom of her dress and commenced to caress the smoothly warm contours within.

"Tonight the *Governor Moore* drops down to the forts."

"Oh, Léon, why?"

"Because those sacré Yankees have broken our chain. They sent the *Pinola* and the *Itasca* under our guns and snapped it. 'Twas a damned courageous exploit, even for Abolitionists."

"Oh, Léon! Are you really going into battle?"

"Undoubtedly," he smiled, pulling her across his chest in order to cradle her in his arms. "No one doubts that the Yankees intend to try passing the forts."

Kitty sighed and made no protest to his further exploration of her garments. When Archie had got his orders, she'd been so numbed she hadn't understood, or responded to, his unusually fervent advances. And Archie now lay dead in far-off Tennessee.

"But why should the Unionists run such risks? Even if they should win through, they are doomed now that the *Mississippi* is launched and ready to fight."

At mention of the ironclad's name she experienced a small twinge; to her Sam Seymour and the *Mississippi* were synonymous.

"She's launched all right," Duchesne admitted, "but two of her engines are still incomplete, and thus far not one of her battery is mounted. Sam is beside himself, but can accomplish nothing for the moment."

Kitty raised anxious eyes.

"Well, then, you still have the *Louisiana.*"

A bitter laugh escaped him. "The *Louisiana* remains unmanageable and is so poorly designed that at best she can serve only as a floating battery. Still, in that capacity she should prove valuable, since our experts declare that not a single gun mounted by Farragut's ships can penetrate her armor."

The Creole then dwelt at length on the encouraging fact that, thus far, Fort Saint Philip, as distinct from Fort Jackson, had suffered no damage from mortar fire.

When the church bells began to ring eight, Duchesne lifted his guest and carried her towards an outside stairs leading to his little library.

"*Hélas, ma petite côlombe.* Barely have we time to—read a single chapter of our favorite book."

"Barely time, my sweet?"

"Our unfeeling Navy has ordered the *Governor Moore* to sail at half after nine."

When gently he lowered Kitty upon a divan overwhelmed by towering shelves of books, she commenced to tremble strangely, unwillingly, much as she had the night before Archie Pingree's company had gone swinging off down that muddy lane to board the troop train. Right now Kitty was visualizing her young husband as he had leant over the rear platform, waving his cap and devouring her with his eyes.

Why must she be doomed to suffer another such ravaging farewell? Veins gorged, her heart pounding, she almost sleepily looked upwards to find her gaze dominated by Léon's half-buttoned sky-blue tunic. Lord! Lord! How handsome he was! Her arms swung up, pulled his dark head down, down until his cheek bristles bruised her lips.

"Darling dear," she whispered, her lips to his ear. "I love you so! Do you, can you realize that you are going into battle—and what that can mean? You—you might be killed. That can happen, Léon. I know."

With an airy gesture he waved away the suggestion. "Others may die, but not I, *mon ange.* Our love is too great."

Her hands framed, imprisoned his face. "Please answer me truthfully, Léon, just how much do I mean to you?"

She felt the waxed end of his mustache bend, then break to the violence of his kiss. "Everything in this life, Kittee. Surely you must believe that?" he murmured in a surprised tone.

"Then in that case," she faltered, thinking of Sam Seymour's bitter warning, "aren't you—aren't you going to ask me something?"

"But I have," he cried gaily. "So, ma chère, let us waste no more precious time."

She raised shadowed, suddenly stricken eyes. "No. You know very well I don't mean that. Surely, you can't have imagined that I'm—a—an easy woman?"

His eager, radiant expression abruptly dissolved. "What a delightfully unpredictable thing it is! Nom de Dieu! Whatever gave you such an absurd notion?"

"Oh, Léon dear, please." Her white cheeks suddenly flamed into unaccustomed color. "Can't you understand? I—well, I have considered that because these are wartimes our—our—relations—oh, how shall I put it?—as a, well, a—a—sort of honeymoon in advance. When are we to be married?"

Duchesne sat up, appeared genuinely astonished. "Married? But my dear, you are a widow, une femme du monde. Kittee! Kittee! Don't look at me so. Surely you must have understood about this, our little affaire?"

"I seem to have been dense. What has this meant to you?"

"What but a mutually pleasurable association of mature persons in need of companionship during difficult times?"

"Oh, Léon! Léon! No more than that?"

"Infinitely, but were I to marry an American my father would disinherit me, and I have no private fortune." In her eyes he read a world of pain and shame. But why? Why? This was no green girl.

How understanding Sam had been! Despite herself Kitty emitted a small hurt cry. "Oh Léon! I can't have been wrong. We've—we've got to be married!"

Quickly he seized her by the shoulders, but not roughly. "Kittee, what do you mean? Are you pregnant?"

"I have every reason to believe so," said she so faintly that he hardly heard her.

Duchesne stood up and went over to look out upon his moon-flooded courtyard. "In that case, Kittee, I am most regretful. I shall, of course, make the usual provision for you and this child which you say is mine."

" 'You say?' " Kitty sat up, eyes ringed and lips set in a rigid and anguished rectangle. "Whose else could it be?"

The Creole continued to view his patio, but commenced to do up his tunic and silvered buttons.

"Possibly 'tis a sprig of my old friend and shipmate, Samuel Seymour. *Enfin, ma chère.* Have not you lived but a floor apart for several months? Surely there was some midnight traffic on those stairs?"

"I think you'd better say nothing more," Kitty murmured in a small, dead voice. "It appears that again I've made a silly fool of myself."

She had darted across the library and disappeared downstairs before he could even wheel about. By the time he got downstairs he found his front door wide open and her bonnet and cashmere shawl abandoned on the hall settee.

He started in pursuit, but gave up at the entrance to Dumaine Street because Kitty's long-limbed figure had disappeared and it was high time to be reporting aboard the *Governor Moore*. Panting a little, he re-entered his *pied-à-terre*.

When he returned to New Orleans, he determined to reassure dear Kittee with a magnificent pearl necklace—yes, he would even give her a small house of her own on Rampart Street. That should adjust the matter—generously.

Yet it would not. Hand on doorknob, he halted, utterly dumfounded.

"*Bigre!* It cannot be that I—Léon François Saint-Juste Duchesne—actually have fallen in love with this simple little American widow?"

The question remained unsolved even when he crossed the *Governor Moore*'s dew-soaked gangway and stiffened gravely to salute the quarterdeck.

XXV

MOVEMENTS OF THE C.S.S. Manassas

AT THE END of nearly five days that nerve-racking, never-ceasing, rain of mortar bombs bursting on Fort Jackson finally came to an end.

"Some sixteen thousand eight hundred shells," Commander David D. Porter reported to his blue-clad superiors, "have been fired into that fort by my mortar boats. There has been considerable damage done."

The sudden silence at first seemed unnerving to the weary, half-deafened gray gunners emerging from casemates within their battered fort.

"Now, mebbe, we kin score!" growled a black-bearded battery commander. He, like most of the garrison, had tried to range the Union mortar fleet lying hidden behind the bend, but could not. The intervening forest rendered it impossible for the artillerymen to see their targets. Besides, the trajectory of their field pieces prevented the lobbing of shells above the woods. Only mortars could accomplish that—and there were no mortars in either fort.

The significance of this somehow-alarming silence was not lost upon certain captains commanding the Confederate men-of-war lying at anchor just upstream and around a bend behind Fort Saint Philip.

The night of April twenty-third–twenty-fourth was one of the most impenetrable blackness. Lieutenant A. F. Warley could recall no darker. It was perfectly suited for an attack.

That young officer, therefore, did not retire to sleep aboard a tender alongside, but remained smoking a reflective pipe on the iron whaleback of his command, the C.S.S. Manassas. Slowly, his eye traveled over dew-spangled sloping plates towards the hood-like gunport, then on to a little jackstaff rigged above his craft's heavy, wickedly pointed ram. For a patently improvised war engine she thus far had accomplished much and had fared well, despite her single little nine-pounder gun and fragile quarter-inch armor—if such properly could be called armor—and her overburdened engines.

His short-stemmed pipe glowed under a sharp inhalation revealing Warley's intense, alert eyes, and generously wide mouth.

Now that the eternal report of shells bursting high over the bluffs across the river was stilled, this night appeared preternaturally quiet. Very clearly Warley could recognize not only sawing and hammering going on to repair Fort Jackson but even individual voices and the barking of a dog.

While fanning away a halo of mosquitoes, Warley briefly studied smoke rising in lazy, sable ribbons from the two tall funnels of his command. His crew, sleeping aboard the *Phoenix*, tender-tug alongside, lay sprawled about her decks shrouded by tarpaulins and snoring manfully. Yonder, huddled under separate awning, slept the ram's two pilots Levine and Wilson; under another slumbered the *Manassas'* First Lieutenant Frank Harris and the ram's engineer officers, Weaver and Dearning. On all these he was prepared readily to rely when the imminent, deadly issue of battle hung in the balance.

A little chilled, Warley arose and, heels ringing softly upon the *Manassas'* iron skin, walked aft along a removable wooden catwalk. Idly, he regarded the occasional sparks rising from the twin funnels to dance, mingling with heavier fumes emitted by the State Navy's gunboat, *Governor Moore* and the River Defense ram *Resolute*.

Nearer to Fort Saint Philip, he knew, were berthed the *McRae* and the *Jackson* of the regular Confederate Navy; then, although he couldn't see them, there should be three units belonging to the Army's controversial and thoroughly insubordinate River Defense Flotilla.

Lord, what a mess was here! Yesterday the unmaneuverable *Louisiana* had been towed over to a new position, just upstream from Fort Jackson's water battery, where she could sweep the river and protect a nest of fire barges.

Across the river, hammers kept on slamming away like huge nocturnal woodpeckers and lanterns swung and blinked, suggestive of demented fireflies. When darkness lifted he found he could just recognize the spars of the Army's *Breckinridge* and the State Navy's *General Quitman*.

Warley spat reflectively over the side. Were the experts correct in declaring that the wooden sides of the Union ships could never, at short range, withstand the terrific pounding of shore guns.

The situation here, he reminded himself, would not be comparable to the problem present at Port Royal Inlet where Commodore Du Pont's Federal warships had found plenty of room in which to maneuver and so to outrange the Confederate land batteries. Let only one or two big ships, like the *Hartford* or the *Mississippi*, sink in midstream and their wrecks unavoidably must block the progress of their consorts, to immobilize them long enough to allow the forts to fire withering blasts at point-blank range.

Warley worked aft, listening to the current *lap-lapping* at his ram's stern plates. Um. From the flagstaff dangled a smoke- and weatherstained Confederate naval flag. Of course, it should have been lowered at sundown, but there had been many more important considerations to occupy a commander's mind.

Had he really recognized Commander Seymour aboard the *McRae?* He hoped he'd been mistaken because Sam's presence there would indicate that no hope remained of mounting the *Mississippi's* guns in time for the impending action.

What other old and dear friends were upon this Stygian river tonight? How many of them might be aboard those grim Northern men-of-war lying below the bend? Nearer at hand were Huger and Read aboard the *McRae*, and McIntosh commanding the *Louisiana*.

Of late he'd grown right friendly with bulldog-jawed Commander Kennon of the *Governor Moore*, but, for some reason, he'd never been able to cotton to Captain Grant of the *General Quitman*. Maybe it was because he talked too much about fighting and hating all Northerners; Grant reminded him of certain ladies who talked a mighty good bed, yet seldom graced an unofficial four-poster.

Steam hissed comfortably from an escape valve rigged between the *Manassas'* two funnels and, up on the bluff above sleeping gunboats, some mockingbirds commenced warbling as if to celebrate this cessation of mortar fire.

Yawning, Warley reckoned it must be nearly three o'clock—time to summon Lieutenant Harris and rout out his firemen—what with the poor grade of coal he'd been issued, it required an unconscionable time to get up steam.

Warley's foot was reaching for the *Phoenix's* rail when, high in the heavens, exploded a gigantic star of flame—a mortar shell which threw into momentary relief the pockmarked western façade of Fort Jackson. Hardly had the report of that bursting shell come slamming across the river than four horizontal flashes attested the fact that the gunners in the Water Battery were on the alert.

Like a kennel of disturbed watchdogs, more and more cannon growled over yonder, until, in a few instants, pandemonium had shattered the previous unearthly stillness.

Warley cupped his hands, shouted over the uproar. "Manassas men! Get aboard, all of you! Quickly, quickly!"

They dropped, heels clanging, onto the ram's deckplates and then scrambled down a narrow hatchway into the hot and oily-smelling gloom below. Instants later came the reverberating clatter of fire-box doors being slammed back, then the rushing scrape of coal shovels at work. Voices boomed queerly within the hull.

Rubbing their eyes, Lieutenant Harris and Pilot Levine came crowding into the tiny conning place situated just aft of the Manassas' single gunport.

"Prepare to cast off!" Warley shouted. "Throw over the catwalk and cast loose the tender."

The cannonading downstream was swelling as if the War God had pulled out a diapason stop on some Titan's pipe organ, causing a succession of deafening, crashing salvos. While waiting for headway steam, Warley, by the uncertain glare of bursting shells, got his first glimpse of the enemy. Some ocean-going man-of-war, still far downstream, was preparing to find her way through the gap opened in that futile chain barrier.

"Time?" he snapped. In preparing an official report such details were of first importance.

"Three-thirty, sir," Harris shouted. "Shall I make note of it, sir?"

"Aye, aye." Warley then whistled down the engine room tube and, ascertaining that the Manassas' boilers had raised steerage pressure, ordered half speed ahead. Smoothly, silently, the long, low-lying hull slipped out into the current less than ten minutes after the alarm had been raised.

"Mr. Pilot," announced Warley, "we'll stand downstream and ram the first enemy vessel we sight."

To feel the ship's fabric throb, to hear the soft panting of the engine urging her on towards an unknown fate tautened Warley's nerves. Due to the ram's unique construction, bow waves foamed up over her seegar-shaped bow, nearly reached the threshold of her gunport.

He recognized orders being given by his officers below, also the heartfelt curses of stokers complaining about the bad air and heat; all the same they fed pitch and tallow into the *Manassas'* fire boxes until the pressure gauge's dancing black needle rose and rose towards a scarlet line marked "Danger."

All of a sudden Harris, who had been staring intently into the murk, yelled, "Port! For God's sake, port hard!" Pilot Levine whirled his stubby wheel over just in time to escape the path of a vessel rushing furiously out of the dark.

She was Confederate. Everyone could see her flag clearly revealed by banderoles of orange flame spouting from her smokestacks, but there wasn't time to speculate on her identity. The three officers crammed into the *Manassas'* conning place discovered considerable difficulty in determining what lay ahead—despite the blinding flashes of cannon being fired at all levels. Warley rang for half speed, attempting to orient himself. He felt he had better because, upon the bluffs, whole batteries were letting fly simultaneously, causing the smoke-veiled night to quiver and quake under the thunder of their reports.

"Now comes an answer," thought Warley. In the iron-protected conning place it was relatively quiet, but the ram's officers recognized a deeper, more sonorous note; heavy guns nearer to the Mississippi's swift running surface were firing evenly, creating a deadly undertone in this symphony of conflict.

"There they are, sir!" Levine burst out suddenly. "My God, there's a big one coming up to starboard. Shall I steer for her?"

In quite an ordinary tone Warley said, "Pray do, Mr. Levine, and try to strike her amidships."

Through acrid-smelling layers of burned powder smoke drifting above the river, all at once could be seen a whole series of bright red and white lights— Always one above the other—evidently night signals for Federal vessels.

Warley slid back the armored hatch above, enough to let him stick out his head and make sure that his own blue light was bright and shining. He got a faceful of water from the wake created by the ship which had just passed. Waves surged up the Manassas' foredeck like swells over a half-tide rock, and fine spray splashed into the conning place, drenching all three officers.

"Mr. Harris, pass the word below that we are about to ram," Warley ordered. "Make sure our piece is loaded and its crew ready, then come back and report to me."

Much like a surfaced whale, the Manassas churned further out into the center of the river straight towards two superimposed lights above a jet blur against the sable background.

Warley felt his throat muscles stiffen, for from downstream came the distinctive woosh!—woosh!—woosh! of threshing paddles. Could this be one of those infernal River Defense gunboats? Hardly. Yonder beat was too powerful, too deliberate. Harris returned, cap gone and jaws working steadily on a chew of tobacco. "All secure below, sir." His face loomed queerly in a half light created by the binnacle lamp.

Vivid parallel streaks of fire began raking the night in the direction of Fort Saint Philip; no doubt now that an enemy was approaching. The ram's steering wheel creaked and protested when Levine, with Warley's help, ground it over, altering the Manassas' course into a ponderous flat arc.

No ship of the Confederate squadron could match this vessel in size, so, beyond a doubt it must be one of the Federal fleet. Rapid calculation suggested that this might be the Federal Mississippi, the only sizeable paddle ship reported to be with the Union fleet. Was it ironic that ships on both sides were named Mississippi?

"Hold hard below!" Warley bellowed down the speaking tube. "We ram inside of a minute."

Promptly came the ringing clang of furnace doors being slammed to, the clatter of hastily dropped shovels. The stokers and gun crew below must now be thrusting wrists through leather handholds nailed to the former tug's framing; only thus could they avoid being hurled, with perhaps fatal results, against the boilers or interior structure.

Wet-smelling air poured through the view slit, together with wisps of gunsmoke. Warley found it increasingly difficult to see the enemy, so dazzled was he by a continuous pattern of gun flashes.

As in a dream, he glimpsed another ship following his intended victim, watched her sides spurt flame.

Where were the other Confederate ships? The limited angles of observation prescribed by his ram's design prevented such knowledge. For all Warley knew he might be steering right into the path of some onrushing man-of-war. In magical suddenness the black bulk of the U.S.S. *Mississippi* materialized above the low-lying ram, her yards a faint tracery visible thanks only to some conflagration rising astern. Details of the enemy's hull and superstructure became starkly revealed, even spume flying from her mighty paddle boxes.

Yelling something unintelligible, Levine ground his wheel slightly to port and directed the black mass of the *Manassas* straight at the enemy vessel.

"Hold hard!" Warley had time to shout just before his beak struck the U.S.S. *Mississippi* aft of her paddle box and caused a grinding crash like that of a dozen tall trees simultaneously felled. Warley and Harris were slammed hard against the conning place while the ram shuddered and bucked to a stop with her whole fabric groaning and crackling.

"Fire!" Warley gasped. "Fire, Mr. Weaver!"

Into the steam frigate's towering, dripping side the *Manassas'* single cannon suddenly blazed, hurling a shell equipped with a time fuse into the Union ship's vitals. When it detonated it must create a shambles of her boiler room.

Robert Levine shouted with a hysterical note in his voice, "Back! For God's sake back your engines, Mr. Warley. We'll—" His voice became lost in a furious, tremendous blast of sound because the U.S.S. *Mississippi's* whole starboard battery had let fly to drench her attacker in sulphur fumes, scorching gases and whirlwinds of sparks.

So great was the heat that Warley's mustache and brows writhed and smoked. Even as he listened to the familiar sound of the guns being run in for reloading, Warley managed a stiff smile on deducing that the Federal's guns could not, for the moment, be depressed sufficiently to hit the low-lying hull of his command! Her terrific broadside apparently had accomplished no more damage than to carry away the *Manassas'* starboard smokestack.

Warley collected his reeling wits, gave the order to back, and was overjoyed to feel the ram's engines throb powerfully; the former tow boat's screws, eleven feet in diameter, drew her swiftly clear of the stricken U.S.S. *Mississippi*.

Warley received a momentary impression of shattered planks fringing a gaping hole and of water gushing into it before the Union ship vanished into the smoke-shrouded darkness with paddles still churning regularly. In order to avoid the possibility of another broadside delivered at effective range, Warley ordered his ram passed under the frigate's stern.

"Christ! That was a good one!" grinned Harris.

Levine vented a strangled cough. "Hope we ain't started no deck plates. It sure was a mean lick we give her."

Reports from the engineers indicated that, apparently, the blow had caused the *Manassas* no perceptible damage.

"Where away, sir?" the pilot shouted. All three officers still were deafened by the terrific concussion of that broadside fired just above their heads.

"Take her downstream," Warley directed. "Our forts must have crippled some Yanks by this time and we'll finish them off."

Harris yelled, "Look! Look to port!"

Another huge black blur was bearing down on the slow-moving ram.

Eternal, agonizing instants ensued. It seemed impossible that the *Manassas*, never a handy craft, could escape being run down. The stranger—she turned out later to be the U.S.S. *Pensacola*—was faster than her predecessor and fairly surged along.

By the glare of some burning ship which was lighting the whole river, the Federal man-of-war let fly the only gun she could bring to bear—her forward pivot gun. Scant feet high of its target the projectiles screamed by, then the tall sloop bow loomed right overhead.

By less than ten feet Warley's little ram managed to escape the *Pensacola's* murderous rush. As it was, she swung and bobbed in the enemy's wake like a piece of driftwood while a solid sheet of water surged over the *Manassas'* whole length, gushed through the viewing slit and spurted through those openings designed to repel possible boarders with boiling water.

Choking, blinding billows of wood-, gun- and coal-smoke then enveloped the *Manassas*, and briefly isolated her amid a world bereft of horizon or sky.

"How does she steam?" Warley yelled down to his engineers now stripped to the waist and gleaming like animated bronze figures.

"Eight knots, sir!" Weaver bellowed back. "That's about all, too, the draft's failing. Are the funnels secure?"

"Starboard one's shot away."

Then a vagrant air current suddenly swept aside a baffling bank of vapors to reveal huge areas of dancing, lancing flashes off either bow.

"We're between the forts, sir!" Levine yelled. "Hope to God they recognize us."

But they didn't. Purple curses escaped the ram's officers when a roundshot from Fort Saint Philip struck the *Manassas'* lightly armored back a glancing but savage blow which caused her to shudder and heel away over. Again came the keening scream of a ricocheting projectile. *Bong!* Then a shell burst right over head, its fragments causing the ram's whole hull to resound like a beaten gong.

"God above!" Warley yelled. "Those bloody fools are trying to sink us. Come about! Come about!"

But to turn the sluggish *Manassas* against the current was easier said than done. Meanwhile, to make matters worse, the gunners of Fort Jackson joined in punishing their own vessel.

Cursing and praying, the ram's crew heard several shots strike and glance off. Two great holes, however, were punched through the remaining smokestack, further decreasing draft and the *Manassas'* speed.

When, finally, the ram had completed her laborious turn and had started back upstream, Warley momentarily deserted the conning place to inspect his engine room.

He entered an area in which ghostly figures, tinted amber by the lights of kerosene lanterns, appeared and disappeared through clouds of oily-smelling steam.

Chief Engineer Dearning, stripped to the waist and black as any of his coal heavers, had to be tapped twice on the shoulder before he would turn his head. Thanks to the panting labor of cylinders and the loud gurgle caused by water passing along the hull, it was practically impossible to hear anything, especially when coal scoops went rasping over the iron floor or struck their edges against the fire-box door frames.

"Everything working all right?" Warley demanded, half-smothered in the hot and fetid gloom.

"Those last shots must have started some plates," Dearning shouted through cupped hands. "We'd best not ram again. Listen."

Warley, stumbling aft, was shaken to hear sounds as of a miniature cascade.

"Have you sounded the hull?"

"Haven't had time," Dearning panted, using waste to free his eyes of sweat. "My God, that there gauge is down five more degrees, sir. Can't you clear away that wrecked funnel? I've got to get more draft!"

"Not a chance. We're in the midst of the Federal fleet or so it seems. What else can be done?"

The chief engineer thrust a purple, blackened face close to Warley's ear. "Nothing but pray. If them Yankees hit t'other smokestack we'll not travel much further. There's hardly draft enough now to keep the coal gas out."

"I'll try to sheer out of action long enough to clear away that stack." Warley clapped Dearning on the shoulder and spoke encouraging words to his shaggy, black-faced stokers. "You're doing fine, boys! We've knocked hell out of one of their big frigates and we've just begun to punish 'em. Keep up the steam."

At the same time he tried to recall whether he'd heard any explosion from that shell fired into the U.S.S. *Mississippi's* bowels, but couldn't.

With head still swimming from the engine room's infernal heat, Warley was glad to find himself back in the overcrowded conning place.

Harris gave the hour as four-fifteen; a little less than an hour had passed since the *Manassas* had slipped out of her berth.

The bald head of Menzies, the relief pilot, snapped about. "Yonder comes another and a big one, Christ A'mighty!" His voice rose sharply. "Look! They got them fire rafts ablaze and one of 'em's fouled the enemy for sure!"

"Which is she, sir?" Harris demanded, making another entry in his mental report.

"Either the *Hartford* or the *Brooklyn*," replied the *Manassas'* commander. "We'll have full speed ahead, Mr. Harris. The enemy's so occupied with that raft I don't think her people have noticed us."

Again the command was passed, "Stand by to ram!" and again the crews scrambled to their handholds. Those in the cramped little conning place were treated to the memorable sight of a furiously flaming barge muzzling under a big steam sloop's beam and flinging fiery lassos at her yards and rigging. Men in dark uniforms could be seen attempting to pole away the menace or to play hoses on their own sides.

During that fateful interval during which the *Manassas* bore down upon her enemy the pre-dawn sky had become a palpitating pattern of brilliant scarlet, vermilion and orange-white flashes. The noise became terrifying and all but unbearable.

Again sounded the awesome crunch and creak of overtried timbers, and tortured groans from the *Manassas'* fabric preluded a blast of steam rushing up from below. Shrill screams began to assault Warley's ears even before the *Manassas'* shell gun was fired for a second time.

"Back! Your engines, back!" Levine was shouting. "Them fire rafts is drifting down on us!"

Dearning's head materialized amid whirling gray vapors. "Cap'n, we daren't back, shock's unseated our goddam' engine."

Warley cupped both hands. "Try reversing, anyhow. You'll maybe pull our engine back onto its base."

While waiting, the ram's commander directed a pungent curse upon John Stephenson and his civilian engineers. In the Old Navy an engine never became unseated. Amazingly enough, the pull of those overpowerful propellers jerked the displaced engine more or less back into its original position.

The enemy steam sloop promptly repeated the U.S.S. *Mississippi's* tactics and fired a broadside, with more telling effect because one of its shots ripped apart plates protecting the *Manassas'* back as if huge tin shears had been at work. An instant later followed the heart-stilling crash of some hollow metal object striking the side.

"There goes our other goddam' smokestack," Levine growled. "Now we're really fouled up!"

Howls of pain and livid curses revealed that the ram's little nine-pounder had jumped its carriage and mangled several gunners.

Menzies turned a drawn and colorless face. "Well, Cap'n, reckon this here hooker's about done her turn."

The commanding officer made no reply; he was too busy watching the *Brooklyn* so prettily outlined by the fire barge. Had she begun to list slightly to starboard? By God, she had! Definitely so. Delightedly, Warley patted the sweating steel skin of his command. "Not so bad, old girl! We've crippled at least two of those big bastards."

Down the speaking tube he yelled, "Make all possible steam, Mr. Dearning. We'll attempt to proceed upstream. Don't want those damn' forts blasting us again."

The *Manassas* proved able to push her crumpled nose upstream only a shade faster than the current ran.

Meanwhile the sky brightened until now forest-crowned bluffs on either shore were revealed in silhouette; then it became evident the whole river was dotted by enemy ships, some fighting off fire rafts, some engaged in artillery duels with the forts or with Confederate men-of-war. Here and there blazing wrecks sent pillars of smoke and flame soaring upwards, but what ships these had been, or whose, was impossible to tell.

"What's going on up ahead, sir?" Harris presently demanded. "Looks like a single vessel is being attacked by three others."

Warley snatched up his field glasses, studied the action a moment, then snapped, "It's our *McRae*. Gentlemen, we will proceed immediately to her assistance."

Levine's unshaven jaw sagged. "Assistance? Christ A'mighty, Cap'n, it's us needs assistance! We cain't do nothin! Our only gun's overturned and we cain't raise speed enough to ram a snail."

"That will do, Mr. Levine." The expression in Warley's red-rimmed eyes looked dangerous. "You are here to con this vessel, I to command her."

Quickly enough, the Federal ships spied their new enemy. Two medium-sized steam sloops promptly left their companion—and the *McRae*—blazing furiously away and came charging downstream.

Warley snapped, "Mr. Levine, steer for the nearer enemy. We will attempt to take her with us."

The pilot shook his head, shouted, "Hell's fire, no, Cap'n. This is plain suicide. We can't—"

As if to support Levine's protest, a violent explosion shook the *Manassas* from stem to stern and sent steam roaring through the escape valve an instant before engineers, coal passers and gunners scrambled from below coughing, gasping and hauling along three insensible members of the shell gun's crew.

"Coal gas, Captain," choked Dearning. "Ain't enough draft."

Ignoring long-range and therefore futile musket fire from a Union gunboat, the *Manassas'* crew clambered out onto their ripped and shot-pitted deck to lie wheezing, helplessly watching the ram lose headway until finally she swung broadside to the current.

Coughing amid foul fumes pouring into the conning place, Warley took the wheel and himself guided the faltering *Manassas* towards the river's eastern bank. Luckily, she retained just sufficient steerage way to permit her grounding on the rim of a swampy little bayou.

Tears poured down Warley's grimy features, but he commanded crisply, "Stand by to abandon ship!" Abandon ship? Alas, no other course remained if he wished to save these men who cheerfully had risked their lives again and again. Already one of the enemy was changing course, so that in a matter of minutes she could send a full broadside crashing through the *Manassas'* paper-thin armor.

Tenderly the crew eased their disabled fellows into the warm river water, then dragged them ashore to safety among the masses of tall green reeds.

"Where's the skipper?" panted Engineer George Weaver.

"Dunno. Ain't come ashore yet, has he?"

Lieutenant Warley had not, because at that moment he was struggling to hack through his dying vessel's delivery pipes. By sheer will-power he clung to consciousness and defied the noxious gases below long enough to toss flaming armfuls of oily waste into the fuel supply and among the riven timbers forward.

Even while ranging shots from the Federal cruiser began to raise silvery, poplar-like patterns from the shoal, Warley carried on deck his orders and signal book.

His head was spinning so wildly as the result of concussion combined with coal gas that he was scarcely aware of shaking his fist at the on-rushing man-of-war and screaming, "We'll get you bastards yet!"

Harris and Weaver waded out and dragged him ashore barely a moment before some fluke of the current dislodged the *Manassas* and freed her to drift blazing, helpless but yet somehow unconquerable, towards the battle raging in ever-more vicious intensity downstream.

XXVI

Swaying, the Scales of Fate

To every armorer, carpenter, engineer and rigger toiling with the desperation of men attempting to reinforce a crumbling levee, spates of rumors hourly arriving from downstream proved maddening. No one knew what to believe—the incredibly good reports or equally fantastic evil news.

Sam Seymour, gray-faced and stripped to an undershirt and greasy gray trousers, alternately grinned and groaned while personally directing the assembly of a pivot gun's iron carriage.

Of only one cheering fact could he be sure; it was an enormous advantage to have on hand this trained ordnance crew from the East. Another inspiring thought was the knowledge that although much, so much, remained to be done before the Mississippi could steam down to crush the invading fleet, Flag Officer Farragut's armada had no Monitor along to protect it from annihilation. Irad's shade momentarily came to stand by his brother's side. A good thing that Irad had died without knowing that his beloved Merrimac's ravages had been thwarted effectively by John Ericsson's Monitor, that miserable little "cheesebox on a raft."

When, with dawnlight, the dull thunder of those cannon downstream was achieving a diapason crescendo Sam encountered Lachlan Brunton before a cook tent whither he had repaired to gulp a few draughts of scorching black coffee.

"Those propeller shafts turned up yet?"

"Yes," the Scot replied, his red and swollen eyelids blinking like those of some nocturnal animal suddenly exposed to full daylight. "I just might develop enough power wi' two engines to maneuver if only we are granted time to slip one shaft into position."

The Scot's jaws, working steadily on a chunk of cold corn pone, moved the fringe of red bristles standing out along them in a series of wave-like undulations.

"Tell me, Sam," Brunton demanded through a fine spray of yellow crumbs, "is yon rumor indeed credible that the Confederate Command has sent *three* separate naval units against the Northerners?"

Sam shivered under more than a cold gust off the lead-black river. He shrugged, replied miserably, "I fear so. You see, we've the *Louisiana* under McIntosh, Warley in the *Manassas* and Huger commanding the *McRae* to represent our Regular Navy. Also there is the Louisiana State Navy to be counted. My good friend Duchesne is probably fighting right now under Bev Kennon, commanding the *Governor Moore*. Can't recall the name of that other State vessel."

"She's the *General Quitman*," supplied a grease-blackened engineer officer at Brunton's right. "Some fellow named Grant commands her."

"That's right," Brunton growled, lighting a charred corn cob pipe at the cook fire. " 'Twas him delayed delivery o' my propeller bearings through some daft requisitions."

Upriver came speeding a flight of mallards which promptly veered well away from Mr. Millandon's meadow because of forge and cooking fires blazing there and raising sooty clouds to mingle with sour-smelling mists hanging low over the shadow-ruled river. Mechanically, Sam's eyes followed the course of these waterfowl until they lost themselves in the dim light.

How wonderful it was thus to repose oneself even if for but ten short minutes! Pray God these current reports of wild rioting and insurrection in the city would prove untrue. It wasn't in the least reassuring to imagine Robbie and Louise, to all intents and purposes alone, barricaded in that big, vulnerable and nearly empty house on Conti Street.

"Say, Sam, what's the whole truth about that crazy River Defense Flotilla they claim belongs to the Army? Can we expect cooperation from them?" demanded wiry and dark-browed Lieutenant Pegram.

Sam shook his head, swallowed more coffee and winced under its heat. He needed to dispell this confusing, deadening sense of fatigue.

"Maybe, but I doubt it, despite the fact John Stephenson's river-rat captains have hired away plenty of good engineers, deck hands and equipment. Of course, a miracle may take place if those damned, ignorant and independent river captains graciously decide to honor Commodore Mitchell's commands."

Pegram, his mouth full, stared bitterly at a heap of rivets heating on a portable forge set up on the great ironclad's afterdeck. The rhythmic flare of its furnace tinted the dew-dampened plates a brief crimson then faded, then revealed the armor again.

"Isn't it just hell to be up here with all that fighting going on downstream?" Sam demanded. "And to think of poor Mitchell's trying to fight the Old Navy with three different and damned independent units!"

As, stiffly, Sam descended the bank to labor again aboard that scow upon which the ironclad's gun carriages were being readied, he wondered how gay, brave Alex Warley might be making out in his beloved Manassas. Certainly that successful, seegar-shaped ram must serve as a prototype for many a Confederate man-of-war?

What of the C.S.S. McRae? Sam felt particularly curious concerning the role being played by that slim, trim man-of-war amid the naval engagement now raging in ever-increasing fury below helpless and terrified New Orleans. The McRae, of course, had been fitting out at the same time as the Sumter; unfortunately, she had been completed too late to avoid being bottled up by the Federal blockade sealing the mouths of the Mississippi. Certainly, the Regular Navy ships Louisiana, Manassas and the McRae would give good account of themselves.

He was puzzled to predict what the Louisiana State Navy vessels might accomplish. Certainly the Governor Moore, with Bev Kennon and Léon Duchesne, both ex-Regular Navy officers aboard, would not fight clumsily nor in vain. What Alexander Grant, in the General Quitman, might do remained anybody's guess.

A raging sense of frustration seized Sam. In God's name why must this great, long-anticipated engagement find him, a top-flight gunnery officer, lingering on the river bank and working like some damned day laborer? Subconsciously, he knew that no sensible excuse existed for his being anywhere else. The Mississippi's ordnance officer must remain on hand, for, at any hour now, might come orders to hoist in that great warship's battery. Already he'd placed some broadside carriages aboard, together with all the ammunition and a small number of projectiles.

Surely the forts, reinforced by the Confederacy's three flotillas, would deny passage to the Union's vulnerable wooden fleet for at least another thirty-six hours?

"Oh, God, please, please!" he prayed thickly. "We have worked so hard. Please. Grant us this little time."

Stiffly as a sleepwalker, Sam strode past a leather-aproned armorer plunged into the slumber of complete exhaustion; the fellow lay with bald head pillowed upon no softer object than the iron wheel of a gun carriage.

Down at river level resumed the resonant *clang-clang!* of mauls driving red hot rivets home in the after-gunport frames. Tackles whined and creaked, men cursed and mules coughed amid the lifting river vapors. The work went forward more furiously than ever now that daylight was increasing. Now, more than ever, did the fate of the C.S.S. *Mississippi* lie, lifting and falling, on the scales of Fate.

XXVII

Captain Simonds

"Een my time," Captain Mike Simonds was explaining to George, his son, "some tough crews I have mastered on thees river. Yes. But where Johnny Stephenson found these hell-scrapings, got me beat— plenty."

Together with the first mate, a big Irishman named Cochrane, Simonds and George, duly listed as second mate, lingered on this former sea-going towboat's bridge.

The *R. J. Breckinridge*'s upper works having been sheared away, the two from this elevated position could view the full depth of cotton bales built in tiers as high as the walking beam's lower half.

"Pa, what happened at your captains' council aboard the *Warrior*? You've looked mad like a wet cat ever since."

Cochrane interrupted, "Ah-h! 'Twould have made a mouse wroth to watch that there parcel o' big-mouthed baboons jibber, curse and talk big, as if they could fool people into thinking they wasn't scared half to death."

"So that was the trouble?" George Simonds commented. "These

deck hands we got below act scared half out o' their dim wits; though maybe they'd be brave enough in a saloon brawl."

Meditatively, Captain Simonds stroked a full and graying black beard. "They ain't used to fighting thees way, no more than any o' them blowhard captains." He jerked a contemptuous, broad thumb towards a line of dark hulls barely visible below Fort Saint Philip.

"Way they wuz talkin'," Cochrane rumbled, "wuz nothin' short o' traitorous. Mike, did ye hear that McCoy slob swear he'd sink himself before he'd take orders from the Navy?"

"He only repeat what Johnny Stephenson he say las' night."

The Irishman spat resoundingly over the rail. "He's looney. My God, Mike, to hear him ye could believe we wuz fightin' the Confiderate Navy along with them cold-butted Yanks."

Hammerings in Fort Jackson came ringing down from the heights with telegraphic clarity.

"What happened at the council, Pa?" Young George Simonds insisted.

"Lovell, that beeg Army General in New Orleans, he send Johnny Stephenson orders he must obey the Navy Commodore Meetchell. When he hear Stephenson he speet like scalded cat, so too, Hooper, Pheellips, McCoy and the other reever captain. They say, 'To hell weeth Lovell, Meetchell, everybodys! We fight Yanks when we goddam' ready to. Damned to the Devil weeth Navy gold braids and saluting, reporting and keesing the foots.'"

Up to the bridge floated a snatch of ribald song, then a sudden squall of rage, the sound of trampling feet and blows. A big voice was snarling, "Like hell I'll stand watch!"

"Blast yer ugly eyes, you'll take yer turn like the rest o' us."

"Yeh, you carp dung, and who aims to make me? Christ A'mighty! Them sojers will leave us know if them bum-blistered Abolitionists show fight."

"Cappen Simonds shore will crawl yer hump when he hears." That would be Townshend, a vicious Kentucky riverman who when even half drunk would boast of the half dozen murders he'd committed.

"Muck Cappen Simonds," snarled a one-eyed fellow named Morton. "Ain't no greasy Guinea give Dan Morton no orders."

For so large a man, the Greek could move extraordinarily fast—as certain of his enemies had learned to their sorrow. Black beard bristling, Simonds hurled himself into the *R. J. Breckinridge*'s fore-castle.

"Where ees son-of-a-bitch said that?" he glowered, hairless bullet head drawn deep down between his shoulders. Only sullen looks answered him.

"So, he not talk so brave to Mike's face, heh? Fine pack o' slob-birds I take into a fight."

"Sez you, Mister," cried someone from the background. "We'll have a fi' dollar raise er this here hooker don't stir tomorrey."

Simonds recognized the speaker, dove in and grabbed the collar of his greasy, homespun shirt. "You want five, heh? Well, here ees five and five more." Twice he drove his fist smacking into the fellow's leathery features.

An ominous surge forward did not disconcert Mike Simonds. A round-house swing caught one man full on the mouth and sent him reeling back; then a blade glittered. Not for nothing had Michael Georgi Popalogolus Simonides survived an education on the Piraeus waterfront. Spinning about on his left leg and at the same instant lashing upwards with his right foot, he bent suddenly so far forward that his finger tips touched the deck. As a result, the heel of his heavy, hob-nailed boot caught the man wielding the knife squarely under the chin and snapped his head back so violently that he sank, shuddering queerly, onto the deck.

Simonds picked up the knife, snarled at Townshend. "Now, you pees-ant, get these bastards up on decks!"

"Sure, Boss, sure. Take it easy," cried the riverman backing away.

Roaring strange oaths Simonds then strode over and fetched a pair of prostrate figures some savage kicks in the ribs. "Now," he bellowed, "you remember who ees boss over thees sheep? Heh?"

Grinning, husky young George Simonds greeted his father on the foredeck, but below decks the would-be knife-wielder had groaned and turning on his side gasped, "By Jesus, I'll carve that Guinea bastard's liver for this."

When, at three-fifteen, that single mortar shell burst, preluding the Union attack, the *R. J. Breckinridge* stirred like a disturbed ant hill.

"Where that damn' mackerel-eating mate?" Simonds roared.

"Here, sir." Cochrane was buckling a pistol as he ran up.

George took the wheel. "What are the orders, Pa?"

"Johnny Stephenson he say wait until we see some damn' Yankee ship deesable', then we mus' ram and seenk her." He whistled down the speaking tube to the engine room. "You down there, Hogan? Get up goddam' steam, queeck, queeck!"

A blast of sulphurous profanity was his only answer.

"I say get steam up queeck. You, bosun, stand by to cast us off."

The men of the River Defense Flotilla collected in small knots about the deck staring in frightened awe upon that display of deadly pyrotechnics in the sky.

"This heah ain't no place for Mrs. Beasley's boy!" yelped a gangling, barefooted youth; then, as easily as a yearling buck, he vaulted the rail and disappeared among the bushes.

Simonds caught up a double-barreled fowling piece charged with buckshot.

"Get away from rail," he roared, thick neck swelling. "Next one tries go near eet gets shot."

The hands below promptly moved away from the bulwarks; they knew Simonds' threat was far from being an empty one. Like sleep-walkers, a handful of artillerymen detailed to handle a field piece lashed to the afterdeck were turning out in a deliberate, dazed way.

Because, thus far, no clouds of spark-laden smoke had begun to issue from the Breckinridge's tall smokestack the captain once more whistled down the engine room speaking tube. He got no reply.

"George," he growled, "I go see what that no-good Hogan ees doing."

"Maybe, Pa, you better lug along a pistol. Want me to come, too?"

"No, you and Cochrane watch reever, maybe find what ees happenings. See? Ees Manassas leaving berth; McRae maybe come next. Watch. See which way they steam."

"Sure thing, Pa." Although the boy's intense jet eyes looked like smudges amid the pallor of his features, his hands were steady as from a drawer in the Texas he pulled a long-barreled, five-shot Colt's forty-four.

A terrifying display of fire power was commencing to manifest itself downstream and again mortar shells arched lazily up—up, then plunged, trailing sparks until, finally, they burst over Fort Jackson.

"Maria!" breathed young George. Somewhere in that smoky gloom lurked enemies; well-trained, well-equipped enemies, ready to shoot and kill. Imagine watching a huge cannon swing in his direction! Swallowing hard, he recalled how his friend Dimitri Poulgas had looked when he'd got that hit in the chest during a hunting trip.

Captain Simonds, stepping out on deck, noticed that something had begun to burn downriver and was flaming so brightly that the whole sky throbbed.

"In few minutes," he decided, "I weel take out thees sheep and hont me a Yankee. By Saint Leo, they owe me two fruit steamers!" He prayed, however, that the forts might sink most of the enemy's big ships. "Kyre Christos! All I want ees wan leetle one I can sink weethout getting sunk." Then he made his way down through dim, musty and kerosene-smelling gloom to the engine room, his big Colt's cocked and ready. They were a bad lot below, very tough.

"Christ!" Cochrane, listening at the engine room speaking tube, had recognized the brief staccato roar of a shot, then two more, followed by a wild jumble of strident voices in which he heard someone growl, "Reckon I've settled that old bastard."

"Bub," said Cochrane, "your pa's in trouble. Let's go."

From that drawer beneath the pilot's table, George Simonds produced a pair of pistols which weren't much—just two small cap and ball derringers. These he gave to Cochrane. Heart pounding, George started down the ladder ahead of Cochrane who seemed only too pleased to yield precedence to his junior.

When George reached the main deck, the boy turned and started for the forecastle but advanced only a single step before the blast of a shotgun fired at very close range almost blew him apart. Briefly, George Simonds flopped about the deck like a newly landed fish and emitted queer, thick, gurgling noises. Then his mangled body went limp.

"Got the pup o' the Guinea, too," Townshend called from the shadows, while Cochrane retreated hurriedly into the Breckinridge's wheel house. "You kin come up on deck, Hogan."

"Good heavens, man, what have you done?" A slim, girlish-looking sergeant of Volunteer Artillery had come clumping up, nervously clutching a carbine. Gulping, he stared upon the body blackly draining blood across the deck.

"Killed the bastard, that's what. Wanta make anythin' of it?"

The sergeant tried to bluster. "By whose orders? Captain Simonds?"

Hogan, at the head of a swarm of savage and well-armed deck hands, appeared at the main companionway. "Cap'n Simonds? He's resigned fer keeps."

Everyone guffawed.

"Then, sir," shakily demanded the boy sergeant, "who is in command?"

"Me." Hogan swaggered forward, a bowie knife in one hand and Simonds' revolver in the other. "And I think you and yer boys better play soljers ashore." Hogan jerked his thumb towards a plank gangway rigged at the prow of the River Defense ship. "Git! Haul outta here!"

The militia consisted of only six youths in cross-belts, kepis and ill-fitting light brown uniforms. Hopelessly confused, the volunteers complied readily enough and went crashing off along the shore.

Townshend waved a whiskey bottle. "He'p yerselves, ye ring-tailed wil' cats. Reckon we'll find more o' this in the Texas."

Hogan cocked a bloodshot eye at the river and the battle commencing to assume shape out there. "Say, boys, ain't much use riskin' a bellyful of Abolitionist shot with nawthin' to show fer it, is they?"

A chorus of "noes" answered him.

"Wal, after we get done rummagin' about this old hooker, wouldn't it be just a damn' shame if she was to take fire?" He flung a hand in the direction of that roaring blaze. "'Pears to me like the *Warrior*, acrost the river yander, already's found trouble gettin' under way."

No one paid the least attention to George Simonds' slight, incredibly flat-looking body except to curse when, in looting, they slipped on his blood.

At the end of twenty minutes the *R. J. Breckinridge* commenced to pour smoke from her portholes, then to spout hungry, yellow-red tongues of flame matching those of other River Defense vessels such as the *Warrior* and the *General Lovell*.

XXVIII

THREATENED CITY

BECAUSE GANGS OF river rats, deserters and masterless Negroes, emboldened by that slowly approaching cannonade, had begun to pillage shops and homes, Tina Brunton set her jaw and loaded Lachlan's fowling piece just as she had insisted he teach her. The business of looking into the bore of a double-barreled shotgun, she calculated, should discourage most would-be looters; they were cowards, else they'd be doing their part on the river or in the forts.

Since dawn of April the twenty-fourth, New Orleans had existed in turmoil. Everyone could hear the heart-stilling crash of distant salvos, the boom of single guns and the alarm bells clanging on and on so senselessly.

During the morning public apprehension mounted and those few hardy persons who had gone to work returned in order to protect their homes from lawless invasion. The louder the sounds of battle, the larger grew mobs of semi-drunken ruffians and harlots roaming the deserted streets and squares.

Three houses away from Lachlan Brunton's home, a gang had broken down the door to accompanying screams from the household. Here and there certain units of the Home Guard and the Foreign Legion did attempt to maintain order and shot several plunderers out of hand. These had lain in Thalia Street ever since, dead and unsightly. Another departing looter had collapsed in the gutter further away.

Broad daylight had hardly reached the threatened metropolis than Maggie Schniewind appeared, herding her numerous brood and lugging a shawlful of hastily collected food and clothing.

"I daren't stay near the waterfront any longer," she gasped. "It's awful. All the warehouses, arms and liquor stores are being ransacked. When they broke in downstairs at our place, I grabbed the kids and ran out the back."

She commenced to sob softly, her tears mingling with sweat running down her plain, freckled features. "Mary preserve us! I wish I knew where Gus is right now."

"God will look after Gus—and Lachlan. He will," came Tina's quietly positive assurance. "I know it, sure as I breathe. Here is Lachlan's pistol. Can you fire a pistol?"

Maggie gulped. "I guess I can cock it and pull the trigger; just let anybody come near my children." Gingerly, she accepted the weapon. "What does Lachlan say about the fight downriver? Will the forts drive them back?"

"Lachlan I have not seen in three days," Tina replied, while wiping dry the younger Schniewinds' plentiful tears. Living like this wasn't to be endured for long. Everything was out of joint. No food, no order, no knowing what might happen at any minute.

Because of frequent hurricanes, this house, like so many in New Orleans, had been equipped with heavy shutters of live oak braced by iron bars; they should afford fine protection against any except an organized assault.

Tina's chief concern lay in her rear door which, for some reason, was flimsy and locked but imperfectly.

"What have you heard?" Tina demanded. "I have not stepped out-of-doors since yesterday."

Maggie repeated rumors that two River Defense rams had come rushing up, panic-stricken, to report that several Federal gunboats had successfully passed the forts.

Tina's coral-pink lips flattened themselves. "Then our *Mississippi* will drive them back, all the way back to the Delta."

Maggie cuffed her eldest son for trying to snitch a cold yam from a dish in the pantry. "Then she's been completed?"

"Oh, I am sure she has," Tina declared. "They have been working on her like mad people. Lachlan told me—"

Out in Thalia Street arose a frightening series of yells, whoops, and drunken cries. Peering through a crack in the shutters, Tina beheld the approach of a veritable saturnalia. Descending the street was a throng of horrible, savage-appearing men and bestial, half-clothed females. One harridan had wrapped herself in a pair of yellow silk window curtains, another cavorted about in a bedraggled ball gown of sapphire-blue silk.

Shrieking bawdy songs, they were prancing along behind as piratical a crew as had appeared in New Orleans since the days of the Lafitte brothers and Dominique You. One of the leaders, a beetle-browed man, pointed to a house directly opposite the Bruntons' and, immediately, half a dozen ruffians dropped their plunder to hurl their weight in unison against door panels which promptly gave way.

In cold horror, Tina watched the mob leader wheel about to stand peering at her own well-painted home. "Maggie, pick up that pistol. I think they are coming over here."

The Irish girl, instead of obeying, buried face in hands and commenced to shrill, "Jesus, Mary and Joseph, preserve my poor innocent little children!"

Brunton's wife kicked Maggie so soundly on the rear that she grunted and picked up the pistol while Tina leveled the duck gun waist-high. Whether its charges would carry through the heavy panel she had no idea, but she intended to fire when the first blow fell against her door panels.

"Ah-h, the hell with it," a hoarse voice grunted. "Door looks too damn' strong."

When the tumult actually commenced to diminish down Thalia Street, Tina felt her knees loosen under this incredible relief. She had started towards the kitchen only to be appalled by a resounding crash in the direction of the rear door.

"Come quick! Quick!" Tina reached her kitchen in time to glimpse a panel of the back door flying in, to create a bright frame for several black and sweaty faces.

"Adam is in danger," was her only thought while throwing the fowling piece to her shoulder.

"Get out of here, you black trash! Get out, or I'll shoot!"

One of the raiders uttered a breathless, cackling laugh and, reaching through the broken panel, commenced groping for the bolt.

"Shoot! Shoot!" Obediently Maggie raised her pistol, clutching it with both hands. She was pointing, all right, and trying to fire, but couldn't because she hadn't remembered to cock her weapon.

Like a tremendous black spider the hand fumbled for then closed over the bolt.

"Lie down, Maggie!" The instant the Irish girl sank crouched on all fours Tina rushed forward, pulled the trigger and the shotgun filled her kitchen with noise, flame and smoke. Like an invisible giant, the recoil sent her reeling sidewise and at the same instant snatched the fowling piece out of her grasp.

Deafened and appalled at the tremendousness of the report, Tina stood swaying helplessly, her ears affronted by a scream of mortal pain. As in a trance, she perceived that where that sable arm had been, there now existed only a ragged hole framed by hideously bright splotches.

"Christina, you must act! You are not yet safe," her inner consciousness warned. "That gun you must reload. Others may come." The shotgun she discovered lying but a few feet behind her. Somehow she had discharged both barrels at once.

"Oh—e—e! Ooh—e—e!" Maggie was raising a horrible keening cry.

"Schweig!" Tina screamed. "Schweig, du grosser Esel!"

Maggie Schniewind kept up her insensate squalling until Tina snatched up a saucepan of cold soup and hurled its contents full into her face.

Beyond the door a thick weak voice croaked, "Oh, Lawd, Lawd! I'se dying! Lawd Jesus help dis po' nigger. Lawd, Lawd!"

Not until she had recapped and reloaded the duck gun did Tina Brunton peer out into her back yard. Two figures occupied its neat brick walk. One of the would-be looters, an Indian half-breed, lay on his back, stone dead; the Negro was crawling off on his knees with his sound hand clutching a shapeless, pinkish mess of tendons, flesh and shattered bone which had been his right arm.

Glassy-eyed, Tina watched him disappear through the back gate at the end of a brilliant trail of blood.

During the day the barricaded householders heard musketry in various directions and, towards sundown, regular volleys rattled Tina's windows and reverberated through the deserted streets.

"Volley firing must mean that troops of some kind have appeared," Tina breathed. "Thank God! Even if those soldiers are Yankees."

Nothing remained save to scour the house for food, maintain a vigilant guard and pray that her husband was safe. Somehow, Tina could not even visualize a future which excluded Lachlan Brunton.

In the back yard, thousands of thousands of bluebottle flies were exploring the half-breed's corpse.

XXIX

Louisiana State Navy

To both Captain Beverly Kennon and Commander Léon Duchesne, it appeared that the Mississippi River was crammed with fighting ships and that visibility was growing progressively worse. Smoke from five or six vessels blazing at the river's edge, smoke from the thudding, roaring guns compounded by fumes discharged by the glowing fire boxes of forty men-of-war near by, created a strange, unreal and blinding atmosphere through which the speedy paddle wheel gunboat, *Governor Moore*, was forced to proceed.

Thrice, dim and ominous shapes bore down upon, but eventually rushed by the State warship. Once, however, an ignited fire raft began to spread its orange-red glare over the river hulls could be distinctly discerned through the shifting veils of smoke.

To distinguish friend from foe Duchesne discovered was next to impossible, but, because of the C.S.S. *Manassas'* unique design, he recognized the little ram plowing downstream towards a tall Yankee sloop. Presently, she became lost to sight but he could hear guns banging away amid the murk.

Stripped to a white cotton shirt and uniform trousers, Beverly Kennon ordered the *Governor Moore's* wheel ported and conned the former towboat towards the river's eastern bank in search of Blue gunboats. His quest was quickly satisfied when, quite without warning, a tall ship appeared. She undoubtedly was a Yankee because of the bright red and white recognition lights showing at her foretop mast.

"Prepare to open fire!" Kennon bellowed down to Henderson, a gaunt and stringy individual who had served aboard the *Governor Moore* in peacetimes. Shielded by cotton bales, the *Moore's* gunnery officer waited tensely beside that heavy thirty-two-inch rifle gun mounted on the foredeck.

Aside from Léon Duchesne and Henderson, two other officers were serving aboard the State gunboat. They were Robert Haynes and

French Frame. Of these four officers Henderson and Haynes commanded a detachment of field artillerymen manning the nine-thousand-ton Governor Moore's two unsighted and unbanded rifle guns mounted bow and stern.

Duchesne, delighted to find himself entirely cool and self-possessed, reported the course of the enemy vessel pounding up from starboard. Light from the burning Warrior and Breckinridge suddenly disclosed her identity. She proved to be a small gunboat—the U.S.S. Cayuga.

Léon's mouth suddenly went dry. Dieu! Why was Henderson's gun crew so damned sluggish? Before they could get the Governor Moore's pivot gun trained, the Cayuga veered and fired at terribly close range. Two of the Federal vessel's shots screamed harmlessly by, but one cannon ball splintered the Governor's port paddle box and another punched a great jagged hole out of her funnel. Not until then did the Governor Moore's forward gun vomit a great flood of red-gold flame and hurl its thirty-two-pound ball straight into the Cayuga's black-painted stern.

Even while Henderson's high-pitched voice began to direct the reloading of his gun, another enemy ship surged out of the smoke and, at a range of thirty yards, the U.S.S. Oneida promptly lashed the little State cruiser with a devastating hail of canister.

Fortunately, most of the enemy's spiteful, leaden balls thudded into the protecting cotton bales or rattled against the side like giant hailstones.

Again baffling, disconcerting smoke clouds closed in, isolating the Governor Moore and eclipsing all view of the enemy.

"Really hit that Yankee," Kennon observed tensely. "Wish some of our Regular Navy roosters had been there to watch. Wonder where our ships are?"

"Can't imagine," Duchesne replied, standing very straight beside the wheel. "I've been expecting to sight the Quitman any moment. I hope Grant hasn't pulled foot. We'll never hear the end of it if he has."

"Put your helm hard about, Quartermaster; don't fancy running into cross-fire from the forts."

Duchesne envied chunky little Beverly Kennon's calm manner, and hoped that he was betraying none of his own lively fears. The awful eerie screech of stray roundshot passing overhead, the whining, dry-sounding sigh of grape or canister kept on making his finger tips tingle and his mouth go dry.

Some unknown man-of-war went threshing by in the opposite direction, another paddle-wheel steamer by the sound of her.

Once the Governor Moore had started back upstream she encountered the wreck of the Defiance, another River Defense gunboat. She was blazing like a used Christmas tree tossed on a bonfire.

"Mon Dieu! Look, Kennon! Look over there!" Duchesne could not avoid clutching Kennon's arm. Out of the gloom had materialized the hull of a tall steam frigate showing white and red lights at her foretop.

"Down! Lie flat everybody!" Kennon bellowed, anticipating the enemy's intention of yawing and firing a broadside.

For Henderson's gun crew the warning was given just a second late, or possibly, they were too occupied in training their piece to obey in time. They were blasted into Eternity amid a blinding sheet of flame and screaming canister. Solid shot of large calibre also ripped huge sections out of the State cruiser's wooden bulwarks and sent her cotton-bale armor spinning high into the air. Under the impact of that murderous broadside the Governor Moore staggered and, had she been a propeller vessel, she must have heeled far over on her beam's ends.

Billows of hot gases singed Duchesne's mustaches and free flowing hair and his ears rang as if boxed by a giant.

Rallying his senses, the Creole perceived that concussion had blown Kennon across the wheel house with such violence as to knock out his wind. As for the pilot he lay inert and dripping blood from a gaping wound in his forehead.

Another Confederate gunboat must have appeared on the Federal's opposite beam, for at once the big frigate veered away under the erroneous impression that she had finished off the Governor Moore. While this was far from the case, every man of the twelve who had been serving the forward gun had either been blasted out of existence or stretched upon a deck littered with splinters and fragments of human flesh.

"Too big for us," Kennon gasped, dragging himself over to the idly revolving wheel. "Mr. Duchesne, go below and take command of the forward gun. Commandeer any men you need."

"Aye, aye, sir," Duchesne snapped just as he had back in Annapolis. Several rungs had been shot out of the bridge ladder, so he was forced to drop a long yard onto the deck and so landed on something softly yielding; it proved to be the lower half of a man. Having vomited suddenly, violently, Duchesne felt better. He ran aft, en route conscripting men for a new gun crew based on five artillerists from the stern pivot gun.

Coughing amid acrid smoke given off by the blazing Defiance, the replacements followed the tall young Creole forward to shove aside the mangled bodies before commencing to reload the big thirty-two pounder.

Meanwhile, with smoke streaming like ghostly pennants through punctures in her funnel, the battered State cruiser once more gathered headway.

Struggling to fight down further nausea, Duchesne ripped off the gay, light blue tunic in which he had swaggered about so many balls and bars and helped drag aside the bodies.

"Fetch sand," he directed. "Can't keep footing on this mess."

A gray-haired artillery sergeant out of the Old Army told off two loaders, two spongers and four tackle and levermen.

"I will sight this piece and cut fuses myself," Duchesne announced, his black eyes snapping. "You stokers can pass powder, fetch shot and tail on to the training tackle when needed.

"Cast loose and provide!" he barked. Then in staccato accents, "Shift pivot left. Serve vent and sponge. Load!"

Thus, at the end of ten minutes, the Governor Moore's miraculously undamaged gun once more was readied for action.

Léon was amazed to learn how readily the exercise-commands returned to him. This thirty-two-inch rifle could, and, by God would, do some mighty execution before all was done.

"Must be nearly half past four. Should be light soon," Duchesne decided, peering up at the flame-spouting forts. "Damn this cruising about in the dark."

Silently, and without any warning, a ship showing red and white lights surged out of the gloom and let fly at the little State cruiser. This time it was the Moore's rear deck that suffered under a pitiless rain of canister. Five more men died there, and as many more fell wounded.

"They're really cuttin' us down, suh," drawled Lieutenant Haynes up in the pilot house. "How many were we when we started out, sir?"

"Ninety-three all told. Where've you stowed the wounded?"

"In the cable well, sir. Who was that last one?"

"Read the name *Pinola* on her stern," grunted Kennon, fumbling at the flap of his holster. After stepping out onto the wreckage of his bridge, the Captain sighted carefully and shot out a distinguishing blue light burning at the Governor Moore's masthead.

"Don't seem to be any but Yank ships around," he remarked with a tight grin, "so there's small use advertising our loneliness."

Gradually, but perceptibly, daylight commenced to dilute the darkness and presently found the Governor Moore's paddles driving her upstream in pursuit of two half-seen gunboats. Soon her officers thought to recognize the furthest as their first antagonist—the big steam frigate *Pensacola*.

"The *Mississippi* will soon settle her hash," Haynes predicted to his reorganized after-gun crew.

"Then they've finished her?"

"Sure," someone called. "They got guns into her yesterday and she's been moved down to the city."

"You sure of that?"

"Yep. Bosun in the *McRae* told me so. He ought to know."

Smiles relaxed the drawn faces all about. "Just wait until them damn' Yanks tangle with her," cried a young compressor man. "They'll get a bellyful in jigtime."

Duchesne thought it strange that, if the mighty *Mississippi* indeed had been completed, neither Kennon nor himself had been so informed. Still, local communications, never very good at best, during the past week had deteriorated to the point of non-existence so the great ironclad really might have been placed in commission. He prayed so.

While the light improved and frightened waterfowl commenced to speed past the Governor Moore, her walking beam teetered and her paddles thumped and swished fast, faster. Meanwhile the State cruiser's crew rearranged their cotton-bale armor as best they might and otherwise repaired damage wrought by those crushing broadsides delivered by the Pensacola, Cayuga and Pinola.

Occasional planks and pieces of wreckage began to drift by, then part of a wheel house and shattered small boat—mute testimony of combats taking place further up this great, glassy river. The only other Confederate vessel thus far sighted by the Governor Moore's company was the Stonewall Jackson, a cotton-clad of the River Defense Flotilla and she was fleeing upstream as fast as she could steam. This, then, was the first of those two vessels Kennon had been pursuing; still further upstream was steaming another and a larger man-of-war. Although it remained too dark to identify her colors, Kennon decided she must be an enemy because her funnel was mounted forward of her mainmast.

Deliberately risking shots from the panic-stricken Stonewall Jackson, Kennon ordered a white and a red light to his masthead before taking in his flag, just as his command overhauled the Stonewall Jackson thumping along about a third of a mile away on their starboard beam.

The Governor Moore might never have existed for all the attention Captain Phillips paid her.

"Let's hope we can bring that Yankee sloop to action opposite the Szymanski Battery," Kennon muttered. "Then, maybe, the Stonewall Jackson will come up and lend a hand."

Before long, Kennon felt reasonably certain that yonder swift Yankee gunboat was not a steam frigate at all, but probably the Varuna. If so, she must be finding trouble in her engine room for, under normal conditions, a vessel of the Varuna's class easily could outdistance a former towboat.

Once the two gunboats were cruising less than half a mile apart Kennon directed his deceptive white and red lights doused and rehoisted the Confederate flag. At once the Varuna—it was indeed she—swung hard-a-starboard, let fly with her rifled guns—and missed!

Carefully, Léon Duchesne sighted his piece then stepped back and yelled, "Fire!" The sergeant jerked his lanyard, whereupon the whole foredeck quivered under the pivot gun's recoil. Clouds of rotten-smelling and dirty-colored smoke briefly enveloped the gun crew, then were whirled away. Livid curses escaped the blackened and sweat-streaked men about the big pivot gun. By a few but vital yards their shot had fallen short and now the Varuna, spouting sable smoke from freshly stoked fires, was circling back to attack her slightly smaller antagonist.

As the Union ship turned, so also did the Moore, but in a tighter circle. Kennon's intention to ram became obvious. It was while the two vessels were drawing rapidly together that Duchesne perceived an error committed in mounting the Governor Moore's forward gun so far abaft the knightheads. He could not sufficiently depress his piece without its becoming blanketed by the Moore's own bows! All the while the Varuna maintained a deadly discharge, killing men and knocking her enemy's bulwarks and sides into flinders.

"Ahoy there, Duchesne!" Kennon bawled down through his speaking trumpet. "You'll wait and fire as we ram!"

Duchesne's men, huddled under the scant protection of the cotton bales, watched the Federal ship grow larger and larger until her spars seemed to tower directly above them.

"Duchesne! Fire through our bow if you must!" Kennon yelled as, again, canister from the enemy's eight-inch guns came whirring like gigantic iron bees killing three men of the forward gun crew.

Duchesne, trembling like a whipped thoroughbred, saw the old artillery sergeant execute a curious sidewise leap, then disappear through a gaping, splintery hole in the bulwarks.

"Now! Fire, now!" Duchesne could hear Kennon imploring so he gripped the lanyard and, praying that he had ordered the muzzle sufficiently depressed, jerked hard on it. Ensued a tremendous crash marking a rupture of the State cruiser's bow which allowed the thirty-two pounder's shell to rip into the Varuna's vitals just at the instant the two vessels collided. Whatever effect her shot might take, the Governor Moore's ramming proved so effective that she rolled the Federal vessel far over on her beam's ends and sent cascades of water gushing into her ports and wounded side.

There were no faint hearts aboard the Varuna, either; even as she righted, her crew fired both rifle guns into her assailant and a small cannon, mounted on her transom, was handled so effectively that it slew five more of the Governor Moore's dazed and nearly exhausted company.

For a moment no one realized that Captain Kennon had ordered his command back out into mid-stream and was steering straight for a line of Federal warships steaming doggedly upriver. The prospects proved too much for Mr. Duke, a civilian engineer officer pressed into duty as helmsman.

"You gone crazy, Cap'n?" he screamed, blood-flecked features working convulsively. "We've no men left! Damned if I'll let you murder us all!"

Mr. Duke swung so suddenly as to drive Kennon's bulldog head against the wheel-house wall with sufficient force to stun him. The engineer immediately ground the gunboat's helm hard-a-starboard, but already the enemy ships—big, *Hartford*-class vessels—opened fire at long range. One of their very first shots dismounted the *Governor Moore's* forward gun and flung Léon Duchesne violently to the deck, semi-conscious and quite helpless because of a severe gash inflicted across his right knee.

More salvos came screaming across the river but the *Governor Moore* kept on firing her after gun. She was much like a failing champion boxer who, disdaining to quit, suffers blows which can be neither anticipated nor avoided. A shot struck the State cruiser's walking beam, spraying heavy splinters of iron about quite as effectively as a bursting shell.

In the depths of the wounded gunboat sounded a chorus of deep-toned shrieks then an engineer, with skin peeling from one side of his scalded face, reeled up from below screaming, "Surrender! Surrender for Christ's sake, Cap'n! Cylinder head's split!"

That the *Governor Moore*, no matter what her immediate fate, could fight no more was a fact of which Léon Duchesne was only dimly aware as he sat slumped against an undamaged segment of bulwark attempting to fashion a tourniquet out of his handkerchief and a jagged splinter.

At length he succeeded in checking that deadly flow from his knee but he must have lost more bright arterial blood than he had suspected because he felt surprisingly contemplative and at ease. He even waved a red-smeared hand at Beverly Kennon who, wildly disheveled and glaring through jet hair tumbling over his eyes, appeared on the foredeck in company with two scarecrow figures. Together, they managed to raise the tattered remains of a jib. This provided enough way to ground the *Governor Moore* on a sandbank some half mile below the wrecked U.S.S. *Varuna*.

Tirelessly Kennon ranged his battered ship, seeking out wounded men and ordering their mates to lift and carry them ashore.

At length he bent over that slight, blood-splashed figure on the now-dangerously sloping foredeck. "How are you feeling, Duchesne?"

"*Merci, tout va bien, mon Capitaine.* I will be all right," the Creole replied sleepily; but this wasn't true. All his strength was required to keep tight that vital tourniquet. Gradually his mind clouded until the morning sky paled unnaturally and he felt his body being lifted, up, up, up, till he seemed to be floating thousands of miles above the earth. Therefore, he neither saw nor heard the end of the valiant little *Governor Moore.* With her ragged ensign still flying, she burned until the flames reached her magazine and blew her into history and glory.

XXX

STILL-BORN

ABOUT MIDDAY OF April the twenty-fourth a steam launch panted up to the C.S.S. *Mississippi* bearing a wild-eyed naval officer who demanded an immediate conference with Commander Sinclair. From his tragic expression and anxious manner those at the giant ironclad's gangway deduced that important elements of the Union Fleet must have accomplished the impossible and run past the forts.

Hammers, mauls and wrenches which had been noisily at work up to that instant were allowed to fall silent and an oppressive stillness spread over the great ship.

Aboard the *Iatan*, a group of haggard officers in greasy work clothes stood staring, incredulous and miserable, at one another across a long table which, in happier days, had supported meals for first-class passengers. Lieutenant Commander Samuel Seymour, having been at work on an ammunition scuttle when the news came, appeared late. He was hollow eyed and unwashed and wearing bits of sawdust and little chips in his brown hair and side whiskers.

Hands trembling and features atwitch, Commander Sinclair read, then let fall, a sheet of paper handed him by a very thin young naval lieutenant gaunt with sleeplessness.

Above angry curses arising from the ironclad alongside, Arthur

Sinclair drew a deep, sighing breath, then said: "Gentlemen, we are herewith warned that an enemy squadron has passed Forts Jackson and Saint Philip in force and are at this very moment reported to be steaming for New Orleans."

"What!"

"Listen to our orders from Flag Officer Whittle." Sinclair smoothed the dispatch and read in accents so thick and halting that it seemed he must be translating a difficult passage from some foreign language: "You will at once prepare the *Mississippi* to be towed upstream out of danger from the enemy. You will also load aboard the tenders her battery, including all such other gear as may be needed to complete her, and depart for Baton Rouge."

The buzzing of bluebottle flies sounded loud out of all proportion as various implications sank in on civilian and naval constructors alike.

"God help us. And all we needed was two more days!" growled Asa Tift.

"Where are the tenders?" Ivens inquired of the messenger.

"Flag Officer Whittle stated that he is dispatching two steamers to tow you upstream, sir," replied the courier. "They should arrive very shortly."

By a palpable effort Commander Sinclair pulled himself together and gave directions that all essential gear be readied for transportation aboard the rescuing steamers. He foresaw that it would not improve matters to weigh down the already ponderous and utterly inert iron-clad.

"Shall I attempt to mount at least some of the guns, sir?" Seymour demanded. "Might be needed to defend her."

"There is not sufficient time, sir," Sinclair snapped. "Merely prepare your ordnance for transfer."

"Why not at least put the ram's rifles aboard?" Lieutenant Robert Pegram suggested. "Perhaps they could be mounted under way?"

"The tow must be kept light as possible," Nelson Tift explained in a tired voice. "It is going to take powerful engines to haul her against this new current."

Everyone at Mr. Millandon's landing was miserably aware that heavy spring rains, falling further up the Mississippi Valley, had increased the river's normal four-mile current by at least a knot. Had they not for the past two days watched clay-colored waters eating at the bank and carrying off chunks of debris at a terrifying rate of speed?

Weary constructors, tired armorers and the complement of officers from the East worked like mad in selecting essential items of equipment and machinery which later could be put into position at Baton Rouge, Memphis or maybe Fort Pillow.

All day long the crews toiled. Sick at heart, Sam Seymour supervised the removal of his guns and their carriages aboard a scow together with that precious shot collected at the cost of so much time and labor. Like everyone else who had sweated and planned over the *Mississippi* and had watched her take shape and come partially alive, Sam worked as in a nightmare.

" 'Tis the Devil's own luck!" complained Brunton. "But for those tardy propeller shafts I could have had the engines turning two days back."

"I can't believe the Yankees got by the forts in any condition to fight," Sam kept repeating to Lieutenant Carey. "Damn it, Clarence, I saw those forts myself! They've whole batteries of eight- and ten-inch Columbiads, plenty of rifles and howitzers—one hundred and sixteen well-protected guns against unarmored wooden ships struggling against this cursed current!"

"That five-day bombardment from the mortar fleet must have turned the trick," Carey suggested gloomily. "Let's get busy."

Lieutenant Dawson flicked sweat from his brow. "Even so, it'd have been a different story if our astigmatic and self-satisfied Navy Department had let Hollins send down our whole Regular river fleet. As it is, there ain't enough left at Memphis to accomplish much."

Everyone kept peering downriver to glimpse the smoke of those expected two steamers but it was not until late in the evening that the *St. Charles* and *Peytona*, only middle-sized river steamers, came churning up alongside the helpless *Mississippi*.

Immediate recriminations broke out when Commander Sinclair and his naval officers cursed the river captains for their inexcusable tardiness. These, livid with rage and in blasphemous language, swore that they never had received orders to move upstream until mid-afternoon. And where had they been since? demanded the outraged Regulars. Because of wild riots and the looting general along the waterfront, Captain Bell swore he had been forced to recruit a crew

at his pistol's point. Even so, he had collected but half the men he
needed.

By lamplight, the constructors and regular crew toiled all night
stowing aboard the St. Charles the most valuable of their tools and
equipment.

The river captains proved so unwilling to cooperate that Sinclair
in desperation finally ordered the Mississippi's crew to adjust lashings
securing the Peytona and St. Charles to either beam. He even sent
aboard some of his own engineers to make sure that the river boats
kept up a sufficient head of steam. As a further precaution he posted
grim-looking sentries beside the gangways to keep the steamboat crews
from running ashore and mingling with a fast-dispersing army of laborers and mechanics.

In the early dawn the river boats fired their boilers and prepared to
tow, once the ironclad had been cast free of her moorings. Sam, tired
as never before, stood near on the Mississippi's bow watching the oily-
looking river current begin to take hold, propelling the precious man-
of-war down towards the Federal fleet.

The St. Charles blew a furious blast on her whistle then her stern
paddle wheel commenced to lash the amber-hued water; an instant
later the Peytona followed suit.

Seymour and the other men dotting the two-hundred-and-seventy-
foot deck felt a measure of relief at determining, by means of cross-
bearings taken on shore objects, that the ram actually had begun to
move upstream. Their joy soon became dissipated, however, for once
the main force of the current gripped all three vessels, they lost headway no matter how hard the river boats panted, strained and threshed.
The armored monster's dead weight was too much; foot by foot, the
trio commenced to be carried downstream!

In agony Arthur Sinclair roared, "Steamboats ahoy! Steer back into
shoal water then pass a hawser ashore. We will have to find more tow-
ships."

A little later the Peytona was cast loose and, conveying Commander
Sinclair, the Tift brothers and Lieutenant Commander Seymour, she
dashed down towards New Orleans; her speed seemed arrow-like after
those laboring struggles to overcome the current.

To Sam's amazement the river proved to be alive with traffic; steamboats which had lain idle for months reappeared with decks blackened

by passengers and freight. The *Flora Belle, Dew Drop, Alec Scott* and half a dozen lesser packets were turning their low bows northwards. Gradually, clouds of blue-gray smoke grew denser above the last bend concealing New Orleans.

"My God!" cried Asa Tift. "Those damned Yankees must be burning the city!"

Furious outcries burst from a Marine detail crowding the *Peytona's* steadily vibrating foredeck.

"Naw!" corrected Bell, lean jaws working hard at a chew of tobacco. "Yonder ain't nothin' but cotton burnin'; mob set it afire last night. What you Navy fellers are going to see in New Orleans ain't pretty. Ain't no law or order nowheres. Them flatboat men and thugs hev gone plumb crazy. Troops been firing into mobs since sunup."

Not only were small hills of cotton ablaze but also burning river steamers and ships of all sorts lifted vast pillars of flame into the morning sky. The masts and smokestacks of vessels already sunk projected above the current. Pirogues, smacks and small boats of all sorts were scurrying about in search of, or bearing away, plunder from sheds, warehouses and homes penetrated by the lawless.

When he saw a knot of men reeling and swaggering along the levee Sam's heart seemed squeezed by a chill hand. With such packs of human hyenas roaming unchecked what might not prove the fate of the weak and defenseless?

Certain steamboat captains, ruthless enough to find and drive aboard a skeleton crew, were loading panic-stricken refugees, but only those who could pay their way at exorbitant rates. Again and again, Sinclair and Seymour hailed for assistance. Couldn't these rivermen understand that the priceless, victory-assuring *Mississippi* stood in dire need of assistance? Threats, bribes and appeals to patriotism or cupidity alike achieved nothing.

Once ashore, the naval party became engulfed by swarms of wild-eyed would-be fugitives. The Yankees were coming, ready to level the Crescent City, they cried; eager to exterminate her population and rob, rape and ruin without compunction. Not one steamboat captain could be found willing to offer more than specious excuses or sullen defiance.

To Sam it was horrifying to behold such shameless, naked greed and selfishness.

Hot, furious and desperate, the Mississippi's officers ranged far and wide, trampled by fear-maddened crowds or threatened by rapacious shipmasters. Brief bursts of musketry from the heart of the city became more frequent.

All at once the crowds quit fighting towards the waterfront, hesitated, then began driving, hauling or carrying their possessions away from the river.

"They're coming! The Yankee ships are coming, damn them!"

Standing bruised, bleeding and battered on the Peytona's spar deck once more, Sam Seymour witnessed the appearance of a long line of trim topmasts and taut yards moving beyond the gull-whitened roofs of warehouses dotting Slaughterhouse Point. From the tops of that sinister array streamed the once well-beloved Old Flag. There could be no doubt that, in a very short while, the Union fleet would arrive off New Orleans ready to bombard the terrified metropolis with its ponderous batteries.

As if mesmerized, Sam watched the armada round into full view, black hulls bright in the morning sun and directing sable clouds of smoke high into the heavens. How many of yonder vessels could he not recognize at the first sight! Sam experienced a stinging in his hot and weary eyes. Yonder cruised the tall-sided Brooklyn, the ironically named Richmond and the Federal Mississippi; then the Pensacola and, flying Uncle Davy Farragut's long, blue pennant, the flagship Hartford. Smaller, and moving in a parallel column, steamed lesser Federal men-of-war such as the Iroquois, Cayuga, Seneca, Pinola, Wissahickon and others.

As became a trained naval officer, Arthur Sinclair made an instant decision. To river captain Bell he snapped, "We will return upstream."

"Like hell I will," the fellow protested. "Ain't I already passed up a young fortune to help you? Look at all them folks fightin' to come aboard."

Sinclair uttered a terrible curse. "If you don't order this craft cast off immediately, I'll blow you into two pieces, Mister, and praise God for giving me an excuse!"

Thus, about midday, the Peytona returned to join the St. Charles and the motionless ironclad. To the Confederate Mississippi's officers it proved agonizing to view their ship and see how completed she appeared from a distance with armor gleaming dully through a sudden downpour.

Since the ironclad couldn't be saved, she had but an hour or so to live; everyone knew it. Sam Seymour's blistered hands closed on the rail of the *Peytona* in terrible, futile and impotent revolt at what must be done.

Was it for this that so many unselfish men had racked their brains and strained their sinews? Was it to this end that countless telegrams had sped to Richmond and back, that train after train had rumbled westwards, creaking under guns and armor? Gone for nothing had been these endless months and weeks of inspired labor. Now no one would ever know what brilliant naval history might have been written by this cold, silent and helpless giant.

Despite himself, Sam turned aside and commenced to sob softly, then wept with great racking spasms that shook him to his waist.

The Regulars were efficient about their soul-killing task of destroying the most powerful man-of-war yet constructed on the American continent, but Commander Sinclair's voice broke when the moment came to order ignited combustibles piled at critical points aboard the doomed ironclad.

In sickened silence the Confederate *Mississippi's* crew watched their still-born vessel drift out into the river and commence to turn clumsily this way and that, yielding to the current's vagaries.

Lachlan Brunton choked and buried his shaggy red head in his arms when, for the first and only time, he watched smoke commence to rise from the ironclad's squat funnel.

She was spouting flame through all her gunports when the river steamers later dragged her out to sink in mid-stream where the Abolitionists might not be able to raise her.

Once the ironclad's outline had dwindled to a smoldering speck on the river's broad bosom, Commander Sinclair blew his nose, wiped his mustache and then summoned his officers.

"Gentlemen," said he heavily, "I conceive it to be our duty to return to New Orleans. Since no more Confederate naval vessels exist in this vicinity we will tender our services to General Lovell. Perhaps we may assist him in defending the city."

XXXI

The Ambulance

Rain sluicing down in silver-lead torrents for nearly thirty hours assisted in putting out a majority of the fires which, during nearly two days, had been blazing in various quarters of New Orleans. The weather also accomplished much more towards dispersing the rioters than frightened and untrained squads of soldiers.

The city's riffraff, maddened and rendered reckless by liquor looted from various warehouses, had run riot all the night of the twenty-fifth of April, leaving scattered bodies, smashed doors and windows and gutted houses as evidence of their savagery.

As Sam hurried along Camp Street, Commander Sinclair's parting admonition rang through his aching head. To his handful of dejected subordinates landing at the foot of Tchapitoulas Street he had said, "If this city can no longer be defended, gentlemen, it is our principal duty to make good our escape. Trained naval officers will be in even greater demand later on. This loss of New Orleans does not by any means doom our Cause to disaster; should you doubt me please recall how many stinging defeats were endured before victory was won by General Washington and his armies."

It had been a grim, weary and rain-soaked group which had debarked from the *Peytona*, for in their sunken eyes lingered visions of the flame-spouting *Mississippi* drifting helplessly down away downstream.

Under his stiff rubber coat Sam shivered, felt water trickling down his neck from the brim of a wide felt hat. This narrow street he was following must have been the scene of wild disorder for everywhere lay stones, bricks and sticks. A body lay across a gutter effectively damming it and creating a large muddy pool. The dead man, a thin undersized fellow, Sam realized, wore the white cross-belts and dark blue uniform of a private in the Foreign Legion.

Further along he came upon the wreck of a delivery cart immobilized because of a broken wheel. Every now and then he encountered small parties of troops shuffling dispiritedly along with heads bent against the lashing rain. Soon Sam became aware that all these units were marching in the same direction, eastwards away from the levees and the menacing muzzles of the great cannon aboard Farragut's grim, trim men-of-war. Anchored well out in the river, they swung restlessly to the current, as if impatient to loose death and destruction upon the fallen port.

To Sam's query a mud-splashed young captain sighed, "General Lovell has ordered all troops to quit the city. Did you know that the Yankee Admiral has promised to level it if an immediate surrender is not made?"

"But, damn it, sir," Sam growled, dashing water from his hat brim, "aren't you soldiers going to make some kind of a defense?"

The young captain's lips tightened, but his shoulders sagged still further. "We haven't a chance. Our commanders don't seem to know where anybody or anything is. If those forts and the Chalmette Battery couldn't stop those damned Blue coats, I reckon there isn't much hope of our doing so." He nodded and splashed on after his men.

"I'd best report at Naval Headquarters," Sam told himself wearily. "Maybe they'll have orders of some kind. It's hell, this not making a fight of some kind."

From a handsome residence down a side street issued a series of terrible, shrill screams—to which nobody paid the least attention. Broome Street he found peopled by refugees of all sorts, lugging pitiful bundles of possessions through the smoke-heavy twilight. In some faubourgs people could be seen bargaining or fighting for the use of any vehicle able to turn a wheel.

Every so often a coach or carriage would come clattering along, usually crammed to capacity with white people. Valuable slaves clung to doorsteps of the vehicles or retained a precarious hold on the roof.

Nearer the center of New Orleans the throng of hurrying, obviously panic-stricken citizens grew denser. Soon it became almost impossible to get across such principal east-west arteries as Shell Road, Canal and Toulouse Streets.

Many people seemed to move in a species of daze, only speaking to beg information or to spread increasingly appalling and utterly groundless rumors. All that they were sure of was that Federal troops would commence landing at dawn with orders to shoot on sight every male over eighteen years of age.

A wild-eyed householder had heard first-hand that the women of the city were to be collected and parceled out for the carnal satis-faction of troops now being fetched upriver under the command of Massachusetts' sinister and cockeyed Major General Benjamin F. But-ler. Lurid reports circulated, too, that a general uprising of slaves was taking place and that this or that plantation had been plundered and burned.

The St. Charles Hotel's lobby presented a distressing spectacle of pandemonium and terror-stricken aimlessness. Wild-eyed guests were rushing hither and thither, attempting to learn when and where refugee trains might be leaving, and offering small fortunes for trans-portation to them.

In line with Sam's expectations, the only order issued by gray-faced but imperturbable Commander Whittle was to the effect that all naval personnel must board a special train departing from Jackson Depot at four o'clock on the morning of April twenty-sixth. Naval officers were at liberty to fetch along body servants, baggage and any members of their immediate family.

"What finally happened to the *Governor Moore?*" inquired some-one as Sam and some fellow officers started downstairs. "I heard she put up a most gallant battle against impossible odds."

"She was sunk," growled Lieutenant Pegram, "like every other ship of our force. If only those lily-livered cowards commanding the River Defense Flotilla had done more than run, scuttle or burn them-selves! Just let me lay hands on one of those loud-mouthed river rats!"

By all accounts Sam deduced that not a single gunboat of that amorphous fleet had fired a shot with the one exception of the *Stone-wall Jackson* and she had destroyed herself immediately after her senseless ramming of the already-shattered *Varuna.*

Candles and lanterns flashed eerily about the St. Charles' dim lobby—gas having long since been turned off—but the hotel's huge bar remained crammed by melodramatically talking militia officers, many of whom were hopelessly drunk.

Out on the street Sam found that the rain had lessened to a fine drizzle, but the pungent reek of burning cotton still stung one's nose.

He determined to head straight for the Cottier home on Conti Street, especially since packs of thugs and ruffians were commencing to venture outdoors again now that rain had abated.

Keeping him company, for want of other occupation until train time, strode Lieutenant Dawson whose long sensitive features remained set in an expression of ominous disgust.

"I aim to shoot the first person I see looting," he announced. "It's plenty bad us getting licked like this, but for these damned human vultures to feast on our defeat—well, I'm not going to tolerate it!"

An officer wearing the Louisiana State Navy uniform joined them. "My name's Lanier," he said. "We may as well keep together, don't you think? There's no telling what may happen. It was terrible downriver," he continued. "They blew up the *Louisiana* just after the forts surrendered and brought in some survivors of the *Governor Moore*. The whole west end of town is running riot."

"Wounded from the *Governor Moore*? What's being done for them?" demanded Sam.

"Nothing at all, damn these cowardly civilians to hell. I've been trying to come across a wagon to haul some of our badly wounded out of the rain. Right now they're lying about the levee like logs."

When, a moment later, a delivery cart appeared clattering along at a brisk trot, Sam leaped out into the street and grabbed the bridle of a powerful bay. "Get down!" he rasped at a big, fat-faced fellow occupying the box. "And get down, quick! Damn your eyes!"

"Like hell I will! This is my horse and wagon," roared the driver. "Let go that bridle! I'm to get five thousand dollars if I get this stuff of Mrs. Legendre's away."

Swearing fiercely, Dawson swarmed up onto the seat and, by means of a single, well-planted kick, sent the cursing, furious driver sprawling onto the muddied cobbles. Immediately the two other naval officers climbed up to settle upon a huge load of bundles and draw longsnouted Navy Colts.

Sam took the reins and, by circling through residential districts and paralleling main arteries, reached the levee far more quickly than he had dared to hope. On the levee at the foot of Bartholomew Street a pair of smoky lanterns revealed a double windrow of motionless figures over whom a few tarpaulins had been rigged. The majority, however, still lay exposed to the sifting rain.

Lanier cried suddenly, "That's a *Louisiana* uniform over there! We've found my party. These are the *Moore's* men over yonder."

Sam whipped up, sent the wagon splashing over towards a knot of light-colored uniforms.

"Thank God, it's Lanier," called somebody out of the darkness. "We'd just about given you up."

Sam unhooked one of the wagon lamps and went striding out onto the levee, demanding, "Where are the most gravely injured?"

Dawson and a group of volunteers meanwhile cleared the wagon's body of everything save several bundles of linens which they hastily converted into improvised mattresses and coverlets. A bespectacled civilian physician who looked as if he had not slept in days caught Sam's arm and guided him towards the right end of the line.

"The most critically hurt are here," he said. "I am afraid we'll lose most of 'em if they can't get immediate treatment."

As gently as possible the silent, sunken-faced wounded were lifted up into the cart—too far gone to groan or make comment. The fourth patient, however, seemed to rouse from a deep sleep and peer about. Suddenly the ghost of Léon Duchesne's voice mumbled, "And how are you, friend Seymour?"

Sam caught his breath. Duchesne was so pallid, so shrunken-looking that he appeared all-but-lifeless lying there under a muddied patchwork quilt, with once-martial mustaches drooping over his rain-wetted cheeks.

"My God, Léon! How badly are you hit?"

"One remains to observe the cost of defeat," he gasped. "It's my leg, I've lost all feeling in it." He actually managed a smile. "Sam, do you suppose you could have me taken home? I expect Émile, my servant, will still be around; he will know what to do. Ought to, he's had plenty of experience with mornings-after."

Rain puddles left behind on the levee shone scarlet with more than the lantern's light when, at length, the improvised ambulance rolled away to a chorus of groans from those left behind.

"Hang on, lads, we'll soon return for you," Lanier called. He then turned to Sam. "Where away?"

"To Commander Duchesne's home off Bourbon Street. It's directly on the way to the Methodist Hospital."

Thus it came about that, around nine of the evening, Léon Duchesne returned home and felt vastly comforted by the familiar aspect of the soft yellow façade of his pied-à-terre.

"What a way to return," he remarked painfully. "Last time I was carried in like this was after the King Comus Ball 'fifty-eight." Curious, he had never before noticed the presence of a small cherub peering out from among the gilded scrollwork at the top of his hall mirror.

Sam directed that the long figure be deposited in the drawing room upon a settee upholstered in ruby damask. Perhaps this choice of a resting place was just as well since a scarlet thread of blood had mounted the front steps, followed the hall and then had led straight over to the settee.

Lanier nodded, patted the wounded man's shoulder. "I'll better be getting along to the hospital. Good luck, Duchesne. See you later, Commander."

Sam nodded but didn't look up. He was too busy inspecting a crude tourniquet rigged above a mass of hideously stained cloth which once might have been the sleeve of a man's shirt. Um. The pressure could not have been eased in hours Sam guessed after a quick glance at the shiny, plum-colored thigh.

"Not pretty, eh, mon ami?"

"No, Léon, not pretty. Is there a doctor anywhere in the vicinity?"

"Dr. Brouillard, but I doubt that he is available."

"Anything I can do to help?" Dawson inquired, just as Émile, the butler-valet, came pattering in on broad bare feet, his face gone yellow-gray through fright.

"Oh, M'sieu! Quel désastre!"

"Late, as usual." Duchesne managed a faint laugh. "Go fetch a bottle of cognac. I—I remain chilly."

Sam wiped fingers on the lining of his dripping rubber coat. "You've lost a powerful amount of blood, my friend, and you'll require constant care. I wish I—"

The Creole blinked, raised a powder-blackened hand and beckoned. "Émile, just you run around to the Carondelet House—"

"No!" Sam objected. "Let Dawson go, he stands the better chance of getting there. Émile, you go find a doctor—any doctor, but quickly."

"What shall I do when I get to the hotel?" Dawson's tired

gray eyes looked huge by the light of the candles Émile had ignited.

"Please convey—my admiration and—and—compliments to Mrs. Pingree," Léon whispered. "Tell her I implore her understanding—that—that I require—immediate attendance. Bring her back with you, Monsieur. You *must!* Do you understand?"

Towards midnight they gathered in Léon Duchesne's gay little salon beneath crystal chandeliers and tall mirrors which multiplied infinitely whole rows of dancing candle flames. Doctor Brouillard could not be found, but the Reverend Doctor Kincaid of the Third Episcopal Church was in attendance.

Fortunately he had studied medicine before entering the ministry and so was completing his physical ministrations when the front doorbell jangled and a sound as of wind rushing through dead oak leaves filled the corridor. Kitty Pingree, hair streaming wildly over the shoulders of a heavy cape, came flying in and darted over to the settee.

"Oh, Léon, my poor darling! My own sweet love." The muddied hem of a nightdress appeared beneath the cape when she flung herself onto her knees beside that tall figure crumpled under a concealing blue woolen blanket. "Everything will be all right now, dearest. I am here to care for you."

Over her shoulder she cried to the men standing silent and sober-eyed above her, "I'll save him, Sam, I'm not a doctor's daughter for nothing."

When Kitty bent lightly to kiss the stricken man's colorless lips, Sam stole a sidewise look at the Reverend Doctor Kincaid and was dismayed by the almost imperceptible shake of his head.

"Émile," Duchesne gasped, "must you always need prompting? Pour cognac for Madame Pingree and these gentlemen." His dark, intense eyes gone cavernous, he called Sam forward.

"Yes, Léon. What is it?"

The ghost of a smile plucked at Duchesne's mouth. "Once we attended—wedding—Brunton's, remember?" A long sigh escaped him. "You were best man—then. Will you act again—if—if you, my Kittee, will accord me the enormous honor of becoming my wife?"

Kitty turned aside, quivering, her features white. "I—I, but do you really love me, Léon? This is—not just pity?"

"With all—my heart and soul, *chèrie*. Everything—I—I—"

"In that case," quietly interrupted the minister, "I think we had better not delay."

The Reverend Doctor Kincaid, wise with years, said nothing further, only motioned forward the three other figures, then reached into the tail of his long black coat for that Bible from which he seldom was parted.

Against the undertone of Émile's heartbroken sobbing, they gathered about the gaily-hued settee. Kitty Pingree knelt, overshadowed by the two officers standing at rigid attention in their muddied and wrinkled uniforms. In a low tone the Reverend Doctor Kincaid commenced, by the dancing candlelight, to read the marriage service.

When he had done, he said, clearing his throat, "Dearly beloved, while it is customary for the groom to kiss the bride, I believe in this instance the proceeding had better be reversed."

Léon Duchesne staring blankly up, felt the warm pressure of lips upon his, then whispered, "Be kind to our little one— *Ah, Seigneur Dieu.*" Then his life escaped in a weary, sibilant sigh.

XXXII

RETREAT

THAT CONSIDERABLE RIOTING must have taken place in Conti Street was inescapable. The wavering and uncertain light of a lantern carried by Commander Samuel Seymour revealed shards of broken glass, bits of smashed pottery and all manner of abandoned plunder littering the cobbles.

Near the corner of Marcus Street two bodies lay blackly sprawled beneath a wall. Above them a series of white splashes that could only have been bulletholes suggested that these were looters caught and executed out-of-hand by some military unit.

Conti Street, however, was far from deserted by the living. Like embodied shadows Negroes of all ages could be seen slinking into alleyways or shuffling along through the night, bent under nondescript bundles and heading as a rule in an easterly direction.

Through an open window Sam heard a woman sobbing over and over. "They've killed poor Willie, they've killed poor Willie!"

As if oblivious to such mundane troubles, a church clock not far down the street severely sounded three sonorous strokes to remind Sam that he must drive his aching legs still faster. So weary had he become that he experienced only few of the dreadful apprehensions which normally would have tortured his imagination on recalling that Louise and his son, for two whole days, had been defenseless and exposed to the perils of this mob-ruled city.

When he noticed an ominous black rectangle where the Cottier's door should have presented a smooth white surface, his breath came in with a sharp click and he broke into a lumbering trot.

"My God," he choked.

Not only Louis Cottier's house but the two residences adjoining it had been broken into. A small heap of smashed furniture lay smoking feebly and giving off a faint red glow; further on more loot, apparently abandoned in haste, created a jumbled pyramid before the entrance.

Panting, sick at heart, and conscious of a burning sensation back of his eyes, Sam noticed that all glass was gone from the ground-floor windows. Successive, sickening waves of despair shook him.

Why hadn't he forgotten discipline sufficiently long to have hurried here straight from the landing? All this could not have happened very long ago. Horrible mental pictures of Robbie lying murdered, of Louise's dark beauty revealed, pawed and then defiled swam in his agonized imagination.

"Louise!" he cried. "Louise, for God's sake answer me!" His big voice caused the whole dripping, smoke-tinctured street to resound, but only resulted in causing a party of armed Negroes to run away down a side street.

Drawn pistol ready and with his lantern throwing erratic amber-yellow barbs of light in all directions, Sam scrambled over a heap of sodden carpets and curtains abandoned in the doorway to stand peering into the Cottier house now smelling of spilled liquor, wet cloth and the heavy, musty odor of blood. Whose blood? He shivered and swallowed convulsively on nothing.

"Louise! *Robert!*" His voice echoed and re-echoed through the dim darkness. It proved quite a task to pick his way over debris littering the hall until he came upon the corpse of a man at the foot of the stair. The body lay in a wide pool of blood, with head propped against the lowest step, staring blankly upwards, while with both hands clutching a wound taken above the heart.

"Louise!" Sam's voice rose to the pitch of a scream as his mind struggled to refuse what his intelligence suggested. At a sudden rustle he spun about, leveling his Colt's in time to glimpse the family's big tiger cat go scurrying across the plundered dining room.

"Louise? Robert?" By exerting a supreme effort Sam got a grip on his nerves and forced himself to listen, but only the sullen *drip-drip* of water falling from the eaves, and a few distant shots rewarded him.

Holding his lantern high, Sam then stepped over the dead man and climbed a wide stone staircase. On the first floor, only a trifle less of disorder prevailed. Splashes of ink, of filth had stained the upstairs sitting room's powder-blue walls.

Although he had never been above the ground floor of this house, he knew, nonetheless, that Louise's room was situated at the end of a passage to his left. Skin on the backs of his hands tightened at a soft *thump* and then a scraping sound. Again he readied his big Navy Colt's. That noise could have been made by no small animal.

"Who's there?" he called when the scraping was repeated. Hurriedly, he plunged down the hallway after clambering over the remains of a broken bed.

"Come out of there!" he ordered. "Come out, or I'll shoot you down."

To his ears came a muffled exclamation, then his heart soared.

"Sam! *Sam!* Is that really you?"

"Are you all right? I—I—" He blundered forward as the door before him swung back to reveal Louise dropping a long-barreled fowling piece. She flung herself, sobbing, into his arms.

"Robbie! *Is Robbie safe?*"

"Sleeping. He's exhausted. It has been terrible here. Terrible." Louise had placed a candle in the center of her bedroom floor beyond that heap of furniture with which, evidently, she had barricaded her door.

As if to resist some fearful force threatening to tear her away, Sam's arms clutched her soft, palpitating figure and his lips bruised her tremulous ones.

"What a nightmare has ended," she sighed. "I have been praying for you night and day, mon âme, and truly believe that through God's grace my love has sheltered you."

Presently he tiptoed over to kiss his son, crumpled and looking so very small in the midst of Louise's great canopied bed. Straightening, he drew a deep breath and passed a dazed hand over his forehead before pulling out his watch.

"Sam! Why do you learn the time?"

"My darling, I expect it will be difficult for you to understand why I can't linger here with you."

Incredulous, she stared at him from great eyes round as those of a cat hunting at night. "You would leave me—us?"

"I am ordered to board a train for the East at four o'clock; it leaves in a very short while," he explained heavily. "Will you collect some clothing for Robert?"

Louise continued to stare a long instant, then, as if breaking a trance, smiled and stood straight. "I think I can find a portemanteau large enough to hold enough clothes for us both."

"Both!"

The glory in her eyes was the most lovely thing he had ever beheld. "Certainly, my darling. You cannot imagine that I would linger behind?"

"But—but—" he protested, incredulous. "This is your home. There is this house to be protected."

"The Federal troops will be landing with daylight," said she, busy at a chest of drawers. "Besides, my brother Étienne is in town."

She came to him, placed hands on his sodden shoulders. "Do you recall what Ruth, the Moabite woman, said? 'Wither thou goest, I will go; and where thou lodgest, I will lodge: thy people shall be my people . . .'"

Haggard and unbearably weary, Sam held her at arm's length, demanded harshly, "Can't you, won't you realize, darling, that with me only danger, poverty and discomfort are in store for you?"

"That is of no importance," she cried, lifting her face to his. "What I know is only this. Although defeated, our people—yours and mine—

have not been beaten! They will go on fighting until a final Victory is won. How can I, at such a moment, turn aside?"

His arms folded her cruelly close. "Come then, my dear. So long as there remain women like you to sustain our Cause, we can never falter."

Finis

DATE DUE

GAYLORD			PRINTED IN U.S.A.